TO RUDY HAWZA —

IN HONOR OF YOUR

OLYMPIC WALKING

CAREER.

ALL THE BEST —

[signature]

The
IDEALIST

THE STORY OF BARON PIERRE DE COUBERTIN

A HISTORICAL NOVEL

○ ○ ○ ○ ○

GEORGE HIRTHLER

RINGWORKS
PRESS
ATLANTA

MMXVI

THE IDEALIST
The Story of Baron Pierre de Coubertin
A Historical Novel
Copyright © 2016 by George Hirthler
All rights reserved. This book or any portion thereof
may not be reproduced or used in any manner whatsoever without the express written permission of the publisher except for the use of brief quotations in a book review.

Published in the United States by Ringworks Press, Atlanta
The Ringworks Press symbol is a registered trademark of Ringworks Press, LLC.
Printed in the USA on acid free paper
First Printing, 2016
Deluxe edition ISBN 978-0-9974759-2-0
Trade hardbound edition ISBN 978-0-9974759-0-6
Softcover Edition ISBN 978-0-9974759-1-3
ebook edition: ISBN 978-0-9974759-3-7
ISBN 978-0-9974759-0-6

10 9 8 7 6 5 4 3 2 1

www.coubertintheidealist.com

To Jason and Jamie,
the radical and the muse
in the middle of my heart

—*and*—

For all those who labor
in the Olympic Movement
to build a better world

PREFACE

by Thomas Bach,
President, International Olympic Committee

*"The Olympic Games are ... a pilgrimage
to the past and an act of faith in the future."*—*Pierre de Coubertin*

The Olympic Games are in a constant and continuous quest to revitalize and renew their history. In every edition of this global celebration of humanity—as each generation of rising athletes aspires to make their mark—every event on the competition schedule has the potential to rewrite the history books.

As the world watches, we place each new feat in the context of its history-making predecessors. The legends of the past take their place on the podium with the victors of the present. Every medal is a triumph of the human spirit, a milestone for all humanity. Every edition of the Olympic Games symbolizes the universal values shared by all humankind—and confirms that united in our diversity we can make the world a better place through sport.

But it is not so often we have the opportunity to celebrate the origins of the Olympic Movement itself—that indelible campaign by Baron Pierre de Coubertin to resurrect the Olympic Games after 1,500 years in obscurity. With *The Idealist*, however, we have a chance to do just that. George Hirthler's historical novel transports us back to our modern origins and reminds us of the soaring idealism that motivated one relentless aristocrat to create a celebration of humanity the entire world could embrace.

In reimagining Coubertin's life, Hirthler not only pays homage to our founder, but gives us a portrait of a man for whom no sacrifice was too great, no challenge too high, no goal too distant. With its evocative prose, *The Idealist* reminds us of the debt the Olympic Movement owes to *le Rénovateur*. It is only because of his ambition, vision and tenacious drive that the Games are still extending their reach and still uniting our world in friendship and peace through sport.

George first told me of his intention to write a book about Coubertin in 2011. As I monitored his progress over the last five years, I had high hopes for this book. Now that it is in print, I believe those who venture into its pages will discover a new source of Olympic inspiration in the unforgettable story of the first modern Olympic dreamer.

"*I strive, in relation to other men, to discover the nature,*
if not the necessity, of my difference from them. Is it not precisely
to the degree I become conscious of this difference that I shall recognize
what I alone have been put on this earth to do, what unique
message I alone may bear, so that I alone can answer for its fate?"

—Andre Breton, Nadja, 1928

"*No modern institution so important as the Olympics owes*
its existence so fully to the actions of a single person ...
Moreover, for all the vast changes that have accrued
to the Games since their first celebration in 1896, they still
bear indelibly—from their flag to their official ideology—
the stamp of Pierre de Coubertin."

—John J. MacAloon, This Great Symbol, 1981

"*We shall not have peace until the prejudices which now*
separate the different nations shall have been outlived.
To attain this end, what better means than to bring the youth
of all countries periodically together for amicable trials
of muscular strength and agility."

—Pierre de Coubertin, 1894

PRELUDE

THE STORM

Lausanne, Switzerland, 1937

A dark morning storm swept across Lake Geneva, spilling down from the French Alps in torrents of rain that washed the streets of Evian and rolled across the wide water north toward Lausanne. Down at the shoreline where the high hills of the city dropped to the water, just behind the Gothic seventeenth-century Château d'Ouchy, an old lone rower pointed his ten-foot skiff into the coming cloud front and pulled against the oars. His boat pulsed into the rough, freezing waters and the rain lashed his wool Breton shirt, soaking his white hair and the thick brush of his mustache. The wind raised goose bumps on his forearms, which were thinner now but taut with sinews that still gave him a firm grip. Within minutes, he was gasping to fill his seventy-four-year-old lungs with fresh air and give his muscles the oxygen to keep going straight, but the wind was strong and he quickly wore down. Buffeted and pushed, the skiff turned sideways against his will. He pulled harder on the right oar—his right arm had always been stronger—and began to turn in a wide circle, first retreating but soon coming around again—and again—to drive into the wind and draw a small measure of joy from the effort against this natural adversary sent down by the gods.

He would not be denied his morning workout, so he persisted, turning circles for a half hour before heading back to shore as the storm weakened. Dragging his skiff onto the rocky bank, he looked south toward France, his beloved mother country, and warmed briefly as a ray of sunlight cut through an opening in the clouds. For a fleeting moment, he imagined he saw the signature summit of the highest peak, Mont Blanc.

HOPES AND FEARS

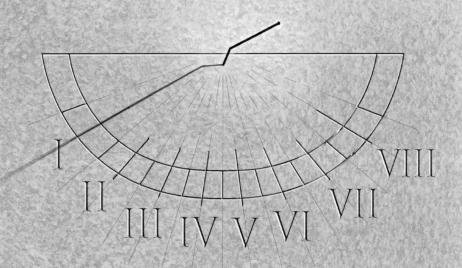

1

THE LETTER

O n a cold January day in Paris, Jacques St. Clair, the leading sports writer for *Le Petit Journal*, was contemplating the image of the Matterhorn, searching for the right way to end his story of the baker from the Latin Quarter who had climbed Switzerland's highest and most dramatic alpine peak a year ago in a daring solo ascent—"just to see what the world looked like from up there."

Leaning back in his slatted wooden chair, feet up on the desk, ignoring the cacophony of the newsroom, St. Clair fingered the silver chain around his neck, twirling and catching again and again the gold pendant of a single bicycle wheel. He pondered the motivation of a bread maker who spent his days kneading dough for his neighbors while dreaming of risking his life for vistas only visible from the top of the world.

"For you, Monsieur Jacques," said the mail boy, interrupting the writer's reverie and dropping a letter on the stack of papers next to his old Olivetti typewriter. Without breaking his relaxed pose, St. Clair reached over and picked up the letter. It was postmarked Lausanne, not that far from the valley of Zermatt where the baker had started his ascent. Resisting the distraction, St. Clair dropped the letter and went back to his pendant, looking for the next literary handhold to lead him to the end of this particular story.

He was thirty-six at the time and had gained some prestige for the quality of the stories he wrote, particularly the profiles of sports champions, active and retired, and those, like his baker, who stepped out of the everyday to pursue the heroic. He loved the milieu of sport—its sweat, its risks, its obstacles, its triumphs, the adulation it engendered. It was in his blood. A decade and a half earlier, he had been a promising competitive cyclist, winning two stages of the Tour de France at the peak of his athletic career in 1923.

And St. Clair still took pride in his physique, which was stockier and more muscled now, but fairly fit. His old editor, Edgar, said it was obviously the power of his body that gave his writing its vigor. He was five foot ten with a large chest that extended like a shelf from his round and solid shoulders. Somewhere in his French bloodlines there must have been a German or a Scandinavian—his hair was blond and thick and rose from his head like the bristles of a stiff brush. He combed it forward in an unfashionable but distinct style. His eyes were hazel, and his jaw provided a strong frame for his handsome visage.

He'd likely still be an athlete if it weren't for the diary he had kept on the Tour that year. Spotted by a journalist, it was the diary, when it was published, that had opened the door into writing. Without much hesitation, St. Clair had parked his bike and moved from the peloton to the middle of a throng of editors, reporters, typists, and copyboys in the equally hectic and crowded newsroom of *Le Journal* on rue de la Fayette. The diary offered painful descriptions of the agony of the mountain stages, especially St. Clair's collapse on the Col d'Izoard, where the champion, Henri Pélissier, who rode for Automoto, seized the lead in an act of sheer dominance. The writing revealed a literary talent for long-form features that quickly lifted St. Clair above the competitive hustle and fray of daily deadlines.

He gained popularity and prominence in writing about Johnny Weissmuller and Duke Kahanamoku, the American gold and silver medalists in swimming at the 1924 Paris Olympic Games. Rising quickly, he became *Le Journal's* lead Olympic writer, which led to significant assignments at the Games in Amsterdam in 1928, Los Angeles in 1932, and Berlin in 1936. In the German capital, he was mesmerized by the brilliance of Jesse Owens and aggravated by the symbolic clash of the Olympic rings and the Nazi swastika.

As his career developed and his talent regularly took him to the front rows of sports history, St. Clair felt a growing desire to write something of more significance. He wanted to find a literary challenge that would take him beyond the confines of the celebrity profile and give him a chance to test himself in the realm of a book, a literary marathon he thought of as the *Tour de Page*. He longed for a journey through a story of chapters that unfolded like a staged race, one after the other, with the same unpredictability that sport presented.

It was this ambition, the desire to see his name on the cover of a book that the letter from Lausanne surprisingly spoke to. The moment after he sliced it open, St. Clair knew this was the opportunity he had been hoping for—a chance to break away from the pack and ride off toward the mountains alone, to find his own path to a dramatic solo summit. The envelope contained six pages, all filled with the neat scrolling script of a Dr. Francis M. Messerli, who had, according to the date, started the letter a week before on New Year's Day, 1937. As he read, St. Clair felt his muscles tense in anticipation. Line by line an old familiar feeling took hold of his body—as if a clock were counting down to the start of a race.

Dear Monsieur St. Clair:

Although I seldom see your work on the day it is published, I have been an avid long-distance reader of your stories for more than a decade here in Lausanne. We have Le Petit Journal *sent in each week in part because I have developed a particular affection for your literary portraits, which often touch me like paintings do.*

But it is your reporting on the Olympic Games, which I consider the finest published anywhere, that has moved me to write to you now. I believe we are near the end of one of the greatest stories in the history of modern sport, the story of a life of epic struggles and heroic determination that has been largely overlooked by the world, even though it produced the greatest spectacle of sport we know— the Olympic Games.

It is, of course, the story of Baron Pierre de Coubertin, a Frenchman from Paris like you, a man whose singular idealism and visionary force brought the Olympics back to life after 1,500 years and helped move sport onto the field of national passion where it thrives today.

For twenty-nine years, I have been one of Coubertin's closest friends and allies—and I have also been his doctor. Across that period, I have watched his fortunes decline while those of the Games have risen higher and higher. And in the last year, after the controversial success of the Berlin Games, I have seen another change—and I'm afraid if we don't record his memories for posterity soon, they will be lost to us forever.

I have asked the baron again and again, even begging once or twice, to write his full autobiography. Despite his promises and his undeniably prolific capacity to write about anything, he has not filled a single page of prose toward this goal. A few brief anecdotal memoirs he drafted some time ago for the International Olympic Committee, which he founded, hardly tell the full story.

So this letter is dispatched with a certain sense of urgency. I have set aside funds for a writer in residence to get the baron's story written. I'm hoping you are that writer. Please let me know if you are interested; if so, we will make arrangements to move you to Lausanne to begin the work as soon as you are available.

The letter went on to convey more detail, but that, in essence, was the offer Jacques St. Clair was left to consider—an offer to move to Lausanne to work for a year at full salary on a book about the Frenchman who had reached back through time to resurrect the ancient Olympic Games for the modern world.

St. Clair knew who Coubertin was. He had first seen the little man at the 1924 Olympic Games in Paris, he remembered. But it wasn't actually at the Games, he thought. No, it was during a ceremony at the Court of Honor at the Sorbonne, a moment commemorating the thirtieth anniversary of the founding of the Olympic Movement. The date was June 23rd. He recalled the image of Coubertin walking into the arched, columned court in a long-tailed tuxedo, a top hat in his hand, side by side with the president of the Republic of France, Monsieur Gaston Doumergue.

St. Clair leaned back in his hard chair for a moment, picking up the Automoto squeeze ball he kept in the pile of papers and books stacked around the Olivetti. He squeezed without counting—one hundred squeezes a day was a long-lost goal—and let his thoughts drift back to that day.

St. Clair had been at the ceremony to meet and interview Charles Paddock, the American sprinter from Texas glorified as "the human cannonball." Paddock had won the 100 meters at the 1920 Antwerp Olympic Games after the war and had set the world record at 10.2 seconds a year later. St. Clair remembered Paddock had been there to see Coubertin—to thank him for helping promote a world sprinters' tour.

St. Clair had waited for Paddock while the event unfolded, paying little attention to the dignitaries and their speeches. At the time, that side of the Games—the organizational effort, the committees of old men, the history and archives—held no interest for him, even though he loved history, particularly the history of Paris. But now this story—the story of this small, aristocratic Frenchman pushing forward an enormous event of modern pageantry, an idea that was embraced by the world's greatest athletes and heads of state—this story of how the Games actually began and became the foreboding spectacle the Nazis had turned them into the year before—this could be fascinating.

He breathed deeply and squeezed the ball hard, holding his excitement at bay as he recognized that Coubertin's story would take him out of the arena he had been working in—into a broader game of politics, finance, and some international intrigue, he was sure—while allowing him to maintain the connection to the heroes of sport who had fueled his work until now.

Messerli had been persuasive in appealing to his desire to write something significant. "This story cannot be contained in the margins of a newspaper profile or told with justice in the pages of a magazine," Messerli had written. "It needs a writer whose heart pulses with sport and whose talents and ambitions are equal to the tasks of rendering the imprint of one of the most important lives of our times."

Messerli had left a telephone number and indicated that once he and St. Clair struck an agreement, he would secure an apartment for the year and send a package of books and documents for background.

It was the middle of the afternoon and St. Clair's story of the Matterhorn baker was due in the morning, but he had only the conclusion left and it could wait till late tonight or the first thing tomorrow.

He had to share the Lausanne letter with his American fiancée right now. He lifted the gold wheel to his lips and kissed it before letting it fall back under his shirt. Juliette had given it to him one month ago to mark the anniversary of their third year together. She had called it a good luck charm, and he would tell her it had been spinning in his hand when the letter arrived. She would not believe their good fortune. They'd been talking about traveling and thinking about moving for months, their hearts set on a new adventure. Donning his heavy jacket and tucking the letter inside, he folded his tablets and papers into a canvas satchel, pulled on his cycling gloves, and headed for the street below where his new De Dion-Bouton Course with the three-speed *dérailleur* was locked inside the building's entrance.

2

OLD FRIENDS

Behind the glass wall of La Nautica, the art deco steel-framed restaurant on the back of the Château d'Ouchy, two men stood eight feet above the ground at the top of a granite staircase, watching Pierre de Coubertin pull his skiff up onto the rocks on the Lake Geneva shoreline. Amid the white linen, crystal, silver, and thematic nautical effects hanging on the walls of the restaurant, they gazed out as the old rower tied up his boat and looked back at the stormy sky that had drenched his morning exercise just as the sun broke through.

"He must be freezing. He probably should have waited an hour for better weather," said Dr. Messerli. The balding but fit forty-nine-year-old was Coubertin's closest friend in Lausanne.

"He never has the time to wait," replied Émil Drut, the manager of the restaurant and another of Coubertin's oldest friends. Twisting the end of his long, curled mustache, he said, "I'm going down to meet him." Walking away, he dusted a trace of white flour from his black coat sleeve.

As Coubertin stepped through the stone-arched opening of the staff door on the back of the Château d'Ouchy, dripping wet, Drut was there to greet him, handing him a large towel and holding out a cup of coffee.

"Thank you, Émil. You're always too kind," Coubertin said. "Is the doctor here?" They moved into the staff changing room, where the baron had left his clothes, as usual, in a small locker Drut provided for his convenience.

"Yes, Dr. Messerli and I were watching you row from upstairs, making a few notes on your technique."

"Well then, it should be clear to both of you that I'm ready for Henley this year." Pierre looked at him with a half-smile before reaching over and patting Drut's paunch with the back of his hand. "But you've got some work to do, Émil, if you're going to make the Ouchy juniors."

"I'll stick to my regimen here ... pulling corks from bottles," Drut said, turning toward the stairs, leaving Coubertin to change.

A little while later, Dr. Messerli heard voices across the restaurant and looked up from the sports page of *Le Matin* to see Pierre and Émil chatting amicably and moving toward him. Messerli reflected on how Pierre was always kind to everyone. No matter what he was feeling inside, his interaction with people was invariably bright, just as it was at this moment with Émil—despite what Messerli knew Pierre was going through.

And, despite the twenty-five-year gap in their ages, something in Pierre had touched Messerli's heart on the day they met in 1908. It wasn't just that he was *le Rénovateur* of the Olympic Games. His presence and charm, the way his character and essence emerged so large from such a small frame, set him apart as someone unique. Messerli's affection for the man, and to some degree his fascination with him and his lofty ideals, had only grown stronger as their friendship deepened across the last twenty-nine years. Few days went by now without some interaction between them. In some ways, though he wasn't formally part of the International Olympic Committee, Messerli had become the true keeper of the flame of Coubertin's vision. They had launched the Olympic Institute of Lausanne in 1917, which combined athletics and education for the working man. They had established the IOC's Olympic Library together in the 1920s and '30s and were still working on it—sorting Pierre's voluminous personal letters from the official ones.

As Émil took his leave, Messerli stood and greeted his old friend and mentor.

"Hello, Francis. Good of you to invite me to such an early meeting."

"I have something to talk to you about."

"Not my rowing, I hope."

"No, but I watched you today, my friend, rowing in circles again. You're like a stroke victim who can only turn in one direction." He regretted the joke as soon as he said it, but smiled anyway since there was no taking it back.

"A little dizziness is not a stroke, Dr. Messerli," Coubertin said with a half-smile. "And if you read more Jung than Freud, you'd know the circle is a symbol of perfection. I like making circles."

Messerli preferred Freud's cerebral analytics while Coubertin put more weight in Jung's more intuitive interpretation of dreams and symbols. It was a current subject of debate between them. Coubertin liked challenging the doctor in the medical field, where his own expertise was limited and required research. Messerli didn't take the bait this morning.

"I have something to tell you." Messerli lowered his head and cast a serious gaze as he filled the baron's coffee cup. "I may require a significant investment of your time in a major project I'm launching across the next year."

"So," Coubertin replied without hesitation, "you've found a writer for my story."

"Not yet, but I'm anticipating a response."

"And from whom are we waiting for this response?"

"Jacques St. Clair."

"Well," Coubertin said, a lift in his voice. "If it's St. Clair, I will certainly make the time."

Messerli exchanged a conspiratorial glance with his friend—they had mastered the look over the years to convey an acceptable plot—and then both smiled. As their breakfast was served, Messerli thought about how Pierre's face had aged over the last three decades, how the lines above the eyes had lost their fight and drooped into a state of sadness. He knew the fire still burned inside, somewhere, but the sparkle was not shining through as it had for so many years. The once-black hair was now silver white. The distinct kindness of his empathetic gaze made Pierre approachable, and his rosy color made him look good for his age. But the doctor was fearful his health was failing. Messerli suspected Coubertin might be gravely ill. There had been spells, dizziness, fainting, and the occasional lapse of memory. Messerli knew that if this life story were going to be written with the insights only Coubertin could offer, it had to be written now.

"There is one point, Francis, that I must insist on. We're not going to tell St. Clair about Geneva."

"What? You're going to lie to him?" Messerli had hoped Coubertin wouldn't impose any conditions on the agreement, but it seemed the baron wanted to exert some control.

"I'm living a lie, Francis. I don't want the story to be dominated by my ruptured marriage or Marie's instability."

"You won't be able to hide it. He's bound to find out."

"I've hidden it successfully from others."

"Not people you were meeting with on a regular basis."

"I'm going to structure the interviews so it's not that difficult."

"What about the baroness—she won't hide it. Nor will she be able to disguise her anger."

"Yes she will. We've already discussed it. She's agreed that I'll stay at Mon Repos when I need to. This is her legacy too. She's willing to keep up appearances."

"It's a tangled web you're weaving, Pierre. I'd strongly advise against it."

"Your opinion is noted."

"How long do you think you can keep this ruse up?"

"As long as I need to. I have to make sure it feels right before I disclose everything."

"Well, you're not dropping out of this project once I move him here. I'm committing to a year."

"Do you think it will take that long?"

"Yes, Pierre, this is a real biography we're talking about. Not the superficial account in your *Memoirs*." Messerli was frustrated, but determined to hold course. He figured once St. Clair arrived and established a rapport with the baron, the old man would gain the confidence to tell his story in full—and reveal the truth.

○ ○ ○ ○ ○

What Messerli hadn't told St. Clair was that until just days before the doctor had composed and sent the letter, Coubertin had been a completely unwilling subject. It had taken more than six months to convince the aging baron that his story needed to be told—and that it had to be written by someone else.

Messerli had first proposed the idea of a biographer just after the 1936 Games in Berlin. While he never said so then, the idea was meant to give the baron a fresh impetus, to provide his friend with a new, uplifting goal, a chance to focus on his achievements rather than on the specter of the Nazis' success and their lingering designs on the Games.

Coubertin had been horribly conflicted over the extraordinary spectacle as the Games unfolded in Berlin. On the one hand, he was elated that the Olympic celebration had begun to reach the global dimensions he had envisioned from the beginning. He was joyous that more young people than ever were now competing—3,956 athletes from forty-nine nations had marched into the opening ceremonies, nearly a thousand more than Paris had drawn in 1924, the last Games he had presided over. Coubertin liked to repeat those numbers and occasionally write them down to consider their import as if they held some secret promise. At the very least, they indicated the growth of the Games.

But overriding that recognition and the good that came from the competition was the awful, undeniable fact that his Olympics had been turned into a compelling and wholly detestable propaganda platform for the Nazis, who had proven highly adept at manipulating the symbols of peace to cover and sanctify their own ends.

Coubertin had declined Hitler's repeated invitations to attend the Games. The chancellor had offered his private plane to fly the baron to Berlin. Hitler had even sent Carl Diem—one of Coubertin's oldest German sport allies—in his chauffeur-driven Mercedes-Benz as a final attempt to persuade the old man to come to the Games. Although he pointedly refused, Coubertin did record a radiogram for the opening and sent a message of congratulations for the closing. He was trapped in defending his great creation against the threat of political boycotts and the calls for the end of the Games after the Nazis' monstrous propaganda effort. But he did speak to the young, as he always had.

"And you, athletes, remember the flame lit by the ardor of the sun, that came to you from Olympia to shed light on us and to warm our age. Guard it jealously deep within you, so that it still burns bright on the other side of the world when you gather to celebrate the twelfth Olympiad in four years on the far-off shores of the great Pacific in Tokyo."

Otherwise, he kept his distance, knowing his presence would undermine the IOC's flagging authority. Once the flame was extinguished in Berlin, Coubertin fell into a mad depression for more than a month. Messerli knew he needed to find an antidote to lift his friend's spirit. The idea for the biography came to him then, but Coubertin was completely implacable in his resistance.

One night as they were dining together at la Grappe d'Or, a small, elegant restaurant off rue de Bourg, Messerli broached the subject again.

"I have no intention of entrusting my life story to anyone but myself," the old man said as Messerli gazed at him in the soft candlelight. But even as he spoke, his conviction was weak, his face shadowed in resignation. He didn't believe in his own story anymore.

"Pierre, my friend," Messerli started, a bit incensed, "you're not going to write it yourself—you're too caught up in your numerous projects, for God's sake. You're an incessant creator. Your ideas flow nonstop, but you're not disciplined—you're always trying to do more than you can. And that's why I'm worried. Who knows how much time we have left? We've got to find the right writer, and you've got to commit the time to take him through your life and work."

"My work?" Coubertin asserted with a distinct and unfamiliar note of bitterness. "My work is gone. It's all in the hands of a madman. My great dream is now the property of a fascist dictator who—"

"What are you talking about, Pierre?" Messerli asked, thinking the old man had turned paranoid. "Hitler has had his day in the Olympic arena. He isn't a threat any longer."

Coubertin looked at him, his face swelling with sadness as the story emerged.

○ ○ ○ ○ ○

Just a week before, Coubertin had left his apartment at Mon Repos, leaving the baroness and his daughter, Renée, bickering again at breakfast, and walked down the stairs to the offices of the IOC, a separate suite of rooms provided, just as his apartment was, at the largess of the city of Lausanne.

Mon Repos was an old château with estate grounds in the heart of Lausanne, a four-story mansion in a gated park shaded with century-old trees along a private drive. The municipality of Lausanne had purchased it some years before for public events and administration, with an apartment reserved for visiting dignitaries. Financially strained, Coubertin and his family had lived there for six years.

When he walked into the IOC offices that morning, Godefroy de Blonay was waiting for him, as he often was. A Swiss baron whose family owned the Grandson Castle, Blonay had been recruited by Coubertin to the IOC in 1899 as Switzerland's first member. He started the Swiss Olympic Committee and guided the development of the Lausanne Congress in 1913. And in 1915, when the baron moved the IOC headquarters from Paris to neutral Switzerland to ensure their security during the war, their friendship deepened—and Blonay served as interim president of the IOC while Coubertin returned to France to defend his country. With their shared aristocratic heritage, common love of sport, and devotion to the work of the IOC, they were natural allies.

But in 1920, when the IOC formed its first executive board—an effort to help make the organization more professional and move away from Coubertin's more or less autocratic rule—a rupture developed as Blonay gained authority as that board's first secretary general. It wasn't long before a power struggle erupted—and the women's issue became the fulcrum point the board used, in part, to loosen Coubertin's grip and push him toward retirement. Coubertin stood opposed to having women compete in the more strenuous competitions, particularly track and field events, while the board aligned with those espousing, even agitating for more women's events. Ironically, the last Games Coubertin oversaw as president—Paris 1924—witnessed the dramatic expansion of Olympic competition for women. Coubertin retired the next year in Prague, and Blonay became the chief liaison between Coubertin and the new president of the IOC, the Belgian count Henri de Baillet-Latour.

Somehow their friendship survived—and they had now spent years working together, off and on, along with the younger and more energetic Messerli, sorting out and cataloging all of the historic archives that Coubertin had shipped to Lausanne in 1915. After years of interaction, often intense and emotional, Coubertin knew Blonay well and could read his moods. If something needed to be said but couldn't be, or if some secret was being withheld, Blonay sometimes locked his jaw into rigidity, pressed his mouth together, and bit his lips while averting his eyes when Coubertin questioned him.

On this particular morning, all the tics and twitches were present. "What's wrong, Godefroy?" Coubertin asked. "What have you heard? Is there something Baillet-Latour needs?"

Coubertin was always anxious to provide his counsel to the president and the IOC's leadership, even when he knew it was unwanted. While he admired most of what Baillet-Latour had done to keep the Games on track through Amsterdam and Los Angeles, Coubertin had quickly recognized that the IOC and its president were outmatched by the National Socialists once they came to power and took over the organization of the Games. While giving lip service to Baillet-Latour's demands, they played him like a puppet under a master marionette. In Nazi hands, the Berlin Olympic Organizing Committee became a public relations platform for Joseph Goebbels, Hitler's minister of propaganda. The Games were forged in a crucible of international controversy and accusations of racism against the Nazis, with threats of boycotts dominating the headlines. Much to Coubertin's quiet embarrassment, the values of the Olympic Movement were compromised as the Nazis succeeded in putting on the most self-aggrandizing event in history.

Despite all the criticism that befell Baillet-Latour, Coubertin felt some sympathy for his old Belgian colleague; he knew he had tried, fruitlessly, to keep the Germans in check. He attempted to ensure the rights of all athletes were protected throughout the celebration and that discrimination was kept at bay. He failed on all fronts. Now that the Games were long over, the Germans remained more involved than they should have been, seeking, it seemed to Coubertin, a far greater role in the future of the movement than former organizers deserved.

Blonay bent over behind the desk that separated them, lifting some files from the floor, avoiding eye contact, biting his lip.

"It's nothing that concerns you, Pierre. Let's just focus on these files from Le Havre." They were going through every file in every box, one by one, sorting out the personal papers Pierre had mixed in with the official documents over the years.

"It's the Germans, isn't it?" Coubertin said, eliciting a swift look of confirmation from Blonay. He was surprised, no doubt, or suspicious that the baron might have heard something already.

"Baillet-Latour and I spoke over the weekend. A German delegation came to his office in Brussels and proposed a few ideas for the future."

Coubertin's heart sank as his fears rose. He looked up at his friend, hoping his resignation wasn't fully apparent. Blonay most certainly wanted to tell him the full story—that their movement was under threat from the Nazis. Controlling the Olympics had always been a struggle and always will be, Coubertin thought.

"Who was in the delegation?"

"It was von Halt, von Tschammer und Osten, and Diem."

Coubertin knew who they were. Dr. Ritter von Halt was the Nazi who had led the Berlin Olympic Organizing Committee and become a German IOC member. Hans von Tschammer und Osten was president of the German National Olympic Committee. Carl Diem was its secretary general, once an ally and dear friend of Coubertin's who was now trapped by history and serving the will of the National Socialists. The Olympic torch relay from Olympia to Berlin had been Diem's idea, and it was carried off brilliantly. Nevertheless, Coubertin regretted Diem's opportunism even as he understood the pressure on the man, who was extremely capable.

"And what was it they proposed?"

"They were there representing Hitler," Blonay said. "It was his ideas they were presenting."

"Yes, of course, they were speaking for the Führer," Coubertin said, his displeasure evident.

"Hitler has commissioned his architect, Albert Speer, to design a new Olympic stadium, with even more grandeur than the one that held a hundred thousand in Berlin. They're essentially planning to create a permanent home for the Games, a modern German Olympia."

"Oh my God." Coubertin tried to laugh at this ridiculous notion, but he was closer to tears than laughter. He felt so powerless. "And what did Henri say to this?"

"Henri is not the man he once was," Blonay said frankly, "not even the man he was a year ago. There's more. It was all outlined in a paper presented by Diem."

Coubertin listened in disbelief as Blonay told him Hitler intended to move the IOC headquarters to Berlin and completely rejuvenate the organization by appointing new leadership. Hitler planned to create a new Olympic celebration, manipulating the symbolism of the Games to serve his own ends. Coubertin took each despicable idea as a rejection of the principles of the Olympic Charter and the values that had guided the movement since its founding. And yet Baillet-Latour had evidently approved the concepts in whole, without objection.

Oh, Henri, Coubertin thought, my protégé, my friend, what have you done?

As Baillet-Latour's physical strength had faltered and weakened, Coubertin knew his presidency had weakened as well. To have even allowed such abhorrent ideas into discussion—and then to not have dismissed them immediately—was pure cowardice. Baillet-Latour had lost all perspective. Even though the Nazis had controlled him during the Games, he had on occasion asserted the authority of the IOC, demanding at one point the removal of their anti-Semitic signage and getting his way. Coubertin knew Henri had once directly rebuked Hitler over a point they had argued, telling him as they entered the stadium that under the five-ringed flag, this ground was now Olympia—and in Olympia, the IOC ruled.

Whatever resistance Baillet-Latour had once shown was clearly gone now. Coubertin well knew that the obvious successors to IOC leadership, the most influential gatekeepers waiting in the wings—Sigfrid Edström of Sweden and Avery Brundage of the United States—were both enraptured with the power of the National Socialists. They both tended to sympathize with the Nazis' arrogance if not their philosophy.

Coubertin dropped his head. The future of his Games belonged not to its rightful heirs, but to those who envisioned the world under the Third Reich.

○ ○ ○ ○ ○

"So you see, Francis," Coubertin said, looking across the dinner table at Messerli with defeat in his eyes, "what started as a great movement for peace through sport has become a tragedy in the making."

Messerli felt the anger rising, a vehement voice inside saying this can't be. All the years and effort and money and vision that Coubertin had invested in this movement could not now become the property of the Third Reich. No, it couldn't be, he couldn't let it be.

Incensed that the fighter in Coubertin—the most relentless battler and smartest political operative Messerli had ever known—was throwing in the towel, Messerli spoke more loudly than he intended, taking the baron by surprise. "The greatest tragedy is not that Hitler has control of your Games for the moment. No, the greater tragedy, as I see it, is that your story has been lost and that the meaning of your movement is threatened. It is time to rally, Pierre, not quit. You're a genius, my friend, and the world needs to know it." At that moment, Messerli realized he was speaking the truth—and that Pierre's story, the biography Messerli had in mind, was far more than therapy for a fading leader. He suddenly realized he had to produce this book *now*, that the story itself might be the best weapon the IOC would have to fight the Nazis for control.

"Ah, Francis," Pierre said, "you are among the best of men and certainly my best friend, but we're two old men sitting around a table—well, one old man relying on the excessive generosity of a slightly younger old man, just keeping up appearances. There is nothing left for me to tell ... and my story won't make a difference now."

"It will, Pierre, and not just now, but for a century to come," Messerli said with conviction. "Yes, you're broke, yes, there's little hope right now, and yes, you're faced with an overwhelming enemy. But what you've done, the ideal you've created, is far greater than the destructive power of a political movement that seems based on hate."

"We both believe, Pierre," he continued, "and I only believe because you have convinced me of it, that this great movement will one day reach into every town, village, and hamlet on earth. And when it does, I want to be sure your name is known."

3

JACQUES AND JULIETTE

edaling hard on his De Dion-Bouton, Jacques St. Clair raced across the Seine on the pont au Change and coursed through Place Saint-Michel, the January air numbing his fingers, his lips stiffening in the breeze. He scarcely felt it; dashing like a courier on a mission, carrying an epistle that held a promise he would soon share with the woman he loved.

Juliette, he knew, would be painting in her atelier. Either that or she would be singing in the shower. Her mother was an actress in Philadelphia and had taught her daughter to love Broadway show tunes. It was one of Juliette's most endearing characteristics—she was always ready to perform. They lived in an apartment on the sixth floor of a building on rue de Medicis. The front overlooked the Luxembourg Gardens, where they'd met three years ago just weeks after she had arrived from Philly. But it wasn't the view that had made Juliette insist on this place, more expensive than they had planned. No, it was the back room with the French doors and large windows that captured the afternoon light. It was the best room in the apartment, and Juliette immediately claimed it as her studio.

As the gardens came into view, St. Clair remembered the morning they met.

"Why are you circling me?" she had asked on the third day in a row that he had deliberately ridden near enough to make eye contact with her, violating the common courtesy most cyclists extended to those walking the paths through the Luxembourg.

18

He had watched her walk on her morning rounds for a week, noting how she kept a quick pace and threw her hips wide for speed. Her gait looked a touch exaggerated and drew some stares, which she didn't seem to mind. She wore a beret, but her short, tight jacket and pants told him she was an American. Her outfit accented the lovely shape of her derriere, which caught St. Clair's eye the first time he cycled past her on the way to work. He watched her at a distance at first, wondering about the backpack she wore, and then saw her stop a few times to pull out a sketch pad, sit, and go to work. Once he watched her for a while at the Fountain of the Observatory, sketching the Jean-Baptiste Carpeaux statue of four women holding up the world. Although he rode by repeatedly, he couldn't capture her attention. Finally, after no success driving by and smiling at her, he began to circle her, drawing progressively closer with each revolution until she stopped.

"Well, since I'm a Frenchman, it was important that you spoke to me first," he said, stopping and straddling the bike as she looked him over.

"Oh, you're French," she said. "I thought Frenchmen were more sophisticated in their approach to women. Shouldn't you be offering me a new purse or some kind of seductive gift?"

He laughed. "Yes, I'm French, and you're an American—and I would gladly give you a seductive gift if I could afford one."

"Oh, so you have no money?" she said, breaking into a wide grin. She looked at the bike, which was clean and glistening, and his clothes and tie, which he hoped suggested a profession at minimum. He would later learn that she hadn't met any Frenchmen her age yet, just a few old men from her mother's expat circle—and that her art classes weren't scheduled to start for another week.

"Well, maybe *un peu*—a little bit, but—"

"Well then, maybe I'll speak to you again tomorrow," she said, walking away.

He let her go. But the next day at almost the same time and place, he was circling again, and she appeared glad to see him.

"I have found enough change to buy you a cup of coffee," he said.

"You'll have to do better than that," she said, striding off.

"Well, tomorrow is payday," he said, following on his bike. "Perhaps I can squeeze in a croissant."

She stopped and turned to look at him more closely again, as if trying to decide if he were handsome enough for her. "And who pays you?"

"*Le Petit Journal.*"

"Ah, you're a newspaper man, then?"

"A sports writer," he said, using an American term.

"Then let's meet tomorrow for a coffee and a croissant," she said, turning to go.

The next morning they walked over to a tiny café by Saint-Sulpice a few blocks from the garden. They talked for two hours. That night, they met for dinner, and they had been nearly inseparable ever since.

○ ○ ○ ○ ○

St. Clair parked his Dion-Bouton and entered the building. Rather than ride the lift, he climbed the six flights of stairs, fulfilling a daily promise to exercise wherever he could, and entered their apartment.

"*Bonjour*," she called from her studio as he walked in, dropping his satchel and coat and pulling out the letter. She was seated on a sofa with a sheet draped over it, stained a hundred times by her careless brush. She looked at the work in progress on an easel before her and then back at him.

"What's that?" she asked, extending her long, fine paintbrush like a pointer, circling the tip in the direction of the letter. She stood and moved to him.

"This? This is our future," he said, kissing her as she took the letter and smudged it with a blue thumbprint. "Are you interested, mademoiselle," he asked, "in an adventure to a far-off land where your canvases will be filled with new vistas and your lover will write an important book?"

She plopped back on the couch and unfolded the pages, looking at Messerli's script, and quickly became absorbed in the story. "Yes, of course I am. This sounds like a marvelous opportunity."

While she continued reading, St. Clair turned to the kitchen counter and uncorked a bottle of red.

"Baron Pierre de Coubertin," she said. "I don't think I've heard of him."

"You're not alone. But like millions of others, you do know what he has done."

"The Olympic Games, of course—and I see the point this Dr. Messerli is making," she said, waving the letter. "But is this a good story? What's it about?"

St. Clair sat next to her, nudging her aside, hoping none of the paint on the sheet was still wet. He had carried into the office a good many color swatches on his ass without knowing it—and had, therefore, been the butt of one too many jokes. He put two short, round glasses on the low table covered with her tubes of oils, cans of brushes, blades, and rags, and filled them both with Côtes du Rhône.

"I think it could be a great story," he said. "He's a very small man like Napoleon, but he moved mountains to resurrect the Games. I'm not sure if he's a hero yet, but I'm pretty sure this could be a heroic story."

They raised their glasses in a toast and drank to all the possibilities. They had been talking about the idea of traveling together for some time now, and they had actually planned a route down through Switzerland to Rome. She was ready for something new—maybe even more than he was.

"How soon can you leave *Le Journal*?" she asked. "When will you talk to the doctor? If we can make a break, I'll start packing right away."

○ ○ ○ ○ ○

Messerli was surprised at how quickly St. Clair—and his American fiancée—agreed to his proposal and made their travel plans. Barely three weeks later, at the end of the first week in February, the doctor cleared a few days on his schedule. That morning, instead of going to his office at the University of Lausanne, where he was head of the School of Medicine, he had stayed home. After a leisurely brunch with his wife, who left to watch over their granddaughters, he spent a few hours collecting his thoughts and making notes for St. Clair. He didn't intend to tell this seasoned journalist how to approach the biography, but he did want to suggest a way to approach Pierre. He wondered how St. Clair would react to the notion that part of his responsibility was to inspire the old man, to provide a little therapy along with the writing.

The time came to meet the writer. After donning his overcoat, bowler, and gloves, he grabbed his walking stick and pocketed the key to the cottage he had rented for St. Clair. Inside the front door of his town home, he took a quick look in the coat-rack mirror before heading out and was glad the hat covered his balding pate. His clean-shaven face was too fleshy, he thought, but he still felt young and vital. He smiled at himself, pleased he had drawn St. Clair and his fiancée to Lausanne for what could easily be the most important project he'd ever undertaken.

Messerli walked at a good pace from his town house near the Savoy Hotel up the hill of avenue d'Ouchy, under the railroad overpass to the avenue de la Gare, and left to the train station in the center of Lausanne. The streets were full of people and cars, buses, and trolleys. He nodded to people he knew and even to strangers, a practice he had picked up from Coubertin, and entered the great hall of the train station at precisely 3:00 p.m., glancing up at the giant clock mounted beneath the pediment of Le Grand Gare. With ten minutes before the arrival of St. Clair's train, Messerli moved casually to the back door and glanced across the platforms on the eight tracks covered with waiting crowds. A woman was kneeling nearby, daubing her child's tears with a tissue. He strolled over to the kiosk against the back wall and considered the case of croissants, *pain au chocolat*, and *beignets*, fingered a copy of *Le Matin*, and glanced at an international headline he had read that morning, another report on Neville Chamberlain's campaign for prime minister of Great Britain.

The train arrived in a roar on the fourth track. Messerli watched the passengers disembark, recognizing at once the young blond countenance and athletic look of St. Clair, wrapped in a tight black jacket, wearing a beret, and effortlessly carrying two thick suitcases as if they were filled with air. St. Clair looked around for someone familiar and made eye contact with Messerli, who waved across the tracks as the journalist smiled, set his suitcases down, and turned back to the train, reaching up to help a young woman in a long red coat step down, another small suitcase in her hand and a large purse over her shoulder. She looked up as St. Clair spoke to her and gestured toward Messerli. The doctor was immediately struck by her beauty and the glow of her smile as she waved in friendly anticipation. St. Clair hopped back on the train and emerged with a shiny bicycle balanced on his shoulder. He bore it with a practiced ease as he picked up the suitcases, moved to the stairs, and disappeared with his fiancée.

Messerli was there to greet them as they came out of the tunnel, offering his hand to St. Clair. "Monsieur St. Clair, it is a pleasure to meet you."

"Dr. Messerli," the young man said, his eyes glistening with excitement, seemingly impressed with the stature and distinguished appearance of his host. "Please call me Jacques, and may I present my fiancée, Juliette Franklin."

"So pleased to meet you, Mademoiselle Franklin. May I please …" Messerli reached for her suitcase and turned them both toward the exit, making small talk. "I trust your travels were comfortable."

"Thank you, sir," she replied sweetly. "Yes, the trip was pleasant. And it's certainly a pleasure to meet you. We've both anticipated this moment"—she paused to draw him in—"as if it were an answered prayer."

St. Clair laughed, and Messerli saw that her reference to piety was a quip. Perhaps she liked to play the comedienne. The doctor grinned. He was pleased. They were both polite and friendly and, despite the distance and wearying train travel, excited to be here. He could sense immediately that they were both deeply pleased with the opportunity.

Outside, Messerli guided them into a cab and they headed for Ouchy. "Let's get you settled into the apartment I've rented on the lake. I hope it suits you."

"I'm sure it will," St. Clair said. "We're quite happy to be here."

On the short route to the lake, Messerli learned a little more about Juliette's arrival in Paris, her painting, and how Jacques had "accosted her" with his bike in the Luxembourg Gardens just after she got off the boat from Philadelphia.

From the road where the taxi left them, they carried the luggage down a set of stone steps through a garden to a small outbuilding on the side of an impressive château. As they approached the salmon-colored two-story structure between high, well-groomed hedges, Messerli guided them on the path around the house, where they emerged on a grass terrace with a low stone wall. From this perch over the treetops on the falling hill below, the views of Lake Geneva and the Alps across the water were breathtaking. Behind them, a set of French doors opened onto a patio of pavers inlaid in the terrace. A round iron table and chairs sat on the patio.

"Oh my God," exclaimed Juliette. "This is utterly gorgeous! Is this our little house?" Messerli laughed at her enthusiasm, and Jacques quickly set down his bags and bicycle to receive her excited embrace as she skipped over to him.

"This was the gardener's house," Messerli said, leading them in through the front door, "but the Zwiefels, the family in the château, who happen to be my patients, decided to turn it into a guesthouse last year."

"It's perfect," St. Clair said as he and Juliette looked over the kitchen and the brocaded furniture and peeked into the bedroom. Beams ran across the ceiling of the bright central room, which drew in the sun's glow through the French doors.

Juliette fingered the heavy country print on the drapes at the doors and gazed out in disbelief. Without taking her eyes from the view, she said, "Your letter to Jacques, Dr. Messerli, was a thrill to both of us, since we were hoping to find an adventure, a new direction for our life together."

"Well," Dr. Messerli said, "we all have a mission before us—" But before he could continue, Juliette was at his side, hugging him and kissing him on the cheek.

Blushing a touch, he excused himself. He urged them to get settled in and arranged to meet St. Clair in the morning at the café at the Hôtel Angleterre. "Just follow the path down the hill and turn right at the seawall. It's only a few blocks away."

As he crossed the patio on the way back up to the path, Messerli glanced at the French doors and saw the young couple in a deep, romantic embrace. He headed to the office quite confident that St. Clair would have no trouble making the adjustment to life in Lausanne.

4

THE VISTA

When he woke and opened his bedroom curtains the next morning, Messerli beheld the brilliance of a bright blue sky that gave the surface of the lake a shimmering aquamarine dazzle. He dressed quickly, had a coffee, kissed his wife goodbye as she was coming down to the breakfast table, and headed off to collect St. Clair for their meeting.

"Change of venue," he said to St. Clair at the Café Angleterre. "I want to show you the site where Pierre and I had our first meeting—on a brilliant sunny day like this."

They took a taxi up to the Abbaye de l'Arc, higher on the Lausanne hillside, and walked out onto the terrace café, where the panoramic view of Lake Geneva and the Alps was even more spectacular. They could see east to the end of the lake and the Fraubourg peaks where the valley opened up toward Verbier and Zermatt and the Italian border to the south. And to the southwest they could see rows of white mountains staggered in the distance, their majestic shoulders obscuring the glories of Mont Blanc as they marched toward Grenoble and the South of France beyond it.

Messerli seated himself at a table on the terrace and ordered chocolate croissants and cappuccino while St. Clair settled in next to him, facing the stunning landscape to the south. Out on the lake a flock of seagulls swirled around a few fishing boats bobbing gently on the glistening water.

"How's the place? Everything okay, Jacques?"

"I'm not accustomed to having a client," the writer said, "but I already feel a deep sense of gratitude for what you've done and what you've provided. If this is the life of a writer in residence, then this will be my profession from now on. Juliette and I could not be happier—and I am truly looking forward to meeting Baron de Coubertin."

"Well, your availability and commitment to this biography mean the world to me." Messerli decided to dispense with the courtesies. "I don't know what protocols you'd like to follow, but I'm assuming we'll establish a schedule of interviews with Pierre, then you'll begin to write and we'll confer and review what you do. Eventually, his life story will take shape. Does that sound reasonable?"

"That's the method I would have recommended if you'd asked me," St. Clair said. "I've built my career doing profiles based on interviews, but I'll also have to do a significant amount of research for this book."

"I'm sure you will. The IOC archives are at Mon Repos in the heart of the city, where Pierre lives and keeps an office. And Pierre is an encyclopedia—and not just on sport. He's written a three-volume history of the world, *l'Histoire Universelle,* so there are few subjects he isn't conversant in to some degree. He started out with an exceptional Jesuit education in the classics and he has never stopped learning. Erudition may be his greatest strength."

"That's quite obvious when you look into his publishing history," St. Clair said. "In addition to the Olympic books you sent me, I have copies of *The Evolution of France under the Third Republic* and the novel he wrote under the *nom de plume* Georges Hohrod, *One Rally*, which seems to be fairly autobiographical—plus a few dozen articles from *Le Figaro* and others. He is impressively prolific."

"Yes, he is—or he was," Messerli said.

They both paused and took in the view.

"Dr. Messerli," St. Clair began, "I've been thinking about how to approach this book since your letter arrived. On the surface, it's easy to think of this as the story of the man who created the world's greatest sporting event. Given the rising prominence of the Olympics, that's a story worth telling since so few really know much about him. That appeared to be the intent of his *Olympic Memoirs*—which was clearly not his best effort. But it strove to establish, rightfully, no doubt, that he was at the center of every major milestone in the history of the movement. You cannot read it and reach any conclusion but one: without Baron Pierre de Coubertin, there would be no Olympic Games today."

"I think that's a justifiable conclusion. Don't you?"

"Yes, I do, on the basis of the documents and story we have today. It's even more evident in his *21-Year Campaign*, which is a better piece of writing. I'm not suggesting that I'm in any doubt about the authenticity of either story, but we have work to do, and that work will involve looking deeply into the origins of the baron's idea of the modern Games—and the movement."

"Agreed. I think that's part and parcel of the work ahead. But the larger story from my perspective is the story of the man. His life, his vision, his work."

"That's the very point I was trying to make," St. Clair said. "The Games are the easy part—the sporting record is all there—it's the story of the man who created them that holds the mystery. We'll have to examine his motivations, the ideas and forces that shaped his values, the society he was born into, the fading power of the aristocracy, and the birth of the Third Republic and how that affected him."

Messerli was excited by the scope of St. Clair's interest. "You're obviously thinking this should be a very thorough history of his times, an in-depth biography."

"Dr. Messerli, my entire professional life has been wrapped in the here and now, in the details of the moment as it unfolds in the arena. It's been all about the immediacy of sport. The knockout punch. I've moved here to change all that, not only because I think the Coubertin story is as important as you think it is—I do—but because the broader challenge interests me. I want to see if my talents are equal to the *Tour de Page* we're talking about, and if I can make the leap from sports reporter to a writer capable of a major biography."

"It seems my letter arrived at just the right moment."

"The timing could not have been more propitious."

"Well then, it's as I hoped it would be," Messerli said. "Our interests are fully aligned."

"I think that's true," St. Clair said, "but just to be honest, I want you to know that I'll follow the story where it leads. There's something very tragic in the current circumstances of his life and it reminds me, sadly, of so many sports profiles I've written over the years—stories of great athletes who fall on hard times after their careers are over, after their gifts are gone and the sounds of the crowds have faded away."

St. Clair's description of the fading hero produced a jolt of emotion in Messerli and he had to stare at the vista and concentrate to keep his eyes dry. He was filled with an affirmation that the work they were launching was part of his life's purpose—and he was already certain that St. Clair was the right writer. But he also felt a shadow looming, even in the sunlight, a knowing sadness that they were starting this journey a little late, maybe too late to complete it. He collected himself and said, "Well, it's clear you've already looked beyond the pages of his books. That's encouraging."

"I know people in Paris who know him—or knew him—and know some things about his life today," St. Clair said. "They all seem to respect him, but they consider it tragic—his wife is evidently unkind to him and I understand he's basically broke."

Messerli grimaced. "Your friends in Paris are right. He's lost everything, financially and personally. It's true his wife hectors him and deprives him of even pocket money. His son is mentally retarded and his daughter, his one hope, is too often under the influence of the baroness. He calls them the Cat and the Bird. They're living at Mon Repos—an old château owned by the city that Lausanne basically provides for them at no cost. I don't know what they'd do without it."

"That's tragic, but I'm going to have to interview the baroness—she's half the story."

"That's complicated, Jacques. She's very mercurial, sometimes unstable. I'm not sure she'll cooperate. Her anger ... well, let's just say she can be very vehement."

"She must have a softer side."

"Yes, she can put on a show in public—but Dr. Jekyll seldom appears. It's Mr. Hyde most of the time."

"That's a cruel analogy. But I've dealt with lots of difficult characters over the years—and I can't write this story without her. Even if she's filled with rage. Makes the story more interesting."

Messerli had an anxious moment, wondering whether he had made a mistake, but the notion passed quickly. He didn't believe the baroness would undermine the story—she had a legacy to protect as well. And even if she tried, the truth would rise. And the truth would elevate Coubertin's reputation. He decided then and there that he would support St. Clair fully, wherever the story took him. The important thing was to get the book written. "I understand," he said. "I wouldn't ask you to compromise your professional ethics."

"I'm glad to hear that, because this biography is going to have to answer a simple but very tragic question."

"Which is?"

"How did a man who gave the world so much end up with so little—or more to the point, how did a man who gave the world something so idealistic end up in such a sad personal state?"

"I think, when you start the interviews, you're going to find—despite the current circumstances—the story of his life is filled with inspiration."

"I'm sure that's true. But what happened to his family?" St. Clair asked. "They were rich, weren't they? Doesn't the IOC have a fund? It seems they should. He is the founder."

That note of compassion was exactly what Messerli was hoping for. "It's all gone," he explained. "He's not close to his brother, Paul—in fact, they're alienated. Paul sold the Château de Mirville five years ago, which broke Pierre's heart. As a boy, it was his favorite spot in the world. His wife's money is depleted as well—she had a respectable inheritance when they were married. And no, the IOC is basically a volunteer organization. There's no real fundraising. A few of the IOC members tried to provide some money, but Pierre won't accept financial charity. He knows that we keep accounts for him at several restaurants—like the Croix d'Ouchy—so he can entertain guests. But otherwise he resists any gifts."

Messerli moved on toward his point. "Physically, he appears to be strong. He stays in shape, does rather strenuous exercises for his age, but he's been weakened psychologically by the continuing blows to his personal esteem— and the threats to his great work."

"Threats to his great work? What threats?"

"I'll get to that, but first I want you to consider his state of mind. Think about it. He came from a family of aristocrats with a fortune that should have lasted for a few more generations, but he exhausted it all pursuing his great campaign for the Games. And now he can't provide for simple things. He can't find any paying work. Can you imagine how humiliating it has been for him to search for a job—and be turned down everywhere?"

"For an aristocrat that *would* be humiliating. Where has he looked?"

"He talked to a few bankers and some old industrialists who politely declined his entreaties," Messerli said. "Closer to home, he even tried to secure a spot managing the Lausanne Palace Hotel, which hosts a good number of Olympic guests—and they turned him down." He paused, letting the gravity of the situation register with St. Clair. "And that leads to something else I wanted to discuss with you—not a favor exactly, but something I think could be important to Pierre."

"Go ahead," St. Clair said. "We're going to have to be completely open with each other."

"I think your interviews can serve a dual purpose. I think they can be therapeutic," Messerli said. "Our first objective, of course, is to record his memories and write his biography. But the interview process itself can be ... no, should be, therapeutic for him—at least that's my hope. Do your work. Take him back through the halls of memory—as far back as you can—and have him re-create the life he's lived, and try to encourage him, psychologically, through the process."

"I understand. I'm not a therapist, but I know what you're asking for. I've seen the interview process work that way a good number of times, especially with older men whose glory days are long forgotten. They do respond to the interest."

"I want him to think about what he's accomplished," Messerli said, "rather than what he's failed to do. I don't like to say this, but I'm confiding in you and I want you to know your work here is urgent. I have a sense he's nearing the end, and the situation developing in Berlin is stealing his final thread of hope. It seems the Nazis have laid plans to take control of the IOC and make the Olympic Games a permanent celebration of the Third Reich. Pierre feels helpless to confront either the leadership of the IOC, who give only lip service to his counsel, or the Nazis. God help us if they take control of the IOC."

"That's the threat, is it? It's that serious?"

"Yes, it's that serious. I don't want to tell you how to do your work. God knows you're one of the most acclaimed sports writers in the world, and I don't want you pandering to him. But if there's any way for you to give him the sense that you—a writer I know he deeply respects—also respect him and believe the world needs to hear his story, that could help. We need to restore his belief in himself and give him a mission that will carry him toward the future."

"Certainly, Doctor. I'll do what I can. The depth of my interest is genuine— and it's already grown significantly just talking to you. Now, if you don't mind, I want to start the interview process. I've got a few questions for you."

Messerli had wondered if St. Clair would take this approach. "Fine. What would you like to know?"

"I'd like to start today with a little background on your relationship." St. Clair took out his notebook and a pen. "Tell me about the first time you met."

Messerli looked out at the lake again and remembered sitting at this very spot with Pierre. They had met a few days before, as he recalled. "It was a Friday afternoon in October of 1908, and I was in the gym at the Gymnastics Club of Lausanne teaching a class. I remember the scene quite clearly."

As Messerli began to describe that first encounter, it pleased him to see St. Clair taking detailed notes—notes that were later drafted into one of the first passages of Coubertin's biography:

Francis Messerli, a twenty-year-old medical student, was turning in circles in the middle of a group of boys jogging on a parquet floor in a wide arc around him as they warmed up for a lesson at the Gymnastics Club of Lausanne. In the next hour, he would run them through a series of calisthenics, tumbling, rope climbing, rings, and parallel bar exercises. Messerli was tall, with an athletic build, and in good condition from his own gymnastics practice. Dressed in a white gym suit and canvas shoes, he had a full head of dark hair over a clean-shaven, square face. The fact that he was in this gym on a Friday afternoon, volunteering as a coach for a group of local boys, told something of his values, and of his appreciation for sport.

"Come on, boys, pick it up. Five more minutes," he said, looking at the stopwatch dangling from his neck. The pace quickened. His commands were respected because he was the son of Arthur Messerli, the Swiss gymnastics champion who brought fame to this club as he earned plaudits on the national and international stage.

Halfway through the session, while the boys were taking turns doing mounts and dismounts on the parallel bars and Messerli was spotting them, the double door to the gym opened, squeaking as it always did. Messerli glanced over his shoulder to see a small gentleman enter, hat and walking stick in hand, and take a position against the wall, observing without interrupting.

At the end of the workout, as the boys were stacking the mats in a pile by the wall, the man approached Messerli and introduced himself. "Hello there," he said. "That was an impressive lesson, particularly the reverse dismounts."

"Thank you, sir," Messerli replied, shaking his hand. "Do you know gymnastics?"

"A little," the man said. "I'm Baron Pierre de Coubertin and I'm delighted to make your acquaintance, young man."

"Francis Messerli, sir," he said, and just then he realized he knew the name. "Are you *le Rénovateur* of the Olympic Games?"

The gentleman smiled broadly. "I am indeed. Have you followed the Games in London this year?"

"Yes, I have, particularly the gymnastics competition."

"Ah yes. Braglia, the Italian, was splendid in the all-around. Your students would have loved him."

Surprised that he was suddenly in an Olympic conversation with such a prominent man, Messerli fell back on the obvious question. "What brings you to Lausanne—and to this gym?"

"I'm here on a scouting trip at the invitation of Godefroy de Blonay—perhaps you know him? His family owns Grandson Castle."

"Yes, my father knows him and his family. He's head of the Swiss Olympic Committee."

"That's right, and with Godefroy's help, I'm planning to organize an international Olympic congress here in a few years. I've come to look over the facilities and learn what I can about how sports are organized and administered here. I heard this was one of the finest clubs in Lausanne."

"Well, thank you, sir," said Messerli. Impulsively, he asked, "Have you met the mayor?"

"I have not yet had the pleasure," Coubertin said, raising his eyebrows.

"Perhaps I can help with an introduction or two. I do know the sports community here quite well."

"Excellent. Do you have time for a cup of coffee and a brief discussion?"

"Not today—I'm on my way to a meeting of the student union. I'm studying medicine at the university. But tomorrow morning I'm free."

"I'm staying at the Beau Rivage. Could you call on me there?"

"I'd be happy to."

That night, Messerli couldn't escape the feeling that he'd been granted access to the high courts of international sport, a heady feeling for a young man with such a deep family connection to gymnastics. The next morning, when he picked up Coubertin at the Beau Rivage Hotel in Ouchy, he felt as if he were on a mission, and it was almost a sacred duty to help *le Rénovateur* pursue his Olympic goals. Messerli took the baron by taxi up to the archery club, the Abbaye de l'Arc, to show him another dimension of Lausanne's greatest quality—the vistas of Lac Leman and the Alps to the south.

As Messerli told the story of their first encounter—how Coubertin had spent an hour asking questions and taking extensive notes about the sports structure of the city and his own club—he hoped St. Clair was beginning to understand that the baron was an athlete of organization. He was a master planner, a man with the drive to create schemes and strategies to implement his vision step by step, a producer who arranged every detail to ensure the moment was right.

After several hours, Messerli found himself growing a bit impatient with the recollections. He realized how quickly interviews could digress into minutiae. But he felt he had formed a bond with St. Clair, a kind of business partnership overlaid with a personal connection. He had no doubt he could trust the man. His writing always strived to bring out the good in people, and Messerli felt certain St. Clair carried a large reservoir of good within as well.

As they were wrapping up their first long session together, Messerli stood, stretched his arms above his head, hunched his shoulders, and waited for St. Clair. They walked around the building in silence, descending the steps toward a taxi waiting to take them back to the city.

St. Clair spoke at last. "Dr. Messerli, if you don't mind my asking, why are you doing this? I've seen people rally before around their old athletic heroes when they fall in decline or go broke, but I've never seen anyone go to this length."

Messerli stopped at the bottom of the steps, considered the question for a minute, then looked squarely at St. Clair. "I owe him so much," he said. "He opened up a new world for me. He's taught me more about life, values, sport, and friendship than anyone. He's made my life far richer than it would have been without him. And he's given our world something rare—sport with a global mission. But it's probably a lot simpler than that. The truth is he's my best friend, and I don't want to lose him. When you meet him tomorrow, I think you'll understand."

5

THE MEETING

S t. Clair sat inside the Angleterre, watching as Messerli and Coubertin approached, walking along the quay across the street, waiting for a few vehicles to pass before crossing. Standing in the winter sunlight next to Messerli, who stood around six feet and carried two hundred pounds on a wide frame, Coubertin appeared to be even smaller than St. Clair remembered him on that day in Paris in the tuxedo. He was five foot three, shorter than average, but he looked at least a foot shorter than Messerli as they moved in tandem toward the café. After they entered, however, Coubertin's stature seemed to grow as he inhaled deeply and his face broadened into a wide and graceful expression of pleasure. He had his gloves off and held his walking stick on his left as he moved swiftly and directly up to St. Clair, holding his eyes while nodding and greeting him with a gracious note of aplomb.

"So I am finally in the presence of the great sports writer from Paris," Coubertin said. "I have been anticipating this moment."

St. Clair rose and took his outstretched hand. "Well, sir," he said, "any greatness in this room belongs to you alone."

The old man nodded again, glanced at Messerli, and laughed. "A charmer as well, I see."

Messerli shook St. Clair's hand and gestured for them to sit.

Coubertin continued in the same vein. "Well, Monsieur St. Clair," he said, "in my assessment—and I have managed to study the art of sports writing for some years now—your work stands alone, so I am pleased that the good doctor here has somehow persuaded you to come to Lausanne to help me with my memoir."

"That's very kind of you, Baron de Coubertin. Please call me Jacques."

"I'd be delighted to, Jacques, if you will reciprocate. I'm Pierre to my friends."

St. Clair noticed that the frock coat Coubertin unbuttoned was slightly worn, its velvet collar frayed at the edge, and that the fedora he placed on the table had obviously served him well for many years. Despite the aged fabrics, he was impeccably attired in the style of a true French gentleman, with a gray wool suit over a waistcoat, a starched white collar folded over the Windsor knot of his tie, and black boots nicely polished though cracked from years of wear. As Coubertin laid his arm on the table, his white French cuff just clearing his jacket sleeve, St. Clair's eye fell on the black cufflink that matched the color of his buttons. His nails were unpolished, not manicured but neatly cut, his white mustache was perfectly trimmed, and the hat hadn't disturbed his neatly parted hair. The scent of a pleasant aftershave wafted by.

"It's an honor for me to have the chance to work with you," St. Clair said, "and, hopefully, to write the story about how you managed to resurrect the Games and how this international movement came into being."

"It's a long and detailed story," Coubertin said, "with a good deal of educational theory and reform and the standardization of sport. Quite frankly, despite your gifts and Dr. Messerli's determination"—he paused and grimaced—"I'm not sure the world is really interested."

"You'll get no argument from me that if we focus on educational theory and if the structure of our story covers the evolution of the rules of rowing"—St. Clair motioned out toward the lake—"there isn't going to be much magic on the page—"

"Well," Coubertin interrupted, "in the halls of Henley, the superiority of the coxed versus the uncoxed eight can certainly generate a heated debate."

They all laughed lightly at the esoteric distinctions of sport.

"True enough," said St. Clair, "but that's not the story I've come here to write. I want to write the story of a man who gave everything he had to impart to the world a vision for celebrating together what I believe you call 'the eternal springtime of youth.'"

"And you're telling me there's magic in that story?"

"There's more than magic. There's truth," said St. Clair, and Coubertin's eyes narrowed. "And that truth is threatened right now, which gives us some drama."

St. Clair decided to do what he often did in interviews with older subjects who expressed doubt—he decided to make physical contact. He glanced briefly at Messerli, then leaned forward and put his hand over Pierre's forearm. "I know a little about your personal life at this point—not much, but I've read your *Olympic Memoirs* and your *21-Year Campaign*. I'm fairly well convinced that the humanity of your story—the struggle, the isolation, the odds and opposition you had to face, even at times the humiliation—would have sent most men away crying. But you, like a great athlete, never quit, never let any defeat deter you from your goal—and that goal, in my opinion, is worthy of the recognition I hope the story we develop will ultimately deliver."

"Well, my young friend," Coubertin responded, breaking the weight of the moment, "I see you have a passion for your work. I very much appreciate those sentiments. What did you think of my *Memoirs*?"

St. Clair took a moment before answering. "Let me be honest. They provide a fairly good basis for the behind-the-scenes administrative work you did. They answer some questions *prima facie* about your commitment to education. They give me a superficial sense of how you organized the Sorbonne Congress and resurrected the Games, of who was in the room, and of how you created the atmosphere. Over the years, I can see what drove the host city decisions, why you staged the larger congresses when you did, and how you determined their content. I can even see the growth and, to some degree, the personalities of the IOC. But the real story is missing. Dr. Messerli is right."

"You're saying it's too factual and not sufficiently personal?"

"Yes, that's exactly what I'm saying—it's time to write the full story of your life, the story of the man behind it all, the man who gave his all to resurrect the Games and ensure that they survived."

"The story of the man behind it all? As I've told Francis more than once, I think that's a story the world has left behind."

"Why do you say that?"

"Look at my life right now, Jacques. It's not a pretty picture, not a portrait of great success."

"We're in the midst of a great depression. A lot of people have fallen on hard times through no fault of their own."

"I'm just a bit worried my story will detract from the story of the Games."

"The Games have a life of their own. Look at Berlin; even in this worldwide economic morass, they sparkled with theatrical charisma and produced one of the greatest stories of athletic triumph and political manipulation of our times."

"They were controversial, to be sure."

"Yes," St. Clair continued, "and the level of historic controversy they generated showed, more than anything, how important they are to our world."

Dr. Messerli had been sitting quietly aside, listening with interest, but now he leaned forward and interjected: "They *are* important to our world, Pierre, and they're *your* creation. That's why your story needs to be written!"

"Here's what I want to know," St. Clair said. "What possesses a man to believe he can launch an event the whole world will be drawn to? What forces shaped the mind of a man who sought to build an enduring set of values into a sporting event—and who conceived of a global movement to sustain that event and ensure its duration? Why did that man insist on linking education and sport into a symbiosis that turned out to be its great distinction?"

"Those are big questions, Jacques," Coubertin said, "and they probably will take a full biography to answer."

"I've got a lot of questions in that vein," St. Clair said, "all to help me understand the answer to the question, Why? Why you were compelled to do what you did? And I also want to know what role Paris played in shaping your view of the world. I need to know what was going on inside of you in reaction to the world outside, especially the city you lived in, because I believe that period—the beginning of the Third Republic and the Belle Époque—was a highly inspiring time."

"Well," Coubertin said, "it has been a while since anyone has sought to probe so deeply into my past. Where shall we start? I suppose we'll be spending a lot of time together?"

As they carried on, St. Clair was delighted that Coubertin seemed to be in full agreement with him on all the larger points. Without further ado, they established a working schedule, agreeing on three days a week—mid-morning till mid-day since Pierre didn't want to start too early or work too late. St. Clair also proposed they should find the time as their work developed to have dinner together every now and then, adding an inviting social engagement to the tasks at hand.

"I am blessed," St. Clair said, "with an American fiancée who is a gifted painter. But painting is the least of her talents. She loves good food, good wine, and good conversation. And she is very much looking forward to meeting you."

After an hour, they had covered all the issues and planning necessary. They agreed to meet the next day to commence with their first interview, with Messerli joining them.

"Let's take a walk along the quay," Coubertin said, clearly pleased and energized by this first meeting. "But please excuse me for a moment."

As Coubertin went to the toilet, the doctor expressed his appreciation, speaking softly. "Thank you, Jacques," he said. "You did more for Pierre today than the entire Olympic Movement has done for him in the last five years."

"Given what you said yesterday, I thought it would be best to start right in with the encouragement. Hope it wasn't too much."

○ ○ ○ ○ ○

Sweeping, landscaped lawns rose on the hill across the street from the seawall, collecting the afternoon light in deep shades of green as St. Clair and Coubertin walked along the waterfront under an interspersed row of plane trees. "I've been told you were a successful cyclist before you became a writer," Coubertin said, "and that you gave up racing to work for *Le Petit Journal*."

"Yes, that's true. I won two sprints on these powerful legs in the 1923 Tour de France, but I couldn't keep up with the climbers. And losing was torment, especially to Pélissier, who liked to taunt everyone."

"Sport without sportsmanship can be demoralizing," Coubertin stated, ever the teacher. "But how did you make the move into journalism? I heard it was an instant transition, which is unusual."

"I got lucky. The diary I was keeping did the trick."

"A diary struck the interest of *Le Petit Journal*? Tell me how it happened."

"We had just finished the grueling Col d'Izoard climb, and that night, I was sitting on the terrace of our hotel, my legs and back still aching. I was trying to scratch out a few impressions of the moment when Pélissier sneered at the rest of us in the lead pack, stood on his pedals, and rode off as if he had gears we couldn't reach. I was bent forward, leaning over my little notebook, when I smelled cigar smoke and sensed someone hovering over me. Old Edgar Perrine, the *Journal*'s Tour writer, who became my friend and editor, was looking over my shoulder and reading my open diary, which I snapped closed."

Coubertin laughed. "That's classic sports journalism," he said. "Spying on an athlete writing in his diary."

"Actually, I wasn't offended and I wasn't exactly uncooperative," St. Clair admitted. "Edgar said the last line he read sounded rather good and quoted it back to me verbatim: 'Pélissier looked right through Bottecchia's disguise and saw the weakness in his eyes.' When he asked if he could read a page or two, I handed the diary to him. He sat and ordered a beer, and within a few minutes said he wanted to run the story of the climb in the *Journal* the next day."

"So you were published while you were still racing?"

"Exactly. And Edgar came back the next night and said they wanted a story from me after every stage. My diary suddenly had a formal deadline. It was only a couple hundred words and it was easy for me. But as soon as I started it, I began to lose interest in the race. I was more focused on finding a story in the peloton than competing. I'd ride next to the leaders early or look for someone struggling or take off after a breakaway to see what developed. And other riders started telling me things," St. Clair explained, excited to be telling his story to someone who could appreciate it as few others would.

○ ○ ○ ○ ○

Listening to St. Clair tell his tale, Coubertin took the full measure of the man for the first time. He could easily see the strength of an athlete's frame. St. Clair wasn't that tall, but he was stocky and somewhat thick, more like a rugby player than a cyclist. He had the chest of a bull, like Zeus taking Europa, Coubertin thought, legs that could pummel the pedals for hours, arms like steel shafts. He possessed real power, signaled by the jut of a jaw that could certainly take a punch. And yet, his visage was clearly kind. His blond hair softened his face and his eyes held empathy, a genuine human interest emphasized as he lifted his brow and produced the hint of a grin when he asked a question, anticipating the intrigue of the answer.

Standing next to him, Coubertin did not feel small but rather empowered by the presence of a new friend. Still young enough to be an athlete if he chose to, Coubertin thought, yet seasoned enough as a professional writer and arbiter of sport to add credence and drama to Coubertin's story. Physically, St. Clair would have the stamina. Professionally, he'd have the skills. Intellectually, it remained to be seen if he had the merit.

"That's a great story," Coubertin said, stopping and turning to face St. Clair, "as so many of your stories are. Tell me briefly about your Olympic experience. You've covered eight editions of the Games, by my count, winter and summer. Did you go to the United States?"

"Yes, I went to Lake Placid and Los Angeles."

"Two trips or one?"

"Two. And the trip to Los Angeles forced me to miss the last ten stages of the Tour de France that year. But I'd seen enough of the Tour over the years, and I didn't want to break my string of Olympic Games."

"I'm glad to hear you're that devoted to the Games."

"They're the pinnacle of sport as far as I'm concerned. You really have created the greatest arena we know."

Coubertin smiled in gratitude. "What about your family, your mother, your father? Are they living in Paris? Any sisters and brothers."

"No, I'm an only child. Mother is still in Paris. We lost Father."

"Oh, sorry to hear that. What happened?"

St. Clair turned away from Coubertin without answering and looked across the lake at the mountains. "You really get the most beautiful vistas here in the late afternoon."

"Yes, we do. They're inspiring." Reticence noted, Coubertin reached out to shake St. Clair's hand again. "I've got to get up to Mon Repos now," he said, "but I'm certainly looking forward to continuing our conversation tomorrow. I'll see you at the Café Italia for lunch."

○ ○ ○ ○ ○

St. Clair was only a short walk from the cottage and went directly home with a sense of excitement. He felt as if he had been admitted to a small but exclusive society of men who wanted to shape history—and one who had changed it. Juliette would want to know every detail of his meeting with the baron. When he came up the hill to the terrace, St. Clair was surprised to see the curtains drawn across the French doors. As soon as he opened the door, he breathed in an aroma of sandalwood and had a visceral response, knowing their conversation about his meeting with Pierre would have to take a back seat to romance. The living room was shadowed but flickering with the golden glow of candlelight.

"*Bonjour,*" he called, certain that Juliette was about to surprise him in some way. She didn't answer. She was a free spirit, a true bohemian at heart, and when she lit the candles and burned the incense, she had only one thing in mind.

He moved toward the bedroom but then heard the whisper of a kiss behind him. Juliette stepped out of the shadows of the kitchen with a glass of wine in her hand, the long tresses of her black hair spread alluringly across her shoulders. She was wrapped in a rather short apron, and as she turned slowly it was soon clear that the apron was the only thing she was wearing.

$$5$$

THE PAST

The next day, on a cold but bright February afternoon, Messerli and St. Clair arrived at the same time at the brick and glass front of the Café Italia, exchanging greetings as they walked the passage to the entrance. St. Clair held the door for the doctor and bowed as his new employer walked in.

They were greeted by the wondrous aroma of fresh garlic and the lovely Gabriella, the daughter of the owner and chef, adorned with a red-and-white checked apron around a traditional Italian peasant dress.

"Gentlemen, I believe you're meeting Baron de Coubertin," she said. "Please come with me." They followed her to a side porch covered with a trellis of vines, only partially enclosed but kept warm by a small fireplace.

Coubertin was waiting for them at a table, looking at the label of a bottle of Brunello di Montalcino the chef had sent to him as soon as he was seated.

"They say a prophet is without honor in his own land," Coubertin said. "But this prophet, if you'll excuse the immodesty, is not without a good bottle of wine thanks to Luciano, who insists we must drink well at lunch today."

"He has great affection for you, Pierre," said Messerli, informing St. Clair that they often met at this restaurant for lunch.

Beyond the pleasantries, once the bottle was opened and decanted and the glasses filled, Coubertin insisted on welcoming St. Clair by offering a toast he had made some years before when he had birthed the Olympic Movement. "I want you to hear this because it was originally inspired by a moment of great joy back in 1894—the moment we were sure the Olympic Games would live again."

St. Clair held his hand up as Coubertin lifted his glass, and the baron waited while he retrieved and placed his open notebook on the table, anxious not to miss the quote.

Looking at St. Clair, the baron repeated one of his favorite old lines: "I lift my glass to the Olympic idea, which has traversed the mists of the ages like an all-powerful ray of sunlight and returned to illumine the threshold of the twentieth century with a dream of joyous hope."

"Well said, sir," St. Clair replied, thinking how appropriate it was that the first Olympic words Coubertin quoted to him took in two millennia.

They chatted about the dinner banquet at which Coubertin had first offered that toast, which was held one night in Paris during the week-long congress where the Games were resurrected. St. Clair then steered the conversation toward Coubertin's ancestry, wanting to establish the serious intent of this first formal interview.

"Now, if you will," St. Clair said, "why don't you begin by telling me something about your family and your name."

"I came from a family of artists and diplomats with a bit of royal heritage," Coubertin said, obviously prepared. "My paternal grandfather, Julien Bonaventure de Coubertin, was both a gifted violinist and a successful military leader who became France's first ambassador to Brazil—"

Dr. Messerli interrupted. "Don't start in the last century, Pierre—take him back further. Tell him about Felice di Fredi. Start at the beginning. In the vineyard. Put your hands in the dirt, and dig for something worthwhile."

As Coubertin looked at his old friend, he smiled and his eyes brightened into a laugh. He looked away for a moment, casting his glance at the fire crackling a few feet away. His forehead wrinkled as he spoke. "So you want the drama, do you? You want the story to emerge from the earth—as it surely did?"

"What's important to me," declared St. Clair, holding his pen poised over the thin tablet, "is to get a sense of how you think of the past and to hear the tone of your voice and the cadence of your speech when you talk about such personal things as your family and your heritage."

"The past," said Coubertin, "means everything to me. It is where I found the future." He paused and St. Clair looked up and caught Coubertin staring pensively at his fingers guiding the ink across the page. St. Clair knew writing could have an effect on a subject, particularly someone who spent so much time putting his own thoughts on paper.

"Please continue."

"In my family, the past was always consciously present—not just the recent past, not just the preceding generation, but the ancient past," the baron said. "The world of antiquity reached out to us again and again and called us to service even as society was plunging headlong into a new age. We lived in a world of insurrectionists, but my family, the Coubertins, well, we were resurrectionists. We brought the past back to life.

"Felice di Fredi, one of the earliest ancestors I know of, was an Italian winemaker, a Roman of some means. He had a vineyard on the Esquine Hill, on a lovely site right where Nero's Golden House—the Domus Aurea—had been when Rome ruled civilization. He was having a shallow well dug at the bottom of a slope where he thought he might find water. At the end of the day on January 13 in 1506—yes, we know the exact date—he walked down the rows of vines to check on the well's progress. His men were gone, the dirt piled up next to a pit that was dry. To test the soil, he stepped down into the pit and thrust his walking stick into the dirt at his feet—and to his utter astonishment it plunged without resistance right up his wrist, into what must have been an empty space. He retrieved a shovel and broke through to discover the fractured top of a vault of bricks."

As Coubertin paused, St. Clair felt the moment of intrigue take hold. He scribbled across the tablet, furiously recording the moment, nearly verbatim, in a personalized form of Duployan shorthand he had created long ago.

"Excited by the mystery of what lay beneath his feet," Coubertin continued, "Fredi rushed back up to his vineyard house, lit his largest lantern, and dragged a wooden ladder down to the dig. When he clambered back down into the pit and opened more of the roof, he knew he was looking into an ancient room— what might have once been the chambers of a Roman emperor."

"Down went the ladder ..." Messerli injected.

"Yes, he lowered the ladder and found good footing," the baron said, "and carefully, with some trepidation, he took a few tentative steps down into the darkness, holding the lantern low. The light filled a small, vaulted chamber strewn with debris, a broken stone bench against one wall, empty granite shelves on another, some large broken vessels, nothing of note, but there was an arched doorway through to another chamber and another beyond that. Fredi cleared the way of dusty cobwebs and in the fourth chamber, he was startled to see a large white marble face contorted in agony. Staggering in disbelief, he held the lantern higher and studied the face of Laocoön, portrayed by the sculptor at the very moment when he realized the serpents were too strong and would destroy him and his two sons."

"Laocoön? The priest of Troy?" St. Clair asked.

"Ah, you know your Virgil. That's a good sign," Coubertin proclaimed.

"*Arma virumque cano*,'" said St. Clair, reciting the opening line of *The Aeneid*, "of arms and the man I sing."

"Well," Coubertin said, smiling, his pleasure obvious. "It appears our discussions will be wide ranging."

"But please continue," said St. Clair.

"Fredi had found a brilliant marble sculpture—*Laocoön and His Sons*—undoubtedly at one time the property of Nero, depicting the assault by the sea serpents Athena had sent to punish Laocoön for trying to reject the Trojan Horse and warning the people of Troy that it was a trap. Do you know the work? It's in the Vatican Museum."

"I think I've seen an illustration," St. Clair said. "Is he standing with one son on each side and the serpent wrapped around them all?"

"Exactly," said Coubertin. He and Messerli exchanged a glance.

"There is no question, Pierre," Messerli said, "that you have a highly literate athlete here to help you shape your memoir."

St. Clair looked down, pleased with their recognition. They were erudite men and it meant a lot to him.

"I can tell you every detail of the discovery and the statue and the family history that followed," Coubertin continued, "because it was the subject of one of my father's finest early paintings, exhibited in the 1846 Paris Salon. It hung throughout my youth at the top of the stairway, just outside the door to his atelier in our Paris home. And also because we made a trip to Rome in the summer of 1869 when I was just six, not only to visit the Vatican to gaze upon the *Laocoön* but also to visit Fredi's tomb in the Church of Santa Maria in Aracoeli at the top of Capitoline Hill."

As St. Clair scribbled notes in shorthand, he already had a strong sense of how this scene would unfold when he drafted it for the book.

Thunderstruck with excitement at his discovery, Fredi scrambled back up to his villa, nearly shouting the story to his wife, who followed him around the house in disbelief as he washed up, changed, and ran out the door. He headed straight for the Church of Santa Maria in Aracoeli to share his excitement with the priest and to see whether they could summon the pope himself.

Father Geron, the portly priest who had baptized Fredi's children and depended on his tithe, would not call on the Vatican until he had seen the miracle of Laocoön himself. And so Fredi led the second of at least five treks into the vault that night, followed each time by a parade of progressively elevated personages, religious and public, as word of the discovery began to spread throughout the city.

With Father Geron's help, Fredi pulled together a crew of workers and monks in the middle of the night who began to clean up the vaults and prepare an appropriate entryway for the pontiff. Guards were posted along the villa road to hold the gathering crowd back from the vineyard.

By first light of morning, Father Geron and Fredi were at the Vatican. They were granted entry into the Papal Library, and preparations were made for a visit by the pope and his entourage that afternoon.

It was agreed that Father Geron would make the initial introductions when the pope arrived but Fredi would guide the tour into the vault, which now featured a ladder nearly as wide as a staircase, a string of lanterns along the ceiling that lit the space well, and a long runner of old red carpet that led to the statue itself, now cleaned of centuries of dust and polished to a high white gloss—far more striking than the day before.

When the pope's train of horse-drawn carriages made its way slowly up the villa road through the crowds of awed and curious peasants, the commotion grew and Fredi felt as nervous as a man on trial. In the din of noise as the coaches passed and the crowd got a look inside, a name was suddenly on everyone's lips; it raced up the side of the road ahead of the procession. It reached Fredi's ears before the carriages made the top of the hill: a name revered by all in the art world, the name of the pope's own genius, Michelangelo.

And there he was, stepping out of the pope's coach first, the great, tall man with the square, granite-like head, black curly hair, broken nose, deep-set eyes, and alarming glare, his swirling cape enlarging him as he turned back to offer the pope his hand.

Adorned in a simple black cassock with a wide belt at the waist, Pope Julius II stepped out of the ornate gold-and-white six-horse carriage fully prepared to descend into the earth. As Michelangelo turned the pope toward the villa gate, Fredi took in the impressively embroidered coat of arms on his belt and gazed up at his short shoulder cape and white skullcap.

Just as Father Geron was about to step forward to offer his greetings, the pope called out, "Where is Felice di Fredi?"

"He is here, your Excellency," replied Geron, bowing and extending both arms toward Felice, who also bowed as the pope approached.

"I understand you have unearthed a great treasure, my son," the pope said, extending his ringed hand and raising Felice out of his bow. "And word has reached me from Father Geron"—the pope nodded toward the priest in recognition—"that you are a faithful servant of the Lord and a pillar of the Santa Maria congregation."

"I hope, your Excellency," Fredi said, regaining his composure and smiling brightly, "that you find the Laocoön as impressive as I did. When I found it in the fifth chamber of a vault below these vineyards, I felt as if I had been transported back into the pages of *The Aeneid* by the spirit of Virgil himself."

"Well then," said the pope, "with such an invitation, I can hardly wait to see it myself, but I think we shall reserve the final judgment on its quality to our dear Michelangelo."

The big man looked hard at Felice as they tramped through the villa gate toward the rows of grape vines. "Have you found a signature on the sculpture?"

"No, we have not," Fredi said, leading the way.

Lifting his glass, Coubertin took a good gulp of the Brunello and finished the story with a flourish.

"When they emerged from the vaults, Michelangelo pronounced the sculpture the greatest work of art the world had ever seen. While there was no signature, he attributed it to three sculptors from Rhodes—Agesander, Athenadoros, and Polydoros—all of whom were mentioned in the writings of Pliny the Elder in the second century BC. Michelangelo confirmed, as did Pope Julius II, that it had indeed been in the possession of the Roman emperors down to Nero. He also called it *The Death Struggle of Laocoön*, a name that never took hold but came to me as a boy through the stories of my father and grandfather, family legends enhanced by three centuries of proud descendants.

"As a guest at a dinner with the pope and several cardinals a little later," Coubertin added, "Felice di Fredi wisely gifted *Laocoön and His Sons* to the pope and the Catholic Church, and within days it had been unearthed and carted off to take a place of honor in the Vatican's Belvedere Court. In return, the Pope Julius bestowed upon Fredi a series of honors and a papal stipend that enhanced his stature within the community and added to the glories of the family name."

After the drama of the *Laocoön* story, Coubertin and St. Clair spent the rest of the afternoon tracing the baron's full lineage. His earliest known ancestor, Pierre de Frédy, Seigneur de la Motte and chamberlain to the king, who was perhaps Felice di Fredi's French uncle, was granted a coat of arms and invested with nobility by Louis XI in Paris in 1477, twenty-nine years before Felice's discovery and papal honors.

A long succession of successful aristocrats in the Royal Courts of France and distinguished leaders of politics and business ensued. In 1577, Jean Frédy, who earned great wealth by capitalizing on the booming spice trade, purchased an estate in the Chevreuse valley just south of Versailles and acquired the seigneur de Coubertin, giving the family the name it carried forward. In the early 1700s, the naval commander, François Frédy, then captain of the King's Ships, gained riches through the West Indies Company and built the Château de Coubertin in the Chevreuse, placing it in the sphere of the Palace of Versailles, which the Sun King, Louis XIV, would build later that century. While most of the family survived the 1789 French Revolution, Henri Louis de Frédy had the misfortune to fall under suspicion at the age of seventy-three. Having drawn too close to the royals as they tried to escape, he was beheaded in the bloody moment of terror that took the much younger Marie Antoinette.

It was at the Château de Coubertin that Pierre's paternal grandfather and his father were born, in 1768 and 1822 respectively. Remarkably talented as a painter and a violinist, Pierre's grandfather, Julien Bonaventure Frédy de Coubertin, was equally gifted on the military and diplomatic fronts. He survived the dangerous and rapidly shifting political sands of his time and achieved a great measure of distinction under both the empire of Napoleon and the monarchy of Louis XVIII—no easy feat. A trusted cavalry officer on Napoleon's general staff, he was named counsel in Cuxhaven and Oldenburg by the emperor. By the time the monarchy was restored in 1814, Julien had married Caroline de Pardieu, whose family traced her heritage back to the Crusades. Moving swiftly into the new king's circle of leadership, Julien was named a Knight of the Legion of Honor. Impressed by his rare combination of creativity and executive authority, Louis XVIII appointed Julien as France's first ambassador to Brazil, where he served from 1818 to 1820 and established a Royal Academy of Fine Arts in Rio de Janeiro. Upon his return, the king made him a hereditary baron in 1821—and that was the title his grandson, Pierre Frédy de Coubertin, proudly inherited.

While not as ambitious, Coubertin's father, Charles, pursued his art with real passion. Raised at the Château de Coubertin with his own studio, Charles Louis de Coubertin rose as the family's finest painter, acquiring a town home in Paris and moving to the city in the 1840s, where he exhibited at the Salon de Paris for the first time in 1846. He married Marie Gigault de Crisenoy later that year.

Coubertin's mother's family descended from the French aristocracy and included Viking kings as well. Rollo, the first Duke of Normandy, hailed by his men as a fearless warrior, was part of her bloodline—and her son's. Marie was the daughter of the Marquis de Mirville and inherited the Château de Mirville in the Caux region, which had been in the family since the sixteenth century.

There were more ancestors of distinction to detail, but St. Clair was satisfied with the content of the interview and the work accomplished in one brief afternoon.

"I can give you a set of papers to trace the family lines in the detail you need," Coubertin said, "but I hope today provided you with a good start—and at least the beginning of my perspective on the past."

"It was an auspicious start," said St. Clair, "both figuratively and literally. Tomorrow let's leave the lineage behind and jump ahead to your boyhood."

"Ah," said Coubertin, "my childhood. Well then, our journey will take us into *le vieux Paris*—the old Paris—as it slowly became the Paris of modernity, but the ancient past will not leave us alone for long."

"Gentlemen," said Dr. Messerli, "duties at the university and the hospital will take me away from this most enjoyable assembly for the next few days, but in my opinion, this is precisely the path you should follow in your work."

"Francis, as always, I am deeply indebted to you for arranging all this," said Coubertin. "Giving an old man an opportunity to tell his story may just be a new kind of medicine."

Walking back down the cobblestones of rue de Bourg—the shadows deepening as the early evening light faded—St. Clair was haunted by the image of Laocoön struggling with the serpent and Coubertin's depiction of the past reaching out and wrapping him in its unrelenting embrace.

7

THE NIGHT

Lausanne fell quiet under the deep shades of a starry, cloudless night, a city of solitude drawing into itself with the predictability of a Swiss watch approaching the witching hour. The cool wind rising from the lake rustled the bare branches and bushes in the park around the Villa Mon Repos, the impressively gated green enclave near the heart of the city. The soft murmur of the breeze played to no one in the empty paths that wove through the park. A single flickering light burned behind a third-floor window of the neoclassical façade of the old château, barely illuminating the small bedroom where Pierre de Coubertin sat alone on the edge of his bed, bent over, rubbing his sore feet. They hurt every day now, whether he walked or not. It seemed very few patches of earth these days were forgiving to his step.

The room was sparsely furnished with only one fine piece that belonged to him, a four-drawer chest on clawed feet with a bowed front and gilded bronze braces running up the edges, its braided golden drawer handles falling like festoons around the inlaid colors of the handcrafted marquetry. When he looked at the woodwork, it still evoked memories of his aristocratic youth and his father's insistence that beauty could be found in the tiny, delicate forms of craftsmanship as surely as it was visible in the grand scale of the sculpture and architecture across their beloved city. He'd had the dresser shipped from Paris in 1919 when he sold the family home at 20 rue Oudinot, his final loss of major property in a long slide away from the elegant, moneyed life he had once lived. Several other pieces of furniture occupied the small, monastic cell of his room—a nondescript stuffed chair and ottoman, the single bed with a few old, flattened pillows, a washstand, and a table for books beside the bed—all owned, like the Villa Mon Repos itself, by the city of Lausanne. He lived as a guest now in a world he had created, and while he never failed to express his gratitude, it was increasingly harder for him to do it with any true sense of sincerity.

The top of his dresser held several framed photographs, a small jewelry box, and a candle stand with three flickering flames before a nicked and fractured wooden mirror that filled the room with some light. He had been sleeping alone in this room off and on now for more than a year since the baroness had thrown his things into the hallway outside their larger and more ornately furnished bedroom next door. Their marriage was broken. These days, her anger seldom abated, her tone was always accusatory, her moods erratic, yet she slept well behind the wall between them. Their daughter, Renée, was across the hall. She was still affectionate with him when they were alone, still freely showed the deep admiration his wife once possessed for him, but in her mother's domineering presence she was too intimidated to express her love. Their mute and insensate son Jacques and his caretaker occupied rooms at the back of the floor. Coubertin's love for him was a deep abyss of sadness.

The candlelight jumped and Coubertin looked up at the single painting hanging in the room, a large image of his father's that covered the wall separating him from the baroness. It was a scene of mythic reality his father had created in 1896 to celebrate the rebirth of the modern Olympic Games. The robed figure of Victory was seated on a throne in a classic Greek temple atop a wide stairway above land and lakes, with athletes and other people gathered before her to honor this new tradition. He knew every aspect of the scene—every brushstroke and nuance of color, every poised prop, expression, and stance of its figures—and each spoke to him with a kind of melancholic reassurance that what he had done with his life was meaningful. Alone in his room at night, this was his only talisman, his constant touchstone and sole reminder that his quest had its grail, that he had been chosen for—or perhaps cursed with—a mission that would have consequence. There was usually little solace or comfort in his ruminations on the painting, but on this night, as he rose to snuff the candles, he looked at the outstretched arm of Victory and wondered whether she had beckoned Jacques St. Clair to Lausanne to help him through these difficult days.

Lying in bed in the shadowless room, the paraffin still hanging in the air, he thought about St. Clair's face, still young enough to be an athlete, no creases or crow's feet, but alight with the desire to know a story that had never been told properly, or maybe even honestly. The blue eyes so intently focused, the pen held so expectantly in the hand, knowing with a certainty sadly missing in most young men that he was on a mission of significance. Thinking about the day, a day spent in his ancestral past yet very much in the present moment, Coubertin felt a surge of energy in his spirit, like an awakened sense of purpose, a measure of strength brought to the game by a new partner. As tired as he was, shifting to his side to relieve a dull ache anchored in his back, he felt that something so long missing was returning like a comet on the edge of the infinite night, a tiny glow, a barely discernible sparkle headed this way. But it was not in the blackness of space where this light appeared—no, it was on the black edge of his own iris. There was light once again in the eye of *le Rénovateur*.

GLORY AND RUIN

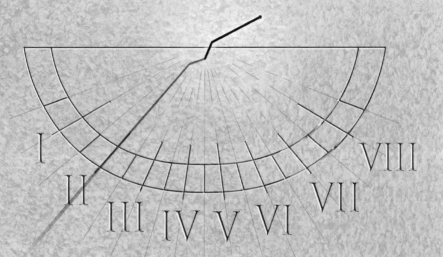

NOTES AND DRAFTS

By the end of February, three weeks after arriving in Lausanne, St. Clair had secured a small office on the second floor of a building overlooking the winding gray cobblestones of rue de Bourg, just up from the Place Saint-François. The room was functional but sparse, with a swivel chair at a long, narrow table pushed up against three casement windows, which were deeply set into a cracked plaster wall. The space provided the solitude he needed to work through his extensive interview notes and interpret the shorthand he had resurrected to try to accurately capture Coubertin's eloquence as it spilled rapid-fire from his lips. Glancing at his scribbles, he hammered at the keys of the Olivetti, which sat in the midst of a spray of notebooks and papers, adding page after page to the neat stack of a manuscript that was already showing some substance.

Other than a single light fixture in the middle of the ceiling, a dirty red Persian carpet on the floor, and a tall, thin vase on the windowsill surrounded by a bed of fallen rose petals—a neglected gift from Juliette—the room held nothing else but books. Along the floor against the wall sat about twenty dusty, aromatic volumes Messerli had given him, plus a growing stack of old magazines, newsletters, circulars, and files from the International Olympic Committee. Most of the publications were from the hand of Pierre de Coubertin, including the very dense and impressive *Universal History* published ten years earlier when Coubertin was sixty-four. St. Clair would have to acquire a filing cabinet or some shelves soon.

As he prepared to pack up and walk over to Messerli's office at the University of Lausanne, St. Clair lifted a few freshly typed pages of verbatim notes and wondered, as he read and heard the baron's distinctively nasal voice in his mind, if he could preserve the first-person perspective in a few passages—creating something of a stylistic innovation between the third-person narrative he had already started and the spoken dialogue he and Coubertin had engaged in.

"Mine was a childhood of wonders, spent between our Paris hotel on rue Oudinot in the 7th, where I was born, and the two châteaux of my grandparents ... in the valley of Saint-Rémy-lès-Chevreuse by Versailles just south of Paris and the Château de Mirville in the far north of Normandy near the English Channel. I was raised in a privileged world of fascinations and dreamscapes both urban and rural. On the one hand, a Parisian world of culture, refinement, painting, music, fashion, literature, history, and religion, framed by a family who believed in the greatness of the French monarchy and ached for its return. On the other, a forested land of magical paths and lakes, horses and boats, and fragrant fields of kind farmers whose children loved to play just as I did.

"I was born as *le vieux Paris* was beginning to disappear. Under the Second Empire, Baron Haussmann, the Prefect of the Seine, was given vast authority by Napoleon III to redesign and rebuild the city, which is just what he did, transforming the old medieval labyrinth into the capital of modernity just as I was growing up.

"Our home on rue Oudinot was in the École Militaire Quarter of the 7th arrondissemont, only a few blocks south of the expansive grounds of Les Invalides with its Golden Dome, the hospital and church that Louis XIV had built for his wounded and recovering soldiers at the end of the seventeenth century. After Louis commemorated the dome in 1706, which was instantly recognized as one of the world's finest architectural masterpieces, a grand migration of decorated generals, wealthy officers, heralded aristocrats from the Marais, royal court patrons, politicians from the Vendôme, and nouveau riche merchants and businessmen swept into the environs. With bold and exaggerated bidding, they bought up every inch of the open fields and old city blocks around Les Invalides and the great military parade grounds of the Champs de Mars in front of the École Militaire, where the Eiffel Tower was erected 180 years later. They engaged in an unprecedented competition to see who could design and build the most opulent country mansions, the now famous family 'hôtels' of Paris's remarkable patrimony.

"In Versailles and then again at Les Invalides, the Sun King had signaled there should be no limits on architectural magnificence and artistic expression in any field of endeavor in France. Our national destiny had a creative aesthetic. A hospital for veterans should be marked by the inspiring beauty that adorned the monarch's own palace. It wasn't only the church that had cultural responsibilities as a repository of art. The government and the military should not be constrained by modesty but should strive for grandeur and glory in the edifices they erected. Like the popes and the Medicis in Italy, Louis XIV saw the ennobling possibilities of art and culture and created an industry to engender it. It was a fine time to be an architect, a painter, a sculptor, a builder, a mason, or a maker of jewelry, ornaments, or furniture. There was no end to the work.

"The monarch had set in motion a trend toward the splendid and the lavish. And soon the old narrow streets of the Saint-Germain-des-Prés echoed with the clamor of demolition and the hammer of development. A new Paris was about to emerge, a neighborhood of personal palaces the likes of which no city had ever seen."

○ ○ ○ ○ ○

As he walked up rue de Bourg, a section of the manuscript in his shoulder bag to show Messerli, St. Clair thought about what he had achieved so far in Lausanne. From his perspective, the interviews were going well, and he felt he and Pierre had established a strong, personal rapport, a level of trust more engaging and certainly more intimate than St. Clair had ever had with an interview subject before. He was not sure whether this was a natural part of the book-writing process, which required deeper and longer conversations, or whether he and the baron had simply taken to each other because of their shared devotion to an intellectual interpretation of sport. He didn't know whether Coubertin had always opened up and embraced people as he had St. Clair, but he doubted it—he certainly knew Coubertin was not averse to conflict when he disagreed with others, even his friends.

They'd had about ten one-on-one sessions since their first interview with Dr. Messerli, whom St. Clair was updating every few days. The sessions hadn't been strictly chronological, but they had mostly focused on the broad story of Coubertin's youth, his upbringing, and his education. St. Clair had decided to show Messerli a piece of that storyline today, a piece that began in the countryside of Mirville.

He was a little boy, smaller in stature than the farm boys with whom he played in the fields and woods around the sixteenth-century Château de Mirville, the family castle in Normandy where Charles and Marie loved to take their four children from May to August to escape the heat of Paris. Pierre was charming, eloquent, and well liked as a boy by all the farmers and servants who labored in the pastures and small towns that had been part of the sphere of the Château de Mirville for centuries.

Pierre's maternal grandfather, Étienne-Charles Gigault de Crisenoy—who, like Pierre's paternal grandfather, also bore the hereditary title of baron and carried the Legion of Honor for his distinguished military service—decided to make the beloved family estate part of his only child's dowry when she became betrothed to Charles de Coubertin in 1844.

His mother loved the people of the village as much as she loved Jesus. In fact, she studied medicine by candlelight so she could help cure their ills and serve their needs. The people came to the château as if they were visiting a doctor's office, shambling up shy and bent and grateful for any attention, presenting their fevered and bruised rag-clothed children with hope in their eyes. Pierre's mother nursed them with her remedies, food, faith, heartfelt sweetness, and good advice. And when she heard someone was too sick to come to her, she went to them in their rough-hewn homes with stone and wooden walls, mud floors, and hay roofs. Sometimes she took Pierre and his sister, Marie, to watch her work and to teach them what her father had taught her—that they must take care of the people who worked for them and sustained the farms and towns around the château.

"Mirville is your birthright but it is also your responsibility," Baron de Crisenoy had told his daughter. "You must care for those who care for this castle and the commune that gives it life."

On those country childhood mornings, Pierre would wake early when the gates at Mirville creaked open as the workers arrived. He would push out the heavy shutters of his second-story window and look down, excited to see the servants' children already running around the gravel courtyard. Before he finished dressing, the mouthwatering aromas of the stove were crawling up the stairway from the kitchen. He would have his crêpes and fruit and cream at the big table next to the stove with the other children simply because he wanted to be with them. When they were done they would run out after him, past the stables and over the stone bridge to the woods. And it was there, running, jumping, and climbing trees, that Pierre discovered that even though he was small, he had a surprising physical advantage. He had strength beyond his size in his arms and legs, which gave him a growing sense that his body was perfectly proportioned and balanced. He could run faster and longer than the other boys, tricking them easily with his quickness and avoiding their grasps when they wrestled, and he could keep a ball away from them with his feet with some ease.

He relished physical contact and had a competitive streak. He realized later that it had developed naturally because his two older brothers, Paul and Albert, had played rough with him and tickled him and swung him around from the time he was a baby—and taught him to box, wrestle, swim, and row on the Mirville lake in his little boat, the *Tam-Tam*. They schooled him in all sorts of ball games, put him on guard with their sabers or épées, and put the reins of their horses in his hands as soon as he was ready to ride. He was fearless on horseback when his brothers took him out—he loved to gallop and jump and leave them behind, a little jockey who reveled in flying above his steed and moving with the rhythm of the animal, hearing its breath and feeling the excitement of its beating heart.

When he was young at Mirville, he found a joy in life that came through the games they played; he would stay out until the bell rang at dark and his playmates had to go home. When he was inside, his mother broadened his mind with language, literature, and music. She was fluent in English and he learned it with ease, delighted that he and his sister could speak in a tongue his father didn't understand. And his mother taught him to play the piano while his sister strummed the harp. He resisted at first, but the music came naturally and he took pleasure in the easy dance of his fingers. His father took him to the studio and taught him to draw and paint. There were many nights when Pierre looked up from his book and found the entire family engulfed in reading, stimulated by a library full of great French literature and works on art and the ancient world. He was bright and read with a felicity more advanced than his siblings when they were young. He was fascinated by the imagery of the classics, The Iliad, The Odyssey, and The Aeneid—all things of ancient Greece and Rome. He took pride in paging through stories and papers of family history with both his parents, beginning to understand that the Coubertins served a role in a great nation.

His earliest memory of those halcyon days in Normandy was a whitened image of the shoreline at Étretat, the artist's colony on the coast of the English Channel thirty miles north of Mirville where poets, writers, painters, and musicians filled the bistros, bars, hotels, and salons—and where his father sometimes rented a house to move the family to the beach for a week so he could paint the sea. Pierre recalled a vivid but ethereal moment, sitting on a blanket on a sunlit beach with his mother and sister, his hands on the warm pebbles, his teenaged brothers Paul and Albert splashing in the surf not far away. Before them, covered in a billowing white smock under a straw hat, his father stood at an easel gazing off at the great arch of stone rising from the relentless waves in the Channel beneath the cliffs above the town. Palette in hand, his painting box sitting on its rickety legs, he was re-creating the magnificent sculpture of nature known as L'Arche, la Porte d'Aval, a subject rendered by hundreds of artists in the course of time—by Courbet, by Monet, and later, by Pierre himself as he walked along those cliffs and grew to love that same indelible scene.

The family traveled less often to the greater and more prestigious Château de Coubertin in the valley of Saint-Rémy-lès-Chevreuse, just south of the Palace of Versailles, the property of Pierre's paternal grandparents, Julien Bonaventure Frédy de Coubertin and his wife, Caroline, who was the daughter of the Marquis de Pardieu. Although Charles kept a studio there, the very studio where he had learned to paint as a child, he preferred the vales of Normandy and the small villages where his wife, Marie, and her family were so beloved by the people of the commune. When they were there, the château was theirs alone, a family home free of the social obligations and political intercourse of Paris—and free of the strife that sometimes arose between Charles and his mother in Chevreuse. Although Pierre was close to both his grandparents, he felt the strain and tension between his grandmother and his father, who, perhaps in rebellion, chose to be a painter when his heritage had called for a military or political career.

Nevertheless, Charles was most adamant about cultivating an interest in the family's history in each of his children, so he arranged grand family adventures to Rome during certain summers. Since no single train connection existed between Paris and Rome when Pierre was a boy, the family traveled with a dozen trunks by train and carriage over the Alps on long and tiresome treks, but his father was insistent on the duties they had to perform. Although the alpine villages they passed through in springtime were charming and filled with the fragrant scent of hibiscus and bougainvillea, Pierre was delighted when his mother suggested they take the train straight down to the coast at Marseille and board a ship for Rome. It was the route Pierre preferred and would later take on his Olympic missions.

In walks about Rome with his father, Pierre was thrilled to learn the history and meaning of the ancient ruins, and he marveled at how long the legacy of the emperors had endured. In the Coliseum, the Arch of Constantine, Baths of Trajan, and especially the glorious expanse of the Forum, Pierre felt the power of life, not death, and embraced the living spirit of the past of the Senate and the People of Rome. With his vivid imagination, he expected Cicero to step out from behind a column at any moment, toga falling from his expressive arms as he lectured on liberty—and Pierre was always on alert for the approaching thunder of Caesar's army marching back into Rome yet again. His father walked him all over the city, into the voluminous magic of the Panthéon, across the Piazza Navona, past the flowing Trevi Fountain, and up the Spanish Steps to the Villa Borghese and the Galleria, where he touched Bernini's magnificent *David*, the sling that slew Goliath stretched by the marble arm. Site by site, scene by scene, Pierre began to understand that behind this great patrimony, behind this once vibrant explosion of human creativity, there was a society of ideas, a society of culture that valued artistry as the ultimate expression of life itself.

And it was in Rome that he first felt the historic pride in the name he possessed— Pierre Frédy de Coubertin—as he recognized among these timeless works of art not only the imprint of his long-ago ancestors but the prestige of his own father. On the walls of the Vatican Museum he beheld one of his father's most acclaimed paintings, *The Pontifical Cortege*—a twenty-four-foot-long canvas depicting a parade of Catholic dignitaries in full regalia, a historical record of the start of a religious conclave that had been commissioned by Pope Pius IX himself in 1868.

Nothing, however, moved Pierre as powerfully as the moment he entered the Vatican's Pio-Clementino Museum, guided by his father, and stood before the white marble miracle of *Laocoön and His Sons*. Although he had seen the sculpture depicted in his father's paintings and had heard for years the stories of Felice de Fredi's discovery and his presentation to the pope, he was unprepared for the emotional immediacy of the statue and the arresting impact of its artistic hold. The pain on Laocoön's face and the agony of knowing his sons were about to die moved Pierre, as it had moved so many, to want to reach out and join the battle—to free the priest and his progeny from the serpent.

When his father explained that it was the discovery of the *Laocoön* that had led Pope Julius II to start the Vatican Museum in 1506, which became the greatest repository of art in the world, the boy felt as if the blood of history itself were flowing through his veins.

They stepped out into the gardens of the Cortile del Belvedere, and his father told him it was in this magnificent enclosed courtyard that the museum had actually begun. For it was here that Pope Julius II placed the *Laocoön* and then added two other masterpieces from ancient Greece: the *Pythian Apollo* and the massive *Torso of Antinous*. Over time, this trio had attracted tens of thousands of visitors and had become the church's motivation for collecting more sculpture and art for the glory of God.

As they did on every trip to Rome, the family climbed the long stairway up to the threshold of the Church of Santa Maria in Aracoeli on the Capitoline to pay their respects at the gravestone of Felice di Fredi, which was embedded in the base of one of the church's ancient columns. Pierre's father would always get on his hands and knees and use a rag to clean each and every engraved letter. As he polished the family legend, Pierre would put his fingers against the cold marble to feel the chiseled edges of the old name. When they left, Pierre always begged to walk across the terrace to Michelangelo's beautiful Piazza del Campidoglio, which the boy loved for the grandeur of the giant equestrian statue of Marcus Aurelius.

Dr. Messerli removed his glasses, laid the papers down on his desk, and sat back in his chair, gazing for a moment across the wide plaza at the front of the university. He turned back to St. Clair and held his eyes for a few seconds before speaking, seeking a way to express how much the passage stirred him.

"I didn't know that the discovery of *Laocoön and His Sons* was the start of the Vatican Museum, or anything about those boyhood visits to Rome. This is extremely moving for me, Jacques. I can already tell it is going to be the kind of life story I was hoping for."

"I'm glad you feel that way."

"When can I read more?"

"I'll give you another batch in a few days or perhaps next week. I have a good start on what happened to the family during the war in 1870 and '71—a few really impressive stories about his mother's fearless nursing, and how his father walked him around Paris after the Commune was crushed to show him what they lost and what France would have to rebuild."

"Excellent!" Messerli looked at his calendar for a moment. "You know, this could be an exciting week in Lausanne. We've got that dinner with Avery Brundage, the head of the American Olympic Committee. He's on his way from London right now, I think."

"I know. Pierre told me he sent Brundage a telegram and asked him to come down."

"I'm glad you're going to be there," said Messerli. "Brundage is like a bull. He can be overpowering. I'm not sure how he'll respond when Pierre starts in on that German proposal that Baillet-Latour has embraced. The baron has become rather angry about it."

"Isn't Brundage sympathetic to Hitler?" St. Clair asked. "And what about Carl Diem—isn't he coming too?"

"Most people think he is, yes. And I'm guessing Pierre will have something to say about that. I think Diem is coming the week after next or possibly next month. Pierre wants to handle him alone."

St. Clair lifted his shoulder bag and started toward the door. "Thank you, Francis."

"One more thing," Messerli said. "My wife and I are planning to have a dinner party Sunday night the week after next for Pierre and Marie and a few of our friends, and we were hoping you and Juliette could join us. The baroness doesn't get out enough, and I'm sure she'd enjoy meeting you and your vivacious American."

"A party. That sounds delightful. Juliette will be thrilled. Should I assume we'll be drinking a little champagne?"

"You can count on it, Jacques. Doctor's orders."

9

THE ATELIER

Before leaving his office that afternoon to head home for a drink with Juliette, St. Clair found a few pages of notes on Coubertin's memories of his father's painting studio. He knew Juliette would be interested. They were planning to walk down to the Angleterre for dinner later that night.

"What did you talk about today?" Juliette asked, leaning back in a paint-stained shirt that had once belonged to him, her hair half spilling out of the clawed clasp she used to keep it on top of her head. They were sitting on the sofa having a glass of wine.

"Mostly the siege of Paris and the War of 1870—he called it the end of his childhood."

"Must have been awful."

"Traumatic, but things weren't so bad in the École Militaire where they lived. Oh, I almost forgot. Three or four sessions ago, he told me all about his father's atelier and artistry, and I just finished typing up the notes." St. Clair pulled the pages from his bag.

"He was a formal religious painter, right?" she asked, looking at the pages.

"Yes, at the insistence of his wife," St. Clair said, heading for the bathroom. "Go ahead—read it while I get ready to go to dinner."

"My father's atelier was on the top floor of our house, up five flights of stairs. It ran across the back of the building side to side and had a wide wall of windows over a balcony facing north. The near north view was dominated by the Dome Church of the Hôtel des Invalides, and since my father considered Louis XIV the height of civilization, he never tired of linking his work to the monarchy. He always set his easel perpendicular to the windows, saying his paintings were bathed in the golden light of the Sun King's Dome. He managed to ignore the fact that some of the glow of the Dome may have come from the spirit rising from Napoleon's crypt below, a theory I occasionally brought up to chide his obsessions after I became an adult.

"When I was a boy, you could tell a good story of the history of Paris from our roof. Before the neighborhood was built up, you could glimpse the spires of Notre Dame and the dome of the Panthéon. Across the Seine you could see the Arc de Triomphe, the new Palais Garnier opera house, the Hôtel de Ville, and the foundations of Sacré-Coeur up on Montmartre. Later, of course, we could see the Eiffel Tower rise over the rooftops as it reached its spectacular heights.

"When my father was younger, concentrating on his career and establishing himself in the Paris Salon, Paul and Albert were not allowed in the studio while he was working. But my sister Marie, whom he greatly favored, softened him up, and when I came along, I was welcome to keep him company at any time. He kept drawing pads and even a small easel for me. Marie and I became two of his favorite models and we famously appeared, along with him, in one of his greatest works, *The Departure of the Missionaries*, which was in the 1869 Salon.

"When I was a boy I loved being up there watching him work. There were paintings or studies or sketches on every wall. The wall on the east end above his work tables and cabinets was reserved for his best, his chosen work. It was covered from floor to ceiling, which was about twelve feet, in the manner of the salon exhibitions. And when I entered my teens and my talent for illustration developed a little, I even enjoyed sketching in his presence. We had a good dialogue, and while my views of the world evolved in opposition to his, we remained very close.

"My father would deny it because he was such an ardent loyalist, but there was a time when I believe he had strong Republican sympathies. Around 1847 or 1848, he traveled to Algiers, Egypt, and Jerusalem and experienced life, I believe, on a different level. His artistic subjects were common people on the street and in the souks, and guides on the pyramids. When he came back to Paris, his first major painting, by far my favorite, was called *At the Cabaret*. It was an intimate and personal portrait of five working-class men playing cards at a table, cravats around their necks. It captured a scene of real life, as if my father was responding to the call of Baudelaire—to paint life as it was, not as he imagined it. That might have been anathema to him later, under my mother's influence, but early on, I think he had sympathy for the struggles of the working man. What is particularly striking about *At the Cabaret* is the way the light falls through the leaded-glass window and illuminates the red beret and face of the man looking forward from the back of the table. That red beret, the red cap of liberty, was still a symbol of revolutionary France in those days.

"What comes back to mind even before the imagery is the sensational smell of turpentine, which was faint in the mornings but filled the studio and hall in the late afternoons when he opened the cabinets and began to clean his brushes. Even the oil paints had curiously alluring odors, some of poppy seed and walnut and linseed oils, which smelled so good they were nearly edible. He had tinctures, powders, and glass tubes of pigment. He even dyed his own colors on occasion, but he enjoyed the trips to Blot's Painting Emporium on rue Saint-Honoré, where he could spend hours discussing the merits of a cerulean blue or an old vermilion while I waited and played with Monsieur Blot's dogs, a curly-haired poodle and a rough-coated Airedale.

"I still have the old wooden paint box he used in Mirville in those summers *en plein air*. I brought it back to Paris as a keepsake after he died. I don't know why I've kept it, just couldn't seem to let it go. I shipped it to Lausanne when we sold the house on Oudinot in 1919, after the war. Such a beautiful home, so central to everything. It broke my heart to sell it, but my work was in Lausanne then and I needed the money."

"It has a sad ending," Juliette noted as she changed for dinner. She stopped for a moment to watch Jacques shave in the small mirror over their sink.

"Yes, his life after Paris always seems tinged with a measure of sadness," St. Clair said, thinking about a poignant moment when Coubertin spoke about letting go of his life in the City of Light. As soon as the baron mentioned selling the house, he became vulnerable and hesitant. He suddenly seemed his age, overtaken with fatigue. The vibrant memories of his youth, which had filled him with such joy when he'd first brought them back, dissipated quickly in the face of the hardships he had suffered after losing the family home he treasured.

10

THE WAR

T he next morning, St. Clair arrived at his office early and spent a few hours typing up his notes on Coubertin's recollections of the 1870 Franco-Prussian War.

"My childhood essentially ended when I was eight, which is when I became, by necessity and by circumstance, a young adult. War brought change to my family, to Paris, and to France. It introduced a level of disruption and anxiety that was, in many ways, the death knell of the ease and fantasies that had filled my days before the war. The war was the beginning of my adult education. What I saw and heard then, in the near panic in my home and the chaos of the streets, pushed me toward a serious bent and made me, I believe, a lifelong seeker of alternatives to violence and armed conflict. Yes, I was angry for my country after the defeat by Germany, and when I was young I did want to see our pride restored through glorious conquest, but that period passed as I awoke to the intellectual and moral possibilities of life in a peaceful society.

"On the day I turned eight, January 1, 1871, Paris had been under siege for 105 days and the people inside the city were starving, all two hundred thousand of them. The Franco-Prussian War, launched by Napoleon III the summer before, was a disaster from the start. When Napoleon and eighty thousand French soldiers were captured at Sedan that September, we all knew it was only a matter of days before the Germans reached Paris. They laid siege on September 18, cutting off all supplies and travel in and out. On January 6, they turned their canons on the city.

Some of their artillery landed in the Latin Quarter, hitting the Panthéon and the Sorbonne and horrifying all of us on the Left Bank.

"My brothers, Paul and Albert, were serving with the National Army at the time, and they were with the troops inside the city. Both were officers, so they were able to keep my parents apprised of events and offer some protection. Our home was in the École Militaire anyway, where the presence of the army was particularly pronounced. My parents tried to maintain a level of normalcy in our home, having Maude—our live-in maid—serve dinner every night, with my sister Marie and me at the table. Father continued to employ the servants, even our coachman, Henri, though we weren't taking the coach or horses out into the city.

"On the night of my birthday, the family made the usual fuss and gave me a new saddle and riding boots—and I played the role of the surprised child, but I knew I wouldn't be riding Cyrano, my favorite horse, for some time. That night when the cake was served, my brother Paul arrived, his face gripped by the tight strap of a plumed regimental hat, his blue, gold-buttoned uniform crossed in a red sash, a silver sword swinging in its sheath at his side as he strode into the room in high boots. He hugged me and wished me a happy birthday, but quickly turned to give news in hushed tones to my mother and father. I heard them talk of troubles up by Montmartre with rebellious Parisians and continuing losses in every battle with the Germans.

"I was sent to bed but crept back down the stairs and heard everything, as I usually did. My brother told of the houses of the rich being pilloried and burned.

"Several months later, when the Commune took over the city and the barricades went up, General Thiers withdrew the National Army to Versailles, recognizing that a battle in the streets, at a time when the soldiers of the National Guard had already betrayed their oath and sided with the Communards in the riots and chaos, was probably doomed to fail. Paul and Albert moved out of the city with the troops, which filled my mother with dread. She relied on their presence for her sense of security. Still, some protection was nearby, which I think saved us at the time. A battalion was stationed in the École Militaire to protect the army's property, and when a barricade went up on the boulevard des Invalides just a few blocks south of rue Oudinot toward Montparnasse, it was cleared away quickly by a few platoons and the cavalry.

"The trauma of the war instilled in all of us, I think, a deep desire for social order. The chaos of the Commune and the barricades, Frenchmen killing each other without reason, citizens accused of crimes that were fiction, persecuted because of their status or simply by being in the wrong place at the wrong time, the insanity of the blind devotion to a color, and the cruel inhumanity of the powerless once they gained power—it all seemed so insane. The lessons of those days and the sense of fear that touched my family were burned deeply into my being.

"France disappeared into a social frenzy of mob violence and vengeance against imagined wrongs, and Paris became an inferno of vicious acts, a city under the control of a populace without compassion or conscience."

It was late in the afternoon at Mon Repos. They were almost finished for the day, Coubertin standing and buttoning his waistcoat, when St. Clair asked him if he had witnessed any violence himself, had seen any fighting, or knew of acts of heroism during the war.

He stopped buttoning and let his chin fall to his chest. "I saw enough blood in one day during the siege to know I never wanted to see war up close again," he said, sitting back down. "And yes, I did see an act of heroism. We had a hero in the house."

Coubertin spoke without pausing for an hour.

"During the siege, before the Commune forced the family to hide inside, my mother felt a calling to help where she could. Although my parents were very protective, since I was the baby of the family, she took me out into the city as she sought to serve the sick and the wounded. Before we went out, she put on a white nurse's uniform and hat, then wrapped a white armband with a red cross around her arm, and another around mine. She insisted it was very important that I keep the armband on all the time and never lose it. She called me her 'orderly' and ordered me to get things when she was working in a clinic.

"We always moved fast when we hurried through the streets, trying to avoid the rush of people, carriages, and wagons bearing wounded soldiers. The image I remember most clearly is the number of Red Cross flags above doorways. They hung from balconies and on makeshift flagpoles, sticking out into the street in all directions. As the war raged outside the city, it was as if every open building had been converted into an ambulance—the name for any medical facilities set up as a small hospital. I remember seeing flags of the Red Cross flying on the Odéon, the Comédie-Française, and the Invalides, of course, but also on schools, bakeries, cafés. They were everywhere. Even after the war, when I walked with my father through the city, we once pulled a half-burned Red Cross flag from the rubble of the Tuileries.

"The first two or three times my mother took me with her, we went to the same destination, a small apothecary on rue du Dragon off Saint-Germain. A Dr. Antoine worked there with some nurses, mostly treating soldiers who had found their way back to their own neighborhood and families, cleaning and dressing wounds, but also sick men and women and feverish children with all sorts of maladies. The apothecary had a good stock of supplies, and my mother had some medical training so she knew how to use a number of medicines. She was quite good at calming and comforting the ill and applying stinging medications or soothing lotions and salves. She could stitch up a wound, and I helped by keeping the water clean and hot and by giving her new rolls of tape and gauze from the shelves in the back.

"My father always objected to my mother's work and they argued about it over dinner, but he couldn't stop her when she evoked the Lord and insisted it was her religious duty to the people and to France, that the blessings of Jesus on our family required this service. She was never fearful and felt God would protect us from harm, which even I knew was a leap of faith.

"One afternoon in the apothecary, two men brought an officer in on a stretcher, his old mother crying beside him and appealing to Dr. Antoine to rescue her boy, whose blue and red uniform was bloodied. They lifted him onto the table in the middle of the front room where the doctor tended patients, just inside the window, which was usually packed with the faces of curious people. As Antoine calmed the mother and led her back out the door, my mother unbuttoned the officer's coat, noticing the edge of a card sticking out of the breast pocket. She stripped him down and began cleaning a bloody shoulder wound as Dr. Antoine went to work, probing for a bullet. The officer grimaced and woke, fear on his face, mumbling something about America. Antoine spoke to him softly, using an ether rag to put him to sleep.

"When they finished, my mother pulled the card from his coat and showed it to Dr. Antoine. It read, 'If I am wounded, please take me to the American Ambulance.'

"'Where have the Americans set up their ambulance?' my mother asked.

"'On the avenue de l'Impératrice. It's an impressive hospital. All the soldiers want to be taken there because the Americans learned how to treat the wounded effectively in their own Civil War.'

"'What do they know that we don't?'

"'I'm not sure, Marie,' Antoine said, 'but if you'd like to work there, I could arrange it.'

"Dr. Antoine respected my mother's skills and appreciated her devotion to his clinic, but he knew she wanted to do something more. So he recommended her to his friend, Dr. Thomas Evans, who had set up the American Ambulance—and it was there, on one long and devastating day, that I saw in my mother a measure of courage I did not know a woman could possess. She was like Joan of Arc to me after that day, bloodied but defending France by rescuing those who fell on the battlefield."

St. Clair was moved by Coubertin's recollection of a harrowing scene from his mother's work at the American Ambulance and immediately drafted a passage of the scene to show Messerli.

Even though the city was under siege, Charles de Coubertin left for a few days with an escort provided by his sons and traveled down to Chevreuse to see his father, who was in critical condition. It was a weekday morning and Pierre was playing in the parlor when his mother called him and Marie down to the hallway. Wearing her nurse's hat and armband, she was standing with Henri, the coachman.

"I'm working today at the American Ambulance and I don't want to leave you two here. Get your coats and put these on." She handed them their Red Cross armbands.

"Where is it, Mother? Are we taking the coach?" Marie asked.

"It's across the Seine on the avenue de l'Impératrice and no, we're not taking the carriage."

"But that's too far to walk," Marie said.

"Marie," their mother replied, touching her daughter's cheek. "It's not too far. Henri will escort us, but we can't take the carriage. I don't want to put the horses at risk. So many people are starving. We've all heard the stories."

In the four months of the siege, the two hundred thousand people left inside Paris became increasingly desperate as food supplies dwindled. Family pets and street animals went into the ovens first—and then rapacious, hungry mobs began pulling horses out from under their riders in certain parts of the city. Carriages and cabs were overturned and left on the streets as their horses were led away to slaughter. The stables of some hotels and châteaux had been raided. Even the animals in the zoo—all of them, including the elephants—were eventually eaten.

They walked the two miles to the American Ambulance in formation behind the formidable Baroness Marie de Coubertin, holding her head high and asserting her authority as a woman on a medical mission. Henri walked only a step behind, pulling Marie and Pierre along to keep up. They crossed the Seine on the pont d'Iéna as the baroness warded off aggressive street merchants and beggars, parting crowds with her urgent look and steadfast pace. Passing through the Place du Trocadéro they moved up the avenue de Malakoff and then turned onto the avenue de l'Impératrice. Running between the Arc de Triomphe and the Bois de Boulogne, it was one of the great wide boulevards of Paris, lined with private palaces and international embassies. Pierre beheld the tented encampment of the American Ambulance covering the wide lawn of the American Legation on the south side. The large gray and brown canvas tents, stained by oil, were arrayed in enormous rectangles end to end like the halls of an exposition. A train of horse-drawn carriages moved under military escort up and down the avenue and crowded into a congested funnel at the front of the tents. Smoke rose from fires and stoves, and Pierre noticed that some of the stoves had pipes that ran into the sides of the tents, heating them, although he didn't find it that cold.

Through a jumble of wagons, carts, and open fire pits with black pots of water bubbling furiously, his mother led them toward the largest tent. The grounds were rutted and muddied by the wagon wheels and an army of nurses and others scurrying back and forth. As they drew closer, Pierre saw soldiers lying in the carts, some still and traumatized, some moaning or crying out in pain. Men were lifting them one by one and placing them on stretchers, which they carried in and out of the tents.

The Coubertins reached the open flaps of the largest tent; Pierre's mother motioned for them to wait. "I'm going to find Dr. Evans," she said softly, trying to comfort her children. "He's going to teach me triage."

Impulsively, Pierre grabbed Marie's hand and pulled her forward while Henri was looking away, and they entered the tent just behind their mother. She didn't try to stop them, and Henri followed.

It was warmer inside, heated by the pipes from the stoves, yet ventilated. Pierre felt a chilly breeze on his cheek. Before them a long, straight aisle of planks separated the beds on the left from supply stations and work tables on the right. Teams of white-frocked doctors and nurses were working on the wounded at a number of stations, but other soldiers were lying in wait, clearly desperate to be attended to.

The baroness surveyed the room and seemed to take it all in with both awe and understanding. Just as she stepped forward to inquire after Dr. Evans, the flap at the far end of the tent flew open. With a shout the head nurse rushed in, followed by men bearing several stretchers and a doctor in tow. As they approached the Coubertins, the head nurse paused and sent the stretchers down a row, then turned to the baroness with a severe look.

"I'm Betty Jean Russell and this is my hospital. I know you're here to help, but you're not doing us any good standing there—and you're going to have to get rid of these children."

"I'm Marie de Coubertin," the baroness answered. She turned quickly to Henri and Marie, who was starting to cry, and said, "Henri, take them home and watch them carefully."

"Dr. Campbell," Nurse Russell yelled, "here's your new assistant, Marie." She shoved the baroness toward the row of tables where the doctor was waiting. Then she turned and bent before young Marie, wiping away a tear. She smiled at Pierre and said, "Your mother is doing God's work here." She spoke with a choppy American accent and had a large red birthmark on her cheek; a mop of curly locks spread from the white crescent of her hat. But there was comfort in her voice, and as Henri herded them out of the tent, Pierre looked back to see his mother running a white cloth down a bloody arm she was holding up from the table.

When Madame Coubertin returned home mid-morning the next day, Pierre and Marie were stunned by the blood on her clothes. She dropped her cape in the hallway and they followed her up the stairs, where she collapsed on her bed without undressing.

11

THE WALK

The interviews on the war had occupied a few afternoons at the beginning of March. While it was still crisp and cold in the mornings, spring was coming early to Lausanne, and green was emerging on the plants and trees. To get away from the office for a day, St. Clair and Coubertin met for a long lunch and afternoon discussion at La Nautica, Émil Drut's restaurant behind the Château d'Ouchy. They had an exquisite view of the lake beneath the budding plane trees that filled the park behind the docks. All day long, ferries traversed back and forth to Evian, France, or up and down the lake to Geneva and Montreux. St. Clair made a note to take Juliette for a cruise to France one night.

Émil smiled as he hovered over them, ensuring his friend had everything he needed. "Ah, with the great writer again," he said. "And how is the story coming, Mr. Jacques?"

"Pierre is a master storyteller, Émil, so my work is quite easy. I just take notes. See?" St. Clair held up his notebook to tease old Drut, and Coubertin laughed. It seemed every time Émil came to the table—and he came again and again—he always loitered and sought to read what St. Clair was writing.

"He's just as curious as the rest of my old friends," Coubertin said. "They're all protective of me because they think I've been mistreated."

"Certainly some justification for that," St. Clair said. "Let's get back to work. I think we've talked enough about the war."

"I agree. Once General Thiers put down the Commune and my brothers were stationed back in Paris, our lives started to return to normal."

"What I've been wondering about is the following year. You started at Saint-Ignace in 1874—when you were eleven—but what happened in that period between the end of the conflict and your start at the new school?"

"Actually, that was a very significant time for me—and for my father," Coubertin said. "My grandfather, Julien, died during the siege, and I'm not sure my father ever felt right about the way all of that ended. In any event, he suddenly took a great interest in teaching me the history of Paris, and because of that we drew very close."

"You mean he sat you down and taught you the history of the city?"

"No, he took me on walks. And to tell you the truth, although I studied history all through Saint-Ignace, through the École Libre, and all of my adult life, these walks were the best history lessons I ever received."

"How did they start?"

"It wasn't long after the Commune was crushed and order was being restored again," Coubertin said, recollecting the times. "While my mother was still visiting the hospitals and tending the sick, taking my sister more often than me, I began to ask my father questions about the war and why Paris itself always seemed to shed so much blood."

"One morning as my father painted in his atelier, I was sitting nearby, trying to read Stendhal's *Sentimental Education*, which was a bit above my level but not too challenging. I had just come across a violent description of the 1848 revolt in Paris, a scene of troops firing on the revolutionaries and slaughtering their own, and it provoked me to wonder what my father had been doing then. He was twenty-six then, a young married artist who had just returned from a grand tour of the Orient. Here he was now, nearing fifty, and the streets of Paris were once again stained with the dried blood of patriots and anarchists, just as they had been in his youth. I wanted to know why.

"When I looked up with the question on my lips, I hesitated because my father seemed nervous. The studio was filled with sunlight. It was a lovely spring morning, the wall of windows illuminating the room, a day to be optimistic. But I could sense my father wasn't making any progress on his painting. I recognized the motions, a constant shift in the angles of his head, looking up, then back at the canvas, then away. He'd step back, then forward, then abruptly to the side. I knew he was about to end the session as he tossed his palette aside and picked up the turpentine rag. Something was on his mind as he walked to the window, rubbing the paint from his fingers. I joined him, getting a whiff of the turpentine.

"We looked across at the old stone wall behind our courtyard, at the high locust trees that were always late to bud, to the Golden Dome of Les Invalides, which we wouldn't see if the trees were fully leaved, up to the azure depths of the sky, as fine today as the brightest blue oil on his palette.

"'Father,' I asked, 'why did Paris have to go through another bloody revolt like it did when you were young? The soldiers shooting the people?'

"He looked down at me with soft eyes full of sympathy, seeing the Stendhal open in my hand and realizing, I think, that the traumas we'd seen had left my heart and mind unsteady and wondering—just as they had troubled him. He knelt down and took me by the shoulders, our faces only inches apart, every whisker in his fine beard and mustache in exactly the right place, and a faint hint of coffee beneath the cologne he wore.

"'Ah, my son, my precocious young son.' He ran his hand through my hair and spoke to me, not as a boy, but as someone who had seen war and witnessed the damage it had done. 'It is hard to be a child,' he said, 'in a nation that has yet to grow up. Our city is the heart of France and France is still trying to find her way in this turbulent world. I must teach you as much as I can about Paris, about the old Paris that is disappearing so quickly. The city you were born into is not the city I grew up in. I doubt that there has ever been so much change in one place at one time. But I think, Pierre, that you're ready to see it as it once was and to look ahead, perhaps, to what it may yet be.'

"He took the Stendhal from my hand and laid it on the windowsill before drawing me to him in a reassuring hug. Then he stood and said, 'Let's go for a walk.'"

○ ○ ○ ○ ○

Holding Pierre's hand, Charles de Coubertin stood back as their coachman, Henri, stepped past them in the arched passageway between their courtyard and street and pulled hard on the massive wooden door, swinging it wide as father and son emerged onto rue Oudinot. Twenty paces to their right, their narrow street opened onto the wide boulevard des Invalides, which was busy with clopping horse carriages, soldiers, and citizens moving past. Only two blocks beyond, they could see the green spring blooms of the plane trees bordering the Invalides Esplanade. Charles turned to his left and led Pierre along the winding cobblestone road into the old neighborhood, passing the fashionable town homes on rue Monsieur to the left and the St. Mary Clinic on the right. They stopped at the tables of the Roux Family Boulangerie at the corner of rue Vaneau, where Charles bought his son a petit scone and exchanged pleasantries with Monsieur Roux.

Passing the tailor shop where Charles had his suits made, they crossed rue de Babylone and followed rue Vaneau a block farther to rue de Varenne. Everything looked as it should—no signs of the terror of the Commune or the conflicts that had visited these tight old quarters. At the corner, the baron turned his son to the right and looked down at him.

"Before we go closer to the Seine where the fighting was rampant, I wanted you to see the glories that were France in a single home. We're going into the Hôtel Aramount," he said, leading Pierre along the sidewalk until the wall to their right curved inward to the impressive front gate, a massive arched entryway set in a concave wall of rusticated granite blocks and adorned on each side with a niche holding a mythological figure, one with a sword, the other with a harp. A soldier guarding the gate gazed at them as they stepped up, and Charles presented a card. He directed Pierre's gaze up to the pediment, to a statue of a muscled hero rescuing a woman, his arm raised in victory and his noble virtues captured forever in marble. A French flag and another with a coat of arms flurried against the blue sky. "The Aramounts want the world to know they'll defend our country," said Charles, indicating the beginning of his lesson.

They entered the immense courtyard, huge by comparison to their own humble hôtel, as a gold-trimmed six-passenger phaeton carriage with silver-spoked wheels turned slowly to the clip-clop of horseshoes and crossed before them, disappearing into the stone stables on their right. The cobblestone grid of the grand court led to the foot of a sweeping oval staircase, ascending around and between two pedestals topped with roaring lions. The powder white marble façade rose two stories to a balustrade that rimmed the roof like a crown, barely concealing the domes rising at each end of the house. A colonnade completed this *mise-en-scène*, truly a stage for performances. A balcony of iron and gold projected out from the arched glass doors on the second floor. The perfect lines, harmony, and artistry of the scene were disturbed only by the frightening faces of three mythical gargoyles carved into brackets beneath the balcony, glaring down in fixed expressions of anger designed to scare off any unwanted spirits.

Charles watched his son taking it all in, moving his gaze from side to side to absorb what his father wanted him to see.

"Can we go in?" Pierre asked.

"Of course, we can," Charles said, heading up the stairs. "The Aramounts are away but our families have been friends since his father served with your grandfather in Napoleon's army."

Charles had already taken Pierre inside the soaring Dôme des Invalides. He had guided him through the voluminous grandeur of the Panthéon and other grand buildings, including the Sistine Chapel, but he had never asked him to observe or study the atmosphere and effect of opulence in a private home like this.

As they stepped inside, they entered an interior world of immediate aesthetic effect. Amid a circle of fluted columns that defined the inside of the hexagonal entrance, the black-and-white tiles of the granite floor glistened like a polished stage. Like a conductor, Charles motioned with an open hand up the monumental marble staircase before them, which was banded in a black-and-gold railing of alternating metal shields and urns beneath the banister and led to a theatrical scene from the aristocratic past. The entire wall above was a mural of a royal party in progress, with women in resplendent gowns and men in finery laughing and drinking and leaning forward over an ornate balustrade to welcome each new arrival.

"This way, son," Charles said, laying a hand on Pierre's shoulder to guide him to the right. As they swept through a magnificent paneled doorway and a mirrored antechamber toward the golden glow of a bejeweled chamber, Charles harkened back to the past.

"In the early part of the century before Napoleon fell at Waterloo," he said, "Tallyrand and Aramount vied for social prominence in the Faubourg Saint-Germain. This street, rue de Varenne, represented the height of Paris fashion. It was in this very room—the Golden Salon—that your grandfather Julien often entertained the Aramounts' dinner guests with his violin."

They passed through double doors into a room beneath a rotunda—a room almost completely encrusted with gold. The wide chamber was formed by eight arched alcoves recessed from the walls, alternating as thresholds for filigreed mirrors or windows. Calling his son to his side, Charles pointed to the top of the alcoves, a series of ovoid vaults set off by golden pilasters fringed with a tracery of fine vines and carved laurel wreaths. In every other one, a statue was set in a cartouche formed by the quarter sphere of the ceiling. Patiently and carefully, the baron described the symbolism of a *rinceaux* of delicate acanthus leaves, which were repeated everywhere—honeysuckle and rosettes wound in volute strands of golden pearls embedded in the edge of the wood, egg-shaped symbols of fertility, every inch pleasing to the eye, every detail expressing the luxury of that world.

Charles felt he was in the midst of a world in danger of disappearing—and he wanted his son to see what he saw. "Take it all in, son," the baron said, admiring the artistry himself. The room was topped with a domed ceiling soaring above a circular hedge of glimmering gold arabesques. The walls were covered with paintings of sylvan settings with dreamy winged men reaching for reclining beauties surrounded by seraphim, scenes of natural love and peace in wooded landscapes of an idealized past.

In the middle of the room, Charles tapped his foot on the inlaid parquet-and-ivory floor and did a little dance for his son, spinning around a long dining table set for a party of twelve, playing an invisible violin and humming a pretty song as the boy looked on, smiling with obvious amusement. "This, Pierre," the baron said, "was the world your grandfather inhabited, not as a central player, but as a friend granted access in recognition of his military prowess and his musical skills."

As they left, Charles asked whether Pierre understood what he was trying to teach him.

"I think so, Father," the boy said. "Our family was once part of this world, a world of kings and their courts of royalty, a world where we were welcomed into rooms of gold."

Charles couldn't have been more pleased with his son's response. "You're a gifted boy," he said, "truly precocious. But that was only the first half of the lesson today."

Leaving the rarified atmosphere of the Hôtel Aramount, they hurried up rue de Bac, the baron's pace now more insistent. The lesson was about to change. As they crossed the intersection of the boulevards Saint-Germain and Raspail, Charles didn't pause for even a second to take in the view Haussmann had created. That would come later. Rubble was strewn on the road ahead, and smoke rose above the buildings on rue de Université and rue de Lille. As they crossed rue de Université, the baron glanced down the narrow trench of the street; it looked like a deep gutter, piled with debris and overturned wagons and stones. Smoke seeped out of some distant windows, the residue of a riot. As he guided his son around the corner at rue de Lille, the scene was even worse. A barricade of rubble had been built over horse carts turned on their sides, blocking the long rut of the street beyond. "This is what the Commune left behind," the baron muttered, looking up at the façades of several grand mansions that had been torn open. Grimacing at the scene and gasping at the acrid smell of the ruins, Charles picked a path ahead toward the Hôtel de Pomereu, which the rebels of the Commune had ransacked and burned.

Ahead, several soldiers were watching a group of laborers move in and out of the open ruin of the Pomereu gate, each bearing trash and stones and throwing them onto a pile on the street. The baron led his son between the fallen walls into the grand court, where two gentlemen, dressed in tailored overcoats, hats, and cravats were supervising a larger group of workers. They nodded at the baron as he and Pierre passed. Ahead, three men were trying to upright a grand *coulée de gala*, a once beautiful red carriage. Behind them the carcass of a horse lay half exposed in the doorway, still harnessed in a small covered phaeton whose roof had been ripped to shreds.

"Pierre," the baron said, "come with me." They stepped over broken glass and shards of sash as they climbed the stairs and entered the torched, blackened doors of a nearly destroyed opulent family hôtel. A stone mason and his crew were already rebuilding the blocks around the entrance, preparing the frame for a new door. Inside, the mansion was structurally similar to the Aramount, with a grand staircase on the right, but the walls were blackened with soot and the great chandelier lay on the floor in a tangle of twisted metal and shattered crystals.

"The Pomereus fled before the Commune riots started," Charles said, directing the boy around the debris, "which is one reason their mansion was attacked." As they moved toward the antechamber, Charles reached down and unhinged a small crystal obelisk from the fallen chandelier, carved into a small diamond-like point, and handed it to Pierre. "Take this, son, and every time you look at the light reflecting through it, remember what you saw here."

They moved through the first room, strewn with more broken glass and overturned cabinets, tables, and chairs before entering another large room that once glowed golden. Charles froze, gazing up at the vaulted ceiling, which was burned open, a charred black frame for the blue sky above.

Looking down, the baron scowled at the inventory of damage. A statue of a Greek ruler lay at the foot of its pedestal, arms broken, the head with a crushed granite nose lying six feet away against the base of the wall where it had rolled. A pair of golden cherubs were untouched on the cornice above, but their twins from across the room lay in pieces on the floor below. What remained of the ceiling fresco, once a gorgeous scene of inlaid panels that told a story of French history, was now burned and smeared with black soot. A portrait of an honored ancestor was torn across the body, hanging out of its splintered golden frame. Mirrors shattered but still in their frames presented fragmented images of the whole dismal scene.

Frowning in anger, the baron said nothing. He merely took his son's hand and guided him back out of the room, out of the hotel, across the courtyard, and back into the street. They headed for the pont Royale and crossed over the Seine.

"I want to see the Tuileries," Charles said on the bridge, where they stopped for a few seconds to take in the small plumes of smoke still hanging in the air over Montmartre and parts of rue de Rivoli, and, more tragically, over the Hôtel de Ville. "My God," Charles exclaimed, "they burned down the town hall."

In ten minutes of fast walking, they passed by the Louvre on the right bank of the Seine and came upon the former Royal Palace of the Tuileries, now a smoking pile of stone beneath the haunting skeletal structure of the building. A motley trickle of men and women moved among the debris, picking through the ruins, hoping to find something of value. Charles stood in silent disbelief, mourning the lost glories of the *Ancien Regime*.

"It's hard to believe what we're seeing," Charles said as they took in the scene. "What in God's name possessed these rebels to torch this beautiful palace?"

"Look, Father," Pierre kicked aside some rubble and pulled on a piece of red cloth. A torn sheet broke free, a piece of fabric with half a white cross stitched on its front. "The Red Cross was here," he said. "Mother will want to know."

Charles hailed a passing coach cab and took Pierre up to the Church of Sainte-Marie-Madeleine. They entered and sat in a pew. Charles prayed for some time before he led Pierre down the front steps and to the Restaurant Durand, where they sat outside with a full view of the Place de la Madeleine.

"Charcuterie, please," said Charles.

It had been a long afternoon for St. Clair, and Coubertin was at the end of the story that had become a touchstone in his relationship with his father over the years that followed. Neither ever forgot the experience. In fact, they gave it a name—the Walk of Glory and Ruin—and they referred to it nearly every time their recollections turned back to that day, or when some point of France's grand architectural patrimony arose. It was the first in a series of walks his father had led him on, each filled with an insight of one kind or another.

The shadows outside had lengthened to the east as St. Clair continued to make notes on everything Pierre had recalled. He could see the old man was tired and needed fresh air, but he had one more question.

"What happened after that dinner at the Restaurant Durand? Did your father ever express the anger he was feeling or explain what it all meant from his perspective?"

Coubertin sighed. "Oh yes, he made sure I understood what he was trying to teach me." He reminisced further.

"My father sat in silence for a while, looking at his charcuterie, still simmering with anger over the ruins he had shown me. He was an artist, yes, but not a fading sensitive painter averse to confrontation. He raised two army officers and believed the monarchy had led France to greatness—and like so many Frenchman of his time, he wanted that greatness back again. He had little stomach for the cries of the revolutionaries for the rights of man when all he saw of revolution was the kind of destruction we had seen that day. He sipped his red wine and we looked at each other across the table. I could see the fire in his eyes; his anger was palpable.

"He saw I was anxious, that his reaction and silence had worried me, and like the caring man he was, he responded and remembered that he had taken me for this walk to teach me something he considered important.

"'Pierre,' he said, 'we have seen two sides of France today.' He paused to consider how he could explain his perspective to me. 'A side of glory and a side of ruin.'

"The waiter brought a small wooden bowl with two green apples to the table, and my father smiled in thanks. He pulled out a pocketknife, opened it, and proceeded to peel the apple, slicing off a nice chunk of the flesh and offering it to me on the extended point of the knife.

"'I wanted you to see, son, that man is at his best when he gives full rein to his creative instincts and draws the inspiration of artistry from his soul—and man is at his worst when he gives rein to violence and runs with the mob in search of blood, a fiery torch in his hand. Art brings out the noble aspirations of man; violence pushes him back toward the cave. One instinct elevates society, the other destroys it. If you want to celebrate the rights of man, build a cathedral to democracy, don't burn down the mansions of your neighbor.'

"My father fell quiet again, and I didn't know what to say. The sweetness of the apple filled my mouth, even as his words tinged the moment with bitterness.

"'I can't imagine what the future holds for France, son, or what it holds for you—but something has to be done to give this nation political stability, to stop the insanity of Frenchmen killing Frenchmen. Maybe your generation will find a new path back to the glories we once held so dear.'

"He looked out longingly at the pillars of the Madeleine, and I followed his gaze to the façade of a Greek temple that evoked the classical achievements of the past."

12

THE ARTIST

One morning in early March, a month after they arrived in Lausanne, St. Clair was in the kitchen, brewing coffee, cooling down from a morning run, waiting for Juliette to awaken. Thinking about his upcoming session with Coubertin that day, he anticipated learning a few things about Avery Brundage, the controversial head of the American Olympic Committee. They were scheduled to have dinner with him that evening, and St. Clair was trying to imagine how the baron would interact with one of the young lions of his movement. He was also wondering how he was going to corner Brundage for an interview before he left town.

Juliette emerged from the bedroom in her bathrobe and fluffy slippers. "Pour me a cup, please," she said, pulling open the drapes, filling the room with light and illuminating the canvas mounted on her easel. She gazed out the window and turned as Jacques brought her coffee.

"How'd you sleep?" he asked, bending over and kissing her neck, catching the sweet scent of her unwashed hair.

"Like a baby. But look at this, a nightmare in oil," she said, gesturing toward the canvas, a fairly ordinary depiction of the extraordinary mountainscape they looked at every day. She had painted it straight away, a realistic composition without any of the daring colors, brush strokes, or imagination that marked her best Parisian cityscapes, many of which were focused on statues and architecture. St. Clair was beginning to worry that she wasn't challenged or inspired here, and he knew that could be a problem.

"This is my third landscape in the last two weeks," Juliette complained. "I can't look at another vista—and I don't want anything to do with a still life, a vine, a flower, or a shard of pottery. I need to paint people."

"Well then, paint people," St. Clair said. "You haven't looked up that art class Dr. Messerli told you about. You haven't gone up to the Place Saint-François and sketched the Swiss coming and going. Perhaps you just need to get out and start interacting with the locals. What happened to that sequence of glass studies you were working on before we left Paris?"

"The abstracts? This isn't the place for abstracts, Jacques. I'll tell you what I need—I need to meet Pierre and discuss something with him. You've kept him to yourself long enough."

"I'm not keeping him to myself. You've met him." He moved to the table and pulled the cloth cover off a basket of croissants.

"That introduction on the sidewalk hardly counts. And yes, you *are* keeping him to yourself." She settled down across from him and smiled. "Every night you come home with these stories about his life—things maybe no one else has ever heard—and I don't even know him."

"Well, Dr. Messerli and his wife are having that party the week after next and you'll be meeting everyone there."

"I don't want to wait for that party—that's not my point. You've entered into a whole new world, looking at the entire life of a man and a worldwide movement he launched. I want to meet him to see what he's like—and I also want to paint him."

"You want to paint Pierre? Is that what you want to talk to him about?" St. Clair was surprised. Juliette had never shown any interest in portraiture.

"Yes. There's a lot of symbolism in his world, connections to the past, ancient myth, young people, political leaders, great athletes, flags and pageantry and celebration." She went back to the doors and looked out at the vista she was tired of painting. "I'm wondering what I'm going to see in the eyes of a man who has lived in the middle of that universe."

"Ah, I get it. You want to step into my world and share my adventure."

"Yes, Jacques, I admit it. I want to see what this little genius of sport is all about too. That's what you've called him, isn't it, genius of sport?"

"Sometimes. That's what I'm thinking of calling the book."

"Well, you've got me intrigued. Not only that, he comes from a family of artists. He might enjoy having his portrait done, maybe in very contemporary Olympic style."

"Olympic style?" St. Clair asked. "What's that? All right, I'll bring him up here after lunch and you can ask him about it. I'm sure Pierre will love talking to you."

St. Clair got back earlier than expected, without Coubertin, and heard Juliette singing in the shower. He knew the song, "Give My Regards to Broadway," an old American tune she had learned from her mother as a child and often reprised while shampooing her long locks. He tiptoed up and yanked open the shower curtain, startling her, and she quickly pulled the curtain across her body.

"Is Pierre here?" she asked.

"No, he couldn't come up," St. Clair said, smiling and reaching for the edge of the curtain teasingly. She frowned. "We've got this dinner with Brundage tonight and I suspect there may be a couple of meetings to follow. He said he'd love to meet you for lunch after Brundage leaves town. He's suggested Friday— on the patio at the Croix d'Ouchy. I told him you were in love with Paris and wanted to hear his stories of growing up in the 7th."

"Well, that's partly true," she agreed as St. Clair left the room.

In seconds he heard her pick up the next verse:

Say hello to dear Coney Isle, if there you chance to be.
When you're at the Waldorf have a "smile" and charge it up to me.

St. Clair smiled as he sat down and pulled out his notebook to read through what he had just written. As he opened the book to that morning's notes, he remembered the sparkle in Pierre's eye when he told him his charming American fiancée, a painter, wanted to meet him. He was thinking how much Pierre was going to enjoy Juliette's company, just as she hit the chorus and sang loudly,

Give my regards to Broadway, remember me to Herald Square.
Tell all the gang at Forty-Second Street, that I will soon be there ...

13

THE INDUSTRIALIST

oubertin, Messerli, and St. Clair rose together to greet Brundage, who arrived with some bluster, peeling off an expensive belted raincoat, shaking it free of rain, and handing it with his hat to the maître d'. Brundage was a large man, Messerli's size, and he immediately strode around the table to lean over and embrace Coubertin—awkwardly given the differences in their sizes, but with clear and genuine affection. Pulling back a step, he stood straight up and clasped the baron's arms in his big hands, smiling and gazing intently at the little man.

"You look very good, Mr. President. You retain a robustness in your cheeks that all younger men must admire." He turned with Coubertin's introduction to shake St. Clair's hand with a nearly crippling grip.

"The great Jacques St. Clair," he said, with a burst of air that caused St. Clair to blink. "Here doing God's work, I understand." He winked at Coubertin and moved quickly around the table, greeting Messerli with a hug and a booming "Francis" that turned a few heads.

As they settled into their seats, St. Clair noted that Brundage waited for Coubertin to speak. "It's good to see you, Avery," the baron began. "I'm glad you were able to come." The waiter appeared with a bottle of wine for Coubertin's inspection. "I've ordered a bottle of Château La Dominique Grand Cru of St. Émilion, which I hope is to your liking." He looked at Brundage with a sidelong glance.

"Is it a 1930?"

"Indeed it is."

"As always, your taste is exquisite, Mr. President. I'll be delighted to share that Bordeaux with you."

"How was your trip down from London?" Coubertin asked.

"Uneventful," Brundage said. "I bring you warm greetings and regards from Sigfrid and"—he paused, looking pointedly at St. Clair—"a number of ideas that we believe worthy of your consideration."

St. Clair heard a clear deference in Brundage's tone as he addressed the restorer of the Games. It was a deliberate, dutifully expressed respect from a man who, it was well known, was not accustomed to bowing before anyone and could in fact be quite combative. He was a highly successful American industrialist, a construction magnate with a taste for fine Asian art and French wine. In Olympic circles, he was known for his adamant passion for amateurism and his devotion to Coubertin's Olympic ideal.

St. Clair knew his story. Brundage had competed on the American Olympic team at the 1912 Stockholm Games, placing sixth in the very tough pentathlon won with ease by Jim Thorpe. Although it was twenty-five years later, he appeared to have maintained some interest in exercise. His body was toned, its broad, stocky structure symbolizing, to St. Clair's eye, the strength of an American football player. He sat upright like a soldier, moving his shoulders and his square, fleshy face together to convey his full attention to each speaker. His hair was receding and combed back, with touches of gray on the thicker sides. He wore delicate wire-rimmed glasses that added a note of thoughtfulness to the blunt look of his round nose, full lips, and clean-shaven cheeks. He was elegantly attired in a dark gray suit with stylish topstitching along the edge of the lapels, and a blue regimental tie offset by a white button-down shirt. His manners seemed impeccable.

"Mr. President, with your permission," Brundage said, placing a small red velvet bag with drawstrings in the middle of the table, "I've also brought you a small gift."

Coubertin seemed to hesitate for a moment. St. Clair wondered if his *savoir faire* had escaped him given the serious business on his mind. But he quickly recovered, leaning forward with a grin, reaching for the velvet bag. St. Clair watched with fascination as a ritual unfolded before him. He knew the tradition of giving small gifts, as an expression of affection or appreciation, had become an endearing social custom within the Olympic family. Messerli claimed Coubertin had started the ritual himself, and Brundage had become one of its most avid practitioners.

Coubertin unwrapped an exquisite ivory figure, a hand-carved image of a Japanese samurai about four inches tall. It rested neatly in his hand as he examined it. "Beautiful, and so delicately carved." He handed it to Messerli.

"It's a *netsuke*, Mr. President, a popular historical form of miniature sculpture in Japan. They're highly desired collectibles."

"Thank you, Avery," Coubertin said.

As St. Clair learned during the course of the dinner, the baron had asked Brundage to meet with Sigfrid Edström and discuss at length Coubertin's proposal on how to address the threat to the IOC emanating from Berlin. Messerli later made it clear that Coubertin recognized Brundage and Edström as two of the most powerful members of the IOC at that point—clearly destined for future leadership roles if Baillet-Latour's health continued to fail. St. Clair knew that several things about Brundage—and a few about Edström—irked Coubertin, and the baron was not one to hide his displeasures. Although he was no longer in control of the IOC, St. Clair knew he was determined to rescue it from the disastrous trap the Germans had set. He wondered when the baron would address the issue.

As the dinner progressed, Brundage described at length how successful the Berlin Games had been and what a hero Jesse Owens had become back in the United States. Brundage was pushing hard for some recognition that he had been right all along and that any discussion about the American team's participation—which had produced a firestorm of protest in the United States and nearly a boycott—had been counterproductive.

Coubertin interrupted. "Yes, it was certainly an efficient competition. The Germans are always strong on logistics." He sat back in his chair, reserved and polite. "But it was a military celebration as much as anything. All those uniforms, just politicizing sport and using our Games to elevate the image of National Socialism."

"I would say it was more than simple efficiency," Brundage said, "and the promotion of National Socialism was kept at bay."

As if a switch had been thrown, something happened to Coubertin at that instant. He assumed a larger presence, his posture became more pronounced, and he seemed to lift himself higher with his elbows on the table. St. Clair was suddenly aware of a transformation in his aspect—the baron quickly became more assertive and emerged again from his old beaten shell as an energized leader. The man who had once possessed the force of will to control everything around him, to move mountains, shape circumstances, and motivate people to recognize their role in the greater good—that man was suddenly there again at the table.

"First of all, Avery," Coubertin said, "your defense of the American Olympic team's participation in the Berlin Games was morally right."

St. Clair glanced at Messerli, and it was clear the doctor was equally absorbed by the emergent force of the old man. Coubertin chose his words with purpose.

"I applaud your relentless obstinacy in ensuring your national team was there.

The Germans we chose to host the Games were not the Germans in power three years later. But we cannot allow the Games to be subject to national political changes on either side—the hosts or the teams—and expect them to survive." He paused for emphasis before delivering his next words with some force. "But both you and Sigfrid have been too sympathetic and certainly too lenient in placating the Nazis. You especially, Avery, crossed the line and ignored some very legitimate complaints about the exclusion of Jewish athletes—and not only from the German team. As I see it, you may have set the stage for Baillet-Latour's capitulation. I know he had been strong on some points with Hitler—demanding the removal of offensive signage—but he has become weak."

Brundage was quick to defend himself. "Mr. President, they did a brilliant job organizing the Games. The pageantry was arresting, and the torch relay may be the greatest of all modern sport innovations since Athens."

"I'll give you that, Avery," Coubertin said. "They're masters of symbolism, and the torch relay is a wondrous expression of the eternal character of the Olympic spirit. However, regardless of their resources and their promotional abilities, we cannot let the International Olympic Committee fall under their spell or, God forbid, their control."

St. Clair could see that Brundage was chagrined, but the industrialist backed away, refusing to challenge his president. He nodded and clearly seemed to register the fire in Coubertin's eyes.

"I agree, Mr. President," Brundage said, his tone lower, more humble, "and so does Sigfrid. We do not take this threat lightly."

Coubertin did not let up. "Did you know that Diem was presenting this proposal to Baillet-Latour in Brussels?"

"I did not. But I did know, even before the Games were over, that Goebbels and Hitler had discussed the possibilities of a permanent home for the Olympics—and investing more energy into the Olympic Movement."

St. Clair was stunned by this revelation as Coubertin pursued the point with exasperation in his voice. "You knew about this? You discussed it with them?"

"No, it wasn't a discussion. It was only a passing conversation, and I told Goebbels in no uncertain terms it was completely out of the question. I made it clear that the rotation of the Games among the capitals of the world was an inviolable principle of the Olympic Charter."

Coubertin pulled back from the line of criticism. He had made his point and seemed certain that Brundage was on his side. "So what do you think we ought to do now, Avery?"

"Well, first, we have to reject the proposal from Diem through the executive board. We will not confirm Baillet-Latour's encouragement."

"A postal vote by the executive board?"

"As soon as I can arrange it," Brundage said. "I'll speak with Blonay tomorrow."

"And what should we do about Diem?" St. Clair was fascinated, realizing the decisions at hand could determine Olympic history.

Brundage's response was blunt. "We'll do whatever we have to do to take him out of the Olympic Movement."

Coubertin responded quickly. "I'd rather sacrifice Lewald if it comes down to it—if someone has to go. I assume we can't touch von Halt."

St. Clair was surprised by Coubertin's move to defend Diem by offering up Theodore Lewald, who had served as the president of the Berlin Olympic Organizing Committee.

"The Nazis will certainly protect von Halt," Brundage said. "But Lewald is vulnerable."

Coubertin spoke up. "I don't want to undermine Carl too much or put him at risk with his masters. He's been productive and faithful over the years, but I'm sure that in that system he's had to fight for his survival. I think he's become an opportunist out of necessity—and now he seems to have compromised everything he believed in. I'm going to ask him to come to Lausanne—and I won't be easy on him."

"He won't be able to stop their grand designs," Brundage said.

"No. But we will," Coubertin said. "You'll drive the vote to reject through the executive board, and I'll ensure Carl knows there's no hope that this plan will ever be approved. He'll take the message back to Germany."

St. Clair felt the tension abate as the conversation turned to Jesse Owens. Coubertin complimented St. Clair on the feature he had written about the friendship between the black American and the blond German long-jumper Luz Long. The table was of one mind that their friendship symbolized the core mission of the Olympic Movement—to bring athletes together across all of the international boundaries that divided them.

As dinner ended, Coubertin insisted Brundage and Messerli agree to join him for a strategy session the next day in the IOC offices. When they left the restaurant, they stopped in the street to say their goodbyes. As Brundage and Messerli walked away, Coubertin tugged on St. Clair's sleeve to delay his departure.

"I want you to be there in the morning, Jacques," the baron said. "This may be one of my last real Olympic initiatives and you might as well witness it. I'm not quite through with Avery yet." St. Clair nodded in agreement, aware that the fire was still burning in Coubertin's eyes.

14

THE COMMISSION

he next morning, St. Clair headed up the hill to Mon Repos early, eager to watch Coubertin, Brundage, and Messerli in their strategy session. The goal, St. Clair knew, was to plan a course of action against Diem and the Nazis. Since Blonay had taken ill, St. Clair figured Dr. Messerli would assist Coubertin in coordinating his strategy with his young leaders.

Brundage was clearly taken aback when St. Clair arrived, glaring at him for a second and narrowing his eyes in suspicion. As they pulled chairs into a circle in front of Coubertin's desk, St. Clair sensed he was sitting in on a true moment of Olympic history. The three men were dressed formally in suits with vests, but the meeting had an intimate aspect, especially when Coubertin deliberately pulled his chair closer and bumped Messerli to close the circle so their knees were nearly touching.

After some banter about last night's wine and their resulting sound sleep, Coubertin took control. He started with what sounded like a bit of sentimental reminiscence, but it clearly had another purpose.

"Avery," he asked, "do you remember Father Didon?"

"Of course," Brundage answered. "Although I never met him, I know his words, *Citius, altius, fortius!* Didon's famous slogan."

"Yes, he loved his Latin," Coubertin acknowledged, "and we owe much to his memory. He was staunchly onside in my battles with Paschal Grousset as we were fighting to reform French education back in the 1890s."

"I think I remembering reading in your *21-Year Campaign* that he helped introduce your sports program into French schools, correct?"

"That's correct," Coubertin stated. "Didon believed deeply in the moral value of sport, and he was first to implement my ideas in full. It was a great success. And he and I often trained together when I was refereeing rugby matches. He had the stamina to go a good six miles without stopping, even though he was stocky—built a bit like you though smaller."

"I didn't know he was athletic. I don't often think of priests in cassocks as athletes," Brundage said, looking surprised—and he was probably as curious as St. Clair was about where Coubertin was headed with this story.

"Yes, he was a surprising man in many ways. He was one of the most eloquent and powerful speakers of his day. He could lift a room to its feet with inspiration—and he could speak with moral outrage. He once delivered a speech at an awards ceremony I had arranged for his students and their parents. It was 1893 or '94 if my memory serves, and I'm certain it was an assembly at Saint-Julien. He'd heard there were certain racist sentiments being expressed in the school community, and he would not stand for it. Before his spellbound students and their uneasy parents, with unparalleled boldness he launched a frontal assault on the *bête noire* of the day, anti-Semitism, calling it by its real name, racism. His irony was biting—and he sought to destroy a bias that had no right to survive in God's precincts."

Coubertin stopped as he noticed Brundage staring down at the floor. "Enough of the memories," he said. "Let's get to the business at hand."

Everyone looked directly at Coubertin, waiting to see what he would say next. He once again engaged Brundage's gaze.

"First of all, Avery," he began, "I need your assurances that I have your complete devotion—and in fact I also need you to vouch for Edström and straighten him out if necessary. Both of you, despite your friendship with von Halt and your sympathies with the Nazis, must recognize the threat this Berlin idea poses to the future, to the independence, and to the very autonomy of the Olympic movement."

"I understand, Mr. President," Brundage said, the folds of his forehead creased deeply in thought. "I'll fight with all my energy to defend the independence of the Olympic Movement."

Coubertin leaned over and put his hand on Brundage's knee. "This is a real threat, Avery, and I need you to help lead us through it."

"I'll do whatever you think is right." He seemed somewhat flushed, St. Clair thought, that his devotion had been called into question.

Coubertin sat back up. "The first thing we have to do is take Baillet-Latour out of the conversation. We need a letter from Henri to Hitler and Goebbels.

He'll copy Diem, von Halt, and von Tschammer and let them all know he has formed a small commission to assess their proposal in detail."

"Good idea," said Brundage. "I like the notion of a new commission. Baillet-Latour is obviously pliant since he agreed to the terms of their proposal so readily. Shouldn't be a problem to get him to agree to a new commission."

"You won't be asking for his agreement," said Coubertin. "You'll be *telling* him precisely what we're doing—to a point."

"Me?" asked Brundage. "Why would I be telling him?"

"Because you and Edström have done the most damage by encouraging his sympathy for our German hosts. It's essential that Baillet-Latour see this ruse for what it really is—a coup d'état of worldwide sport. And you're the perfect man to educate him. He won't resist you. You'll leave for Brussels as early as you can—no time to waste."

Brundage shifted in his chair and crossed his legs. St. Clair could see he was uncomfortable—absorbing orders that left no room for objection. "I'll have to change my departure from Paris, but I can make the adjustments. I'll get Edström on the telephone after our meeting and see if he wants to meet me in Brussels."

"That would be smart," Coubertin said, nodding. "He'll need a full briefing on our strategy—and we'll add a note to the letter about the meeting between the three of you in Brussels." Coubertin pulled a letter out of his notebook, already composed. He looked it over and handed it to Brundage. "I'd put it at the end of the first paragraph. And this letter needs to be written in Baillet-Latour's hand."

Looking at the letter, Brundage said, "The Commission for the Future of Olympism—I like the title."

"You should, since you're a member."

Brundage continued reading from the letter: "I have asked Baron Pierre de Coubertin, the honorary president for life of the International Olympic Committee, to chair the commission, which will be comprised of Avery Brundage of the United States, Sigfrid Edström of Sweden, and Dr. Francis Messerli of Lausanne, who will serve as its secretary. I have full confidence in their abilities and judgment, which combine both historic perspective and a clear view of the future needs of our movement and its ideals. They will assess your proposal point by point and make recommendations on all appropriate actions to our executive board in September, which will in turn put its own recommendations to a vote before our membership at next year's IOC session in Paris."

"I didn't realize we had scheduled a session for Paris," interjected Messerli.

"We haven't," said Coubertin. "This is simply a strategy to move Henri aside, bless his heart, and ensure we maintain control while we sort out how to deal with these bloody opportunists."

A host of other points were discussed, including skiing rules, commercialism, and a loud debate on amateurism. Coubertin attempted to rebuke Brundage for his rough treatment of Eleanor Holm—whom he suspended from the U.S. team for drinking on the ship to the '36 Games—but eventually gave up the argument when Brundage refused to yield the point. St. Clair recognized this was another strategic move, not as important to Pierre but a chance to give Brundage some ground on a different issue.

After the meeting, St. Clair asked Brundage for an hour of his time the next morning, and he agreed. He was leaving on the train for Geneva at nine o'clock and asked St. Clair to meet him at the Lausanne Palace at seven.

15

THE PHILOSOPHY

W hen St. Clair arrived at the Lausanne Palace the next morning, Brundage was seated at a table along the wall of windows at the back of the lobby, near a black grand piano. The industrialist wore the same polished wingtip shoes and gray pin-striped suit he had worn at dinner, but with a blue shirt and red tie. He cleaned his spectacles by steaming them over the hot cappuccino, a clever gesture St. Clair had never seen before. As they spoke, their voices carried softly in the pleasant acoustics created by long, elegant drapes and plush carpeting.

"I understand Francis Messerli talked you into moving here to work on Pierre's biography," Brundage said.

"Yes, I was interested in the story and delighted by the opportunity," St. Clair replied. "I live with an American painter, and we were looking for an adventure to take us out of Paris when the doctor's proposal arrived."

"Ah, I see. Messerli is a good man, a loyal friend, and he's doing invaluable work for the Olympic Movement by motivating Pierre to tell his story."

"Dr. Messerli told me you helped with a fund for Pierre, a stipend to help him out financially."

Brundage looked out the window. "Well, we've tried. We collected $5,000. He wouldn't accept it. Instructed us to hold it for his family after he's gone. He's barely getting by. As I understand it, the baroness controls the funds, what little they have, and I don't think she gives him much. It's sad and completely unjust. He's basically broke."

St. Clair wondered if she was as cruel as everyone said. "Couldn't you simply put him on a retainer with the IOC, give him a weekly paycheck?"

"If you understand Pierre, his commitment to Olympism, his class, his family, his background, you'd know that accepting money from the IOC would be a betrayal of everything he's worked for, the standard of service he set for himself and all of us. You don't get in this movement to make money. You follow his example and sign up to serve the world through sport. He'd rather die with nothing than betray his legacy. Principles, ideas mean everything to him. That's why he's been such an extraordinary leader."

"How do you assess his contribution to the Olympic Movement and the restoration of the Games?"

"Invaluable, inestimable—the movement is inconceivable without him." Brundage spoke with conviction and passion, obviously committed to Pierre's vision. "He is central to everything that's happened since 1894; he is the one and only constant. If you take him out of the equation, remove his will and drive, the Games would not have gone on, the movement would not have lasted. He put everything he had into the Olympics: his family fortune, his energy, his ideas, his literary talents. The Games are his child. They belong to him—not the Greeks, not the French—they're solely his, and now ours, because he has bequeathed them to us."

"Yet a number of other attempts were made to resurrect the Games before he came along."

"That's true," Brundage admitted, "but you can judge them all by their results. William Penny Brookes was a great man, but he did what he did for the people of Shropshire, not for the world. Zappos's attempts in Greece? Valiant effort, but ultimately it didn't endure. None of them had Pierre's genius. He saw the global potential. And he created the system—with the national Olympic committees, the international sports federations, the IOC, and even the continental games—that ensured the movement would endure."

"Why hasn't he had more recognition?"

"The spotlight always falls on the athletes and ultimately the heroes, not the organizers—and certainly not the administrators. You know better than most that the press loves the hero's story. Outside of a small circle of aristocrats, businessmen, and professional organizers, it's an invisible movement. But someday the world will hear Pierre's story—and understand the contribution he's made. Your work may prove essential to that goal."

"I hope it does. What do you think I should be focused on in that regard?"

"Olympism," he said without hesitation.

"Coubertin's Olympic philosophy?"

"Yes. His philosophy of friendship and peace through sport—it's the greatest distinction our movement possesses. Ask him to define the Olympic ideal for you, the ideology of sport he created. It reaches from individual human excellence to international understanding and peace. It's as full of hope and aspiration as anything I've ever encountered."

"You seem to be one of its strongest advocates, and yet you were very close to the Germans?" St. Clair couldn't help but wonder how a man who seemed so interested in defending Coubertin's philosophy could have been so sympathetic to the Nazis.

Brundage glared at St. Clair before finally saying, "Look, I'm not perfect. You heard Pierre last night. But he knows I'm as committed and as passionate about the Olympic ideals as anyone on earth. I will carry on his mission and will try to be as unrelenting as he has been."

He paused for a moment, then picked up the point. "You know, Pierre's life is the lesson that every athlete must master to succeed. You've got to be relentless. That's Pierre in essence. Relentless. Unstoppable. A force of nature. A little man with a huge spirit—and a vision for building a better world."

"And your work?" St. Clair asked. "Do you have aspirations to succeed him?"

"How's the book coming?" he asked in return, clearly wanting to deflect St. Clair's question.

"His story is fascinating. Right now we're talking about his youth, his experiences growing up, what his mother and father taught him."

"How's his health?"

"I'm not a doctor, but he is still rowing regularly and he walks everywhere."

"Glad to hear it. When will I be able to read something?"

"Maybe next time you return to Lausanne."

"What's your timeline for finishing the first draft?"

"We're here for a year as guests of Dr. Messerli. My plan is to work from now until the fall probing as deeply as I can into Pierre's life before he launched the Games. From 1896 on, the historical record is pretty robust."

"That's true. It's all documented," Brundage agreed.

"I want to get as deep as I can into the forces that shaped his ideas."

"I think the Paris Universal Exposition in 1889, when the Eiffel Tower was built, had a major influence on his thinking."

"No doubt," St. Clair said. "The exposition was the most formative international event in his life—but his ideas on education and sport were already in place before that."

"Well," Brundage said, rising, "I can't wait to read your book. What are you going to call it?"

"Just between us?" St. Clair said, folding his tablet as he stood to shake the man's hand. It would not hurt to have Brundage feel he was being taken into a confidence.

"Sure."

"I'm thinking the title will be *Genius of Sport*."

"I like it," Brundage said. He turned to leave, raising his hand in a wave without looking back.

As he walked off, St. Clair was left to consider his contradictions. The big man had just offered him more insight—in a brief interview—into Coubertin's character and seminal role than anyone else had. He had shown true affection for the founder—and had been adamant about the philosophy of Olympism as the greatest gift Coubertin had given us. And yet, he had clearly been too sympathetic to the Nazis and certainly too dogmatic about amateurism. Before leaving the Lausanne Palace, St. Clair composed a few thoughts about Brundage, deciding it was the authority of the Nazi power structure and the efficiency of their organizational effort that proved irresistible to him. It couldn't have been their ruthless repression, St. Clair thought—not for a man who was clearly committed to Coubertin's vision of building a better world.

16

THE MAP

fter Brundage departed, St. Clair turned back to the biography and reviewed his notes on Coubertin's childhood. He wasn't sure how much attention he would give to Coubertin's walks with his father in the end, but he decided—since Pierre mentioned there were a dozen walks—to spend one more session talking about them before moving on to Saint-Ignace, the school that shaped Pierre's teen years.

St. Clair and Coubertin were in the office at Mon Repos, and the baron was idly paging through papers behind his desk as St. Clair began the interview. "Let's talk briefly about the other walks and the things your father taught you."

"I'm not sure I can remember the details of each walk," Coubertin said, gazing at the ceiling. "We covered a lot of ground. We went through the major landmarks—Les Invalides, Napoleon's Tomb, the Panthéon, Notre Dame, the Place des Vosges, even Versailles and Chevreuse—"

St. Clair interrupted. "No, not the sites, not the architecture—try to remember what he was trying to teach you."

"Ah yes," Coubertin said, "there's one lesson I'll never forget."

"One morning, as we were finishing our breakfast, before we left for another walk—I remember we were going to look at the Roman ruins in the Latin Quarter—my father pulled out an old map of Paris and delicately spread it on the tablecloth, brushing away crumbs and moving a few plates and some silverware. It was an old work on parchment, yellowed and frayed at the folds and edges, a collectible that had been kept among the family possessions and handed down.

"'Your grandfather gave me this map some years ago,' he said.

"'Did he take you on walks like ours?' I asked.

"'Yes, he did. And he gave me a perspective on how Paris had developed, which he might have learned from his father as well—I can't remember. But this map is from the middle of the eighteenth century, maybe 1750, even before my grandfather was born.'

"I climbed onto my chair so I could stand above the map and clearly see the bird's-eye view from the elevation the artist himself worked from.

"'What do you see?' my father asked. It was his favorite question, an instruction to look closely, and a phrase that still echoes in my head today. He was teaching me to look deeply, beyond the surface—not only at the scene in front of me, but at the meaning behind it.

"I looked closely, not wanting to respond until I saw beyond the obvious. The Seine was the dominant feature, curving sinuously through a city whose churches and small buildings and narrow streets were rendered in black ink. My eye was drawn not to the islands in the Seine, not to the wide boulevards, which were very few, not to the cathedral of Notre Dame, the Tuileries, or even Les Invalides, which was so near to us now, but to the intriguing web of tight, curving streets that wound around and into each other in a maze of twisted passages and dead ends.

"'I see a maze,' I said.

"'That's good, son.' Paris was a maze, a crazy labyrinth that had grown from the Middle Ages in a convoluted matrix of alleyways and side streets that had no order. They blocked out air and light and confined people in prison-like hovels, the garbage and odors of city life assaulting them moment by moment.

"'That's what your grandfather showed me when I was young, but as a soldier his lessons weren't about building a better city for the citizens, they were about opening up the city streets to give the army access to the revolutionaries who threw up the barricades and blocked off streets and entire sections of the city.'

"'And burned the houses of the rich?' I asked him.

"'Yes, and burned the homes of those they resented,' my father replied. 'What else do you see?' He took the map from the table and laid it on the floor so I was much higher above it. 'Do you see any patterns?'

"It was suddenly clear to me. 'Yes, I see circles, not perfect, but circles inside circles,' I said, recognizing a number of dark lines that made the map of Paris look like a group of irregular O's, one inside the other.

"'Precisely,' he exclaimed. 'Those are the seven walls of Paris—the walls that mark the expansion of the city from the time of the Romans forward. You can see just how it grew.'"

At that moment, as he was taking notes, St. Clair was surprised by an angry shout from the hall. Coubertin's head shot up.

"Pierre!" a woman's voice called as the sound of approaching footfalls grew. "Where are you?" Her tone was indignant, harsh. The door swung open and in stepped a woman who could only be the Baroness Marie Rothan de Coubertin, her face pinched in wrath, her ire rising when she saw St. Clair. He recognized her from photographs and was surprised that she showed no embarrassment at her intrusion.

"Good morning, dear," Coubertin said pleasantly. "This is my friend, the writer Jacques St. Clair, whom I've told you about. We were"—he paused and looked at St. Clair—"just about to take a walk."

"I don't care where you're going," she said, refusing to be diverted.

St. Clair stood and faced her, expecting a greeting, but she ignored him.

"Have you been in my purse?" she asked accusingly, glaring at Pierre.

Coubertin blanched, his eyebrows lifting and his face drooping with sad resignation. He avoided glancing back at St. Clair. "No, dear," he said, "I have not."

She was a short, sturdy woman, dressed in a white blouse with a tight collar and billowy sleeves and a full black wool skirt that spread to the floor. Her brown hair was rolled up into a neat cone; her petite face, aged and slightly reddened in anger, was not unattractive.

Perturbed by his response, she nevertheless recovered briefly as they all stood there awkwardly. "Pardon me, Monsieur St. Clair," she said. "I was not aware ..." Her voice trailed off, but then she looked back at Pierre, sneering. "Stay out of my things." She spun around, slammed the door, and stomped back down the hall. Another door slammed and Pierre turned to St. Clair, crestfallen, searching for an explanation.

"Women," said St. Clair, hoping to ease them out of the moment, still in shock. "It's never easy, is it?" It would be miserable to live with a woman like that, he thought.

Coubertin nodded with a half-hearted smile. "She has become obsessed with money." Putting on his coat, he picked up his cup and finished off his coffee. "Let's go for a walk and talk about this later."

They walked up the hill past the cathedral and into the wide plaza before the grand façade of the university as Coubertin finally begin to regain his composure. The embarrassment hung over them like a pall shrouding the sun, and St. Clair knew the best way to break the spell would be to dig back into their interview. "Let's have a drink and wrap up the session before we lose the thread," he suggested.

Once Coubertin had a few sips of wine, he shook his head and moved quickly back into the story the baroness had interrupted.

"That morning my father and I walked over to the Latin Quarter and the ruins of the Roman baths. He gave me his perspective on why the Romans settled on the Île de la Cité—it was the natural protection of the Seine, of course—and that gave me a sense of the original dimensions of the settlement. He told me the boulevard Saint-Michel was once part of *le cardo maximus*, the road that led to Rome, and not more than a block from there, in a garden behind the small church of Saint-Julien-le-Pauvre, he showed me a large rectangle of dark gray stone leaning against a wall. It measured about nine feet long, five feet wide, and probably a foot thick. He asked me to guess what it was. I studied it for a while, finally seeing the pattern of scars across its surface, and I gazed at them until I realized they were the ruts of chariot wheels.

"'It's part of the Roman road,' I proclaimed, and my father was delighted that I had deduced the answer. He said this was only half the width of the road. The Romans made it twice as wide so two chariots could pass or turn around without going off into the soft side. And as far as anyone knew, this was the last piece of Roman road in Paris.

"That realization somehow filled me with a vague sense of loss, a slight hint of regret that I could never know all the things that had come before. Important parts of the past were disappearing every day and I didn't want to lose them.

"When I tried to express my worries, my father said he understood, but he wanted me to know that the past would never reveal all of its lessons. 'Every day of history hides a million secrets we will never know,' he said.

"And then he walked me to the Cour du Commerce Saint André, the old passage off Saint-Germain, and showed me the base of a tower from one of the oldest walls in Paris, the wall built by Phillip Augustus in the thirteenth century.

"It was later, over lunch, that my father told me something I would never forget, because it forged in my mind a truth I would much later come to think of as one of the central lessons of history. He was in fine form that day, far more eloquent than usual.

"'Our city, my son, is a place made of rings, the walls of centuries, spreading in ever-widening concentric circles formed by the push of history and the fate of heroes, each successive generation placing its blocks over the old foundations. We live among the memories and ghosts who cannot and will not leave the quarters that gave birth to their stories. We live with the poetry of the dead singing to us across the boundaries of time. In our city, my son, the geography is spiritual and mythic and historical all at once. Paris is the muse of the metropolis—the artists all feel it. They're drawn into the invisible cloud of its glories, hoping to touch a passage of inspiration, a link to the spark that makes greatness available to all men. There is something here that feeds the vision, fuels the soul, and uses artistic hunger to mobilize what's new.'

"'There are times when cities flower,' my father said, 'when man blossoms and the world becomes a different place. It happened in Athens and Rome in the ancient world, in Florence in the Renaissance, and here in the Enlightenment. I have a feeling it may be surfacing here again, that we may be on the verge of a new epoch, a new day, a new consciousness. I don't know if I'll see that day, Pierre. I am a Royalist, not a Republican, but I can see from history that the circle of inclusion is always expanding and the rights of man are pushing past the barricades again. In a way, I am locked in a prison of my own making—the small cell in which I make my art—constrained, unfortunately, by my beliefs when I see so many new faiths emerging. But, this is the path that life offered me—and your mother—and I gladly embraced it.'"

17

THE ÉCOLE

In the middle of March, no more than a week after Brundage left town, Messerli found a package of drafts on his desk for review. St. Clair had attached a note on top saying he was particularly pleased with the piece on Saint-Ignace and Father Caron, and he had begun to think about how to integrate Pierre's own writing into the work. Messerli closed his office door, put everything aside, and eagerly began to read.

Every Sunday morning, the Coubertins took a short walk together to church. From their door on rue Oudinot, Pierre remembered, the front door of the church was only 227 steps away. They turned right at the corner of the boulevard des Invalides, beheld the grand image of the Golden Dome, and walked a block to Saint Francis Xavier, a historic Jesuit church with twin bell towers rising on each side of the cross on the gable above the arched entrance. From the street, granite stairs that spanned the edifice led up to the massive wooden doors that were bolted, banded, and studded with black iron and carved with rosettes and Catholic symbols.

Just as she had pushed her husband toward the celebration of faith in his paintings—a move toward tradition that served the family well when both Napoleon III and the Vatican acquired his paintings—Pierre's mother ensured the family's piety was sustained in weekly worship at Saint Francis Xavier. As Pierre and every Jesuit-taught child knew, Saint-Francis was one of the six brothers who had joined Ignatius of Loyola in founding the Jesuits in 1584. They all took vows of poverty and committed themselves to serving every order of the pope without question, "that we may be altogether of the same mind." As a boy, Pierre could recite some of Loyola's *Rules for Thinking with the Church*, but even then, his intellectual acuity prevented him from fully embracing the Jesuit disciplines as his mother and father hoped he would.

With two older sons already in the military, Charles and Marie believed Pierre might find his way to the priesthood, but his keen mind, endless curiosity, and independent spirit stood in firm opposition to their aspirations. When Pierre's father inserted him and his sister Marie into one of his most famous paintings, *The Departure of the Missionaries*, everyone in the church saw it as an expression of priestly hope. Pierre, however, knew his father understood him well, even then, since in the painting, the boy was looking back at the viewer, distracted, and not at all engaged in the ceremony the scene depicted.

While Les Invalides Church had a historic claim on the soldiers who trained and served at the École Militaire just a few blocks away, Saint-Francis drew a good contingent of soldiers as well. Every Sunday morning the pews in Saint-Francis were filled to capacity with the colorful uniforms, plumed helmets, and bicorne hats of both officers and infantry. While the priests conducted the services and the litany of voices filled the vaulted sanctuary, Pierre studied the varied regimental designs and insignia proudly displayed by the soldiers all around him. After church, he would announce to his father—or to Paul and Albert if they were present—that this week five battalions and twenty companies were represented in the congregation.

At a young age, Pierre embraced the Christian faith and sensed the presence of the Holy Spirit among the congregants. He was often moved by the blend of patriotic fervor and nationalistic pride that infused the rituals and sacraments of a religion rooted in the marriage of the military and the church. When hymns of celestial battle and earthly conflict were sung, voices booming with their loyal French commune, he swayed and felt the pull of God and country on his grateful heart. He knew that a calling was stirring in his soul, a calling to serve the greatness of France, he thought. But as he grew and studied the Gospels and the story of Jesus and began to understand the power of love, a quiet conflict began to simmer in the depths of his being. He would not speak of it to his family—and he would never betray the great military tradition of his grandfather Julien and his two brothers should his country need him—but he began to wonder if the dual symbolism of the bell towers of Saint Francis Xavier, the army and the church, really belonged together. He began to see Jesus's message of love and service in a different light, along a different path, one that led away from armed conflict.

○ ○ ○ ○ ○

A year after the Franco-Prussian War, toward the autumn of 1872 when Paris was beginning to recover from the combined disasters of the Germans and the Commune and to rebuild under the Third Republic, Pierre's mother gathered her family around the dinner table and announced that the Jesuits were going to build a new school for elite students on rue de Madrid on the Right Bank. Given the quality of the priests who were going to teach there, Marie Crisenoy de Coubertin had no doubt the École Saint-Ignace would quickly gain status as one of the city's most esteemed academies for future leaders.

"And we're going to enroll Pierre in its first class," his mother said just as Pierre lifted a silver soupspoon to his mouth. He was stunned by the news. "You'll start as soon as the doors open," she declared.

"But I like this neighborhood, Mother, and even Father says I'm doing very well at the College of Vaugirard," Pierre argued, thinking primarily of the first kiss he had just experienced with Antoinette, a charming raven-haired girl who lived on the sixth floor of an apartment building on Les Invalides Esplanade, just a block away. "I don't want to change schools."

"Well, son," said his father, "there's no doubt the Vaugirard Jesuits deliver a fine education. They did well by Paul and Albert, but this is a new school with some very fine teachers by all accounts. They're going to be very strong in the classics and I know you'll be vitally interested—if not inspired—by living there."

"Living there?" Pierre said, his voice rising. "You mean I'd move to the school?" He looked between his mother and father, who glanced at each other from opposite ends of the table.

"Well, yes, Pierre," his mother said adamantly. "It's an absolute privilege to have the chance to live and learn at Saint-Ignace."

"What? Pierre can't move!" exclaimed Marie, sitting across the table. She looked surprised, anxious, and angry all at once. "He's my little brother. He can't move," she pleaded.

"Pierre is at the age," his father said, "where decisions about his future must be made. Let's not forget all the virtues a Jesuit education delivers." He lifted his glass. "And let's not argue but rather toast the extraordinary opportunity for this young Coubertin to begin fulfilling his destiny."

As they raised their glasses, Pierre thought of that moment at dusk the day before with young Antoinette on her balcony. Her parents not yet home from work, the Invalides Golden Dome glistening in the setting sun over her shoulder, Pierre leaned in and closed his eyes and their lips met in the sweetest sensation he had yet known. Why do I have to move now, he wondered.

"I've asked Father Caron to come by to meet you, Pierre," his mother said. "He'll be here tomorrow morning."

Still smarting at the notion of having to change schools, Pierre sat glumly on the sofa in the *étage noble*, gazing out the back windows at the old locust tree over the wall. He wondered when the weather would break so the gardeners could turn the earth and plant rows of vegetables in the long field beyond the tree. The fireplace crackled to his right as his mother, sitting in the armchair in front of him, her back to the windows, tried to get him to focus on the details she was sharing about the new Jesuit school. She seemed to know everything.

"It's a fine building, son, with an arched colonnade running along rue de Madrid," she said. "The dorms and the classrooms will line each side of the interior courtyard, and the chapel will be on the east end."

"Who's the headmaster?" asked Pierre, although he had heard rumors.

"It's going to be Father Michel Telhard, who was over you at Vaugirard last year."

Pierre was happy to hear that Telhard would be his headmaster—again. He was a robust and joyful man who believed in forgiveness more than punishment, who was known to love a good debate, and who appreciated every bright intellect God sent his way.

"And the Father we're going to meet? Where is he from?"

"Father Caron is a dynamic teacher and a lover of antiquity, which is why I wanted you to meet him. He studied history at the Sorbonne before he entered the monastery at Avignon."

The bell downstairs clanged and Maude, the maid, went to answer it.

"That must be him," the baroness said, rising. "Now, Pierre, please show the appropriate respect."

"I'll behave like an adoring acolyte, Mother. Don't worry." Pierre stepped around the couch as the stairway began to creak. Father Caron was following Maude up to the *noble étage*.

A head full of thick, dark hair appeared at the stairhead, then a handsome, smiling face above broad shoulders. Father Caron stepped into the room, standing upright, a tall man, trim and fit, with a large leather book braced easily against the dark wool of his soutane, which was drawn tightly around the waist with a black sash. As the baroness moved to greet him, extending her hand, Pierre locked eyes with Caron, and in that instant he began assessing the priest as a potential ally or opponent.

"Welcome, Father," his mother said. "We're so pleased you could come."

"My pleasure, madame, to meet you in your lovely home." He glanced with an approving nod at several of the religious paintings on the wall. "And a further pleasure to have a chance to meet a most promising student—as I understand it—even before the school is built."

"Thank you, Father. We are quite proud of Pierre."

"Pleased to meet you, sir," Pierre said, stepping forward to shake Father Caron's hand. The priest did not bend forward or act as if he were meeting a child but simply tilted his head and extended his hand.

"My pleasure, Pierre."

At close range, Pierre noticed three buttons sewn into the cuff of the cassock, a mark of quality mirrored by the topstitching on the short cape over his shoulders. His white collar was freshly starched. The sheen of a row of large brass buttons, each bearing the image of the Jesuit cross, descended down the face of the robe. As they took their seats, Maude served coffee and set out a tray of fresh madeleines. Pierre noticed that beneath his cassock, Father Caron's heavy black boots were dull and scraped a little, a comforting touch of humanity he was glad to have spotted.

Without saying a word about it, Caron carefully set the big leather book on the floor, leaning it against his chair so Pierre could clearly read the gold lettering on the spine, *History of Ancient Art*, along with the writer's name, Winckelmann. Pierre didn't know the book but thought it curious that a French priest would bring the work of a German author to their home.

Pierre listened as Father Caron gave his mother an update on the progress of construction at the school. It seemed the first class might be allowed to move in before the work was fully finished, which would present only a minor inconvenience and would not distract from their studies. The priest spoke with confidence and some animation, using his large hands in an endearing style like an Italian. He sat straight up and swiveled easily in the chair to ensure he was not leaving Pierre out of the conversation. When he turned toward the baroness, Pierre gained a sense of the physical strength of his arms and back. He wondered whether the priest practiced sport.

And then the man shifted his torso, casting his focus fully on Pierre. "I have heard from good sources that you're deeply interested in ancient history. Is this true?"

"Well, Father," Pierre said without a pause, "given my family's deep roots in France and Italy—and my dear parents' devotion to the church and tradition—I suppose it's not surprising that I have a passion for the past. Yes, I'm intrigued by ancient history."

"Any period in particular?"

"In particular," Pierre replied, "I have an affection for ancient Greece and Rome, for the literature, theater, philosophy, and"—he stole a quick look at the oversized leather book, and when he looked back, he noted the crinkle of a conspiratorial smile barely registering at the corner of Caron's mouth—"and, of course, for the art of the ancients and the Renaissance."

"And I understand you've been to Rome."

"Oh yes. My father led us on a pilgrimage to Rome at the time of the Vatican conclave. We went to St. Peter's, the Sistine Chapel—everywhere. We paid our respects to our forebearers, and I had a chance to see the classical art among the ruins."

"You are very fortunate, Pierre," said Father Caron, "to have a family who has cultivated your appreciation for the ancients and who are now seeking to ensure that your God-given gifts and talents—which appear to be abundant already—are developed to the full extent of God's glory."

Pierre had not expected to be moved by this encounter. But Father Caron's words—his sincerity, his tone, and his empathy, and indeed, the very fact that he acknowledged talent in Pierre already—moved him. He felt a now-familiar stirring, a calling, perhaps, to a mission rooted somewhere in the past. Before he could recover enough to say thank you, the priest moved on.

"Now I have a confession to make, Pierre, and this is something your mother knows already." He smiled broadly as he made the point, as did the baroness, whose motherly pride had swelled at the Father's kind comments. "I too have a passion for the world of our Greek and Roman ancestors. I have a deep love for the expression of human creativity, and I believe, as did Johann Joachim Winckelmann"—he lifted the great book and laid it on the table between them with the cover turned to Pierre—"that the ancient Greeks reached a pinnacle of artistry that few, if any, have matched since their time."

As Pierre's eyes followed his hand, Father Caron reached across the edge of the large volume and pulled it open to a page he had marked, revealing a lavish illustration of one of the greatest masterpieces of ancient Greek sculpture.

"That's the Belvedere Apollo," said Pierre, happy to recognize a work he had seen in the Piazza del Belvedere on the family's journey to Rome.

"And I'm sure you know what's on the next page."

"*Laocoön and His Sons.*"

Caron turned the page and sat back as Pierre absorbed Winckelmann's masterful illustration of the statue uncovered by the Coubertins' famous Italian ancestor, Felice di Fredi.

"Pierre," Father Caron said, "I'm going to be teaching several classes in the classics, including one on Winckelmann's theories, and I want you in them. I think we'll delve deeper into the history of art than any Jesuit school ever has. This will be a journey, Pierre—not simply a course of study—but an adventure through the corridors of human creativity for the glory of God and the benefit of those with a heart to learn."

Pierre looked up. "Father, that's an adventure I'd like to take." He rose and beckoned Father Caron to come with him. The baroness excused them as they climbed the stairs to his father's studio, stopping in the hallway to study the painting of Felice di Fredi gifting the masterpiece of *Laocoön and His Sons* to Pope Julius in 1506. Even at his young age, Pierre could sense it was a spiritual encounter for the priest.

As if to corroborate Pierre's thoughts, Father Caron said, "I'm certain it is God who has led me to this family."

After Pierre had guided Father Caron through the studio, explaining each of his father's paintings, they spent the rest of the afternoon side by side paging through the Winckelmann book, and before they turned the last page, Pierre was as certain as the priest that Saint-Ignace was where he belonged.

○ ○ ○ ○ ○

Pierre and his classmates were hardly a year into their studies at Saint-Ignace, in the fall of 1874, when Father Caron entered the room in a state of excitement. He announced they would be closely following the German archaeological expedition in ancient Olympia, calling it a chance to bring Hellenism to life in the classroom. Caron was good friends with a Jesuit from Germany who was part of the Ernst Curtius expedition team. He had promised reports on any major finds or progress—and young Pierre, only eleven at the time but already a star student, found the prospect inspiring.

"We're not going to wait for the excavations to begin, however," Father Caron said. "As part of our curriculum in the classics, we're going to start reading Pausanias's *Travels in Greece*." He held up a copy to emphasize its promise. Over the course of that winter, he brought in a French translation and passed it around, having each student read a page of the description of the ancient world, and he had the class work on translations from the Greek as well.

The German archaeologists spent every winter for the next six years in Olympia—another expedition each year. And every school year, Father Caron had Pierre's class read the reports of what the Germans discovered and compare any facts they found to the ancient descriptions. The first few years were dominated by the statues from the pediments of the Temple of Zeus and the extraordinary metopes that graced the cornices. It was the third year that produced the most thrilling discovery of all when word reached the class—in a letter from Caron's Jesuit friend—that Curtius's team had discovered the *Hermes of Praxiteles*, an ancient sculptural masterpiece. They found it exactly where Pausanias had described it—on a plinth in the Temple of Hera. It was well preserved by layers of soil nearly fifteen feet deep.

History had indeed come back to life at Saint-Ignace—and Pierre de Coubertin was to recall in his *Olympic Memoirs* more than fifty years later the impact it had on his growing imagination:

> *Nothing in ancient history had given me more food for thought than Olympia. This dream city, consecrated to a task strictly human and material in form, but purified and elevated by the idea of patriotism which there possessed as it were a factory of life-forces, loomed with its colonnades and porticos unceasingly before my adolescent mind.*

Pierre graduated from Saint-Ignace at the top of his class in 1880, ready to find his path in the world. He knew he would deeply miss the priest who had helped shape his intellect and driven him to master rhetoric. His gratitude was so deep it could fill the fountains of Versailles, he thought, and he remembered one of their last conversations before graduation.

"Father, I feel as if there is something I'm meant to do, something for France," Pierre said. "I don't know what it is, but I know I have to search for it."

"You should search for it, Pierre," Father Caron replied. "But if it's a calling, it will find you. You needn't worry. Whatever it is, it will find you."

ART AND LOVE

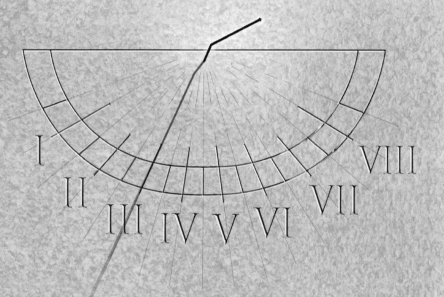

18

THE LUNCHEON

J uliette woke early on a late March morning with an elated feeling, a lightness in her mind, a touch of happiness in her heart. St. Clair was already gone as she stepped out of bed with vim. Today she was going to meet *le Rénovateur*. Out on the patio, as the sun rose and boats raced across the sparkling lake, she painted for an hour, experimenting with skin tones on an old man's face. She started with a sketch, etching in the lines of age around the eyes and creating the impression of a thick, broad mustache. She worked the brush into the oils. Not so easy, she thought, trying to move from dark to light tones, but she knew she had time to figure it out. It was sunny and breezy and she was exhilarated about meeting the baron. She wasn't quite sure why she wanted to enter Jacques's working world, but the idea of painting a portrait of the founder of the Olympic Games was persistent. She had even had a dream in which she was in Paris, painting a distinguished, aging aristocrat seated in a gold-framed rococo chair, red drapes hanging behind him in a studio from the last century.

In the early afternoon, she donned one of her favorite blue dresses with frills around the décolletage. For a finishing touch, she clipped a red rose from the vase in the kitchen and pinned it to the wide brim of her white straw hat. Leaving a little early, she walked down to the quay for a look at the boaters and the ducks before heading to the Château d'Ouchy. Walking up the hill, she considered something Jacques had suggested the night before.

"Listen," he said, "when you do meet him, why don't you ask him why he was against women competing in the Olympics."

"What? Don't you think that might offend him? I don't want to get into an argument in our first conversation."

"No, to tell you the truth, I don't think it will surprise him. I'm sure he's been asked hundreds of times, but probably not so often by a beautiful young American."

Juliette smiled. "We'll see. If it seems right I'll do it, but I want him to sit for a portrait—and I won't compromise that goal."

She arrived at Croix d'Ouchy a few minutes late, climbed the steps, and went inside. Peeking around the corner from the dining room, she spotted Coubertin sitting alone on the patio, reading some papers laid on top of a valise, a bottle of red wine already uncorked and waiting.

"Baron de Coubertin," she said as he looked up, "I'm Juliette Franklin." She extended her hand.

"Enchanté," he said, rising quickly. "Please call me Pierre. I am so pleased to finally meet you." He bent to kiss her hand. "I can't believe Jacques has kept you hidden all this time."

Juliette was momentarily surprised she was taller than he was, but his grin and his manner immediately set her at ease as she leaned in for the customary three kisses, a Swiss social gesture she was beginning to enjoy, his mustache tickling her cheek. Then he graciously pulled back her chair, a gentleman at work.

He was still smiling brightly as they sat, and while his mustache covered most of his grin, his face was filled with amusement. "I apologize for opening the wine before you arrived, but I got here a little early to catch up on some correspondence. They know me well here, so I'm always right at home."

"Not at all. May I join you?"

"So," he said, pouring her a glass of light burgundy, "I understand you have a deep love for Paris."

"I certainly do. I moved there for the city as much as the art."

"Not for love?" He gave her a mischievous glance.

"No, not for love. I am indeed a romantic, but the love was an unexpected benefit."

"Then let's toast to the unexpected," the baron said, lifting his glass.

"Jacques tells me you come from the 7th, the École Militaire."

"Yes. Do you know the area?"

"Well, I'm more familiar with the Faubourg Saint-Germain from reading Balzac, but I've spent a good bit of time at the Rodin Museum."

"Studying his sculpture?"

"Yes, and drawing inspiration for my painting."

"The museum is only a few blocks from my home—or the home where I grew up on rue Oudinot. I can become wistful thinking about it."

"You no longer have the home?"

"Alas, we had to sell it not long after we moved here. Right after the war in 1919."

"Do you miss Paris?"

"Of course I miss Paris," he said, twisting a tip of his mustache, staring absently at the wall of old vines over the trellis on the side of the patio. "I miss France. The absence is ever-present." He turned back to her with a thoughtful expression. "But when the war broke out, I had to find a safe home for the Olympic Movement—in a country not engaged in the hostilities—and with de Blonay and Messerli, two of my most loyal colleagues, here to support the work, Lausanne became an obvious choice."

She hadn't expected such a serious turn in the conversation so quickly, but Pierre was clearly in interview mode after all the hours he had spent with Jacques, his past very much present in his thoughts. She paused, uncertain of what to say, but he seemed quick to sense the need to move on.

"And how did you become interested in Balzac?" His face brightened.

"My mother—she had a love of French literature and particularly the social manners and fashions of the salon. The magnificent artifice, she called it."

"Ah yes, the salons were a world unto themselves. I enjoyed a few years of that magnificent artifice myself. I could have been a minor character in Balzac. Who was your favorite?"

"The Duchess of Langeais, without question."

"Ah, *La Comédie humaine*. Quite deep. And tragic."

"Yes, it was tragic, but I loved the frivolous descriptions, the dinner parties, the social settings, the couture of the Faubourg Saint-Germain, all the things Balzac held up to ridicule. The costumes and the vanity were to my liking as an artist."

"Not the retiring Sister Theresa of the Carmelites?"

"The tragedy of the love affair was moving, and it was admirable that the duchess wouldn't compromise, but the world Balzac rendered—the scenes of that particular Parisian life and times—that was what captured my imagination."

"And millions of others," he said. "That's the world and the arrondissement I was born into. We'll never see the like of it again. Balzac was a giant."

Suddenly, Juliette was possessed of a thought, a way to charm the baron and move his heart—and perhaps bring a little magic into his life. She wondered whether she could find the right dress for the dinner party Messerli was throwing.

"I'm quite looking forward to the party Dr. Messerli is hosting next weekend … a chance for all of us to get together."

"Yes, Francis puts on a splendid dinner party—not quite the Faubourg Saint-Germain in its prime, but it's certain to be a sumptuous affair."

The breadbasket was empty when their meals arrived—croquettes of shrimp for her and lamb chops for the baron—and Juliette decided it was time to broach the subject of the lunch.

"I know Jacques told you I am very much interested in painting your portrait."

The baron stopped slicing his lamb and leaned back in his chair, raising his knife and fork like small flagpoles in each hand. He looked at Juliette anew.

"I knew you were painting—and Jacques did say you were bored with landscapes—but why would you want to—"

"It's not out of boredom, Pierre," Juliette interjected. "Every night Jacques comes home and tells me something new about your world, about your life, the ideas you had, and it's fascinating."

She watched his expression. The lines around his eyes grew more definitive, and under the brush of his mustache she saw his lips compress.

"Your story has already taken up a great deal of space in my imagination," she continued, "and you are *le Rénovateur* of the Olympic Games … so it's not really surprising that I would want to paint you, now, is it?"

His hesitation turned into a long pause, a moment of serious thought. Finally he spoke. "Well, mademoiselle, I'm flattered. But to put it delicately, is there not the matter of your qualifications? I haven't seen your work—although Jacques has of course sung your praises, and Francis has said you're remarkably talented. He loves your landscapes."

She shifted uncomfortably, thinking he might reject her. But before she had a chance to reply, his face lifted in a smile and he continued. "At any other time, I might ask to view your portfolio. But fate, it seems, has sent you and your gifted fiancé to me. You've given me a chance to recall the chronicle of my life in an unhurried exploration, a pace of memories that any man might enjoy. Of course, I will sit for you, my dear, because I find you charming, beautiful, and intelligent—and because I want Jacques to know your participation can only strengthen our work."

She was thrilled and felt something Jacques had often described, a sense of privilege at being admitted to a small but important circle. "Thank you so much," she said.

"My father was a painter," he added, "and I have a love of the arts almost as deep as my love of sport. If you want to paint my portrait, Juliette, we will find the time."

Juliette felt the creative affirmation she had hoped for. She now had a mission of her own, a mission that would demand that she push her artistry to a new level. "We're going to get to know each other quite well, Pierre," she said, and deciding to express her confidence, added, "and I'm going to paint your portrait as no one ever has."

They stayed at the restaurant for another hour and a half. Juliette did most of the talking, and he seemed content to listen and gaze at her countenance, perhaps absorbing the energy of her youth. She asked to see his family photos—to see his face at every stage of life—telling him that when she was ready she would start with a series of sketches, studies of his face, then move onto the canvas and into color only after she felt confident she could capture his essence. They agreed it would be convenient for her to sit in on Jacques's interviews occasionally and start her sketches while Pierre responded to his questions—assuming Jacques agreed.

By the end of the lunch, Juliette felt she had established a level of connection and trust between them that would allow her to open the one subject over which she knew conflict might arise. "May I ask you something about the Olympics?" she said at length.

"Of course. Ask me whatever you'd like," he answered, sipping his third coffee.

"Well, I hope I'm not being too forward, but I'm puzzled about something. I followed the Olympic Games in Los Angeles and was quite inspired—as I think many American women were—by the wonderful performance of Babe Didrikson."

He nodded, and his eyebrows drooped slightly as if he knew what was coming. "Yes, she was quite amazing."

"I'm glad to hear you say that—to me her athleticism is undeniable. But Jacques has told me you stood firmly against women competing in the Games."

"I'm afraid that's true, Juliette."

"But why? Since you've given the world so much, why deny women their place at the starting line?"

"Well, I could tell you—as others have written—that I'm a product of my times, that my mind was formed in a society that diminished the role of women and put them in their place. And some of that would be true—the influence of heritage, mores, social customs. But I'm afraid my thoughts were molded more by the ancient model I resurrected—even though I adapted it to modern times. And, well, observing girls and young women collapsing in high-level athletic exhaustion … that bothered me."

"But Babe destroyed those myths," she interrupted, saying it more adamantly than she intended. She could see he was stung.

"It's true, my defenses are weak. Even though we had women competing in swimming, archery, and tennis between Paris and Stockholm, I stood against their entry into the more challenging athletic events. Even when the executive board was telling me I was falling behind the times."

Juliette had never been one to mince words. "You were, Pierre, and that's unfortunate," she said gently.

"Well, the fact is, no one is perfect, least of all me. I was wrong and I paid a price. You may know—perhaps not—that my position on women in the Games became one of the issues that pushed me toward retirement."

"You could have changed your mind," she said.

"I was never against women in sport," he said. "That is, I was never opposed to exercise and games in schools for girls—and I was of course fully committed to egalitarian education for women and men. That's all on record."

Juliette let the argument die, disheartened a little that he had confirmed the vestiges of an outdated attitude. As she was deciding it wouldn't matter, that she wouldn't allow it to interfere with her work, he moved a little toward repentance.

"I suppose you're just going to have to find it in your heart to forgive this old man for a few of his foibles," he said. "Obviously, I was out of step with the times."

"Well, you may still be a little bit out of step, but the times have moved on and there are women in your Olympics today. So maybe I will be able to forgive you—someday," she teased.

"I can only hope my old attitudes don't end up coloring your work."

She laughed and they rose to leave.

19

THE TANDEM

St. Clair had been surprised during the dinner with Brundage to hear Coubertin mention that he had been a rugby referee and trained on long runs with Père Didon. One afternoon in late March, he asked Messerli about it when they were reviewing his drafts on the war and Saint-Ignace at his university office.

"Yes, Pierre attained real stature as a French referee. I think he quit after he blew the final whistle at the National Rugby Championship match in Paris— maybe 1891 or '92, just before his Olympic proposals."

"He must have been a fairly good athlete."

"Oh yes, very competitive. He was very fit when I first met him in 1908," the doctor said, looking up over his reading glasses and laying the Saint-Ignace draft on his desk. "This is excellent, by the way," he added, tapping the papers. "I'm going to show you a file of correspondence between Pierre and Teddy Roosevelt you'll find interesting."

"The American president?"

"Yes, they were friends. The baron met him at the New York Athletic Club on one of his first U.S. college tours, I think, another introduction by William Milligan Sloane of Princeton—have you talked about him yet?"

"No. I've read about him but we haven't reached that point yet."

"No matter. They met years before Roosevelt became president. But when he was, Roosevelt invited Pierre to stay at the White House on more than one occasion."

"That's remarkable! What was the correspondence about—the St. Louis Games?"

"Eventually yes, but most of it is more personal. They were both very interested in physical fitness and sport in education—and Roosevelt had a vision for building a robust nation."

"Was Roosevelt by any chance a disciple of Thomas Arnold too?"

"Not sure, but I know the two of them often compared notes on exercise. In one letter, Pierre documents an experiment he did in 1903, I think, to assess the impact of a hard day of workouts. In the hot sun on the French Riviera, he did six straight hours of competitive exercise and sport—running, tennis, fencing, boxing, cycling, rowing—"

"Cycling," St. Clair said, his interest immediately heightened. "Did he cycle much?"

"Oh he loved to cycle. When he first came to Lausanne, I was part of a cycling club, mostly young students, and Pierre would ride with us—he was in his late 40s, but he could hold the pace along the lakes. He was usually in the back on the climbs."

"Really?" St. Clair said, a thrill running through him. "He rode with you?"

"We used to go along the lake and roads to Geneva, the other way to Montreux, up to the hills to Grandvaux, into the mountains. He loved climbing up to Grandvaux—not very hard for us, but a real accomplishment for him."

"Grandvaux," St. Clair said. "Where is that?"

○ ○ ○ ○ ○

When St. Clair asked Coubertin about it later, the old man recalled his cycling days and Messerli's club with a good laugh.

"I miss those times," he said, "the rides, the routes, the climbs." He had fond recollections of his favorite ride. "I think the longest and hardest trek we took was up to Grandvaux for lunch and the views. I remember the effort with some measure of pride. It was perhaps among the most strenuous but finest days I had as an athlete. Even though I was older, I was able to stay with the main group as we wove our way up the mountainside. The lunch and the wine that afternoon, the camaraderie after the climb, the sun and the vistas, all made me wistful that I hadn't played more team sports. Memories can be deceiving, but the pleasures of that day remain very much alive for me."

After the baron told St. Clair that he had never made it back up to Grandvaux—still one of his favorite places above Lac Leman—St. Clair had an idea. For several weeks after that, he rose early and took his three-speed De Dion-Bouton out for climbs that lasted an hour, journeying as far as three hours on the weekends. Juliette tried to ride with him a few times, but he wouldn't slow down and left her struggling on small hills before they had even made it out of Ouchy.

St. Clair was already fit, and it didn't take him long to work himself up to a state of climbing confidence. He then set off to visit several cycling shops in Lausanne and found what he was looking for at a place called Cycles Piguet at rue du Tunnel 8—a tandem cycle, a two-seater with two sets of pedals chained together on an extended frame with a stoker handlebar attached to the back of the post under the front seat. St. Clair lifted it and was pleased that the bicycle was not that much heavier than his Dion-Bouton.

"Can you put a new sprocket and a three-speed *dérailleur* on this tandem?" Jacques asked.

"I don't see why not," said Monsieur Piguet, a middle-aged man dressed in a mechanic's apron. "Be glad to try it. It will take long wires. Can you come back on Monday?"

They worked out the price and the details—and that Monday evening St. Clair brought Juliette back for the initial test ride. She was wobbly for a second, but caught on and laughed as they went up and down the street in front of the shop. Jacques picked up speed and worked the gears. As they rode home, St. Clair chatted happily, anticipating the day when he and Coubertin would ride together up through the vineyards to Grandvaux.

20

THE PHOTOGRAPHS

A t the beginning of April, Juliette accompanied St. Clair up to Mon Repos for her first visit to Coubertin's office. When they entered the park, she was impressed by the grounds, the landscaping and flowerbeds—to say nothing of the edifice of the old château. Walking up through the greenery and emerging into the half circle of large urns around the fountain at the entrance, she paused to take it all in. Long-stemmed lilies stood above their bowls, colorful splays of impatiens spilled down from the footwall, a rainbow shimmered in the fountain's spray—and Juliette was absorbed by the beauty of the scene.

"Jacques, this hardly looks like the home of someone under financial strain," she said, pulling him toward the fountain.

"Well, none of this belongs to them."

"Still, it's not what I expected after your stories of empty pockets."

"They do what they can to keep up appearances, Juliette—don't be cruel. They're living on the largess of the city, and it isn't easy for him."

"I'm not being unsympathetic, Jacques. I love that little man. I'm just surprised, that's all."

Inside she stopped to admire the statues, the fluted columns, and the handsome sunburst mosaic on the floor. "He's never far from ancient Greece, is he?" She followed St. Clair up the stairs.

The door to the office was open when they walked in. Coubertin was standing behind his desk, a delicate young woman in a lovely pale blue dress beside him, her hair pinned up but not perfectly done. They were holding several photographs above a black box sitting open among Coubertin's papers. He was smiling broadly but the young woman looked up tentatively, a glimpse of fear passing across her face as she tried to smile.

"Ah, the great French writer and his lovely American painter," the baron said, taking the woman's arm lightly and guiding her around the desk to meet them. "Jacques, Juliette, may I present my favorite person in all the world, my daughter, Renée."

"So pleased to meet you," said St. Clair. Renée extended her hand but dropped her gaze bashfully.

"Pierre," said Juliette, deliberately moving forward to take Renée's hand, lifting her chin and looking directly into her eyes, "you didn't tell us you had such a beautiful daughter." Renée demurred but smiled, her genuine warmth apparent. The baron laughed with delight.

"It's nice to meet you, Juliette—and you, Jacques," the young woman said. "Father is always singing your praises."

"A few even well deserved," the baron rejoined. "I believe you two were born in the same year," he said, nodding at both the women.

"Oh my God!" Juliette exclaimed. "Finally, a woman my own age in Lausanne. I've been hoping to find a girlfriend."

Renée's expression changed—her eyes widened and she raised her brows, as if she didn't know how to react, suddenly looking a little frightened by this new American.

Her father's response was immediate. "Renée and I were just going through a box of old family photographs," he said. "I was thinking that Renée might help Juliette sort through a few of these while Jacques and I pick up the interview."

Juliette moved to the desk and looked down into the box, and St. Clair followed. Layers and layers of photos were piled up in disarray. She picked up two photos—both with large groups of men and women fanning out behind the baron and baroness on the steps of a formal entrance, all in suits and ties and elegant dresses. What a treasure trove of imagery, she thought. It was exactly what she had been hoping for.

"That's the IOC session in Paris in 1924," Coubertin said.

Renée added, pointing, "And that one is in Prague."

"Do you know the setting for all these photographs?" Jacques asked.

"Most of them," Renee said. "Our family is devoted to Father's Olympic work."

"What I really need," said Juliette, dropping the photos and digging for a few more, "is a formal pose, something closer up."

"This is my favorite formal portrait," Renée said, handing Juliette a framed print that had been buried on the desktop. It was a photo of the baron from the shoulders up, his head tilted, a smile turning up the corners of his mouth, his eyes crinkling with charm.

"This is perfect," declared Juliette.

Renée appeared pleased. "I can show you all of them," she said.

"Why don't you take Juliette to the Rouge Room and look through the box," the baron suggested.

Although Juliette had hoped to sit in on the interview that day, she saw the look of uncertain expectation in Renée's eyes. "Good idea," she said, smiling at Coubertin as Renée gathered up the loose photographs and put the lid on the box. Juliette followed her toward the staircase.

○ ○ ○ ○ ○

St. Clair and Coubertin were swiftly engaged in the corridors of the old man's memories. Their conversation delved into Coubertin's decision—after Saint-Ignace—not to follow his brothers into a military career. He dropped out of Saint-Cyr Military Academy in a matter of months. At his father's insistence, he tried studying law at the Sorbonne for a few years, but he finally decided to follow his heart and enrolled at the École Libre des Sciences Politiques. The Po, as it quickly became known, was a new school started by the intellectual leaders of the Third Republic—Hippolyte Taine and Émile Boutmy—to prepare France's next generation of political leaders and diplomats. Coubertin knew that Jules Simon, one of France's former prime ministers, often lectured there—and he had been as interested in studying with Simon as he was with Taine.

"I'm not sure we've covered the chronology fully here," St. Clair said. "If you started going to the Po around 1883 or '84—and began building your relationship with Simon there—what were you doing in the early '80s, after you left Saint-Ignace?"

"I did two years of law school at the Sorbonne and took the two trips to England we discussed."

"Yes, but that wouldn't fill five years—what was your life focused on then?"

Coubertin suddenly grinned and bounced in his chair as if delighted by a memory. "Well, I did spend a good bit of time with a certain poet, but I'm not at all sure I want to go into that period … let's call it the salon years."

"A poet in the salons of Paris?" St. Clair asked, surprised by the twist and intrigued by what could be a literary sidelight. "What poet? What was his name? Don't tell me, Rimbaud?"

"No, not Rimbaud, although he once had a bloody tumult with Rimbaud. His name was Jean Aicard."

St. Clair recalled the fleeting reference in Coubertin's *Olympic Memoirs* to June 23, 1894. "The poet who delivered the ode in the Sorbonne the night you resurrected the Games?"

"The one and only."

"Well, this is a surprising turn."

Just then a light knock on the door interrupted the conversation, and a boy in breeches and a cap stepped in as the door opened. "Telegram for Baron de Coubertin," he said, approaching the desk and handing a folded piece of paper to the baron as they exchanged smiles.

"Hello, Jean-Louis," said the baron, rising and reaching into his pocket. The boy looked over at St. Clair and smiled as he accepted a coin from Coubertin.

"Thank you, sir," the boy said, touching the brim of his cap. "Two more telegrams to deliver," he said politely, hurrying out the door.

The baron sat on the edge of the desk, opened the telegram, and said, "Looks like Brundage has gotten Baillet-Latour to agree to the delay stratagem." Handing the telegram to St. Clair, Coubertin added, "The letter has been sent to the Germans telling them the commission has been formed." He rounded the desk and sat back down, shuffling through another stack of papers. "Looks like I've got some work to do."

St. Clair read the brief statement out loud. "'HBL agrees with all points. Letter signed and sent to von Halt, von Tschammer and Diem. Edström informed. All await direction.'"

Coubertin said, "I've already drafted letters on our next steps to Baillet-Latour, Brundage, and Edström, which we'll send this afternoon." St. Clair realized that in the past week or so, Coubertin had been treating him more like a collaborator than his biographer.

The baron lifted the first letter and held it up, reading it in part while glancing at St. Clair. "In the meantime, I want to summon Diem to Lausanne immediately so we can make sure von Halt et al. understand the import of the commission's work. Can you take a telegraph down to the train station for me?"

"I guess so." St. Clair was reluctant. "But I don't want to lose time on our interviews today. We agreed we would spend at least half a day on the book."

"That's true," said the Baron. "Why don't we go down to the telegraph office together and find a place to talk?"

He dropped his head and inscribed the message to Diem, then read it aloud. "'Following receipt of commission letter from Baillet-Latour, please confirm terms with DOC and meet me in Lausanne earliest. Await your arrival plans. PDC.'"

For the next hour, St. Clair waited impatiently while Coubertin added lengthy notes to his letters to Brundage and Edström and then finished up two or three other pieces of correspondence before they said goodbye to Renée and Juliette, ensconced in the Rouge Room, and walked down to the telegraph office. It was nearly two hours later when they finally stopped for lunch at the Café de la Gare to continue their interview.

"Listen, Jacques," said Coubertin, "I apologize for the delay, but this issue won't wait and you know it. This is a serious threat and we've got to deal with it. You have to understand and, in fact, you have to help me with this. If the Germans take control of the IOC ..."

"I do understand," said St. Clair, who had ordered a bottle of red, knowing the wine would help the baron make the move from the intensity of the present to a time more than fifty years removed. "But I've been here for two months and we're just getting into the 1880s. At this rate, I could be here all summer and we'd just be getting on the boat to Athens in 1896."

Coubertin laughed loudly. "Well, Jacques, it took me a lot longer than that to get to Greece," he said with a smile, taking a drink of wine. "But that's not true. We've bounced all over—and we've talked informally about many of the Games' highlights covered in the histories. I'm of the opinion, my friend, that we've made some very good progress. You've been through my family history. Francis told me you summarized my youth quite nicely. We've talked through my university days—"

"Briefly," St. Clair interrupted.

"Yes, but you've got the highlights. And you've interviewed Brundage, so I'd say you're making very good headway."

"Nice of you to be so optimistic, Baron. But there's a lifetime to cover and I feel a certain need to move the story ahead so I can get more writing underway."

○ ○ ○ ○ ○

When St. Clair returned home later that night, Juliette was sitting on the couch in a bathrobe, her hair still wet from the shower. She had a bottle of sherry open and was leaning over the coffee table studying an arrangement of loose photographs she had placed in rows.

"Look what Renée gave me." St. Clair dropped his satchel and retrieved a glass.

"Gave you?" he asked, sitting, kissing her, and taking in images that seemed to be a chronological depiction of Coubertin's life.

"I meant to say, *loaned* me. Isn't this fascinating?"

"Yes, but I thought you were after portraits, pictures framing his face."

"Well, I was—but I've got more," she said, lifting a folio he hadn't seen. "As we went through the box, I thought you'd be interested in these—and when I said it might help you—Renée insisted I show them to you."

"What was she like one on one?"

"Tentative at first, diffident, a little skittish, not good at eye contact. I don't think she socializes that often. She warmed up, though, once I got her talking about the pictures, and by the end of it, we were almost best friends. We're going to have lunch."

"Is this his father's atelier?" St. Clair asked, picking up a small image with a white serrated edge. It focused on the back of a painter standing at an easel in a long, tailored suit coat, a wall of paintings directly in front of him, his face turned in profile to a source of light through a wall of windows to his left.

"Yes, that's Pierre's father in their Paris home."

"Just as he described it."

"Here's one she loved from her mother's family estate in Alsace."

"Ah, this must be Luttenbach-près-Munster. Pierre has mentioned it only in passing," St. Clair said, looking at an informal family portrait at a picnic at the edge of woods. Pierre was in a wool suit and boots, the young Renée standing between his legs, her mother and grandmother in full dresses looking on, and their son, Jacques, a stocky boy in a French naval playsuit, gazing off. "Did she say anything about her brother?"

"No—nor did she say anything about her mother. She seemed intent on staying focused on her father's work. She seems to know his life quite well."

"These are superb," St. Clair said, noting how Coubertin was always more or less front and center in a series of group shots, obviously of IOC leadership. "Look how he ages from this desk shot—I think that's in Athens with Vikelas— to this one, which must be in Prague, for his retirement speech." I've got to include some of these in the biography, he thought.

"Yes," said Juliette, curling her arm around St. Clair's shoulder, nestling close. "They're superb and certainly deserve your full attention. But that can wait till morning—you've got more pressing things to do right now."

21

THE PARTY

St. Clair had been waiting for more than an hour, it seemed, while Juliette dressed for the Messerli party. She would not let him into the bedroom or bath so he sat on the couch, slowly paging through a stack of French cycling magazines that Edgar had kindly sent him from Paris. Edgar was the only one from *Le Petit Journal* who wrote him with any consistency or expressed much curiosity about how the book was coming. He tried to keep St. Clair abreast of events back home. His letters were mostly about cycling, especially the Tour de France, and rugby, but increasingly they'd been filled with ominous notes about Germany and the sad state of France's political leadership. "No will, no vision, no muscle," Edgar had written.

St. Clair lifted his glass of Bordeaux and barely wet his lips. He had been sipping this one glass forever, it seemed, but he intended to stay sober at least until he met the guests at Messerli's party.

"What's going on in there?" he asked loudly for the third time. "We're going to be an hour late—and I don't want to be rude."

"An hour is not rude, it's fashionable," she shouted back, her voice suddenly rising as the door opened and she swept into the room like an apparition.

St. Clair was shocked. She was dressed in a voluminous green silk gown, tightly pinched at the waist, spreading like an umbrella down to the wide circle of its hem. She looked like a nineteenth-century courtesan.

He stood, uttering, "Oh my God," in sheer disbelief. Her beautiful face was powdered pure white, with the brightest red lips he had ever seen and touches of rouge over her cheekbones.

She extended her hand without saying a word, and he took it and turned her around to absorb the details of her costume. Her raven-black hair was neatly shaped into a high crown that nested above her head and made the most of her long, elegant neck. Her bare shoulders were covered with a pink chiffon shawl, crimped and crisp enough to stand on its own, and her décolletage was framed in a ruffled lace that St. Clair found arresting. But her eyes, which were always alluring, were now divine, their deep violet color offset by thick black eyeliner and lashes and a perfect purple shadow. She was bejeweled with sparkling crystal earrings and a necklace that Madame Pompadour might have worn.

"Juliette," he said, still gazing in stunned appreciation, "I don't know what to say ..."

"It's not Juliette tonight, Jacques," she said. "I'm the Duchess of Langeais, and I promise an evening you won't soon forget."

○ ○ ○ ○ ○

Twilight was setting in when St. Clair knocked on the door of Messerli's town home. He stood aside to allow the "duchess" to enter first. The maid who opened the door reacted as St. Clair had anticipated—her mouth literally fell open and she lost her composure, quickly moving aside as the duchess advanced.

As Juliette swept through the broad foyer into the Messerli's warm parlor with St. Clair striding in behind her, the effect was mesmerizing. Everyone stopped sipping their aperitifs. Coubertin and his wife, Marie, looked up from their conversation with another couple, champagne glasses in hand, and froze, their gazes fixed on the apparition suddenly commanding center stage.

The impression on the doctor himself was amusing, St. Clair thought. "Mademoiselle Juliette," Messerli mumbled, clearly taken aback, "perhaps you've thought we were hosting a masquerade ..." He seemed about to apologize when he saw the delightful smile on his wife's face. Their grandchildren giggled and stared in amazement.

Juliette's gown rustled as she moved directly toward the baron and baroness, the fullness of the dress brushing the furniture and the legs of the guests, creating a *swish-swish* of crinkling silk that filled the silence and softened the gasps.

St. Clair was proud of his fiancée. Once she'd captured everyone's attention, he stepped forward, lifted her white-gloved arm by the hand, and said, "Ladies and gentlemen, may I present the Duchess of Langeais."

"Ah, Balzac," said the baroness unenthusiastically.

"I have traveled down from Paris for this party for only one purpose," Juliette proclaimed in her duchess role, turning slowly and gracefully to draw each guest into her spell. "And that purpose is to meet the man of my dreams, Baron Pierre de Coubertin—and, of course," she said, bowing slightly, "to meet the lovely baroness by his side."

The baron bowed deeply and rose with a sparkle on his laughing face. The baroness forced a smile, the doctor laughed, and the guests burst into applause. Their voices rose with a gaiety as the glorious past of Paris came to life before them. St. Clair could only watch in admiration as his fiancée stayed in character, blatantly seductive and deliberately out of place. No one seemed to mind. Without hesitation, Coubertin offered his arm as if he had been invited to the courts of Louis XIV. Juliette held the center of attention with little effort, moving with the baron to meet every guest—and as he made the introductions, she invented story after story connecting each of them to Talleyrand or Pompadour or Cyrano de Bergerac or some other great personage of legendary France.

As St. Clair watched, a literal reincarnation of a French princess lifted the spirit of the party into a spontaneous play. In a kaleidoscopic swirl, Juliette played to her admirers and led them, elated, with the laughing baron on her arm, through the library toward the dining room, its polished place settings visible through the archways.

In their wake, the baroness drifted over to the fireplace, withdrawing from the gaiety. St. Clair waited for a minute and then walked over to her.

"Monsieur St. Clair," she said, greeting him but stiffening slightly.

"It's good to see you again, madame," he said, not sure what to expect from her but pleased to see the trace of a smile as she turned to watch the revelers. Her face was marked by the deep lines of a prolonged sadness, but he could still see in her countenance the early beauty that must have attracted Pierre. In her twenties, when they'd met, her lips must have been as full as her saucer eyes were pronounced. He had seen the pictures with her hair tautly pulled away from a round face that was attractive, if not beautiful.

She looked at him, her eyes softening. "Your girlfriend has quite an imagination. Did you help her with the costume? It's quite good, you know, and would have worked well in its day. I'm surprised she knew how much he loved Balzac."

"No, madame, I was nearly as surprised as you were when she emerged from the boudoir after holding me at bay while she prepared. I was asked to help only with some last-minute powder and the chiffon wrap."

"It's a charming performance that reminds me of a much happier time, part of the world in which Pierre and I circulated when we were young."

"Ah," St. Clair said, "that's a world I'd love to hear about." He was hoping to find a way to open her up.

"Monsieur St. Clair," the baroness said, looking directly at him. "The circumstances of our first meeting were not ... perhaps I should apologize." She hesitated and he was swift to interject.

"No need to apologize, madame. It would have been better had I arrived and been properly announced."

"We've been under an unusual level of strain for some time," she said.

St. Clair waited, knowing she was suspicious, always on guard.

"Our life—the life we have now ..." she hesitated, holding his gaze. "It's not the life I expected when we set out on this great adventure—his great adventure—all those years ago."

The opening he was hoping for. He moved to stand in front of her, his back now to the party so they were engaged face to face. "Madame Coubertin, the book I'm writing about your husband, his life and his vision ... I don't think I can create the full story without *you*—your memories, your reflections, your perspective on the experiences you shared ... the dreams you had ..." He stopped, uncertain. Had she really shared Coubertin's dreams?

"There were dreams, monsieur, dreams that came true but only after long struggles. And there were disappointments—many, many disappointments. You certainly recognize that, don't you?"

"Yes, of course. But for me to paint the picture fully, to bring to life the long journey of your lives ... well, I need to have the opportunity to talk to you in great detail. When, where, and how did you meet, what was your world like then?"

The hint of a smile creased her face and her eyes lifted. She raised her hand, her fingers touched her lips. "In the beginning, he brought joy and laughter to my world." She paused. "We could talk about that—those days." The smile vanished, the suspicion returned. "But there are things I don't want to talk about, things I won't talk to you about."

"I understand, madame," he said. "But the memories you're comfortable talking about will help color in a world ... that's nearly as long gone as the time Juliette has tried to bring back tonight."

"I'm not sure," she said. "Perhaps I'll talk to you. There's very little about his story that I don't know," she said intriguingly. Abruptly she looked away and raised her voice. "And speak of the devil. Here he is."

St. Clair turned as the baron stepped up to them. "Come, Marie, you're missing a marvelous moment," he said. "Juliette is quite the entertainer," he said to St. Clair as they headed to the salon.

The Duchess Juliette greeted them. "And lest we forget our manners, ladies and gentlemen," she said in an exaggerated voice of sophistication, "let us recognize that we have among us tonight one of France's most distinguished writers—the Balzac of sports, the Flaubert of the bicycle, the Stendhal of the Olympic Games, a veritable Jean-Jacques Rousseau for the common man's athletic nobility—and my rather unfashionable escort, the charming Monsieur Jacques St. Clair."

○ ○ ○ ○ ○

It was very late on a highly spirited and starry Sunday night. The three men had moved together out the back door and were lounging now in cushioned chairs on Messerli's terrace, shadowed in the after-dinner glow of lights from inside the house. The air was crisp, the city quiet, the three of them slightly drunk and still grinning from the dizzy gaiety and inspiration of a party that had drawn the baron into a circle of revelry none of them could have anticipated as the evening began. Coubertin had ended up at the piano after dinner, trying to play a few Broadway show tunes Juliette insisted on, and finally turning to a more somber but lovely Chopin nocturne, which toned down the hilarity that Juliette was once again trying to provoke and returned the evening back to a more traditional dinner party among new friends.

St. Clair and Messerli puffed on cigars and sipped on iced Amaro Averna, the doctor's preferred digestif. St. Clair flicked an ash and posed a question that instantly wrapped them again in the conspiracy to recall and record one man's history. "Francis, do you know the question Pierre's father asked him over and over when he was a boy?"

"Of course I do," Messerli said. "I've read over the passages on Pierre's youth several times. 'What do you see, son?'"

Coubertin smiled. "He would have loved seeing what I saw this evening."

"Well, what I want to know," St. Clair said, "is what do you see when you look into the future? Into the future of the Olympic Movement?"

The baron's brow crinkled and he twirled the end of his mustache as he looked at St. Clair. "Is this a good time to dive back into an interview?"

"A few questions won't hurt," St. Clair said, taking out a small notebook.

"That's a good question, Jacques," Messerli said. "We haven't really spent much time over the years speculating on where the Games might go, but when you think about it, they lasted for nearly twelve centuries in ancient Greece, and we're only in the fourth decade now."

"The future is a mystery," Coubertin said. "That's obvious ... but it isn't hard to speculate, if that's what you want."

"It is," said St. Clair. He waited as *le Rénovateur* began to talk about the possibilities.

"Let me tell you first what I saw when I started," Coubertin said. "I saw the possibilities of a worldwide network of three interdependent organizations, all forming one international family of sport—the international federations to guide the development of each sport, the national Olympic committees to develop the teams that would compete in each edition of the Games, and the International Olympic Committee guiding it all, ensuring that the values of sport and the ideals of excellence and peace we've nurtured for so long are preserved and protected and taught to every athlete who earns the right to be called an Olympian. I saw the possibilities of every Olympian becoming an ambassador of those ideals, leaving the Games as a hero, carrying that message back home, sharing it with the rising generation of competitors to come, a ceaseless and perpetual movement of ideas and ideals through time, athlete to athlete, generation to generation, on and on forever."

"Well, that is happening now, isn't it, to some extent?" St. Clair asked.

"Not as I envisioned it. It's still a possibility because, as Francis said, we're still at the beginning, but the educational emphasis has been lost to a large degree—my early colleagues would be appalled," he interjected without explanation. "And the cultural dimension, which was always as important as sport to me—well, we never got that right."

"Set aside what's wrong for a minute," St. Clair said, "and tell us what you see ahead."

Coubertin looked at St. Clair, his eyes softening in reflection. "See far, speak frankly, act firmly ... When I dream about the future, I see stadiums built that will rival the ancient Coliseum in Rome for pure awe, houses of sport that will become symbols of friendship and peace, landmarks of where the world gathered for the Games. There will be masterpieces of design on the intimate level of Stockholm's stadium and palaces of even greater extravagance than those the Germans so recently produced. Not because we want luxury or need it—we don't—but because cities will want to honor the movement and lift its stature before the world.

"The Games will move relentlessly through time and space across all the continents. We are now headed to Asia for the first time to celebrate the Games of Tokyo 1940. The Olympic Movement will eventually cross all the borders that divide mankind. It will reach into every country and spread the philosophy of Olympism through host cities and their education institutions. The flame—being passed along city streets and burning in the cauldron at the Games—may one day become the ultimate symbol of the community we hope to create.

"Sport will prosper and grow through a system of events and leagues that strengthen continental and national teams and play. They'll set the stage for heroes with Olympic aspirations and inspire young people with dreams of their own. As the Games grow larger—and that trend is clear and unstoppable—and as they attract more journalists and more news coverage, the academic community will become increasingly involved. Someday, we'll have psychologists and sociologists examining the meaning of the Games, and economists assessing their import.

"The prestige of hosting the world will grow and the competition for the Games will become more pressing. Someday, all the world's greatest capitals will line up against one another for the right to raise the five-ringed flag and light the cauldron above a new stadium in their cities. On that day, whenever it may be, my spirit will rejoice—for that will mark the day when the influence of the movement has reached a pinnacle of respect in our world—and that day, I believe, will be only the beginning of the real influence of the Olympic Movement."

22

THE BARONESS

After two more persistent invitations, St. Clair was delighted that Marie de Coubertin had finally agreed to an interview—but not at Mon Repos. For their meeting, she selected the restaurant at the Hôtel de la Paix, a short walk for her and a brief climb for him up the hills of Lausanne on his De Dion-Bouton. It was an overcast and wet April morning as St. Clair stepped into the foyer of the hotel and spotted the baroness just entering the café through the far door on the corner of rue de la Paix. While he peeled off his damp jacket, he watched her shake and close her parasol before being shown to a seat in a booth along the front windows. She wore a dark hat and coat over a collared white blouse and carried a large handbag on her shoulder. She seemed agitated as she sat.

"Good morning, Baroness," he said, approaching the table.

She offered her hand and he took it briefly, but she quickly withdrew it. "Good morning, Monsieur St. Clair. I hope you didn't get too wet coming up here."

"The rain was light, madame, and I'm quite used to it," he said, placing his notebook and pen on the table between them. "I cycled to work every day in Paris regardless of the weather."

"My husband told me you once rode in the Tour de France?"

That's a good beginning, he thought. This must be her nice side. "Yes, in my early twenties I thought I might have a career as a professional cyclist."

133

"But the life of a journalist had more appeal?"

"As a cyclist, I had limitations that were obvious. I knew I could only go so far. The writing, though, is like a journey without boundaries—it's almost impossible to predict where it will take you."

"Like this morning? Here you are meeting with an old baroness who has little to say on a gray, rainy day."

"Well, to be honest, madame, there's nowhere I'd rather be."

"You can't be serious," she objected, a faint smile on her lips. "You'd prefer an old baroness to a young duchess?"

"I do admit Juliette can be quite entertaining, but you possess half of a story I'm just beginning to grasp, I think—and without your voice in the mix, that story will never be complete."

The baroness paused as the waiter set out two cappuccinos and a tray of sweet cakes. She looked out into the dark gray sky at the building tops that faded into the mist on the hill below. "It's complicated for me, Monsieur St. Clair, because it's hard to look back. I know what you want me to tell you—all about the heroic effort to resurrect the Games—"

"No," St. Clair interrupted, "I don't want a packaged story neatly bound. I don't want a charming portrait if there was no charm. I want you to tell me as honestly as you can what happened when you and the baron met, how you started out on the course that led to the Olympics, and where that course has taken you since."

"I have great admiration for my husband and his achievements," she said, sounding apologetic rather than defensive. "And I do feel a responsibility to protect the legacy he's created. But had I known where we would end up—had I known what it would all lead to ..." She hesitated. "I'm not sure I would have ..."

At that point, she stopped because St. Clair had picked up his pen to make a note. She stared at his hand, clearly conflicted. When she looked up at him, her blue eyes seemed to be filled with doubt.

In a tone he often used with people who were reluctant to talk, St. Clair said, "It will be a year or two before the writing is finished on this book. So we have plenty of time to talk about the things you want to discuss—and to figure out how to address those things that seem too difficult right now. Why don't we simply begin with your family? Your childhood?"

As soon as St. Clair shifted the subject to her family and her background, the baroness relaxed her shoulders again and sat back in the booth, taking off her hat and unbuttoning her coat. "My father was Gustave Rothan," she began, stirring her cappuccino, "a wonderful man who served Napoleon III as a European minister during the last decade of the Second Empire. He wrote a masterful six-volume diplomatic history after the Franco-Prussian War."

Once she started it was as if she'd been waiting to tell *her* story for half a century. She constructed a voluble narrative about her past that was rich in detail. St. Clair had to write fast to keep up, but his shorthand was now more polished and swift than it had ever been. He drafted her story later that day.

Marie Rothan came from an old, moneyed Alsatian family of the Protestant faith that had owned the Château de Luttenbach in the lush, mountainous valley of Munster, west of Colmar and south of Strasbourg. It was a fine, large estate with a grand stone castle fronted by a famed copper dolphin fountain and extensive gardens in the back enclosed by impressive arched walls. Known for its hospitality to aristocratic travelers, it had once played host to Voltaire and attracted adventurers who loved to hike and roam through the remote but beautiful French forests that seemed to stretch endlessly in every direction. The village of Munster was only a half hour away by coach, but the château gave every guest a feeling of pleasant isolation in a magical, natural world.

The serenity and tranquility of the landscape belied its political volatility. On the border between Germany and France, Alsace-Lorraine was a treasure desired by both nations and had been a source of simmering hostility for centuries. With its four broad, vineyard-feeding rivers—the Moselle, the Saar, the Rhine, and the Rhône—it had been the grand prize of the Franco-Prussian War: taken in triumph by Germany in 1871, it was brought back to France through the Treaty of Versailles that settled World War I.

Marie's father, Jean Georges Gustave Rothan—who was born in 1822, the same year that Pierre's father, Charles de Coubertin, was born—must have been moved and inspired by the political history of the region, for he found his calling in international diplomacy. With a passion for peace, a personal cachet, and decisive intelligence that marked him as a dashing figure, he found great favor in the courts of Napoleon III and represented the Second Empire on ambassadorial posts to Prussia, Turkey, and Italy. His reports arrived in Paris with a clear and compelling literary force that earned him ever-greater respect, and he rose to prominence as a plenipotentiary minister with the power to negotiate and sign state contracts, agreements, and treaties.

As a man of letters from a cultured family, Rothan took advantage of his diplomatic position to visit the finest museums and galleries wherever he traveled. During long-term posts and assignments in Berlin, Frankfurt, Constantinople,

Florence, and Rome, he sought out the leading art collectors and dealers and engaged in salon debates on painting and sculpture. Gradually, he refined his tastes and acquired a personal art collection of some significance. A love of fine painting and the pursuit of small masterpieces became his lifelong avocation and second passion—after diplomacy.

Not long after he married Marie Caroline Braun, a vivacious French-German beauty of Upper Rhine descent, they moved to his new ambassadorial residence in Frankfurt am Main, where their only child, Christa Anna Marie, was born in 1861. To their delight, young Marie picked up German as quickly as French and showed a proclivity for learning and a passion for ideas that matched her father's.

But what seemed like an idyllic vocation for a young ambassador and his family turned progressively more stressful and frightening as the old political hostilities rose again in the 1860s and the emperor began to imagine that he was as gifted as his Uncle Napoleon had been at military strategy. It was a conceit that his nation would pay for with a loss of lives, property, and international prestige from which it would never quite recover.

In feverish communiqués in early 1870, as Rothan prepared to preserve his art collection by hiding it in a warehouse near Paris and protect his family by moving back to the Château de Luttenbach, he repeatedly warned Napoleon III to back away from any aggression against the Germans. He reported that their armaments and army were much deeper and stronger than the emperor's intelligence indicated—and that the Germans were ripe for a fight. He forcefully recommended maintaining the peace and promoting long-term prosperity through trade. Alas, finding a minor offense in a Spanish communiqué, Napoleon III declared war—and the tragedy of Sedan, in which the emperor and his eighty thousand troops were captured in a Prussian rout, became the great bloody stamp of failure on France's military record. The Second Empire collapsed quickly as the Third Republic struggled to rise in the chaotic atmosphere of the capital. Knowing that the Prussians under Bismarck would march on Paris, Rothan felt his family would be safe in Luttenbach, but his intelligence was wrong too and they were soon evicted, though spared any harm, by the invading Germans.

Having made their way back to Paris after the eruptions of the Commune when order was somewhat restored, the Rothans were overjoyed to find that their friends and servants had preserved their home near the Place Saint-Georges from any damage or theft. Recognizing that his political career was over—blackmarked as a political pariah by the fledgling Third Republic—Rothan sought solace in his art collection and decided to begin writing his memoir. He also discovered a great source of joy right in his home, as his daughter, Marie, now twelve, began to take an interest in the art he had collected.

"All the art had been packaged in crates and stored in a warehouse in Auteuil," the baroness continued, now having a glass of Swiss white wine from the commune of Aubonne and picking at the charcuterie board St. Clair had ordered. They had been talking for nearly three hours. "My father had the crates brought to the house a few at a time. We had a large luggage room between the mansion and the stables, and it was there that we pried open each crate and carefully unwrapped every piece of art.

"My father wanted to do all the work himself, without the servants but with my assistance alone. I'd hand him a crowbar and try to brace the crates against a trunk while he forced open the wood, and sometimes"—she laughed a little—"I would use all my strength to try to pull a nail out of its hold with the claw of a hammer."

"How extensive was his collection?" St. Clair asked. "How many paintings did you unpack?"

"I'm not exactly sure, but we were working together across the entire summer and into the fall—months of unpacking and hanging the work in this room or that, taking it down if he didn't like the effect or the light, repositioning pieces. It was an extensive collection then, and he continued to build it until he died in early 1890. I can tell you this: when my mother and I sold the collection through the Galerie Georges Petit on rue Saint-Georges in May of that year, there were 256 paintings listed in the catalog—but let me come back to that."

"Tell me about the paintings and your interest in them as a young girl. Which were your favorites?" This interview is a pleasure, St. Clair thought. The baroness wasn't so difficult after all.

"We were in no hurry that summer," the baroness remembered, her voice soft and her eyes wistful. "Every painting had a story, which my father wanted me to hear, and every painting brought us closer. Before we started working together that summer, he had always been a strong presence in my life—a figure of great authority and a parent, yes, but not an affectionate father who doted over his daughter. He was an ambassador, and while he took pride in my language skills and schoolwork, he was an important figure in an Imperial world, always preoccupied and caught up in political intrigue. He left it to my mother to raise me, and she was wonderful, to be sure, and powerful in her own right, but that summer, the plenipotentiary minister of France became a true father, and my love and respect for him grew with every painting he pulled out of those crates.

"Imagine the education I got—my father was very well read. With each painting, he discussed the intent of the artist, the style of the painting, the symbols embedded, art movements, political context, the provenance of each piece, even its economics, and sometimes the frame. Through his discourse, I learned about the Dutch masters, the greatest French painters of the royal courts, the Italian giants of the Renaissance, and even the lesser known but equally impressive Germans. All of this was invariably woven into an enchanting tale as he told me what he saw and what he loved about each piece. He would always start with the story of the artist.

"But he was teaching me far more than the history of art that summer. The experience was emotional, personal and familial in the best sense, an enlightening bridge between generations that had centuries of shared cultural dimensions. He told me each piece of art was a member of our family, a sister or brother to me. 'Wherever this painting goes when it leaves our home,' he said, 'our family will always be part of its provenance. It will carry our name into the future. When we took it in, we extended its life and guided it somehow on its way.'"

"And what was your favorite painting, Baroness?"

The answer was immediate: "My very favorites were two pieces my father hung in my bedroom because I loved them so much: *The Allegory of Painting* and *The Allegory of Music*, by François Boucher. He was a master of the French style in the eighteenth century, perhaps the most famous court painter under Louis XV and a devoted friend of Madame Pompadour, the king's infamous mistress. We know her beauty best from his painting. But the two pieces I favored were filled with the magical moment when the muse touches the artist, rendered in the symbolic presence of cherubs and eternal feminine beauty. Would you like to see them, Monsieur St. Clair?"

"Yes, of course—you still have them?"

"No, they were sold at auction when my father died, and it was the end of the whole collection. But I've kept a memento." Reaching up behind her head, the baroness took a golden locket from around her neck, hidden beforehand by the ruffles of her collar, and opened it to reveal a miniature cloisonné with the two extraordinary scenes—which brought her descriptions to life.

"Impressive," St. Clair said. It was remarkable that the memories of that summer were still so vivid to the baroness.

"This locket is a small measure of my father's many gifts to me. In the 1870s, his collection became quite well known in the art world of Paris and beyond. Paul Mantz, the editor of *La Gazette des Beaux-Arts*, came to the house and wrote two long pieces that celebrated the Galerie Rothan—which he described as one of the finest private collections in France. After that, there seemed to be a constant stream of guests who flattered their way into our home."

"Hardly sounds like the life of a retiring diplomat."

"No, it was an exciting time, stimulating intellectually, inspiring culturally, and often surprisingly filled with fun," she said, smiling at a memory.

"Recalling something humorous?"

"Yes! Once, a very wealthy gentleman who had quite a collection of Bouchers asked to see the two *Allegories*. My father turned to me and declared, 'Well, they belong to my daughter, Marie—and she keeps them in her private gallery. You'll have to get her permission to see them.'

"The man laughed but took the suggestion to heart and appealed to me with a great show of respect, praising my discernment in keeping the Bouchers apart from the major collection. My brief tour proved a great success, and so my father made it *de rigueur* for all tours!"

"Your father must have been a great man," St. Clair said.

"I think he showed his true greatness in the years that followed," the baroness replied. "That late stage of my father's life—which started in the collapse of the Second Empire and saw us fleeing like refugees from the family château at Luttenbach into an uncertain future in an unstable republic—turned out to be his best years. When he turned to writing, he found a new sense of liberty. He produced a comprehensive and much-praised political history of the empire, and that was highly satisfying to him. His six-volume *Souvenirs Diplomatiques* sold well for years and restored some of the respect he had lost through his association with Napoleon III. While my father was on the outside of political power, he was not alone. A wide network of former Imperial officers and administrators gave him a strong social community. And he found personal peace at home. They were happy times."

○ ○ ○ ○ ○

It was late afternoon and the baroness was still talking. Suddenly she halted, and St. Clair followed her gaze out the window. The rain had stopped and the sky was bright gray, still overcast but lightening. Across the street, Coubertin and another man, tall and skinny but about the same age, came up the steps from the small pocket park and turned toward the Place Saint-François. They were talking animatedly, both dressed in morning coats and top hats and using their umbrellas as walking sticks. The tall man had a hesitant gait, as if his knees were untrustworthy, and appeared to be frail.

"That's Lucien Drussard, one of Pierre's oldest colleagues from Paris, probably here on IOC business," the baroness said. "He's still with the French Olympic Committee, I believe."

"A French colleague from how long ago?" St. Clair wondered whether Drussard would be a good interview subject.

"Oh, from the very beginning, I'm sure. In fact, he worked with Pierre on the formation of the Jules Simon Committee in 1888—the very first sports committee that Pierre created and controlled. Drussard played a key role in pulling all the running clubs together."

St. Clair was surprised at the immediacy of her recall of the Simon Committee and Drussard's role in it—because, he assumed, that work predated the beginning of their courtship by some years. He wondered just how much she knew about Pierre's early career. "Perhaps I should interview Monsieur Drussard."

"Yes, you should," she said, suddenly shifting in her seat, as if she was ready to leave. "Do you want to go after them right now?"

"No, no, no, no." St. Clair reached across the table and placed his hand over hers, trying to be reassuring, not wanting to lose her. "We have so much more to cover—the times in which you met Pierre and what you thought of his Olympic idea—but let me ask you something else, briefly." He hoped that by this point she was beginning to believe she could trust him.

"Maybe another time, monsieur. I must really be going." She began to gather her things.

"One more question, please?"

"All right, if you insist."

"When you identified Drussard, I was a little surprised that you knew of the role he played in 1888. Didn't you and Pierre meet and begin dating in the 1890s?"

"Well, no. We began our romance and public courtship not long after my father's funeral in 1890, but I had known Pierre for years."

"You'd known him for years? When did you first meet?"

"At an art auction," she said, "with our fathers, maybe in 1878 or '79."

"Well, that's a surprise to me. Let's go back to the beginning, then ..."

"Monsieur St. Clair," she said as if beginning an apology, "I really must be going. We've spent much more time talking than I thought we would. Perhaps another day?"

○ ○ ○ ○ ○

After the baroness walked away under her small parasol, St. Clair decided to see if he could track down Coubertin's old friend, Lucien Drussard, at the Lausanne Palace, where the baroness had said he was probably staying. He walked the two blocks from the Hôtel de la Paix, passing through the crowds of late-afternoon commuters at the Place Saint-François before reaching the grand façade of the hotel.

The baroness had guessed correctly; Drussard was registered at the Palace. But he did not answer a call to his room. St. Clair was leaving a note for him at the front desk when the lanky old man stepped out of the elevator, a cane in his right hand, and moved slowly down the stairs, holding the rail while his top hat bobbed up and down.

"Pardon, Monsieur Drussard," St. Clair said as the man righted himself and looked askance at him. Drussard's eyebrows furrowed in the search of something familiar.

"*Bonjour*, monsieur," Drussard said. "How may I help you?"

"I'm Jacques St. Clair, Monsieur Drussard." The man's eyes brightened immediately.

"Ah, Pierre's new friend, the great sports writer from Paris."

"That's kind of you, sir." St. Clair extended his hand, which Drussard accepted with an awkward left-hand shake.

"Pierre told me all about the work you're doing on his biography. I think it's a wonderful enterprise, and Pierre is certainly energized by it."

"Thank you. I was wondering whether I might interview you about the early years in Paris and your work with Pierre back then?"

"Those were great times," the old man said, "and I'd enjoy talking with you, but I'm running a little late for a meeting that promises to turn into a long dinner, and I'm leaving for Paris early tomorrow."

"Too early for a cup of coffee?"

"Yes, unfortunately, but I'll be back in three weeks, perhaps a month, and I'd be happy to meet with you then. Send me a note in Paris—Pierre has the address—and we'll set it up."

"I'll do that," St. Clair said as the old man began to move around him toward the door. St. Clair walked beside him. "If I sent you a few questions, do you think you might have time to answer them?"

"Not certain, Monsieur St. Clair, but you can try." Without saying goodbye, he walked gingerly to the rotating door as the bellman stepped in to help him.

23

THE AUCTION

St. Clair met the baroness again a few days later at the Hôtel de la Paix. They sat in the same booth, in the front window, and the day was overcast once again. But she had come prepared to talk and to tell him the story of the day she met Pierre in 1878 when he was fifteen and she was seventeen. The draft flowed later from his notes.

In the courtyard of their home on the Place Saint-Georges, her father helped Marie Rothan mount the step up into the caliche, looking up at her with undisguised pride. She patted the folds of her elegant white silk dress as he sat beside her on the cushioned bench, his gray suit pants and black coat contrasting with her gown in the dapples of the afternoon sun.

"The Hôtel Drouot," Gustave Rothan said to his coachman, who quickly popped the reins and made a clicking sound that produced a sudden surge as the bay lurched and pulled the coach forward, its low wheels spinning across the cobbles.

Minutes later, they arrived at the hotel on rue Drouot. Her father offered his arm to Marie as they passed through the lobby into a ballroom crowded with well-dressed men and women moving in groups along the walls of the room, perusing the art and objects that would soon go on auction. The middle of the room, under the candlelight of an enormous chandelier, was covered with two sections of neatly aligned seats, all facing a low stage at the front and divided by a center aisle. The famous auctioneer, Charles Pillet—the *commissaire-priseur* of the moment—was leaning forward, his arm resting on the podium where his gavel waited, discussing a point with a tall bearded man who, Marie noticed, was accompanied by a younger man, perhaps his son—a short but handsome boy. He was taking in the commotion of the room when he spotted her and offered a discreet nod as if they knew each other. But she didn't know him, and she raised her head and turned away. Soon, however, curiosity overtook her. They seemed to be the only two young people in the room, so she found herself glancing back in his direction once or twice, each time noticing that his gaze was still fixed on her.

Her father caught the eye of the auctioneer, who broke off his conversation and waved them over. She resisted looking back at the young man as her father led her to the stage.

As they approached, Pillet straightened up and said, "Gustave Rothan, I don't believe you've had the pleasure of meeting Charles de Coubertin."

"Ah, Monsieur Coubertin, it's a distinct honor," Rothan said, extending his hand as they shook.

"And mine as well, sir," said Coubertin. "I've heard much about your collection."

"And I know and admire your work," said Rothan. "In fact, I once bid on *The Departure of the Missionaries.*"

"I'm flattered," Charles said. "May I present my son Pierre."

Rothan reached out and shook Pierre's hand, then said, "And this is my daughter Marie." Looking at her, he continued, "This man, Marie, is Baron Charles de Coubertin, one of our leading and most devout painters, and his son Pierre."

As she was forced to turn and look directly into Pierre's dark, protuberant eyes, the auctioneer distracted their fathers by loudly interjecting what a great pleasure it was to have two such handsome young aristocrats present for today's exciting sale.

Marie extended her hand to Pierre, noting he was slightly younger than her. With a sparkling smile and a charming manner that surprised her, he took her hand, bowed from the waist, and said, "So pleased to make your acquaintance, mademoiselle. It's nice to find someone at the Hôtel Drouot from my own generation."

Addressing her father, Pierre said, "May I have your permission, sir, to give your daughter a better look at the art that is about to go on the block?"

"Of course," said her father, smiling back. "I'm sure Marie will be quite interested in your perspective on the best pieces."

With that, the senior Coubertin nodded and the fathers turned back to their conversation. Pierre offered his arm, Marie took it with only the slightest hesitation, and they set out to circle the room. Let's see what this boy knows, she thought.

They came to a painting by Jacques-Louis David, a comparatively loose, smaller study for his celebrated *Napoleon at the Saint-Bernard Pass.*

"Do you know David's work?" asked Pierre.

"Yes, I do." She looked closely at the brush work in the composition. "I love this study because I do think his equestrian portrait is the most dramatic of the emperor—and certainly conveys his sense of himself."

"*Napoleon Crossing the Alps*," Pierre said.

She was going to recite the well-known fact that the portrait was fiction—that Napoleon had actually crossed the Alps on a mule—but refrained from showing off. She wondered if he knew.

"A master of neoclassicism," said Pierre. "My father studied with François-Édouard Picot, who studied alongside David and painted with him, so we know his work quite well."

"And which paintings do you like best?"

"Of Picot's? My favorite is L'Amour et Psyché."

She knew the painting—two nudes in a canopied bed. "No, not Picot's—and certainly not so much nudity," she replied, a bit piqued. "Which of David's paintings do you like?"

"Oh, you do know your paintings. Well, I think *The Death of Marat* is David's finest piece, bringing so much light to a dark theme, and I love some of his later work, particularly *Venus Disarming Mars*."

"*Mars Being Disarmed by Venus*," she corrected. "Yes, that's a beautiful work."

"It evokes an age I've been enchanted with for years."

"Do you mean the age of mythology?" she said, laughing teasingly.

"No, but I do love mythology. The world of ancient Greece is my obsession."

They moved along the wall, exchanging views and comments on each painting and object. Marie looked at him more closely now, surprised by the ease with which he described the work. Eventually, they turned a corner into an antechamber, where a roped-off column under a beam of light presented an ancient Greek amphora with wrestlers leaning into each other.

Pierre was immediately fixated by the object. As he leaned in to examine the black paint on the golden-brown urn, he asked without looking at her, "Have you been following the German excavations of ancient Olympia?"

As soon as the baroness uttered the word *Olympia*, St. Clair felt that sense of discovery he knew so well as a journalist—a kernel of new information. "Wait," he said. "Pierre spoke about ancient Olympia on the first day you met? In 1878?"

"Yes—is that surprising?"

"Well, the general story is that his idea to restore the Olympic Games emerged in the early 1890s. So it seems a little early."

"That's true. But back then he wasn't talking about the idea of restarting the Games, he was only talking about ancient Olympia—which wasn't all that unusual at the time. Like so many young Jesuit students, he was obsessed with the ancient Greeks and Romans. In their lessons, the Jesuits painted an idealistic portrait of the ancient world, and the more imaginative students—Pierre was certainly among them—were literally transported into the past. Pierre became a modern Hellenist. And because of who he was—a very sports-minded and athletic young man who would go for long runs in the Bois de Boulogne from the time I knew him—he was particularly taken with ancient Olympia. You should ask him about it. He references it in his memoir. He and his favorite teacher at Saint-Ignace, Père Caron, followed the German excavations very carefully."

"Yes, I've talked to him about Saint-Ignace and the German excavations, but I was just surprised that he spoke to you about it when you first met."

"Well, ancient Olympia was always on Pierre's mind—as was the ancient Greek model of education based on the gymnasium."

"So you and Pierre had a continuing relationship throughout the years—and you were part of his campaign to bring physical education into France."

"No, not exactly. Pierre and I became quite close the year after we met at the Hôtel Drouot. When our families started socializing, Pierre and I began to spend time together and a natural attraction developed. For a year or two, we were almost inseparable," she said. "I think we could both see the future and knew where it was leading. But then there was a break," she said, a sigh of resignation in her voice.

"And just as quickly as it began, it was over. I didn't see him again for a decade," she said, "until my father's funeral in 1890. He helped my mother and I prepare Father's collection for the auction at Galerie Georges Petit. It wasn't long after that we rediscovered what we once had and we were in love again."

St. Clair ordered their lunch. And then they talked for three more hours, driven by his indefatigable interest in the details of her life, hardly noticing as the sun broke through the clouds and Lausanne shimmered in the aquamarine gleam of the lake in the late afternoon.

From St. Clair's perspective, the baroness was an excellent interview subject. Where was the monster, he wondered, thinking Messerli had misled him. But then he recalled her anger that day at Mon Repos—and her reluctance at the party, her lack of joy. A strange mystery, he thought. As she talked away, St. Clair was amazed by the fluidity of her memories. It was as if a floodgate had been opened. The most interesting revelation came when the baroness explained why she had ended her affair with Pierre.

"Pierre was just a boy of fifteen when I met him—and I was only seventeen," she began. "But he was as charming and as smart as any man I'd encountered. His eyes were large and pronounced, almost bulbous—but deeply affecting,

I'd say, especially up close when he fixed them on you. They were such a deep, deep brown they were almost black, with a nearly invisible line around the pupil, and that made them somehow seem full of sincerity. When he looked at you, you felt as if he were absorbing you. And he was very muscular in a surprising way. Although he moved with an easy athletic grace, he was small, and so you didn't have an immediate impression that he possessed a muscular frame. The first time I hugged him, in my room, I put my hand on his shoulder and dropped it along his arm—that's when I felt the strength. Those arms were like rocks. Even years later, when we went to Luttenbach and walked through the woods, he could pull himself up into a tree like an acrobat. He was very gifted physically.

"But what bound us, truly, was the world of art, which came to both of us through our fathers. Our cultural experiences gave us an intimate connection from the very beginning. It was emotional, because art can be so personal, and it was intellectual, because we talked about painting and sculpture and the traditions in which they fit with far more knowledge than nearly anyone else our age. That connection was very inspiring—to meet someone of my own generation whose cultural passions were as real as mine and as rooted in a family commitment to the arts.

"He was Catholic and I was Protestant, and at the time, that mattered more to my father and mother than to me, but it was somewhat of a barrier. The truth was that I had a full social life—and then I met someone else."

"You mean another suitor?"

"Yes, someone a little older."

"Who was the other man?"

"It doesn't matter, but his name was Pierre Augustin Melachoir, and his family lived in a large hôtel near the Park Monceau. He had a fabulous British carriage with an enameled black finish and a large family crest emblazoned in gold on the door. My girlfriends all loved him. He was the best dancer among the social set I knew at the time. Pierre was persistent—and deeply disappointed, I know. I hid from him and refused to meet him when he came to the house. I was young, and the world was filled with dazzling men."

24

THE RIDE

S t. Clair said goodbye to Juliette while she was still in bed, reluctantly drawing away from her languid kiss and lingering arms. He wrapped two baguettes, some cheese, a bottle of wine, and a canteen of water in a tablecloth and stuffed it all with a towel into his saddlebag. Leaning the tandem bike against the cottage, he tied the bag between his seat and the handlebars Coubertin would grip. St. Clair was dressed for cycling in shorts that reached his knees, a short-sleeved shirt over a tighter long-sleeved one, and low black cycling shoes that fit nicely on the metal pedals. It was a lovely morning in mid-April.

He set out on the tandem, which was just a bit heavier than his De Dion-Bouton, and worked up the hill from Ouchy to Mon Repos. It was a short climb he had made a few dozen times, and on the tandem he was only a little slower, so he arrived relaxed and in a light sweat at nine o'clock as he had promised. He dried himself off and waited to cool down before he went in, then took the stairs up two floors to the sign on the office door, COMITÉ INTERNATIONAL OLYMPIQUE. He knocked lightly and went right in. Coubertin looked up from behind the desk where he was writing a letter and had already piled up a stack beside it. He rose and came around to meet St. Clair.

"So we're going for a ride, are we?" he asked, smiling at St. Clair, who was a little winded from the stairs. Noting the perspiration, Coubertin laughed. "I see you're feeling the effects of our hilly terrain. Are you sure you can bear the weight?"

"With a little help from you I'm sure these pistons will carry us to the Grandvaux." St. Clair smacked his thighs. He was looking forward to the challenge.

Coubertin wore loose cotton pants made for exercise and a blue Breton pullover, both fine, but he had on leather boots that looked too heavy for cycling.

"How about this?" the baron asked, holding up a four-button herringbone jacket with a belt in the middle.

"Too heavy, Pierre. You can wear it if you want, but once we get going I'm sure you'll want to unbutton it or take it off."

"All right, I'll leave it behind. But don't count on too much help from me."

St. Clair wasn't counting on any support. He just wanted to give the old man a good ride to a place he hadn't seen in a while.

As they mounted and pushed forward on the two-seater, it lurched left and right in wobbly twists through the gravel in front of Mon Repos. But St. Clair was pleased with the immediacy of Coubertin's response as they fell into rhythm with their movements. Within ten turns of the pedals, they had balanced the tandem and accelerated out to the firmer ground of rue de la Manche and leaned into the turning lane. They moved at an easy pace through the village and Coubertin pedaled well, not straining or pushing too hard, but giving enough energy to offset some of his weight. St. Clair gripped the handlebars and was able to power the cycle forward without much difficulty while staying in his seat. He knew at once that with Coubertin's modest effort he could carry them up the 2,500-foot ascent that would take them to Grandvaux.

Out of Mon Repos, in the sunlight of a beautiful spring morning, they glided downhill toward the waterfront and were soon clear of the city, passing through farmland and glades of groomed trees, the green fields of Pully and Lutry glistening with dew and rising mist, foothills swelling upward to their left, and crowns of dark forest above the vineyard fields they soon broached. As their breathing settled into the rhythm of cycling, they drew the crisp air into their lungs, and St. Clair felt the exhilaration of exercise. The sensation the baron called the "joy of effort" came quickly, and St. Clair wondered if the old man shared the feeling. And then he worried about the baron's stamina. This is much more strenuous than the rowing he's used to, he thought.

"How's it going back there?" St. Clair shouted.

"I think I'll make it," Coubertin hollered. "Feeling okay so far."

"Hold on," St. Clair said, standing on the pedals and riding harder, demonstrating his cycling skills as they moved through several switchbacks and crested a hill. He settled back down into his seat when they hit a flat stretch.

During the hour-and-a-half ride, St. Clair had no trouble powering them all the way up to Signal de Grandvaux, where they pulled into an inn with a café that Coubertin knew. Coubertin peeled off his Breton and stretched as St. Clair unpacked their bread, wine, and cheese. They sat at a table outside on the edge of a field that fell away into the trees below, looking out on the finest vista St. Clair had seen so far. They weren't at cloud level, but they could see more of the first shoulders of the French Alps, where the range of peaks spread like the pointed white helmets of an army moving down toward Italy and the south of France.

They sat quietly for a while, breathing deeply, St. Clair checking to make sure Coubertin had handled the climb without too much strain. "How are you, Baron?" he asked at length.

"I'm fine, Jacques—lost in my memories. As we were riding, I was looking over your shoulders and remembering the road ahead. I remembered pushing up these hills years ago with Messerli's mates. The conversation and laughter were always enjoyable—and so were the hijinks of an acrobatic Spanish rider named Paolo who could lift his front tire off the ground and sprint on one wheel. What I remember most though was bearing down and pushing as hard as I could to stay up with the best of them.

"I never expected," the baron continued, "to come back up here on a cycle—or at all for that matter. It's exhilarating to be out in the sun like this, enjoying the clean, cool breeze, taking in the beauty. I owe you—and I owe sport, for there is no doubt it is sport that's brought us here."

"Yes, it is. I wanted to share a true moment of sport with you."

"You're an athlete, Jacques, and you wanted me to witness your performance. I have—and it was magnificent. One of the finest I've experienced in years."

At that moment, St. Clair felt a tremendous sense of satisfaction, an affirmation from the ultimate voice of judgment that he had done something right, something good, something that touched the virtuous heart of sport. He realized then that he had wanted the baron's approval. He had wanted to display his athletic prowess and gain an honored place in the deep corridors of Coubertin's sporting memory.

As he looked at the baron, the kindness of the old man's smile told him there was now a different bond between them—the cherished bond of friendship through sport.

St. Clair took out his tablet and began to ask Coubertin a few questions about his own athletic past.

"Jacques," Coubertin said in a voice filled with affection, "I don't want to talk about sport right now. We can come back to that. I'm much more interested in the long conversations you've had with your most recent interview subject."

"The baroness?"

"Yes, Jacques. You've spent more time talking with my wife than anyone has in the last forty years. Was she pleasant?"

"Completely. A pleasure for the full two sessions. Very polite, no anger at all."

"That's amazing." The baron seemed incredulous. "I want to know what you talked about."

"Well, I was going to ask for your recollections of the events she described to me."

"Of course. I'll be happy to give you my take on anything you discussed. Did you talk to her about when we met?"

"Yes. In great detail."

"How much detail?"

"Do *The Allegories of Painting and Music* ring a bell?"

"Indeed—her paintings. It sounds like you broke through, Jacques. No one has seen that side of her in years—at least not privately. That's more impressive than your climbing ability! Now tell me what she said about the first time we met."

An hour later, back on the tandem, they flew down the long hill together, back to Mon Repos. Even after the ride, the baron was as persistent as St. Clair had ever seen him, digging for detail after detail about the baroness's memories. He wanted to have dinner and then meet again the next day. Finally, he was ready to provide St. Clair with his version of his first encounters with Marie Rothan.

25

THE BEDROOM

I t was just after lunch when Coubertin and St. Clair sat down at the sidewalk café at the Angleterre. Coubertin had been impressed by the baroness's recall and her wistful memories of the good times they had once enjoyed.

"Where do you want to start?" he asked. "Should we go back to the first time I met her?"

"Yes, I think that's a good idea."

"Very well. But first, Jacques, I've got to say thank you—again. If you knew how unhappy my wife and I have been over the last decade, maybe longer—and you really don't—you'd be able to understand how important it is for me to know she can still recall the love we shared. And do it pleasantly."

"You're welcome, Pierre. She was quite clear she loved you deeply."

Coubertin looked out at the horizon across the lake, seemingly absorbed in that thought. "Now, what's your question?"

"Do you remember the day you met Marie at the Hôtel Drouot?"

"Ah yes, of course—I distinctly remember that day." Coubertin's eyes were bright. "It was 1878. I was fifteen and she was a very mature seventeen. The auctioneer introduced our fathers and they, in turn, introduced us—and I was smitten from that moment on." A grin flickered across his face. "What was the point that surprised you again?"

"That you spoke to her about the ancient Olympics on the day you met."

"It's not really surprising at all. That was the year after the Germans had discovered the *Hermes of Praxiteles*, right where Pausanias said it would be. That was also the year of the Paris Exposition—the year I looked into the eyes of the Statue of Liberty face to face."

"You'll have to tell me about that later—but what do you remember about Marie?"

"She wore a full white dress with a silk shawl and a fancy feathered hat that rode perfectly over the crest of her brunette hair. She had full lips, rounded, rouged cheeks, and the fiery blue eyes of an intellect. And truth be told, she had a broader perspective on the history of French art—no, that's a bit limiting; I would say she had a much broader knowledge of the art world than I did at that point—and I had grown up under the tutelage of a painter."

"She wasn't my first romance, but she was my first serious love—and she became the enduring love of my life."

When the auctioneer Pillet hammered the podium and called the room to order, Pierre was sorry to see that Monsieur Rothan and his father were sitting on opposite sides of the room. He reluctantly said goodbye to Marie, expressing hopes they would meet again soon. She demurred, leaving him with no promise. He was not at all sure he had captured her interest, feeling it must have been obvious he was trying to compensate for the gap in their ages by acting more mature than he really was. He was still a student at Saint-Ignace, for God's sake, and she was about to enter the University of Paris.

As he sat with his father across the room, five rows back from Marie, he couldn't stop thinking about how clumsy he had been in their exchange. At one point, commenting on a work by Delacroix, she had spoken in flawless English. His spoken English was good at that point, but not as good as hers, and he'd apologized, learning in the process that she had attended finishing school in Brighton, England, where Queen Victoria summered, and that she had mastered the language in short order.

Pierre watched with interest as Monsieur Rothan bid on and secured a drawing by the Italian Giovanni Battista Brambilla and was disappointed when his father, looking at his pocket watch, elbowed Pierre abruptly, rose, and headed out of the hotel.

In the big coach on the way home—his father liked to take the six-seat barouche to any significant social gathering, and the Hôtel Drouot art auctions certainly qualified—they sat on the bench, each looking out the windows as they rolled down boulevard Haussmann toward the Opéra. Pierre glanced over as his father removed his top hat and rubbed his forehead, squinting as if he were in some discomfort and sighing deeply.

"Are you all right, Father?" Pierre asked.

"Yes, I'm fine. Just tired and, quite frankly, a bit disappointed by the bidding at the auction today. Prices are falling. It seems all the talk is about the Impressionists and their show," he grunted, "*The Salon of the Refusals*. What a ridiculous name for a salon. This world of ours just never stops changing—and it's hard to know where it's going."

This was his father's usual refrain. It would lead to complaints about the political instability of the republic and the ever more pressing need to bring back the monarchy—a bankrupt notion with no hope of success.

But Pierre had another conversation in mind, and at that moment he decided that seeing Marie Rothan again was his first priority—so he launched a strategy to be sure his father made it happen.

"Well, I thought Monsieur Rothan paid a decent price for that Brambilla."

"Yes, but it was not a major work. The David sketches drew only forty thousand francs and they were worth twice that."

Without warning, the carriage took a high bounce at the pont Royal, and Pierre and his father were suddenly suspended; they crashed into each other as they scrambled to hold their places on the soft bench.

As they laughed, Pierre said, "Sometimes you've got to be a gymnast to take a coach across the Seine."

"Ha! Well said, son." The elder Coubertin clearly enjoyed the joke.

"I heard from Marie that her father has quite an admirable collection."

"Yes, that's what Charles Pillet told me. Supposed to be very impressive, all hung in his home at the Place Saint-Georges. He did invite me to call on him. I have half a notion to go see it."

"Really, Father? Well please let me know if you're planning—to—" Pierre stumbled, surprised that the idea of a visit was already in place. "I'd like to join you."

Charles looked over at his son. "I suppose you would," he said, smiling. "She is quite attractive."

Pierre, chagrined but hopeful, returned his father's smile.

"All right, I'll arrange it," Charles said. "There's evidently a piece in the *Gazette des Beaux-Arts* on the Rothan collection. I think it's by Paul Mantz. Why don't you see if you can find it in my back copies?"

They rode quietly until reaching boulevard des Invalides when Charles spoke again. "Don't get your hopes too high, Pierre. Monsieur Rothan may have a fine art collection, but politically, he's no visionary. He served under the ludicrous regime of our minor emperor, and even worse, they're Protestants."

"Once we got home," the baron said, "it took me about ten minutes to find two different stories on Rothan's collection in my father's dusty stack of *Gazettes des*

Beaux-Arts. He was just settling onto the settee in the *noble étage* with a drink in hand when I joined him and began to page through the stories. Paul Mantz, a very prominent art critic, praised the collection, which piqued my father's interest. Before I left him he was muttering that he must see *The Flight into Egypt* by a German—Esslinger, I think."

○ ○ ○ ○ ○

Coubertin's recollections of the romance that followed—and ended after a year—took St. Clair a good while to sort out. He typed up a few pages of Coubertin's verbatim memories of the visit to the Rothans—and then drafted a scene for Messerli's review.

"About three weeks later, if my memory is accurate, my father, mother, and I were standing in the main salon of the Rothans' house at the Place Saint-Georges enjoying a drink. The house wasn't as ostentatious as the old mansions in the neighborhood, but it was impressive, with a fine courtyard, a ceremonial entrance, and a terraced garden out back. The salon was not that large but the ceilings were twelve feet high, and Monsieur Rothan had converted it into a private art gallery in the manner of the Paris Salon, with work hung all the way up the walls.

"After a brief tour, my mother and Madame Rothan went out to a small gazebo and my father drew 'the Minister,' as he now addressed him out of respect for the collection, back to an equestrian painting that impressed him. Marie and I followed. It was actually an early study by Théodore Géricault, a lovely, loosely brushed composition for his later masterpiece, *L'Officier des Chasseurs de la Garde Imperiale Chargeant.* My father was very interested in the impression left by the brushstrokes.

"'Although the composition must have been carefully drawn, the brushwork was obviously quickly done, in a moment of inspiration,' Father said, his finger tracing lines near the surface. I leaned forward to look more closely, as did Marie, and we were both aware our sides were casually touching. 'It's very much in the style of the Impressionists today, which indicates to me their work is a bit unfinished,' he said.

"Monsieur Rothan harrumphed his agreement, two traditionalists passing their predictable judgments. 'You won't find any Impressionists hanging in this salon.' Marie and I exchanged glances that indicated a mutual disapproval. We both admired the Impressionists.

"'Pierre,' said the Minister, 'Marie happens to have a private collection of several pieces by Boucher, which I'm sure she'd be pleased to show you.'

"Marie smiled at her father and nodded demurely. 'Why yes, I would, Father. Thank you for the suggestion.'

"I extended my arm and Marie guided me, with apologies. 'I'm sure you'll find my little *Allegories* a tad boring, but I've loved them since childhood.'

"'Please don't think I'm so predictable,' I said as we took the first step up toward her boudoir. 'I happen to have a taste for allegories.'"

St. Clair drafted the scene that followed, knowing Messerli would like it.

The rising wall along the curving staircase was lined with dozens of Rothan's paintings, a diverse and colorful collection of portraits and landscapes, heroic and mythological scenes, all masterfully framed and arranged. Pierre took it all in with a glance or two, but his vision was fixed on Marie's lovely shape, bound tightly at the waist beneath frills and folds of white cotton. As she ascended each new step, the hem of her dress rose teasingly on her trailing leg, revealing for only an instant the pure pink skin of her surprisingly toned calf.

She stopped at the door to her room, turned back to Pierre with her hand on the large gold knob, and said, "This is the room I've had since I was eleven, and I'm afraid it's still decorated for a little girl's sensibilities. You'll have to forgive the setting."

"I'm sure I'll be delighted by a glimpse into your childhood," Pierre said, leaning toward her with his eyebrows raised, taking in her perfumed scent. As his face neared hers, she pushed open the door and they stepped together into the pink privacy of her youth. Light spilled into the room from an alcove of windows on the left, draped in ruffled curtains that partially enclosed a cushioned seat covered with all manner of dolls and pillows and a stack of books tucked neatly against the glass. A four-post canopied bed covered in sheer, opalescent fabric sat directly across the room and evoked in Pierre an immediate wave of desire.

Just then Marie, standing with her back to the mirror of a low vanity that gave Pierre a view of both sides of her at once, raised her arms in a V pointing to the wall above her and said, "Behold, *The Allegory of Painting* and *The Allegory of Music.*"

Pierre forced his gaze away from her alluring pose and absorbed the color and content of Boucher's brilliant compositions—mythological, cherubic, symbolic, and gorgeously feminine by every measure. Suddenly, before he could say anything or even knew what he was doing, he stepped directly to her. Their eyes locked and his arms encircled her waist as she lowered hers around his neck—and their lips came together in their first kiss, a moment that had filled his imagination since he'd first beheld her at the Hôtel Drouot.

After lingering for a few seconds in the anticipated sensual pleasure of their embrace, she pushed him away and giggled coquettishly. As she turned away, his eyes lingered on the enticing declivity of her breasts. He hoped she had not noticed.

"Now don't be so forward, Pierre," she said. "Impudence and desire never make a good match."

She was right, he knew, because the physicality of his desire was nearly overwhelming, so he calmed himself and followed her to the window seat.

She carefully arranged a few pillows and they half reclined into the intimate alcove, facing each other across a space she set and controlled. But he knew he could lean forward and, if she did the same, their lips would meet again.

"You're young and impetuous, and you have much to learn," she said. "But you're handsome and fit, and you're certainly more cultured and educated than most young men I've met."

"Well," Pierre replied, not shy about again taking in the sensual shape of her décolletage, "I have to admit that my knowledge of art—and perhaps my appreciation of it—is a sadly inadequate match to yours. I'm hoping you'll take it as a personal mission to help complete my education—in all the forms of art we might enjoy together."

"Oh, indeed, you want to learn? Well," she said, leaning forward slightly as he matched her move, "we're going to have to set up a schedule of classes because there's so much to teach you."

Their lips met again, and it may well have been the sweetest moment of Pierre's young life.

○ ○ ○ ○ ○

It was a beautiful summer and Pierre was in love. Across that fall and into winter he and Marie grew closer and shared the intense intimate affections and pleasures of two privileged teenagers with free access to their family hôtels and to coaches with footmen who would drive them anywhere in the city. For Pierre, the love affair produced a devotion and deep commitment that led him to think the future was unfolding in the surprising new alignment of their families. But for Marie, the experience meant far less—more an enjoyable flirtation with a young, inexperienced suitor—and it hardly overtook her consciousness as it did his.

Pierre worked hard through his final two years at Saint-Ignace and secured his baccalaureate, achieving the distinction of being elected top of his class. He also stood for the examen d'honneur, all while struggling to hold Marie's attention and devotion. Pierre had seldom met anyone outside his school who shared his experience and his views so fully. Culturally, they had both been raised to appreciate the arts, admire the finest paintings, and understand their traditions. Intellectually and politically, they had each made a separate break from their opposing family traditions of monarchy and empire, with each recognizing and embracing the egalitarian spirit of the new republic. Still, they strove to respect and maintain the social fabric of their aristocratic heritages. They wanted to preserve its privileges and liberties as they matured into the young adult world of Paris.

The couple might have made that journey together were it not for the difference in their ages. At that age, two years is a significant difference. After that first kiss, Pierre, at fifteen, made it plain he wanted to spend as much time with Marie as he could—but she, at seventeen, had far more freedom and a circle of friends that included several other interested suitors. For the Rothans, an endless stream of invitations and social opportunities arrived from the cohort of officers, administrators, ministers, and officials who had once run the Second Empire—men who were out of favor but hardly out of touch. And while the art world beckoned her as well, it was the temptations of another world altogether that lured Marie—the world of the salon, where the scions of the aristocracy mixed freely with the rising bourgeoisie and the nouveau riche and competed for the attention of Paris's next generation of beauties. While the cabarets and clubs of the demimonde created new levels of entertainment and sexual enticement, at the high end, Parisian society moved to the rhythms of life in the salon—which was a life that for now, at least, Pierre was too young to enter.

During his senior year at Saint-Ignace, when he knew he was losing Marie, Pierre nevertheless occasionally took the coach to the Rothans' on the weekends unannounced, his heart rising in anticipation of finding Marie ready for a ride to the Bois or down the Champs, as she often had been the year before. But when the servant opened the door and expressed surprise that Pierre didn't know that Marie was off with someone else—whose name was freely offered if asked—Pierre began, finally, to understand that life had dealt his heart its first amorous pain. Only later did he realize she had openly set the stage for the end of their brief courtship, dropping hints that he, socially inept at the game at hand, had simply missed.

"Pierre, please, not next weekend, maybe next month," she had said, and he remembered other hints: "I'm just not that interested, Pierre." "Oh wait, no, I can't. I won't be here." Feeling the shock of disappointment again and again, he recoiled, as a man must, from the dream that she would be forever his.

Pierre resolved then to learn and master the ways of the world. After Saint-Ignace, he would throw himself into the nightlife of Paris. He would try his hand at the social life of the salons, where his brother Paul and his grandfather Julien had charmed with their poetic and musical skills, shining like stars in the orbit of the Faubourg dinner-party circuit. He would bide his time, for he was still too young to gain an invitation to that privileged world, but when the time arrived—when he turned twenty—he would be ready.

HEART AND SOUL

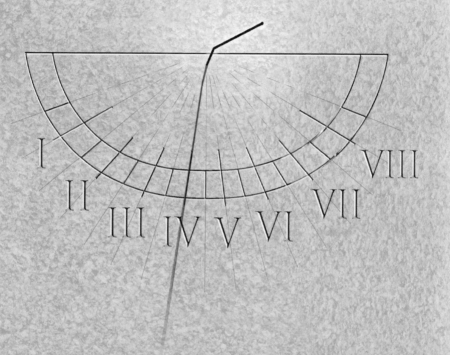

26

THE SALON

While it might not have been germane to the larger story of Coubertin's work in education reform—or the founding of the Olympic Games—St. Clair took an interest in the social life that Coubertin developed in the early 1880s in Paris. The baron tried to dismiss it as a fleeting period of frivolity, but as May began St. Clair's fourth month in Lausanne, the writer wanted to know more.

"So by your own account you attended at least one hundred dinner parties, almost all of which included dances?" St. Clair asked, wondering about the veracity of such a claim. He knew that in those days—in the early stages of the Belle Époque, Paris had indeed had a vibrant social calendar and the salons were legendary, but he was surprised Pierre was now claiming to have danced his heart out for several years.

"You don't believe me?" Coubertin asked, feigning disappointment.

"Well, one hundred parties in a couple of years—that's a lot of socializing. Not to mention the expense ..."

"The expense?"—Coubertin waved away the implication—"No expense was spared. That was never an issue for those striving for social prominence. Hosting a dinner party was as much a competition as Olympic sport, believe me."

At St. Clair's insistence, Coubertin recounted a series of elaborate dances in the finest homes of Paris. The names of the hosts—Sagan, Varennes, Schickler,

Rothschild—and his dance partners rolled easily from his memory. St. Clair was pushing for details when suddenly the baron stopped.

"Wait a minute. I kept a scrapbook—and I think it's right here," he said, springing up and leading St. Clair down the Mon Repos hallway to a closet stacked full of boxes. Coubertin perused the labels on a few shelves before finding what he wanted. From a dusty old cardboard box he pulled a red leather book with an image of children playing on the cover. Every page of the album was filled with two, three, or four invitations pasted in, all surrounded by illustrations in his own hand: birds, men in top hats, ornamental staircases, theatrical performers bowing across the page. Lists of the women he had danced with were inscribed next to many of the invitations. The last few pages of the album contained a list of his favorite dance partners between the years 1882 and 1885. St. Clair counted them—there were more than thirty women listed.

"Seems you were quite the *bon vivant*," he said.

"Well, I had a certain style on the dance floor. It was a good time to be young, Jacques."

Coubertin returned the album to the box and St. Clair remarked, as they walked down the hall, that he had enough notes to draft something about the party circuit—and about the baron's transition into and out of that life.

On the advice of his brother Paul, who had long since left the more youthful side of the salon scene—the gatherings given to games, recitations, and parties—for the stuffier dinner discussions with generals, politicians, and the nouveau riche, Pierre decided to enter the social scene as every young Parisian did in those days: on horseback.

Twice a day a cavalcade of the shiny carriages of the well-to-do, with coachmen attired in livery matching the colors of the coats of arms emblazoned on their doors, streamed down the Champs-Élysées and avenue de l'Impératrice toward the Bois de Boulogne. Once in the morning and again in the early evening, the bridal paths along the avenues filled with riders on horseback, the young and the aspiring mixed with the established and the escorted, matrons and patrons of the art world accompanied by their cockaded and well-plumed aides. Their ultimate destination was the avenue of the Acacias and the requisite stop at Le Pré Catelan or Le Grande Cascade, the iconic French restaurants in the park. The rituals of the ride were far more than mere showmanship, far more than a statement of equestrian skills. The promenade itself was a procession of status. In a society that had little time for sport and athleticism, it seemed ironic to Coubertin as he trotted along on his new chestnut steed, Plato, that the social life of the elite was rooted in equestrian interaction. Everyone who was anyone, it seemed, took a ride.

On his first Sunday afternoon ride—the pinnacle of the weekly processions—
he was moving with the parade along a bridal path in the Bois when he heard his
name called from a crowd picnicking on a lawn beneath a lovely grove of acacias.
As he pulled up to say hello, he took note of the large, shiny black barouche with
four horses in the rig and a golden coat of arms affixed to the door. His Saint-
Ignace classmate, Maurice Dubois, was happily lunching with the Princess Sagan,
an illuminating presence at the time among the young, rich hostesses of Parisian
nightlife. Introductions were made and, keeping it short as Paul had advised,
Pierre begged forgiveness and rode off to keep his appointment with Duke de la
Rochefoucauld at the Jockey Club.

○ ○ ○ ○ ○

Within the week, the engraved invitation arrived, his name rendered in a
handsome calligraphy on a fine linen envelope, its weight increased by a large
red wax seal stamped with the same stylized S Coubertin had seen emblazoned
in gold on the side of the carriage in the dappled light of the Bois. "The Princess
Sagan requests the pleasure of your company at the Salon de Sagan on Saturday
…" He filed the invitation in a slot on his desk and smiled at the thought of such a
swift social opening. He would have to remember to thank Paul.

○ ○ ○ ○ ○

In the open caliche, Pierre waited in a short line of coaches to reach the grand
staircase of the Hôtel Sagan. As they drew nearer, he stood on the floor of the
carriage, snapped his waistcoat to straighten the wrinkles, took several running
steps, and made a daring leap toward the first plateau of the staircase. He landed
expertly and turned to observe, with some satisfaction, the gaping stares of the
drivers and guests in the waiting carriages. Amid flickering flames of torches
around the entrance and servants dressed in Indian robes holding goblets of
wine, he danced quickly up the stairs and into the crowded foyer, where richly
costumed men and women were peeling off their coats and handing them to a
row of servants.

He made his way through the antechamber into the gracious gold glimmer
of the salon, already crowded with about fifty people gaily raising toasts to one
another and chatting amicably in small groups, but most looking beyond their
immediate conversations to see who had arrived and to discreetly observe their
own gilded images in the tall mirrors that lined the back walls of the room.
Mingling with the scents of the lavishly perfumed ladies was the inviting incense

of the kerosene lamps and paraffin candles—along with a palpable aroma of pleasure. Grand stone fireplaces provided warmth on each end of the room. Draped from a high curtain rod, luxurious brocaded velvet spilled down to form archways around the glass-paned doors that opened onto a terrace overlooking elaborate gardens.

Pierre took it all in as he lifted a flute of champagne from an elegant tray covered with chocolate favors bearing the mark of the princess. He spotted a few friends across the room, and as the crowd parted momentarily, he noted a large knot of people surrounding the Princess Sagan herself. She was laughing, an infectious trill that sparked an outburst of mirth across the room.

"Hello, Maurice," Pierre said, approaching a group of young men who opened their circle to admit him.

"Ah, Pierre." Maurice shook his hand. "Nothing like a ride in the promenade to open the doors to the finest salons, eh?" Maurice introduced Pierre to the circle, two of whom were friends from school.

"I've heard the princess always manages to showcase an entertainer or two," Pierre said.

"Oh yes," said Maurice. "I think she's got a poet primed for us tonight—not to mention the usual charade—in which newcomers are often called upon."

"Well then, I guess I'd better get some advice on my skit."

As they laughed, drank, and chatted, Pierre felt comfortable in the setting, although the levity of the evening produced an immediate sensation of frivolity— and frivolity was not Pierre's preferred milieu. He broke away and wandered about, exchanging greetings with those he knew, making eye contact with a few appealing strangers, but even as he made the effort to mix, he began to wonder if he belonged among this set.

The delicate chime of a hand-held bell rang softly in a doorway, where the tall captain of the servants announced dinner. The crowd immediately began to move into the dining room, savoring the aromas from a table the size of a small ship, absorbing a dazzling array of flaming candelabra and glistening crystal goblets, the sheen of fine china, and the glint of silver amid a floral presentation of fine orchids and calla lilies. As the guests were seated, a small army of servants swept in with decanters of lush ruby wines and small plates of shrimp and salmon paté.

Pierre was seated between Charlene Chevan, a young blonde his own age, and, to his surprise, Esmeralda Costes, the favored aunt of the princess and a paramour of princes in her day. The wine flowed and the evening unfolded in waves of conversation and hilarity that swept through the room under the invisible baton of the princess, who showed remarkable poise and grace, Pierre thought, in orchestrating the table talk.

The pretty, bejeweled Charlene fluttered her eyelashes and spoke with a coquettish flair that was instantly alluring, but she proved no match for Esmeralda's sharp ripostes and whispered counsel. The younger woman soon turned away from Coubertin to concentrate on the older man to her left.

"Don't be disappointed," said Esmeralda, noticing the cold shoulder. "There's far better fare ahead for you if you're patient."

"Your encouragements, madame, are certainly appreciated," Pierre said as a burst of laughter turned them toward the far end of the table. A red-haired beauty had the room's attention, raising her glass to the princess as she said, "Well, I didn't mean for the double chin to be a direct reflection of the general's double cross, but I must say it's a delightful interpretation."

The crowd roared its approval—but Pierre was transfixed by the lady of the moment, who returned his stare with an even gaze, holding his eyes long enough to tip her glass to him and offer an enchanting smile before turning back to her immediate company. The color of her hair seemed to shift in the light from red to titian to auburn and back.

"That's Jennette Montaigne," said Esmeralda. "She's the poison pen *du jour*, with a marvelous sense of humor in her caricatures."

"Aha," said Coubertin. "She's the one who's been skewering the great men of the Third Republic in *Figaro*."

"Yes, she is, but I'd say any proclamation of greatness is premature, Pierre—and Jennette is certainly a worthy adversary for their fatuous policies."

The dinner went on as Esmeralda described the various guests—"a philanderer, a rogue, a rising star, a rare principled banker, an excellent equestrian, a master builder, a spice merchant, a seductive jeweler, and an arts patron." Her often caustic commentary made the evening progressively more entertaining. Just before they parted company, Esmeralda said, "I wouldn't be surprised if you were called upon tonight, Baron. I hope you're as entertaining as your brother Paul was. We miss his spirited poetry."

"Oh, I'll never live up to Paul's stagecraft," Coubertin said, "but if called upon, I will perform."

○ ○ ○ ○ ○

A half hour later, as the guests flowed out of the dining room into the drawing room, the princess paused, stretched out her arm, and tilted her head slightly, gazing at a gentleman who was not as polished and refined as many of her other guests. Insouciantly pointing at him, she curled her fingers, beckoning him across the room.

He swaggered forward, his thick head of hair swept back and up inelegantly, his dark, unkempt beard encircling a square, handsome face, full lips framing a gleaming smile. His eyes were inflamed with the adventure of the moment. His coat was a rough brown redingote, several seasons out of fashion, and his pants were baggy and untailored. Yet he commanded the room with some ease by the force of his physical presence—he was built like a bull. Pierre noticed his unpolished boots, more suited to riding than the salon.

Reaching for the princess's hand, the stranger raised his arm and hers like a pose from a waltz. Turning slightly to smile at the attentive crowd, he spoke in the voice of a performer: "Do you wish me to sing a poem of your elegance, beauty, and charm, some missive of the heart rhymed to show a man's appreciation?"

He stepped laterally and she began to turn with him, both moving forward as they defined a circle in the middle of the room. The crowd in turn encircled them with the same gay ease, listening carefully as he continued his praise: "An appreciation of the stellar gifts God has bestowed upon these parts?"

"As you wish, my good man," the princess replied as they spun slowly, evidently happy to act out her part as the cynosure of the hour, "since you have at your command the tools of the libertine and the liberty of the poet."

"Be it known," proclaimed the man, gazing in histrionic awe at Princess Sagan's fine bouffant, which Coubertin realized later was the key to his rhyme, "that the world at my fingertips is now as golden as the morning sun rising over the far blue sea, that my eyes are now blinded by grace, and that my blood is filled with gratitude. The meaning of the moment has slipped away, beyond my grasp—my faculties pleasantly lost—as I behold the profound magnificence of the woman who allows me, now, to call her Princess."

Pierre watched in admiration as the man pronounced a poem:

> She is my muse and my sage,
> and tonight she's our bacchante;
> her dazzle leaves me humble,
> though I want to be gallant,
> for she sees much more than mortals,
> and she's always au courant.

For a moment, Pierre was distracted by Jennette Montaigne's profile, which appeared to him as a cameo across the moving crowd, only to disappear as quickly. He turned back to the audacious performance just as it concluded.

> The minstrel, the poet, will come sing her praise,
> the swordsman, the archer fall prey to her gaze.

The jester and king will admit they adore
the charms described by your humble troubadour.

Indeed, the troubadour ended cleverly with a long, sweeping bow as exaggerated and charming as Molière might have done on his best night on the stage. The applause was spontaneous and punctuated by loud shouts of "Bravo!" The princess bestowed a kiss on each cheek and moved to her seat on a mock throne, slightly elevated on a small riser at the side of the room. As she scanned the assembly in search of another form of entertainment—calling a magician forward—Pierre asked Esmeralda about the poet, whose persona impressed him far more than his verse.

His name was Jean Aicard, a poet, novelist, and adventurer from Provence who had come to Paris some years before and had recently achieved a certain fame among the fashionable set by delivering spontaneous compositions celebrating the scene he happened to be part of at any given time. As it would turn out, that night was the beginning of a long friendship between Pierre and Aicard.

The magician performed a few card tricks, making several coins disappear in his hands and drawing some laughter with a seemingly endless silk streamer that too obviously flowed from his sleeve. He produced an egg from the nest of the princess's fine bouffant, an unfortunate trick that drew a disheartened groan from the guests.

"Pierre?" the princess called. "Pierre de Coubertin—where are you?"

She was summoning him, no doubt, to show off in the manner that his brother, Paul, once used to establish the Coubertin name as a gold standard for salon entertainment.

"Here I am, Princess," Pierre said, stepping forward. "What might your pleasure be?"

"Cher, cher," she said. "Would you kindly lead us in a game of charades?"

"I understand that charades are your favorite?" Feeling the butterflies common to so many performers, Pierre calmed himself, drawing confidence from his older brother's coaching, knowing he'd be ready at the moment of this public debut.

"Indeed," she said, "the theater pleases me most of all."

"A play it shall be then." Pierre turned to the crowd. "As I act out a scene for the pleasure of our hostess, you'll need four things to solve the riddle of my pantomime: the name of the play, the author, the character being played, and to win this round, the exact scene depicted by the charade."

Pierre had prepared for the moment with a scene from one of the most popular plays to come out of Paris. He bowed before the princess on one knee, closing his eyes and imagining the scene as he had seen it when he was a young boy at the Théâtre Historique, Alexandre Dumas's own playhouse in the Marais.

Standing, he reached up and moved his right hand through the air along an imaginary shelf, taking hold of an invisible object, pulling it back and turning his hand as if to examine it. He brought it down, all eyes following his gesture, and laid it in his open left hand. His next movement clearly suggested that he was opening and paging through a book.

"It's a book," a woman yelled.

"A play based on a book," shouted a man and Pierre immediately smiled and pointed to the fellow, indicating that was correct.

Les Misérables was immediately suggested along with a host of other plays adapted, including *The Count of Monte Cristo*, which was close since it was also by Dumas.

Pierre shook his head and moved to his next scene, knowing it wouldn't take this crowd long to solve this first riddle. That had been Paul's advice. Have three scenes from three plays ready for a charade: make the first easy to engage the crowd, make the second funny to get them laughing, and make the third one difficult to showcase your virtuosity and cultivate their appreciation.

He held out his hands, open palms facing out, then turned his head and raised his brows with an expression of grave concern as if he were holding off an advancing enemy. Next, he slapped his right hand on his left wrist and drew an imaginary sword, extending his arm and flicking his wrist. Murmurs and guesses begin to rise as he used the sword to point at three imaginary opponents.

"It's d'Artagnan fighting the Three Musketeers," someone cried. A chorus of shouts signaled acclamation, but Pierre raised his hand, indicating the guess was wrong and that there was more to come. And then, nearly leaping, he quickly reversed himself with a twist of his head—and then pantomimed a broader battle in which his original opponents were on his side.

"Ah. D'Artagnan and the Three Musketeers are fighting Cardinal Richelieu's guards." The acclamation grew louder this time, and Pierre bowed with a smile as applause lifted the room.

"That is correct," he said. "It's Dumas. It's *The Three Musketeers*."

"Another scene, Pierre," said the princess.

He bowed toward her. "As you wish," he said, planning his second charade. It was to be a humorous piece from Molière's famous *School for Wives*, which played the Comédie Français every other year. He was about to begin when a clicking sound behind Pierre suddenly captured the attention of the room, creating a hush as the exuberant guests fell silent. Turning toward the steady rhythmic ting of steel on steel, Pierre saw the mad poet standing on the raised hearth of the fireplace, his eyes gleaming as he clanged the blades of two swords he had drawn from their mount over the mantel. Pierre guessed at his intention before he pronounced it.

"If you're going to portray a scene from Dumas, at least give us some swordplay," he shouted, tossing one of the épées toward Pierre in a high, inaccurate arc. Pierre kept his eye on the handle, stepped left, and pulled it out of the air with ease. He deftly whipped the blade in a series of circles and swirls to suggest his skill—which was quite advanced, thanks to years of training at the hands of his brothers.

While the crowd murmured its approval of this improvisation and the princess uttered, "Oh my," giggling slightly, Pierre wondered what the poet had in mind. Nonetheless, he raised his épée and assumed the stance of a fencer at the ready—point out, free arm curled behind his head, a wide smile on his face.

"En garde," yelled Aicard, grinning wildly as he leaped from the hearthstone in a fancy balestra, closing the distance between them swiftly and moving into a basic advance that was more of a theatrical lunge than a threatening attack. Pierre expertly parried.

For the next five minutes, they filled the air with the sound of steel, a conversation between the blades—parry followed by counterparry and ripostes, attacks, and counterattacks ... a dance of practiced moves demonstrating the skills of both men without threatening either. As they became used to each other's style, they gave signs and signals allowing them to perform a choreography familiar to all advanced fencers.

With a slight nod to the left by Pierre, Aicard read correctly the move called for, and they each performed a fléché and a croisé, back to back, creating the tension and drama of a real match. As Aicard began to tire from the exaggerated advances and retreats required of the performance, Pierre guessed that he wanted to clash in a beat. He nodded and they both advanced, their blades sliding easily up their hilts. As their hand guards clashed and their faces came within inches, they smartly pushed away. Catching the signal of a dropped eyebrow from Aicard, Pierre turned his back and made a full circle just as Aicard did, putting them face to face as both pointed their swords down and away, indicating the end of their performance. They bowed to loud applause and then met in the middle for a congratulatory handshake.

In short order, the party moved into a large ballroom where an orchestra awaited and the dancing began. Before Coubertin could locate the object of his desire, Jennette Montaigne, whom he desperately wanted to meet, he found himself, at the insistence of Esmeralda, spinning around the dance floor with Charlene Chevan in his arms, the first of many coquettes lined up as a dividend of his successful social debut.

At one point he saw Mademoiselle Montaigne leave the room with a tall, dark-haired man. She was so absorbed that he failed to catch her eye. Then he saw Aicard wandering out with two women in tow, one on each arm. Nevertheless, the joy of the evening lay before him, and he proceeded to embrace it with good spirits.

The crowd was much diminished by the time Pierre left the dance floor and went out on the terrace to catch his breath. When he stepped into the soft shadows just off the ballroom, he heard laughter at the far end of the house, near the rounded glass wall of the observatory, and spotted Jean Aicard, bottle and glass in hand, leaning on the balustrade and talking with two women.

As Pierre approached, Aicard said, "Your fencing is polished, my friend. I take it you consider yourself a sportsman?"

Pierre laughed and introduced himself to the women, Émilee Derain and Giselle Bodette, both strikingly beautiful but closer to Aicard's age than Pierre's, perhaps in their mid-thirties. "Something of a sportsman," he said, "but far less entertaining than you."

"Oh, no entertainment, please. I'm afraid I've fallen into a sad scene, and I know I'll have trouble facing myself in the morning after that garish performance."

"Au contraire—I thought you were quite skilled." Pierre did wonder how a poet and novelist could have become such a party favorite.

Émilee had quickly moved into the observatory and now returned with a glass. "Brilliant, and certainly a great success with the princess," she said.

"Damn the princess," said Aicard, splashing cognac into the glass for Pierre. "I've been distracted, but tomorrow is another day. *Santé*," he said, lifting his glass to Pierre, taking his measure with a telling gaze, his forehead wrinkled in concentration. "Do you like to ride?" he asked.

"I love to ride," said Pierre. "And you?"

"My father kept horses in Provence. Shall we take in the Bois de Boulogne tomorrow afternoon?"

THE PAINTED HOUSE

Even after he had written the scene, St. Clair remained curious about Aicard's technique. "How did Aicard do it, Pierre—how did he deliver that poetry so spontaneously?"

"He was a master of rhetorical invention," Coubertin said. "Jean simply called it living poetry. He had a gift for language and a *joie de vivre* that demanded he seize the moment. His voice had a resonance and tone that made it mesmerizing. It spilled effortlessly off his tongue, a stream of language that defined the scene you beheld. The poetry wasn't always great, but I haven't encountered anything like it since."

"Did you ever ask him about it?"

"Yes. He once told me it was easy for him—that he knew he could trust his talent to deliver words when he opened his mouth. And I watched him write more than once ... he could fill the page almost as quickly as he could move his pen."

"I know his work at a distance," St. Clair said. "I believe he was popular at one time, but never in the first ranks of literature."

Coubertin looked away and gazed out the window of Mon Repos. "Jean rode his talent like he rode his horses, without ever trying to discipline it or push its full potential," he said. "His social success, unfortunately, diminished his reputation as a serious poet. He was ostracized by a group of very progressive and, I thought, very jealous writers and artists—that coterie that had forged a counterpoint cultural identity through Impressionism, the Salon of the Refusals, and symbolist poetry. Rimbaud detested him.

"Jean's entire world was a departure from mine, but once I entered it, I was fascinated. He was a tireless socializer and seemed to know the salon circuit as well as the minister of culture. He never lacked for invitations or social opportunities and would have been higher on the social registry if it weren't for his drinking. He had a wild side, which, to be honest, I quite enjoyed. The salons were one thing, but they never satisfied his Dionysian appetites, and he introduced me to a good number of cabarets and clubs. He kept two different flasks in that big redingote coat. The drink never slowed him at all and I was witness to more than one inspiring poetic performance when I knew he was, as we used to say, beyond the pale."

St. Clair looked at his notes, remembering another question he wanted to ask. "Did you ride with him in the Bois de Boulogne the next day?"

Coubertin thought about it for a moment. "No, not that day. We did ride together quite often—and once raced around the lake for a stake of 100 francs— but he didn't show up that morning, so I decided to ride up to Montmartre to look for his house."

Early the next morning, just after breakfast, Pierre saddled Plato, his chestnut and the largest, strongest, and fastest horse in the family stable. Handsome enough for a portrait, Plato had a white diamond along the length of his nose and white boots that complemented his burnt orange coat and rusty mane. Pierre made it clear to their coachman, Henri, that Plato was for riding only and should never be harnessed into a carriage.

He rode out across the pont d'Iéna and up to the Arc de Triomphe where Aicard had promised to meet him at eight-thirty. After waiting for some time, Pierre dismounted and let Plato graze on the south side of the Place de l'Étoile, watching a few mounts coming down rue de Monceau in hopes it would be Aicard. At nine, Pierre decided to ride up the avenue—thinking he would encounter Aicard coming down from Montmartre. But he didn't, and eventually Pierre passed through Pigalle and rode up to the small square in the town. He asked for directions and was told to ride rue de Flore for a mile and look for a dirt road on the left at the edge of the cemetery.

In the morning light, Pierre rode past ramshackle houses, fields, and farmlands stretching east beyond the rising white façade of *Sacré-Cœur*. When he reached the cemetery, he stopped at a high perch and looked back down across the falling landscape where the city of Paris unfolded to the south. Funnels of smoke rose from thousands of chimneys across the city as Pierre gazed at the familiar landmarks below—Notre Dame, the Panthéon, Les Halles, and the Dôme des Invalides in his own neighborhood. A woman with a basket of flowers approached the gate of the cemetery along the road where Coubertin had stopped, and he asked, "Do you know where the poet Jean Aicard lives?"

She looked up at him, lifting a hand to shield her eyes from the sun, and said something indistinct about a color palette, then pointed back up the road, indicating a little twist to the left.

Animals and farmers were stirring in the fields Pierre passed, and the road wound up a little knoll as the place came into view. He was not expecting the wild appearance of Aicard's house, but it amused him as he realized he had understood the woman's words after all. The poet lived in an old two-story wooden farmhouse on a hillside. A porch surrounded three sides of the structure, and the walls and porch railing were painted in swatches of color that formed a pastiche not unlike a large palette of mixed hues. The house looked like a colored quilt, all patches, not perfectly squared. It was surrounded by a short wooden fence that enclosed a garden overgrown with weeds along the side of the house, above which some staked plants grew. Several vines of grapes and tomato plants grew along the fence line. Beds of squash, carrots, lettuce, and potatoes covered the ground. Beyond the backyard was a barn that had long ago been whitewashed judging from the green moss at its base, but had since been painted with swaths of color even bolder than those on the house.

Pierre dismounted and lashed the reins to the fence as the front door opened. Aicard emerged, pulling his suspenders up over a natty blue-striped Breton, unkempt and still sleepy. A young woman in a peasant dress followed him out with a straw basket in hand, and he swatted her on the backside as he yelled to Pierre, "Come in, my friend! It's good to see you found your way up the hill."

Pushing open the gate, Pierre stepped onto a path with irregular paving stones covered in moss and crossed by vines. "*Bonjour*, Jean. I thought we'd agreed to meet at the Arc and ride to the Bois."

"I believe you're right," Aicard said, shaking his head. "I was distracted by a bottle of absinthe and the lovely charms of my housekeeper, Genevieve," at whom he gestured.

Stepping onto the porch to take Aicard's outstretched hand, Pierre turned to watch Genevieve pull up some turnips and onions and a few potatoes, shake off the dirt, then drop them into the basket.

Returning, she smiled at Pierre. "It's not often we see a gentleman in these parts."

Ignoring the insult, Aicard said, "Let's have some breakfast, Pierre. And then we'll ride up the hill to a place I think you'll love."

Following Genevieve into the house, they entered a central hall with a room off each side and a stairway just ahead. Pierre glanced into the room at the right and saw a young, long-haired man sitting up and rubbing his eyes. His boots sat in the middle of the floor and his toes were sticking through his socks.

"Pierre, this is Charles, a half-assed painter but a very good horseman. He's from Aix-en-Provence and has come up here to follow Cezanne and his ilk. Charles," he said as the man rose, "this is Pierre de Coubertin, an actor and a fencer from the 7th who keeps his appointments."

Pierre laughed. "I'm not an actor, I'm an orator." He shook hands with Charles, who looked Pierre's own age. Pierre took note of the Impressionistic style of the numerous paintings hanging or leaning on the walls and propped up against the furniture. They all looked quite good, experimental but professional—still lifes, landscapes, and village scenes. Nothing struck him as having the power of the Renoir or Cezanne that had enthralled the public. But they were clearly the work of young painters seeking a new way, not driven by the ambitions of the salon, at least not the traditional salon. The room across the hall was filled with an equal number of paintings surrounding an unmade bed with an iron frame.

"Are these all Charles's paintings?" Pierre asked as they walked past the stairs into the kitchen. Genevieve was at the stove, adding garden vegetables and bacon to an iron skillet.

"No—we've got four young painters working here now. A few in the barn out back. Two from Provence, one from Grenoble, and one from Paris. They keep me amused and in touch with life."

Coubertin drank a cup of coffee while Jean ate a plate stacked high with fried vegetables and scrambled eggs and prattled on about the state of art in France. "Do you have any idea of how to get the Third Republic to provide more support for young artists? They're eating all my income," Aicard complained.

Pierre had no solutions to offer, but he was inspired to find himself inside the home of a working writer who gave what he could to support young artists at the beginning of their creative journeys. While Aicard told him about one promising young painter who still lived with him on occasion, Coubertin thought about the world he had just entered. As a boy at Mirville, he had spent time in the homes of the farmers whose children he had played with, and as a young noble he had been in the homes of tailors, printers, bookbinders, bankers, bakers, and leather tanners—all manner of bourgeois homes—but seldom as a friend sitting at a kitchen table. He had been raised in the house of an elite painter and knew the world of aristocrats far better than he knew the working class, and he had never ventured into a place like this, something akin to an emerging creative community. He breathed deeply, savoring the aroma of charred fried potatoes and strong coffee, and wondered at the small miracle that had led him from his first salon to this poet's humble but marvelous home.

After breakfast, Pierre, Jean, and Charles ventured out to the barn, behind which was a four-stall stable with a slanted roof built against a high stone wall covered with moss and lichen. Three dogs began barking and racing around wildly as Jean and Charles saddled their horses. Genevieve brought out a satchel, which Jean threw over his shoulder while she stuffed a few bottles of wine and some cheese and bread into the saddlebags. Charles fastened a painter's box, an easel, and a canvas across the back of his horse while Coubertin went out front to mount Plato.

They rode until Jean turned onto a trail through the woods, a well-trod path shaded beneath a canopy of oaks and maple trees. After a time, they passed out of the woods, crossed a slight incline, and curled back onto a flat opening with a grassy patch and a rock surface that gave them a vista of the entire metropolis below. Charles set up his easel and began to work *en plein air* on a scene of *Sacré-Cœur* in the left foreground, above the sprawl of the city. Jean threw Pierre a blanket, uncorked the wine, and unwrapped the food as they spread out on the grass. From his satchel, he pulled out a notebook and pen but didn't open it. They stood together and gazed over the city, then sat and relaxed, casually recalling and celebrating their surprising triumph with épées before the princess. They laughed hard, and Coubertin confessed he was relieved that he hadn't had to perform a scene from *The School of Wives*, which he wasn't certain he could have pulled off.

At Jean's prompting, Coubertin recounted some of his family background. After a while, Jean turned the conversation to his own ambitions.

"Every time I look at this place from up here, I think about the secret lives entwined in every house and building and street below. The human drama is all the same, as Hugo says, the struggles of the rich and the poor not so different."

"*Les Misérables*," said Pierre. "The fall from grace awaits every man."

"The fall from grace awaits every man ..." Aicard repeated. "I believe you have a little of the poet in you."

"No Jean, I don't hear the voice of Calliope in my head. I haven't been touched by the hand of God to write poetry as you have, but I am yearning to find a form of art of my own—"

Jean cut him off, almost shouting. "Ah yes, the yearning! The affliction of the soul, the inescapable condition of life for the sentient among us. The burning inferno from which there is no respite."

"What's your yearning, Jean? Are you trying to build an art colony up here on your farm?"

Aicard laughed, tilting his head back and then pausing to absorb the site of Paris yet again. "No, Pierre, I've been lucky. My family wasn't rich, but my father, who was a respected journalist and a great horseman, arranged for a good education and my poems were recognized for their promise when I was still in school. My first books, which celebrated life in Provence, sold well and I ended up with more than enough money to move to Paris and become a serious writer. I bought the farm a few years ago to keep horses, and then a distant cousin who wanted to paint needed a place to stay. When he got here he made friends—and suddenly I had a boarding school for young artists, which provides me with lots of interesting companions for drinking and debating."

"And entertaining, I'm sure."

"That's the tragedy of it, Pierre," the poet replied. "The easy debasement of the gifts, the insouciant deception of popularity, the sucking vortex of the class you come from, the gifts waiting beneath the layered petticoats, offered in the dance of seduction to which no man is immune. It's easy to be entertaining," he added. "It's hard to be disciplined."

"But the yearning never leaves, does it?"

"No, it's there right now." He looked directly into Coubertin's eyes. "I have a yearning to write a great novel about this city and the times we're living in. About the changes we've seen, the disappearance of the old medieval labyrinth, and the truly magnificent boulevards that emerged from the destruction. About those who fight to save what's old, seem to lose everything they believe in—but then come to love the beauty of the city and the new life that springs from their loss."

Coubertin was moved by the notion of a beautiful life emerging from a great loss. "I love that idea," he said, "not just the redemption, but the naturalism of it, like a seed in soil, the black dirt giving life to the red rose, a thing of beauty emerging from nothing."

Jean looked at Coubertin for a moment. "Yes, there is a naturalism to urban life. It's never as artificial as it seems. And what about you, Pierre, what's your yearning? Will you become our next great master of charades?"

"God forbid," Coubertin said, laughing. "I'm not sure where the future will lead me, but I do have an unfocused desire, an ambition to find something for my talents—whatever they may be. I'm not sure I'm looking for a mission yet, but I am looking for an idea." He didn't know how to tell Aicard—or didn't feel inclined to yet—that he wanted to help create a new future for France, to help build the Third Republic into a nation worthy of all honor.

Just then, Charles yelled, "Look!" They followed the tip of his brush, which he pointed toward the south. Two large balloons were rising over the Champ de Mars, just to the right of Les Invalides in Pierre's neighborhood.

"Balloons rising on the wind," said Aicard. "They can carry you above the struggles, but only for so long—as old Gambetta learned when he escaped the Prussian siege."

Pierre got to his feet and went to examine the painting Charles was working on, noting he used the brush not in strokes but in daubs that formed a series of colored dots that gave shape to the imagery and objects in the scene: the stunning new basilica of *Sacré-Cœur* formed by a thousand points of white, blue, and gray.

When he turned back, Jean was leaning over his notebook, writing furiously in longhand. As Pierre approached, Jean reached into his satchel and pulled out a clothbound book he tossed to Pierre. "I brought this for you. Hope you find it interesting. Sit and relax." Coubertin looked at the cover of the novel, La Vénus de Milo, by Jean Aicard. Responding to his expression, Aicard said, "It's the story of the discovery of the masterpiece. Given what I've heard of your family's history, I thought you might like it."

And so it was that Pierre began a friendship with the poet and novelist Jean Aicard, who would become his favorite riding companion, most honest interlocutor, and enthusiastic guide to the nightlife of Montmartre. That afternoon, as the sun crossed over Paris and the shadows moved like the hands of a clock, Charles painted and Jean wrote tirelessly in his notebook while Pierre sipped wine and absorbed, for the first time, the true literary gifts of the poet who had charmed the Princess Sagan and her salon.

28

THE SKETCH

I t was mid-morning on a mid-May day when Juliette arrived at Mon Repos, the sky slate gray under slowly drifting cumuli—but from her perspective the day was full of bright promise. In minutes, she would begin her first session sketching Pierre in preparation for the painting she had talked him into. She stopped at the circular turnaround that bordered the garden at the front door of the mansion, observing the pleasing arrangement of flowers and decorative urns. She imagined an image of Pierre in the setting, which harkened to an earlier age, but dismissed it quickly as too artificial for his portrait. Her mind was alive, full of ideas and scenes for the background of the composition she was going to create around his graceful deep brown eyes and distinct mustachioed visage. At the moment she was favoring something along the lines of da Vinci's *Mona Lisa*, with the baron centered in the foreground, his face and shoulders in full color detail with a distant city and Greek temple on the far horizon at head level. She had secretly begun to fantasize that her painting of Pierre, which she hadn't even begun, would become the trademark cover of the book Jacques was writing. She could visualize stacks of them, neatly arranged with her portrait spotlighted at night, in the windows of her favorite Paris bookstores.

Leaning to her side to pull open the heavy castle door, Juliette entered the foyer. She paused for a minute to admire the sculptures set in their niches and the sunburst mosaic on the floor. A setting as elegant as the baron himself, she thought. Carrying a large sketchpad under her arm, she climbed the stairs to the third floor. Stopping at the office door, she could hear Jacques and Pierre talking. She knew they were working through another interview, and they planned to continue talking while she observed and sketched her subject. Not an ideal beginning from her perspective—she would have preferred to have Pierre frozen in a single pose—but she was happy to get the process under way. Moreover, she wanted to hear their exchange since it might reveal a character trait or point of interest she could convey.

"Good morning, gentlemen," she said just as Jacques finished a question about something he called Pierre's motto.

"Aha," Pierre proclaimed, springing up from behind the desk, "the lovely Duchess of Langeais has seen fit to join us." Jacques stood as well but Pierre reached her first. They smiled in mutual delight and kissed three times, and then Pierre removed some books and papers from a chair for her.

Juliette set her things on the floor. "I hope you don't mind the interruption." She looked around, taking in the top of the desk, the credenza and shelves behind Pierre's chair, the *objets d'art* on display, and the bookcase across the room, which contained a few dozen curios of Pierre's Olympic past. "I promise not to disturb your conversation. I just want to get my sketches started."

"Nonsense," said Pierre, returning to his desk. "Feel free to join in the conversation. As an *artiste*," Pierre exaggerated the word, "you may have insights we workmen completely miss."

Juliette glanced at Jacques. He looked annoyed—he had stressed to her that very morning she should let the interview roll on uninterrupted. "I was just asking Pierre about the personal motto he adopted, 'See far, speak frankly, act firmly,'" Jacques said. "It's on his *ex libris* bookplate, you see."

He handed her one of Pierre's books, open to the inside cover and a label that combined the slogan with an image of an old Greek temple. She took the book and stared at the image for a second, feeling some confirmation about her concept for the portrait. "Lovely," she said.

Pierre seemed more animated in Juliette's presence, staying attentive to the artist as she settled in. When she was ready, holding the large pad up at an angle from her lap, pencil beginning to move over the paper, Coubertin turned to Jacques, sitting straight up to provide the right profile. His conversation was more deliberately expansive and philosophical.

"The term *visionary* is usually reserved for those who see into the future with some accuracy, spot the trends, recognize the patterns of where society is moving, and then propose actions, reforms, or business ideas that advance successfully, sometimes against others' perceptions. I don't think this province of foresight or prophecy belongs alone to intellectuals, political leaders, or artists," Coubertin said, tilting his head in a quick nod at Juliette. "My motto is specifically meant to encourage everyone to look beyond the day—to see far— not in simple geographic terms, not only as a mariner studying the horizon with a telescope, but as a man—or woman"—another nod—"looks for meaning beyond what is visible, beyond the superficial."

"What do you see?" asked Jacques, smiling. "Your father's favorite question."

"Ah yes. What Solomon said was true—there's nothing new under the sun. My father made me look for meaning and I'm encouraging everyone to do the same."

"And you think everyone is capable of seeing more than they do?"

"Yes, I do. Most of us drift through life without examining the visual content of our experience beyond the obvious—or interpreting the events of the day to understand their context better. I want people to see in the most illuminating terms, from the personal to the national and even to the international. I came of age in a time of immense change at every level of society—industrial, economic, political, cultural, social. Some saw the changes as opportunities, others were crushed by them. I think there's a broader opportunity for those who take the time—and create the habit of mind required to try to see, truly and deeply, what the future holds. It's what Messerli and I sought to teach in the Institute of Physical Education of Lausanne."

The conversation went on for an hour and a half. The baron rose, gesticulating as he talked, then walked around and peeked at Juliette's sketches, before sitting to pose again. He had become noticeably more voluble in her presence and spoke with more energy. Without noticing it, they moved past the lunch hour as Coubertin continued to speak forcefully on a variety of subjects. Juliette was looking down at her pad when Pierre suddenly stopped speaking mid-sentence. There was a catch in his throat, a small choke, and when she looked up, he was ashen white, sitting back in his chair with a hand weakly clawing at his chest— then he slumped to his left and seemed to pass out.

"Oh no!" Juliette cried.

"Pierre!" Jacques yelled. "Are you all right?" He dropped his tablet and moved quickly around the desk, taking the baron's shoulders and resting him against the back of the chair.

Just then Pierre revived, letting his hand drop away. He said nothing, bowing his head for a few seconds and then breathing sharply as if catching his breath, sucking the air in deeply. His chest and shoulders began to rise in a pronounced fashion. Finally lifting his head, he rested it against the chair, opening his mouth to draw in more air.

"Yes," he said weakly, recovering. "I'm all right. Just lost my breath for a minute. It's nothing."

It was something, of course, something serious, and Jacques insisted—against Coubertin's muted protests—that they stop for the day.

○ ○ ○ ○ ○

Jacques and Juliette left together and walked a few blocks to the small park across from the Hôtel de la Paix. They sat on an iron bench between two trees groomed to look like giant cones in the perfectly landscaped green space, which they had to themselves that afternoon. Under the overcast sky, the lake faded into the mist as they looked to the south, and they sat quietly for a few minutes ruminating on the experience they had just shared, an intimate morning with an old man who had become the locus of their lives. Jacques was already living in a consciousness shaped by the time span of Pierre's life and work, and now Juliette had engaged in an imaginative world borne completely on the wings of the Olympic spirit incarnate in the little French aristocrat. Although they hadn't discussed it yet, she knew there was something critical about the time they were spending with Coubertin. Their work was not simply about a book or a painting—it was something more.

St. Clair was visibly shaken, his head turning from side to side in swift denial of a silent conversation. Juliette knew he was worried about the old man's health and watched with concern as he rubbed his forehead and dragged his hand down his face, his fingers spreading over his nose and mouth, covering a deep sigh of exasperation.

"What if he … what will we …" Suddenly he jumped to his feet. "I've got to talk to Dr. Messerli. This is awful." He paced back and forth. Juliette didn't know whether Pierre was at grave risk or whether it was just a fainting episode, but she knew what was troubling Jacques. His father had died when he was young—thirteen, she thought. Jacques would never discuss it, and always changed the subject—and she now realized that Jacques had developed a relationship with Pierre that had certain father–son characteristics. She knew Jacques loved Pierre's approval. Watching him, she realized his anxiety was only growing.

"Honey," she called to him, "please Jacques, come sit. It was just a fainting spell. We both know his health is fairly robust—you even—"

"We don't know that," Jacques said, shaking his head. "Francis always said there was an urgency to the book." She stood and stepped into his path and embraced him, holding him tight, forcing him to be still. He buried his face in her shoulder, choked back a sob, and finally relaxed. They sat back down on the bench in quiet contemplation.

Finally Jacques spoke. "Let's see what you did," he said, pointing at her bag.

Juliette pulled up her sketch pad. She lifted the cover and opened it so it lay flat across their laps. Jacques looked down at four full sketches of Pierre's face, two in profile, one at an angle, and one frontal view, all roughly formed with loose lines for the hair and chin and several darkened with more detailed pencil work. The delta of wrinkles reaching out from the corner of his eye, which became more pronounced when he smiled, was perfectly captured in one of the drawings. There was a charming aspect of age to each of the renderings.

"He really is an old man," Jacques said, caught up in the images she had captured. "The years have recorded a certain truth in his countenance. He's got the energy of youth at times, but there are moments when he gives into his years, when the fatigue arrives and seizes control."

"It's sad, in a way, that we're just getting to know him now," Juliette said, "because I think he's unique, maybe uniquely gifted."

"He is. But I think you're just beginning to sense the truth of what Dr. Messerli told us from the beginning in that first letter," Jacques said. "If we don't get this story down now, it will be lost forever."

"Do you think he's really sick?" Juliette asked, her voice touched with worry. She lifted the pad and turned the page, revealing her next sketch, which she laid before them.

"I don't know. I hope not." Jacques looked at a more fully formed and larger face with those absorbing dark eyes staring right at him in full rendered detail. "These are wonderful," he said, leaning over and kissing her cheek. "You're really seeing into him, already touching his being."

Juliette smiled with pleasure at Jacques's praise. She turned her head down again to look at the drawing she had done. She traced the ridge of his aquiline nose with her fingers. "I feel something when I'm with him that I haven't felt anywhere else," Juliette said. "It's not like he's a saint or a spiritual presence; it's more that I feel I'm tapping into a source of wisdom."

"I don't think it's wisdom you're feeling. But there is definitely something that flows from him if you're open to it. I've been thinking about it for the last month, and I really believe it's a form of inspiration."

"Inspiration," she repeated. "Yes, it is, but not a bolt, not like an epiphany. It's more like a low, steady stream that fills you with a desire … a desire to do something better or perhaps something important."

"I think after all these years of pushing and struggling to bring the ancient ideal of the Olympics back to life, after so many thousands of meetings and speeches and events and proposals and changes—so much struggle and so many battles—that Pierre has actually become the idea he's been advocating for so long: the idea that we can all reach for a level of excellence that may seem beyond our grasp. It seems to live within him, and it just flows out to anyone who spends time with him."

"The Olympic Games do that, don't they? They fill people everywhere with that desire," Juliette agreed. "That desire to reach higher. Maybe that's what he's giving us."

"Maybe you're right. Maybe that is exactly what he's giving us." St. Clair stood and began to pace again.

29

THE STRATEGY

A few hours later Juliette and St. Clair were at home, sitting in somber solitude on the sofa. After they returned from the park, St. Clair had tried to reach Dr. Messerli but hadn't gotten through. He'd grown progressively sullen, distant, and impatient with anything Juliette asked or said. He was now reviewing his notes, fidgeting with his pen and tablet, grinding his teeth, and biting his lip in a way Juliette had never seen before. She was penciling around her sketches, absentmindedly drawing while keeping an eye on him. A bottle of wine was open, but neither had an appetite for dinner. They weren't speaking— at least not in a sustained way.

The telephone rang and broke the spell. St. Clair leaped up to answer it.

"Dr. Messerli," he nearly shouted, "Pierre collapsed today. He passed out in the middle of a sentence. For a moment I thought he had died." He paused as Juliette came up behind him to try to listen in, placing her hands on his shoulders. "No, no, no—I'm not exaggerating. It seemed like more than a fainting spell to me."

Juliette heard what Dr. Messerli said next. "Well, I just talked to him and he seemed perfectly normal, Jacques. In fact, he was enthusiastic. He said you had a good day and Juliette was there sketching away." St. Clair's shoulders dropped and Juliette felt him relax.

"Really?" he said, his voice rising, nearly cracking. Juliette now knew for certain that his connection to Pierre was far deeper than she had guessed. "Are you sure? It seemed like he was … I don't know, but he choked before he passed out."

"Whatever it was, Jacques, it passed."

"But you need to check on him now."

"Listen," Messerli said, shifting the subject, "Pierre is fine. He wants you and me at Mon Repos for a meeting first thing tomorrow. Carl Diem is en route from Munich with Hitler's response to Baillet-Latour's letter."

"All right," St. Clair said, not reacting at all to this stunning news. "I'll meet you there."

Messerli added a final reassurance. "Jacques, I'll get there before you and take a good look at Pierre. Come up about nine."

When St. Clair hung up, Juliette hugged him and then asked the questions she knew he should have asked—questions that would force him to focus on the work: "Are the Germans responding to Pierre's plan to evaluate their proposals through the Committee on Olympism?"

Yes, exactly," he said, "the Commission on the Future of Olympism."

"Does Pierre think this is a serious threat?" Juliette continued, pushing her fiancé to clear his head. "I mean—the Germans are powerful."

St. Clair hesitated before picking up his wine and facing her. "Yes, of course. Pierre sees it for what it is—a blatant attempt at a coup, an assault on the independence of the International Olympic Committee—and he won't stand for it. It's a very serious matter."

$$\circ\ \circ\ \circ\ \circ\ \circ$$

The next morning, Messerli was waiting for St. Clair on the landing of the grand staircase at Mon Repos. "He's fine," the doctor said, extending his hand.

"What was it?" St. Clair asked. "It was shocking to both of us, especially Juliette."

"Basically, it was what everyone calls a swoon," Messerli said. "Do you want the medical term?"

"Yes." St. Clair stopped at the top of the stairs.

"It's known as *vasovagal syncope*, basically a fainting spell. The latest work by Sir Thomas Lewis indicates that most often full consciousness is lost for an instant, but full recovery is swift."

St. Clair took out his notebook and had Messerli spell it. "That's all it was?"

"Yes, Jacques, he's perfectly fine. No loss of memory, no sign of stroke."

"Then there's nothing to worry about?"

"I didn't say that," Messerli said. "This isn't the first episode, and late last year I'm fairly certain he did have a mild stroke. But let's go in now. We can talk about it later—he's anxious to get started."

As he followed Messerli up the stairs, St. Clair felt as if the ground had shifted, as if he were near the edge of a precipice, as if his rope had frayed and he was barely holding on to a lifeline. His thoughts flashed back to a day in a park in Paris. He was riding a bike behind his father. They were coming to a gate onto a street. He held down the anxiety and moved through the door Messerli had opened.

"*Bonjour*, Jacques," the baron said, shaking St. Clair's hand as they entered the office. "Don't be worried about that little episode yesterday. I'm just getting old, and if I don't get enough sleep—well, Father Time can be a stern reminder."

"If you say so," St. Clair said, looking the old man in the eyes, searching for the truth. Coubertin diverted his face. St. Clair noticed a copy of Baillet-Latour's letter to the Nazis on the desk as he and Messerli took seats opposite Pierre.

"I assume the president's letter served the purpose?" Messerli asked.

Pierre picked up the letter. "We'll know when Diem arrives with Hitler's response, but I think our letter makes a strong case. Henri must have come to his senses and recognized that the proposals he approved are a grave matter for the IOC."

"Did he follow your draft?" Messerli asked.

"Almost verbatim," Coubertin replied. "The Commission for the Future of Olympism has been established. Von Halt, von Tschammer, Diem, and, I suppose, Hitler and Goebbels all know about it by now."

"Good," said Messerli.

"Good?" Coubertin said. "It's only a stopgap against the most serious threat we've faced since the end of the Games in Athens—when King George wanted to host the Games permanently in Greece."

Glad to be in interview mode again, St. Clair made a note to ask about that battle at the end of Athens. "You've faced a lot of challenges over the years," he said.

"That's the truth," Coubertin said. "The Olympic Movement has never been bereft of enemies. The gospel of peace tends to attract the violent. But this is like a self-inflicted wound. I don't know what Henri was thinking when he agreed to their nine-point plan. Moving the IOC headquarters to Berlin, allowing that anti-Semite to appoint new members, removing every ounce of autonomy and independence the membership has fought to preserve for forty-three years, making Germany the permanent host of every Olympiad—it's unthinkable."

He picked up the letter only to throw it back down. "We may have created this committee as a bit of a ruse, but the future of Olympism is absolutely at stake here."

Coubertin paused for a moment and rubbed his forehead with his fingers. He looked at both of them, fixing those nearly black eyes on each of them in turn.

"Francis, Jacques, I have to rely on the two of you to do a few things before I meet with Carl face to face."

"When exactly does he arrive?" Messerli asked. "Is he coming alone?"

"Yes. He's traveling by himself, thank God. It would be a lot more difficult to deal with von Tschammer."

"He is a cold bastard, isn't he?" Messerli said, immediately looking abashed at his lapse of decorum.

Coubertin nodded. "His train arrives about four this afternoon and he's staying at the Beau Rivage. He'll undoubtedly be expecting me to extend the usual courtesies—as I typically have—and meet him at the hotel for a drink if not dinner on his first night in Lausanne. But I want to make him wait."

"For how long?" Messerli asked.

"Until he's sweating with discomfort," Coubertin said. "We are suspending the collegiality of the IOC with Diem and his Nazi friends until further notice."

"We can't just treat him as a persona non grata," said Messerli. "He's an old friend."

"Oh, we won't ignore him," said Pierre, "but we won't show him much respect. Let's face it—he's on a mission from a man who wants to seize control of the IOC and the Olympics—and he has a message to deliver. Any hint that he might not be able to complete that mission—to start to rebuild cooperation with us—he'll take as a major threat. And that's bound to make him nervous."

"Carl does have a tendency to worry," Messerli agreed.

"You would too if you were in his position—that's our first strategic advantage."

Coubertin and Messerli had both known Carl Diem for years, and they briefed St. Clair quickly on his background. He was a brilliant sports administrator, an intellectual with a sharp mind and seemingly indefatigable energy who had helped redirect German sport away from its public obsession with the nineteenth-century Turner movement, a form of mass calisthenics.

"Carl was a godsend when he first showed up at our session in London around 1908, I think," said Pierre. "He was bidding for Berlin as the 1916 host, and he had put together a great plan. He was impressive, a very fit athlete himself. He's a big man, Jacques, physically imposing, as you'll see. And he would have done a brilliant job organizing the 1916 Berlin Games if the Great War hadn't erupted. But once Hitler took power in 1933, he became an opportunist. I think his personal commitment to our ideals are shallow at best."

As a young man, with a dedication that matched Coubertin's, Diem had driven Germany toward a national engagement with modern sports. He had pushed for the formation of sports clubs across the country and had served as a powerful voice in ensuring Germany's full participation in the Olympic Games after the war. But the National Socialists had used him, leading him on with the promise of power and support. In a spark of genius, he invented the torch relay, playing to the symbolic lust of Goebbels—but also successfully creating a dazzling new Olympic tradition. Ultimately, Goebbels reduced Diem's power but kept him on the committee for the 1936 Games. Diem had become Germany's go-between with the IOC and had lost his usual verve for decision-making and commitments. The Germans knew Diem was completely devoted to Coubertin, loyal to a fault, and they had sent him to Lausanne several times before the Games to talk the old icon into attending. In declining every invitation and mode of luxurious transport, tuning down Hitler's private plane and limo, Pierre knew he was hurting Diem, but he refused to go to Berlin.

Realizing St. Clair was taking this all down as notes, Coubertin said, "Jacques, we'll talk about this later for the book. For now let's focus on how we're going to handle Carl."

St. Clair looked up at Pierre. "I'm not going to lay aside my pen at this point, Pierre. I need to capture everything we're doing—and I'll need a full account later of those invitations from Hitler."

Without argument, Coubertin simply pushed ahead. "I want you both to meet him at the train station," he said. "And Francis, as soon as you're face to face, I want you to give him a stern look, man to man, and say bluntly, 'Carl, what the hell have you been trying to do behind Pierre's back? Are you out to destroy the Olympic Movement?'"

"You want me to challenge him immediately?"

"Yes, confront him. Show him your indignation, your anger," Coubertin said with resolve. "Get yourself worked up in advance. It'll take him aback. Make sure he knows I think he's betraying me."

"He *is* betraying you," Messerli responded, "which is all the more surprising because we all know how much admiration he has for you."

"Admiration has become a disease in Germany today. Carl doesn't think he's betraying me or the IOC. That's the point of the challenge. And Jacques, don't wait for Francis to introduce you. Introduce yourself. Interrupt if you have to. I suspect he'll know your name. In fact, I'm sure he knows about the book we're working on, but emphasize that you're here on assignment from *Le Petit Journal*."

"You want him to think I know everything he's done, everything they're trying to do," St. Clair said, figuring it out.

"Yes. We'll put the weight of truth behind your pen. Ask if you can interview him tonight. And if he says he's going to be meeting me, cut him off." Coubertin hesitated for a moment. "No wait. Francis, you correct him. Just say I'm too busy to meet him tonight—maybe tomorrow."

"I actually do want to interview Diem for your story," St. Clair said. "He is Germany's leading Olympic historian at this point, right?"

"Oh yes," said Coubertin. "He can offer a good deal of background. He's been our confidant for years. It's a shame that he's put himself in such a position."

"I think what you said earlier is true, Pierre," Messerli noted. "I doubt that Carl's had much of a choice."

On that note of compassion, St. Clair saw a cloud pass over Pierre's face. Both men felt something deep for Diem, even though they knew he had betrayed them. They conspired for a while longer, and then Coubertin asked Messerli to report in after they had dropped Diem at his hotel.

30

THE NIGHT CLUB

S t. Clair enjoyed the stories of Coubertin's friendship with Aicard, enjoyed writing about the man and his spontaneous ways, and was contemplating making him a major figure in the biography, linking the passage of years between Coubertin's first forays into adult life and the night he launched the modern Olympics in Paris.

Aicard and Coubertin met in the small square of Montmartre early Saturday evening and took a table outside the Café de la Artiste, watching as several painters and potters packed their canvases and crafts into carts and wheeled them away, leaving the center of the village to those arriving for the nightlife. A pleasant din of music wafted from the bar across the way, softened by the laughter and conversation of the café.

"Now that is what the word *beauty* was meant to describe," said Aicard, gesturing at two well-coiffed women strolling by on their way down the steep steps to the lower village.

Pierre nodded his agreement and said, "Cheers," lifting the frosty Parisian Aicard had insisted on ordering when Pierre had confessed he'd never had one. "Hmph," he said, tasting the too sweet concoction of absinthe and crème de menthe. "Do you actually like the flavor of this?"

"Of course not, but it's essential to your education. You'll be ordering a good number of these for the ladies we're going to meet tonight and I want you to know what you're feeding them."

"Well, a sip would have done fine."

"No, that's not the point. I want you to feel the effect. We'll be drinking vodka or red wine, but these Parisians are nearly as potent as they are popular."

"Where is it we're headed?"

"We're going to walk down to Le Chat Noir in an hour or so, and you're going to enter my world."

○ ○ ○ ○ ○

As a full moon rose over Paris, Aicard led Coubertin on the grand tour of the clubs of Montmartre, covering Le Chat Noir, the Cabaret Au Lapin Agile, and the Moulin de la Galette with its double windmills. Amid waves of music and light and the jostling bumps of dancers and revelers in every club, Aicard was recognized by doormen, proprietors, clientele, waiters, and a host of friends. He knew his way around every interior like an architect, familiar with backrooms and alcoves, the places to go when the best seats were taken. As Aicard bought round after round, Coubertin made no attempt to match the poet's consumption, but even with a measure of reserve he was unable to resist the infectious, boisterous joy produced by this assault on his senses.

Aicard introduced him to a half dozen dance partners throughout the night, but they were always on the move and Pierre never had more than a single dance with any of them. They worked up a good sweat in the heat of the clubs, only relieved when they went out into the street to head to the next dance hall. It was well past midnight when they emerged from the Moulin de la Galette, both breathing deeply of the fresh cool air.

"Enough of the tourism," Aicard shouted, walking rapidly through the crowded streets. "You've hit all the big shows, Pierre, now it's time for the crème de la crème, the club of true aficionados."

"Where are we going?"

"My favorite place, a little off the main." He turned into an alley shadowed into near darkness. "Just up here," he said, beckoning. They turned again and Coubertin saw at the end of the passageway a door illuminated in blue light under a scalloped awning. A large man in a dark suit turned toward them as they approached.

"Ah, Jean," he said, "welcome."

Pierre followed his friend through a short hall that opened into a high, wide room with a vaulted ceiling. Inside, the club was a swirl of lights and heat and sexual energy, music blaring loudly from a bandstand at the far end of the room and a master of ceremonies, more like a comedian than a chanteur, half singing and shouting into a megaphone. A troupe of voluptuous women, each painted with white powder and rouge, wildly swirled and lifted their dresses on the wooden dance floor, thrusting their surprisingly nude buttocks out in brief flashes that drew outbursts of yells and whistles from the raucous crowd. A thin balcony, jammed with men and women hanging over its iron railing, encircled the room above the dance floor, and on each side of the room, rows of tables beneath the balcony led back through pillared supports to a mirrored bar with plush seats and banquettes against the back walls.

Pierre felt the effect of the scene immediately, the alcohol stirring his passion as he followed Jean through a jostling throng of men and women to a table on the side of the dance floor. A handsome man in a short black tuxedo greeted them and pulled the chair out for Jean.

"Is this acceptable, monsieur?" he said with a bright smile.

"Yes, André—as always, a delightful view. This is my friend Baron Pierre de Coubertin. Pierre, this is André Delatré, the proprietor and our host for this evening."

"Pleased, André." Pierre reached to take the man's hand in a brief shake, noting the perfect proportions of his face, the silken sheen of his thick black hair, and the fully waxed points of an impressive mustache.

"Garçon!" shouted André, raising his arm, and immediately a waiter in a white waistcoat was at their side as their host moved through the crowd to greet another personage. Jean ordered vodka.

"No doubt how he found his way into such an entertaining trade," said Pierre, leaning into Jean's shoulder to be heard above the din.

"He's had to fight the ladies off every day of his charmed life. His first establishment was a simple brothel, but a man of imagination always sees the possibilities beyond the bedroom."

The vodka arrived and Jean poured them each a glass. With a quick *Santé*, he threw his back quickly while Pierre took a more restrained sip.

The first loud song ended and another kicked in, bringing a surge of dancers from both sides of the room out onto the floor, some men grabbing wildly for the troupe of female performers as they attempted to recede to the stage. The entertainer began to sing. The song was obviously a popular hit, familiar to the patrons, who sang along as the pace of the music quickened. Pierre watched the crowd move with gyrations practiced and polished in some cases and raw and inept in others. Jean rudely pointed and laughed at a large, awkward man attempting to impress a younger woman.

As the throng shifted, Pierre caught glimpses of the tables across the room and noted a good number of women sitting together or alone, some rising against the mirrored backdrop to take a hand of invitation. The music was infectious and

Pierre had an urge to dance, but he was constrained by the thought that this wasn't the waltz and he might be lost in the free-form frenzy before him.

The table tipped a little as Jean stood and said, "I see a flower that needs plucking." Pierre watched with amusement as Jean swayed a little, shouldering his way rather roughly through the group behind them to arrive at the table of a stunning young woman in a bright pink dress.

When Jean leaned in, the woman leaned back, clearly not offended since she grinned and laughed with her friend, but curious as she took in the rising black wedge of Jean's unique hairstyle. Once she fixed on his appealing countenance, she was on her feet, and they moved directly toward Pierre; she threw a telling glance back at her friend before they moved onto the dance floor.

Pierre hesitated for only a second before rising, the bottle of vodka and glass in hand, and making his way toward the other comely lady.

○ ○ ○ ○ ○

"That night we ended up in a coach with two women and a bottle of whiskey, if memory serves," Coubertin said, shaking his head. "And we spent the rest of the night at Jean's colorful farmhouse."

"Quite a departure from the salon scene," St. Clair noted.

"Entirely different—but that was just the beginning of a long string of Dionysian adventures better forgotten than recalled. For every dinner party and dance in an elegant rotunda, there was this other side of life, a bit crazy but nearly irresistible. I'm not particularly proud of that period because I wasn't very productive at all, just totally absorbed in the social life. In fact, it robbed me of my discipline."

"How did you get it back?"

"Love brought it back. I fell in love with a woman who loved the nightlife but was more interested in ideas and conversation than the drunken side of our debauchery. Her name was Jennette Montaigne, and she was a brilliant caricaturist."

"A caricaturist? Wasn't she the redhead you'd seen at Princess Sagan's salon?"

"Yes, that was her."

"Did you meet her again at a salon?"

"No, I met her at a nightclub. Jean introduced us."

31

THE GERMAN

ow did he react when you met him at the train last night?" Coubertin asked St. Clair as they waited for Diem in the IOC office. The baron had made Diem wait all day at the Beau Rivage without word. Late in the afternoon, he finally sent a messenger to the hotel to summon the German to the Villa Mon Repos for a meeting at five o'clock sharp.

"Exactly as you predicted."

"Did he show any anger at all?"

"No," St. Clair said. "He did show a great deal of disappointment. It took him a minute to understand what was happening. Francis stood still in the train station and waited for him to come up from the tunnel, and then refused to return his smile or shake his hand. He looked concerned and confused, and when he dropped his hand, Francis lit into him."

"Did Francis deliver the point on betrayal?"

"Oh yes, very clearly—and Diem repeated the word, saying, 'Betrayal? What betrayal?' And then he turned his head as if looking behind him, considering what do to."

"Poor Carl," Coubertin said. "He knows he's in for a tough time here, but it's the trip home that will weigh on him."

"I introduced myself and he did know my name, but then Francis cut the conversation short and let him know he'd be dining alone—and then we left him there. It was rather tense, and I forgot to ask him for an interview."

"You'll have time, and he'll be looking for an ally—or at least someone to talk to."

Taking a seat behind his desk, Coubertin instructed St. Clair to pull one of the two guest chairs over to the side so Diem would be sitting alone. They heard the German come up the stairs and knock on the door at precisely five. The room seemed immediately smaller when he stepped in, hesitating at the door.

Coubertin rose and extended his hand. "Have a seat, Carl. I wish I could say it was good to see you."

"Well, sir," Diem said, dropping his valise in the chair and enfolding the little man's hand in both of his, "it is good to see you." He gave a forced smile and reached up to remove his bowler. He wore a gray suit with a red tie bearing a black swastika in a white circle.

Coubertin glared at him, saying nothing for a half minute.

"I understand you're somewhat upset with our proposal," Diem finally uttered, trying to put empathy into his voice.

"Your command of the language is better than that, Carl," Coubertin said forcefully, no empathy returned. "I know you realize that 'somewhat upset' is a gross understatement."

"I'm not sure why you don't see the benefits of the idea the Führer and the minister are offering."

"You're not sure, Carl?" Coubertin's voice was still controlled, but rising. "Not sure why I would feel betrayed by an idea that would completely compromise the autonomy of sport? You know damned well that I've fought to preserve our independence for more than forty years. Don't be disingenuous with me."

"But Berlin would bring new energy and resources to the movement—"

"Carl!" Coubertin was shouting now, cutting him off. "Stop the palter. You're only deceiving yourself. This will destroy the Olympic Movement and turn the Games into even more of a political instrument than Goebbels has made them. The Führer is a dynamic leader, but the jury is out as to whether his is a good or destructive dynamic—and a growing chorus of voices sees a very serious threat to peace in this Third Reich."

"The critics are misinformed," Diem said, raising his voice with some conviction.

"Time will tell, but there's no debate about the rising opinion. Let me tell you what's happened to me. You know I refused every offer to go to the Games last year." Coubertin paused to glance at St. Clair to make sure he was recording this point. "I know why you wanted me there—as a prop, a publicity tool, another symbol for Riefenstahl's films. But I did defend the Games, even praised Hitler. *L'Auto* sent a Paris correspondent down here after the Games to get me to denounce the entire festival, but I refused. I had no choice. I called Hitler a forceful leader and said they were the best Games ever—and I was savaged back in France. Labeled a fascist in my own country. Others followed, but I stood my ground, defending the success of the Berlin Games and the work of the organizers, even when the questions violated my lifelong commitment to all sport for everyone. I know there was anti-Semitism, pushed offstage but still persistent. It was the triumph of athletic talent that I defended. I defended you, Carl, and this is the reward I get—an assault on our movement, a play for control."

"Well, we can alter the points of the proposal. I'm sure we can find common ground."

"No, we can't, Carl. Let me tell you why. The proposal you, von Halt, and von Tschammer made to Baillet-Latour, which he inexplicably seemed to agree to—that proposal is clearly destructive to the future of international sport and to everything we've built. I don't see how you can view it any other way. Moving the headquarters of the IOC to Berlin, changing the rules by which IOC members are elected so Hitler can have a free hand in appointing his minions to membership, ending the rotation of the Games among world cities and hosting them exclusively in Germany from this day forward—all this is worse than what the Greeks wanted in 1896—much worse! The Greeks did actually have a historical claim. The principle of rotation is necessary to ensure the future and global popularity of the Games. You must know this; you must see this."

"Pierre, please," Diem said, "I believe the Games in Berlin served to strengthen the Olympic Movement, and I believe the ideas on the table will help push global sport to a new level of glory, carrying your great legacy farther than ever."

"I'm sorry, Carl." Coubertin's tone was softer now. "But it's clear to us"— he motioned toward St. Clair, who had not stopped writing—"that you've sacrificed your own principles and your devotion to international sport to serve your puppeteers. You've done some great work for us—the invention of the torch relay is pure genius. But your proposal can only be seen as betrayal. You are this close"—Coubertin held up his hand and showed the smallest possible space between his finger and thumb—"this close, to becoming persona non grata in the Olympic family. It's only your years of service that restrains me now, but my enmity is growing quickly."

In the silence that followed, St. Clair watched Coubertin glare at Diem while the German looked down and away, searching for some way to respond to the old man's onslaught. St. Clair supposed it was only Diem's admiration and respect for the baron, and probably love, that kept him from leaping up and thrashing him.

"Now, Carl, if you don't mind, I've got things to do," Coubertin said with deliberate condescension. "Please leave us, and we'll reconvene tomorrow to discuss our formal response to your proposal. I'll have a letter for you to take back to Berlin."

○ ○ ○ ○ ○

After Diem left, Coubertin's fierce demeanor changed. He was crestfallen, and he held his hand up for silence. St. Clair watched in disbelief as the old man leaned forward, buried his disconsolate face in his hands, and gasped a couple times as if he were sobbing.

"That's the end of one of my longest friendships," he finally muttered, getting up and leaving the room. He came back in a few minutes, wiping his face with a damp washcloth. Seeing the fatigue in Coubertin's body when he collapsed back into the chair, St. Clair realized that the task of berating Diem had drained all the strength the baron had. Not because it had been difficult—although it had—but because friendships formed in the Olympic world, built over time and over borders in the spirit of a common mission, are implanted deeply in the emotions.

"I'm sorry that was so hard for you," St. Clair said.

"It was more than difficult, Jacques. I haven't been that hard on anyone in more than a decade."

"Well, he had it coming."

"Yes, but that doesn't make it any easier."

"Have you written the letter you're going to give him to take back tomorrow?"

"Yes, but at this point, it's nothing more than a postponement—it simply says our committee will deliver its recommendations to the executive board in October."

"They'll have to accept that, won't they?"

"Yes, but I have to give Carl something more to take back to his masters."

"What? You don't owe him anything more."

Coubertin fumbled around his desk for a bit and pulled a folder from beneath a pile.

"I've been keeping a secret, Jacques. No one knows this yet—except you, now—but I'm planning to leave my personal archives to the Germans, basically to Carl. Their university system, their devotion to scholarship, what they've done over the years from the archaeology at Olympia and their research on the ancient games …" He paused as if to let his words sink in. "Add it all up and they've done as much to preserve the Olympic ideal—despite their political manipulation and this latest subterfuge—as anyone."

St. Clair was incredulous. "Are you serious?" he said, appalled that Coubertin would reveal such a move after the confrontation he had just witnessed. "I—I can hardly believe this. You're going to entrust your archives to them, knowing what they're proposing?"

"I know, but this is something Carl has promised to invest in—and take care of for me—and I know he will. They're building an Olympic library in Berlin."

"What about France? Surely your papers would be better off in Paris, where you launched the movement."

"France? I don't need to tell you how often they criticize me. *L'Auto* basically implied I had become a fascist given my defense of the Berlin Games. Four years ago on my seventieth birthday, I got telegrams from all over the world, but nothing from France."

"But you love France, Pierre, and …"

"That's not the point, Jacques. They won't invest in the kind of international study center that Carl will create. They don't have the funds. And I don't have any high-ranking proponents left in Paris. Drussard's the only one left—and he has no power."

"But what if there's war?"

"Oh, there will be war, Jacques. We can't predict when, but it's coming again. I'll have the IOC's archives here in Switzerland—and mine will go to Berlin."

St. Clair surmised that Coubertin, bereft of resources, was ready to align with anyone who could protect his archives. The thought depressed him. "I hate to say it, but it sounds like you're hedging your bets—and making a bad decision."

"I've got to find the best way to preserve the record."

"Does Francis know about this?"

"He'll understand. He knows the level of German Olympic scholarship."

"Jesus, Pierre, I don't know …" Looking down at his notebook, St. Clair found an exit. "Let's talk about the day Hitler's limousine showed up at Mon Repos."

"I don't want to talk about that now."

"Why not?"

"Because Carl got out of that long black Mercedes-Benz that day dressed in jack boots and his full Nazi uniform. It was a side of him I had not seen before and hoped never to see again."

32

THE CARICATURIST

St. Clair drafted the story of Coubertin's love affair with one idea in mind: he wanted Juliette to be moved by it. He gave it to her late one night in May and sat on their sofa drinking wine while she read it through. The fact that she didn't put it down until she was finished was a very good sign.

After a year of indulgence in the nightlife of Montmartre, Coubertin met the woman who became his passion and drew him away from the regular revelry.

Late in the evening on a summer night in 1884, Aicard was leaning across a table in Le Chat Noir, trying to speak above the music and dance floor noise, his boozy breath blowing across Pierre's face, but Pierre was looking past his friend, his gaze fixed on the redhead he had seen but missed meeting at his first salon.

He had a clear view. She was sitting in a banquette against the back wall, the mirror behind her reflecting her full red mane, drinking and chatting with two other women. As he watched, she picked up a tablet and appeared to make a few notes with a rapidly swirling hand.

"There's a true beauty in that back booth, Jean." Pierre pointed at her, not mentioning he knew who she was. "I haven't seen red hair that bright in years."

Aicard fell back in his chair and turned around to look. "Aha, that's Jennette Montaigne. They call her Jennette the Red because she draws blood with her pen. You've seen her caricatures in *Figaro*. She's very talented, but quite temperamental from what I hear."

"Do you know her?" Pierre asked as the noise level rose with a new sing-along and dancers poured onto the floor.

"What?"

"Can you introduce me?" he shouted.

Aicard rose and signaled the way, indicating he would follow Pierre. "Don't get your hopes up, my friend," he said. "I doubt you'll end up back at my house with her."

"If I end up anywhere with her," Pierre replied, "I'll be happy."

The closer they drew, the more he was taken with the fine lines of her face and the contrast between the sheen of her thick tresses, which she wore piled on her head, and the soft alabaster of her skin. Her black dress covered her shoulders but was open at front beneath a small ruffled collar. He could see, as they approached the banquette and she leaned over to speak to the women sharing her booth, that she was petite, a point that gave him a thrill of anticipation.

"Hello, Jennette," Jean said as he and Pierre approached the banquette like men ready to order drinks at a bar. Pierre smiled and stared at her—perhaps impolitely, he thought, but he couldn't help himself. She looked up and fixed her riveting blue eyes on him. At his sides, Pierre's hands trembled slightly; he breathed deeply, rubbing his thumbs and forefingers together to still them.

"Hello, Jean," she said without looking away, a grin showing she was game. "Who is this handsome man you've brought to me?"

"A whirlwind of intellect," Aicard said, sweeping a hand toward Pierre, "a rider always a furlong ahead, a dashing madman with a painter's soul and a heart drenched in wine—this, Jennette, is a forlorn admirer who won't take another breath until you show him you care." Playing along, Pierre bowed deeply before her as the poet concluded: "May I present Baron Pierre de Coubertin, who boldly sought this introduction."

Jennette extended her hand and Coubertin lifted it delicately to his lips. Her skin was soft and warm, and she moved her fingers over his and took hold, not letting go.

"Jean exaggerates, of course," Coubertin said, "but he spoke the truth when he said you took my breath away."

She laughed loudly, then introduced her friends, and they squeezed together to make room for Jean and Pierre.

Her tablet was a small sketch pad on which Pierre recognized a profile of the club's impresario, Rodolphe Salis, with his bearded chin distorted and his handsome nose oversized to capture the essence of his charm.

"I don't come up here that much anymore, Jean," Jennette said. "But there's a piece coming in *Le Charivari* on Rodolphe, and I wanted to see him in action again before I started drawing."

"It looks as though you're off to a quick start," Aicard said, motioning to the tablet, which she quickly picked up and put away. "So where have you been lately? I know you've been as busy as a red beret on the barricades."

She laughed again. "You've been keeping up with the news."

"I love every face you draw, and I've been seeing a lot lately."

"Figaro is always pushing for something new," she said.

"Jean tells me," Pierre said, "that politics is your true métier—and the arts are secondary." He wondered if she remembered the moment they'd first seen each other at the salon. He wanted to ask her but held back.

"Well, writers, poets, and painters tend to be my friends," she said, "so I can't be as merciless with them as I am with republicans."

"I know you wield your pen like a sword, and your sarcasm really hits its mark."

"Speaking of swords," she said, loud enough for Jean to hear, "I seem to recall that you two put on quite a show for the princess last year."

"That was no act, my lady," Aicard said, deliberately leaning in close to the two women between them. "I was on the attack"—he put his arm forward and mimicked a thrust—"and Pierre's life was spared only by his own swashbuckling swordsmanship."

Jennette turned toward Pierre again, smiling and speaking softly. "So, what does a swashbuckler do when he's not entertaining?"

The music changed to a slower beat, and Pierre took his cue from the moment. "Well, he dances on occasion. Would you do me the honor?"

"I don't dance on first dates," she said, "but sharing the company of a poet and a baron a while longer sounds appealing. Gentlemen, I'm a little hungry, so why don't we find our way to a quiet restaurant where we can get to know one another?"

○ ○ ○ ○ ○

Several dinners followed as Coubertin and Jennette drew closer, but she held him at a frustrating distance. While he waited, he studied her caricatures intently. She drew very much in the manner and tradition of the great André Gill and Honoré Daumier. Business and political scandals were her forte. He worried when she was remote, hoping it wasn't the cursed difference in their ages that made her so secretive. He was twenty-one and he guessed she was close to thirty. He was sure she found him attractive, and he was certainly falling in love with her. For several months she seemed intent on keeping Pierre on a schedule that protected her private life from their interaction—but then there was a sudden change in her tone and she opened herself to him.

"Boulevard Haussmann in the 8th," Jennette yelled to the driver as she and Pierre climbed into the carriage on their way to her apartment for the first time.

Pierre reached for her and started to pull her across the upholstered seat, but she resisted with a charming nod and smile, saying, "Pull back on those reins, Baron. I need a moment."

She opened her large bag and took out her pad, which she opened to the last sketch she had done. Taking pen in hand, she tried to write as the coach rumbled over the cobbles of Montmartre.

"That's impossible," Pierre said. "You can't draw in a carriage!" The coach bounced and swayed as if providence intended to emphasize his point.

"I'm not trying to draw, just making a note for my editor about Carnot, our beloved minister of public works."

"Don't you ever quit?" Pierre asked.

"Of course, now and then. I'm not obsessed with my work."

"Rumor says otherwise."

"Well, rumor can drop dead. You caught me at a busy moment."

"There's romance at hand, darling," he said. "It's time to set the pen aside."

She raised her eyebrows and shook her head, giving him a cross look. "We'll see about that, Monsieur Coubertin."

"That would be Baron if you're using titles."

"All right, Monsieur Coubertin," she said again, ignoring his taunt. She folded the tablet and dropped her pen into the bag. "Let's see just how romantic you are." She reached up and put her hand behind his head, pulling him down, opening her mouth as their lips met.

When they entered her building, Pierre was surprised by the compressed space and the poor illumination provided by a few small gas sconces. Two secured and elegantly designed doors enclosed a tight vestibule with nothing more than an umbrella stand and a wall of mailboxes. Inside, there was no lobby at all but rather a stunning innovation: the doors to a residential elevator. A traditional stone staircase curved up into the shadows around the wire fretwork of a steel elevator shaft, embedded with the thematic artistry of a set of stylized fleurs-de-lis and rinceaux.

Pierre could feel Jennette's eyes on him as she pressed the button and a mechanical chorus erupted from above and below, the motorized cables inside the cage moving up and down in unison as the cabin descended toward them.

"Well," he said, "you're full of surprises. I didn't know they had lifts in apartment buildings yet."

"My father pushed for it after he first rode the elevator at the Trocadéro."

"Ah, at the 1878 Fair."

"Exactly," she said. "This is really his apartment—or was, I should say. He hardly comes to town any longer."

The lift arrived with a clang, and Jennette pulled open the accordion doors and the second set behind them. Pierre gripped the handle and let her move into the small cylinder first, which was mostly shadowed since very little light passed through the metal web. It was scarcely large enough for the two of them, and she stood against the back wall waiting for him to enter. He pressed in against her as the accordion doors snapped shut behind him, their faces just inches apart.

"You're going to have to close the second door," she said, "or the lift won't rise."

Without turning, he reached back and groped for the handles, leaning more fully into her as he pulled the two doors together with another clang. Jennette reached for the panel of buttons, finding the top one. The elevator lurched, and they kissed again as it rose slowly to the sixth floor.

○ ○ ○ ○ ○

When they entered her apartment, she led him directly into the main room, which had a portrait of her father over the fireplace, its mantel covered with family photos amid a spray of feathers. She dropped Pierre's hand and began to undo her scarf, flinging it onto a crowded coat stand as she walked down the hallway.

"Make yourself at home," she said, disappearing into the shadows. A light went on down the hall as Pierre circled the sofas and tables in the center of the room to take a closer look at the drawing table set against the wall. French doors filled with ornate leaded glass were set under a long transom. He could faintly make out the shadowy balcony beyond. On the drawing table, which had a long tray of pencils and paraphernalia attached to its side, he looked at a set of sketches of Minister Carnot now in the works. The length of wall over the table was covered with earlier drawings. Several framed magazine covers featuring her illustrations were obscured by the pages tacked over them. Pierre recognized Simon, Ferry, Napoleon I and III, Haussmann, Hugo, Flaubert, Manet, and Zola—all perfectly skewered to emphasize some point of their ego or stupidity. He lifted a sheet of paper to look at a framed cover of *Figaro* featuring Otto von Bismarck—with a hilariously large head and a gunboat between his legs like a child's riding horse. He laughed heartily.

At the sound of glasses clinking, he turned as Jennette approached with drinks in hand. Sheathed in a silk shawl over a lace camisole, she leaned in to kiss him softly, handing him a Pernod, which they had often drunk together.

"It's a good thing you're not a politician," she said, touching her lips. "That mustache is begging for a rendering. It's entirely too long."

"It's a treat to see your work in its unfinished state," he said, grinning. "Do you ever draw something that compliments your subject? Every one of these emphasizes a flaw."

"I'll move to flattery when our leadership abandons its incessant stupidity." Abruptly she reached up and pulled the clasp from her hair. She shook her head and her red tresses spilled down.

Impulsively, he moved forward and encircled her waist with his free hand, kissing her with the passion he could not restrain—and she responded in kind. Pulling back, she led him down the hallway to her bedroom, where candles were already lit and a soft duvet welcomed them.

○ ○ ○ ○ ○

Later, as they were lounging in bed and she was doodling on a tablet, Pierre rose and wandered about the place, examining her possessions, books, jewelry.

"Nosy, aren't you?"

"Just curious," he said, noticing two dumbbells sitting on a small two-step bench in a recess between the boudoir and the doorway to the kitchen. "What's this?" He bent to pick up the twenty-pound weights. "Are you trying to build up your muscles?" He looked at her, curling the weights with an easy flex.

"Those are my father's, who was something of an exercise buff. I don't know why I haven't gotten rid of them—did you see his pull-up bar?" She pointed toward the door opening.

Pierre turned to see a metal bar mounted across the doorway, about seven feet up, he guessed, realizing her father must have used the two-step bench to reach it. He set the dumbbells down and moved the bench into place.

"My father could do twenty in his prime," Jennette said, sitting up with interest as Pierre stepped onto the bench, facing her bed. "Do you think you could do that many?"

"Twenty is a lot." Pierre reached up. The bar was about a half foot above his reach. "You can count," he said as he leaped.

She laughed with delight. "One, two, three ..." she counted as he pumped quickly and lifted his body effortlessly, raising his chin almost all the way above the bar, smiling broadly as he showed off. "Eighteen, nineteen, twenty—*mon Dieu*, you're good!"

He grunted for the first time with the effort, pulling himself up now with less speed, his forehead still clearing the bar.

"Twenty-seven, twenty-eight ..." she called out with real amazement. "That's more than Robert ever did."

Pierre didn't know who Robert was but was glad to surpass him. "Thirty-five ..." she said, and he could feel the strain intensifying. He was determined. Finally, she shouted, "Forty!" and he dropped down to the bench and sprung across the room to dive into her bed, gasping in pain.

"That's most impressive, Monsieur Coubertin." She leaned on his heaving chest and gave him a quick kiss. "I think you've set a record for the apartment."

"Who's Robert?"

"A British lord," she said. "I won't lie to you, Pierre—he is my heart-song, but he left me to go back to London two months ago, and I'm not sure I'll ever see him again. We've been lovers for the past three years and I will love him forever—but he's the past and, for the moment, at least, you're the present."

"Well then, let's make the most of the present."

Juliette stopped reading. She leaned over and kissed Jacques. "I love it and I love you," she whispered seductively in his ear. "Let's make the most of *this* moment."

33

THE LECTURE

I n mid-June 1937, Dr. Messerli announced that Pierre had been invited to give a lecture in the great hall at the University of Lausanne to celebrate the forty-third anniversary of the founding of the modern Olympic Movement. Coubertin graciously consented, then cleared his schedule and canceled a few interviews with St. Clair that week to prepare. Early on the day of the lecture—June 23—the baron broke his seclusion and invited St. Clair to two meetings he had scheduled, one with two new IOC members and the second with Paavo Nurmi and a delegation of Finnish Olympians who had come to pay tribute to the founder. After the discussion with the new members, who wanted Coubertin's advice on building the Olympic Movement in their countries, St. Clair and Coubertin waited an hour for Nurmi, who must have arrived late in Lausanne and did not show up.

"We'll see him later, I'm sure," Coubertin said, granting a hero a little leeway.

The lecture was set for Wednesday night at seven. Deciding to make an afternoon of it, St. Clair and Juliette set out at four to walk up the long hill from Ouchy. Juliette carried a roomy cloth shoulder bag that held one of her sketch pads. On rue de Bourg, St. Clair steered Juliette into the Aubonne Chocolatière and bought her an expensive box of truffles, which she absolutely could not resist. St. Clair had to close the box after she devoured half the sweets.

Winding their way up the hill, they passed the cathedral and reached the open expanse of the cobblestone Place de la Riponne, the largest plaza in Lausanne. The neoclassical façade of the Palais de Rumine, which housed the university, stood to the east. They sat at a café on the south side, drinking a bottle of Saint-Julien from the Médoc, watching the people rush about at the end of the day. The sky was clear, the weather balmy. They had a good view of the impressive Italianate edifice of the university, stained dark brown by years of stormy weather, but still imposing between its twin bookend towers. They watched as a number of cars and taxis began to pull up, dropping off local notables, including, St. Clair guessed, the robed figures of the university's provost and a bishop.

He spotted and pointed out Paavo Nurmi and his two Finnish compatriots as they strode across the plaza. Finally, Dr. Messerli's car arrived with the baron and baroness. St. Clair called for the check as Coubertin and his entourage slowly climbed the stairway. At the top, the old man stopped and turned to gaze back over the city, watching the public move through its routine for a brief moment.

St. Clair and Juliette hurried across the plaza and arrived as Coubertin and the baroness passed through the large front doors and began their slow ascent up the long, arched tunnel of the grand staircase with Messerli at their side. As they reached the platform of the atrium, in the magnificent vaulted opening at the foot of the dolphin fountain, Coubertin stopped and St. Clair became aware of a growing murmur. Following Coubertin's excited gaze, he looked up to see throngs of young people leaning out of the arcade that framed the upper story, twenty columned openings on the level above them, hundreds of young faces looking down at the baron in expectation, if not awe.

The doctor guided Coubertin and the baroness up to the next flight of stairs to the Aula, the Grand Amphitheater. St. Clair lingered for a minute. "This is the kind of recognition he should have everywhere," he said to Juliette, turning her up the stairs. They entered the amphitheater just as Coubertin and Messerli were escorting the baroness to a seat in the front row, which was occupied by a number of IOC members and several other dignitaries. The two then made their way to the stage. St. Clair wanted to sit in the middle of the auditorium, but Juliette insisted on moving closer to the front so she could see the baron more clearly as he delivered his message.

St. Clair was pleased to see that the great hall was nearly full—perhaps five hundred people—including a good number of boys in their teens who were seated together in groups that suggested classes or teams. It was a very good turnout for a Wednesday night, he thought, suddenly certain that Messerli had used his position and professional network to fill the room.

The provost stepped to the podium and, tilting the silver grill of a microphone toward his chin, offered a few remarks explaining the university's pride in hosting a series of public lectures. His voice echoed against the high walls and vaulted ceiling, which had the proportions and acoustics, if not the decorative details, of a small cathedral.

"We are honored tonight to welcome to the University of Lausanne a man whose work has been crowned in the celebration of ten Summer Olympic Games and four editions of the new Winter Olympic Games. While many of us here in Lausanne know him or recognize his distinct features as he walks our city streets or rows in his skiff on Lac Léman, it is not so often anymore that we are graced with his presence in the podiums where he was once such a prominent figure. We are delighted to have Baron Pierre de Coubertin address us tonight—and offer his perspective on the past, present, and future of the Olympic Movement he launched in Paris precisely forty-three years ago today. To properly acknowledge his achievements and to put them into the proper historical context, I'd like to invite our own Dr. Francis Messerli, the head of our School of Medicine, to formally introduce the baron."

Two groups of boys spontaneously sprung to their feet in applause as Messerli rose, but they quickly recognized that this was not his night and sat back down as he held his hands out, calming them with a smile and barely suppressed laugh.

"You'll have to forgive the enthusiasm of a young group of gymnasts," Messerli said. "They're all very excited to hear the story of the Olympic Movement from the founder himself."

As Messerli begin to talk, Juliette took out her sketchpad and St. Clair opened his notebook, scratching out a few points about the provost and the general atmosphere in the room.

"We are proud to have with us tonight the great Paavo Nurmi and a group of Finnish Olympians who achieved true distinction on the field of play," Messerli said, motioning with his hand for the men to rise as he named them all. "Paavo Nurmi ranks as the greatest medal winner in Olympic history. Between Antwerp in 1920 and Amsterdam 1928, he won twelve medals in all, nine gold and three silver, an achievement that stands alone. He is the only man ever to have held world records in the mile, the five thousand, and the ten thousand meters simultaneously. Paavo would tell you that the sacrifice required to become an Olympian—to make your national team—and to finish on the podium, takes a level of personal discipline, drive, and motivation that is out of the reach of most men. There have now been nearly four thousand Olympic medalists, heroes all in their own way—but I believe that none of them have had to reach the level of commitment or sacrifice that it took *le Rénovateur* of the Olympic Games to put our greatest festival of sport on the world calendar."

Messerli spent five minutes on the baron's background and the milestones of his career, touching on the difficulties and enemies he faced along the way, helping the audience understand they were in the presence of a man who deserved their highest esteem and a good measure of gratitude. St. Clair made notes on the enemies who Messerli named—as if they were members of an exclusive Olympic Hall of Fame of Adversaries: Paschal Grousset, the fierce communard who had stood against his efforts to reform the French school system; the Greek politicians who tried to reject the first Olympic Games; Albert Piccard, the commissioner of the Paris World's Fair of 1900, who had undermined Coubertin's efforts in organizing the second Olympic Games that summer; and James Sullivan, head of the American Olympic Committee, who had tried, more than once, to seize control of the Olympic Movement.

"Against all odds, Pierre de Coubertin gave our world its greatest celebration of human solidarity—an international movement that promotes peace and produces friendships through sport. Please join me in welcoming to the podium the illustrious son of France and Lausanne's leading citizen, Baron Pierre de Coubertin."

The applause became a standing ovation as Coubertin made his way to the podium and waited for the crowd to quiet. Messerli had more than accomplished his job, St. Clair thought, going a little too far, perhaps, but making the most of the opportunity.

"Ladies and gentlemen," Coubertin began, "I hope you all have the honor of one day being introduced to a public audience by a friend whose devotion knows no bounds, whose loyalties are as unshakable as the rock on which this university rests, and whose faith in your ideas—in this case, the future of Olympic sport—is full of unbounded enthusiasm. If you are ever so lucky to enjoy such a moment, you will know then what it has been like for me to have a friend as good as Dr. Francis Messerli for the past twenty-nine years. Thank you, Francis.

"Tonight, as we celebrate the history of the Olympic Movement, which, at forty-three, is still much younger than me and many of you, I want to look at history in a broader sense and tell you how I think the Olympic Movement fits into the times in which we live. I want to talk about how, in so many ways, the Olympics can help us see the promise of the past and push for its fulfillment in the future.

"If you'll kindly indulge me, I will not recite for you the history of the Games, the heroic feats, or the eternal verities of sport. I'd like to begin, instead, with a story from my youth.

"When I was a boy, Paris underwent a massive transformation. In the decade before I was born, the Prefect of the Seine, Baron Haussmann, was empowered by Napoleon III to rebuild the city. My father, who remained a staunch monarchist till the day he died, had a grudging respect for Haussmann's vision and wanted me, from an early age, to understand just how the city of my birth had changed from the old, choked metropolis of his youth, from a city of narrow streets and a medieval labyrinth of hovels to the capital of modernity we know today, with its wide boulevards, stunning Beaux-Arts architecture, and captivating vistas. He took me on walks about the city to point out the transformation but before he did, he laid out a century-old map of Paris and had me look at it, asking over and over a simple question, 'What do you see?'"

Like the rest of the audience, St. Clair listened intently as Coubertin wove the tale of his walks about Paris with his father. Although St. Clair had heard the story before and had written about it, he was surprised when Coubertin turned his focus on the old walls—the seven circles of Paris that represented the progressive expansion of the city, each new wall encircling people who had been living on the outside.

"It was many, many years after my father took me on those walks," Coubertin said, drawing his conclusion, "that I began to understand that the successive construction of each of those walls reveals the central lesson of history, the inexorable truth of past, present, and future. If history teaches us any one thing, it teaches us the lesson contained in those walls—and the hundreds of thousands if not millions of walls built in towns, villages, and cities throughout the world since ancient times. And that lesson is this: that the circle of inclusion is constantly expanding and cannot be stopped. Walls, which are so often viewed as a symbol of exclusion, have long served as a means of inclusion as well.

"Sometimes those circles expand dramatically—not physically or geographically, but conceptually, legally, compassionately—as they did when the American colonies declared their independence from King George and established the rights of life, liberty, and the pursuit of happiness for all their citizens. As they did when the Third Republic reached out to the very borders of France and its colonies to include all of its citizens in liberty, equality, fraternity.

"With each generation, more people gain the rights and privileges of citizenship. Women's suffrage is the most recent breakthrough, but more are coming. And we can see them clearly in the realm of sport, in the meritocracy of the arena, where the gifts and talents of every man are, in fact, the only currency that counts, the only ticket required for participation. At the Olympic Games, kings and paupers race side by side in the spirit of fair play and the equality of competition.

"That is what my friends and I saw in the possibilities of the Olympic Games— an opportunity to expand, through sport, the circles of inclusion across all the borders that divide us. Aside from the personal benefits that exercise and competition deliver to the individual, we saw the possibilities of sport with a social purpose. We saw an opportunity to push back the social, political, and economic divisions that make us adversaries in other realms; we saw the ability to dissolve the class distinctions that separate us in society, the possibilities of uniting our world in equality on the field of play, a meritocracy open to all, a republic of muscles. As I once wrote, 'On the playing fields, men are no longer enemies or political adversaries, but only fellow players, playing the game.'

"Above all, given the generations I grew up with, we saw in sport the possibilities of friendship—and the potential of creating a new worldwide movement that would become a strong and vital ally for peace. The circles we sought to build were circles of friendship and peace that revolved around sport. The five Olympic rings, which represent the continents, are really five great circles of inclusion through sport. We have pushed those circles across the borders of more than fifty nations today—fifty countries that now have their own national Olympic committees. And well beyond the end of my life, the Olympic Movement will continue to push those circles all the way to the ends of the earth."

The baron paused, breathing deeply, St. Clair noted, his shoulders rising as he prepared for the home stretch.

"Now, let me tell you why I think our movement has the power to reach that far," he said, a new level of conviction entering his voice, "why I believe the promise of Olympic sport is unlimited, and why I believe we are still only at the beginning—still in the infancy—of the possibilities we have unleashed.

"There are those who say that sport can only do so much—that it cannot create peace. But I say it can—it can make a vital contribution to the process of peace and help us all build a better world. Sport is most powerful when it is driven by a social purpose, when it is linked to education, and when it conveys the values at the heart of the Olympic ideal. And what is that ideal? Let me define it for you."

At that, St. Clair quickly turned a page in his notebook as a spark of excitement rose inside him—thinking a revelation might be at hand, something he had not heard before.

"I see the Olympic ideal in five stages of realization," the baron continued. "It starts with the personal and moves to the universal, from human excellence to mutual respect, from mutual respect to the flowering of friendship, from friendship to international understanding, and from international understanding to a desire for peace. In this way, sport can make a contribution to peace.

"It begins with a commitment to human excellence on the most personal level. As every Olympian will tell you, a commitment to athletic excellence entails discipline, drive, perseverance, endurance, a hard-headed denial of distractions, and a refusal to let any obstacle or injury stand in the way of your ultimate goal. There are always injuries, setbacks, sidetracks, and delays, of course, but excellence can be achieved only through the denial of every challenge. An injury is an enemy to athletic excellence.

"So, Olympism calls us to a state of mind—what the athletes now call an attitude of pride—that holds the focus on the highest standard of performance possible. In the Olympic realm, those who achieve excellence rise. They rise past their local and regional competitors to face the finest athletes from across their nation. Once they make their national team and travel to the Olympic Games—and march in the Parade of Nations at opening ceremonies, they have already brought honor to their country. They have become Olympians.

"And when they step onto the field of play, against the champions of other nations, against the very best the world has to offer, my idealism tells me there will be mutual respect. When I line up in the lane next to a man from the other side of the world, of course, I want to beat him, but I cannot help but respect him. For he has had to make the same sacrifices, has pursued his goals with the same unfailing dedication that I have. Whatever our differences, we are brothers in sport, champions near the top of a pyramid that has only a few more stones above us. We will push each other toward greatness, to the top of the podium that stands above the entire world. As the Greeks said, 'There is no greater honor than what a man achieves with his hands and feet.'

"Out of that respect, friendship sometimes flows—and when it does it may flourish in unusual ways and with profound meaning. With us tonight is the great Olympic journalist from *Le Petit Journal* in Paris, Jacques St. Clair. He has written eloquently about the friendship that developed on the field of play in Berlin between Jesse Owens and Luz Long. If you know their stories, you know how unlikely that friendship would have been in any other realm but sport—the grandson of an Alabama slave and the epitome of the blue-eyed, blond-haired German superman. To think that Luz Long—under orders from the Third Reich to win at all costs—provided Jesse Owens with the encouragement and practical advice to win the long jump gold medal—while Long himself fell to second place—is to believe in the best possibilities.

"It is not much of a leap from there to think that those Olympians will return home and plant the seeds of international understanding between their nations in the circles they travel in. And how much further must faith carry us to think that one day there will be one hundred thousand Olympians carrying the torch for peace in their own nations?"

The baron stopped speaking for a moment, and St. Clair realized he wanted the audience to dwell on the possibilities that there just might be some truth to what he was saying.

"Ladies and gentlemen, I am an idealist—someone who believes in the best possibilities in every situation, someone who has faith in the positive potential of every idea, who sees the alternatives to failure, who aims high. I'm not always an optimist anymore, but I am an idealist still. And it is the idealism at the heart of the Olympic Movement that I believe in with all my being."

Coubertin paused before closing with a simple note of gratitude. "Thank you so much for listening to me tonight."

The applause was immediate and thunderous. Coubertin lingered at the podium, his head panning back and forth as he looked across the room to take in the waves of public appreciation. Watching from the audience, St. Clair wondered if this might be among the last public nights the baron ever enjoyed.

34

THE OLYMPIANS

S t. Clair stood behind Coubertin and listened as a crowd of admirers surrounded him after the speech and thanked him, one by one, for his talk—and his life's work. St. Clair could see that the old man was filled with gratitude at the response. He asked each person in turn for his or her name, and was gracious with the deep throng of Messerli's young athletes who were last in line. Nurmi and his friends waited patiently until the baron was finished and then proposed that Pierre join them for a drink in the bar at the Palace Hôtel. At first he demurred, feigning fatigue, but Nurmi persisted and he finally agreed. St. Clair thought the emotions of the moment made him more amenable to a social celebration—and looked around for the baroness to see if she too had drawn inspiration from the night, but she was gone. No goodbyes, no congratulations, no shared joy.

Messerli departed to get his car and promised to join them at the bar. In a few minutes, the Finns and Pierre were coursing down rue Madeleine to the old town, with St. Clair and Juliette trailing behind. Coubertin led the way through the revolving doors of the Lausanne Palace and up the steps into the low light of the Havana Bar, where Messerli was waiting. They settled into a circle of maroon leather chairs with brass tacks gleaming down the arms. Pierre sat against the wall with Messerli and St. Clair on either side and the Olympians across a low table. Drinks came quickly, and several bowls of nuts were rapidly diminished. Juliette sat quietly at the end of her table, drawing the scene on her sketch pad.

"I take it, Juliette," Pierre said, "you're going to record this illustrious gathering for posterity." The others all looked her way.

"Just a few impressions," she said, "but I'll be sure you all get copies if it turns out to be a masterpiece."

Pierre chuckled and turned back to Nurmi as St. Clair opened his tablet. The conversation began with a round of compliments on the speech, and Nurmi proposed a toast.

"For everything you've done for us," he said, "for the athletes of the world, and the generations to come, we just want to say—thank you."

"You've honored me already, Paavo," said Coubertin. "Your presence tonight made this anniversary far more meaningful."

It was clear to St. Clair that Nurmi and his colleagues had some questions for Pierre, something they wanted to talk about, but the baron preempted them with a question of his own. "Tell me about your lives and what you've all been doing."

"We're all still involved in athletics in one way or another," said Nurmi as his colleagues nodded. "We teach, we coach, we encourage, and we try to inspire."

"It's good to hear that you've stayed involved in sports."

"We're all committed to the Finnish Olympic Committee," Nurmi continued. "We attend the annual assemblies, and each of us tries to help build the team."

One of Nurmi's colleagues, Armas Kinnunen, finally spoke. He was a thin, taut man with curly hair, another Olympic runner. "When we see young talent, we push them to develop, and we've all found that the Olympics—the idea of becoming part of our national team and representing our country—can serve as a strong motivator."

"Is there that much recognition of the Games among the young people of Finland now that you're all retired?"

They laughed. "Oh yes," Nurmi said. "Running remains at the forefront and there's a good bit of interest in a dozen other Olympic sports. But there's also a lot of anxiety in the schools right now, and it's beginning to affect the turnout."

"Rumors of war?"

"Yes, there's a lot of worry about what the future holds. The young are distracted. But what's interesting is how much the anxiety has brought to light the whole idea of peace through sport."

"You wouldn't believe how interested our students are," said Kinnunen, "when we talk about the Olympics as a foundation for friendship and peace."

"Now you're inspiring me," Coubertin said, letting his head drop for a second. "That's music to my ears," he said, still looking down and breathing deeply. "It's the kind of report I wish I was getting every day from around the world."

They were all suddenly aware the old man was tired, but Nurmi evidently didn't want the conversation to end. "So, Baron," he said, "we've been talking about you and the Olympic Games without a break it seems as we've traveled the last three days—and now that we're here with you, we have three questions we'd like to ask."

"Of course," Coubertin replied. "I'm at your disposal."

St. Clair took note of Nurmi's face, which was square and seemed open and honest. He had a broad forehead, wide-set eyes, a prominent nose, and very few wrinkles—although he was forty, he looked as if he could still compete. With his glowing cheeks, his admiration for *le Rénovateur* was unmistakable.

"Thank you," Nurmi said. "First, what was the greatest athletic performance you ever witnessed? Second, what was the greatest single sporting event you've witnessed? Finally, how did the whole idea of peace through sport come to you? What was it that drove you to make peace and friendship the real foundation for the Olympic Games?"

"Hmm," Coubertin murmured, pressing his lips together in concentration. "The first two are easy, but there's no simple answer to the third. It was the evolution of an idea over the course of five years."

St. Clair wrote a note to himself to explore the evolution of peace and sport with Pierre and to discover the concept's point of origin.

Coubertin looked up, seemed to will himself to rally, and said, "Well, you, Paavo, certainly rank at the very heights of Mount Olympus and are without question the greatest runner I've ever seen on the track. And with all due respect to Jacques's reporting, I did not see Jesse Owens in person. But I was once witness to a performance so dominant and so decisive that I can only think of it, even now, a quarter century later, as an athletic miracle."

They all looked at him in anticipation, but St. Clair knew the name that was coming.

"Jim Thorpe," the baron said, "was the greatest athlete I ever saw. He had a reservoir of stamina that no one could match, the strength of a bull, the balance and agility of a dancer, the speed to sprint with the best, and the ability to do everything well. The decathlon was meant to be the most difficult contest in the Games, essentially to determine the world's greatest all-around athlete. The pentathlon was meant to be a rough and rugged prelude but a tier below, testing a different set of skills. To win either was extraordinary. To win both at one Games—nearly unthinkable.

"How he did that remains inexplicable even if you witnessed those gifts in action as I did. He simply excelled at everything. The javelin, pole vault, sprints, hurdles, even the shot put. In that stadium in Stockholm we were right on the edge of the field, an intimate setting that gave you a heightened sense of his brilliance. You could see the sweat dripping off him as he ran by, out front in the fifteen hundred, pulling away. No one could touch him—he ran away with everything.

"He was a humble man, but perhaps the most gifted natural athlete we'll ever see. I'm sure you all remember that at the awards ceremony, when King Gustaf hung the medal around his neck and proclaimed him the world's greatest athlete, he famously replied, 'Thanks, King.'"

They laughed in agreement, and Coubertin provided a personal anecdote. "One afternoon I went to see Thorpe, unannounced, on the ship where the U.S. team was staying—which happened to be, I'm just now remembering, the SS *Finland*. It was moored at Gamla stan, the old town of Stockholm, just down the waterfront from the royal palace. Thorpe unfortunately wasn't on the boat. I ended up talking to his cabin mate, Abel Kiviat, who took silver in the fifteen hundred meters even though he held the world record. A great young fellow, best Jewish distance runner of the era. He told me that on the passage from the United States, everyone on the team ran around the ship training like mad, but not Thorpe. Most of the time, Kiviat said, he sat in a deck chair, relaxing and smoking cigarettes. Even his teammates marveled at his ability."

The baron paused to take a drink, and Nurmi used that as a signal to order another round. Messerli had a glass of ice water brought for the baron.

"Thorpe's legend is fully deserved," said Nurmi, taking the opportunity to raise a controversial issue. "I find it detestable that the IOC stripped him of his medals because he was paid to play baseball." His angry tone was barely veiled. Nurmi himself, St. Clair remembered, was declared ineligible five years earlier and prevented from running in the Los Angeles Olympics over a disputed payment he once received. This was personal.

Coubertin did not seem taken aback by Nurmi's change of tone, nor was he evasive. "Yes, the politics of amateurism are anathema to clear thought within the IOC. It's the longest-running controversy we've had and remains the bane of sport today. Class distinctions die hard, particularly when the purists who count themselves among the privileged gain power." Coubertin held his fist in front of him and nodded in agreement with Nurmi, who seemed gratified with that response.

"And what would you classify as the greatest Olympic event of all time?" he asked.

"There can only be one beginning to any enduring tradition," Coubertin said, "and the Athens Olympics of 1896 will always hold that distinction. We sailed to Athens with the expectation of a miracle—and the Games did not disappoint." He paused, looking at each member of the party individually. "All of us who were there were filled with anticipation that through the rituals of the Games we would experience a mystical connection to the ancient world. It arrived on the fifth day, and it was the resurrection we were waiting for— that indescribable jolt of magic when the present and the past meld and break through the veils of time and eternity takes hold. That ancient mystical encounter was carried toward us across the centuries on the shoulders of a single runner in the fustanella of a Greek peasant as he led the marathon into the stadium, a farmer with a country on his back. Spiridon Loues bore the fervent hopes and dreams of a nation that saw in his victory the full restoration of the grand glories that once belonged to Greece alone. The acclamation of the people as he coursed along the route lifted the city itself to a level of patriotic bliss and an infectious spirit of public joy that engulfed us all. In that most symbolic of all events—heralding memories of the legendary Greek victory at Marathon and the heroic sacrifice of Phidippides—Loues covered twenty-six miles and fifteen centuries, closing the gap between space and time. The emotions and elation of that moment can never be repeated. History completed a fifteen-hundred-year cycle in that single event—and it produced a level of national pride the likes of which the world will never see again."

When the baron finished, his fatigue was even more evident, but he stayed where he was—determined not to disappoint the legendary endurance runner and his colleagues, all of whom were obviously devoted ambassadors of the Olympic ideal. He looked at Nurmi and waited.

"What I'm most interested in," said Paavo, "because I'm always trying to give young people a relevant story that's true, is how you came up with the idea of making peace—or putting peace at the foundation of the Games."

Coubertin looked over at Messerli, then at Juliette and around the circle. "As I said earlier, there's no brief answer to that question. It was an evolution of thought that occurred over some years."

"Well, I'm still interested," said Nurmi. "I was hoping for a story I could take back and tell my students."

"Well, if you want a story, I believe I can give you a sense of where the connection between sport and peace originated—and how it became essential to my Olympic plans." They all sat back as Coubertin began a story he called *The Poet, the Princess, and the Statue.*

St. Clair wrote quickly to capture every word, ran out of paper, flipped his tablet over to fill in the back of the pages. He was certain this story belonged in the book.

SPORT AND PEACE

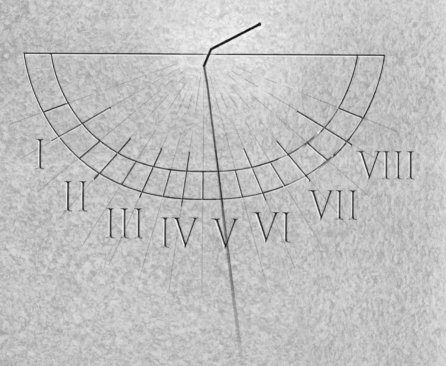

35

THE OLD ALLY

A few days later, returning from Mon Repos on a hot afternoon in late June, St. Clair found an envelope from the Lausanne Palace stuck at eye level into the door jamb of the cottage. The uncertain scrawl took him a minute to figure out. The note read: "Have just arrived from Paris for a week. Meet me Friday morning at nine in the hotel lobby. Lucien Drussard." This was good news. Drussard was an aristocrat like Coubertin. They had met at university and were friends and allies in the earliest days of Coubertin's campaign. St. Clair believed he would be an exceptional source.

St. Clair told Juliette about the note over a glass of wine as she stirred a fine brown broth on the stove. "I think he's going to be a key to the story of Pierre's first forays into education reform."

"Drussard?" she said, trying to remember. "Ah yes, another ancient sports relic, right?" she laughed. "The tall, skinny one?"

St. Clair grinned. "Don't be disrespectful. He's no relic. He's still involved with the French Olympic Committee, and he must be in his mid-seventies like Pierre."

"I'm beginning to think you're spending all this time with old men just to make yourself feel younger!"

"They do make me feel younger," St. Clair admitted, "but I've got you to make me feel older."

"I know. It's shocking how much men age in their late thirties," she joked. "I may need a replacement soon."

St. Clair moved quickly around the counter and grabbed her wrists, turning her toward him. "We'll have no talk of replacements here," he said, kissing her before going back to his wine.

○ ○ ○ ○ ○

At the Lausanne Palace, Drussard pulled up his cane and took St. Clair's arm as they turned up the steps under the coffered ceiling. "I can still walk everywhere," the old man said, "but it's good to have a steady hand on the stairs."

On the landing, St. Clair shifted and took Drussard's arm, guiding him around a marble table holding an enormous vase of fresh-cut flowers, becoming aware of the man's frailty. Drussard's step was uncertain and St. Clair could feel the bones in his arm and elbow, as if his hands were wrapped around a skeleton covered only by fabric. Leading him around the piano to the second set of stairs, St. Clair glanced quickly at the old man's hand and saw the bulging veins rising over the bands of tendons and bones—like a leaf that had fallen to the ground—a translucent blue shading of blood beneath the skin.

Once they were seated—in the same chairs in which St. Clair had interviewed Avery Brundage four months earlier—old Drussard had enough energy to laugh at the memories of youth that flowed effortlessly from his lips. Seeing the sparkle in his eyes and the joy in his face, St. Clair laughed with him when he described his first impressions of Coubertin.

"The first time I saw him, I thought, who is this loud-mouthed little Napoleon? We met in the midst of a debate in a lecture hall at the École Libre des Sciences Politiques—the Po, as we called it—in a class being conducted by the very eminent Jules Simon, who had been prime minister the decade before and who we were all trying to impress. It was 1883 or '84, and I was on my feet making a case from my seat in a small amphitheater when I was interrupted by a classmate standing on the far end of the row behind me. He was a little man, seemingly fit, in a neatly tailored suit, and he gave the impression of being fearless. He was quick to his feet, had a penetrating voice, and spoke with an eloquence that indicated he was both gifted and well schooled. You knew you were up against a formidable debater. Even though he countered a point I was making, he did it with a finesse I found appealing, and I took a liking to him almost immediately. He had verve and style—a cultivated public persona even then—when we were what, in our early twenties?"

"Sounds as if he was a spirited young man. What was the argument about?"

"It was a point, I think, on the status of priests in the French education system.

The church had controlled education in France for far too long, most agreed. But there was continuing value in their schools and teaching. I had made the point, contrary to the reforms under Prime Minister Jules Ferry from a year or two before, about the importance of maintaining and not rejecting completely the influence of Catholic priests—Jesuits, Trappists, Franciscans—in our education system. I didn't fully embrace the new phalanx of Black Hussards that Ferry promoted. It was a standard position and I was arguing the case primarily to ensure Jules Simon knew where I stood. But Pierre, who I quickly learned was a great admirer of Ferry and his reform movement, offered a riposte and actually used my name, even though we had not been introduced."

"Can you remember what he said?" St. Clair asked.

The old man looked up in thought, gazing at the massive teardrop chandelier sparkling above the floral profusion in the middle of the room. His lips pulled back tight, he looked down and then seemed to remember. "I think he said something like 'Perhaps the good Monsieur Drussard, who clearly shares our affection for the priests who gracefully schooled us, would admit there is much to learn from scholars who aren't compelled to begin every lesson with a reading of the Holy Scriptures.'"

Drussard stopped for a moment, watching St. Clair as he recorded the old man's words in his quick shorthand. "I was surprised," he continued, "since it was just the beginning of the year and the class had met only once or twice before, that he knew my name. After class, when we talked, I discovered that he knew the names of every one of our classmates—far better than any of our professors, I'm sure. I had never met a student like that."

Now the memories came to Drussard in a rush, and he became more animated as he talked, edging forward to make sure St. Clair recorded each point. "We went for drinks later that week and I learned a good deal about him in our first long conversation. He wasn't at the Po so much to learn as he was to push forward a mission. He was already set on becoming a leader of the education reform movement in France. He had very compelling arguments for the changes that were needed—he seemed to know everything about the gradual and radical changes that were instituted through Victor Duruy under the Second Empire, Jules Simon when he was prime minister, and Jules Ferry when he served as both prime minister and minister of public education in 1880. Pierre saw continuity where others saw chaos. He saw the evolution of France's education system in very clear historical terms. He believed that the universal education Ferry had mandated in 1880—and the creation of the National Ministry of Education in that same act—put us on the threshold of a new era for France. I learned a great deal from him when we discussed those changes and his vision. We became close during that first year, socializing, drinking, and discussing the lectures in the evening over dinner."

"Was he focused on introducing sport into education then?"

"No. He'd been to England only once at that point, and the sport focus came through his second or third trip. But I remember that he worshipped Thomas Arnold, the Rugby headmaster who brought sport into the English schools. And when he visited Rugby, in 1885, it hit him like a revelation. He came back from that trip and told me he had had a vision. That memory is clear to me because we went to Victor Hugo's funeral not long after he returned. He must have been twenty-two years old at the time—we're the same age. At Rugby, he had what some call an epiphany, partly spiritual in his case. It was a social insight linked to the evolving role of the nobility at the time. It clarified everything, gave him a specific sense of purpose—to harness the emerging international popularity of sport for the benefit of France. Our nation was way behind the times in giving sport the place it deserved in education. And of course, as I'm sure you know, he was an athlete himself. Pierre loved sport and had a thirst for competition. He was always looking for a match of some sort. I was a runner then and we took to racing and running together, playing tennis, and riding horses. He also fenced and even loved to box."

They talked for two more hours and made an appointment to meet again the next morning at the same spot. After that meeting, St. Clair returned to the cottage to draft a few scenes capturing Drussard's recollections of Pierre's early interaction with Jules Simon and the night Pierre had introduced him to Jean Aicard. But before he got to his notes from Drussard, St. Clair drafted a quick introduction on the Po that he would use as the opening to this section.

The École Libre des Sciences Politiques—the Po—was founded in 1872 by Émile Boutmy, Albert Sorel, Hippolyte Taine, and other leading French intellectuals, including former political leaders of the Third Republic, to help shape a new vision for France's future—and prepare the next generation of the nation's political leaders and diplomats. They sought to create a new school of thought and birth new ideas and solutions to the country's social, political, and economic problems by gathering the finest young minds of future generations—with admissions based only on merit, an egalitarian view to intellectual capability—under the tutelage of the day's most gifted teachers and leaders. In this theoretical meritorious mix, the rising sons of the bourgeoisie, the emerging opinion leaders of social discourse, and the scions of a fading aristocracy could argue the future of their country with those who had recently stepped away from the offices of power or were mounting fresh campaigns to return to the reins of state.

It was an unusual academic experiment and opened once again an opportunity for Coubertin—as Saint-Ignace had in a far more limited way—to step to the forefront of education and enter into face-to-face dialogue with those who were helping to shape France's future. This was an experiment in education at the highest levels—and Pierre de Coubertin, who already believed that education was the key to the future of France, had found a milieu in which he could articulate, test, and refine his own theories. More importantly, he could engage with the powerful as he sought to find the right role for the ambitions that burned hot in his heart and mind.

$$\circ \; \circ \; \circ \; \circ \; \circ$$

Tall, skinny, and dressed like a gentleman in a tailored Prince Albert coat that hung open unbuttoned and unbelted, Lucien Drussard lingered in the hall outside an amphitheater in the Po, waiting for his friend Pierre to wrap up a post-lecture conversation with Jules Simon. They had agreed to go for a drink at the new Café de Flore on the Saint-Germain, where Pierre wanted to introduce Lucien to a poet from Provence. Nodding at a few passing acquaintances in the marble-floored corridor, he fingered a golden chain hanging across the front of his waistcoat and lifted his pocket watch into his hand. They were running late, but it didn't matter since they'd be drinking together past midnight. Lucien had an even temperament, and once the classes of the Po ended for the day, he slipped quite easily into the mindset of a man of leisure.

Glancing to his side, he looked through the doorway to where Pierre stood at the front of the room, leaning against Simon's table. The old man, his pate shining between two tufts of gray hair that extended from the sides of his head like curled brushes, was stuffing a stack of papers into a valise while listening intently to the energetic flow of Pierre's conversation. The young man gesticulated, raised his hands, turned them over in an appeal. Looking over the glasses perched on his long, full nose, Simon nodded in apparent agreement. He stepped from behind his table and extended his arm, inviting Pierre to join him as they turned toward the door. It was an intimate gesture that surprised Lucien. Simon continued to talk, his arm around Pierre's shoulders as they moved across the front of the amphitheater. Watching them approach, Lucien had the feeling their conversation was about more than classwork.

"Monsieur Drussard," said Simon as they came through the doorway and Pierre approached him. "What are you gentlemen up to tonight? Out and about?"

"Well, sir," said Lucien, "we're actually preparing for a debate with a representative from the southern provinces."

Pierre laughed. "We're going to have a drink with my friend, Jean Aicard."

"Ah yes, a fine writer," said Simon. "Pierre, we'll continue this conversation tomorrow and I'll look forward to your proposal." With that, the former prime minister of France spun on his heel and made his way smartly up the hall.

"Proposal?" exclaimed Lucien. "What scheme have you launched now?"

They left the Po and walked up rue de Guillaume to boulevard Saint-Germain, turned right, and walked two blocks to the Café de Flore.

Lucien's curiosity wouldn't relent. "On the way out, he had his arm around you like a son. Looks as if you know each other pretty well already."

"That's just the way he encourages us, Lucien. But it's true, he's taken an interest in an idea I have and we've had a good number of talks about it."

"You and the prime minister, eh? Talks?"

Coubertin stopped outside the café and looked up at the old church of Saint-Germain-des-Prés across the boulevard. "Yes, talks—the last one in his study with snifters of brandy. That's the purpose of the Po, isn't it? To put the best minds together?" He turned to walk in, but Lucien grabbed him.

"In his study?" Lucien's voice rose in surprise and competitive disappointment. This was clearly a victory for Pierre over all of his classmates. "What have you proposed?"

"Well, it's a simple idea, really. Since one of the missions of the Po is to carry on Taine's legacy, I've proposed an update to Taine's *Notes on England*—specifically the fourth chapter, his perspective on English education."

"Ah, that book is about twenty years old, isn't it? Do I sense a trip in the offing?"

"If I have the right papers, the right letters of introduction, I'll go this summer. I've already given Jules extensive notes about the points we should be investigating."

"Jules?" said Lucien, incredulous that they should be on a first-name basis.

"Yes, Jules," said Pierre, rubbing it in. "We share a view on the evolution of education, Lucien."

Lucien was left speechless as Pierre looked down the side street where the patrons left their horses and carriages. "Aha, there's Jean's horse," he said, pointing to a handsome bay. "Let's have some fun, my friend." Coubertin held the door of the café open for Lucien.

Aicard was waiting at the bar, just taking a glass of red wine from his lips when Pierre introduced them.

"Just as advertised, Lucien," Aicard said, smiling and squeezing Lucien's hand in a powerful grip. "As tall as a tree and as skinny as a twig."

Trying to squeeze back but losing the battle, Lucien took in the profusion of hair rising above Aicard's head in all directions, his glistening eyes, his rough riding pants and outdated redingote coat. Freeing his hand, he wondered what had possessed Pierre to form a friendship with such a man. "Good to meet you as well," he said, putting his hand behind his back to flex his fingers. "Pierre speaks highly of your writing and conversation, not to mention your riding."

"Indeed, thank you, Lucien. Pierre is a natural promoter," he said, handing them each a glass of red. "He tells me you can handle a horse as well, but we'll see about that on Sunday night if you care to join us in the promenade of the rich and promiscuous."

"Jean believes," said Pierre, lifting his glass in a toast, "in a theory, not yet proven, that the ladies in their carriages in the Bois on Sunday nights are there only to pluck men off their horses."

Jean laughed in a burst, and Lucien felt a jolt of electricity at the image of being pulled into the back of a big carriage by a beautiful countess in a fluffy gown. He quickly understood at least one aspect of Aicard's allure.

"I have a table for us near the kitchen door so we can keep an eye on the help," Jean said, taking the neck of a bottle in the same hand as his glass while he reached up to guide Lucien by the shoulder.

Once they were seated, Aicard abruptly began describing himself to Lucien, as if a further introduction were required. "I am a republican, Lucien, as I'm sure you've noted by my egalitarian openness. I like to mix with the hoi polloi and the nobility. I've discovered that a diversity of life experiences are essential to my craft as a writer."

"Ah yes," Lucien said, "the oft-proclaimed theory that there is no substitute for experience in writing. A notion I've long considered bereft of force—used by some writers to justify outlandish behavior."

"Perhaps that's because you have not yet had enough real-life experiences or because you don't know how to recognize true insight. What writers are you talking about?"

Pierre was leaning across the table with a wide grin on his face, clearly enjoying the early parry. He wasted no time in upping the ante. "Jean, you should know Lucien has a particular taste for the science fiction of Jules Verne and believes *Twenty Thousand Leagues Under the Sea* to be among the finest literary achievements."

Lucien tilted his head back with a confident smirk, proud of his literary predilections, but Aicard frowned, saying, "I won't go so far as to call science fiction an abomination. Jules Verne is not a bad man, but you cannot call that writing literature. It's nothing but postcards from imaginary worlds, children's fairy tales from a place no one will ever inhabit."

"Well then," Lucien said, lifting his glass diplomatically, "I'll tell Captain Nemo to scratch you from our next dive." Aicard and Coubertin laughed, and Lucien shifted away from further dispute. "We've found our first point of disagreement, but since our mutual friend here recognized that we have much in common, let us explore a more amenable subject."

"What did you have in mind?" Aicard asked, just as a young waitress arrived at the table with a basket of bread and a bottle of water.

They all glanced up, uttering, "Merci, mademoiselle," in unison. Lucien paused for a moment as she turned away, then said, "Women, Jean. I'd like to talk about women, a subject I understand you have a certain mastery of. As a younger man, I am always willing to learn."

○ ○ ○ ○ ○

As the night wore on and the wine flowed and the men bonded, Lucien felt as if he had been welcomed into a new fraternity of the gifted and raucous, a rough rider and a gentleman. While Pierre laughed rapturously at Aicard's raw force and bawdy eloquence, Lucien's thoughts turned back to the image of Jules Simon with his arm around a potential protégé. The contrast between that man and the one at the table fascinated him, and he wondered how to reconcile this moment of joie de vivre with the political import of Pierre's ambition.

"Pierre," he said, his tone serious, "are you going to tell us about the mission you and Jules Simon were discussing today?" Turning to Aicard, he added, "You should have seen the two of them, Jean, like father and son—the illustrious former prime minister of France with his arm around the shoulders of young Pierre."

"Sidling up to the powerful again, Pierre," said Aicard. "That's a predictable move for a representative of the recently deposed nobility."

"Well, I wouldn't say we're completely disenfranchised, my friend." Pierre sat back and stretched. "And I do believe the former prime minister, and perhaps the current one, share that view. Despite your desire to drag us away into debauchery, we may yet have some useful role to play in this floundering republic."

"Simon did seem enthused about your idea," Lucien asserted.

"Well, I'd say that Jules Simon, perhaps more than anyone else in France today, has the vision—and the connections—to help us define a new role for the nobility. As far as my idea goes, Lucien, it's a long way from fruition, but I'm certain I've captured his interest and believe I'll soon have his endorsement. He wants me to go meet William Henry Waddington."

"That's heady company—the ambassador to Great Britain," Aicard said. "I should say I'm not surprised. The drive of the nobility never wanes."

"If it's the drive of the nobility that's motivating Pierre, I'd say more power to him. We've only been at the Po for a year," Lucien said, "and no one else seems to have caught Simon's attention the way Pierre has. Waddington, for God's sake—that's a prime introduction."

"We'll see," said Coubertin. "It does hold some promise. Simon tells me he has quite a sports background—he attended Rugby and Cambridge."

○ ○ ○ ○ ○

In their second session, Lucien told St. Clair he had kept a journal in the 1880s and had reviewed a few entries in anticipation of these interviews. He took out a piece of paper and looked over some notes. "Jacques," he said, "there are three things I wanted to emphasize—three things I think are critical to understanding Pierre's motivation and determination in those days. The trip to Rugby and the vision he had there. The meeting with Gladstone that followed it. And—"

"Gladstone?" St. Clair looked up when he heard the name and interrupted Drussard. "William Gladstone, the British prime minister? Pierre met with him?"

"Yes, that William Gladstone," Drussard said, impatient to get his third point out. "And Victor Hugo's funeral, which, you may know, was the first state funeral orchestrated under the Third Republic."

"That's an intriguing set of events," St. Clair said. "I want to hear all the details."

"And I will provide them. But first, I want to make sure you have a real sense of the impact Pierre had on Simon and those around him."

"You said yesterday that Pierre had a force of personality that was undeniable."

"Yes, that's part of it. But it was the substance of his thinking. Even though he was young, he had a kind of authority based on the power of his ideas—and his ability to express them, I'd say. It was interesting to watch him mix with Simon and the other professors and government authorities outside the Po. He approached them all as equals, fearlessly, as if his ideas were at least as good as theirs. And they all responded as if he were their equal. Pierre could present his concepts with such force and conviction that you knew immediately they were going to succeed—and that it was important to work for their success.

"Even then, I had a sense we were going to make history—and I signed on to the cause wholeheartedly. We were going to reform the French education system together. There were only a few of us then, but the movement spread quickly, and Pierre began writing—and Simon eagerly read what he wrote. His second book, *L'Education Anglaise en France*, did far more than update Taine. That single publication gave us the power to reorganize French sport. Pierre saw the opportunity and seized the opening with a brilliant stroke—the formation of the Committee to Promote Sport and Physical Education in France."

"The Jules Simon Committee?"

"Yes, Simon was its titular head, but the power belonged to Pierre," Drussard said. "It gave us some authority over dozens of French sports associations, and it opened the door directly to Jules Ferry. Simon took Pierre to see him."

"Was Ferry prime minister at the time?"

"No. Ferry left office a year or two before. But he was head of the organizational effort for the 1889 Universal Exposition—and as it turned out, he and Simon wanted Pierre to help with their work organizing the exposition. They needed talent and energy—and Pierre was a font of both."

For the next few hours, St. Clair wrote steadily as the old man gave him one story after another—covering Simon, Waddington, Ferry, Rugby, Gladstone, and the Hugo funeral, each full of a few anecdotes and personal insights. Finally, his voice began to sound fatigued.

St. Clair looked up just as Drussard fingered his watch fob, checked the time, and said, "I've got to go, Jacques. It has been a great pleasure reliving these moments with you."

St. Clair assented even though he didn't want the conversation to end. He helped the old man out of his chair and they left the Lausanne Palace. Once they were outside, Drussard insisted on walking without assistance. Like a longtime athlete recovering his form, he stood upright, put more effort into his stride, and moved up the sidewalk toward the Place Saint-François with an air of certainty, his cane reaching out and clicking on the pavement with each step. The sky was gray and the cobbles wet, but Drussard was steady. He was on his way to a meeting with two men from the Union Cycliste Internationale and two others from the Fédération Internationale des Sociétés d'Aviron. Business as usual in Lausanne.

They stopped for a moment along the side of the church, out of the way of the swarm of passersby. Drussard leaned against the cold stone wall of the church and thought for a moment while St. Clair waited, knowing a few final thoughts were coming.

"What you're doing is important, Jacques," Drussard said. "It's important to tell Pierre's story so more people can understand what he has done for the world of sport."

"Thank you, Lucien. I appreciate the time you've given me—and I hope I can call on you for a little more if need be."

"Of course, Jacques, anytime."

They shook hands and St. Clair watched the lanky man in a suit and top hat walk slowly up the cobbles of rue de Bourg. He moved away deliberately, keeping his head tilted, eyes focused on the ground, gradually fading into the crowd as his top hat bobbed around the corner and out of sight.

Turning toward home, St. Clair thought about the frailties of memory and the tragedy of how in every moment of every day, the stories of the lives around us— some mundane, some heroic, some filled with passion, some with deceit—were being lost as the old and aging took their final steps into the night.

36

RUGBY, GLADSTONE, AND HUGO

On an early London morning in 1885, Pierre took an open cab to the Euston train station, tipped the coachman liberally, and called a porter to help with his portmanteau and two other black trunks. In first class, he watched the English countryside roll by as the sun burned the early-morning mist off the farm fields. Neatly tended hedgerows, fenced pastures against wooded glades, and wide, open green spaces with herds of cattle and sheep and horses in corrals flew by. The continuous stops at towns and villages such as Hemel Hempstead, Leighton Buzzard, Wolverton, and Long Buckby hardly broke his reverie.

He was fixed on his destination and an encounter he had long imagined, not a material meeting, but a connection with the spirit of the great man himself, Dr. Thomas Arnold. In the landscape of his mind, he saw the playing fields of Rugby School covered with teams of boys in whites and colorful school caps running and shouting. The cloaked figure of the doctor stood on the sidelines, watching in approval.

On the platform at the small brick station house, as a porter loaded his luggage onto a cart, Pierre admired the hand-carved script on the wooden sign that read Rugby. The name evoked something meaningful in his heart, linked as it was to the birth of a sport he loved, something that had occupied a fervent part of his dream life since he'd first encountered the story of Arnold's legend in *Tom Brown's School Days*, which appeared as a serial in the pages of *The Journal of Youth* when he was a fifteen-year-old at Saint-Ignace.

"So this was the second leg of a brief trip where you had planned to cover a group of boarding schools and universities?" St. Clair asked. "And what was your specific mission on this trip?"

Coubertin thought for a moment and said, "Yes, it was brief, but it was my third trip to England. I had already been to Eaton, Harrow, and Charterhouse. I'd also returned to London for a few dinners and meetings, and I was intending to go from Rugby on to Cambridge and Oxford, at minimum. It was the continuation of the research I was gathering for a book on English education—and its lessons for France."

"But your plans changed at Rugby?"

"It was a turning point, the realization of a new direction," Coubertin said. "I haven't had many experiences like that in my life. I discovered my true purpose in a flash of insight—and decided to go right back to London."

Coubertin quickly fell into a routine in Rugby, going to the school in the morning, holding interviews and appointments with the headmaster and various members of the staff, and observing the students exercise and play games in their gym classes. He spent his afternoons in the library and the archives, going through the records of Dr. Thomas Arnold's years. On the second day, he became fascinated by the notebooks of the schoolboys, who had recorded the invention of the game of rugby during a football match.

As Coubertin read, he absorbed the story. On a hot afternoon in the summer of 1833, a student named William Walter Ellis, frustrated with his inability to dribble the football as effectively as his mates, violated every rule of the game in a creative outburst. Picking up the ball, he ran toward the goal, past teammates and opponents who, excited by this break in decorum, chased him down and tackled him. Within several years, the students of School House, including the son of the headmaster, Matthew Arnold—destined to write world-famous poetry—recorded and revised the rules of the new game of rugby on the lined pages of a workbook.

Examining the original penciled script of that first set of rules, Coubertin marveled at how such simple shifts in a game played with a ball on a field of grass between two goals could open a seemingly infinite number of options and appeal to boys with different talents, body types, and aspirations.

It was inspiring to imagine schoolboys given the liberty to invent a new game out of an established tradition. What freedom, thought Pierre. What a brilliant atmosphere to cultivate for learning.

As he finished his writing that afternoon, he felt as he often did at the end of a fruitful day of discovery. He felt the urge to run. He went back to his hotel, changed, and set out on the five-mile cross-country course the classes used, gaining new perspectives on the campus and the glades beyond. The next day, he participated in two games of football and a game of rugby with the boys, then treated himself to a fine dinner in town that night.

○ ○ ○ ○ ○

On his fourth day in Rugby, on his way to School House, the first building on the campus, Coubertin walked up High Street, passing the bakery and shops already teeming with customers—the shopkeepers began to look familiar and offered nods of recognition to the French gentleman passing by. He gazed up at the crenelated towers of School House, which evoked memories of King Arthur and the Knights of the Roundtable. He knew the boys loved Sir Walter Scott and the literary heroes he embedded in England's storied past. Walking through the gates, Coubertin crossed the small School House courtyard where Dr. Arnold had played games of "fives" with the students. A few boys were heading to class—neatly dressed in blue jackets and neckties with book bags over their shoulders. On the groomed lawns behind the buildings, Coubertin beheld again the same scene he had seen on his first two mornings at Rugby: boys in their whites scattered in groups, squads, teams, and classes across the great open fields of play—dashing after balls, shouting at one another, halting at the whistles of their referees, and tackling forcefully at the instructions of their coaches. Another team of boys was emerging from the field house on the far left, lining up for morning stretches and calisthenics as their coach pointed to the formation from his perch at the top of the steps.

The voices that rose at a distance were faint, but their tone carried the joy that the boys of Rugby were feeling at that moment—as voices had from the fields of every school he had visited, just like the voices of young men at university. On the fields of play, the pressures of the classroom bled away, the stress of studies, discipline, and deadlines faded to the sidelines as the joy of effort—a phrase Coubertin would patent as his own—took hold and the youngsters reveled in the physical delight of play, drawing inspiration from the heart and soul of sport.

Under a cloudless morning sky, the scene before him captured the essence of English school sport. It was as if the whole town were an arena. The tradition of sport seemed to bleed into the red brick of the field house on the left, the larger gymnasium on the right, and across the roads into the Victorian buildings on campus and the houses of the townspeople beyond. The sounds of sport were as natural here as the beds of flowers at Coubertin's feet, which ran along the road to the back of Rugby Chapel. He gazed at the chapel, its tower encasing the bell that would call the boys to devotion later in the day—a place consecrated in his imagination by the memory of the greatest English educator of all. It was fitting, he thought at that moment, that the chapel stood at the top of the great sporting field like a citadel over a kingdom, with the king himself, Thomas Arnold, resting beneath the cold stones of its foundation.

As he walked onto the still-wet field, heading toward an appointment with a rugby coach and young team captain, Pierre made a note to return to examine the chapel later.

○ ○ ○ ○ ○

At the end of the day, under a sky streaked with beams of orange and red from the western horizon, Coubertin walked along the fence on Baby Road. The retreat was under way on the great green expanse, with boys trotting back toward the field house, the games of the day settled until tomorrow. Across the way, he looked at the classic façade of the library, its peaked dormers and arched windows framed in white stone and patterned red brickwork.

Reaching the top of the green and the Queen's Gate, where Victoria herself had once entered the sporting lawns of Rugby, Coubertin turned along the walled road to the rear of the chapel. The services were long over now, and the chapel would be empty. He stopped for a moment to take in the design of the new church tower, which had recently been completed in 1882. It rose in alternating bands of red-and-orange brick and white stone that reached for the sky in a conical peaked belfry with three arched openings on each side. The back of the chapel was dominated by stained-glass windows that mixed the story of Christ with the heritage of England in the finest mythological traditions.

At the base of the tower, a small door was set into the buttress, which Coubertin knew was the door by which the headmaster entered to access the pulpit directly and deliver his messages to the assembled class. Pushing the door open, he stepped into the still, quiet sanctuary of Arnold's past, looking over rows of pews split by the center aisle. The walls were inset with gray headstones bearing the names and epitaphs of the generations of distinguished men who had passed through the halls of Rugby. The silence of the chapel was the august sound of tribute, tradition, and hallowed memories.

A small set of stairs curved up to the elevated pulpit on the right of the chancel. Coubertin left his satchel in a pew and stepped into the pulpit, overlooking the room where a giant of education had first expressed his philosophy, where the holistic ideal of body, mind, and spirit had reached a modern pinnacle early in Arnold's career. He imagined the scene of the boys listening in anticipation to the esteemed man's oratory—so clearly evoked in *Tom Brown's School Days*.

Coubertin laid his arms on the podium where Arnold would have placed his notes, noticing for the first time that the lectern was a wooden carving with the head, breast, and wings of an eagle facing the congregants, its back an open board with a shelf for papers. The ideas pronounced here were meant to soar from the wings of the bird—a metaphor any boy would recognize.

Earlier that afternoon, Coubertin had read a brief summary of Arnold's philosophy, handed to him by one of the coaches he was interviewing. It stated that Arnold's first objectives were the cultivation of religious and moral principles, followed by the code of gentlemanly conduct, and then, and only then, the development of full intellectual ability. In the world Arnold created at Rugby—a model of education that was destined to sweep across England and around the world in a wave of influence—the pursuit of ideals and ideas were balanced so that the boy became a fully rounded man, aware of his responsibilities and his abilities in the wide scope of life. A motto appeared at the end of the paper that portrayed the character of the ideal student as Arnold saw him: "He awakes every morning as if everything is an open question."

Wondering if he could follow in Arnold's footsteps and add innovation to innovation, Coubertin looked down and saw a name engraved in the granite floor just a few yards from the altar. Stepping down from the pulpit, he walked over to examine the inscription. Sir Thomas Arnold, it read, and Pierre felt a surge of inspiration as he looked up at the cross suspended over the altar. At that moment, he felt something like a wave of heat rise through his body. His face flushed and he yearned to hear the headmaster's voice.

The room darkened a shade as the light dropped away behind the stained glass, and the silent atmosphere deepened as he looked down again at Arnold's name engraved in the worn granite. He kneeled to touch the stone, his fingers tracing the shallow letter forms. Suddenly he remembered his father kneeling beside him as a boy in the Church of Santa Maria in Aracoeli in Rome, his fingers feeling the name of his ancestor, Felice di Fredi, in the cold headstone—and the sensation of that memory rushed at him again. A realization swept over him that he was on his knees at that very moment before his destiny, that the longing in his heart had led him here, and that a calling had been waiting in this chapel at the intersection of his desire and Arnold's legacy.

He stood and looked again at the cross, the eagle over the pulpit, and the complex beauty of the intricate woodwork of the ceilings. He had a heightened sense of the importance of this tradition and the integration of spiritual values, of a code of conduct and educational ethics at the heart of sport. He knew he was standing on the threshold of a new age of sport and knew as well, with even more certainty, that he was standing in its very cradle. He knew now he had discovered the essence of his mission, a mission rooted in education reform but fueled with the rising power of sport.

As Coubertin walked out of the chapel that day, he felt as if he had discovered the direction his life was meant to take. At last, he understood the root of the ambiguous longing he had felt in his heart for so long. He knew now that he wanted to import the joy of sport into the schools of France—and he reflected on how much better his own education would have been if only Saint-Ignace had had a great green on rue de Madrid. He knew beyond any doubt he would have excelled at the games boys played. But he knew with even more certainty that his classmates would have discovered something else, something vital about themselves when they raced out of their locker rooms, left their studies behind, and began to learn what their bodies where capable of when freed from the constraints of the classroom. They would have learned the great lessons of teamwork, cooperation, self-sacrifice for the greater good. There was no reason why the boys of France should not have that experience in school—and so many reasons why they should.

When Pierre returned to his room, he found a telegram from Simon: "Gladstone has agreed to see you on Thursday. Check in with Ambassador Waddington in London."

He could hardly believe the timing. This was providence. He was going to see the prime minister of Great Britain, not for the purpose of the interview he had originally asked Simon to arrange, but now to present his theories on the core civil strengths of the British Empire. He began to pack immediately, wondering how he would ever thank Simon for arranging this meeting—and for having this much confidence in him. He was only twenty-two, after all.

"How did Jules Simon convince Gladstone to see you?" St. Clair asked, curious about the connection.

"They had been prime ministers at the same time nearly a decade earlier. They'd interacted regularly on international affairs and developed something of a strategic partnership, which, Jules told me, became a genuine friendship. But it went sour, as so many political relationships do, in a disagreement over colonial conflicts. Nevertheless, Simon put the request in at my urging—through our British Embassy. I went there, hoping to meet Waddington, but he had unexpectedly left for Paris that morning."

"And Gladstone still accepted the appointment with you?"

"I had a feeling he saw it as a simple gesture, a step in the restoration of a once valuable relationship."

"Where did you meet?"
"At the office Gladstone kept at Westminster."

○ ○ ○ ○ ○

On the train back to London, Coubertin wrote furiously, melding his theories about Britain's character into a cogent argument he intended to present to Gladstone, an argument that contained the best of everything he had observed on his visits to Eton, Harrow, Charterhouse, Winchester, Wellington, Rugby, Oxford, Cambridge, Kings, and a half dozen other places he had investigated. His idea was that games that took root in those preparatory schools grew into sporting traditions at the universities—and from there extended their worth and influence into the very foundations of the British character, the core strength of the Empire, the building blocks of society and social integration. What Arnold had built was not a system, not a factory, not an educational enterprise; it was a state of mind rooted in the muscle of the nation, the collective muscle of every individual deployed not with brute strength, but with the values of cooperation, interaction, and respect that shaped the particular qualities of England's civil society.

Gladstone was the most prominent and resolute political authority on Britain's preeminence and civil stability. Now serving his second term as prime minister, he was a bulwark of tradition and one of the most forceful leaders on the global stage. Coubertin breathed deeply, still amazed at the honor and the opportunity to present his theories to such a political giant.

Later that day, having passed through a legion of secretaries, assistants, and administrators, all of whom seemed to cast accusing glances at him, Coubertin was ushered into a surprisingly small office. He found himself alone with His Premiership, who was too busy with paperwork to look up from a massive desk, but seemed to signal with the flourish of a pen that his guest should take a seat.

Coubertin sat and looked across the desk. It was hard not to stare in fascination at the familiar overweight figure with the oft-caricatured visage. His face was creased in a permanent frown, with two large folds dropping from the bridge of his large pugnacious nose to the corners of his downturned mouth. His skin was embedded with deep thought lines, a grid imprinted by the stress of bearing the cares of an empire across a fifty-year career, and his willowy white hair fell away from his pate, shooting out this way and that, not quite unkempt but almost too fine to be held in place with a brush. His demeanor was impatient—he was obviously not a man given to smiles—but when he finally looked up his eyes shined with true intensity, and his presence, like a living monument of Victorian might, made it an honor to share the room with him. He spoke before the exchange of courtesies.

"Simon is doing well, I take it, enjoying his years behind the rostrum, lecturing the future republicans on how life should be lived?"

"Yes, he is fine and appreciates his stature as elder statesman at the Sorbonne and the École Libre. He sends his best regards."

Gladstone grunted. "Hard to fathom why, after ten years without a word, he thought he could call on the spot and gain an audience for an acolyte."

Coubertin ignored the slight and spoke with all the power and authority he could muster, trying to steady the quaver in his voice. "He knew you would either confirm or reject a theory I've developed, a philosophical position on how the core strength of the national character of Great Britain was formed—and formed in turn the foundational might of the British Empire."

"He assumed I'd be interested in your theory?"

Coubertin tried not to flinch as he emphasized the superiority of England over France. "I've developed a theory about the formation of the personal and social strengths of a nation that built the world's most civilized society while expanding its unrivaled hold on a growing global economy—all at a time when my country went through four revolutions, three monarchies, and two empires, finally falling into a republic, nearly by default. I have been searching for the key to your country's admirable stability."

"Very well, let's hear this theory of yours, then."

Coubertin laid out his thoughts on the brief but seminal career of Thomas Arnold, describing the direct lineage of Arnold's character-building curricula, the self-determination and teamwork ethic he implemented, and its immediate and vast spread across the campuses of England's school system. Coubertin defined the character of a modern Englishman in Arnold's terms: spiritual, muscular, cultural, sociable, and ready to work for the greater good while playing a role in the nation's destiny. He drew distinctions between the antiseptic and intellectually driven classrooms of France and the Hellenistic whole-man development of English education. Without pausing, he summarized his theory that it was the character-building nature of competitive sport in the schools that contributed, perhaps above all else, to the stability of English society and the ease with which each new generation of British leaders and workers were acculturated and assumed their place in the social order. When he finished, Coubertin felt as if he had done justice to his ideas and had effectively held the great man in the spell of his rhetorical logic.

Gladstone ruminated and looked away, raised a hand to his forehead and rubbed the corners of his skull. He picked up his pen, opened an appointment book, and flipped the page to the next day. Coubertin could see that the agenda was packed with one meeting after another, but Gladstone carefully put a line through an 11:15 appointment and wrote Coubertin into the crowded space left.

"Plan to be back here tomorrow at 11:15 for a brief discussion. I'm intrigued by what you've said, but I want to give it some reflection and discuss it with a friend. On the surface, it appears to be valid, but it's a new idea, at least to me, and original enough to merit full consideration."

And then he bellowed, "Farnsworth!" The door opened almost immediately, and one of his assistants strode in.

"Sir," he said.

"I'm postponing the meeting with Perry tomorrow to accommodate Mr. Coubertin's busy schedule," he said.

"Yes, sir."

With a dismissive wave, he bent back to his desk, but as Coubertin moved to leave, he looked up and said, "Give my best regards to Jules, and tell him he has a standing invitation to dinner when he's next in London."

The following day, the meeting was terse but fully satisfying as Gladstone complimented Coubertin on the originality of his observations and the ideas he presented. The prime minister said simply, "I believe your theory is wholly accurate, and you can move forward with the data you've developed."

As Coubertin walked back to his hotel that afternoon and approached the court of St. James, he could hardly escape the notion that destiny had somehow touched his life. With seeming ease, the doors had opened to one British and two French prime ministers, each of whom in turn had encouraged his vision and his work. Although he was still at the very beginning of his journey into education reform, the notion that he had been chosen for this particular mission rose in his thoughts and stayed in his consciousness for some time, and he remembered the words of Father Caron as he left Saint-Ignace: "Yes, you can search for your life's work, Pierre, but if it's a calling, it will find you."

○ ○ ○ ○ ○

Coubertin took Gladstone's advice. He moved forward, filling notebooks with ideas for how to adapt Britain's schoolboy sports to the French education system. By the time he returned to Paris, he had the makings of a full manuscript in hand. In writing it, he had followed Taine's lead, taking up where Taine had left off and trying to define for himself the theories about the nature and benefits of physical education—basic ideas about sport at school, how it should be organized, how much of England's system—*le régime Arnoldian*, as he named it—should be adapted wholesale, and what parts should be modified. He looked back on what Victor Duruy had done with the modest introduction of physical exercises into the French curriculum under the Second Empire, but it was all military exercises, and those weren't suitable or inspiring or character building in Coubertin's opinion.

Like Arnold, he wanted to find a formula to give boys some freedom to organize their own events—and he longed for the competition that comes only from games. The German methods of mass calisthenics, which the Turner movement had launched and Friedrich Ludwig Jahn had turned into a social force, only led, in Coubertin's assessment, to social conformity—and not to free creative thought. His reasoning constantly led back to the conclusion that Arnold was right—and that Arnold's ideas were right for France. Coubertin felt a wave of patriotism as he thought about delivering to French children the spirit and wonder of life he had first encountered in the serialized stories of *Tom Brown's School Days*.

For the next month, he concentrated on preparing the full draft of a book for Jules Simon's review. He was intent on getting Simon to embrace what he had written—perhaps even pen an introduction for him. He knew one of the keys to reaching Simon was to position the work on the foundation of what Taine had written in *Notes sur l'Angleterre*. There was no shadow of doubt in the convictions Coubertin had developed about what French education really needed. It was all there in Taine, clearly framed and ready for development. He wrote out in careful cursive a summary of the best passages of Taine and pinned the paragraph on the wall of his room:

> The English pupils have at the most six working hours a day, in contrast we have eleven, which is not sensible. A good part of the day is spent in the open air, without any kind of sequestration, the boys going free in the fields, waters, and woods. An adolescent needs physical exercises. It is against nature to force him to be all brain, a sedentary bookworm. In England, athletic games, fives, football, running, rowing and, above all, cricket take up a part of every day. Pride plays an important part; each school tries to beat its rivals and sends teams of players and oarsmen, picked out and trained, to play and row against the others.

When Simon read through the first hundred pages of Coubertin's book, he said, "It's time to meet Hippolyte Taine and get his advice on where to go next."

A few days later they took a carriage together to Taine's house in the Latin Quarter. The old man was fading and didn't rise from his chair, which sat in a recessed bay of windows with three chairs in a semicircle facing him across a round tea table. Knowing he was in part preaching to the choir, Coubertin began his brief with the mandate to establish equality if not an equivalency between physical and intellectual education in all French schools—public and private. He paid tribute to Taine's early observations and gave the old intellectual an overview of the potential of student associations, fields, pools, and gymnasiums built at schools across France. He outlined a program of training for coaches, rules to guide each sport, and basic criteria for legislation that would ensure access for every child, not just the privileged. When he wrapped up, Taine breathed deeply, looked to Simon, and said, "Finally, the energy of the next generation applying itself to our ideas."

Basically embracing everything Coubertin proposed, Taine turned the discussion to ideas for popularizing sport across the country, and they talked about it without coming to any conclusions. Taine closed the meeting by asking Simon and Coubertin to return on Sunday for the salon he and his wife hosted, saying he wanted to give Pierre a chance to express his ideas before an audience of people who might not be so sympathetic, but who might help him promote it if they embraced it.

As they took the carriage back to the Po, it was clear to Pierre that they had established the makings of a significant partnership in education reform. It was a heady day for Coubertin and a good day for Simon as well, who told Pierre he felt he had helped launch the career of a protégé with enormous potential. He already had several ideas for how to apply Coubertin's energy and talents to other aspects of his current work.

Within a matter of months, Coubertin's essays on sport and education were appearing in Le Play's publication, *Le Réforme Sociale*, major papers, and sport magazines. Coubertin even launched his own publication, *Le Revue Sport*, and managed to turn out about sixty pages a month, almost all in his own hand. As the ideas flowed, the direction of his mission clarified.

○ ○ ○ ○ ○

In May of 1885, France fell into a state of national mourning when Victor Hugo died. There was a palpable sense of loss in every one of Coubertin's circles. His father and Jules Simon, political opposites, both praised Hugo's contribution to French culture and his uncompromising principles.

"He had integrity," said Charles de Coubertin, turning from a painting to look at his son, who had come up to the studio with a copy of *Figaro* in his hand, the headline mourning the loss of a French hero. "Any man who would leave France for Guernsey just to protest the pretender to the throne is a man of great character."

"They're going to give him a state funeral," Pierre said, "a public procession from the Arc de Triomphe to the Panthéon, where he'll be interred."

Charles looked out the window at the Golden Dome of Les Invalides. "The Panthéon? Well, he was a great writer—and in France ideas are worshipped."

Later that day, Coubertin saw Simon in his office at the Sorbonne, where he also lectured. "He was a great republican above all else," Simon said. Hugo had served in the parliament of the Third Republic after returning from his self-imposed exile. "And I always admired his poetry. *Les Contemplations* are masterful. But *Les Misérables* and *Notre-Dame*," he said, shaking his head, "entertaining—but filled with too much pathos for my taste."

"I enjoyed all of it," Coubertin said. "He deserves the Panthéon. 'To the great men, the grateful homeland.'"

"Yes, it's good to add to the creative intellectual representation among the *hommes d'honneur*," Simon said. "I've been invited to walk behind the casket. Would you like to join me?"

Coubertin was stunned by the invitation—another affirmation of Simon's personal commitment to him, but he had planned to attend with Jennette and Jean. "Of course, it would be an honor. Could I bring a few friends?"

"Certainly. Give me the names and I'll add them to the registry for the honor procession."

○ ○ ○ ○ ○

Pierre was amazed at the scene before him as he, Jennette, Jean Aicard, and Lucien Drussard made their way through the crowd to an area the gendarmerie had roped off for dignitaries. To honor this son of France, the Grévy administration had draped the Arc de Triomphe in an enormous black muslin shroud. As if to signal that all the glories of this day belonged to a poet, Napoleon's charioteers on top of the Arc were completely wrapped in black. Like a cape spilling over the shoulder of a soldier at attention, the black scarf covered the left side of the Arc. Inside the great arch, above the *catafalque* on which Hugo's body rested, stood a three-story cistern, a handsome, shiny vessel of honor as beautiful as any small ornamental vase, topped with a rising finial. It was filled, Coubertin assumed, not with the ashes of a lost soul, but with the national treasury of Hugo's stories. Jean was stopped at the entry by a gendarme, but after some confusion, they were admitted as the procession began to form. They lined up, arm in arm, a few rows behind Simon and a throng of republican politicians on the plaza west of the Arc's grand passage. At the front, behind a corps of flag bearers, two black horses began to pull a massive black hearse draped in honorific curtains down the *Champs-Élysées*. Pierre exchanged solemn nods with Simon, Jules Ferry, and William Henry Waddington, whom he still hadn't met, all standing in a line of former prime ministers just behind the current one, Henri Brisson, and the president, Jules Grévy. It seemed the entire parliament was out in force for the revered man's funeral, and the Champs was lined on both sides with crowds deeper than anyone had ever seen. Every window and balcony was packed with people straining to catch a glimpse of the hearse. The next day, newspapers would report that more than two million had turned out to pay their respects.

A stage had been built on the front steps of the Panthéon and was festooned with black drapes and flags. Grandstands encircled most of the plaza out front as the carriage bearing Hugo's corpse pulled up to the stage. Leaving Simon and his group to the VIP seats on stage, Pierre led Jennette and his friends up to the top row of the closest stands. They stood in place as trumpets sounded a fanfare and the coffin, covered in the Tricolor—the republican flag—was pulled from the hearse and borne up a ramp and onto the stage by a group of writers that included Émile Zola and Anatole France. People pushed and squeezed into the Panthéon's plaza, and rue Soufflot was quickly closed off as the crowds stretched all the way back to the fence at the Luxembourg Gardens.

"Even the realists and opinion makers bow before the old poet," said Aicard, watching Zola and the other pallbearers take their seats on the stage.

Lucien leaned over and spoke to Jennette. "Are you going to illustrate this scene?"

"Yes, of course," she said. "I'm working on a new drawing of Hugo for *Figaro*. I'm going to portray him as a hero—and honor him."

"And what about the politicians standing with him right now?" asked Coubertin.

"They'll get a pass today," she said. "They're picking up a little of Hugo's reflected glory."

As the speeches began, Coubertin realized that seeing the leaders of the Third Republic stand together to pay their respects to a writer did, indeed, enhance their stature in his eyes. He believed a society with these kinds of values, a society that put artistic expression at the height of its culture—such a society had a future worth building. Hugo was worthy of the full measure of their respect, of course. His voice had lifted the spirits of France in the midst of some of its most devastating times. In some ways, his stories preserved hope for the next generations. They were written to elevate and protect the rights of man—every man.

When the Tricolor rose to half-mast in honor of Hugo's life, Coubertin felt a new wave of patriotism sweep over him. He wanted to lift the Tricolor as a banner over his own cause—a cause that would take the education experience of French children to a new level of openness and joy, an initiative he was certain Hugo would have embraced.

Later that night, as they sat in a bar on Saint-Germain remembering Hugo's life and work, the toasts flowed freely. "He was a sentimental bastard but he was a great man," Aicard said, holding out his glass of Pernod so they could all toast, looking at each of them in turn.

"Victor Hugo may have died, but romanticism is still alive," Coubertin said.

37

THE PAINTING

With Messerli's help, Juliette had secured a small painting studio with slanted windows built into the mansard roof of a building near the cathedral. The windows looked out at the Gothic tower of the great church and captured the north light to her satisfaction. At her direction, two workmen had built a two-step platform against the back wall and hung a long pipe from the ceiling so she could drape it with various backdrops. She had several rolls of cream, pink, yellow, blue, and red cloth stacked behind the stage, and she chose a cerulean velvet for the day, saying it would make Pierre's skin tones richer. The workmen brought up a Louis XVI chair that she had found in an antique shop. It was nicely cushioned and covered with a golden brocaded fleur-de-lis pattern, tightly tacked into a finely carved wood frame. The chair sat in the middle of the low stage, offering a perfect view of the cathedral, which was only partially obstructed by the large canvas Juliette mounted on her easel.

An old couch covered with a thick chenille bedspread and a few throw pillows sat in the corner. All Juliette's brushes, paints, knives, and rags were stuffed into a small taboret, and she completed the furnishings with a mirrored sideboard and two floor lamps in the sparse white room.

On the afternoon of Pierre's first sitting, which Juliette had set for two to three hours, Jacques and Juliette made their way up the hill and finished the preparations together. Jacques brought a hot plate and a pot for coffee, some baguettes, cheese, and a bottle of wine.

It was a short if steep walk up from Mon Repos but Coubertin turned up on time, bowler already in hand. He was dressed in a brown wool suit with a waistcoat and tie, his white hair neatly groomed, his thick mustache flaring wide.

"Welcome to the Atelier Franklin," Juliette said, extending her hand in an exaggerated gesture. Coubertin bowed to kiss it.

"So good to see you again, Mademoiselle Artiste," the baron intoned, using a new pet name.

"I hope you don't mind that I'm allowing Jacques to sit in on our first session," she said as St. Clair stepped up. "I thought we would talk, and he so loves to take notes."

"Not at all," Coubertin said, winking at St. Clair as they shook hands, seeing his notebook already lying open on the couch.

Juliette extended her arm and turned the baron toward the stage, explaining what she intended to accomplish first. With a jaunty step, Pierre danced up onto the stage and twirled around the chair. St. Clair noted once again the effect Juliette had on him. He was immediately more animated than usual in her presence. He liked her because she was forward and direct in the manner of most Americans, and because she was beautiful, flirtatious, intelligent, and young. Her storied performance as the Duchess of Langeais at Messerli's party had locked in his appreciation, and now she could do no wrong.

Jacques knew from comments Coubertin had made that the quality of her painting, which he had politely refused to judge, mattered less to him than the opportunity to interact with her. Although the baron had expressed some hope that this portrait, coming so late in life, might be worthy of hanging in the halls of an Olympic Museum at some future date, St. Clair knew he didn't expect the kind of classical work his father might have rendered.

St. Clair had the coffee heated, and they chatted for a while before Juliette insisted they begin, instructing Pierre on the position she wanted. "Can you turn the chair and your body a little more to the left?" she asked, and Coubertin complied.

As she drew an outline of the scene in pencil first, she began a conversation that ultimately led to an Olympic interview as effective as most that St. Clair had conducted—because Coubertin responded to her with a more pronounced spontaneity. But to begin with, the baron had a few questions of his own.

"Juliette, may I ask about your family and Philadelphia?" he said, not looking at her, but keeping his head and eyes fixed on the cathedral's tower rising against the sky, just as she had instructed.

"Of course! But you're going to have to answer my questions as well."

"Fair enough. I'm very interested to know if you are descended from the great Benjamin Franklin."

"Why? Do you a see a resemblance?"

He laughed, and so did St. Clair. "Your beauty gives no hint of a connection," he said, "but the name and the city do."

"My mother always said that Benjamin Franklin was a distant cousin, and my brother, Allen, told everyone at the University of Penn that Ben—he was the only one in the family who called him Ben—was a full-blooded uncle, but I never saw any proof of ancestry."

"Tell me about your family and your education," the baron said, "and how you made your way to Paris—and then into the unfortunate embrace of a sports journalist."

St. Clair grunted from the couch, "Sports journalism is both a modern and prestigious occupation, my good sir. I seem to recall that you once counted yourself among its practitioners."

"Well, yes, as a hobby," said Coubertin, dutifully looking out the window.

"We'll hold the story of how this French rascal got my attention to the end, if you don't mind, Pierre," she said.

"The floor is yours, mademoiselle."

Sketching and looking back and forth from the canvas to Pierre as she talked, Juliette recited a narrative she had delivered to Jacques and friends a good number of times since they had met. "I grew up in Bryn Mar, a lovely leafy community on Philadelphia's Main Line. My father had English roots and was a banker. He took the train into Philly every day and worked in Center City, a few blocks from city hall."

"In the shadow of William Penn?"

"Yes—you know Philadelphia?" Juliette sounded surprised by the reference to the statue of William Penn that stood on the pinnacle of the great clock tower of city hall.

"Only through a friend from Princeton who showed me some of its remarkable architecture. And your mother?"

"My mother was born in the Pocono Mountains in northeastern Pennsylvania and hailed from a Welsh family of coal miners. But she was a beauty with artistic talent and found her way to the Philadelphia Academy of Fine Arts— where I went as well. It's just a few blocks south of my father's office."

"Ah, so that's where they met," Pierre said, listening intently.

"Actually, they met after a play at the Walnut Street Theater. My father was in the audience and my mother was on stage. She started out as a painter but had a certain dramatic flair and had always dreamed of being an actress."

"Does that explain your costumed performance as the Duchess of Langeais?"

Juliette smiled. "Perhaps it does. She acted for five years before my father talked her into the Main Line family life—and they had Allen, then me and my brother Matthew all within six years. She never returned to the stage, but she didn't regret it. Her life was very full, and they traveled frequently to Europe." Juliette paused for a moment, concentrating on the sketch. "But back to your question about the duchess," she said. "I hadn't thought of this before, but my mother kept a closet of all the costumes she had worn on stage, and she and I would often put on little shows for the family. I loved all the finery in that closet. It was pure happiness for me and my childhood friends—little girls dressing up."

"Were you drawn to the theater as well?"

"I only wanted to paint. My mother often said she could act far better than she could paint. For me, the dramatic temptation was never that strong. All the painters I knew in Philadelphia wanted to go Paris—and I did too. I think it started with Thomas Eakins, who graduated from my school around the middle of the nineteenth century and immediately went to study at the École des Beaux-Arts."

"Obviously a very intelligent man," said St. Clair from the couch, a bit bored with the story.

"So there I was in the Luxembourg Gardens, just a month into my Paris swoon, trying to do a great painting of the Medici Fountain, when this handsome young Frenchman on a bicycle started showing up every morning riding circles around me as I walked the paths for exercise."

"So it was sport that brought you together," Pierre said with a laugh.

Juliette laughed coquettishly. "Well, a kind of sport, yes," she said, smiling at Jacques. "Are you tired yet, Pierre?" she asked.

"No, I'm fine," he said. He was still sitting up straight, not yet leaning back or slouching.

The talk went on for another hour, diverted by Juliette to Pierre's memories of his own childhood and the theater life of Paris when he was young. As she shaped an image of Pierre's face in pencil on the canvas, he recalled puppet shows and sailboats in the Luxembourg Gardens and secret games in fields with the coachman's son, Markus. Jacques made notes to circle back on these subjects as Juliette explained she'd want him to sit for her in three-hour sessions at least two or three more times. Finally, she broached the subject St. Clair knew she had wanted to ask him about.

"Pierre, I know you and Jacques have talked about it, but do you mind if I ask you a few questions about the Olympics?"

"Not at all."

"I'm still not clear on how it all began—where exactly did the idea to start the Olympic Games again come from?"

"Aha," he said, "so you'll be doing Jacques's work today. The journalistic instinct has obviously rubbed off."

"She keeps telling me she wants to interview you, Pierre," Jacques said, rising to look at her canvas. "Painting alone is not enough."

Juliette shooed him away, pointing the tip of her pencil at his face.

"Everybody always wants to know the exact moment of revelation," Coubertin said, "the instant of creation. But the idea came from a dozen sources, maybe more. It was in the air."

"And on the ground," Jacques said.

"Yes, that's true." Coubertin elaborated on a few points from a history he knew by heart. "There were several attempts to resurrect the Games, all local or national. A rich industrialist in Greece, Evangelos Zappas, left an endowment to produce new editions of the Olympic Games in Athens—just for Greeks. His heirs organized four Olympics between 1859 and 1890, but they were always a struggle and couldn't be sustained. The Swedes had actually produced Olympian Games as early as the seventeenth century, and the British had had several editions of the Cotswold Olimpick Games under Robert Dover in the 1600s, but they faded as well. The most successful effort was mounted by a gifted doctor and most generous English gentleman, William Penny Brookes, in the countryside village of Much Wenlock in the west near the border of Wales. He held Olympian Games from the early 1850s into the 1890s. He staged a national competition in the name of the Olympics at the Crystal Palace during the 1866 exhibition, but never again reached beyond his village. I met him through my first international sport survey in 1888, and he invited me to the Olympian Games in 1890, where I was honored to present awards to several victors. In fact, it was from Dr. Brookes that I learned of the Zappas Olympics and his earlier efforts; neither were widely known."

"So that's where the idea actually came from—and it was two years later, right, when you first proposed the Olympic Games?"

"No and yes," Pierre said. "The idea for an Olympic Games in France had been proposed by both Georges de Saint-Clair, a close colleague in the early days, and more vociferously by my archrival in the French sports movement, Paschal Grousset—around 1886 and 1887—which is when I first began to discuss it as well. So it was in the air well before the good Dr. Brookes responded to my survey. And yes, I did deliver my first proposal to resurrect the Games in 1892, but it failed miserably. That failure was, however, the genesis of the rebirth of the Games that followed in 1894."

"You had an archrival?" Juliette asked.

Pierre puffed his lips, exhaled loudly, and shook his head. "I'm afraid that's an understatement. Grousset was more than an archrival. He was a cold-blooded enemy—the first in a long line of enemies who opposed and challenged and buffeted me publicly at every stage of the quest to turn the Olympic Games into the international movement they eventually became."

"Well, we're going to have to hear all about this Monsieur Grousset—and all those other enemies—aren't we? But I'm still curious about the origins of your idea for the Olympic Games—Jacques told me you were defensive in your *Olympic Memoirs*, claiming it was all your idea."

Casting a glance toward the sofa, Coubertin said, "Yes, I was defensive. It was a reaction to the fact that during the entire celebration of our first Olympic Games in Athens in 1896, there was not a single acknowledgment or moment of public recognition that I had anything at all to do with the rebirth of the Games. It was humiliating for me and a grave disappointment for Marie. And then claims emerged over the years from various pretenders—and I did want to assert my claim as the sole author."

"But what about Dr. Brookes?" Juliette asked. This time, Coubertin moved in response. He turned and looked at her, then Jacques, and she stopped drawing and stepped out from behind the canvas.

"I doubt the controversies will ever go away," he said. "But it wasn't simply the idea of putting on a sporting event. It was resurrecting an ancient festival whose moral and social influence over society, and even more, over Hellenic civilization, had once been far greater than any institution we know today— perhaps as influential in its time as the church was during the Middle Ages."

Coubertin paused as Juliette went back to the canvas—and he spoke with some emotion and force. "My conception of the Games was never as a sporting event alone, but as a movement of sport driven by values that would help produce a better world …" he paused. "I think you've heard the story already."

When St. Clair finished his notes, he looked up and said, "The international concept of rotating the Games from country to country, or rather city to city, was yours alone, wasn't it?"

"Yes, that was my idea," Coubertin said, "but in some ways that's also a bit misleading. It wasn't just the idea, it was the work that made all the difference— and the work was hard and endless. When I was young, I held my own but as I aged, I was no match for the forces or power struggles the Olympics unleashed."

The light began to fade in the late afternoon as the first long portrait session drew to an end. Pierre began to lean forward, little by little, and had to straighten his back and shoulders every so often to escape the obvious discomfort. Despite her ambition to keep going, Juliette took the cue.

"You've been a marvelous subject, Pierre, and a stirring interview." She stepped away from the canvas and placed her pencils in an open cup on the taboret. Mounting the stage, she placed her hands on his shoulders as he stood. "Thank you," she said, looking directly into his eyes. "You're a wonderful subject—in all ways."

"And you're entirely too kind, Duchess," he said, kissing her cheeks three times. "I won't look at the drawing yet," he said, "not until you're ready to show it to me."

38

THE REPUBLICANS

oubertin rose from the desk, picked up a framed photograph of Jules Simon from the bookcase, and handed it to St. Clair. Simon, who appeared to be about fifty, was seated in the photograph, posed formally in a double-breasted suit coat, fully buttoned with the short, wide flare of overlapping lapels just below his cravat and the thin edge of a white collar defining his neck. He was gazing intently at the source of light illuminating the left side of his face, his mouth fixed in conviction between the round creases of his cheeks. His prominent forehead rose above a face framed by a set of long, bushy sideburns; his hair was brushed straight back into a shadowy sphere.

"He was a great thinker who shaped his age," Coubertin said, looking down at the photo. "One of a handful of men whose intellect and commitment to an egalitarian future molded the Third Republic into a hotbed of liberty and a cauldron of opportunity for everyone."

St. Clair handed the photo back. "Could you have done what you did without him?"

"No, unquestionably not. His name, his endorsement, his engagement in my work were all invaluable. He was seventy when I entered his class, and I was fortunate because I knew he was looking for young talent."

"How did you know what he was looking for?"

"Because I read what he wrote, knew the content of his lectures, read the papers, did my homework." Coubertin replaced the photo on the shelf and returned to his desk. "I knew he was part of a grand education reform movement I wanted to attach my name to—but that wasn't my only interest."

"What was your other interest?"

"I knew he was working with Jules Ferry on the 1889 Universal Exposition—and I knew they were looking for organizational help there too."

"Ferry wasn't prime minister then, was he?" St. Clair asked.

"No, but he had launched preparations for the 1889 exposition when he was in office in 1880 under President Grévy, who asked Ferry to stay on and oversee its development. You can't imagine how important the vision for that fair was to the leadership of the Third Republic. They believed it would provide the ultimate imprimatur of success for the progress France had made since 1870."

"So you were planning to push your ideas on physical education through the exposition?" St. Clair wondered.

"Not at first," Coubertin said, "but that's exactly how our strategy evolved."

"Was Simon deeply interested in sport in education?"

"Yes, and so was William Henry Waddington."

As they collaborated on the development of Coubertin's ideas, Simon began to open doors for his protégé. Not long after Hugo's funeral, while Coubertin still felt the impetus of Taine's approval, he and Simon met a few times to discuss ways of moving forward.

"Sport in education has always been part of our vision, though not the central point," Simon said. "For Ferry and me, it has always only been a matter of time."

They were walking along the side of the Sorbonne, about to part as twilight fell over Paris. "Did you make any specific plans?"

Simon stopped on the spot. "Waddington did," he said, and seemed to realize something. "Damn it. You still haven't met Waddington, have you?"

"No, but not for lack for trying." It had been over a year since Simon first recommended that Pierre meet the ambassador to England, but Waddington's schedule and travels never seemed to line up with Coubertin's requests.

"You need to meet him now—no later than tomorrow. He's here, but I think he's returning to London in two days."

"What's the urgency?"

"He'll understand your emphasis on sport—he's a product of the English system, the epitome of what you're striving for."

○ ○ ○ ○ ○

William Henry Waddington had an old mansion in the Marais on the rue des Archives. Pierre drove the caliche himself and made better time than expected, crossing through the Place Saint-Michel across the Île de la Cité and past the Hôtel de Ville into the heart of the old aristocratic stronghold. Waddington was an odd name for a Frenchman, let alone a recent prime minister and former two-time minister of public instruction, once under Simon. He was the son of an Englishman who had married a Frenchwoman and built a successful fabric manufacturing business in Brittany.

Arriving at the mansion a half hour early, Coubertin pulled the carriage into the open courtyard. A stableman appeared and took the reins as the baron brushed the dust off his suit coat. A maid let him in, leading him through a drawing room into the ambassador's study. Before pulling the double doors closed, she indicated the ambassador was on his way back from the *Élysée Palace* and should arrive in time for their appointment.

Standing in the middle of the room on a Persian rug, Coubertin took in his surroundings, a man's room in every respect. The walls of the room were covered with books in dark mahogany cases, paintings, photographs, and framed documents. A large partners' desk dominated one end of the room, and a divan and four chairs surrounded a low table in front of a fireplace at the other end. Light flowed in from two sets of double French doors, curtained like the proscenium of a stage with the folds of heavy golden drapery. Between the doors sat a waist-high sideboard with a wide surface covered by *objets d'art*, mementos, and ceramics. The wall above it held a series of photo memories of Waddington's life.

Two images immediately captured Coubertin's attention, one of a rowing crew from Cambridge on the Thames and another of three boys wearing white uniforms and school caps in front of the unmistakable tower of the Rugby Chapel. Sport had been Waddington's passion as a young man, and according to Simon, it still was.

Pierre closely examined the photographs of the young and athletic Waddington. He knew the background. Waddington's family ranked among the richest in the community—with their fiber-spinning factories buzzing and minting money twenty-four hours a day near the Atlantic coast of France. Since the local schools didn't impress him, the elder Waddington insisted his son have all the benefits he'd had through an English education and managed to get the boy enrolled in Rugby School in the 1840s. Young Waddington was a bull on the pitch and excelled at all the sports, helping Rugby win several school championships in its namesake sport. He also took a boxing title at 180 pounds and become a mainstay of the rowing team, which helped pave his way to Trinity College at Cambridge. Waddington was one of the eight who beat Oxford in their famous annual rowing competition on the Thames in 1849—the fourth year of the course from Putney to Mortlake. And it was that moment Coubertin saw depicted in the black-and-white celebration hanging on the wall.

He heard an approaching commotion and turned just as the doors flew open and Waddington stormed in, still a large bull in a black cape, followed by two younger men in black suits, one carrying a valise, the other with a pen and open pad. Without any kind of a welcome, Waddington threw his hat and cloak aside and said, while moving to his desk, "Simon thinks very highly of you, Monsieur Coubertin, and says you've got a few things that might interest me, so please take a seat, but give me a moment."

The two men sat along the side of the partners' desk while Coubertin settled into the open seat across from Waddington, who busied himself sorting through a stack of papers, flinging envelopes at random to each of his assistants, dictating orders.

"Now, Monsieur Coubertin," he said, speaking with an impatience and force that were slightly intimidating. "What is the thrust of your ideas?" Pierre wondered whether he should apologize and reschedule as the man glared at him. His face was wide and reddened, and his collar seemed too tight around the thick neck above a barrel chest and powerful shoulders. He breathed through his nostrils. His peppered gray hair was parted and combed close, but his mustache flowed out into thick muttonchops that flared from his jaws.

As Coubertin started to speak, a dry catch caused him to swallow and stutter, and before he could recover, Waddington interrupted.

"Is this about the École Libre? Does Simon need a favor?"

Recovering, Coubertin sat forward and met the man's stare. "No sir, this is about the great campaign for education reform that three of France's most visionary prime ministers tirelessly championed over the last decade."

"I suppose you're including me in that flattering category."

"Simon, Waddington, and Ferry, of course," Coubertin said. "The law that made public education the right of every French child bears the name of Ferry, but any student of contemporary politics knows that without Jules Simon and William Henry Waddington, there would be no such law. The progress was incremental."

"And exactly what is Baron Pierre de Coubertin proposing to add to this great pedagogical achievement?"

It was the perfect question, of course, but Coubertin paused, pulled in his lips to create anticipation, and delivered a single word—"sport"—which caused Waddington to raise his head and his eyebrows as he looked more closely at his interlocutor.

"Sir," Coubertin continued, "I have visited twenty English schools and universities, following in the footsteps of Hippolyte Taine. On the fields of Rugby, I saw the future of French education, and at Cambridge and Oxford, I believe, I may have seen the future of international competition."

The big man rolled forward in his chair and put his elbows on his desk, resting his jowls on a podium formed by his cupped hands. He looked intently at Coubertin. "I think I know your father," he said. "He's a painter, isn't he?"

"Indeed, he is a fine classicist who works mostly on religious themes—at the insistence of my mother." He noticed one of the assistants transcribing their conversation in his notebook.

"Catholics, correct?" asked Waddington.

"Yes."

"I had a discussion with him one night some years ago—at the Luxembourg Palace, I believe," Waddington said. "He's a handsome gentleman, tall, as I recall—had a fine painting on display, something about the missionaries."

"I'm sure it was *The Departure of the Missionaries,* one of his most popular works."

"Yes, that might have been it, but if I'm not mistaken, he does not have much affection for the Third Republic."

"That's very true, sir."

"He's a monarchist, isn't he?"

"Very much so, I'm afraid. He's still hoping for the return of Henry V, the Comte de Chambord."

Waddington rolled back in his chair and roared with delight. "I'm afraid the Bourbons have had a run of bad luck over the last century. And I think Old Henry is dead."

"He is," said Pierre. "I had to endure a long family trek to pay homage at the Schloss Frohsdorf in Tyrol, back when I was fifteen—and he was teetering even then. But that's a small detail in my father's long-term vision. There's always the next heir."

"Ah yes, the Comte de Paris. I see him periodically in London. Ambitious, but lazy. No hope there."

"At my parents' insistence, I've paid my respects on most of my trips to England."

"How does the son of a monarchist, and a hereditary baron at that, become an advocate of education reform in the Third Republic?"

"Well, Monsieur Ambassador, the truth is that I have a passion for France, but my fervor never aligned with my family's vision for my future—or their thoughts about our country."

"Let me guess—they wanted you to become a painter—or go to Saint-Cyr."

"Either would have been preferable by family tradition. My grandfather was a general under both Napoleon and the Restoration, and both of my brothers have distinguished themselves in the military."

"So the Po opened its doors and you met the inestimable Jules Simon?"

"Well, in a roundabout way, that is the story."

"And where did sport come into play?"

"That was always a personal passion for me. I loved to ride, row, fence, box, run, and even wrestle, but we had no opportunities for athletics in the schools. What you experienced at Rugby, which I've now studied first-hand on several trips, is precisely what we need to strengthen our young people, to give them a sense of purpose, and to help the Third Republic fulfill its promise to all Frenchmen."

"Baron, I am pressed for time right now, but Jules was right to send you to me. He knows I believe sport has the power to change lives and create a better society. I'm going to want to know the details of your plans—and specifically how you're going to address the chaos of our current mélange of French sports organizations. I will talk to Jules before I leave for London and see if I can help."

"That would be most excellent, sir. May I have the privilege of calling on you when I'm next in London?"

"Of course. I will open the doors of the embassy to welcome you."

"So once you had Waddington on board, the pace of events began to pick up?" St. Clair asked, watching the baron compose letters at his desk.

"No, it took quite a while," Coubertin said. "The timing is a little hazy. Let's see—there was a long exchange of letters between the three of us—Simon, Waddington, and me. It might have been a year before we had our decisive planning dinner at Maxim's."

"Maxim's," St. Clair said, aware the restaurant was the pinnacle of society in those days. "That sounds like a celebration."

"Simon and Waddington had been reading through parts of my manuscript on sport in education—the book that would eventually become *L'Éducation Anglaise en France*." Coubertin lifted his pen and leaned back in his chair. "We decided to have a strategy session on implementing the ideas before the book was published. Simon suggested dinner. I selected Maxim's."

On the appointed night, Coubertin found himself sitting in a spacious banquet in Paris's finest restaurant with two of France's former prime ministers—and both were focused on helping him develop a new strategy for integrating sport into French education. Waddington suggested that their most important priority—before designing the physical education curriculum for public schools—was the consolidation of France's fledgling and established athletic sports organizations under a single entity, an umbrella organization.

"You have to get control of sports in France. There's no central authority, but there should be. This is the opportunity. Look at Henley and how they control rowing in England."

"How would we do that?" Coubertin asked. "Through a law?"

"No," said Simon. "We don't want to have to endure the political tradeoffs necessary to pass a law granting sports authority."

"Jules is right," said Waddington. "Any attempt at legislation would only delay our goals."

Coubertin was delighted to hear Waddington call them "our goals."

"I suggest we proceed with a three-point strategy," Waddington continued. "First, we identify the finest leader among the most prominent sports associations in France."

"That may well be Georges de Saint-Clair," said Simon. "He's a very fine administrator."

"Good," said Waddington. "Whoever it is, we need to motivate him to partner with Pierre in the formation of a master association, drawing the mess of the current organizations in athletics—cycling, boxing, fencing, equestrian, et cetera—into an umbrella organization."

Coubertin felt he needed to assert himself. "I've had occasion to interact with a few of these federations through the Jockey Club of Paris, and what you're talking about won't be easy. Disputes rule the day. It's a hornet's nest. Every club sets its own rules."

"Well, if sport is going to experience the growth we envision—or have the influence we believe it will—then standards will have to be imposed."

"Agreed," said Simon. "Standards of organization and rules of competition will have to be in place before we propose a school curriculum."

"Second," Waddington said, "the committee I'm talking about—let's call it the French Union for Sport Development and Competition—will have to be headed by a distinguished personage with the prestige to not only draw the participation of the federations but to also keep them in line."

Coubertin listened intently—Waddington obviously knew more about sport administration than either he or Simon did.

Waddington turned his head, fixing his stare squarely on Simon, and said, "Who could we possibly recruit for such a role?"

Simon protested immediately. "My God, Henry, I'm seventy-two years old. What can I possibly give to sport?"

"Stature, theories, ideas, credibility, authority," Waddington said without hesitation. "Come over to London and I'll introduce you to the committee that rules Henley, and you will find your generation in power."

"He's right, Professor," said Coubertin. "Everyone in the sport community would respect your leadership—and the connection to our aspiration of education would be easy for you to address."

Without acknowledging Coubertin's response, Waddington moved on. "Third," he said, "we've got to find a way to connect our drive for physical education in the schools to the Universal Exposition that's coming. Lots of government agencies have been involved since Ferry launched preparations in 1880. We can use the event as a stage for our ideas on the future of sport."

"A brilliant idea," Simon said.

○ ○ ○ ○ ○

When Coubertin completed the manuscript of *L'Éducation Anglaise en France*, which Simon and Waddington had read completely in parts and pieces, offering suggestions but embracing the overall premise, he asked Simon to write an introduction. He knew Simon's name would not only legitimize the content and confirm the theories but would also greatly enhance the reception of the book among the cognoscenti and France's intellectual set. Simon readily agreed, saying he would have a draft ready and would like to meet again by the following Wednesday, a promise that excited Pierre.

At the appointed hour, he sat across the desk from Simon, the pages of his mentor's preface in his hands. As he read, inspiration and gratitude raced from his heart like two sprinters breaking side by side down parallel lanes. With eloquent authority, Simon had proclaimed it was time for the reforms Coubertin was proposing.

Simon painted a dismal picture of the current French student, graduating with his bachelor's degree in hand but unable to speak without coughing because of his ill health and lack of fitness—the direct result of the *surmenage*, the stress and overwork that French schools forced upon their students. He summarized by saying Pierre de Coubertin had arrived with a plan to replace that burden with the benefits of physical education the British had enjoyed and benefited from for years. It was a flattering introduction that would elevate Coubertin's stature in the French education and sporting communities, not to mention in the nation's political leadership circles.

"Now, it is obvious to me that you and I have already accomplished much together," Simon said, his great gray sideburns tilting like wings as he looked over his reading spectacles at Pierre. "And you know as well that my gratitude runs deep for the way you've built on Taine's campaign for education reform—and for how you've articulated in this manuscript a good number of ideas we desperately need in France." He waited for the acknowledgment of his points.

"Yes, of course, and you know that my gratitude runs equally deep for all you've done for me."

"Well, there's something I want you to undertake," Simon said, "something that will require the application of your reporting skills and organizational insights."

"Anything I can do for you, I will." Coubertin was pleased that Simon believed he had the ability to help with, he guessed, some facet of the 1889 exposition.

Excellent," Simon said, "I need your help assessing the current state of preparation for the Universal Exposition—and I may need some assistance with the development, for want of a better word, of the Universal Congress on World Peace that Frédéric Passy and Hodgson Pratt are organizing for the exposition."

"Is there a deficiency in the overall planning?"

"Not so much a deficiency as a need for more hands. Jules Ferry is concerned, but of course he's concerned about everything that has to do with the fair. The prestige of France is clearly on the line—and he wants me more engaged."

"Based on the successes of 1878 and 1865, I'm sure it will be brilliant."

"So you'll help?"

"I'd be glad to help, but there's one complication. I was actually planning to make a proposal to you today on the very subject of a congress at the exposition."

"Oh? What did you have in mind?"

"A congress on physical education. I've been thinking about it since Waddington suggested we find a way to link our education reform ideas with the exposition—remember?"

"Yes, of course I remember."

"Well, I'd like to organize an international congress with leaders in sport and education from around the world."

"Hmm," said Simon, his brow furrowing. "Let me think about how to present this to Ferry."

"I've written a questionnaire," said Pierre, pulling several sheets of paper from his valise. "Here's my idea."

39

THE POET, THE PRINCESS, AND THE STATUE

Under a bright afternoon sun, on the first Sunday of July, St. Clair and Coubertin strolled along the Quay d'Ouchy between the seawall and the row of plane trees that bordered the road, moving away from the corner at the château where people rented flat-bottomed paddle boats that worked like bicycles. Peals of laughter came from behind them as Juliette and Renée, Pierre's daughter, who had become friends of a sort, strolled with their parasols open. The silly ringing laughter brought a smile to Pierre's face, which made St. Clair grateful.

"I'm glad they're getting along," Coubertin said. "Renée needs friends her own age."

"She seems happy, Pierre," St. Clair said.

"Yes, she's in a good period now. So what's on the agenda for this week, my friend? What part of the past does our immediate future hold?"

"I've got enough notes now from you and Drussard to write the sections on the 1889 Universal Exposition—and the baroness has begrudgingly consented to one more interview—but I'd like to delve into the role of the Baroness Bertha von Suttner this week and maybe talk through your battles with Paschal Grousset."

"That's an immense contrast. The princess of peace and the devil himself." He frowned and added, "We can cover the two of them in a couple sessions— what else?"

"I'm thinking of including a series of brief profiles of your major allies and enemies."

Coubertin stopped and looked back at his daughter and Juliette, who were watching the paddle boats and the ducks swimming away from them. "Allies and enemies," he repeated. "No shortage of either, but I'm afraid the balance of power—and certainly the passion—belonged to the latter."

"Good, we'll discuss it soon." St. Clair said. "Right now, I've got something for you to read."

"A piece of my biography?" St. Clair noted the surprise in Coubertin's voice since he had never shown the baron any of his drafts.

"Could be. I finally got around to finishing a draft of the story you told Paavo Nurmi at the palace after your speech—about the poet, the princess, and the statue—and filled it in with the notes you gave me afterward."

"Ah yes, and that's piqued your interest in Bertha's influence."

"Exactly." St. Clair pulled a set of folded, typed pages from his coat.

Taking the papers, Coubertin said, "Let's sit."

They found a bench under the trees, and he began to read immediately.

One day in the summer of 1886, Aicard took Coubertin to lunch off the Champs-Élysées and insisted the baron accompany him that afternoon to the studio of the famous Frédéric Auguste Bartholdi, the sculptor who had created the colossal *Statue of Liberty*, which was then called *Liberty Enlightening the World*. The statue itself, which had been shipped to New York City the year before, was just being mounted on a new pedestal on Bedloe Island in the New York harbor, but Bartholdi was still promoting it.

The carriage left the Champs and headed north toward the Parc Monceau. They were destined for the copper foundry of Gaget, Gauthier & Company, where the statue had been constructed, towering over the neighborhood two years earlier in the odd spidery framework of its scaffolding. Coubertin had taken the tour with Jennette, who knew Bartholdi and had illustrated Lady Liberty for *Figaro*. They had entered the statue through the bottom of her upturned foot, climbed the inside steel framework, which Eiffel had designed, and stood marveling at the sights of Paris from the rim of the torch.

As the carriage rocked on the cobblestones of rue de Courcelles, Coubertin remembered the sense of awe he felt when he first turned the corner that day with Jennette and saw the massive reach of Lady Liberty's arm over the low rooflines. He remembered as well seeing her head and shoulders up close on Champs de Mars at the 1878 World Exposition. He had been on a field trip with his class from Saint-Ignace that day, and he and his classmates had climbed inside the crown.

"Do you remember," Coubertin asked, "the sensation the head and shoulders of the *Statue of Liberty* caused when they put her up on the Champs de Mars in 1878?"

"Yes, I remember looking at that face. It was like standing in the presence of a goddess." Aicard punctuated his point by shouting, "Spectacular!"

Pierre laughed at his enthusiasm. "And why exactly are we going to see Bartholdi? Not that it won't be an honor to meet him."

"I'm writing a poem about the statue, a heroic epic of the creation of the masterpiece."

"You're going to celebrate the friendship of France and America—very good. Is this a commission?"

"No, it's more of a promise. I met Bartholdi some time ago at a dinner and told him I would compose an ode to his great work."

"Am I guessing that you're a little behind schedule?"

"Perhaps, but I didn't set a date. And there's still time. The statue isn't supposed to be finished and dedicated until October."

"That gives you a few months to complete the work."

"You'll like Bartholdi. He's a philosopher as much as an artist, a great republican who wanted to do this statue a long time ago—back when France was still suffering under the empire."

"And why are we going to the foundry and not to Bartholdi's studio?"

"He suggested it. There's a final cast at the workshop, an exact copy about nine feet tall, I think, and I've asked him to explain the symbolism. I need to understand the artistic choices he made, and it'll be easiest to do it looking at the statue."

"And why am I along?"

"There's going to be a young princess from Austria at the meeting, a certain Bertha von Suttner, and I thought you could keep her busy if she got in the way."

"How thoughtful of you. You're using me for my title. I thought perhaps you wanted my perspective on the symbolism."

"Well, that too, if you're not too distracted by the princess."

"Why? Is she beautiful?"

"Not in the classical sense of beauty—and you're too in love with Jennette anyway—but from what I understand, the princess is quite an intellect and has a lot to say about peace."

"Peace?"

"Oh yes. It's a bit ironic, actually. She's working for Alfred Nobel, Mr. Dynamite himself, but she's becoming something of a public figure in the peace movement."

"I wonder if Simon knows her?"

The carriage wheeled inside the gate at Gaget & Gauthier, and Jean and Pierre climbed out. They stood on a street between two rows of buildings, the workshops along the right with low metal roofs, and brick buildings on the left with chimneys above the foundry furnaces, a few spewing smoke into the sky. Metallic dust and black soot covered the ground, doorways, and windowsills. Ahead of them, at the end of the road, an open shed with a high roof bridged the way to an open courtyard where Lady Liberty had stood just two years before.

A short, round man in a plaster-smeared smock with a full beard and long hair emerged from the last workshop door, looked their way, and shouted a greeting.

"Hello, Frédéric!" Aicard called back, waving as they approached him and shook his chalky hand.

They followed him inside the workshop, entering a dim scene of furious disarray and noise, scraps of plaster sculpture, metal, and wood forms scattered everywhere. A small army of men in stained shirts, their sleeves rolled up on muscled arms, were hammering, prying, sawing, bending, screwing, and fitting things together on their work tables or the open floor. Fascinated, Coubertin spotted a full-scale plaster cast of Lady Liberty's hand—the one that held the torch—covered with soot and lying amid a pile of debris far into the depths of the workshop.

Bartholdi was already climbing a short stairway into a brightly lit room with windows against the back wall. Following him, Coubertin and Aicard found themselves in a surprisingly large workroom with drawings of statues and gates and metalwork spread on waist-high tables in the center of the room along with several half-finished clay busts of men on pedestals. Coubertin did not recognize either of the faces being sculpted, but before he could ask, Bartholdi said, "This way, gentlemen," and led them into a hallway in the back wall, down another set of steps, and into a larger, far more elegant room flooded with chandelier light from a high ceiling. The space served as a showcase for a magnificent nine-foot edition of the Statue of Liberty standing on a marble pedestal in full green copper patina.

"This is where we did a good deal of our fundraising," said Bartholdi. "A cast this size has a lot of charisma in such an intimate setting." He fell silent and let them absorb their surroundings.

Pierre looked around. The room was filled with expensive furniture. Large arched frosted windows, which must have fronted an alley, were swathed in thick golden drapes. Wainscoting graced the light yellow-and-pink walls, which held a good number of paintings of sculptures produced at the foundry.

"Well, gentlemen." A lilting voice turned them all back to the top of the stairway as a woman entered the room. "This is certainly a surprise after the grime on the way in." She lifted her full skirt and shook it so the hem waved as she stepped down into the room. She wore a smartly buttoned black jacket over the ruffled collar of a white blouse, and, to Pierre's surprise, on her head was a smaller feminine version of the very top hat he was wearing. A somewhat stocky woman, she appeared to be about forty and in robust health. He doffed his hat as Jean bowed.

She stepped forward and Bartholdi took her hand, making the introduction. "Baroness von Suttner," he said. The title surprised Coubertin since Aicard had said she was a princess. He shot a quick glance at his friend, who was grinning. Another joke at the expense of the nobility.

"This is the poet Jean Aicard and his friend," Bartholdi said with a flourish of his hand, "whose name—"

"Baron Pierre de Coubertin," said Aicard as they stepped forward to take her gloved hand.

"A pleasure, gentlemen, to meet you in the presence of such a marvelous goddess of peace." They all turned again to look at the statue as the baroness added, "I'm sure we're all vitally interested in learning about the inspiration behind your masterpiece, Frédéric."

"I had a chance to climb through the statue a few years ago with Jennette Montaigne, sir," said Pierre, "but I too would be deeply honored to hear the story from you."

"Ah, how is Jennette?" asked Bartholdi. "A shame you didn't bring her. I loved the way she skewered Freycinet last week."

"I'll give her your regards."

"All right, Jean," said the sculptor, "let's start with the concept and why we decided on a figure of liberty."

Bartholdi held them spellbound for the next thirty minutes with a lecture that was both polished and practiced, with pauses for effect and gestures that led the eye directly to one surprising aspect of the statue's symbolism after another. It was a speech the sculptor might have delivered a hundred times to ambassadors, art students, and admiring journalists—and Coubertin realized it would never fail to mesmerize or inspire.

Bartholdi began with the story of Laboulaye's original proposal at a dinner party more than twenty years earlier, in 1865: an idea for a major symbolic gift to America from France to celebrate the one-hundredth anniversary of its independence a decade hence. Bartholdi was only thirty-one at the time, but he was full of artistic ambitions and had already developed the idea for a gigantic statue in the harbor of the French-built Suez Canal, an extraordinary concept he used to bedazzle people.

"I wanted to recapture for the modern world, and particularly for Egypt, the great glory of the Colossus of Rhodes, one of the Seven Wonders of the Ancient World," he said, and Coubertin felt as if a door to a world beyond the reach of mere mortals was opening before him. "But this idea of creating a colossal statue for America seemed even greater."

Coubertin felt nothing but admiration for the boldness of Bartholdi's vision and the huge risks this artist was willing to take to bring his dream to pass.

Bartholdi presented the idea to Laboulaye, who loved it immediately, and they began making plans and discussing concepts. Before long they had focused on a modern version of the Roman goddess Libertas.

"America loved liberty. It was central to their identity. This," he said, reaching into his pocket and pulling out an American silver dollar, which he flipped through the air to Aicard, "this was their first version of Liberty. Note that she's seated. And here's their second, from ten years later." He flipped another silver disk through the air to Pierre, who caught it, knowing it was going to be the full head of the goddess with the band in her hair that read Liberty.

"I wanted all the surfaces to be simple to be sure the focus fell on the symbols. And so we dressed Mademoiselle Liberty in the flowing lines of the *stola* and *pella*, the Roman robe and cloak."

As Bartholdi explained the decisions to crown Liberty with a nimbus featuring seven pointed sunrays that represented the seven seas and the seven continents, Coubertin looked up at the glorious face and wondered if such a goddess could truly inspire unity across the world. Seven, he thought—God's number of perfection. The simplicity of it all. Her forward movement represented freedom from the chains and shackles that lay broken beneath her gown. The book she embraced, engraved with the Roman numerals for July 4, 1776, contained the treasury of the new laws of liberty expressed in the Declaration of Independence. And finally, as Bartholdi reached his hand high as if holding the very torch that Liberty lifted before the world, he said, "The fire of Prometheus, the flame of freedom he gave to man that burns in every soul. A torch to fill the whole world with the light of those who dream of breaking free of all the shackles that bind us."

His eyes fixed on the torch with its static flame, Coubertin tried to imagine the statue rising above the harbor in New York City, a place he had never seen but had deeply imagined. He wondered about the people who would see the colossus as they arrived in America with their hopes and dreams, visitors and immigrants looking up at the promise of the torchlight of a goddess who offered freedom. Amazing, he thought, that such inspiration could be contained in a static form, that the symbolism stamped in metal, inanimate forever, could convey such a vital life force, and that so much drama could have sprung from the mind of one man.

As Bartholdi moved into the engineering details, the fundraising campaign, and how they went about paying for such a colossal cultural enterprise, what struck Coubertin most was how so many people freely rallied to the cause, from the school children who gave pennies to the great industrialist known as the Copper King, Pierre-Eugène Secrétan, who donated every ounce of the copper—128,000 pounds—needed to clothe Lady Liberty in her cloak and robe.

Bartholdi paused for a moment. "Pierre, would you mind entertaining the baroness while I walk Jean through the foundry. It's no place for a lady."

"Of course." Coubertin turned to the baroness and offered his arm, motioning to the furniture in an alcove on the side of the room. "Do you know my friend Jules Simon?" he asked.

She looked surprised. "Yes, of course. Jules is a dear friend. We're working on the peace congress together."

Coubertin guided her to a red velvet sofa fronted by two baroque chairs. They sat side by side on the divan and immediately began talking about their mutual work with Simon.

"I've studied with him, and I've been working with him for a few years—and he recently recruited me to help him review the progress on the organizational effort of the exposition—a task Jules Ferry had asked him to undertake."

"Well then, we're closely connected," the baroness replied. "Frédéric Passy is leading the Universal Peace Congress, and he introduced us a year ago. I think Jules will be giving the keynote speech to open the congress."

"Indeed, he will—and I may be helping him with that speech."

"Oh, so you're a writer?"

"In part—I'm writing a book at the moment on the importance of English education as a model of reform for France—Jules is providing a preface."

"And what's the other part of your work?"

"I've proposed that we add a congress on physical education for the 1889 exposition," he said, "an international congress that will help strengthen our efforts to integrate sport, specifically team sport, into French education. And you?"

"I'm working on a book as well—a novel—in part, like you, because I'm also fully engaged in the peace movement."

"Maybe we'll have a chance to collaborate on the exposition. What's your novel about?"

"It's about war and the irrationality of it all, the devastation it wreaks, and the need for peace." She stared at him. "In fact, it's a call for peace."

"The rumors of war are very persistent," Coubertin replied. "I've seen more than enough of it in my lifetime. Jean said you're working with Alfred Nobel."

"Yes, and I know what you're thinking." She grinned faintly.

"I won't deny my curiosity," Coubertin said, enjoying the moment. "The combination of peace and dynamite does beg an answer."

"He's a peace-loving man and a visionary in his own right. He's made a fortune in explosives and I know he wants to use the money for good, although he's a bit misguided. He thinks he can produce peace by inventing an explosive so destructive it will lead to an end of war—out of fear. I think he's wrong, but I'm glad he supports my work."

"Well, I'd like to support it too. You've already stimulated my interest in the peace movement—and all its possibilities."

She reached over and put her hand on his, speaking like an evangelist. "We live in an age of dreamers, Baron, an age in which anything and everything is possible. It is time to end violence between nations, to find the right way to compete without resorting to conflict and war."

Coubertin was taken with her notion, but before he could respond, Aicard and Bartholdi were suddenly standing over them, asking if they would like to share a bottle of wine. They did, and within a matter of weeks, Bertha von Suttner became one of Coubertin's most important advisers and influential confidantes. Working independently, just one step below the leaders controlling the exposition and developing the peace movement, they began to collaborate and share information and insights that proved critical to their goals—his evolving, hers fixed. They also began to mix socially, often with Bertha's husband, Arthur, an equally passionate advocate for peace and social justice, and occasionally with Aicard, who insisted that they continue to call her princess.

When Coubertin looked up from the pages, his eyes were rheumy. "That's quite a re-creation, Jacques. It's very moving for me—such a vividly drawn memory. It's hard to believe you've built all those details out of my recollections. I wasn't that descriptive of the symbolism of the statue, was I?"

"No, but my research indicates that's how Bartholdi would have described it."

"Well then, it seems my story will finally be getting the full treatment."

Renée and Juliette came over from the seawall, where they had been standing. As Coubertin stood, Renée asked, "What did you think, Father. Did you like it?"

The old man hesitated, composing himself. "*Ars poetica,*" he said, looking lovingly at his daughter. "Monsieur St. Clair has taken liberties with my story, but those liberties are giving it wings. As Aristotle said, 'History is particular, poetry is universal.' This is both."

Coubertin took Renée's arm and turned back toward the Château d'Ouchy, walking ahead of St. Clair and Juliette, who followed closely enough to hear the baron say, "I think the gods have sent Jacques and Juliette to us, Renée. There seems to be no limit to their gifts or kindnesses."

○ ○ ○ ○ ○

Later that night, as they were having a glass of wine in their cottage and talking over the day spent with the baron and Renée, Juliet asked St. Clair about Bertha von Suttner. "So the baroness—or should I say the 'princess'—had a major influence on Pierre's thinking. Was she the one who enlightened him on the power of peace through sport?"

"Not on the power of peace through sport, but on the power of the peace movement of the time," St. Clair said. "He saw the potential of aligning peace and sport—and absorbed the idea that peace could become one of the moral foundations of sport into his thinking. It became a key lesson, if not the ultimate lesson, in the pedagogical role of sport. In his definition of the Olympic ideal— you heard it that night at the university—peace is the fifth ring, the final step from the personal to the universal."

"The fifth ring. I like that phrase, but I don't think I heard Pierre use it that night."

"No, he didn't. That's just something I've been thinking about, a way to summarize his five-point definition of the Olympic ideal."

"Well, I'm very interested in learning more about this *Baroness* von Suttner," Juliette said. "I'm going to see if I can find a copy of that novel she wrote."

St. Clair reached into his satchel and pulled out a file of papers larger than the excerpt he had given Coubertin to read. Sorting through them, he pulled out a few pages and said, "Read this. It's a brief portrait of her life and work. Quite a remarkable and very persuasive woman. Pierre was fortunate to have met her. They became great friends and tremendous collaborators."

Baroness Bertha Kinksy von Chinic was born in Prague in 1843 into a lowly but aristocratic Austrian family that struggled to maintain their social standing after her father's sudden death just before her birth. Raised at a family home in Vienna, she was educated in languages, piano, and voice by a governess who also cultivated her independent spirit. As a young woman, she demonstrated intellectual and literary talents that filled her with ambitions to travel and marry for love, despite her family's hopes that she would elevate their status through an arranged courtship. In her late twenties, she worked as a governess for Baron Karl von Suttner and fell in love with his son, Arthur. Since he lacked the requisite wealth, her family forbade her to carry on the romance—as did his. Brokenhearted but determined to set her own course, she responded to an ad for employment in Paris. In 1875, when she was thirty-two, she took the train to Paris to work for Alfred Nobel. He was forty-two at the time and had gained great wealth through his invention of dynamite. He took an immediate and perhaps romantic interest in the younger woman, whose intellectual and cultural interests stirred his passions, but the job lasted only eight days.

Nonetheless, in their brief time together, rather than work at the secretarial job at hand, she engaged him in wide-ranging conversations focused primarily on the arts and humanities and peace—particularly concepts for how to stop war. The encounter left such an impression on Nobel that they became close friends—and he continued to correspond with and support Bertha throughout his life.

Despite her family's severe disapproval, she returned to Vienna and eloped with Arthur von Suttner. They spent nearly a decade in exile in the Caucasus, where they collaborated and wrote six novels together and where they began a crusade for peace. All this time she corresponded with Nobel, who encouraged her literary and peacemaking pursuits. She and her husband moved to Paris in the mid-1880s to pursue their dual passions and she reestablished contact with Nobel, urging him to put his fortune to work in the service of peace, trying to dissuade him from the notion that a more powerful weapon would engender such fear that war would be unthinkable.

Becoming ever more committed to peace, Bertha joined the London-based International Peace and Arbitration Association founded by Hodgson Pratt. Soon she was working with Pratt and his Paris partner, Frédéric Passy, on the development of the First Universal Peace Congress at the 1889 Universal Exposition, which began with a keynote address by none other than Jules Simon. Pierre de Coubertin was in the audience.

In 1890, her novel *Lay Down Your Arms* created a sensation with its searing, often brutal portrait of the horrors of war. It was a clarion call for peace and helped spread the burgeoning peace movement. At the Second Universal Peace Congress in Rome in 1891, she gave her first major public speech on peace, which established her as one of the most forceful and eloquent leaders of the movement. That same year, her husband founded the Society to Combat Anti-Semitism and they became outspoken critics of the growing anti-Semitism of the time. She helped found the International Peace Bureau in Bern, Switzerland, in 1893 and helped Baron Pierre de Coubertin organize the congress that birthed the modern Olympic Games in the Sorbonne in Paris on June 23, 1894. She believed deeply in his message of worldwide friendship and peace through sport. Through Coubertin's outreach and her influence, Frédéric Passy and Hodgson Pratt were two of seventy-eight honored delegates at the Olympic congress that night. It was again through her influence that Alfred Nobel, who died in 1896, dedicated his enormous fortune to the establishment of the Nobel Prizes, which were chartered to recognize extraordinary achievements each year in fields of literature, medicine, physics, chemistry, physiology, and, most importantly, peace. Von Suttner and her husband worked tirelessly for the cause, helping establish national peace committees in Germany and Austria, where she died in 1914, mercifully, at the outset of the First World War.

"Well, she certainly led an impressive life," Juliette said, laying the pages on the coffee table. "To be that independent and outspoken way back then." She shook her head. "I'm surprised she isn't more widely known."

"A lot of great people from that era have been forgotten," St. Clair said. "In fact, that's why we're here doing what we are right now."

40

THE BARONESS
REMEMBERS

As the summer heat made Lausanne a touch unbearable, the baroness continued to deny St. Clair's requests for another interview. Irrationally, he thought, she remained outraged that he had discussed the details of her recollections with the baron, who had made the mistake of assuming her endearing memories might have somehow brought them closer. She flew into a rage when her husband attempted to discuss his family's first visit to her house. As a result, she refused to sit for another interview. After she turned him down twice, he encountered her on the stairs at Mon Repos. "No, absolutely not. I have nothing more to say about my husband," she said, rushing off. It seemed hopeless until Juliette suggested that he have Renée speak to her. Renée's appeal worked, and the baroness agreed to one more session.

St. Clair had learned over the years that it was best to use a familiar setting with difficult or reluctant interviews, so he asked the baroness to meet him again at the Hôtel de la Paix. Sitting in the same booth by the window where he had first interviewed her, waiting for her to arrive, St. Clair reviewed his notes from their last session more than two months before. Thinking about how volatile and temperamental she could be, he realized he had made a mistake by not following up sooner. "Damn it," he said beneath his breath for allowing so much time to pass after he had built what seemed to be a good bond of trust with her. Perhaps she was discouraged by his lack of attention or gratitude.

When she entered through the side door, she didn't look at all pleased. There was no hint of a smile on her face when she arrived at the booth. Sliding in, she gave no acknowledgment of the cappuccino or cakes he had waiting for her. She left her blue, feathered hat in place despite the fact that it was as wide as a small parasol and a little awkward in such close quarters. Her mouth was tightly compressed, her eyes intense.

"I have to beg your forgiveness, Baroness." St. Clair wanted to reach for her hand but knew it wasn't time yet. No reaction, not the hoped for incredulous "For what?" She simply stared, and when she tilted her head forward to take a sip from her cup, the brim of her hat covered her face entirely.

"I became so caught up in the preparations for Carl Diem's visit, Pierre's anniversary speech, and the interview with Lucien Drussard," he continued, "not to mention the extensive research and writing I've been doing ..." Still no response—just the same cold stare. "I suppose I neglected to pursue the most promising and important interview of all ... you, Pierre's closest and most trusted collaborator." He realized as he said it that despite the overt flattery, it was mostly true.

"Well, I'm here now, Monsieur St. Clair. And I've got other things to do, so please get to the point. And please don't ever ask my daughter to serve as your intermediary again."

"Certainly, Baroness." He looked at his notes, skipping any attempt at a defense of Renée's role. "The last time we talked, we were just beginning to discuss your partnership with Pierre in the founding of the Games. I know the two of you began your courtship in 1890, some months after your father's funeral, but I was surprised that you seemed to know all the details of the work he had done in the previous decade."

"Why are you surprised? You do understand we were full partners in the work—in the campaign—don't you?"

"Well, yes, but I'm speaking of the period between your teenage infatuation and your formal courtship—you seem so familiar with events at which you weren't present."

"It's true. I wasn't involved then, but once we fixed on Pierre's Olympic ambitions—and started planning in earnest—I wanted to know the full history. It was only a year after Paris 1889 when we fell in love again—those memories were still very fresh and he was still engaged with the same circle of players. I made it clear I wanted to be a full partner from the beginning, so I asked him to tell me everything—and we went over it again and again. He agreed it was important for me to know the full story and the people involved."

"So you can comment on the details of his interactions with Drussard, Simon, and Waddington, for instance?" Her chin tightened and she pressed her lips together, glaring at him, and he realized she took his question as an expression of doubt.

"Chapter and verse, if necessary, monsieur, and my memory might be better than his. Let me tell you something ..."

He was certain a lecture was coming, but it turned quickly into something unexpected—her perspective on what they had accomplished. He wrote swiftly as she spoke and had the feeling she had wanted to tell him this all along. "When you launch a movement to change the world, you take on responsibilities that can have devastating consequences," she said, her voice suddenly softening. "No matter how powerful your idea may be, it won't live if you don't invest your life into it, and that's what I agreed to do. Pierre and I were full partners in the vision—and the effort. We were rebels, as he often said. In fact, on the day we were married, when he lifted the veil from my face and leaned in to kiss me, that's what he whispered in my ear—'We'll always be rebels together.'" She paused then, bowed her head, and disappeared beneath the hat, but she continued to speak.

"Like millions of Europeans then, I was fascinated by the classical world. Along with Pierre, I became enraptured with the romance of restoring the ancient Games, giving the world something with timeless permanence—Games between nations—Games that could contribute to peace, building friendships between young people everywhere. It was a romantic idea involving travel to the capitals of the world—a mission that would take us to the corners of the earth, just as my father traveled beyond borders for his country. The idea that the Olympic Movement was going to be our life's work was completely inspiring to me. I felt I was partnering with a great man, a visionary, but there was a price to pay, a severe price slowly extracted over time."

She looked up again, and her expression had changed. St. Clair made a one-word note in the margin—*brokenhearted*.

"But I did not foresee the risks, only the glory. Pierre and I were filled with dreams. Our conversations were about the possibilities of a movement that could unite the world in a festival of friendship every four years. We were dreamers, but we were not unrealistic. Pierre was a detail man, an extremely gifted organizer and as disciplined and committed as any of the great athletes who swept through the Olympic arena. He would never quit or give up his baby." She paused when she spoke of his infant, looked away for an instant, and choked back a groan.

"I knew the work was going to be difficult, putting together committees in every country and organizing major events in distant cities. I had watched Pierre go through misery in 1892 at the Sorbonne when his first proposal to resurrect the Games produced only laughter. But I was so proud barely twenty months later, when the same proposal was embraced with acclaim—because he had the will to make it happen, with only a few strong allies. And then came Athens, and the reality of the difficulties before us became bitterly clear to me for the first time. The public celebration was beyond our greatest hopes and dreams, and the athletic competition was superb. But the personal humiliation, the way the Greeks simply shunted Pierre aside, denied his presence and stole his claim of authorship like brazen thieves in the sunlight—that was shocking and deeply disappointing. I was devastated, and I could hardly understand how Pierre could stand there and take it, then lift his glass at the end to toast the Greeks' brilliance."

She had leaped ahead of St. Clair's story and he was reluctant to draw her back, but he felt he had to. Yet he didn't want her to abandon the passion and clarity she had summoned from those memories. "Take me back again to when the two of you first decided to pursue this dream. What was the source of your motivation?"

There was no hesitation—clearly she had been thinking about explaining her motivations and her role to St. Clair, despite her apparent disdain. "About the time we reconnected—maybe because we reconnected—I recognized our lives represented more than our simple stories. We were both part of the last generation of an aristocracy that still had some power when we were born, but had subsequently been ostracized, denounced, and left without much social credibility in the political power circles of our nation. While we could travel on our wealth and to some extent on our names, the Almanac de Gotha no longer carried the cachet and privileges it once did. There was no escaping the fact that if you had a title, you also had enemies."

St. Clair quickly made two notes in the margin—Almanac = registry of nobility, Enemies = *Grousset?*—as the baroness continued.

"Everyone from our class and generation was struggling then to find their place and role in Paris, in the new France—and it wasn't easy. We still lived by a social code that said you couldn't pursue a career or build a business. *Noblesse obligé* required something more, a selfless contribution to our world. We were trapped in a way and wanted to rebel against that convention, but at the same time we wanted to find a way to honor it, to serve our faded class and traditions—and the Third Republic too. When Pierre and I did get back together, the fact that we were Catholic and Protestant—a taboo for the most part—actually became a badge of honor for us, giving us a chance to make a public statement through our love that said we were not bound by tradition."

She paused then, reached into her purse, and pulled out a compact, putting a little powder on her cheeks, which had blushed. St. Clair took the opportunity to offer a compliment. "The strength of the love you shared is inspiring."

She didn't react well, realizing perhaps that she had been too romantic in her interpretation of their beginnings. "Don't harbor any illusions, monsieur. The man I married and the lives we've led have been largely disappointing. Yes, we've done many great things together—but we've experienced tragedy and loss that can only be laid at his feet. He spent all his money and most of mine on this dream, invested badly, neglected his family at times, and ran off whenever something too inconvenient pressed in on our lives. I will never forgive him, but I will never forsake his legacy and the good work we have done … and in that regard, I am a prisoner of my marriage. Our current circumstances are far from pleasant, as you undoubtedly have recognized."

"And yet, if I may say so, Baroness, you are his greatest defender—and I know part of your anger is based on the way the world has mistreated him."

She looked away again. "You're not wrong about that. I *am* his greatest defender." She turned back to him. "How many times have you crossed the pont Alexandre III in Paris—between the Invalides and the Grand Palais?"

"Hundreds," he replied as an image of the beautiful, ornate bridge rose in his mind.

"There are four shields on the base of the columns of that bridge that represent the four freedoms—and three of them bear the names of great Frenchmen. Can you name them?"

"No—I'd have to guess."

"Frédéric le Play, Félix Fauré, Alfred Picard," she said, a glint in her eye. "Great men, yes, all associated with the world's fairs, but compare their legacies to Pierre's, not in France, but beyond its borders, and I think you can make a strong case that the name of Coubertin belongs on one of those shields—or somewhere just as important."

"I agree. France has never given him the honors he deserves."

"It's not just a failure to honor, Monsieur St. Clair. It's a history of opposition rooted in the distrust so many had for the aristocracy at the time—and it has continued."

"Did it begin with Paschal Grousset?"

"Yes, it did. He was a scathing enemy, vicious in his denunciations—yet quite eloquent. Pierre called him a demagogue who embodied the worst forms of nationalism. He was a master manipulator."

"Did you know him?"

"Only by reputation—as a revolutionary and a writer—but the Coubertin family knew who he was from the uprising of the Commune …" She let the thought trail off as she searched for a memory. "Wait … I did see him once at one of le Play's union meetings—where Pierre spoke. Oh my," she said, interrupting herself. "I had forgotten all about this. I told you I didn't see Pierre between the end of our youthful affair and my father's funeral, but that's not true. I did see him once, very briefly, in a meeting broken up in chaos by Grousset."

"When and where?"

"I'm not sure—middle of the 1880s, '85 or '86, maybe," she said. "A friend of mine, Sophie, was very active in le Play's union. It was in the 16th, I'm sure. Yes, in Auteuil."

○ ○ ○ ○ ○

The street was so crowded with carriages and people in the fading light that the coachman couldn't make further progress. Young Marie Rothan and her friend, Sophie, had to get out of the caliche more than a block from the Hôtel de Auteuil, the town hall of the small village where the Union de la Paix Sociale was holding one of its community meetings. Frédéric Le Play had launched the Unions for Social Peace in the early 1880s, as a social/political organization designed to give the people of the Third Republic—all the people—a broader voice in the direction of the country through a direct channel for input into the political process. The local unions were as popular as le Play himself, who had become a giant of French social action and one of France's most admired thinkers and leaders.

Although she was intimidated by the crowd, Marie pushed ahead, determined to experience a le Play meeting first-hand. As for Sophie, she would have never left—she was a dedicated activist and had talked Marie into traveling to Auteuil for this very meeting. They moved as quickly as they could through the mass of bodies, carriages, and horses clogging the street to the congested throng on the town hall stairs.

"Over here," said Sophie, who had found a handhold on a wrought-iron railing; Marie slipped in behind her as they pulled themselves up the stairs and pushed through the jammed front doorway. Inside, they scrambled forward and made their way halfway to the front, where a podium stood behind a railing on a raised stage. Marie pushed along the wall to a point where two gentlemen in top hats were seated on the end of an irregular row of bentwood chairs.

Marie harrumphed and coughed once or twice until she caught the attention of the gentlemen, to whom, when they glanced up, she and Sophie offered courteous smiles. Doffing their caps, the men immediately stood and offered their seats to the ladies. Pleasantries were exchanged as the first speaker took the podium. Forcefully calling the crowd to order, the speaker iterated a number of calendar items from the month before and the month ahead, and made a few announcements. He concluded by introducing the leader of the local le Play union, who rallied the audience with an intelligent appeal for greater social equality based on what Marie remembered as Christian magnanimity. While the appeal was eloquent and full of compassion, Marie questioned its efficacy in such a motley assembly where very few signs of wealth were evident. Another speaker, less eloquent, tried to build on the theme with a more appropriate emphasis on simple sharing. Roundly applauded, the second speaker stepped back as the floor was opened for debate and comment.

For some time the debate bounced around the room and finally began to focus on the inequities of the education system. Across the hall, a young man gained the floor and stood on a chair, gesturing widely with his arms as he spoke in a voice Marie instantly recognized, a voice that pierced the low rumble with a penetrating aural clarity.

"It is not the task of the people to lead, but to guide," said a neatly dressed young scion of the nobility. "And to guide, they must be educated. The future of civilization—of the society of France—rests today not on the political or economic pathway we follow, but on the direction that education will take. We must focus our energies on opening the doors of the temple of education to all of our people, all of our citizens, to give them opportunities that have so long been denied them, opportunities to learn, grow, and prosper."

"Oh my," Marie said to Sophie, "that's Pierre de Coubertin, a long-lost boyfriend of mine."

She was stunned to see Pierre take control of the room, but that was just what he did, with sufficient force to quell the din. With an extemporary style that drew applause and gruff consents from the assembly at each calibrated pause, Pierre made a series of points based on the notion that the most pressing issue facing France today was education reform. He was advocating that France needed a cultural shift so that children everywhere would be able to take advantage of the mandatory education that had been legislated by Jules Ferry at the start of the decade. Pierre was in the process of proposing a petition when another man with a strong voice responded with great anger and rushed across the room to challenge him, saying they must not allow the nobility to give them any direction on education—or any other issues.

With a fierce countenance and the fervor of a seasoned revolutionary, Paschal Grousset had bullied his way through the crowd to within a few feet of Coubertin, who had shifted sideways on the chair and curled his hands in expectation of a brawl. Another man with wild hair stepped forward to defend Pierre and managed to restrain Grousset, even as he shouted and pointed rudely. "We have rescued France from this vermin more than once—and now we must protect her from their insidious assaults once again."

It wasn't the ideas Grousset was objecting to, it was their author, or rather his class, but the outburst had its effect. The room descended into clamor and there was a rush toward the center, men pushing and threatening each other while the union leader shouted ineffectively for order. Marie and Sophie retreated to the wall and made their way back toward the entry, hoping to squeeze through while others were rushing in.

Just as Sophie pulled her into the doorway and she felt the coolness of the outside air on her cheek, she looked back and suddenly there was Pierre, being pushed through the crowd by his friends. Their eyes met for an instant, and there was a moment of surprised recognition, a second of vague but important recollections—and then, jostled by the tumult, he looked away and she was carried out the door with the crowd. The room seemed to explode into a melee, and the two women hurried off toward their carriage.

○ ○ ○ ○ ○

When she finished with the story of that chaotic night, the baroness finally seemed to fully relax. She stopped fidgeting and gave St. Clair a half-hearted smile, ordered a kirsch, and took off her large hat. "I can't stay much longer, monsieur, but if there's anything important you wish me to address, I'll do my best."

He was acutely aware of how quickly her moods seemed to shift—and wondered how long this pleasantness would last. "Thank you, Baroness. I know it's not easy for you to walk through these memories, but I'm deeply grateful." Turning back a few pages in his notebook, it struck him she might be able to summarize the master narrative of the 1880s for him. Given her clarity and excellent memory, he decided to ask. "I'd like to hear more about how Grousset opposed Pierre's efforts in the schools, but I'm struggling to shape the overall story of his reform efforts and how successful or unsuccessful they were—and how that work related to the 1889 Congress and led to the Olympic Games."

The kirsch arrived and she took a sip, dabbing her lips with a napkin and leaving a light rouge print on the linen. "It's not difficult to tell that story," she said. "As we traveled around Europe in the early 1900s to the Games and IOC sessions and even after the war, I would often provide the wives of new IOC members with a brief history of the Olympic Movement over tea. At Pierre's insistence, I avoided criticizing some of those I would have loved to have taken to task, but the story always seemed to inspire and help new spouses embrace their roles."

"And you included the 1880s in your talks?"

"Of course—it was important for everyone in the IOC to understand that education and sport were indelibly linked from the beginning in Pierre's campaign. I would always establish the premise that he wanted to reform the French education system—attach his name to a grand effort that had been stumbling along for years. And then I would recount the sequence of events between his revelation at Rugby and the founding of the Olympic Games in a narrative that moved from point to point in a logical progression."

"That's interesting. Can you outline it for me?"

"I think so, although it has been a while," she said, and St. Clair felt certain he had asked the right question. "Pierre made a name for himself speaking at le Play union meetings and writing a good number of articles for le Play's *La Réforme Sociale*, but the work really began with his vision at Rugby. He gained great clarity there and returned with a specific focus on sport. Through the École Libre des Sciences Politiques, he began to work closely with Simon, who endorsed his concepts, introduced him to Waddington and Ferry, and recruited him to help with the organization of the 1889 exposition."

"Which is when he developed the idea for the Congress on Physical Education," St. Clair inserted.

"That's right. Two things helped him consolidate power early. His first major book—*L'Éducation Anglaise en France*—and then his creation of the Committee for the Promotion of Sport and Physical Education, which Simon chaired so it became known as the Jules Simon Committee. By the time he was twenty-six, Pierre had become the leading national voice for sport in the schools within the Third Republic. He had some modest early successes building sports curricula into schools, particularly the Monge School and Alsacienne, which already had rudimentary sports programs, but Grousset launched a counter-initiative almost immediately after the Jules Simon Committee was formed—and accused Pierre and his cohort of undermining French sporting traditions."

"So Grousset appealed to French nationalism?"

"Yes, that's exactly what he did, essentially labeling Pierre a traitor to his country. Grousset was his arch enemy—and he was full of vitriol for Pierre. I think he hated aristocrats in general and Pierre in particular. He claimed the baron was poisoning French students with a British sporting affliction, a disease. I read some of his criticism. He called Pierre's most successful school athletic events deplorable festivities. And he set up his own Ligue Nationale d'Éducation Physique, which basically pushed traditional French sports in a direct counter to Pierre's initiatives—and he used a fiery kind of patriotism to attack Pierre, trying to portray him as an insidious betrayer of France. He was pretty effective—he made substantial inroads into the school system and produced very effective annual sports festivals called *lendits* for a few years."

"Sounds like a very skilled opponent."

"Oh yes, Grousset was a true threat, but Pierre developed stronger allies in the government, who probably distrusted Grousset anyway from his days with the Commune. With Simon, Waddington, and Ferry in his court, Pierre ultimately triumphed. Grousset had no place in the 1889 Paris Exposition, and that's where Pierre fully consolidated his leadership role."

"But it sounds as if he stifled Pierre's work in schools to some extent."

"Indeed, he did." The baroness cupped her hand over her chin and thought for a moment. "I think Grousset's opposition actually had a positive impact on Pierre. He began to think about patriotism and nationalism in new ways—and consider their interplay with internationalism. Grousset showed him a side of patriotism that was as detestable as it was xenophobic—but very effective as a rallying cry against any outside influence. Pierre's concept of the Olympic Games was based on the blend of a healthy form of nationalism that can be celebrated in the context of a broader internationalism."

"So I can cheer for my French team when they win silver but still appreciate the achievement of the team that wins the gold."

"That's exactly right," the baroness said, looking at her watch. "The thing to remember is that Grousset's success was short lived—and Pierre was persistent. In 1890, when he met and gained the support of Père Henri Didon, he eventually had great success implementing his program into French schools."

"That's excellent, Baroness, but can we turn back to your overview?" St. Clair was worried about her time. "I didn't mean to divert you from the story, but Grousset will need to have a place in the book."

"I really have to go," she said, putting her hat back on, "but let me compress the rest of the story for you. A year before the Congress on Physical Education, Pierre sent out an international questionnaire to assess the status of sport and physical education around the world. He had more than ninety responses from U.S. clubs, colleges, and universities alone. The responses led him to establish alliances with men in America, Sweden, Germany, Hungary, Great Britain, and Greece—leaders who would later become staunch allies in the campaign for the Games, several among the first IOC members. The Universal Exposition was a great success, and although the Congress on Physical Education was a small event with just a few sport demonstrations, it created an international sports platform that was vital to Pierre's ambitions. When the exposition ended, he sailed for America, toured dozens of universities, solidified his network, and established an enduring friendship with his most powerful partner in launching the Games, William Milligan Sloane of Princeton University ..."

St. Clair was looking at his tablet, writing in his shorthand, when her voice trailed off. He looked up to see her daughter approaching the table.

"What is it, Renée?" the baroness asked sharply.

"Hello, Jacques," said Renée, casting her eyes down to the floor. "Mother, Sonya needs you at Mon Repos." Without explanation or the usual courtesies, the baroness slid out of the booth and hurried off with Renée behind her, glancing back with a little nod as they went out the side door. St. Clair knew that Sonya was the nurse who cared for the Coubertins' son, Jacques.

41

THE UPDATE

St. Clair left the Villa Mon Repos at the end of a hot day in the second week of July and started up the hill on foot, taking his time since he had a half hour before he was scheduled to meet Messerli for a drink on the Place de la Riponne. A week had passed since he had interviewed the baroness, and he felt they had been one of his most productive weeks in Lausanne. Working from Pierre's recollections of the Paris Universal Exposition of 1889, St. Clair believed he had shaped a compelling portrait of Coubertin as a dynamic young man seizing control of his destiny. In the satchel over his shoulder were five chapters of the biography he intended to give to Messerli for review.

As he reached the steep Escaliers du Marché, he stopped to browse a table of books outside one of the small shops along the stairs. He bought a dog-eared copy of *Nadja*, André Breton's surrealistic novel of ten days in Paris, a book he had read some years before in search of a new style of writing and found himself caught up with the mysteries of chance encounters and the theories of discovering true identity. He put the novel in his satchel and continued up the stairs, working his way through a stream of young men and women coming down from the hill after classes.

He sat in a shabby bentwood chair on the sidewalk at the Café Academe, which gave him a clear view of the front door and stairs of Palais de Rumine, and ordered a Pernod. As he waited for Messerli to emerge from the grand façade, he opened *Nadja* and began to read. It wasn't long before the chair beside him scraped the stone, and he looked up to see the imposing figure of Dr. Messerli, his wide smiling face under a black bowler set against the dusky sky.

"So, Jacques," Messerli said, turning the book cover up with a single finger. "I see you're consulting the surrealists to try to figure out the mysteries of Lausanne."

"Hello, Francis. I'm surprised—you know Breton?"

Messerli sat and called to the waiter for kirsch. "There was a point when all the students here were taken with the concept of automatic writing and chance encounter. Here in the serious setting of Switzerland, the Surrealist Manifesto had more impact than the spectacular art of Dali. Kurt Schwitters's collages spawned an entire movement in our art classes."

"Ah yes, the automatic writing. Never led to anything for me—although it's why I picked up the novel in the first place."

"Too bad this isn't a chance encounter, but I'm glad you called," Messerli said. "How's the baron holding up?"

"Very well, actually. He's been rowing quite a bit, walking at his usual fast pace when we take our breaks, and his recollections of Paris 1889 have been his most vivid yet."

"I know he was right in the midst of that exposition, but I don't think we've ever talked about it. What kind of progress have you been making?"

"Very productive. I've got five fresh chapters ready for you to read."

"Excellent. Do they cover the 1889 exposition?"

"Right up to his departure for the United States."

The drinks flowed as St. Clair provided Messerli with a report on his recent interviews with the baron, the baroness, and Lucien Drussard—plus his continuing research on all fronts. Soon, well past the agreed-upon time of one hour, Messerli suggested they have dinner, and he went into the café to call home. St. Clair knew Juliette would understand since interviews often kept him out later than intended, even in the quiet precincts of Lausanne.

They walked out into the night and Messerli said with some enthusiasm, "I know a great spot for *raclette* and *rosti* down by the Tower of Ale in the old city wall. It's a Swiss café, Le Restaurant du Cygne—The Swan—you'll love it."

The old wooden door of du Cygne was set back in a stone wall that formed the corner of the street, and when Messerli pushed it open St. Clair breathed in the delicious aroma of the specialties of the house. The café was below grade, and they stepped down into a sumptuous if shadowy set of small rooms with windows set high in the walls. They were seated in a booth, where Messerli ordered two Cardinal lagers and asked for the wine list.

"Jacques," he said at length, "I think you should begin to compress the interviews on his life in Paris and concentrate more on the high points of Pierre's Olympic journey." When their drinks arrived, he raised his glass and toasted: "To Pierre."

"To Pierre," St. Clair agreed. "Yes, I know it seems I've been taking a long time to get through the early years, but as I told you originally, once we get to the Games the records are rich and deep—there's a lot more documentation to pull from."

"I understand." Messerli searched St. Clair's face. "But there's a clock ticking away in the background."

"Don't worry—we'll get there. Just the other day, I told Pierre that by September we'd work through the first Games in Athens, and after that, we'd push more swiftly through the stories of each successive Olympiad."

"Do you think you can finish the first full draft by the end of the year?"

"Yes, I think so. The hard work of understanding the forces that shaped his life is nearly done."

"You know I'll extend the contract if you need more time."

"That's generous of you. Let's see where we are at the end of the year."

"Let me just say that the work I've seen so far is everything I hoped it would be." Messerli lifted his glass again.

"Thank you, Francis."

The wine arrived, a fine bottle of Pomerol, with a platter of duck hors d'oeuvres sliced as thin as carpaccio.

"There's something I've got to ask you about," St. Clair said. "I had a letter from Edgar over the weekend, and he had heard that Pierre had written something strange in his will—he wants to have his heart buried in Olympia."

"Yes. I've talked to him about it. It's an old French tradition of intellectuals and leaders committed to a cause."

"I've never heard of it."

"It's true. One of his earliest heroes was Gambetta, and Gambetta's heart is in the Panthéon. He told me there's a general whose heart is in Les Invalides, close to Napoleon's tomb—a gesture of eternal devotion."

"So he wants a permanent identification with Olympia."

"Well, given his life, his heart certainly belongs in Olympia—it's the birthplace of his destiny."

"I guess. The heart is the greatest metaphor for what we love most. But how will his heart reach Olympia—who will take it?"

"I don't know."

As the entrées were served, St. Clair reached into his satchel and withdrew a thick package of chapters. "If you'd like to read at dinner, I won't mind." He enjoyed watching others page through his work—and Messerli promptly fingered the stack of neatly typed pages.

"Well, I don't want to be rude, but if you insist, perhaps I'll just peruse the first chapter."

42

THE REFEREE AND
THE TOWER

Messerli was soon absorbed in the first of five finished chapters.

One of Coubertin's greatest strengths as a sports administrator was his mastery of the rules of all the games. He had discovered early that in sport, as in much of life, knowledge of the rules could lead to influence. He knew he could not develop an international ethics of sport—or promote the concept of chivalry on the field of play, a concept he would come to call fair play—if he didn't understand every nuance of the rules of each competitive scenario.

He could see, perhaps as well as anyone at the time, that if sport were to become part of an international exchange, each sport would need a set of rules that worked in every country. The challenge excited him, so he studied the history of each modern sport in turn and learned all that he could of the evolving rules. During his Congress for Physical Education at the 1889 Paris Exposition, he advocated strongly for the international standardization of the rules of each sport. Years later, his knowledge would give him the authority to decisively control the program of each edition of the Olympic Games—from Athens 1896 until he retired after Paris 1924. He never tired of studying the minutiae of sport.

The importance of understanding the rules was brought home for the baron one day in the Bois de Boulogne, where he had gone to watch a rugby match.

○ ○ ○ ○ ○

At the invitation of Alexandre de la Rochefoucauld, the Duc d'Éstissac, a charming and wealthy aristocrat who headed the Jockey Club of Paris, Coubertin attended an amateur rugby match near *Le Jardin d'Acclimatation* one Saturday morning in early 1886. The Rochefoucaulds and the Coubertins had been family friends for several generations, and the older duke had rallied early in support of Coubertin's physical education ideas. Pierre had twice addressed gatherings of the Jockey Club and its influential, sport-minded peerage on the need for integrating sport and exercise into French education.

The green field glistened with dew as sunlight illuminated it. Coubertin was sitting with Rochefoucauld on the top step of a rickety grandstand watching the teams emerge from the field house. He felt overdressed in a suit and silk top hat similar to Rochefoucauld's, while the handful of people on the sidelines were dressed in casual street clothes or sporting gear.

Surprised that Rochefoucauld would invite him to an event of such limited amenities, Pierre stood and jumped a few times on the stands, creating a vibration that shook the entire structure and bounced the duke off his seat.

"Get control of yourself, Pierre," Rochefoucauld exclaimed, grabbing the plank he was sitting on.

Coubertin smiled. "Not exactly the tribune of honor I expected from the Jockey Club. Your friends at Longchamp declined the invitation, I see."

"Well, this is my nephew's event, not mine. I asked you, and you alone, because I know of your affection for rugby—the town and the sport—and I wanted to get your opinion of Gerard's skills."

Coubertin scanned the players warming up on the pitch. "Yes, I see him now," he said, spotting a stocky, muscular young man with curly hair in a red jersey. The uniforms consisted of either red or black jerseys—no caps or matching pants in the British style.

As the warm-up extended and the start time passed, a commotion developed on the sideline with the linesman explaining something to the coaches while spectators gathered around him in a knot.

"No referee," Coubertin said, recognizing the problem as two men emerged—the coaches, he assumed—and walked toward the stands, obviously figuring the Duc de la Rochefoucauld was the ultimate authority on site. Gerard also jogged over.

The coach of Gerard's team spoke first. "The referee hasn't shown up, and we will not have a game without order." Other players stopped their workout to watch the discussion. "It will quickly turn into a brawl," he added.

"This is unfortunate," said the duke. "Is he on the way?"

"We have no idea," the second coach said, "and neither Jean nor I can referee with disinterest."

Pierre decided to intervene. "Do you have a whistle?" he asked. They all turned to him.

"Can you do it?" Rochefoucauld seemed a tad bemused and perhaps impressed.

"Yes, I think so. But can someone lend me a jersey and pants?" Coubertin looked at his soft leather shoes, knowing they'd be slippery on the gras. "And maybe a pair of cleats."

"I think we can suit you up, Baron," said Gerard. "Come over to the field house and we'll get you dressed."

The duke turned to him. "This is very kind of you, Pierre," he said, clearly pleased that a solution was at hand. "I had no idea you could referee."

"I called a good number of games once I mastered the rules at Rugby. Mostly with prep-school boys in England, but I'm sure the men will play fair."

Ten minutes later, Coubertin was bent over on the side of a scrum, holding the ball and trying to catch his breath before he resumed play. For the next hour, he raced up and down the field, using all the strength he could muster to pull the larger men apart when they locked arms around the ball. He managed to keep the game on course with a good pace and flow, calling only a half dozen offsides and a few high tackles. Occasionally he glanced up to see the duke enjoying his calls, particularly his shouts of "Crouch!" "Touch!" "Pause!" and "Engage!" to start the scrums. In the end, the blacks had a final try and edged out Gerard's team 23-20. As Pierre made his way to the field house to clean up, a good number of players approached and thanked him for his officiating. Duc de la Rochefoucauld was full of compliments, further insisting on hosting Pierre for dinner that night.

Coubertin enjoyed the post-match camaraderie. He drew great pleasure from his success, the fact that he could effectively assert his authority in the heat of the moment, managing a competition with tough, muscled, emotional, and often angry men. He had a few bruises, a sore shoulder—having been knocked down when a ball came out of the scrum in his direction—but he knew he wanted to do this again. Refereeing would be a good way for him to stay in shape and close to a league of teams and men who were serious about sport. He left the field that day with one pressing priority on his mind: he had to get into better condition.

○ ○ ○ ○ ○

That night at his desk at home, Coubertin set out a formal running regimen that consisted of a ten-mile loop out of his house in the 7th to the Bois de Boulogne. He was just twenty-three, but he'd already run dozens if not hundreds of times to the Bois and back since graduating from Saint-Ignace. It had been his basic exercise then, along with calisthenics, pull-ups, and some fencing, boxing, and riding—but he had never pursued fitness with the diligence of a true athlete. Occasionally, he'd run alongside other men at the Paris Racing Club, and he knew by sight a few others who circled the lakes in the Bois with some regularity. But as he increasingly saw himself as an entrepreneur of sport, Pierre knew his personal fitness was essential to the integrity of his mission.

He began running regularly in the mornings—either before he started work or mid-morning to take a break from writing. He set a pace, carried a pocket watch, and recorded his times, seeking to document his evolving theories of training and fitness. His new goal was to know precisely how the body responded to exercise over weeks, months, and years.

His body responded and brought his goals within reach, one after another, within weeks. As he trained over the next six years, Coubertin rose rapidly through the ranks of France's leading rugby match officials, reaching his amateur zenith when he stepped on the field before sixty thousand people to referee the 1892 national championship in the Stade de France. The team from the Racing Club of France prevailed over Stade Français 4–3 in that match, and as it ended Coubertin knew he would not referee many more games, although he did come out of retirement for France's first international match—versus New Zealand—on his forty-third birthday, January 1, 1906. His ambitions and his workload forced his retirement, but he would always be grateful for the discipline the role of referee had forced on him. He had gained something far greater than mere physical fitness as he ran through the Bois de Boulogne between 1886 and 1892. His running route had given him a front-row seat to history.

○ ○ ○ ○ ○

Simon had told Coubertin a major decision was pending, and one morning in late 1886 he read the story in *Le Figaro*: Gustave Eiffel, one of France's greatest engineers and the master of modern ironwork and bridge building, had won the competition to design and build the signature architecture landmark for the 1889 Paris Exposition. A great controversy immediately erupted over the winning design, an iron tower that Eiffel and his team had submitted, with a great deal of criticism flowing from the cultural literati and intelligentsia. The design became the talk of the town, not surprising in a city that defined itself as a capital of art and architecture, but the level of public debate—largely a negative reaction to the industrial aesthetic and tapering shape of the tower, was truly remarkable. Although Ferry, Simon, and Waddington reserved judgment and didn't share with Pierre their opinions of the design, public figures like Charles Garnier, who designed the brilliant Beaux-Arts opera house, let the venom flow liberally in the pages of the press. At the head of the brigade of critics, Coubertin was surprised to find Alexandre Dumas, one of France's most beloved novelists, and Guy de Maupassant, one of its finest short story writers. They expressed their outrage in an open letter to the minister of public works, calling the tower "monstrous" and labeling it "without doubt the dishonor of Paris."

But Eiffel was a man of action and within months of his victory, the grounds of the Champ de Mars began to undergo a broad transformation. On his morning runs, Coubertin watched a small army of workers excavate the building grounds nearest the Seine. As months passed, the pits grew deeper, and a set of stone walls rose from the dirt like the remnants of a long-forgotten Roman fortress. By April of 1887, four distinct pits had been dug, each with a matching set of monumental stone and mortar buttresses pointing up toward each other, constructed below ground at an angle that guided the eye upward toward some future crowning point.

Coubertin took to circling the pits and often spotted Eiffel himself below ground supervising the work. As they reached their full height, the walls were capped with extensions of steel rods and braces—some fixed with giant pneumatic pumps that Coubertin assumed might absorb any shocks to the massive infrastructure that was coming. Ingenious, he thought, running toward the Bois, remembering that it was Eiffel who had created the steel fretwork that allowed Bartholdi to adorn the Statue of Liberty with her flowing robes.

For the next twenty-two months, Coubertin marveled as "the Eiffel Tower" rose and imprinted itself in slow increments of steel and iron as the most visible and non-traditional icon on the Paris skyline. In Coubertin's estimation, Eiffel's greatness grew with each new measure of elevation. With the tower rising and the grounds of the Champ de Mars filling with the fantastical architecture of the exposition, Pierre could neither suppress nor ignore the patriotic pride that filled his heart on each run and seemed to fuel steady improvements in his speed and condition.

It seemed that each new level of the tower and the footprint of each new architectural marvel on the Champ triggered a new level of exhilaration in his dreams. Given his position and his growing influence—and his involvement in the fair itself—it was impossible not to take the achievements rising before him as a personal challenge. If this young republic could produce an exposition that surpassed anything the world had seen—and there were growing expectations in Paris this was an imminent possibility—shouldn't his own ambitions reach even further?

As the miles mounted in his log and the reality of the Universal Exposition drew nearer, he felt an increasing sense of his own good fortune. He had been born into a world of privilege for which he was grateful, and although the privileges of the nobility had now passed for the most part, he was even more grateful for the privileges that were unfolding before him through the new liberties of the Third Republic. He could not escape the idea that he was among the most fortunate of men—living in this particular time in this particular city. He felt like a navigator on a great ship heading toward a new horizon, a Columbus on the verge of a new world. He might not have been the captain of his ship, but he felt that on the frontier of sport, the sextant was in his hands.

On those long runs, Pierre discovered something else within himself, a deepening love for the city of his birth, a form of urban adulation bordering on worship. He knew his patriotism was rooted in the geography of his youth—Paris was as much a part of his being as he was an expression of its civilized culture and striving character. The city had filled his family with a love of the imaginative arts and implanted in his soul the spirit of its worldly ambitions. As he ran by the Champ de Mars, he occasionally felt a sense of regret that the magical atmosphere of the exposition was destined to be ephemeral. While the Eiffel Tower would endure, Pierre knew the dazzling architecture of the domed palaces now rising would disappear once their exhibitions were gone. He consoled himself by absorbing the greater magic of Paris itself, recognizing in the ebbs and flows of the seasons the inimitable beauty and never-ending inspiration of the City of Light.

On every narrow street and broad boulevard he coursed through, Pierre found something worthy of his admiration: the detail of a glistening bronze lion's head guarding an entrance or the dazzling life of statuary over an archway. As spring came he caught the scents of lilac and wisteria spilling down in clouds of aroma from private balconies; he marveled at the elegance of the pinnacle of white blossoms standing so proudly on the horse chestnut trees. Like a reporter on the run, there was little that escaped his eye. He found something visually delightful on every run as he traversed the neighborhoods of Paris.

As the exposition grounds on the Champ de Mars sprouted architecture like a particularly fecund forest of the imagination, the Eiffel Tower rose in precise sections that fascinated and exasperated at the same time. Paris's fine artistic sensibilities, exemplified by the grand exuberance of the Beaux-Arts tradition, found the nineteenth-century industrial age aesthetic of the new tower as offensive as the lowly row homes built for the factory workers of London. The furor and outrage seemed to know no bounds as the cultural cognoscenti continued to lead the assault on that "hulking metal beast on all fours," that "odious black skeleton," that "vertical scar on the Paris sky."

While Eiffel ignored the criticism, many sought to rally to his defense, including Jennette Montaigne, who used her poison pen to attack those she described to

Pierre as "the ludicrous reactionaries who sought to hold back the celebration of the Third Republic's undeniable progress." The controversy provided a particularly rich cast of characters for Jennette to skewer in the pages of *Le Figaro, Le Petit Journal*, and even the *Beaux-Arts Gazette*. In one of her finest and largest pieces, she drew Gustave Eiffel fencing with a sword in the shape of the tower, holding back the three musketeers of the status quo: Alexandre Dumas, Guy de Maupassant, and Charles Garnier, all of whom continued to publicly attack Eiffel's marriage of iron and art. She skewered the critics one by one, distorting their features with bulbous noses, small eyes and ears, jaws a caveman would be proud to bear, and invariably small foreheads indicating a lack of capacity for reflective thought. Pierre marveled at her ability to compress and expand the features of a face into completely identifiable public characters, their oversized and exaggerated heads capturing and expressing their hubris on small bodies. Involved as he now was at the executive level in the planning of the exposition, he fed Jennette tidbits of the unfolding controversies and internal arguments, which she quickly turned into pen points of public humiliation. She was always grateful. And when he spotted an illustrative line he had suggested, he felt as if their intimate moments had broad influence. His love for her continued to deepen along with his respect for her inimitable, rebellious artistry.

43

THE ORGANIZATION

Messerli looked up briefly, indicating his approval to St. Clair as he lifted the second chapter and began to read.

With his growing responsibilities as Jules Simon's administrative assistant for the 1889 exposition—and his own Congress of Physical Education—Coubertin found his life suddenly dominated with organizational meetings. At Jules Ferry's insistence, Simon—who had played a prominent role in helping Frédéric le Play organize the 1867 Paris Exposition and had a hand in the 1878 World's Fair as well—took an active role in monitoring the development of the entire event, attending many of the major committee meetings to stay abreast of the overall organization and the planning progress. And Simon insisted Pierre attend with him, take notes, and produce reports and lists of action items. They sat in on the transportation committee and listened to the details of the development of a small railroad that would circle the fair—the Decauville Line—allowing visitors to move from the exhibits on the Champ de Mars to the exhibits on the Esplanade des Invalides. Coubertin filled pages of notes on plans for housing the thousands of workers brought in to build and operate the exhibits, as well as the performers, craftsmen, and belly dancers who would give the fair its exotic atmosphere. They reviewed details of the construction of massive structures of the Gallery of Machines, the Halls of Humanity and the Liberal Arts, the novel national houses from all the French colonies, and the grand agricultural exhibits that would dominate the wide

293

lawns of Les Invalides. Endless contentious debates were held over the installation of the greatest exhibition of painting ever to be mounted—an extravagant version of the Salon de Paris—which would be dominated by paintings chosen to illustrate one hundred years of French artistic excellence, drawing the connection between the first brushstrokes of revolution in 1789 and the full egalitarian canvas of the Third Republic.

They attended sessions for the planning of ticket sales, the distribution of VIP passes, the opening ceremonies, the seating of dignitaries, the management of the press, and the event and programming schedule for the exposition's full three-month calendar. It would ultimately be extended to six months to accommodate the tireless crowds of tourists that relentlessly poured in and would ultimately push attendance to thirty-two million visitors—far exceeding any past exposition. There were more than sixty congresses planned across the three months, including the two Simon and Coubertin were engaged in.

Coubertin found the master planning sessions with Commissioner George Berger the most intriguing, for they were focused more on the overall experience of the spectator—the impressions created, the visions provided, the inspiration offered, and the message delivered—than on the minutiae of the exhibit details. The theme of the exposition was enlightenment, and indeed, its emphasis was on education, but it seemed to Pierre the balance would fall more to entertainment than to schooling. No doubt attentive visitors could learn everything they needed to know about the state of industrial and agricultural innovation in the world, the major trends of architecture and art, the advancements of liberalism, and equality as the framework for government. Tourists could, of course, indulge in the cultural distinctions of distant lands like Egypt, Argentina, Venezuela, Indonesia, and the disparate French colonies of Africa and Asia. But it was more likely, Coubertin anticipated, that Buffalo Bill's Wild West Show—with its retinue of rough riders and sharpshooters, including the deadeye frontierswoman Annie Oakley and her noble collaborator, Sitting Bull, chief of the Sioux Nation—would prove a stronger allure and leave a more lasting impression. By the spring of 1889, you could hardly walk fifteen feet in the city without seeing a large and colorful portrait of Buffalo Bill rearing his golden horse, with a stampede of giant buffalo running right at you.

It seemed every meeting was chaired by a different government official or organizer, and Simon offered a continuing commentary of insights on their management styles, like a talent scout pointing out deficiencies and strengths in various players. Once a week Simon and Coubertin would meet with Ferry, and Simon would provide an overview of progress, pointing out delays and issues and pushing for decisions—and then Ferry would meet with Commissioner Berger, equipped with notes on what had to be prioritized.

Several times, Coubertin complained he had work to do on his own congress and couldn't possibly attend so many meetings, but Simon demanded his time. "This is quite an education you're getting in the art and science of organizing large-scale events," he said. "It's like a degree program in event production, Pierre, so be grateful. There's no university that could teach you what you're learning at my side."

Ferry expressed pleasure in the quality of Coubertin's reports and dispatched him, without Simon, to do a full examination of the development of the exhibits in the Palace of Liberal Arts, which would depict the history and promise of republicanism in France—the full artistic affirmation of liberté, égalité, and fraternité under the Third Republic. That was reward enough to keep Coubertin motivated.

Fortunately for Pierre, Simon's engagement in the First Universal Peace Congress moved along more sanguinely and his responsibilities were minimal. The co-chairs, Frédéric Passy of Paris and Hodgson Pratt of London, were hands-on, effectively directing the overall organization with a cooperative alacrity that seemed to personify the very notion of peaceful harmony. Their meetings moved swiftly through all agenda points, neatly recorded by several secretaries, and Simon relieved Pierre of any reporting responsibilities.

Bertha von Suttner made sure Pierre understood what was taking place. One afternoon, as Pierre and Bertha were standing inside the Palace of Liberal Arts, waiting for Simon to emerge from a private session with Charles Garnier, she gave him an update.

"The growing influence of the peace movement is undeniable, Pierre," she said, speaking insistently as she always did.

They watched workers apply buckets of white plaster to the rock formation of a cave that would serve as the Pleistocene-era home of the Neanderthal man in Garnier's timeline. His exhibit on the History of Human Habitation would span the ages.

"Tell me again why you call it a movement?" Pierre asked.

"Because it's a set of ideas that are spreading from nation to nation—leader to leader—instilling hope that the new forces of internationalism will help our world move beyond conflict and find alternatives to the tragedy of war."

"A movement of ideas," said Pierre. "Seems a bit idealistic in the age of Bismarck."

"We've already moved beyond Bismarck. Don't focus on the old, focus on the young. New ideas need to be planted in young minds. You'll see. The Universal Peace Congress is going to reveal a focus on the young—on educating the next generation in the ideals of peace."

"Are you going to be working through the education systems in each country?"

Bertha took his arm and led him out on the terrace of the palace. "Yes, we are, but Pratt and Passy also want to create an annual international peace congress that travels the world and draws together young people from all nations. Paris will be the first."

"For what? Congresses on peace, lectures, and philosophical discussions every year? That's an aggressive calendar. You can only host an exposition of these proportions"—he swept his arm from the Eiffel Tower across the flowering display of landscaping, the fountains, statuary, and architecture, squinting up at the bright blue sheen of the Grand Dome glinting in the sun—"once every ten years."

"I think they have a less elaborate festival in mind," said Bertha, "but they are talking about bringing young people together for seminars on peacemaking, cultural and artistic endeavors, even sporting competitions among nations."

"Sporting competitions? Annual international sports competitions?"

"Something like that. You'll hear about it in the congress."

Simon emerged then, and as they walked down the steps into the Court of Honor together, Pierre said, "Bertha has just told me that Passy and Pratt have plans for a series of annual international peace congresses with sporting competitions on the side."

"Sport for peace. Why not? We can build international friendships through sport. Pierre," Simon said, "that's an effort worthy of your talent."

○ ○ ○ ○ ○

Coubertin gained other benefits attending all these meetings, of course. His network of contacts expanded geometrically. Everyone seemed to recognize Simon's young confederate. They knew Simon had written the preface to Coubertin's book, and that book—L'Éducation Anglaise en France—had already given the young man a name in France's sports community. People saw him as an accessible ally—and even approached him to present ideas to Simon. Among other insights, he gained an insider's view of the schedule of events. He knew exactly where the organizational problems were, how most exhibits were behind their construction deadlines, and how far behind Eiffel was with the elevators on his tower. He knew the exposition would hardly be ready for its opening on Monday, May 6, but he also knew it didn't really matter. The crowds would turn out, and even if the exhibits weren't all installed, the magic of the environment created—the power and allure of the architecture, gardens, and fountains—would be more than enough to create the kind of irresistible locus in the collective imagination that only such extravagant public events could engender.

With all of his responsibilities, Coubertin was forced to neglect his romance with Jennette, breaking engagements and then showing up late at her apartment for rather hurried, intimate encounters. Although he knew he was putting his ambitions before his love, Jennette didn't seem to mind—and seemed content to embrace love on the run. As the grand opening of the exposition approached, he was looking for ways to draw her into the excitement of his career—to find an opportunity to spend more time with her—and he found it in one of the commissioner's secretive plans. Two days before the grand opening—on a Saturday night after dark fell and no one was paying much attention to their fair grounds—a light test would be performed. Paris was the capital of modernity, and the miracle of illumination—electric light—was coming to this Universal Exposition for the first time on a large scale. To produce what they hoped would be an unprecedented visual spectacle—and a thrill to everyone in the throngs who witnessed it—Commissioner Berger had planned to throw a switch and light up the entire fair on opening night with a hundred thousand light bulbs. The test was planned to ensure the system would work, and Pierre anticipated it would be a spectacular sight.

"I thought I knew everything about Pierre's involvement in the Universal Exposition, but I never heard he had served as Simon's assistant like that," Messerli said, taking a sip of beer and flipping to the third of the five chapters St. Clair had given him. "This is going to be a great biography, Jacques."

44

LA VILLE-LUMIÉRE

With the help of the family coachman, Henri, Pierre loaded a set of small chairs and a picnic table into the boot of the carriage. He purloined one of his mother's finest tablecloths and several candelabra. He filled a case with a chilled bottle of champagne, several bottles of Bordeaux, a few fine blocks of cheese and dried ham and some grapes, then carefully placed the crystal in a soft padded basket. He had prepared his aging parents for a Saturday night out and insisted they stay up past their usual bedtime—but he refused to tell them where they were going or why. Henri had the carriage ready at seven-thirty, and they rode across the pont d'Iéna to pick up Jennette at her apartment. As Pierre helped her into the carriage, she greeted Charles and Marie—whom she knew from a few dinners together— and asked immediately if they knew what the evening was all about.

"We have no idea where we're going," said his father. "Even Henri has refused to disclose our destination."

"Well," his mother said, "it must be some special introduction to the exposition, although we certainly aren't dressed for the occasion." Pierre had insisted they all wear casual clothes suitable for a picnic. The carriage jostled along, retracing its route to the pont d'Iéna. Henri stopped at a lovely patch of lawn on the top of a hill by the Trocadéro, and as he and Pierre busied themselves setting up the table and chairs, Jennette, Charles, and Marie took in the stunning view of the exposition grounds just across the Seine.

"Magnificent," said Charles. Pierre was pleased that his father appraised the scene with the eye of a master painter—and approved.

From their promontory, they had a spectacular view of the Eiffel Tower, now standing in the full glory of a new industrial art aesthetic. Behind the tower, the Court of Honor was enclosed by the three major palaces, each crowned with sparkling turquoise domes, giant faience-tiled spheres that created a glimmering allure in the fading twilight of the spring night. The angle of the view gave them a broader perspective of the fairgrounds than they would have had from the Trocadéro, which looked directly through the arched legs of the tower.

"So, Pierre," asked Marie, "have you brought us here for another dazzling display of fireworks?"

"Not exactly, Mother." He and Henri spread a thick blanket over the ground. "But I believe you'll be more than thrilled by the vision that's coming."

"A vision?" his father said, turning back to the site to look for clues. A string of men appeared to be checking the rivets up and down the full shaft of the tower.

"Yes, Father, you're going to see something no one has ever seen before."

"We've got chairs, so why the blanket?" asked Jennette, smiling.

"Just in case we want to relax." He had placed it there so they could contemplate the stars together after the lights had gone out and Henri had taken his parents home.

"Look at that crowd on the terrace at the Trocadéro," he said, turning everyone in that direction. "Must be something going on here tonight." Indeed, there was a small gathering of people drinking behind the balustrade, waiting, he knew, for the moment of illumination. Even at this distance, he recognized a few men from their planning meetings. The commissioner had sworn everyone to secrecy, but Pierre could see small crowds gathering along the Seine.

As the light faded and they sat around the table watching the magnificent details of the exposition disappear in a slow dissolve, Pierre lit the candelabra and filled the time by pointing out the purpose of the buildings and the overall layout of the fair, with which they were familiar from the incessant newspaper coverage. The city's gas lamps came on and filled the streets along the quay below them with circles of light reflected in the shimmering surface of the Seine. The chugging sound of the diminutive Decauville Railroad rolled across the water and then faded as it rounded the corner of the Invalides Esplanade in a final test run. Amid the gaslights at street level, workers were scurrying around the expo grounds; faint hammering came from inside the exhibit halls, and they heard the occasional metallic growl of the Otis elevators starting and stopping in the legs of the tower, still not ready to lift the crowds up through the iron fretwork.

Checking his watch in the candlelight, Pierre popped the cork of the champagne just before ten o'clock and filled their glasses to raise a toast to what he hoped would be a dramatic and unforgettable moment. Feeling a certain gratitude for the men who had placed him in this position, and for what he knew they all hoped would be a grand and enduring confirmation of the Third Republic's progress, Pierre decided to chance annoying his father with a slightly political toast.

"Henri," he said, lifting another glass of champagne for their coachman, "please join us."

They all stood as Pierre addressed them, lifting their glasses to his. "Mother, Father, Jennette ... may the vision of the Third Republic illuminate our hearts and lift our souls tonight. While I know you don't agree with all my egalitarian sentiments, I'm hoping you are as thrilled as I am by what we're about to see. May the beacon of light that radiates from here tonight bring honor to France and carry the message of Gambetta, Ferry, Simon, and Carnot across the seas. *Santé.*"

They drank and his father looked at him and said, "Well, son, I hope your republic stabilizes and lasts long enough to—" He didn't finish the idea. Suddenly a wave of light streaked across Pierre's face and his father turned as a chorus of amazement—gasps, oohs, aahs, and cheers—rose from the Trocadéro and other unseen quarters as they all beheld a scene of illumination nearly beyond their imaginations.

The Eiffel Tower was painted in strings of light that hung against the night sky like glistening phosphorescent pearls. The beauty of its design was crystallized by tens of thousands of bulbs laced from its broad legs up to its jewel-like crown, which radiated circling lighthouse beams across the rooftops of Paris—as if it were introducing the city to a future of electrical magic. While the tower dominated the scene, the grounds below were filled with their own illuminated fascinations.

"Look at the Court of Honor," said Pierre, and everyone dropped their eyes to the white façades around the courtyard, which looked as though they were emerging from a sea of liquid brightness.

"It's as if the sun is trying to rise through the surface of the earth," Marie said. "Thank you, Pierre, for showing your old mother this delightful miracle."

"This makes the tower look like a masterpiece," his father said. "Its four sections are so clearly defined, and its lines now seem so much more elegant."

Indeed, the grand arches of the tower's legs were outlined in curved strings of light framed like a painting in two broader rectangular strings, which stood dramatically beneath the shelf of the first platform, a much more intense concentration of lights in a repetitive pattern of barrel-like casks that Jennette described as "thirty bottles of crystalline champagne standing side by side, ready to be popped."

"Brilliant," said Pierre.

His father added, "I love the crown."

Their gazes rose again, tracing the narrowing strings of white toward the diadem at the tower's pinnacle.

"That design is truly remarkable," said Jennette, admiring the artistry of the finely placed mosaic of bulbs at the top. "Just below the crown, it looks like a collar above a jeweled necklace."

"Indeed it does," said his mother. "I guess this crown sits on the head of a queen."

Charles put his arm around Marie's shoulders. "Whether it's a king or queen, it's a beautiful moment for France."

And just as suddenly as it had appeared, the light vanished and the ephemeral moment of magic passed. They all laughed together, sharing the joy of wonders to come in a final toast.

"I suppose we'll see this scene every night for the next three months," his mother said. "I think I may have to change my bedtime."

After Henri had packed and taken the elder Coubertins away in the carriage, Pierre and Jennette lay side by side, gazing up at the distant lights of the stars. His head and heart were still filled with the inspiration of the vision. "It's as if God has dropped his celestial canopy on Paris tonight just to show us the possibilities ahead."

"I'll grant you the grand possibilities, but what we saw tonight had nothing to do with God. That was the work of a genius or two."

"Eiffel and Edison?"

"Yes, those two. But forget about them right now, will you?" She leaned into him and kissed him deeply.

"I very much like the way you've presented this extraordinary event in the context of his family—and even his affair," Messerli said. Enthralled by the flow of the story, he picked up the fourth chapter and focused again on the page.

45

THE UNIVERSAL
EXPOSITION

On Monday, May 6, 1889, the grand opening of the Paris Universal Exposition was scheduled for two o'clock at a state ceremony in the Court of Honor. Jules Simon had invited Pierre to join him in the delegation of ministers and officials accompanying France's president, Sadi Carnot, along a parade route from the Champs-Élysées across the pont d'Iéna to enter the court through the great arches of the Eiffel Tower. Pierre politely declined the invitation, saying he wanted to witness the pomp and circumstance—and the arrival of the president's parade—from inside the court itself. Simon was perplexed by the refusal to accept the honor of marching in with the president of the republic—but he understood when Pierre said he wanted to share the moment with Jennette, Jean Aicard, and a close circle of friends. They agreed to meet at the ceremony.

Pierre had secured seats for six in the grandstands from Commissioner Berger's office and had invited Jennette, Jean, Drussard, Georges de Saint-Clair, his partner in putting on the Congress of Physical Education, and Bertha von Suttner to join him. They agreed to meet on the southwest corner of the Champ de Mars near the École Militaire at noon Monday—so they could go into the Court of Honor together through a VIP entrance, avoiding the crush of the two hundred thousand people lined up at the main gates. He was marveling at the full measure of the Eiffel Tower when they began to arrive. An infectious festive atmosphere filled the air as Jennette took his arm and they moved through the gate, walking around the massive gleaming structure of the glass and iron Gallery of Machines—the largest single building in the exposition. As they made their way around its perimeter, Pierre told them what he knew from the meetings.

"It's a dazzling display of architecture, but there's little sense in going inside since there's only one exhibit finished at this point—Thomas Edison's electric circus."

"Well, wouldn't that be worth seeing?" asked Jennette.

"Don't worry—we'll see it later. President Carnot is scheduled to tour the Palais des Beaux-Arts and then visit the Edison exhibit. We'll follow him on his walkabout."

The Gallery of Machines enclosed more than fifteen acres. With Jennette on his arm and his friends in tow, Pierre offered a running commentary on the extraordinary sites and architecture as they made their way across the court and climbed up the grandstands. Scarcely twenty minutes after they were in their seats, the crowd roared as a platoon of cuirassiers appeared on the bridge on horseback and in full regalia, framed perfectly beneath the tower's massive iron arches. As the horses pranced forward in nearly perfect unison, the cockaded helmets of the cuirassiers shimmering in the sunlight, Pierre caught glimpses of the dignitaries marching behind a flock of tricolor flags. A single brigadier general led them across the bridge, his feathery plumes waving above the glint of his breastplate. The Court of Honor was roped off to create a passageway for the procession, and a hundred members of the French Honor Guard held back crowds surrounding the fountains and extravagantly landscaped flowerbeds in the center of the court.

From the height of the small grandstand where they sat, they had a spectacular view of the setting and the proceedings. Looking up they could see the rococo dome shining in the sunlight like the eye of God—crowned by the seven-meter statue of Marianne, the symbolic embodiment of all that France had become and hoped to be.

There was much to take in. The avenues in front of the twin Beaux-Arts Palaces that flanked the Court of Honor were lined with allegorical statues of heroic figures like those on the roofline of St. Peter's. As the parade crossed under the far arch of the tower, Pierre spotted President Carnot; Jules Ferry and Jules Simon walked together two rows behind him and the ministers of his cabinet.

The cacophony of cheers and the beat of the horses' hooves could not drown out the trumpets and timpani that heralded the arrival of the marchers. Pierre's gaze swept from the Eiffel's crown to the lush gardens and still-dry fountains. As he took in the classical cachet of the statuary and the fine lines of the walls formed by the flanking palaces, it occurred to Pierre that France had succeeded in creating one of the most wondrous open-air theaters of all time. The space felt like a cathedral under the sky. The moment held a tangible spirit he was certain everyone present could feel. He turned to Jennette to share his joy, and she met his look and kissed him fully on the lips. This was a moment of national and personal pleasure.

They stood to cheer and Jean reached out and embraced them both—just as the president and his entourage mounted the steps to the festooned stage beneath the central dome. Once everyone was settled, Prime Minister Pierre Tirard led the crowd in a salute to the Tricolor as it was raised and the band struck up "La Marseillaise," which lifted the emotional tenor even higher. This was not the prime minister's show, however, and he quickly turned the podium over to President Carnot, whose first order of business was the dedication of the statue of Marianne. Jean and Lucien rose first to join the wave of applause for the statue that harkened back to Mother Mary, suggesting the heroics of Joan of Arc and looking ahead to a society of full liberty, equality, and fraternity. The president began his speech, and Pierre tried to concentrate on his rhetoric. He heralded the arrival of a new age for all humanity. He offered a perspective of what was worth celebrating on the one-hundredth anniversary of the French Revolution—the rights of man and the impulse toward a republic in which everyone had a chance to speak and be heard. As Pierre had known it would, patriotic pride swelled inside him. He remembered telling his mother when he was young that he had a wild love for France, and he knew at that moment it was still very much alive. As his circle of friends stood close together, Carnot seemed to speak for all of them. The president praised the gains of the Third Republic in its eighteenth year and congratulated his nation on its creative imagination and the soaring heights of its vision, raising his arm to indicate the greatest single expression of that vision in Eiffel's Tower—which drew another roar of approval from the crowd.

When Carnot finished, a few officials brought a large switch to the podium—a prop, no doubt—but the president played along and demonstrated a certain theatricality, exaggerating his gestures as he threw the switch. Another moment of jubilation followed as water erupted simultaneously across the basins of the grand fountains, jets of foam leaping into the air in cross currents that arched over the scene like a natural celebration, spouting from the mouths of dolphins.

Pierre and Jennette hurried down the grandstand and stepped into the president's delegation, moving to Simon's side as they walked up the steps of the Palais des Beaux-Arts.

"Quite a performance," said Pierre, leaning close to Simon's shoulder as Commissioner Berger and the head of the Fine Arts Commission guided President Carnot through the highlights of an unfinished retrospective of a century of the greatest French paintings.

"I thought the cuirassiers were a bit much, but given General Boulanger's supposed threats, they probably struck the right note." Simon paused as Berger explained a gap in the national artistic narrative, whisking the delegation by several blank walls in one gallery they passed through.

The president stopped Berger in mid-sentence, having seen enough of this unfinished masterpiece, and said loudly, "Let's go see the Edison exhibit. I hear it's fascinating."

Inside the vast steel-and-glass Gallery of Machines, which was filled mostly with unopened crates, Berger hurriedly led the way to Edison's fantastically illuminated one-acre exhibition. Even in the light of day, it shined with an undeniable brilliance. And Edison, playing the role of the genius inventor—complete with a full mop of disheveled white hair—stepped forward like a young boy, his waistcoat half unbuttoned, and brushed by Berger to shake the president's hand with great enthusiasm.

While electric light had been his most sensational exhibit to date, Edison was rolling out his next great breakthrough at the exposition—the phonograph, featuring the earliest audio recordings in history. Most people had heard about it, but few had experienced the sensational effect of hearing the human voice and sound effects reproduced by a machine.

Jennette nudged Pierre, and they moved away from Simon to the circle that had formed around Edison and the president, who was staring at the mysterious wax cylinder on the odd machine Edison was describing. As the president watched, Edison lowered a thin metal tube onto the cylinder—and to everyone's astonishment, the music of "The Marseillaise" filled the room, a tenor delivering a clear rendition.

As the anthem ended, Edison showed the president another phonograph with earphones attached. Edison demonstrated how to use the device, then reached out to help Carnot remove his top hat so he could put the earphones in place.

"He's so American," Jennette whispered, almost giggling. "Not an ounce of shyness in that man."

"Yes, he's quite the showman."

The president wheeled around, looking at the crowd with great excitement, hearing something they could only imagine. "Bravo, Mr. Edison," he yelled, not realizing the effect of the earphones on his sense of volume. "Bravo!"

As Edison led Carnot and his entourage into the heart of his exhibit, most of the crowd lingered behind and waited patiently in line to try the earphones at a lineup of five phonographs. When their turn came, Pierre and Jennette faced each other as they heard a deeply resonant but mechanical American voice, say, "Vive Carnot, vive la France, vive la république!"

"That opening must have been a great experience for Pierre," Messerli said. "But as I recall, it was the beginning of the end for him and Jennette, wasn't it."

"Yes, it was," St. Clair replied.

"I'll read the last chapter at home, Jacques, but this is far more than I hoped for. I'm not a literary critic, but it seems to me you're rising to a new level of writing here."

Walking home that night in the heat of July, St. Clair felt the warmth of Messerli's affirmation inside. He knew he was on the right path with the biography—and hoped the doctor liked the chapter on the exposition as much as the previous four.

46

THE EXPERIENCE

Over the next three weeks, as he and Georges de Saint-Clair prepared their Congress on Physical Education, Pierre found the time to escort Jennette to nearly every exhibit in the Universal Exposition. Happy that his parents approved of the Third Republic's triumph, he also took them to the fair for lunch a few times, once to the first level of the Eiffel Tower, where they could hardly stop chattering about the landmarks they could see as they strolled around the promenade.

Of all the exhibits, Jennette loved the narrow passageway of rue de Cairo, a winding Egyptian street in a canyon of stuccoed white walls rising over a *souk* of shops, restaurants, and bars. The street was always crowded with Egyptian boys guiding donkey carts from shop to shop, selling merchandise made by Cairo craftsman, all authentic, all fascinating. Crowded around the base of the Eiffel were the exquisite architectural pavilions of Bolivia, Nicaragua, Argentina, and Mexico, each crafted with unfamiliar design motifs and rooflines that transported visitors into a world of fantasy, a fairy tale of international creativity.

With Jennette on his arm, Pierre walked up to the quay d'Orsay, where France's colonial countries had built pavilions and mounted exhibits that brought their cultures to life through the presence of native artists, chefs, and performers of all kinds. They watched African woodcarvers work their craft on avenue de Gabon, dipped Vietnamese stick bread in fish sauce on rue d'Haiphong, and drank sweet tea while a troupe of tiny Javanese dancers delighted a crowd with stylish costumes and enormous headdresses. They stepped into a Cambodian pagoda, smoked a hookah in a Tunisian casbah, and climbed the minaret of an Algerian mosque.

On the grand esplanade of Les Invalides, they toured the War Pavilion—and Pierre experienced mixed emotions over his pride of French military history and his recent engagements with the peace movement. As they took in the exhibits on agriculture in France and across Europe—Pierre guided them to the viticulture displays and they spent a considerable amount of time with the winemakers of Bordeaux.

Every night, la Ville Lumière came to life, and its incandescence seemed to light up most of the tens of thousands of revelers on hand. The sensuality of the evening was heightened by the exotic sounds, sights, smells, and tastes of a temporal world celebrating the nightlife of distant cultures. Deep on rue de Cairo late one night, Jennette pulled Pierre toward the high-pitched tremolo of an Arabian song accompanied by chimes and drumbeats and Ottoman strings. The melody blended with approving murmurs from an audience sensationalized by the exotic moves of an Egyptian belly dancer—her veiled mouth, hands, legs, and hips stirring fantasies beyond any Pierre had had in the clubs of Montmartre.

Amid this dizzying spectacle, Coubertin saw the possibilities for his future unfolding. On the one hand, he had earned a respected place among the leaders of the Third Republic; on the other, he had found a woman he loved deeply. Every day at the fair, he felt the emotions of both national pride and personal desire course through his heart like the dual pulses of Edison's electrical currents.

While he would sail for North America in August to continue his research into the phenomenal spread of university sport in the United States, he knew he would return to even greater opportunities and personal pleasures. He decided he would ask Jennette to marry him before his departure.

○ ○ ○ ○ ○

Sitting at the Café Angleterre with St. Clair, Coubertin reached the point in his recollections when he had planned to propose to Jennette.

"My God," the old man said. "I haven't thought about that moment for four decades."

"What?" asked St. Clair, "You haven't thought about the moment you proposed to her? Really?"

"No, I haven't—probably because I never did propose. Our love affair fell apart."

"What happened?"

"I could say it's a long story, but it isn't really. Every night we were going home to Jennette's place—riding that little elevator up to her apartment—enjoying Paris in all its glories. And one night we stopped at her mailbox in the doorway and there was a letter in a small envelope from London. I saw the reaction on her face, a shock, then undeniable excitement. She tucked it away and I didn't ask her about it because I'd seen the return address. I knew it was from Lord Robert—the man who had been her lover before we met."

"Did he return?"

○ ○ ○ ○ ○

Pierre and Jennette were due to have lunch the next day, after which they were to meet Georges de Saint-Clair at the Petit Palais to go over the plans for the kick-off session for their congress—but she sent a message saying she couldn't meet, that something had come up and she had to see the editor at *Figaro*. He let it go, but then she canceled their dinner that night and again the next day. Then she simply stopped communicating. He went to her apartment but couldn't find her, and he sent message after message to no avail. The following week, the day the Congress on Physical Education was going to begin with a session called Equitation and the Art of Riding, which she had promised to attend long ago, a terse note arrived: "Apologies, but I cannot come, Pierre."

He longed to hear her voice, even knowing it would rise with uncharacteristic emotion and falter as she told him the truth. He heard the conversation again and again in his mind—and saw scenes he could hardly endure.

"It's Robert, isn't it? Is he coming back to Paris or is he already here?"

"Please don't ask," she would say in a muffled cry.

He distracted himself with the work at hand. The equitation session drew a sparse crowd from the Jockey Club, a reflection of Pierre's waning interest and lack of last-minute promotion—something he usually excelled at. And while he gave a decent talk and worked with Georges de Saint-Clair on stage to demonstrate a number of riding techniques, with two riders on a wooden horse, he wasn't as present as he should have been.

Two nights later, at a crowded reception on the second terrace of the Eiffel Tower—an event staged by Commissioner Berger for a group of publishers and journalists and filled with his exposition colleagues—Pierre turned away from a conversation at the sound of a familiar trilling laugh. Across the room, leaning on the railing, stood Jennette. Her back was to him, and the arm of a tall, handsome stranger—Lord Robert, no doubt—encircled her waist. He started toward her, then stopped as she turned to look into the room. Robert turned with her, and as she met Pierre's gaze, she lost her smile and a crestfallen look shaded her face. The moment was as uncomfortable as any he had ever experienced, and while he yearned to go and confront her, he turned away instead, not back to his colleagues, but toward the stairwell and the long descent down to the ground.

"That must have been devastating," St. Clair said, "and you still had the congress to run."

"The congress wasn't much of a problem," Coubertin said. "Georges de Saint-Clair was a true friend—and he essentially covered for me. He saw the state I was in and stepped up to run the show with the full support of the Jules Simon Committee. I put in an appearance at each of the remaining sessions, and that's about all it was—an appearance. We produced basic seminars on gymnastics, shooting, swimming, rowing, and track and field, mostly walking and running. Our emphasis was always on technique and the need for standardized rules. The École Monge, which at the time had the best sports program of any school in Paris, provided young athletes for a few demonstrations, bringing the discussions to life—with rowing on the Seine and race-walking in the Bois— but we didn't organize any serious competitive events, and frankly, the turnout was disappointing. Our closing session was in a meeting room at the *Palais des Beaux-Arts*—I gave a speech summarizing the results of my international survey on the state of physical education at schools, clubs, colleges, and universities in North America, Britain, and across Europe."

"Did your research reveal any international trends?"

"The primary revelation was the enormous, accelerating growth of sport. It was easy to see a pattern emerging independently in so many different countries—sport was on the rise. It was stronger in the university system of the United States than anywhere else, larger in scale by far than the growth seen in England. It wasn't perfectly clear what the future held, but in retrospect it should have been clear the United States was primed to emerge as the world's leading sporting nation."

"I still don't know how you went through the motions given what Jennette did to you."

"Well, now that I think of it," Pierre said with a slight grin, "I did deliver quite an impromptu piece at the end of the speech, and it was well received."

○ ○ ○ ○ ○

Having covered the details of his research in some statistical depth, reporting on the data that came in from more than 130 colleges, universities, and clubs around the world—the sports played, the number of participants, the organized leagues and competitions—Pierre laid his papers aside. His audience looked at him expectantly. He considered an abrupt departure—thinking he might flee the room just to escape the formality and the trappings of the life that had left a hole in his heart. He wanted to go for a long walk or have a drink—the emotional turmoil of Jennette's betrayal was starting to rise again—but the attendees began to murmur and he realized he had to take control, not only of himself but of the room. He decided to offer his personal interpretation of what all the numbers meant—and he suddenly felt a wave of inspiration on the inside, the pain turning to anger, the turmoil giving rise to clarity.

The ornate, gilded hall in the *Palais des Beaux-Arts* was filled with about a hundred people, most from the Parisian écoles who had been invited by the Jules Simon Committee in hopes of building a stronger school sports system in France. This was the audience he wanted—the very people who could help him implement his program and change the lives of French children. Pierre let the murmur build as he looked out across the room, catching Bertha's gaze. She sat next to Simon, who was looking at the papers in his lap, pen in hand, no doubt making notes for his own keynote speech to the Universal Peace Congress in a few days. Pierre raised his hand, asking for calm.

"Somewhere right now a child is bent over, lacing his leather shoes on the side of a green field," he began, "ready to run onto the pitch and join his friends in kicking a ball around for an hour. It is difficult to make the leap from the simple game they're playing to the foundations that sustain an empire, but nonetheless, there is a direct link. The greatest educator of our time saw the future in those green fields—he saw the potential benefits to society of boys who grew toward manhood while learning the rudimentary lessons of teamwork, the rewards of personal discipline, the character that comes from enduring a loss—as much as the joy of celebrating a victory.

"Sir Thomas Arnold of Rugby saw that and much more. He saw the full potential of sport—not just to strengthen the body, but to focus the mind. Not just to build muscle, but to shape character. Not just to create camaraderie within a team, but to unite a community and fill it with pride.

"Arnold created something unique at Rugby—sport with a social purpose. Sport that fostered the values of friendship and respect, of personal sacrifice for the greater good, of lifting your mates up when they're down and encouraging them—no, inspiring them—to achieve something greater.

"The system Arnold invented—which was quickly adapted and implemented across the entire English school system, from prep to university—turned out generation after generation of Englishmen who were effectively prepared to serve their society, to find their place, their unique role, in helping lift the British Empire to the heights it has achieved. All the while, our own country was stumbling through two monarchies, two empires, three republics, and four revolutions.

"Today, France is on the precipice of something new. The exposition we're part of is a statement about the potential of our new society. What we've achieved as a nation these last eighteen years is admirable—but there is so much more we can do together. Today, our future rests neither in politics nor in religion—but in the direction education will take.

"We have been thoroughly criticized, even attacked, I would say, by Monsieur Grousset and those in his Ligue, for our love of Anglo-Saxon sport, for looking to England for the model we want to install in our schools and the values we want to instill in our children through sport—as if the very notion of placing a British model of success before our children would poison them. But it's foolish to criticize success, or to withdraw into a shell of old and ineffective traditions.

"Thus I say to you—the schoolmasters of France—the statistics are true, the trends are clear. Look at America and the ways in which the power of sport is already lifting that young nation. They have taken the Arnoldian regime to heart. Here in France, we are building a new society—and sport must find its place at the heart of our nation as well.

"The Third Republic is offering the world a new vision and new traditions—and sport must take its rightful place, as it is all over the world. We are entering a new age of sport, dare I say a new age of international sport. It is not difficult to foresee a day when nations will compete on the field of play, when one country will test its skills against the next just as the school in your arrondissement will compete against the next one.

"We cannot and should not be denied our place among the world's greatest sporting nations. But to achieve this end, it is essential that we institute a new model of physical education within our school system. My colleagues and I in the Jules Simon Committee are ready to help—but we need your endorsement and your authority. We need you to throw open the doors of your schools and allow us in—to complete this great education reform that Duruy, Ferry, Waddington, and Jules Simon have nurtured across all these years."

Hearty applause followed the speech. Simon was one of the first to the podium, among a number of people who wanted to shake Coubertin's hand and thank him for the inspiration. "Well done," Simon said, leaning in closely, "and we'll do even better next time. Take a look at this." He pressed a copy of his keynote speech into Pierre's hands. "I'll need you there Sunday night."

After Pierre finished shaking hands and thanking the attendees, Bertha and Georges were waiting at the door.

"Well, we got through it all right," said Georges. "I'm sorry our sports demonstrations were not more competitive, but we did as much as we could."

"I propose we all have a drink to celebrate, gentlemen," Bertha said, taking both of them by the arm and leading them toward the door. As they wove through the pulsing throng of fairgoers in the long hall of the Palais des Beaux-Arts, they passed a room with an exhibition that tugged at Pierre's heartstrings. He stopped for a moment and glanced into the doorway to observe a crowd hovering over Victor Laloux's remarkable re-creation of ancient Olympia, a waist-level model on a wide table with each building, colonnade, monument, pathway, and field identified by the German archaeologists rendered in precise detail. He promised himself he would return for a proper view of Laloux's masterful work before he sailed for North America.

JOY AND PAIN

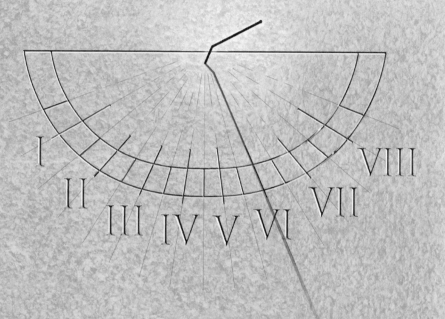

47

THE ATLANTIC

After retreating to the Château de Mirville for a month of isolation and long-walks in the woods—an attempt to purge Jennette's betrayal from his heart and mind—Coubertin took the train from the gare Saint-Lazare up to Le Havre and sailed for New York City on the SS *La Normandie* of the French Line, a two-stack steamer that made the crossing in sixteen days. As he boarded the ship, he felt an immense disquietude rolling inside like the waves of the ocean. The emotional vestiges of his love for Jennette still had a hold on him. As restless and unsettled as he'd ever been, he spent the first evening on board walking the decks and passageways, ignoring the placid ocean vistas while staying as far away as he could from the roving parties and revelers in the bar. He'd have time to mix and drink later—all he wanted at the outset was to be alone and exhaust himself with exercise. After about eight hours up and down all the levels of the ship, he finally felt fatigue entering his body and his mind. He slept from the middle of the night to the middle of the next afternoon.

Pulling a polished deck chair out of a long row, he found an isolated spot on the port side, sheltered from the sun by the overhanging lifeboats, and settled in with a notebook. He intended to assess what he had learned from the exposition—and what he had lost after his five-year love affair with Mademoiselle Montaigne.

He considered his experience as part of the organizing team of the most successful world's fair in history. The Paris Universal Exposition would ultimately attract thirty-two million visitors in six months—a number nearly matching

France's population of thirty-eight million. He made notes as he thought about the staging, the architecture, and the logistics of running and funding such a massive operation for so long—the workers, the housing, the transportation, the ticketing, the ceremonies, the economics, the budgets, and the inevitable difficulties and obstacles. He wrote about how, despite innumerable backroom glitches, missed deadlines, and myriad small failures, it had all come together in a spectator experience of unrivaled brilliance.

He considered the essential role of the commissioner, the executive who had led the development and the implementation of all ideas, with a committee of executives layered beneath and an army of assistants always ready to address the urgencies of the moment. And he thought about the vision of the leaders of the Third Republic—of Ferry, in particular, but of le Play before him, and Grévy, Carnot, Simon, and Waddington—men who had launched an undefined event with the confidence that they would find their way. Men with an unshakable belief that the exposition itself—once realized—would serve as the ultimate stamp of approval on their political philosophy and egalitarian society.

What he had learned—and what he had seen—gave him a sense of the possibilities of organizing and producing an event on a massive scale, an event that would be deliberately temporal, if not ephemeral in its duration, but would exert a hold on the imagination. An event that could inspire a city, a nation, or even the world with its creativity, its cultural significance, its magnitude, and its promise of a future of untold possibilities. He wondered if his passion for sport and physical education might play an even greater role in the development of such an event—and wondered if sport could be its central organizing principle.

For several days at sea he concentrated on writing, making a long list of points to remember and lessons to carry forward from his recent experience. He integrated some of these key points into the questionnaire he had prepared as an interview guide for the American universities he was about to visit: Harvard, Cornell, Amherst, and the University of Chicago among the first. But no matter how hard he worked, how diligently he tried to concentrate, there was no holding back the emotional tides that roiled against his rational thought, and he found little solace in the work. He could not banish the image of Robert's arm around Jennette's waist and the echo of her trilling laugh from his head. For a while, he stopped fighting it and abandoned himself to the slough of the depression that had been haunting him since that night. He was counting on this voyage to give him some relief, to allow time to do its work and the inescapable sea to offer a cleansing. He closed his notebook and lay back, listening to the steam engine's relentless chug, turning the ship's propeller blades and churning the ocean behind it. The sound rolled over him in soothing waves.

And then his thoughts drifted to the hour he had spent alone in the Palais des Beaux-Arts near midnight after Simon's speech—a magical visit to ancient Olympia.

○ ○ ○ ○ ○

At the appointed hour of eleven o'clock, a night watchman, lantern in hand, opened a back entrance to the Palais des Beaux-Arts and led Pierre through the sculptures and exhibits of the central gallery to the entrance of the darkened chamber where the re-creation of ancient Olympia waited. Setting his lantern on the floor, the watchman handed Pierre an unlit lantern and lifted its glass panel, releasing the trapped kerosene fumes. The wick ignited in a small burst.

"I'll be back in an hour," he said.

Pierre lifted the lantern and entered the room. His eye was drawn immediately to an exquisite mural covering the entire side wall, a detailed painting of an idealized scene of Olympia at the height of its glory. In the penumbra of light cast by the lantern, the painting revealed itself in orbs that moved as Pierre approached and walked along the wall. In the foreground, the Temple of Zeus rose on massive columns above its terraced steps, wisps of smoke rising from a pile of ashes at the altar of sacrifice before it. The statuary in the gabled pediment and the carved reliefs of the metopes on the frieze were rendered in full detail. Pierre recognized the twelve labors of Hercules. Across the expanse of the grounds of the Sacred Grove of the Altis, the painting depicted the Temple of Hera and the flowing waters of the Nymphaeum, the monumental fountain set against the base of Mount Kronos. It revealed the intimate beauty of the small temples built as the Treasuries of the Cities that lined the terraced wall at the foot of the mount. The painting showed the entrance to an arched tunnel—the passageway that every Olympian had taken to compete in the ancient Games. The grounds of the Altis were covered with a magnificent display of bronze and marble monuments on great plinths celebrating the triumphs of those who had competed there for a thousand years. Runners and wrestlers and jumpers were shown in training, and everywhere small groups of Greeks in togas strolled or stood gesturing at each other as if they were discussing the events of the day.

In that imaginative moment, Pierre was transported into a landscape he had often dreamed about, seeing it more clearly now than he had ever pictured it, the reality of the past more present than it had ever been—mythical ideas becoming reality.

Turning to the table that held the model of ancient Olympia, he lifted his lantern to cast light over the scene re-created in perfectly scaled three-dimensional form, the landscape as natural as it might look from the wings of an eagle—trees and plants, grassy hills, the dirt floor of the stadium, and paths leading into and out of the Altis.

In that moment, Pierre understood for the first time how Mount Kronos served to define the development of Olympia. Fascinated, he saw how it fit intimately together: the gymnasium on the one side, the Sacred Grove of the Altis in the middle of the walled sanctuary, and the stadium on the opposite side, all arched around Kronos like a crown.

Farther down, the mythic river Alpheios curved around the front of the model where it met the streaming river Kladeos. From the elevation of the sanctuary— only a few yards above the river's surface—Pierre understood how fifteen centuries of floods and quakes had buried it all so deeply in the earth.

He considered the approach of a pilgrim coming through the small village of Olympia, turning down the hill toward the sanctuary, seeing the open courtyard of the gymnasium from above—filled with runners and jumpers and javelin throwers—and then walking past its long colonnades to the palestra where the wrestlers and boxers trained—and the brutality of the pankration drew blood even in practice. Then came the famed workshop of Phineas—the brick structure where the sculptural genius had fashioned the ivory-and-gold statue of Zeus that left every visitor awestruck. Just inside the gateway to the sacred Altis stood the Philippeion, the domed pavilion erected by Philip II of Macedon to commemorate his victory in a chariot race. The sanctuary was dominated by the Temple of Zeus and the Temple of Hera. Taking in the temples, the statuary, the treasuries, the stadium, Pierre imagined forty thousand spectators on the hillside cheering on their favorites. He studied the long narrow roofline of the Echo Colonnade, where the heralds of peace and the trumpeters who started the events had stayed.

He couldn't fail to connect the idea of the Sacred Truce with the peace congress he had attended barely a week before. It occurred to him a mythic connection existed between that ancient truce of the gods, which had once held the power to bring peace in a time of war, and the pleas of Simon, Passy, and Pratt, who, like modern heralds of peace, had called for a cessation of hostilities between the nations. He wondered now if ancient Olympia was tethered to his heart—as it had been since boyhood—by this idea of peace, which he had so desperately yearned for after the wartime trauma of 1870. He read again the description of how the heralds were sent out to proclaim the Sacred Truce, which would run for three months to provide safe passage for athletes to and from the Olympic Games across the empire that was Greece.

Not long after he had heard Passy and Pratt call for annual international gatherings of students as a foundation for peace—gatherings that would include cultural exchanges, education, and friendly sports competitions—he was left to contemplate the idea that sport itself had once possessed the power to calm an entire civilization and cause its warring factions to lay down their arms in light of their passion for sport. Was this an idea whose time had come again?

This Olympia wasn't exactly as he had imagined it as a boy, but it was close. And he found the paintings even more evocative than the model. As he turned away, preparing to leave, he had a premonition and raised the lantern for a last look. He knew that one day he would travel to Greece to visit the ancient ruins—for he was certain there was something waiting for him there.

48

THE TOUR

On a sunny mid-July afternoon, St. Clair took a table on the terrace at the Café Italia beneath the leafy trellis. He was enjoying a glass of white wine when Coubertin arrived, a valise under his arm.

"I've got a few documents for you," said the older man, touching the leather as he sat and signaled for a glass of red. The sunlight dappled the checkered tablecloth and illuminated parts of Pierre's face as he removed his bowler. He looked tired, the lines around his eyes more deeply furrowed, but he was in a spirited mood and seemed happy to have discovered something important.

"Let me guess," St. Clair said. "It's your marriage certificate and the guest book from your wedding."

Coubertin's smile momentarily vanished. "The guest book from our wedding! What an idea. I wonder if Marie has it?"

"I was just joking. But yes, I'd like to have a look at it one of these days. What have you found?"

"Some important government documents." Coubertin pulled papers from the valise, passing them across the table. "The proclamations from the government authorizing the Congress on Physical Education in 1889."

St. Clair tried to refrain from showing his disappointment. He had already written everything he intended to write about the exposition and didn't want to revise it just to reference government support that was a *fait accompli* in the story. "Very good," he said after skimming the documents and placing them in his satchel. "Anything else?"

"Yes, as a matter of fact. Here's the declaration from the Ministry of Public Instruction for my research at colleges and universities in America." Handing it to St. Clair, he added, "This essentially gave me the right to create a letterhead that made my mission official, but here's the best piece I found this morning."

St. Clair took the document and sat up as he realized it was a letter from Jules Ferry to Coubertin, expressing his satisfaction that Simon's young prodigy would be reporting on the state of higher education in the United States. He read Ferry's words aloud: "'We know that your reports will be accurate and factual and will present only what is true.'" Raising his glass in a toast, he added, "That's high praise, Pierre. He must have had confidence from all your reports on the exposition."

The baron lifted his glass and nodded. "Indeed. He knew I needed the research on American trends to refute Grousset's attacks, to counter the notion that my plans were anathema because they were so purely British. I was going to America to broaden the argument and establish the data for international growth."

Looking at the dates of the declaration from mid-1889, St. Clair wondered how Coubertin had managed to line up visits with more than twenty universities so quickly. "So you were able to write on behalf of the ministry and arrange appointments at all the universities you eventually visited?"

"No, not exactly. I did write—and probably gained five appointments—but the meetings on that trip were in large part facilitated by Will Sloane of Princeton."

St. Clair was surprised. "Your colleague from the IOC? So you knew him before that first trip to America? I didn't get that from your *Olympic Memoirs*."

"Yes, I met him at Taine's salon in the summer of 1888, a year before the exposition. And he wasn't simply a colleague. He was my greatest ally—and certainly my closest friend and confidant."

"It sounds as if we're in for a long afternoon," St. Clair said. "Let's start with your arrival in America and circle back to your first meeting with Sloane later."

After sixteen days on the North Atlantic in August of 1889, the SS *La Normandie* made its way into New York harbor, and Coubertin beheld the true magnificence of the Statue of Liberty. In those days, every French ship that entered the port sailed close enough to Bedloe Island to give all the passengers a good look and a chance to pay appropriate homage to the artistic genius of their nation. Shaking off a momentary longing for Jennette, Coubertin marveled at the size of the statue, admiring the large-scale fidelity to the model Bartholdi had shown him. Lady Liberty—as she was already called—looked even more graceful in her monumental flowing robes than he'd anticipated. Mounted on an enormous pedestal the Americans had built—after an impressive fundraising campaign led by the famous newspaper publisher, Joseph Pulitzer—Lady Liberty seemed perfectly positioned to Coubertin.

Gazing up at the face of Liberty, he was transfixed for a moment more, but America awaited. He turned toward Manhattan and took in his first view of America's still young and ambitious metropolitan heart. The image of the city from the water was dark and smoldering, more industrial and less inviting than he had imagined, but once he had disembarked, the energy of the streets and the cosmopolitan mix of ethnicities and languages was everything he had hoped for. Two brawny dockworkers lifted his portmanteau onto the back of a coach, and he was off across Manhattan, gazing out the windows at the shops, storefronts, and painted signs of a surprisingly ramshackle new world. He hoped the experience would help push the image of Jennette Montaigne out of his mind for once and all.

Pierre would be in the United States for four months, with appointments at more than twenty universities on the calendar already. At the recommendation of well-traveled friends in Paris, he was booked for three nights in the Fifth Avenue Hotel, a luxurious enclave that took up the full block between 23rd and 24th Streets at the south end of Madison Square Park. On further recommendations, he had dinner reservations the next night at Delmonico's, famous in Paris for its French cuisine. He would stay in New York City for three weeks to a month, using it as a base of operations for brief trips to colleges and universities before heading to Boston to give a speech. Aside from two meetings at the New York Athletic Club and a few social obligations, he wanted to run through Central Park, see the newspaper skyscrapers near City Hall, pay his respects at St. Patrick's Cathedral, and tour the Metropolitan Museum of Art.

Early the next morning, he walked through Madison Square and Union Square, taking in the irregular hand-drawn signage on the two-and-three-story brick-and-wood structures that lined the streets. On the edge of Union Square, he watched a group of youngsters dancing as an accordion player sang "The Sidewalks of New York." Ragamuffins crowded around a milk station, begging for handouts as he climbed aboard an omnibus headed downtown. He was surprised by the number of bicycles on the street as he traveled south—the two-wheelers were already catching on in the new world. As a writer and sometime journalist, he was interested in the newspaper business, and across from City Hall on Park Row, he took in the Tribune Building, the Potter Building, and the Park Row, all of which housed newspaper operations. Rising above them was the newest and tallest, Pulitzer's New York World Building. A skeletal fretwork a year from completion, it would soon be the highest skyscraper in the city—and yet it didn't seem that tall to Coubertin, who was used to craning his neck up to the heights of the Eiffel Tower.

At a news kiosk on the corner, Coubertin bought a copy of the *New York World* and read an article by Miss Nellie Bly, a Pulitzer reporter who was planning to depart in a few months on an attempt to circumnavigate the globe in a new record time of eighty days—an attempt to prove Jules Verne's fiction could be brought to life.

○ ○ ○ ○ ○

After a few weeks of touring—and several official trips to Amherst, the University of Pennsylvania, and the Catholic University of America in Washington DC, Coubertin took a cab—or a "taxi" as he heard one or two New Yorkers call their horse-drawn coaches—up Fifth Avenue for an appointment at the New York Athletic Club.

He arrived on time for his meeting with William Buckingham Curtis, a legendary boxer, runner, hammer thrower, editor, and sports promoter who still served as chair of the club he had co-founded in 1868. Curtis was among the most influential men in American sport at the time. The year before, as Coubertin had learned from Sloane, Curtis had founded the Amateur Athletic Union, an organization destined to play a seminal role in the development of sport in the United States in the years ahead. Through its combative president, James Sullivan, the AAU was already battling with colleges and universities for control of sports in the young nation.

The City Club, as the members called it, was located at the intersection of 55th Street and Sixth Avenue. As soon as Coubertin entered he was greeted with recognition by the receptionist and led directly up the stairs and into Curtis's office. Sitting at his desk in his shirtsleeves, Curtis was marking up a column of newsprint, which Coubertin recognized as the *Spirit of the Times*, the sports newspaper the tireless entrepreneur had founded. Looking over his reading glasses, Curtis immediately laid down his pen and came around the desk to shake the baron's hand.

"Welcome to the New York Athletic Club," he said, squeezing Coubertin's much smaller hand with a challenging grip, which Pierre returned with force, widening the grin of his host. Curtis was in his fifties, sinewy and obviously still fit.

"I very much appreciate the time you've set aside for me," Coubertin said in crisp English, taking a seat in front of the desk. His language skills would serve him well across this land.

Curtis settled into his chair. "You're preceded by a strong endorsement from Will Sloane, whom I count among our finest members."

"Will has been an immense help to me with his introductions," Coubertin said, "and, of course, with his highly informed view of the rising role of sports in American universities."

"That's not surprising, since Will always has an eye on France." Curtis lifted a few pages of Princeton stationery from a stack of wooden slots on the desk, glancing over Sloane's script. "He's written a good overview of the work you're doing to introduce sports into French education and to survey our collegiate sports scene here. Where are you headed in the US?"

"I'm going up to Boston for the physical education conference—and then touring colleges and universities west to Chicago, south to New Orleans and back up to Princeton."

"That's a lot of miles. Boston is going to be quite an assembly."

"Are you going?"

"No, I've got my hands full here, but I've got Sullivan—do you know Jim?—and several others representing the AAU."

"I know of Mr. Sullivan but have not had the pleasure of meeting him yet."

"Don't presume it will be a pleasure, Baron. Sullivan is as testy as they come."

"In that case, I'll consider myself forewarned."

"If you're around next month, we've got a good competitive program—some rowing and running and boxing—out at our new club on Tanner's Island. I'll be hosting more than five hundred guests."

"Thank you. I read that you opened a summer clubhouse—on the Sound near Pelham Manor."

"You're well informed. It's designed for summer, but we'll use it all year round. Now, is there anything specific you'd like to know about the club or our activities?"

Coubertin withdrew his notebook. "Yes—if you don't mind, I've got a series of questions."

"I'll be pleased to tell you everything I know."

They spent the next hour in a cordial conversation that revealed Curtis's full mastery of the operations of the New York Athletic Club, the array of sports it supported, the competitions it organized and promoted, even the athletic talents and abilities of its members. In his notes, Coubertin recorded dozens of individual and team sports the club featured, from the requisite gymnastics, boxing, fencing, and track and field events to water and equestrian sports, and even mountain climbing.

More importantly, Curtis provided Coubertin with insights into the controversies swirling around collegiate athletics and team sports across the United States and the efforts of university presidents and administrators who were trying to repress the growth of competitive sport in favor of mass gymnastic exercises. "You'll hear from Edward Hartwell of Johns Hopkins in Boston, I'm sure,"

Curtis said. "An absolute blowhard proponent of the dying German system—or is it the Swedish system?"

By the time their meeting ended, well beyond the hour Coubertin had planned for, he was calling Curtis "Father Bill," his cherished nickname as the father of so many American sportsmen. At one point, their talk had turned international when Curtis said, "What we really need is a couple of good competitive teams to come over from England and France for a round robin in rugby. I'd like to see how we'd do against your boys in running, boxing, and maybe wrestling. We'd be happy to host a few meets if you could produce worthy opponents."

After Coubertin closed his notebook, Curtis insisted on giving him a quick tour of the gyms, track, pool, and running rings. As they walked down the stairs to the entrance, Curtis asked Pierre to call him if he passed through New York at the end of his tour. He wanted to hear what Pierre had learned so he could put a story in *Spirit of the Times*, and Curtis wanted to introduce him to several people, including Teddy Roosevelt, New York City's rising star among the young civic leaders and sportsmen.

"Given your interests in sport education, you'll be impressed with what Roosevelt is doing with troubled street urchins—downtown and in Brooklyn. He's using boxing in a couple of gyms he's set up to curb violence and crime. He's clearly turned some boys around."

As he left the NYAC, Coubertin felt exhilarated by Curtis's open embrace, his enthusiasm for all sports, and his willingness to share information and insights. The big man embodied exactly what he'd been hoping to find in the American character. If there were a few more people like Curtis waiting on the road ahead, he knew his trip would be profitable beyond expectations.

○ ○ ○ ○ ○

A few weeks later, he took the train up to Albany, making the connection to Boston—an indirect route but the only option in those days. As he traveled, he ruminated on the world he was about to enter, the emerging world of collegiate sports in the United States. While the popularity of competitive sports had exploded on college campuses across America, most university presidents and administrations feared—as Curtis had informed him—that team sports were undermining education. In fact, Coubertin had appointments on his tour with three of them: Andrew White at Cornell, Daniel Gilman at Johns Hopkins, and Charles Eliot at Harvard. He knew they were all advocates of the more disciplined and less passionate approach to physical education embodied in the regimented exercises of German and Swedish gymnastics. And he knew the Boston conference would be the single largest stage for the continuing debate over which of these gymnastics systems—the Swedish or the German—was best suited to the students of American higher education.

Coubertin also knew the debate itself was already too old-school to be truly relevant. It was already over, even in France. The era of rote gymnastics had passed. Competitive sport was a rising American phenomenon that couldn't be stopped—any more than Thomas Arnold's formula for school sport could be put back in the bottle in England. A new system of physical education had dawned like an all-powerful force of individual liberation and teamwork that would stretch around the world and cast into shadow all those outdated mechanical forms. To Coubertin, sport embodied all the best possibilities of the new international age and should be unleashed to do its work.

As Coubertin passed through the autumn Connecticut countryside, he decided to deliver a speech deliberately dismissive of uniform gymnastics and to take advantage of the opportunity to present *le régime Arnoldian* as the future of sport for all. In his official capacity, he was supposed to report the results of the Paris Congress on Physical Education, including the results of his survey, but a more forceful rhetoric was already filling his head. He decided to repeat some of what he had said in his keynote at the Paris Congress. He was certain many people in the audience would appreciate an endorsement of competitive sport, and he considered it part of his mission to speak frankly about the direction sport should take wherever he could.

The train pulled into Boston's Back Bay Station after dark, and Pierre took a coach to a small hotel he had booked on Huntington Avenue near the public library. The trip took only a few minutes. Surprised by its brevity, he doubled the coachman's tip. He had intended to do a short walking tour that night, but decided to wait until morning to get his bearings and see the campus of the Massachusetts Institute of Technology.

At dinner in the hotel, he made a few more notes on his speech and reviewed the profiles of three of the speakers Sloane had sent. The Boston Conference on Physical Training—an unfortunate name, Coubertin thought, too limiting; it should have been Physical Education—would be chaired by William T. Harris, the U.S. commissioner of education, and would feature speeches by Dr. Edward Hartwell, the director of the gymnasium at Johns Hopkins, and Edward Hitchcock, a Harvard doctor and physical education innovator from Amherst. Although Coubertin had not yet met Harris, he had been introduced to him in letters from Sloane and Simon and fully expected to have a few minutes of conversation with him and perhaps a cup of coffee.

○ ○ ○ ○ ○

Jennette's face moved in and out of the shadows as the coach lurched over the cobbles of Montmartre, the glint of her red mane brushed gently by the night. He wanted her so badly he said her name with an urgency that sounded like a plea. In a whisper she responded, and they fell silent as he reached for her and pulled her in, nestling his face in the intoxicating scent of her hair. He kissed her neck and tasted the vestiges of lavender perfume and something else sweet beneath it. Their lips met lightly at first, separated by the swaying cab. He pulled her closer so they could kiss fully, and he tasted the sweetness of anisette on her tongue, the licorice of love. But he caught the other scent again and it intrigued him.

"What is it you've mixed with the lavender? It's so familiar but I just can't identify it."

"It's your favorite flavor, Pierre," she whispered. "It's oil of vanilla, and I wore it for you." She kissed him again.

A loud knock on the hotel room door woke him from his slumber, and he squinted at the gray winter light bleeding through the curtains.

"Six a.m., sir," said a man's voice through the door. "Your wake-up request."

He mumbled thanks and pushed his face into the pillow, trying to find the lavender scent that had been so distinct in his dream—along with her alluring signature vanilla. He got up, bent over the cold basin, and splashed freezing water on his face, noticing a bar of French Laundry soap wrapped neatly in its dish, the word *lavender* in purple on the brown paper. He sniffed it, wondering if the scent had triggered his dream.

Moving to the window, he gazed out over the campus of MIT and Copley Square just up Huntington Avenue. It was a gray morning and a few carriages, workers and students were already crisscrossing the streets below. Beyond Copley, he could see the four-story classical Greek façade and roofline of the massive red-brick Rogers building on Boylston Street, where he knew Huntington Hall was located. Pulling gently on his mustache and rubbing his unshaven cheeks, he decided the conference would be more than his destination that day—it would be the beginning of his life without Jennette. He would trust in his mission and work to eliminate her from his thoughts and his dreams. The disquietude was already gone. He knew he was beginning to heal. Now, all he had to do was train his will to move beyond her haunting presence—and the training of the will would be a subject loudly discussed, he was sure, in the conference ahead.

○ ○ ○ ○ ○

On his way to Huntington Hall, Coubertin stopped at Trinity Place to look at the cluster of buildings that formed the core of the campus of MIT. He was surprised at how small the campus was, fitting within a city block, but impressed with the reputation and impact the institute had produced in so few buildings. He rounded the Lowell Electrical Engineering Laboratory and headed up Clarendon to Boylston, joining the crowd flowing up the steps of the Rogers building and into Huntington Hall for the congress.

Huntington Hall, like the building that housed it, was part of MIT, but it hosted a variety of public gatherings—political rallies, academic conferences, even traveling fairs and entertainment. The hall warmed quickly as it filled with more than two thousand delegates. Coubertin found a seat along the left aisle in the middle of the room, rising repeatedly for men and a few women as they moved toward the center of the semicircular rows. At nine-fifty, the doors behind the podium opened and the commissioner of education led in the delegation of the morning's speakers.

After brief introductions and recognition of delegates from as far away as California, Washington, Texas, and Louisiana in the south, the floor was turned over to Commissioner Harris for the opening keynote.

Coubertin was not impressed with Harris's initial remarks, comparing the effects of voluntary exercise on involuntary vital organs—or his focus on exercises that relieved brain tensions versus those that didn't. But when he talked about play—the essential role of play in personal development—Coubertin recorded his points as clearly as he could:

"We all know the difference between play and work," Harris said. "In our play, caprice governs, and there is real purpose for the will. Play has its use in education. We are discovering more and more how play is an exceedingly important function; that it is the source of the development of individuality through spontaneity. The individual through play learns to know, to command, to respect himself, and to distinguish between his own impulses and inclinations and those of others. Great strength and individuality grow from play. Nations that postpone play until maturity fail in this respect."

When Harris ended with the idea that nations that failed to grasp the import of play, which Coubertin interpreted as competitive free-flowing sport, would suffer as a result, he felt inspired. He reread his notes and felt a certain vindication as Harris introduced the next speaker, Hartwell from Hopkins. As the applause ended, Coubertin looked down his row and was surprised at the number of notebooks open on the laps of the delegates. Across the aisle, in the rows before him, and all the way up to the back of the amphitheater, people were taking notes on the implications of physical activity as a component of education at every level.

And here now was Hartwell with a discourse on the invaluable role physical development should play in every institution of higher learning in the country.

Coubertin felt the energy of the young republic again and felt privileged to be in the room at this particular point in America's history. Here he was in the midst of a gathering of educators in a nation just beginning to discover and understand the depth of its love of sport and its passion for competition. In Huntington Hall that day, this young colossus of a country was setting a new course for physical education, a course that would help channel its competitive spirit into the development of individual character and fully realized human beings. Coubertin saw the grand possibilities of the moment and pictured the people in the room as the threads of a fabric that would be woven into a great tapestry of sport—a tapestry that would cover the nation coast to coast and inform its future, just as Arnold had helped shape the British Empire.

Hartwell finished and a presentation on German gymnastics began. It was followed by a panel discussion among the morning's speakers, with the proponents of the German system arguing with the proponents of the Swedish system. Hartwell, to his credit, effectively espoused the benefits of competitive sports versus regimental exercise. When it was over, they broke for lunch and Coubertin, pressed into a mass exodus as the delegates spread out around the restaurants of the Back Bay, was unable to spot Harris or the other speakers from the morning. He assumed they were dining privately and determined to track them down at the conclusion of the afternoon session, or after his own speech, if the opportunity presented itself.

He was called to the podium and introduced as the president of the Paris Congress on Physical Education, here to provide a report on the congress and the results of an international survey on sport development. He thanked Chairman Harris and each of the morning's speakers. He apologized for his lack of command of the English language, but then delivered what he hoped was a compelling and eloquent argument advocating the continuing development of physical education and competitive sports at all American colleges, universities, and public schools.

"This morning, ladies and gentlemen," he began, "we heard a rather fevered debate on the virtues of one system of gymnastics versus another. I have news for you from Paris. That debate is over—and the winner is sport. As societies around the world have moved to open the doors of the temple of sport to their children, their students, their men and women, they have begun to recognize the obvious superiority of games and competition—what Secretary Harris so brilliantly described to us this morning as play—over the military regimens or rote exercises we often characterize as gymnastics.

"I stand before you today with the results of a worldwide survey that documents in clear, concise data the rise of sport." He held up a pack of papers for all to see. "I will share these results with you at the end of my talk, but first let me summarize what the international leaders who participated in our congress in Paris in June have come to believe.

"The data reflects a phenomenon that is rising like a tidal wave on the crest of the new internationalism that is drawing our world so rapidly together. That tidal wave is sport, and it is time for us to seize the opportunities that sport so uniquely provides—as a new platform for international concourse and concord. As we look to the future—and the real opportunity that sport presents to education—let us understand the urgency of the moment. As Shakespeare said in *Julius Caesar*:

> *There is a tide in the affairs of men.*
> *Which, taken at the flood, leads on to fortune;*
> *Omitted, all the voyage of their life is bound*
> *In shallows and in miseries.*
> *On such a full sea are we now afloat,*
> *And we must take the current when it serves,*
> *Or lose our ventures.*

"We are at high tide right now, ladies and gentlemen. Sport is rising everywhere. If we want it to serve the greater good, we must harness its powers for education— and for the future of democracy. Sport can inspire the noblest instincts of man, or it can be used to prepare for war. The direction it takes depends wholly on the role it is given in education. If properly integrated and managed, it can serve as a pillar of strength for any great society."

And then, with only a slight pause, he took out the notes from his closing speech at the Paris Congress and began in exactly the same way. "Somewhere right now a child is bent over, lacing his leather shoes on the side of a green field," he began, "ready to run onto the pitch and join his friends in kicking a ball around for an hour. It is difficult to make the leap from the simple game they're playing to the foundations that sustain an empire, but nonetheless, there is a direct link ..."

He went on to lionize Sir Thomas Arnold as the greatest educator of the times and gave him full credit for the strength of the British Empire, which was, of course, undervalued in these precincts. Nevertheless, Coubertin professed that if America continued to adapt *le régime Arnoldian* and the lessons of Rugby to its education systems—as he proclaimed it already had—it could become the greatest nation on earth. Without shame, given the circumstances and the opportunity, Coubertin exaggerated the impact and influence of the Paris Congress and said, as he shared his statistics, that his report was already inspiring the growth of sport in places as distant as Africa and Asia.

All his years in the study of rhetoric helped him immensely in Boston. When he finished with an oratorical flourish that brought the audience to their feet in loud acclaim, Commissioner Harris was the first to the podium to offer his congratulations, shaking the baron's hand with an enthusiasm the entire audience witnessed.

As they parted, Harris insisted they meet for a drink at the end of the day, and Coubertin was approached between every speech that afternoon by men and women who not only endorsed his ideas but also thanked him for building the international bridge of sport between nations. When he met Harris at McGlinchy's, an Irish bar on Newberry Street, he was surprised that Hartwell and Hitchcock were there as well, and they engaged in a long discussion about the tension between sport and study on the college campus. Following the lead of the commissioner, with only a touch of reluctance, Hartwell and Hitchcock offered to support Coubertin in his mission and would remain at his disposal for any information he required. Pierre could not have been more pleased. As he prepared to depart Boston and begin his real investigation of sport in American education, he knew he had struck the right chord with élan and force. After only a few days in the United States, he had established a unique position as an international sports diplomat with the men at the forefront of physical education in this young nation. He wondered if Tocqueville had felt the same embrace and energetic propulsion at the start of his tour years before.

○ ○ ○ ○ ○

While still in Boston, Coubertin had a guided tour of the Hemenway Gymnasium at Cambridge by its director, Dr. Sargent, and witnessed the intense physical examination each student was put through in order to assess and correct their deformities or deficiencies or strengthen their muscles. He watched in astonishment as Sargent put one obviously fit young man through a fifty-point test, measuring strength, breathing, and heartbeat with instruments called a dynamometer, spirometer, and stethoscope. The level of testing and the corrective exercises recommended forced Coubertin to contain a laugh or two, and he concluded that whatever Dr. Sargent was attempting to accomplish had more to do with pure anatomy than sport.

From there, the rest of his four-month trip rolled by with the drive of an extended athletic competition. After Boston Coubertin made his way to Lenox, Massachusetts, where he had an unsatisfying weekend as the visiting aristocrat *du jour* among an exclusive group of upper-crust pretenders who failed to live up to the egalitarian values of America. With great dispatch, he headed back to Amherst, where Dr. Hitchcock led a demonstration of gymnastics set to music. Coubertin marveled at the quaint emphasis on God in Hitchcock's brochures,

which made clear the evangelical role of exercise in the old man's thinking. In all
its forms, Coubertin thought, sport could be molded to meet any ends.

He traveled up to Montreal and visited two universities, then down to Cornell
in Ithaca, where he solidified his relationship with President White and shared his
initial impressions of the hopeless direction that rote gymnastics were giving to
so many in U.S. physical education. He continued on to Chicago, where he stood on
the shores of the inland ocean of Lake Michigan and marveled that a city burned
to the ground only eighteen years before had blossomed into a metropolis of
commercial might. He toured the famous industrial center where Pullman had
made a fortune building railroad cars and tried, with mixed results, to enhance
the lives of his workers with culture, education, and sports facilities. At the same
time, he witnessed the onslaught of urban poverty at Hull House, where he had
long discussions with Jane Addams, admiring her commitment to the poor and
those down on their luck.

In the contrasts of its diversity, America largely lived up to his expectations. As
he rode the rails—which by 1889 comprised nearly one hundred thousand miles
of track—his route defined a large, irregular circle that covered the eastern half of
the country. He went through St. Louis on his way down to New Orleans, crossed
the South, and returned to Washington and Baltimore, his final destination being
Princeton. His journals filled quickly with his impressions of the country, its towns,
its people, and particularly its education systems and the variety of sporting
experience found on campuses.

But the country disappointed him on several other fronts. He was not surprised
to encounter the racial prejudice against blacks he had so often read about, but
the intensity and pervasive nature of the racist culture offended him deeply. At
Tulane University, as he read the founding mission of the great endowment left
by its eponymous benefactor, he saw that it was all intended for whites alone—
and in every facet of social activity he witnessed both the separation and the
disparagement of blacks. As he thought about the Negro question and reflected
on the insults and physical bullying he had seen—and came to understand how
it had all been enshrined in state laws—he wrote that "if the Southern states are
stupid enough to uphold *their* brilliant legislation much longer, one must believe
that they will pay for it dearly in the end."

By the time Coubertin headed to Princeton for an extended stay with the
eminent Francophile professor William Milligan Sloane, he had covered more than
twenty colleges and universities and compiled hundreds of pages of impressions
and raw reports.

49

TAINE'S SALON

L ate on that July afternoon, St. Clair and Coubertin left Café Italia to walk back up the hill to Mon Repos. As they walked, they talked, moving not at Coubertin's preferred fast pace, but at a stroll so St. Clair could take notes. When he stopped to write, Coubertin accommodated him and stood by, answering questions or waiting for him to finish his shorthand.

"When you stayed with Sloane in Princeton in 1889, did you meet many of the athletes on the university's teams?"

"Yes, dozens. Will gave me a good tour of the facilities. I met his coaching colleagues and a good number of professors and their wives, some on his athletic council and some with little interest at all in sport. We watched the football team practice and attended a few intramural games. It was quite an illuminating inside look at the practice of team sport and physical education in America, very much in the vein I had seen at all the other universities. There was an ever-present team spirit and school pride that sprung so naturally from the American character. But the visit wasn't all sport—Will hosted several dinners for me at Stanworth, his home. Lots of lively discussions on education theory, politics. He seemed to know everybody. In fact, he was good friends with Woodrow Wilson."

"You met Wilson?"

"No—he'd been a student there and returned the year after I visited, but I missed him. He became president of Princeton around the turn of the century.

I remember Will saying he was an avid sportsman, might have been captain of the Princeton football and baseball teams during his student days."

"And you said you met Sloane for the first time at Hippolyte Taine's?"

"Yes, at Taine's salon on a Sunday afternoon in 1888, the summer or fall, the year before the exposition—and we had a great discussion about American higher education. In fact, once I met Will, the plans for my tour became much more precise. He provided a lot of insight and direction—and invaluable contacts."

"Did you go to Taine's salon often?"

"Regularly," Coubertin said. "After Simon took me to meet Taine—who had been one of my intellectual idols—I frequented his salon almost every Sunday afternoon. Got to know his wife quite well too. They drew a very broad international collective, lots of academics, writers, and intellectuals."

On a sunny Sunday afternoon, Pierre alighted from the carriage, paid the cab driver, and went up the steps into Taine's townhome on a side street off boulevard Saint-Michel near the Panthéon. As soon as the butler opened the door, the roar of conversation enveloped him. Handing his top hat to the butler, he coursed through the crowded hall, turned through the antechamber, and made his way directly to the main salon, where he knew Taine would be seated in the small alcove at the front windows. Without disturbing the circle around Taine or interrupting the conversation he was conducting, Coubertin caught his eye and nodded his respects before stepping back from the discussion, which seemed to be about a parliamentary bill on hospitals and clinics—a pressing issue, no doubt, but not in Pierre's immediate interest.

He made his way into the dining room, which was packed with small clusters of people on all sides, with two lines of men and women surrounding a table laid out with a sumptuous buffet. Without even trying to eavesdrop, Pierre took note of several discussions as he moved around the table collecting a plate of vegetables, foie gras, and a small portion of pasta. The salon offered him opportunities to drop into circles of conversation on the ineffectiveness of parliament, the slow migration of Paris from gaslight to électricity, the tenor of the upcoming celebration of Bastille Day, and a heated debate on the virtues or threats embodied in General Georges Boulanger, the popular militarist called France's future by many and seen by others as the end of the Third Republic.

Leaning on the column in a doorway, balancing his plate in hand, Pierre observed the flow of people into and out of the rooms and watched for a pattern that indicated someone was beginning to dominate the moment, raising an issue, offering an insight, or creating enough of a controversy to draw attention and silence the other conversations. If Taine stood and spoke, the house would immediately fall into line and listen even more intently if he conferred his intellectual approval by introducing a speaker, as he had introduced Pierre several years before when Simon brought him in. This was the way of the intellectual or academic salon, a social gathering for the explicit purpose of examining ideas, testing them in public discourse, and meeting others capable of mounting eloquent arguments.

A raucous burst of laughter two rooms away turned Pierre's head and split the dense din with an instantaneous gap of silence in which a single phrase floated through the air and reached Pierre. What he heard in a musical baritone, uttered in perfect French with a well-disguised American accent, was the simple phrase "our universities are changing." The subject, of course, spoke to his immediate interests, but he heard something more opportune. Setting his plate aside, he moved in the direction of the voice, which he guessed had emanated from the large glass solarium at the back of Taine's home.

There, amid mottled sunlight and the teeming floral profusion of Madame Taine's horticulture, stood a tall and hefty square-jawed American, a handsome man in a three-piece suit and regimental tie. He was holding forth on the rising standards of higher education in the United States. Pierre stepped into the circle, now three deep, and drew a few welcoming nods as Professor William Milligan Sloane of Princeton University was saying that Johns Hopkins was setting a new course for independent study in the States following a model cultivated by its president on successive trips to Germany—which Sloane proclaimed as the height of academic leadership.

"Hopkins was created for the specific purpose of academic innovation. It is our first post-graduate school, an institution chartered by reformers to lead all of our universities in a new direction. Harvard, Yale, Princeton, Columbia, Cornell—we'll all follow suit."

Pierre listened for a few more minutes and then engaged Sloane in a more detailed discussion of education reform. After a half hour—with Pierre driving the conversation toward the French education system's inability to pivot toward change—most of the others in the circle had drifted away. Pierre had not meant to limit the conversation, but he couldn't help himself, and Sloane appeared fully engaged and intrigued by Pierre's ideas.

"I'm Will Sloane," he said at length, offering his hand and a wide grin.

Happy that it was now just the two of them, Pierre responded with the same informality. "Pleased to meet you, Will. I'm Pierre de Coubertin."

"Why don't we get a glass of wine and find a couple of chairs?" Sloane lumbered forward as Taine's distinctive voice rang out.

Taine was introducing Victor Drury to the crowd. Sloane and Coubertin edged down the hall to get closer and listen. Drury, who had once served as minister of public instruction under the Second Empire of Napoleon III, had recently published an updated edition of his *History of Greece* that included a full description of ancient Olympia based on the German archaeological discoveries.

"Did you follow the German digs at Olympia?" Sloane asked as he and Coubertin settled in two chairs beside a window in a quiet corner of an otherwise shadowed library.

"I did, in fact—my Jesuit class reviewed their annual reports. Father Caron, my teacher, was an enthusiast."

"I'm going to have to acquire a copy of Drury's book."

"You'll have to get in line behind me," Coubertin said, smiling.

"I can wait, Baron, since I have the full reports in German."

"Ah, you read German?"

"I lived in Germany for three years as a student and assistant to George Bancroft."

"Must have been an interesting path that led you to Germany and then to Princeton. I'd like to hear about it, but at the moment, I'm vitally interested in hearing more about the trends in American higher education—and why you seem to know so much."

Two hours later, Coubertin had learned that Sloane traveled in elite academic circles and knew the leaders of many of the best U.S. universities personally. In fact, he was in Paris at the time with Andrew White, the president of Cornell and one of the leading forces behind the founding of Johns Hopkins. White had been at Taine's that afternoon but had left earlier. Sloane nevertheless promised to make the introduction before they left Paris two weeks hence. And Coubertin was inspired by Sloane's reaction to his story. The professor not only endorsed Coubertin's efforts to reform the French education system but was in complete sympathy with his vision of putting sport on equal footing with intellectual and moral development. It was difficult for Sloane to understand why the French had swallowed Grousset's criticism of the British model. Sloane was intrigued by Coubertin's plans for a U.S. tour, and their dialogue became even more animated as the American listed the circle of presidents, professors, and sports leaders whom Coubertin could interview. At Coubertin's invitation, they arranged a dinner for that very evening—and by the end of that dinner Coubertin was certain he had found his first American ally and kindred spirit.

"At the end of that conversation," Coubertin recalled, "I knew what I needed more than anything else—I needed that American verve, energy, and confidence. I needed to get Will and his colleagues to join me in a campaign to harness the power of international sport, to create competitions between nations—and maybe even to resurrect the Olympic Games and make them a modern platform for education."

"You spoke of the Olympic Games that day?" St. Clair thought perhaps they had stumbled upon the memory of the birth of the idea itself—a point in time that had never been crystallized.

"We talked a good deal about the ancient Olympic Games before we left Taine's. Drury's book and the German excavations were the subject of the hour." Coubertin gazed contemplatively at the ceiling. "And we both recognized the importance of international competitions, but I can't say for certain that we discussed a modern Olympics that day."

"But in Sloane, you knew you had found an important ally."

"I didn't realize immediately how important—how central Sloane would become to my work—but well before Athens I knew his was the most meaningful Olympic friendship I ever formed."

As they worked into the night at Mon Repos—an unusual practice for them— St. Clair wondered why Coubertin seldom started meetings early or worked late. The thought passed as they spoke more about Sloane. After a while it became obvious to St. Clair that William Sloane had been *the* primary partner in shaping Coubertin's vision of international sport and competition—integral to the very founding of the Olympic Movement itself. St. Clair decided to dig deeply into the Sloane/Coubertin story.

"Let's go back for a minute to the introductions Sloane made on your behalf on that first American trip. How important were they?"

"How important? Let me give you three names," Coubertin said. "White, Eliot, and Gilman, the presidents of Cornell, Harvard, and Johns Hopkins—all great friends of Sloane, all advocates of international peace, and all ultimately strong supporters of the Olympic Games."

"They were also part of the peace movement?"

"White and Gilman were close to Passy and Pratt and participated in several of the peace congresses."

As they talked on, and St. Clair probed deeper into the details of Sloane's role in those early days, Coubertin rubbed his eyes and slumped more deeply into his desk chair.

"I know it's getting late," St. Clair said, "but let's quickly go through your visit to Princeton and the beginning of your true collaboration. Let's begin with your stay at Sloane's house."

50

THE AMERICAN

At St. Clair's request, the staff at *Le Petit Journal* had sent him a package of research on William Sloane's writings and academic career. The staff had pulled detailed backgrounders from the archives of the *New York Herald* in Paris and the *New York Times* and a few biographies from reviews of Sloane's books from various French papers. Once he read through it all, St. Clair drafted a profile of Sloane, minus his Olympic credentials, that he intended to use in Coubertin's story.

William Milligan Sloane was a prodigy and a polymath, an American patriot by heritage and a true cosmopolitan by temperament. He was raised in a household led by a second-generation Scottish Presbyterian minister who had served as president at three colleges, was a popular professor of systematic theology, and was noted far and wide as a gifted orator. Born in 1850, young Will developed an early love of language and a passion for learning. While his father was a dominant figure in his youth, his mother's family enjoyed even greater social status, tracing their lineage back to the Mayflower in a genealogy shining with Revolutionary-era stars.

His father's gifts soon took the family from its small-town Ohio roots to New York City. In 1855, the Reverend James Renwick Wilson Sloane began preaching from the prestigious pulpit of the Third Reformed Presbyterian Church, a Calvinist stronghold. Like a thoroughbred on a fresh track, young Will worked swiftly through the grades at Martha Washington Collegiate Institute in Manhattan, impressing his father and all of his teachers with the amplitude of his interests and his capacity to master every subject. With his family's encouragement, he entered Columbia University three years ahead of his classmates and graduated with honors and a liberal-arts degree at the age of eighteen. Mature beyond his years, Will headed back to Ohio to teach Latin and the classics at the Newell Graduate Institute in Pittsburgh, launching an academic career that would earn him international distinction.

Ohio could not contain his ambitions for long, and in 1872 he sailed for Germany, following his thirst for knowledge to the academic summits of the universities of Berlin and Leipzig, considered the finest in the world. In Berlin, he became intoxicated with the study of history while mastering the German and French languages at the graduate level. Oriental history, particularly the Middle East, became a new fascination. His dazzling intellect drew the attention of the American minister to Berlin, George Bancroft, who offered Will a position as his personal secretary—and soon they were laboring together to finish the tenth volume of Bancroft's heralded *History of the United States*. Bancroft also introduced Will Sloane to an athletic life previously unknown. Every day, regardless of the weather, Bancroft exercised for two hours at an arduous pace. Sloane was young but he was already too fond of fine cuisine and too out of shape to keep up. Nevertheless, he did visit the gym with Bancroft, lifting weights and sweating off a few pounds of portly excess. The experience ignited in him for the first time a certain passion for sports, not as a player, but as a historian. He was soon searching for sources on the social unity sport engendered and the physical development it promoted—and that set the stage for his engagement in sports when he returned to the United States.

In 1875, Sloane completed his PhD with a thesis titled *Arabic Poetry before the Time of Mahomet*. Doctorate in hand, he began to pack. He had always intended to move stateside in time for the 1876 American Centennial, and Princeton University—through George Bancroft—provided the accommodation, offering him an assistant professorship in languages. In his first year on campus, he taught three languages—Latin, Hebrew, and Arabic—as well as a course in metaphysics.

Not long after he arrived at Princeton, he began a serious romance with Mary Johnston, a beautiful history major, whose great-grandfather, Colonel Davis Johnston, had served on George Washington's staff. Another of her great-grandfathers, Colonel David Espey, was a deputy at the Colonial Convention of 1775, which led directly to the Declaration of Independence—a point of heritage that gave Mary, as she made clear to Will on their first date, the license to rebel whenever she felt constrained. It wasn't long before they were inseparable. Will and Mary shared a love of the past and a vision for America's future. That year,

Sloane purchased twenty-five acres at 20 Bayard Lane in Princeton and began the development of Stanworth, the estate he and his bride would move into the next year. The stone house was designed to Sloane's specifications by a Boston firm—with a sweeping Victorian gingerbread porch—and the grounds were designed by Frederick Law Olmsted, America's foremost landscape architect. Sloane never tired of showing off his house or taking his guests on a bumptious ride around his wooded fields and sweeping lawns in an old donkey cart left to him by the previous owner.

By the early 1880s, Sloane was a rising star at Princeton, teaching multiple languages and courses in world history. While many of the scholars around him were opposed to the rising phenomenon of American sports, Sloane embraced the opportunity to help shape Princeton's sports policies, joining the Athletic Advisory Council in 1881 and being appointed its chairman three years later. Throughout the 1880s, he worked with student representatives and the coaches of Princeton's teams to cultivate competitive disciplines while ensuring that moral and academic development were not undermined by the new craze.

Recognizing Sloane's value and capacity for leadership, in 1883 the university made him a full professor of the philosophy of history, a position that gave him the license to travel broadly across Europe and guest lecture wherever he went. He was in England, France, Germany, and Italy nearly every summer, most often on official missions, but pursuing his own research in the process. His growing aspirations as a writer led him, in 1885, to accept the additional responsibilities of editing the *New Princeton Review*, a literary platform for commentary that served his growing ambitions. In 1888, as he was turning his attentions increasingly toward the history of France, he published his first book, *The* Life and Work of James Renwick Wilson Sloane, a tribute to his father that traced his own intellectual development.

Setting aside for a moment Sloane's involvement with Pierre de Coubertin and the Olympic Movement, the rest of his career was marked by great distinction and literary achievement. His first major work of history, *The French War and the Revolution*, published in 1893, drew high praise from none other than Hippolyte Taine, who said that "Sloane knows France better than any other foreigner." His masterwork followed, a four-volume *Life of Napoleon Bonaparte*, a colossal biography considered both definitive and entertaining. It was published in 1896—but had run first in twenty-six enthralling installments in *The Century Magazine*, which became one of Sloane's favorite publishing vehicles.

After nearly twenty years at Princeton, Sloane moved back to New York City to occupy the prestigious position as Seth Low professor of history at Columbia University, where he was to teach for the next thirty years. One of the founders of the American Academy of Arts and Letters in 1904, Sloane became its second president in 1920 when his friend and colleague William Dean Howells died. Four other books and hundreds of articles flowed from his pen as he instilled his love of history in generations of young students.

He and his wife Mary raised two sons and two daughters. They celebrated their fiftieth anniversary together in 1928, just months before his death in November. His funeral in New York City drew a great crowd of admirers, and tributes poured forth from old and young alike. Remarkably, his obituary in the New York Times made no mention of his long and heroic work to establish the Olympic Movement and put an imprint of moral sport on that global phenomenon.

As a man of the world, Sloane carried his broad frame lightly, and his heart seemed to generate the energy of a small power plant. He stood six feet and weighed 240 pounds, but to almost everyone who knew him, he appeared indefatigable. With a raconteur's wit and a genial enjoyment of life, he parlayed his physical presence into an asset of charm. He was an embracing man in every way, but, when necessary, he guarded his principles and moral vision with a fierce adversarial stance. He was not opposed to engaging in argument or wielding his considerable erudition to put an opponent down. Once he took a liking to you—or adopted your cause as he did Coubertin's—his friendship was steadfast and the full panoply of his skills were at your disposal.

○ ○ ○ ○ ○

Coubertin took the train into Trenton, the capital of New Jersey, and spent two hours in a ramshackle horse-drawn carriage on his way out to Princeton, bouncing through the New Jersey countryside, which reminded him of the patchwork farms of England on a much larger scale. He knew he was traveling back in time to the colonial era when Princeton University was still called the College of New Jersey. It was the fourth college founded in the colonies and subsequently became one of only eight institutions in the prestigious Ivy League.

This was to be Coubertin's last planned university visit and the end of his trip, and he leaned against the worn cushions of the old cab and felt a pang of melancholy enter his soul. Although he longed to return to France and hear the singsong of his native tongue in every mouth—to start his life afresh après Jennette—he would miss this wonderful country, this amazing experiment in liberty and democracy that had managed to do what France could not—endure for a century under one government, even through the trauma of a civil war. America had taken its place in his heart. He wondered how Alexis de Tocqueville and all the other French observers who preceded him had felt as they entered the end of their tours. As he thought back on his four-month American adventure across nearly twenty states and five thousand miles, he was incredibly impressed with much of what he had seen. While everything from the Boston Conference to the energy of the students he had met signaled that he was, indeed, in the midst of a new kind of society, his most engaging memories were anchored in Chicago—mostly in the work of Jane Adams of Hull House. Even in this land of self-reliance, compassion had taken root and the noble aspirations of the helping hand found their place amid that booming engine of commerce and trade on Lake Michigan. And then there was his official mission: he was fully satisfied with the professional level of documentation and notes he had taken on visits to the colleges and universities he had seen so far. He knew he would be able to write an outstanding report on education in America for Jules Ferry and all those yearning for education reform in France, and he knew he would publish another important book on education. The outline of *Universities Translantiques* was already well formed in his mind, and the raw material of the first draft was nearly done. Above all, he thought as the wagon trundled onto a paved road, it was the robust character and personality of the American people that had impressed him most. Everyone he had met took their liberty personally, and all seemed to be searching for the next opportunity, whatever it might be. There was a quest at the heart of the character of every American, it seemed—as if every day did indeed offer a new beginning, not just a metaphorical sunrise, but a literal fresh start to a whole new life if that was what was called for. Optimism was the gilded framework of the American mind.

○ ○ ○ ○ ○

He arrived in Princeton under a twilight sky via Washington Street and took note of the impressive scale of the houses as the carriage moved slowly toward the center of this most American town. He counted a half dozen variations on the three-story clapboard Victorian design, all set at the back of sweeping lawns with wide rambling porches and too many tall gables to count. White paint with black trim seemed to be the preferred color scheme, far less festive than Coubertin had anticipated. Aicard would not approve.

The playing fields of the campus came into view, and Coubertin felt the familiar spark of excitement in his chest. Soon the carriage edged toward the ornate ironwork of Princeton University's front gate, and the handsome stone structure of Naiman Hall appeared, echoes of so many British campuses in its gables and arches.

Under the coachman's pull, the carriage turned left and Coubertin lost sight of the campus. A sharp veer took them down another street, and Coubertin looked ahead to a few more Victorian mansions on even larger lots. At the gate on Bayard Lane, the carriage pulled into the long driveway of a three-story stone mansion with a sprawling front porch, decorated with a necklace of playful fretwork and curlicues, the gingerbread of a master woodcarver. The home had an artist's sense of style.

As the carriage trundled forward, Professor Sloane stepped out onto the porch with a boy at his side, his big hand resting on the youngster's shoulder as they awaited their guest. The boy wore knickers with suspenders and high socks.

As Coubertin stepped down from the coach, he looked up at the great mountain of a man standing tall above him, in shirtsleeves and a waistcoat hardly able to restrain the bulging expanse of his body. With a fully inviting expression, he was obviously pleased to be welcoming a Frenchman into his home. They both laughed before speaking a word, happy to be in each other's presence again.

"Welcome to Stanworth, Pierre," Sloane said, his voice booming. "Son, say hello to Baron Pierre de Coubertin. This is James, Pierre. He's eight years old." The boy bounded down the steps and shook Coubertin's hand aggressively, excitement beaming on his face. "My cousin is the quarterback of the Yale football team," he proclaimed.

"Congratulations, James," Coubertin said, catching Sloane's wink. "That must be a point of pride for the whole family. Are you a football player?"

"I'm a runner," the boy said and, as if to demonstrate, wheeled away and sprinted around the corner of the house.

Sloane stepped down to help the coachman with the stack of luggage. "James was delighted to learn that our French visitor was an international expert in all sports." They shook hands as Mary emerged with a younger daughter. The family embraced their guest as James came back into view around the other corner of the house, drawing praise for his speed. They all lent a hand hauling Pierre's luggage upstairs to a guestroom at the front of the house, just above Will's study.

"Dinner will be ready in about hour," Mary said as she fluffed the pillows on the guest bed. "I hope that's not too early for you, Pierre. We dine unfashionably early to get the children ready for bed."

"Not at all," Coubertin said, helping James position his portmanteau between an oak armoire with a mirrored front and a high colonial dresser. "I'll be delighted to join you."

"It'll be informal tonight, just us in shirtsleeves," said Sloane, ushering the family out the door. "Let's have a drink in my study before dinner."

Once he was unpacked and freshened up, Coubertin went downstairs and knocked before stepping through the open pocket doors into Sloane's study, a room whose walls were covered with shelves of books and *objets d'art* from the professor's travels, with four floor-to-ceiling windows drawing in the fading light across the porch.

"All settled?" Sloane laid his pen aside and rose from his desk.

"Yes, it's very comfortable, Will. Thank you for the hospitality. It's nice to be in a family home after so many hotels."

"*Ce n'est rien*," Sloane said, stepping over to a side table displaying a collection of bottles and glasses. "Bourbon or rye?"

"Let me try the rye since I gave up on the Bourbons at a young age."

Sloane laughed and handed the drink to Coubertin, sizing him up as their glasses touched. "*Santé*," he said. "Pierre, do you mind if I ask—what is your exact height?"

"Five foot three." Coubertin guessed what Sloane was thinking and added, "The very height of a certain emperor."

"Exactly!" Sloane said with a grin. "I take it then that you intend to be the Napoleon of international sport?"

"Yes, but I won't declare myself emperor—I'll take the throne only by acclamation."

"Very wise. Perhaps I can help you engineer the triumph."

As they sat, Sloane spoke in French with a note of the conspirator in his voice, laying out a plan for the week ahead that would include a tour of the campus, introductions to athletes and coaches, a dinner party or two with various professors and their wives, and a few planning sessions on international sport development.

Coubertin assented to the plan and began to respond to Sloane's inquiry about his trip and what he had learned about the state of athletics in the United States— but then Mary called them to dinner.

ooooo

At the table—a long, polished Duncan Phyfe original in walnut under a crystal chandelier—the family listened attentively as Sloane cast Coubertin's mission as a quest to discover the essence of America's sporting character. Mary was engaged and the children were polite as Sloane drew Pierre out on his travels across New England and his college appointments and the obvious conclusions that sport was soon to be a bridge across the ocean, with competitions between distant nations.

"Now, Mary," Sloane said, "Pierre and I are agreed on the fundamental idea that international sport must be built on a moral foundation."

"Well, I would think that's essential if you're going to build on the work you've already begun here at Princeton."

"Then you'll support my commitment to this work?"

"Will it entail international travel?" Mary asked, putting her foremost passion at the center of the question.

"One or two additional trips to Paris over the next few years."

"Then count me in."

"That settles it then," Sloane said. "We'll commence with our first planning session tomorrow. Now, Pierre, I think it's important that Mary and the children learn a bit more of your family history. Would you mind taking us back to the beginning of the Coubertins?"

For the next half hour, Pierre regaled the Sloanes with tales of Felice di Fredi and the discovery of *Laocoön and His Sons*, the chamberlains of the kings, the fortunes built by spice merchants, the beheading of his great, great Uncle Henri Louis de Fredy with Marie Antoinette in the bloody revolution, his grandfather's service under Napoleon and then the Restoration, and his father's success as a painter. He simplified the story for the children and yet made it entertaining for the adults.

As they wrapped up the dinner, Sloane had his wife recount her illustrious American ancestry before launching into his own family's background, a narrative the children had heard before.

"I've read the *Gotha Almanac* and I know something of your distinguished lineage," Sloane said, "so your story did not surprise. But I don't want you to think for a moment that you're in the presence of the hoi polloi, my dear boy. Oh no, the Sloanes are almost, at least in my opinion, part of the American aristocracy, lower echelon, of course. My mother traced our family roots back to the Mayflower, so we are as American as they get. We descended through the Trumbulls, a distinguished line of colonial leaders who became governors and merchants. One son was a member of the Continental Congress and another one, James Trumbull, became a famous painter. If you know the portrait of the Revolutionary Fathers signing the Declaration of Independence, well, that was James."

Credentials firmly established, Sloane kissed the children goodnight as Mary ushered them upstairs and the men moved back to the study.

○ ○ ○ ○ ○

Summarizing the early stage of his relationship with Sloane, Coubertin relayed to St. Clair a brief story about their last conversation in Princeton. "By the end of the trip, we had drawn quite close—and had basically agreed we would collaborate on the development of international sport," he said.

"Had you discussed the Olympic idea?"

"We had touched upon the notion of resurrecting the Olympic Games, although we were more focused on team competitions between two or three nations. Given our mutual interests in ensuring that the development of sport was grounded in education, at that point we were more focused on how to build a set of universal values into sport training and competitions. It was a big question, which we finally resolved a few years later in the philosophy of Olympism. But initially, we were essentially thinking through the ideas that Pratt and Passy had expressed in their annual youth festivals—and friendship became a core part of our long-term mission. We wanted a movement in sport based on cultivating international friendships and fostering peace, which naturally led us—or I should say—led *Will* to a personal realization."

○ ○ ○ ○ ○

After their final dinner at Will's home, the two men retired to the study to wrap up their plans and determine the next steps of their collaboration. Sloane became animated and energetic, moving around the room, brandy snifter in hand, expressing his enthusiasm for their vision.

"There runs in my blood a strong disposition to predestination, Pierre. It's part of the legacy of my Scottish Presbyterian upbringing and it's impossible to deny. So when you arrived in Princeton three weeks ago in that forlorn carriage and emerged with your kindly French countenance and bulbous Italian eyes, bringing to me a calling to help build a moral foundation for international sport, well, sir, it would have been nearly impossible for me not to have heard the hand of providence knocking on my door."

He stopped at the window and looked out at Bayard Lane, lifting his glass in a sweeping gesture to emphasize his point. "If we're to launch a philosophy of sport with the objective of fostering friendships and peace around the world, a movement with a moral at its heart, an ideology of the body meant to strengthen the spirit of mankind, then we must know friendship as well as any two men on earth."

Coubertin nodded in agreement, without replying, knowing Sloane had something in mind. "What is friendship?" the big man continued. "It is devotion, is it not, to the hopes, dreams, and aspirations of another? It is agape and fraternity. It is endless encouragement, shared triumphs and tragedies, mutual respect, the honesty to speak the truth. And most of all, perhaps, joy in the presence of another," he said as he bellowed in laughter.

Then came a confession that Pierre had not expected. "I need a good friend, Pierre, and it's clear to me that you do too, particularly here in America. It may surprise you to know that the faster you rise in the academic world over here, the more isolated you become. And I have always been a bit out of step with my own generation—graduating from Columbia with youth three to five years older than me while my former classmates were just getting through high school. My father pushed me to use my intellect for God's glory, and while I'm not sure God derived much pleasure from my thoughts or academic pursuits, the gifts he granted me brought early attention and accolades. But I had to act the adult before my time, and the camaraderie I longed for was sadly missing from my life."

"Well, your experience in that regard is not unique," Coubertin said with empathy. "While I've made a few good friends across the course of the last decade, particularly one wild poet, the work of education reform and the promotion of physical education can be a lonely endeavor. It's hardly personal. And a lot of my time is spent with aging politicians who long ago lost the taste for personal reverie. There are occasional commiserations, but I've been in America for four months now, and while I've had more dinners than I can count, most have been oriented toward an objective of one sort or another, not personal. I've made a hundred acquaintances, often enjoyable and promising people, but not one genuine friendship—until I met you."

Will walked across the room, his free arm extended, and wrapped the baron in a hug. Drawing back, he said, "Well then, Pierre, our friendship will be the foundation of a new school of sport—and it will become the foundation of amity among nations."

51

THE NIGHTMARE

P ierre wanted to take the weekend off and told St. Clair he was going to Geneva to see some old friends. St. Clair worked on his notes all day Saturday, concentrating on gathering materials on Coubertin's interactions with Dr. William Penny Brookes and Father Henri Didon, two of his strongest allies in the campaign to bring back the Olympics. St. Clair was moving forward at a painstaking pace, detail by detail, but he was deeply satisfied with the work and looked forward to another productive week of interviews. Sunday afternoon, Jacques and Juliette took the two-seat bike down the lakefront and rode all the way to Montreux, where they had a fondue before cycling home. They spent the evening working, then talking and reading together, and they stayed up late making love by candlelight.

St. Clair was still asleep early Monday morning when the telephone jangled. He rose, groggy, and answered to find Dr. Messerli at the other end, his voice filled with urgency. "Jacques, please get up to Mon Repos as soon as you can."

Shocked into full awareness, Jacques assumed the worst. "Is Pierre all right?"

"Yes, he's fine, but he's upset—*enraged*. The baroness has dumped boxes of his books and writing on the curb. He needs help recovering them."

"What? The baroness threw out his writing? How much of it? We need that material—it's the history of the Olympic Movement!"

"I know, and I can't leave the hospital right now. I'll be there in an hour."

St. Clair dressed in a hurry, explaining to Juliette what had happened. "The baroness and Pierre must have had a horrible fight," he said. "It sounds like she's trying to destroy our work."

"Good lord," Juliette said, putting on a bathrobe. "Can I help?"

"I don't know. I'll call you if I need you."

Charging up the hill on the De Dion-Bouton, St. Clair was glad the streets were dry. The sky was overcast but it didn't feel humid enough for rain. Cycling at top speed, he broke into a sweat before he passed under the train bridge, and he was completely out of breath when he raced through the southwestern gate of Mon Repos Park.

As he climbed the path in the park, he spotted Pierre standing amid a pile of boxes, books, and papers on the side of the villa where the trash was usually left. The old man was sorting through and stacking boxes off to the side. He had his suit coat off, and patches of sweat stained his shirt.

"Jacques," the baron said, his voice soft, his expression defeated. "Thank you for coming. We've got to repack these files and move the boxes back upstairs." He had papers in both hands and he waved them at the disarray in front of him.

"What happened?"

His voice was grim. "I'm not sure yet. The caretaker is helping me. He said a car was here last night and a man packed off some boxes."

St. Clair looked into an open box and saw folders of correspondence in Pierre's handwriting on IOC stationery. "Why would she do this? These are historic documents."

Pierre turned away and didn't answer. He sat on a box.

"I don't think I have the strength to carry another box upstairs."

"I'll do it. You need to rest."

"All right," Coubertin said. "Carry these up to the office. I have a key, which I've seldom used, but we're going to lock everything up."

The caretaker emerged from the building; Pierre introduced him as Bernard. Dressed in overalls and a beret, he immediately went back to work. Following his lead, St. Clair lifted a box and followed him up the stairs into the IOC offices. He had moved the furniture away from the back wall and had started stacking the boxes there, next to a closet where early archives were left untouched.

"Bernard, do you know how many boxes are missing?"

"No more than five," he said. "Please don't tell the baron that I carried all of this down to the trash. The baroness ordered me to do it."

"When?"

"Saturday night," he said. "I heard her yelling and came up and found her in the Salon Rouge, alone, crying and shouting that it just wasn't fair."

"Why was she so angry? What happened?"

"I don't know, but when I asked her, she got up and took me up to the IOC's offices. She yelled, 'I want him out of here!' and told me to take all of his boxes down to the curb. I tried to object, but she screamed, 'Right now!'"

Messerli arrived and then Juliette showed up; soon the boxes were repacked and stacked neatly in the office. It was an awkward time for everyone as Pierre settled in behind his desk and said, "I'll have to go through everything to see what's missing. Give me a day or two."

"Where is the baroness?" asked Dr. Messerli with some concern.

"She's not here," said Pierre. "I'm not sure where she is."

"Why did she do it?" Messerli asked.

The room fell silent. Pierre didn't answer. He put his hands on his forehead and leaned on the desk.

"Well, we're going to see if we can track the papers down," Messerli said. He signaled to St. Clair and Juliette that it was time to leave.

Downstairs, they found Bernard in the caretaker's room on the first floor. Messerli made it clear that the IOC records were sacrosanct and had to be protected from the baroness if necessary. "Do you know who carried off the boxes?" he asked.

"I think the car belonged to Monsieur Defleur," Bernard said.

Messerli's eyes narrowed. "We can't let him get away with this."

Defleur was a collector of Olympic memorabilia and had often approached Coubertin and Messerli about the archives. He had an antique store on rue Saint-Laurent.

"Come with me," Messerli said to St. Clair and Juliette. "You can help me with Defleur. Be good to have a journalist along." They got into Messerli's car and drove toward rue Centrale in the old part of town.

"I'm furious," Messerli said. "Why would the baroness stoop to such a low blow? What in the world possessed her to do it? My God, his papers and his books—that's all he has left. She knew she was cutting to the bone."

"It's so cruel, it's hard to believe," said Juliette. She and St. Clair jumped out of the car to follow Messerli into a pedestrian street that turned up rue Saint-Laurent. He was moving at a quick pace.

"I've spent years working with Pierre on the development of the Olympic Library and the archives," he said. "Every single piece of paper is valuable."

The shop, Defleur Antiquités, was on the left partway up the cobblestone hill. The windows were filled with old lamps, writing sets, crystal and silver, ceramics, and a few small chests with ornate woodwork.

Messerli shouldered the glass door open as a bell tinkled. A man wearing glasses looked up from a desk behind a counter near the back wall as the three of them stepped inside. The room held a musty smell of old books, and indeed, books were stacked on tables and in antique shelves against the walls. Dusty, dark-framed paintings hung above. The room was mostly filled with furniture and furnishings from the nineteenth century.

The man stood and greeted Messerli.

"Hello, Defleur," said Messerli, dispensing with any pleasantries. "I suppose you know why I'm here."

"The Coubertin archives?"

"So it was you?"

"Of course it was me. Didn't the baroness tell you?"

"Tell me what?"

"That she gave me the rights to some of the baron's Olympic archives."

"She gave you the rights? That's ridiculous."

"Well, I intend to pay her something once I've had a chance to—"

Messerli interrupted. "You won't have a chance to pay her because I'm taking the archives back. They're the property of the IOC and she has no right to dispose of them."

"Listen, I don't want any trouble," Defleur said, "but I have the rights to the materials she gave me."

"No, you don't," Messerli's voice was forceful as he moved imposingly up to the counter. "This is Jacques St. Clair, a journalist writing about the baron and his archives. We will call the police if necessary."

"Ah yes, the journalist. So you're the one. That's why she was so angry when she called me."

"What?" asked St. Clair, looking at Juliette and Messerli. "The baroness was angry at me?"

"Yes, and she was furious with the baron for introducing you to their son, the retard."

Messerli cringed and looked at St. Clair, who was stunned at this news.

"She said she'd never let you write a word about him," Defleur said. "And believe me, she meant it."

St. Clair was shocked to think the baroness believed he was a threat to their family life. He knew how they felt about their son, naturally protective and loving, not wanting him exposed or embarrassed in any way. The baron had made that abundantly clear and had trusted St. Clair with the truth. "I would never violate their trust or disrespect their family in any way," he said.

"Give us the damn archives," Messerli said, turning back to Defleur, "or I'm going to get the police over here."

At last, Defleur relented. He led them into a back room cluttered with furniture. There, next to a door, was a stack of four boxes, the top one opened, revealing the papers inside. They crowded around the boxes, and Messerli reached in and lifted out a few files.

"My God," he said. "This is Pierre's correspondence. Here's a file on Gebhardt … one on Kemény … another on Sloane. This is critical Olympic history." He shook his head and looked at Defleur accusingly. "What's missing? Have you taken anything out of here?"

"No, not a page," the man said. "I barely got that first box open and took a look at a few files, but it's all there."

"This is all of it? Are you telling the truth?"

"Yes."

"Wait here—I'm going to pull the car into the alley." Messerli opened the back door and stepped out.

St. Clair reached into a box and lifted the heavy file of letters Sloane had written to Coubertin. He started to read while keeping an eye on the boxes.

Defleur fidgeted alongside of him. "So you're writing the baron's life story?"

St. Clair gazed up at him coolly and didn't answer for a minute, waiting until Defleur broke the stare. "It's a confidential matter," he finally said.

He looked at Juliette. She had moved deeper into the room and was fingering the edge of an empty ornate frame sitting on top of some cabinets. "This must have once held an impressive canvas," she said. She rubbed away the dust to reveal gold paint covering a carved floral-and-fruit theme notched in the corner. Spotting a rag, she picked it up and wiped off more of the grit.

"Is this frame for sale?" she asked, the gold glinting beneath her hand.

"Yes." Defleur could scarcely conceal his annoyance. "I want you out of my shop."

They heard the car pull up, and Messerli entered. They carried the four boxes out of the back room into the alley and loaded them into the back of Messerli's car. Defleur insisted he'd taken only four boxes as he had no more room in his car, which was already filled with furniture. But he added that someone else had been there when he left ... another car coming down the driveway, a black Mercedes.

"Do you know who it was?" Messerli asked.

"You'll have to ask the baroness. She may have called someone else."

As they were riding back to the villa, St. Clair tried to explain what had happened to set the baroness off.

"Friday morning when I went up to Mon Repos to meet Pierre, I heard voices laughing out back as I was parking the bike. I walked around to the yard, and there was Pierre with his son kicking a ball while his nurse looked on. I was with them for five minutes before the nurse said they should go in. Pierre introduced me, but Jacques didn't speak, he just smiled a kind of crooked smile and stared at me, his eyes widening. And then when we went inside to go up the stairs, he reached out and took my hand, like a young boy might. When we reached the second floor, just as Pierre turned to go into his office, I saw the baroness standing above us on the landing, watching, and when our eyes met, she gave me a grim look, turned quickly away, and climbed out of sight. I didn't think anything of it, but it obviously upset her. I'll try to talk to her later and see if I can reason with her."

St. Clair didn't tell them how stunned he was by Jacques's lack of coordination. He couldn't kick the ball without swinging his leg at it two or three times. It was an unusual scene to witness—the Baron Pierre de Coubertin encouraging his forty-one-year-old son to play the simplest of games—and a very poignant moment that St. Clair knew immediately would give his story a tragically ironic tone. But he knew now that he could never use it.

○ ○ ○ ○ ○

Pierre was still in the office going through the archives when they got back and stacked the four boxes in place. He sat in the middle of the room in one of the two guest chairs, an open box at his feet, half empty, stacking folders neatly on the other chair. Assessing the files one by one, he was making notes on what he had found.

"Anything missing?" asked Messerli.

"Too early to tell." Coubertin shrugged, appearing now to take the situation in stride. "We're going to have to compare the content to our records, Francis." He smiled briefly. "Just more work for two old librarians." St. Clair knew they had spent years organizing the files and was sure they would eventually figure it out.

"We'll get it done," said Messerli. "Is the baroness here?"

"No," said Coubertin, "but it's probably best to leave her alone for now."

"All right, Pierre," Messerli said. "I'm going back up to the university. I'll call you later."

Juliette gave Pierre a hug and kissed St. Clair goodbye, whispering, "I want that old frame from Defleur's shop for my painting of Pierre."

The baron moved the files from the second chair and St. Clair sat down across from him. "Are you okay?" he asked.

The old man looked up, his eyes tired, his shoulders slumped. "The struggles never end, do they, Jacques? The Cat always wants to scratch," he said. "She'll draw blood whenever she can."

St. Clair knew he was talking about his wife. Although he hadn't yet seen Pierre's diary, Messerli had told him that in his personal writings, Pierre referred to Marie as the Cat and Renée as the Bird. "She was angry at me," he said. "Worried I was going to write about your son."

Pierre shook his head and reached down for another file. "It's beyond anger, Jacques, and it's not you, my friend. It's me," he said with resignation. "There's a very thin line between love and hate in most marriages. When the hardships last for years, when the lash falls as incessantly as it has fallen on us, it's very difficult to find your way back across that line to love. The Cat hates me—and the hatred is deep. She blames me for the loss of everything. All this is pretense now, because the legacy is the only thing that allows us to maintain our sense of dignity."

He lowered his eyes and grew silent. St. Clair could think of nothing to say in such a dark moment. Finally, he reached out and put his hand on the baron's shoulder, squeezing as tenderly and reassuringly as he could, letting the silence last.

Pierre lifted a printed piece from the file, examined it, and handed it to St. Clair, who leaned back to look at it. It was the program for the Sorbonne Congress in June of 1894 during which Coubertin had successfully led the resurrection of the Olympic Games.

"Ironic that this is what she wanted to throw away," Coubertin said, "a record of that pinnacle night. I guess when you look at a life, it's not always so easy to pinpoint one moment that really represents the zenith, but here it is in the life of Pierre de Coubertin. That was the moment, but for the lovely Marie Rothan, once a rebel standing with me in that grand amphitheater on the horizon of a new world, that moment now belongs in the trash."

"I don't think she would throw it all away." St. Clair was not at all sure he had an argument to make.

"She would if she could have her son back. The baby she loved above all."

"What happened to him, Pierre?"

"We'll talk about that later." Coubertin sighed and went back to looking through the files.

St. Clair sensed it would be best to leave the baron to the task at hand. "Shall we take a day or two off? I want to read through these files on William Milligan Sloane."

Coubertin looked up. "Thank you, Jacques," he said simply. "That would be best."

52

SLOANE'S LETTERS

As St. Clair read through the thick file of letters from Sloane, it became clear this distinguished international man of letters had an unshakable commitment to the Olympic Movement. He referred often to the moral values of sport—particularly the idealistic vision of friendships born on the field of play.

The file contained a reprint of an article Sloane had written for *The Century Magazine* on the eve of the 1912 Stockholm Olympic Games—eighteen years after the founding of the Games at the Paris Congress and twenty-four years after Sloane and Coubertin had first met at Taine's. It was titled "The Olympic Idea—Its Origin, Foundation, and Progress," and it appeared in July of 1912, at a time when the American team would have been on its way to the Games of the Fifth Olympiad. Sloane sent it to Coubertin after the Games with a short note saying, "I hope this rendition of our work together over these past two decades meets with your approval."

The article opened with a good account of the growth of sport at the time—by Sloane's estimation more than forty thousand amateur athletes were practicing in the United States and far more in Britain, and hundreds of thousands of spectators thronged to witness their feats—but it moved quickly into an assessment of the founding and purpose of the Olympic Games, which he called "a contest in magnanimity" whose primary purpose was to serve as a "medium of international conciliation."

He recounted the success of the Paris Congress in 1894 as the beginning of the Games and the International Olympic Committee. Calling Coubertin "a man of classical training and spirit," he gave the baron full credit for summoning sport leaders from around the world "to the Sorbonne, oldest of Western universities" to "an awakening of the possibilities of a modern Olympic Games."

Noting Coubertin's travels to the United States to promote the Games, Sloane claimed "in America, he was greeted enthusiastically, winning many valiant hearts to his cause. Here as elsewhere among the select few, the Olympic Idea became almost an obsession," but he also acknowledged the rejection the baron suffered in the earliest days, stating, "The many of course could not find time to bother with an idealist and his strange doctrines. But the small handful in each country was undismayed."

Sloane also revealed his own idealism, saying that by bringing together thousands of young people for amicable competition, the Games promoted friendships that "tend naturally to sweep away the cobwebs of international suspicion and distrust."

In keeping with the tone of respect he showed for the baron in his letters, Sloane said Coubertin was "ever premier in council and the prime mover in actions." In summing up the achievements of the Games through four Olympiads, with a fifth pending, he celebrated the enduring presence of five still-active IOC members who had been there in Paris in 1894, himself, General Balck of Sweden, Monsieur Collot of France, the famous Bohemian novelist, Dr. Jiří Guth-Jarkovsky, and the president, who received Sloane's final accolades.

"These," he wrote, "with many who are dead, and more who are still alive, have maintained the cause against many discouragements, until now it is triumphant. But the lifelong devotion of Monsieur de Coubertin, his tact, his ingenuity, his self-sacrifice in time and money, in short, the qualities of faith and merit, have been the chief reason for the solid establishment of the enterprise."

○ ○ ○ ○ ○

As St. Clair read deeper into the correspondence, he was carried into the early history of the modern Games and found references to a number of conflicts Coubertin had glossed over in his own memoir. As he took notes on each letter and absorbed another article Sloane had written for the *American Journal of History*, three lines of thought emerged. First, it was clear Sloane was an effective counselor for Coubertin, providing him with critical advice on the political issues of sport, shouldering some of the hard work of standardizing the rules of competition—he chaired the commission on amateurism at the Sorbonne Congress of 1894—so that Coubertin could focus on promoting their shared vision of the Games and the larger strategic development.

Second, Sloane was fiercely protective of Coubertin on U.S. soil, ensuring that the aggressive assaults from James Sullivan after the debacles of Paris 1900, St. Louis 1904, and London 1908—all blatant attempts to undermine the baron in order to take control of the movement—were not only parried but ultimately defeated. "Don't worry about Sullivan and Whitney," Sloane wrote in 1912, "they feed from my hand." Caspar Whitney was Sullivan's greatest ally, an influential writer at *Harper's Weekly* and a strident defender of amateurism.

Nevertheless, Sloane managed to control the emergent American Olympic scene with the same authority that he controlled his philosophy of history classes at Princeton. He didn't have to assume authority since he was the original and only IOC member in the United States, yet he bestrode the Olympic sport scene like a colossus across a portal to a new world. His triumph was complete when through his IOC office he appointed the first American Olympic Committee in 1916 and named the grateful Sullivan, Whitney, and Curtis of the New York Athletic Club to executive positions.

Third, Sloane's role was as personal as it was professional. St. Clair found something else in the thirty-year correspondence that touched him far more deeply than the business affairs and sport politics. As the two men aged, the inflection of personal empathy and compassion became even stronger in Sloane's letters. It seemed Sloane knew Coubertin's family and his struggles better than almost anyone—referring to hardships and crises that never surfaced in public light. He wrote of illnesses and sadness and recoveries as if he knew his friend's state of mind almost moment to moment. In a continuous stream of notes full of tenderness and intimacy, Sloane encouraged his younger friend to endure through every struggle.

Sitting on the sofa with the files spread around him, St. Clair said, "Listen to this. This is from the war years—just after Coubertin moved his family from Paris to Lausanne. 'My dear, dear Pierre ... I can't get over the tone of melancholy in your letters ... We're so disheartened that your lovely wife has not recovered yet, but we know she will. She'll overcome this breakdown and will be your full partner again ... such moves are always traumatic and in this case, the war has exacerbated the stress ... Tender love from both of us. Your devoted friend, Will.'"

"My lord!" Juliette moved to the couch and reached for the letter. "The baroness had a nervous breakdown?"

"There are a dozen letters referencing her troubles, and some of them had to do with the children." He read another excerpt. "'We're praying for Renée ... and swift recovery from the operation.' I get the impression she might have had electroshock treatments."

"Oh no! Makes you wonder if the baroness is stable—after what she just did? You don't have to write about these personal traumas, do you?"

St. Clair sat back to consider her question. "I don't know. I don't want to, but I'm going to have to ask him about it. There's nothing of any of this in his writing. Maybe it's in his diaries, but he's not inclined to share those yet."

ooooo

When St. Clair finished reading the files, the personal crises had receded somewhat under the weight of Sloane's overriding focus on Olympic matters and Coubertin's vision. St. Clair had begun to think of the two of them as brothers—brothers of the Olympic spirit, athletes of the intellect, two brilliant men drawn together to form an international aristocracy of the mind, wholly focused on sport.

He was inspired by Sloane's masterful summary of the character of the Olympic Movement and what it had achieved by 1912. He typed up three quotes to discuss with Coubertin:

- *"How far the Olympic Idea may go is not yet determined. Its definition for present uses is sufficiently fixed on the lines of its first appearance: first, to create and strengthen bonds of friendship, such as ought to exist among all civilized nations, by frequent, peaceful intercourse; second, to purify sport, abolish selfish and underhand methods in the struggle for athletic supremacy, secure fair play for all, even the weakest, and, as far as possible, make the contest, not the victory, the joy of the young."*
- *"The Olympic Idea does full justice to all men, for national generosity has made it possible for any athlete who proves his fitness to compete without cost to himself except his time."*
- *"Its membership will change, but not the remembrance of its initial work, which has profoundly impressed both lovers of sport and of mankind. The Olympic Idea has proved a living germ from which already a vast organization has sprung and which has enthusiastic workers and recruits in every civilized country today."*

As he gathered the letters and slipped the files back into his satchel, St. Clair realized Sloane had offered the definitive contemporary judgment on Coubertin's work. More than any other participant in the early stages of the Olympic Movement, Sloane had the intellect, the scholarly discernment, and the comparative context to evaluate the baron's achievements—and St. Clair decided Sloane's judgment was accurate.

53

THE PRAYER

O n the last day of July 1937, as he arrived at Mon Repos one morning to restart the interviews, St. Clair encountered the baroness descending the steps in the foyer.

"I'm glad to see you, Baroness," he began. "I hope you will accept my humblest apologies for—"

She cut him off. "You can't use our son to sensationalize your story. I won't allow it." She sidestepped him, her bottom lip quivering below a sneer. "Jacques represents everything that's wrong with our lives. Do you understand what I'm saying, Monsieur St. Clair?"

"Yes, Baroness, I do understand, and I promise you I will never do anything to embarrass your family. I'm only trying to protect your legacy. You don't have anything to worry about." Even as he said it, St. Clair wondered once again if this was a commitment he could keep.

"Oh, but I do worry," she said, stopping at the door. "We've been interacting with the press for years. I've heard many empty promises before. And as you well know, I've done all I can to protect our legacy."

She spun and exited the foyer before he could say anything more. Through the window, he watched her recede down the path toward the gate on avenue Mon Repos, pacing swiftly away from their conversation. What a walking contradiction, he thought. She had just tried to destroy the legacy she was struggling, in her own way, to preserve. He had so many more questions for her, but they would have to wait. He wondered if he could ever regain her confidence, and in a strange way, her unpredictability gave him hope that he just might.

In the office, Coubertin was clearly distraught—leaning over his desk, head in hands—and made no attempt to feign enthusiasm as St. Clair entered.

"It's been a rough morning, Jacques. The baroness is still angry."

"Yes, I just encountered her on the way up here—and she certainly wasn't happy to see me."

"I'm not sure I'll be much of a conversationalist today," the baron said.

St. Clair found himself impatient at the idea of another delay, but he couldn't bring himself to push the old man at the moment. "Maybe some fresh air?" he suggested.

"Actually, I need more than a little air. I was thinking of taking a walk up to the cathedral. Care to join me?"

"Of course." St. Clair lifted the strap of his satchel back over his head.

As they walked out of Mon Repos Park and turned up the hill toward the cathedral, a silence fell between them, and St. Clair knew, despite being filled with questions about Sloane and his letters, he needed to wait until Coubertin was ready to talk.

When they reached the bridge over rue Centrale, Coubertin stopped. "Let's go down and climb the Escaliers du Marché. I need the exercise."

As steep as it was, they went up the old stairway at a good pace, the baron leading the way to the top of the old city wall. They emerged in front of the cathedral at the small plaza and overlook. St. Clair leaned on the wall and gazed across the lake at France.

"Marvelous view," said Coubertin, pausing for only a second to catch his breath. The walk revived at least a trace of his usual enthusiasm. "I never tire of it. Have you been inside the cathedral? It took more than fifty years to build. It's a masterpiece of height and volume."

"I've not been inside yet."

"Then come have a look. I won't be long."

He followed Coubertin through the massive wooden doors surrounded by a grand arch of carved saints and angels. The cathedral seemed higher and the sanctuary longer and thinner than most St. Clair had entered—although he had little time for religion he was interested in the architecture. He noted it was a good distance to the transept and apse and the stained glass. The soft voice of the priest, who was holding mass for a scattered congregation that barely filled the first five pews, wafted in and out of earshot like the fading echo of a voice across a valley on a windy day.

Coubertin moved down the central aisle, genuflected, and sat in a pew, head bowed. Staying at the back of the church, St. Clair wondered if the old man would find the solace he was looking for. He made a mental note to ask Pierre about his faith and the role it played in helping him cope with the vehemence of his wife's anger and the sad toll of his son's condition.

He waited outside for a half hour before Pierre emerged. They walked back down the *escalier* and settled in for lunch at a small bistro. Pierre ordered an *omelette au fromage* with buttered toast; Jacques asked for a Monte Cristo. From their window seat, Pierre gazed out at the passing crowds. When the wine came, St. Clair opened his notebook. "To better days ahead, Jacques," Coubertin said. "Better days ahead."

Although the baron's smile was half-hearted, St. Clair was relieved they were moving back into their long conversation. "Did the prayer help?" he asked.

Coubertin took a deep breath and sighed, seemingly relieved to be talking about the present and not the past. "Yes. It always helps. Whether it's God providing the solace or it's just the comfort of old familiar rituals, I'm not sure ... but even if it's just an imaginary refuge, after a while, I can feel the peace settling in."

"Is that what they call the peace of the Holy Spirit?" St. Clair tried to avoid any hint of skepticism.

Coubertin looked at him askance. "I know you're not a believer, Jacques— and you have heard me call Catholicism the religion of death—but sometimes there's nowhere else to turn."

"I'm sorry, I know it's a hellish time right now, but I don't want to lose more time. We've got to persevere."

"I'm right here. What's our next subject?"

"William Milligan Sloane."

After an hour of taking notes—mostly confirming what St. Clair already knew—he decided to broach the question of the family crisis. "Sloane's letters carried an unusual note of intimacy—and very often referred to family affairs ... struggles ... medical crises ..." He stopped as Coubertin's face suddenly tightened into an expression he had not seen before. This was new territory. "I have to ask. Did the baroness have a nervous breakdown, Pierre? Was Renée treated for schizophrenia?"

Coubertin's visage hardened further, and he glared at St. Clair with an unforgiving look, reminding him of the animosity he had felt when the baroness looked at him in anger—but then the darkness passed and the baron sighed. "I can't talk about any of that, Jacques."

"That's fine, for now. But we'll have to come back to it. Sloane's letters raise these questions."

"Will and I were very close—and he knew everything my family went through. But those are personal letters—not in the official IOC files. If you want to move on with the interview, let's change the subject."

St. Clair hadn't expected the resistance—Coubertin had never dodged any questions before—but he knew he had pushed the old man as far as he could. "Okay. Let's talk about how you rekindled your romance with Marie after you returned from America at the end of 1889."

54

THE ROTHANS

By the time he had returned to Paris in January 1890 after four months in the United States and a week of holidays with the family in Normandy at the Château de Mirville—Coubertin felt as if he had lost touch with the city and some of his friends. Aside from a long dinner with Simon and Waddington during which he reported on his American travels, he kept to himself for a few weeks in order to finish the draft of his report for Ferry and to complete, at an even more aggressive pace, the manuscript of his third book, *Universitiés Transatlantiques*.

With Jennette out of his life, he decided to wait until the writing was finished to reignite his social schedule—although he called Jean Aicard and Bertha von Suttner to set up a reunion. In the meantime, he went to the Racing Club to get back into shape and to meet with Georges de Saint-Clair. They had work to do in planning the activities for their new Union des Sociétiés Françaises de Sports Athlétiques—the USFSA—created through the merger of the Jules Simon Committee with Saint-Clair's Union des Sociétiés Françaises de Courses à Pied. Their combined successes at the Congress on Physical Education had made them the leading sports development and promotion team in France.

Bertha, her husband Arthur, and Jean Aicard kept him out late over dinner and drinks at Café Flore. While he got a full update on the peace movement—and Aicard's latest literary and social endeavors—Coubertin did most of the talking. His companions were interested in everything he had to say about America, its cities and universities, and particularly about the friendship he had developed with Will Sloane. The fact that Sloane was a Francophile and was friends with

Taine and others made the baron's story all the more relevant and enthralling. Bertha was insistent that he accompany her to Rome for the Second Universal Peace Congress later that year—and he promised he would clear his calendar, knowing that two of his new American friends, White of Cornell and Eliot of Harvard, were planning to attend. More importantly, Bertha reported she was nearly finished with her novel *Lay Down Your Arms*, and she wanted Pierre to read the galley proofs before the book went to press. She wasn't confident the book would be well received, although her husband had nothing but praise for it—as did Alfred Nobel, evidently—so she needed his opinion.

He promised he would start reading the novel the next morning, but when he woke and began paging through *Le Petit Journal* at the breakfast table, he came across a story that filled him with regret—and inadvertently set him on a path that would lead to a new future: Gustave Rothan had died.

○ ○ ○ ○ ○

Shrouded in black, Marie and her mother sat in the front row of chairs, just a few yards away from the casket where Gustave Rothan now rested in a small antechamber at the Reformed Church of Paris—the famed L'Église L'Oratoire du Louvre created by Napoleon for the Protestant minority in an 1811 decree. The rows had filled early as people came by to pay their respects to the great man. Coubertin looked on from the rear seats as many former government dignitaries and friends from the art world stopped to offer their condolences to the widow and daughter, and then turned one by one to bow their heads in silent homage at the coffin. As another old friend turned away, Marie's mother convulsed again in a hushed sob that barely broke the murmur of conversations. Marie wrapped her arm around her mother's shoulders and dabbed at her tears with a lace handkerchief.

Pierre waited for the right moment to approach—and then stood before them, waiting patiently, as Marie whispered words of comfort to her mother. Marie finally looked up.

"Oh, Pierre!" she said, clearly surprised. Her mother turned her head up as well.

"Hello, Pierre," Madame Rothan said. "Gustave would be so pleased to know you came."

"I'm so sorry for your loss, madame." He kneeled before the two of them, feeling his eyes well with tears as he said, "He was a man of destiny and inimitable cultural taste, an exceptional diplomat and excellent writer, and a wonderful husband and father. I was proud to know him."

Her mother began to sob again as Marie said, "Thank you, Pierre," adding as he rose, "It's good to see you again."

At the end of the funeral service in the sanctuary, as people moved away, Pierre saw Marie moving through the flow of the crowd. She caught up with him as he stopped before the door.

"Pierre." She spoke softly, putting her hand on his arm and squeezing it lightly. "I just wanted you to know my mother and I are both grateful you came."

Their eyes met and he remembered what he had felt for her years before. What a beautiful young woman she was, he thought—and still is. The funeral was not the right place to express such feelings. "Of course, Marie. Out of respect for your father, I would never have missed his final service. It brought back so many memories of the sweet times we shared."

Her eyes lit up ever so briefly, then teared. "And I wanted you to know I'm glad to see you again."

Taking the signal, he leaned toward her, looking into her eyes. "Marie, I hope this isn't out of place, but ..."

She looked at him expectantly.

"May I call on you?"

She leaned in and kissed him on each cheek. "Please do," she said, turning back into the crowd, heading for her mother's side.

○ ○ ○ ○ ○

Out of respect for the grieving in her home and the changes he was sure she was going through—arranging a new life for her aged mother—Pierre waited two weeks before sending her a note, asking when it would be appropriate to see her. He had an answer in two days and visited their home on the Place Saint-Georges a month after the funeral.

When the concierge opened the door and Pierre entered, it appeared exactly as he had remembered it twelve years earlier—the same paintings hanging in the same positions along the curving wall of the grand staircase. As Marie stepped from the salon to greet him, he wondered if *The Allegories of Painting and Music* were still holding court in her boudoir.

He followed her out into the sunroom where Madame Rothan was seated at a table going over a large ledger. Papers, notes, and official documents, which Pierre recognized as certificates of provenance for paintings, were spread in front of a seat Marie had just vacated.

"Pierre," her mother said, rising and extending her hand, "it is so good to see you again in our home."

"And it's good to see you, madame, with a smile on your face." Casting a glance at the table, he continued, "I hope I'm not intruding on important matters."

"Oh no, don't concern yourself. There's so much to manage in Gustave's estate, I'm afraid Marie and I have been preoccupied. But I'm glad you're here to distract her."

"Do I need distractions, Mother?" Marie said in a spirited voice. "Well then, I suppose we'll just have to see if Pierre is up to the task." She took his arm and they left her mother to the work.

"I've been wanting to see you since the funeral," Marie said as they went through an antechamber to a glassed-in parlor on the other side of the house.

Pierre was delighted that she had spoken openly, without pretense, and freely admitted her desire. "I would have called sooner, but I was trying to be respectful."

"Respect is important, but I thought you understood my invitation." Sitting on a loveseat, she patted the cushion next to her and he joined her as directed. She rang a bell and asked the maid to select a good bottle of white wine.

"I'll try to be more responsive next time," he said, remembering with a pang how unresponsive she had been when they were young and she'd left him behind. He enjoyed the role reversal but sensed she was still in charge.

When the wine came, she shifted to face him and placed her arm on the cushion behind his shoulders. Her fragrance enveloped him. Lifting her glass, she said, "To the times we've shared, and the times ahead."

"To renewing old affection." He felt a magnetism between them but restrained himself, not wanting to seem forward.

"Can I be honest?" she asked.

"Of course." He turned toward her to express his interest. "You have my confidence."

"I haven't had anyone to talk to in a while, except Mother and a few of Father's old friends. We've been struggling to sort out Father's affairs—and it hasn't been easy."

He wanted to ask about her circle of friends—surely she must have several suitors—but he could leave that for later. "I'm sure it's complicated," he said, wanting to be sympathetic.

"It's both complicated and serious, but ..."

She left the thought unfinished, suddenly leaning forward and kissing him on the mouth. In a minute, they were in a heated embrace, much to Pierre's surprise, but the taste of her lips, her impulsiveness and spontaneity, and the sensation of their passion reminded him of why he had fallen in love with her all those years ago.

Voices and commotion in the next room brought them out of their entwined clinch. Her mother was calling her—someone was at the door. As they stood and straightened their clothes, Marie touched Pierre's cheek. "I'll be at the Rothschild's dinner dance in two weeks," she said. "Will you come?"

"Of course, if I'm invited."

"You will be invited. I'm sorry I have to go, but that's Monsieur Prevoir from Petit Georges Galerie. We're assessing father's collection."

"You're going to sell some of his paintings?" Coubertin was surprised again.

"I'll tell you about it later, Pierre. There's much to discuss."

○ ○ ○ ○ ○

Unbeknownst to Coubertin at the time, Marie Rothan knew far more about him than he did about her. In fact, she had discreetly followed the development of his career in education reform and the sporting world, picking up the occasional tidbit of news or rumor through friends of her father and a social circle that reached into the Paris Jockey Club. Without ever making contact, she had kept tabs on him after that surprising night at the le Play union meeting, where she was impressed by his speech and relieved he escaped the angry attack of Paschal Grousset. She knew about his significant role in the Paris Universal Exposition, his friendships with Jules Simon and the leadership of the Third Republic, and his admirable achievements as a writer, editor, and magazine publisher.

While she thought her interest was simple curiosity about a man who had once been infatuated with her as a boy, a boy whose charms still lingered in her memory, she had to admit it was more than that when a friend at a dinner party told her about the end of Pierre's long affair with Jennette Montaigne—and her heart raced at the news. Although she knew Jennette by reputation, she had no idea the caricaturist and Pierre had been lovers. In fact, while she had quietly inquired now and then about Coubertin's career, she had never sought to delve into his personal life. At the time, in the late summer of 1889, she had been happily seeing a British businessman, Andrew Payne, for nearly a year—and he was seated across the table from her when the story about Pierre and Jennette surprisingly stirred her passion.

Even so, that might have been the end of it if circumstances hadn't conspired to thrust Pierre back into her thoughts. Payne left Paris when his company transferred him to New Delhi, India, leaving Marie without any immediate prospects. She had been planning to move out of her parents' house—perhaps launch a career of her own as an English teacher, breaking the mold she was expected to fulfill—when her father fell ill that autumn and died at the beginning of the next year. The shock sent an ineluctable wave of turmoil through her world as she and her mother discovered the family finances were insufficient to maintain their style of living on Place Saint-Georges. Naturally, her father had always handled the finances—and while he was considered a sagacious art buyer, his passion for collecting had gotten the better of his financial discipline and he had depleted their reserves. He had left them a small fortune, but it was hanging on the walls of their home. They began to plan for an auction, sadly realizing, as they spoke with a trusted friend from Petit Georges Galerie, that the paintings, more than 250 of them, would have to be sold to produce the inheritance they needed.

To maintain a certain social equilibrium in the house, Marie had suppressed her own feelings and ambition in order to give her mother the emotional support she needed as her father lay dying. In the quiet of the mansion at night, she found herself reminiscing about her father and especially his love of art—the deep cultural affection for creativity he had passed on to her. Her reveries deepened as the winter solstice and holidays approached, and she began to think about those early years as the best time of her life—when her ability to speak about his paintings and the history of art with authority had begun to flower, when she had invoked her father's pride by bringing the legacy he was creating to life. And as she recounted the conversations she had about art with the men she had embraced over the years, it dawned on her that only one man had the knowledge and passion for painting that matched hers—only one boy had inhabited the world of the imagination she so dearly loved—Pierre de Coubertin. He was in her thoughts as constantly as any other figure in the weeks leading up to her father's death. The fact that he was Catholic added meaning to her recollections—they shared an artistic link that spanned their spiritual gulf. She had begun to think about contacting him again, about talking to him about the art collection and what it would mean to lose it. When he showed up at the funeral, she couldn't help but feel as if destiny had intervened.

○ ○ ○ ○ ○

He arrived late at the Rothschilds'—having lingered with his father in the *étage noble*, sharing a drink and a discussion about the late Gustave Rothan's art collection. He headed straight for the ballroom, a glittering gold chamber under a magnificent domed ceiling, where the orchestra played a waltz as men in tuxedos and women in gowns whirled with the usual dinner party gaiety. Seeing Marie in the arms of another man produced a pang of regret in his breast. As the waltz ended, Marie and her partner turned toward the bandstand to applaud, and Pierre approached them. He looked directly into her eyes while addressing the man still holding her hand, giving no sign that he knew Marie—and she smartly played along.

"Sir, you appear to be a gentleman of the first rank. Would you consent to allow a baron the enjoyment of a single dance with your alluring partner?"

Politely, the man gathered himself, winked at Marie, and said, "Under different circumstances, sir, I might indulge you, but we have just begun the evening—"

"But the evening is young, Alain," Marie interjected, "and shouldn't I be the one to decide with whom I will and will not dance, baron or not?"

Before a counter could be offered, Pierre stepped boldly forward and embraced her, and the music, as if on cue, rose loudly just as he turned her away, whirling into a series of wide circles with all the other dancers.

"You show great wisdom for such a young woman." Coubertin continued to act as if they were strangers.

"Wisdom has always come easily to me," she said, clearly enjoying the game, "but you should know it's whim, not wisdom, that led to this dance."

"Au contraire, my lady. You are in the arms of destiny. And it is always wise to dance with destiny."

"And what, kind sir, is destiny's name?"

"Baron Pierre de Coubertin."

"Well then, Pierre," she said, turning in perfect unison with him, their bodies pressed together, their faces close, "I'm glad I'm back in your arms."

○ ○ ○ ○ ○

That night marked the true beginning of their romance. Marie and Pierre were falling in love before that first dance ended—and both had a sense their renewed relationship was always meant to be. Pierre's devotion was liberating for Marie, and in turn her love freed him from the haunting sense of loss that had lingered in his soul since Jennette walked away. In the months that followed, Pierre became a constant presence in the Rothans' home, helping Madame and Marie with the difficult work of assessing the value of the art collection and ensuring the provenance of each piece was documented to the satisfaction of Galerie Georges Petit.

The Petit Galerie had become the most prominent in Paris, and the Rothan family had great expectations for the sale. Young Georges Petit had inherited the original gallery on rue Saint-Georges at the age of twenty-two when his father died in 1877, and immediately he began buying the Impressionists and exhibiting a flair for staging themed shows. Since the gallery was only a few blocks from the Rothan manse, Gustave was a frequent visitor, and he was disappointed when young Georges moved the gallery to a larger space. But he understood why, since the young art entrepreneur soon became Paris's leading arbiter of painting. Petit moved the gallery once again to a new hotel he had designed and built on rue de Sèze, then staged two breakthrough shows in 1887 and 1889. In the first, Auguste Rodin unveiled *The Kiss* and three of the figures from *The Burghers of Calais*, creating a sensation and solidifying his reputation as France's master sculptor. In the second, young Petit brought together Monet and Rodin in a brilliant exhibition that became the rage of the cultural scene.

Stimulated by the opportunity and wanting to ensure the best outcome for the Rothans, Coubertin applied all his talents in service to the family. He arranged to have reprints of the Paul Mantz review that had appeared in *La Gazette des Beaux-Arts* in 1874, which called the Rothan house the finest private gallery in Paris, and he provided copies to the Petit Galerie for promotion a month before the sale. After making a study of the collection, he was astonished at its quality.

He was convinced the paintings by David, Steen, Goya, van Dyck, and Bruegel, and *The Allegories* by François Boucher, which Pierre remembered so well, would bring three-quarters of a million francs into the Rothan coffers.

In May 1890, the gallery conducted the auction. Seated together in the crowded house on rue de Sèze, Madame Rothan, Marie, Pierre, and his father watched with sadness tempered by excitement as the auctioneer shouted. The early paintings brought aggressive bidding, and the prices rose. Toward the end of the afternoon, the action slowed, and while there was no doubt Gustave Rothan had done well by his family, the grand total fell just short of the number Coubertin had estimated. Nevertheless, Madame Rothan and Marie would be able to live comfortably in their home—although the walls were now starkly bare, with rectangles of unfaded paint where the art had hung. It was a depressing reminder of the decline in their affairs, but Pierre had a house painter lined up within a week and had Marie searching for tapestries, fabric wall hangings, and replacement pieces of less expensive origin.

○ ○ ○ ○ ○

As St. Clair finished composing the chapter on the Rothans, he remembered a point the baroness had made about the loss of her inheritance—how Pierre had spent it along with his own funds on his Olympic campaign. Going back through his notes, St. Clair found the verbatim reference, which dripped with her distinct bitterness.

○ ○ ○ ○ ○

"I want you to understand, Monsieur St. Clair, that this sale produced a substantial part of my heritage—the legacy my father left me. It was good money, hard earned in the course of a brilliant career and wisely invested with a discerning eye for cultural treasures. I knew each painting by heart and it broke my heart to let them go, but we had to. Father was gone and we needed the money for the house and the servants—and for the life I was going to lead. I held on to that money as long as I could, but now it's mostly vanished on the winds of our Olympic voyage."

55

THE FRAME

On a Saturday morning toward the end of July, St. Clair cycled hard for an hour, west out of Ouchy all the way past Coppet and Versoix to the outskirts of Geneva before turning back. He was still troubled by the baroness's anger and wanted to find a way to persuade her to sit with him again. He needed to regain her trust, if that was at all possible. Racing along the lake, he wondered about the memories she possessed that he had still not heard. He wanted to know—no, he needed to know—about her role in the founding of the Games, her unique perspective on those lofty days at the Sorbonne, and her distress at the humiliations of Athens. If she really felt he was going to betray them, to make the tragedy of their lives even more miserable by making it public, he knew he'd never hear another word from her—but that was a dead end he was not yet willing to accept. By the time he got back to the cottage, he had decided to try a direct approach, to appeal to her for forgiveness—he would become a supplicant—and to appeal to her sense of history. He knew from his first interviews that she wanted to ensure that her side of the legacy would be given its due.

Outside the cottage, St. Clair finished wiping down the De Dion-Bouton as the sun rose mid-morning. He left the bike leaning against the wall, intending to ride up to Mon Repos to look for the baroness later. But when he walked into the kitchen, Juliette insisted on a change of plans.

"You're coming with me today," she said, handing him a cup of coffee. She was already dressed in a lightweight green sweater and long, loose pants he had never seen before.

"And where are we going, your majesty?"

"Back up to Defleur Antiquités."

"Oh no. Why would we go back into that thief's lair again?"

"I want that old frame for my portrait of Pierre."

"What old frame?" For the first time, he noticed a new Swiss hat, an attractive green wool felt with a brown ribbon and feather, sitting on the counter.

"The frame I found when we were recovering Pierre's boxes in that back room."

"I don't remember that." He picked up the hat and handed it to her. "You've been shopping again, I see."

She promptly put the hat on, turned away, and smiled back over her shoulder at him. "Do you like it?"

"Very cute," he said, and indeed it was. The hat sat at an angle, covering only half her hair, its brim rolled lower on one side.

"It's the latest style."

"I'm sure Monsieur Defleur will be impressed."

"You don't have to talk to him. I'll do the negotiations, but you've got to carry that frame up to my studio."

○ ○ ○ ○ ○

An hour later, St. Clair was shouldering the freshly cleaned frame, which was heavier than he had thought it would be, to her studio by the cathedral.

She had talked Defleur into letting it go for a thousand francs, about $40, which she claimed was a very good price. As if he were paying for his sins, Defleur polished it painstakingly to a high gloss, and even St. Clair thought it was quite a find.

"How do you know it will fit?" He shifted it to his left shoulder.

"I think it's exactly right—thirty-six by twenty-four inches. I could visualize that immediately."

By the time they climbed the stairs to her studio, St. Clair had worked up a slight sweat, but he was happy to be helping her. When he rested the frame against the wall, he knew it would fit and knew the painting was going to look extraordinary with those golden garlands surrounding it.

"My God!" Juliette said, leaning the canvas next to the frame. "It's a wonderful match. It's almost as if I chose Pierre's brown suit to set off the gold." They stood side by side, looking at the nearly finished portrait and the ornately carved frame.

"I didn't realize you were this close to having the painting done." St. Clair bent closer to look at the baron's face. "That glint in his eye is perfect."

"Just a touch of white," she said. "What do you think of the Olympic rings floating in the sky like that?"

"Beautiful. It's like his dream hovering up there, as if the gods had sent him on this mission. And I love these old Greek ruins. Is that Olympia?"

"Partly. Part fact and part fiction."

"This is your best work by far, a true breakthrough. I'm really impressed. It will have to be the book cover."

When she didn't respond, he turned to look at her. Her eyes were teary, and she gasped with a hard swallow, then hugged him suddenly, burying her face in his shoulder. "Thank you, Jacques," she said, "for bringing me here … to this … to him."

He held her for a time before pulling away, dropping her hand before going to the window. "Has he seen it yet?"

"No, I'm not quite finished, and I don't want to show it to him until it's complete and in the frame."

"I know he's going to love it."

St. Clair watched a small, familiar figure emerge from an adjacent building, heading toward the cathedral. It took him a moment to realize who it was. "There's the baroness," he nearly shouted, dashing past Juliette, stopping briefly at the door. "I've got to talk to her, but it's really beautiful, darling. Bravo!" he said as he bounded down the steps.

ο ο ο ο ο

He caught up with the baroness at the top of the *escalier* and stepped beside her as she began the descent. He said nothing at first, just walked in tandem with her to the first landing.

At last he spoke. "Do you think you could ever find it in your heart to forgive me?" he said. She stared at him, compressed her lips in an expression of anger, and continued down without a word.

"Baroness, please," he said, following behind her now. "I'm sorry you're angry with me, but I would never, ever betray your trust." No response. He followed her down to the road below the old cathedral wall, then onto the next flight of stairs. One last try. He passed her quickly, stopped on the next landing, and faced her as she came down. "Baroness," he said, desperate for some way to reassure her, "I'm not going to write a single word about your son—nothing. I'm writing *only* about you and your husband. You have my word."

She stopped and stared at him again but still said nothing. Her face was still pinched in a grimace. He knew he was apologizing for nothing, but he needed to win her over. "You've already given me a good part of your story—you and your father in the art world and your first encounters with Pierre—and it will make the book richer, but I need to talk to you about the campaign to resurrect the Games. What you saw, what you did"—he realized he was racing his words and slowed down—"and the experience you had in Athens."

"Bah," she said with a wave of her hand. "Athens was the beginning of the grand disappointment." She paused, seemed to consider something deeply. She looked up. "All right, Monsieur St. Clair, I'll talk to you again. But we'll need to have an understanding—and he can stay in Geneva for all I care."

Geneva? He didn't understand. "Will you meet me again at the Hôtel de la Paix?"

She hesitated, looking at the people moving around them, passing up and down on the stairs.

"Monday?"

At last she seemed to come to a decision. "No, Tuesday at ten in the morning. Promptly," she said in admonition, as if he had been late to their previous interviews. She walked away without a goodbye.

○ ○ ○ ○ ○

It was another gray morning, overcast, humid, and threatening to rain, as they slid into the booth at the front window at the Hôtel de la Paix, at the same table at which they had always met. The baroness busied herself with her purse as if searching for something and then took time fidgeting with her napkin and silverware, deliberately refusing to look at St. Clair directly. When the waiter arrived, she finally looked up, glaring at him as if his very presence were offensive.

"Cappuccino," she said.

"The same with a croissant, please." St. Clair wasn't sure where to begin. "Baroness ..."

She looked at him sharply, her lips tightly pursed, and pointed a finger directly at his face. "Not one word," she said. "Not one word about Jacques or Renée."

"I understand, Baroness—no descriptions, no interaction, no judgments at all. I will, of course, have to mention their births—just as I'll have to describe your marriage."

Her face drooped in resignation and he saw a slight slump in her shoulders. "You know exactly what I'm talking about, monsieur. You will not paint a portrait of a"—she stumbled, searching for the right word—"of an unhappy child or man."

"I will not," he said, "and that's a promise." But even as he said it, he knew he was at least partially lying. Their son, he was certain, was not unhappy. It had been obvious to him that day when they were kicking the ball around that

Jacques de Coubertin lived in a world all his own, a world detached and isolated, perhaps, maybe full of simple thoughts, but not an unhappy one. Nonetheless, he knew that he was going to write about the tragedy of their son—and for now he'd lie about it because he needed more of her perspective. Since she had been so harsh and unkind to him—more than once—he felt no remorse in misleading her. "Let's put that behind us and move on to your story."

"I'm not going to sugarcoat anything, monsieur." She lowered her voice as the cappuccinos arrived. "And I'm not going to sit here all day."

They both took a sip and St. Clair opened his tablet. "I understand, and I'm not asking you to sugarcoat the story." He forced himself to feign patience. "But you mentioned you were partners with the baron in the campaign to revive the Games. Let's get right to the heart of it—how involved were you in the planning of the conference at the Sorbonne?"

"Which one?" She was clearly still angry, but before he could respond, she asserted her position. "I was deeply involved in both Olympic Congresses— first in the 1892 conference, which failed to bring back the Games because the proposal was a little too impromptu, shall we say. And I served as Pierre's planning secretary for the 1894 Congress, which was also in the Sorbonne, and which we all know was a great success. We went to the Olympics in Athens together as a team—and what an exasperating experience that was."

Wanting to be complimentary, St. Clair stopped her, holding up his hand. "Baroness, you've just mentioned the most important period in the revival of the Games—the failed proposal of 1892, the successful Olympic Congress of 1894, and the Athens Games of 1896. Can we cover each of those events in depth?"

"That depends on how much time it will take." She dabbed at her lips with a napkin. "As I said, I don't want to sit here all day again."

"It won't take that long. Let's begin with your recollections of the first failed proposal in 1892. What went wrong? I've heard and read it was a lack of preparation—that the moment wasn't right. That the idea was premature."

The baroness seemed to bristle at the suggestion. "Lack of preparation? That's ridiculous. We were very well prepared in 1892. It was the fifth anniversary of the USFSA. Pierre called our event the 'Jubilee,' and it was very important— the timing seemed propitious. Yes, the 1894 Congress was a larger event with a much more extensive program—and certainly more elaborate staging, but both began in the Sorbonne, both had athletic events, banquets, music, and speeches. I think Pierre will tell you the same thing: the problem wasn't timing, the problem was the audience. We hadn't gathered a sufficient number of international sport figures to respond to the proposal in 1892. We had filled the Sorbonne with a few real leaders, but mostly teachers and students. We didn't have the right international team in place yet. We had calibrated that the level of enthusiasm for the Games in France alone would be sufficient. And we were wrong on that point. There was no disagreement with the Olympic proposal— no real rejection—just a complete lack of understanding and comprehension of the support we would need to move forward. Perhaps we were premature, but we were being encouraged to launch by Bertha, in particular, but also by Henri Didon, Georges de Saint-Clair, and others.

"You're saying that von Suttner and Didon encouraged Pierre—and you—to launch the Games then?"

"I thought you would have known all this by now, monsieur. Haven't you done your homework?"

St. Clair shrugged and lifted his hands, begging her to continue. She rolled her eyes and sighed as if exasperated. Aware of time slipping away, St. Clair leaped ahead to 1894 and the Olympic Congress, but Marie circled back to Bertha von Suttner—to a surprising point that revealed another long-standing slight she had never forgotten.

"You do know that it was Bertha who convinced Alfred Nobel to use his fortune to create the Nobel prizes, don't you, especially the Nobel Peace Prize?"

"I knew she had influenced Nobel, but I didn't know the prizes were completely her idea."

"Well, that's how we understood it." The baroness harrumphed. "Alfred died in 1895, between the Sorbonne Congress and the Athens Olympics, and the Nobel prizes were given for the first time in 1901—and they had an immediate impact and prestige."

"She must have been a remarkable woman," St. Clair mused, sensing the baroness was moving toward a point.

"Yes, she was. Do you know who won the first Nobel Peace Prize? No! What about the second? Or the fifth? Or the thirteenth?"

"No, I'm sorry. I know Bertha won—and Passy won, too, but I don't know the history of the prize."

"Well, you should study it. Frédéric Passy won the first Peace Prize—actually it was awarded to him and Henri Durant, who founded the Red Cross, but that's another point. The second went to Élie Ducommun, the fifth to Bertha herself. Fredrik Bajer won a few years later, and Henri La Fontaine won the thirteenth Peace Prize. You know what they all have in common?"

"They were all part of the peace movement?"

"Wrong. They were all in the room that night."

"In the room? You mean the Sorbonne? At the Olympic Congress?"

"Yes. They were all part of the birth of the Olympic Games. In many ways, the Olympic Movement was born out of the patronage of the peace movement—and Bertha von Suttner, God bless her, was its midwife."

"Five eventual Nobel Peace Prize winners in the room that night. That's extraordinary. I'm surprised this connection has never been publicized."

"We were politely quiet in those early years, sending congratulations to our friends, waiting in hopes our turn would come.

The implication of her remark stunned St. Clair. "Your turn?"

"Are you surprised? I always felt we deserved it ..."—she hesitated and corrected herself—"that Pierre deserved that recognition. The 1910 Nobel Peace Prize went to the International Peace Bureau in Berne, which was well represented that night. In fact, if you'll look at the list of official delegates on the program, I think you'll find 78 or 79 names. Investigate their biographies and you will see that what I'm saying is absolutely true—more than half of them have direct connections to the peace movement of the time."

"So, from the moment of its birth, this movement has been exactly what the baron has always said it was—"

"It has always been a movement of peace through sport. It is an indisputable fact, Monsieur St. Clair. But why hasn't it been recognized as such—why hasn't Pierre been recognized with a prize that seemed to go to everyone else?"

"But he was nominated ..." St. Clair recalled his conversation with Messerli about a nomination just last year.

"Hmph." She looked away, gazing out the window. "Yes, last year, by the Germans, who don't sit favorably with the judges of Oslo. In fact, the prize went to Carl von Ossietzky, a German journalist who fought the Nazis—and was imprisoned for it. Not that Ossietzky wasn't worthy of the prize—but Pierre is certainly deserving. It's an injustice, but it's only one of a hundred we've endured."

St. Clair was stunned—not only by the revelation about her disappointment, and maybe his, in not receiving the Peace Prize, but also by her quicksilver switch to Pierre's defense again. She was a nemesis one minute, an advocate the next. He leaned forward over his tablet, trying to get the Nobel Peace Prize points down, not wanting to look into her eyes.

Suddenly, the light shifted. The sun brightened, and the city outside the window glistened in the clear air while the lake took on a deep blue shimmer. They both looked up, and the baroness reacted as if it were a signal to end the conversation.

"I'm sorry, monsieur, but I can't endure any more of this." She slid across the banquette and was quickly on her feet.

"I understand. When can we meet again? This has been extremely helpful." He rose to say goodbye.

"I'm glad I've given you something to think about." She gave him her signature grimace, turned without a goodbye, and walked straight for the door.

56

THE TRUTH

E arly the next Monday morning—after a late Sunday night laughing and drinking with Juliette—St. Clair crawled quietly out of bed, had a cup of coffee, and took his De Dion-Bouton for a few loops up the hill and back. A fine mist hung in the air, the humidity was high, and it began raining lightly as he circled above the university. By the time he came down rue de la Gare, approaching the train station, it was pouring and he was soaked. He intended to keep going anyway when he caught a glimpse of a familiar figure pushing open the train terminal doors and looking up at the cloud-capped sky. It was Coubertin, and he was carrying a valise as if returning from a meeting. Surprised, St. Clair pulled off the road, wondering why Coubertin was coming out of the station so early on a Monday morning. The old man snapped open an umbrella and crossed the street, moving along the storefronts in the direction of Mon Repos. When he turned up the broad staircase to climb through the town, St. Clair pushed the pedals hard and raced up the hill to be at the gates of Mon Repos when Pierre arrived.

"You're out early," St. Clair said as Coubertin walked up from rue Étraz, huffing a little.

"Yes … an early breakfast with an old friend."

"Anyone I know?"

"No, just a French colleague staying at the Palace."

"Oh, you were at the Palace?"

"Yes, he was leaving this morning."

"Did you walk him down to the train station?"

The question appeared to take Coubertin by surprise. "No, not in this rain," he said, averting St. Clair's gaze. "I've got some work to do before we dive in."

"Okay, I'll see you in an hour or so." As St. Clair pedaled off, he had the sensation that Coubertin was watching him go.

When he reached the apartment, he telephoned Messerli at home.

"Good morning, Jacques. How was the weekend?"

"All fine until Pierre lied to me this morning."

"He lied to you? What are you talking about?"

"I saw Pierre come out of the train station at seven this morning in a downpour. Without saying anything, I rode up to Mon Repos and waited for him. He told me he had been at the Lausanne Palace for a breakfast meeting."

"Why don't you come over and we'll talk," Messerli said. "I knew you'd find out eventually."

○ ○ ○ ○ ○

"It reached a point last summer where Marie was yelling at him all the time—and she seemed on the verge of a breakdown," Messerli said, sitting alone with St. Clair in a small study he kept on the second floor of his house. "He had already moved out of their bedroom—well, she had thrown him out. In fact, she wanted him out of Mon Repos altogether."

"Go on." St. Clair thought about Sloane's letter and the reference to the breakdown the baroness might have had.

"Her anger wouldn't abate, and he was worried about Renée and Jacques—so he found a place in the Pension Melrose in Geneva, which was cheap."

"But where did he get the rent?"

"A friend," Messerli looked away, a willing conspirator. St. Clair knew he had paid—and therefore approved.

"And the baroness? She agreed to maintain this pretense?"

"They established an understanding. She was willing to maintain appearances while you were here working on the book. When circumstances call for it, he stays at Mon Repos."

"Why didn't he just tell me?"

"Why do you think, Jacques? He didn't want the story of his failures—and his family—to dominate the biography."

"Why didn't *you* tell me?"

"I agreed to maintain the pretense until he was ready to open up. He gave me an ultimatum before I moved you down here."

On the way back to the cottage, dozens of images and moments of memory struck St. Clair: Coubertin always out when he looked for him at Mon Repos unannounced, or never there when he arrived too early in the morning for an interview. The Baroness always on her own, coming and going and hardly interacting with Pierre. The weekends away—with friends in Geneva. The occasional sighting of the baron walking through town with a valise in hand. How could he not have known? The lie didn't anger him, but it depressed him and he began to wonder how many more lies there were in the story. *I will find the truth.*

○ ○ ○ ○ ○

St. Clair was surprised by the spare ascetic of Coubertin's apartment in Geneva at the Pension Melrose, just a block away from *Parc La Grange*. It wasn't just a step down from Mon Repos; it was a full staircase below in every respect. Despite the signs of his writing life in the papers, pen, and ink on the small table by the window, there was nothing personal about the place, none of the personal effects or accoutrement that enlivened his office in Lausanne. The acrid smell of spoiled cheese rose from a small table with a hotplate and a basin. The *bain de toilette* was down the hall. It was hard to take, hard to smile, hard not to express grief on behalf of *le Rénovateur*. How could the baron not be depressed, living here?

"Let's go out for a good dinner," St. Clair said, sitting on the edge of the bed, suddenly anxious to escape the pension. "My treat—and I don't want any protest. We're going to enjoy a good bottle of wine."

That seemed to brighten Pierre's spirit as he put on his bowler and a light sport coat. They walked straight up rue du Clos to the shoreline on the Prom du Lac at a good clip. The August sky filled with red and orange shafts of light, and the lake took on the dark blue hues of dusk. A warm breeze heightened their spirits, and St. Clair began to feel better as they ambled into the Jardin Anglais, heading toward the pont du Mont-Blanc.

Pierre stopped on the bridge, gazing at the Île Rousseau, and turned back. "I've got an idea. Why don't we share a fondue tonight? I know just the place— Les Armures in the old town, just off rue de l'Hôtel de Ville."

"Fondue sounds perfect. I'll need the energy for the ride back later." St. Clair realized he and Pierre were engaged in an evasive banter. There was a weight between them neither wanted to touch. "Do they have a good wine list?"

"They do—in fact, I think it was blessed by John Calvin himself," Coubertin said with a laugh. "The Museum of the Reformation is right there, part of the university."

"Geneva is home to many great religious stalwarts."

"They call them bastions here—bastions of the faith."

"Well, we shall drink to their health."

And drink they did, consuming two bottles of wine with two full baguettes and a fiery crock of three cheeses.

Over dinner, St. Clair was reluctant to ask Pierre about why he had kept his Geneva apartment a secret from him—why he had deceived him—these past six months. He decided to wait on the baron. They talked mostly about things they had covered in great detail already—and St. Clair for once did not open his tablet. Pierre asked him how the writing was going, and they even talked about the scores of the rugby games out of Paris from the week before. But for the first time since they had met, a strained silence entered their conversation. Pauses grew longer, diverted eyes more obvious.

St. Clair let the awkwardness grow, waiting.

Finally, unable to evade the strain, Pierre opened up. "I owe you an apology, my friend, and an explanation for why I've hidden my true circumstances all this time."

He began stutteringly, this most eloquent of men struggling to find the words, or perhaps the courage, to discuss the nearly inexplicable reality of his life. "I want to explain something to you that I've never openly discussed with anyone." He paused to look away.

"I'm listening, Pierre. And I'm not taking notes."

When Coubertin looked back at him, his eyes were moist. "You do understand that what happened to us—Marie and me—forced us to live a kind of double life."

St. Clair nodded but said, "No, I'm not at all sure why it was necessary."

"We began as rebels, with the wealth and the will to change the world. After the great triumph of the Sorbonne, we seemed to hold the reins of destiny in our hands. Everything was before us—and we were both filled with the inescapable notion that we had seized control of the future, like a royal republican couple ready to promenade out of the temple before the waiting world."

"I think—" he said, but interrupted himself. "No, I don't think—I *know* I filled her head with dreams and ideas about the accolades that awaited her, that awaited us, when the Olympic Games became everything we both believed they could be. I had no sense at the time that her mental state was fragile—or becoming fragile. When we sailed for the Athens Games, our expectations were high, not only for the event but also for our role in it. But then Athens went awry—the Greeks shunned us, denied us any and all credit for the Games. And while it felt like a betrayal to me—it was devastating to her. She couldn't handle the humiliation of being sidelined. She cried in our room at first—but as the

Games went on her anger grew ... and then she began a tirade that wouldn't stop, saying, 'This is not right, it's just not right, they can't deny you.' She became irrational."

"Why did it hit her so hard?"

"I doubt we'll ever know for certain," Coubertin said resignedly. "I've puzzled over it and think it may be related to what happened to her family during the war when she was young—they had to flee from Luttenbach ahead of the Germans, moved to Paris, and then came the siege of the city. They had to abandon one life for another—maybe that uncertainty fed her anxieties, I don't know, but when Athens ended, our world had changed. Something broke in our marriage. I didn't know it would be irreparable, but it was."

He stopped talking for a moment, hesitant to continue, but then pushed on. "The first breakdown—what they now call a nervous breakdown, came later that year, when she was pregnant with Jacques. I confided in Sloane, whose big heart ached for me—and for Marie. He was the only one who ever understood. He was familiar with anxiety attacks and mental illness. She would withdraw, and then she would go mad with anger and attack me—verbally, sometimes physically."

"When Jacques was born there seemed to be the promise of a new day. I took time away from the Games to spend with her—writing *The Evolution of France under the Third Republic* to stay close to home. I had hopes then, as the movement gained momentum and the second Olympic Congress at Le Havre was coming together, that we would have a normal marriage—and that our dreams would come back. And then on a vacation down in Luttenbach—at her family estate—the real tragedy hit."

"Your son's trauma?" St. Clair asked, knowing he was at last to hear the truth.

"Yes, the trauma. Marie always said it was a sunstroke. But I'll always believe he was born with a congenital defect—that what happened to him would have happened no matter what. We were picnicking in a field on the edge of a grove at Luttenbach. Just Marie, me, and little Jacques. It was a stiflingly hot day. The baby was sleeping peacefully in his carriage when I pulled Marie to her feet and got her to strip down to her bloomers and kick a ball around with me. We played around for a long while, drinking wine, chasing each other—when the blissful summer day was suddenly shattered by a scream, and then a whimper."

"So there was a specific—was it heatstroke?" St. Clair's journalistic instinct intruded but he stopped it.

Coubertin nodded and bowed his head. "Maybe it was. We left the baby exposed for too long."

"But as you said ... it may have been congenital." St. Clair wanted to help.

"We'll never know. But I do know that was the beginning of the end. A life in the public eye filled with the promise of glory and the grandeur of great events—all around an important work. And a life behind closed doors with weeks on end of palpable anxiety filling every room of the house, with Marie screaming at fears and threats unimaginable."

"What about when your daughter was born?"

"Renée's birth should have been a new beginning for us, a chance to start over, and to some extent it was. But as the child grew, Marie's sadness deepened and she became overprotective, perhaps understandably, so that it had the opposite effect. The baby isolated us from each other. She treated Renée like a private possession and left Jacques in the care of a nurse, at first, and then a full-time caretaker.

"Marie went through stages where she would withdraw from me. Something changed in her personality—she was full of fear, always on edge, and treated me like a threat. She always seemed to be startled by my presence. When I came into the room, she glared, and even snarled now and then like a feral cat, pulling the baby out of my sight.

"It wasn't healthy, and I couldn't stand it. From time to time, she would come out of whatever it was, break through like sunlight, and wake some days as normal as she'd ever been. Then we'd have a few months of relative bliss, filling me with a false hope that everything was going to stay all right. But then she'd revert and spiral down into the anger and depression—worse than the last time. I consulted several doctors, and the only one who really understood her condition offered a frightening diagnosis. He said she was on the verge of a nervous breakdown—and either she'd recover from it or repeat the process, breaking down again, and perhaps get progressively worse."

Pierre looked at his hands as he fiddled with the long fondue fork, clinking it against his glass of wine. He grimaced and shut his eyes. The memories were clearly painful, even now.

"That's basically what happened. She had a breakdown, then recovered, and we went out into the world again together, celebrating the developments of the Olympic Movement where we could. She would enjoy it for a time, but then something, usually some small financial pressure that she could usually ignore, or an event with Jacques, or a trip I was taking had to be extended at the last minute—unpredictably, any little innocuous shift could blow up like a stick of dynamite. She had three breakdowns across that decade, and some long periods of illness."

"Were your friends and colleagues aware of this?"

"I sheltered her and kept it all as private as I could. Sloane knew. He was the only one I shared the pain with because of his experience with mental illness in his family—and at the university. He was compassionate. But there were several times when the wives of my colleagues seemed to know why I was suddenly making excuses for Marie's long disappearances. They were kind not to probe. It made the double life possible. I was *le Rénovateur* and they respected me."

"And Renée? How did she fare in such circumstances?"

"Renée's world was never stable and neither was she. She's incredibly strong today—but her childhood wasn't easy. Marie's love was suffocating, she was possessive and unpredictable, moving from a cooing, caring mother to a screaming banshee as quickly as a light turns on and off."

The baron stopped then, saying, "That's enough on the family, Jacques. Marie and I have been estranged for years—but we've kept up the pretense of partnership, as if our marriage were the foundation of strength for the Olympic Movement. We lived a double life that I tried to hide from you."

As they finished, Pierre took a knife and scraped up the crust of the burnt cheese at the bottom of the pot. It came up draped over the blade in a crispy golden shaving about six inches long. Pierre extended the offering to Jacques.

"Take it," he said. "It's the best part."

○ ○ ○ ○ ○

Out on the street, they passed the cannons behind the arches and walked in silence down the Grand-Rue. The night was warm, and St. Clair was conscious of the pall that came over them. He understood that it had not been easy for Pierre to open up and tell him about the double life, and he was grateful. But a conflict tore at him. He did not know at this point how he could possibly tell Pierre's story without including the tragic dimensions of his personal life.

As they walked side by side in the shadows and darkness, the glowing light of the shop windows drew their eyes. Pierre stopped for a moment, gazing at a well-lit display in a toy store recessed in an arcade. He moved toward it and St. Clair followed, saying, "It looks like a little city."

"Indeed," said Pierre, moving so close they both suddenly appeared mirrored in the glass, two men caught in the frame of a night of shared secrets. The image of the two of them together touched St. Clair; he wished he had a photograph of the moment.

"What careful craftsmanship," said Pierre. "Look at the detail—and the color." It was a handsome and intricately constructed scene of a miniature French castle on a hill with fertile farmlands spreading like a carpet from its walls and studded with small farm buildings, fences, peasants at work. The fields were filled with grazing cattle, sheep, and horses—all bordered by a forest and a stream running along the left wall. A squad of cavaliers rode over the bridge in the lower corner, their white pants, blue coats, red collars, and plumed cockades perfectly matching the soldiers of the past. Pierre looked over the castle walls into the courtyard, and in the reflection St. Clair saw his face brighten into a smile.

"The king and queen are out with the people," he said.

St. Clair leaned in and there was the king, in the center of a market with tent tops tilted back to reveal stands full of tiny meats, vegetables, and bread. Wearing a long red robe and a golden crown, he stood like a happy orator, arms raised in a friendly gesture amid an adoring crowd. The queen had her hand extended down to a knot of children taking her gifts with excitement, two already sprinting away with a handful of royal good fortune. The stone structure and buttresses of the castle were realistically rendered, as were the knights on the parapets. Men and women of business and nobility moved in and out of the main gate along the road.

"This is an extraordinary work of art," Pierre said.

St. Clair was bemused that the little man found the scene so beguiling. On each of the walls above the scene were shelves crowded with squadrons of soldiers and representative figures of every class of French society.

"That's Madame Pompadour!" Pierre proclaimed, pointing. "Voltaire and Rousseau," he said with a sense of discovery.

St. Clair stepped back for a moment and watched Coubertin's reflection in the window, watched his friend marvel at the intricacies of an imaginative world.

ALLIES AND ENEMIES

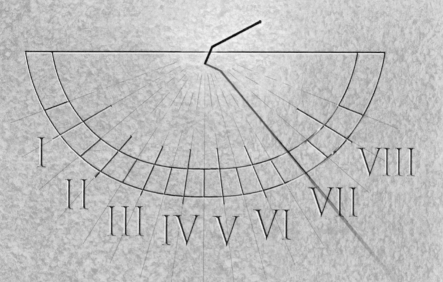

57

THE BREAKDOWN

After their long evening together in Geneva at the outset of August—and after the personal revelations that emerged—St. Clair felt he and Pierre had reached a new level of trust, a more honest and open dialogue. But a career of interviewing people who had often hidden things from him for months—only to reveal secrets in the throes of a confession—taught him the hard lessons of journalism. Such breakthroughs often had a negative side. His subjects had often withdrawn, feeling guilty about giving up secrets they had kept to themselves for years, fearfully wondering what the consequences might be if the truth were uncovered in the light of day, haunted by the loyalties they might have betrayed.

This was a biographer's work, St. Clair knew, persuading people to shed protective layers of deception they had wrapped themselves in—to help them bury the gnawing anxiety, to escape the psychological pain, and to find the comfort every human being needs to live day to day. But he also knew there was a price to pay for drawing the truth out of its hiding place, a cost in resentment that sometimes proved too high to overcome.

For a few days, St. Clair decided to step back and give Coubertin some breathing room, hoping the baron would call him when he was ready to resume their conversation. He busied himself reading through a pile of correspondence between Coubertin and his U.S. university allies, White, Eliot, and Gilman. He noted their gradually increasing advocacy for international sports competitions, student exchanges, and then the launch of the Olympic Games—and, to St.

Clair's surprise, their full engagement in the launch of a series of student debates on France and its history and current affairs. In the midst of building support for his vision of international sport, Coubertin had launched a separate and ambitious academic initiative—an intellectual competition with medals to the winner—designed to ensure American students understood France and vice versa. St. Clair wondered why there was no mention of this in Coubertin's memoirs.

A few days later, he examined another set of letters to and from early IOC members and allies such as Ferenc Kemény of Hungary, General Viktor Balck of Sweden, and novelist Jiří Guth-Jarkovsky of Bohemia.

After five days, his notes mounting and his list of questions growing, St. Clair had to face the fact that Coubertin had withdrawn. On his De Dion-Bouton, St. Clair spent a few mornings and afternoons trying to find him, but the office at Mon Repos was locked or vacant whenever he dropped by. His telephone calls went unanswered, and no response came from notes he slipped under doors. St. Clair began to wonder if he had gone too far—and then he began to feel the personal side of Coubertin's absence. As a journalist, his knowledge of human behavior had given him the liberty to play the waiting game, but his confidence began to erode when he realized his attachment to Pierre was too strong to wait any longer. He missed the old man. He tried calling Messerli but got no answer.

"What am I going to do?" he asked Juliette as they lay in bed one night. "What if his regret is so deep he won't want to talk to me again?"

"Don't be ridiculous. Pierre isn't going anywhere—he needs you as much as you need him—and he's certainly deeply committed to your book. I'm sure he's as excited about the prospects as you are." She rolled on her side and draped her arm across his chest.

"You're probably right, but he's been staying away from me—deliberately—for a week now."

Juliette looked into his eyes. "Jacques, listen to me. If we know one thing about Pierre de Coubertin, it's this: he's no quitter. Yes, he told you things he's probably never admitted to anyone—and maybe he's worried that the truth will hurt his story—but this isn't the end. He'll be back."

St. Clair pulled her down and kissed her, but later, when she was asleep, he was still restless and worried, with negative thoughts controlling his imagination. It turned into another sleepless night. In the morning, his hand shook when he lifted his coffee cup, and he realized he had become unnerved by Coubertin's evasion. He finally reached Messerli and arranged to see him at his office that afternoon.

The doctor was waiting for him on the steps of the university. "Let's get a cup of coffee," he said as St. Clair followed him across the Place de la Riponne.

"Your discovery shook him up," Messerli said as they searched for a table.

"The fact that I found his place in Geneva?"

"Yes. He had grown very confident he could maintain that charade—and when you found him out, well, I think you broke down all his defenses."

"Does he regret that he opened up as fully as he did?"

"I'm sure there's some remorse." They took a table looking back at the university. The plaza and the sidewalks were crowded—a good day for watching the human parade.

"I hope it's not going to be a major break between us." St. Clair watched Messerli's face for a reaction. To his relief, the doctor laughed.

"No, Jacques, it won't be a major break. Pierre was most worried about the baroness. He's never described her ... shall we say, ailments, to anyone. I assured him you weren't about to confide in her."

"Where is he?"

"He's in Geneva, but he'll be rowing at the château early tomorrow. Why don't you come by and join us for breakfast? Perhaps you can get the interviews started again."

St. Clair felt an immediate lift in his spirit. "Thank you, Francis. That's very good to hear."

○ ○ ○ ○ ○

When St. Clair rounded the corner of the Château d'Ouchy and walked through the trees toward the shore of Lake Geneva, he heard voices shouting in alarm and spotted two men waving their arms wildly, creating commotion down by the bank. Breaking into a sprint, he realized the men were Messerli and Émil Drut, yelling to Pierre out on the water. Before he could reach them, Messerli had stripped off his jacket and pushed a skiff into the water—and was now rowing with deep pulls and lunges across the calm surface. St. Clair gasped as he saw Coubertin's boat farther out, and the baron himself slumped forward over his oars, motionless and not responding to the frenzied pleas of his friends.

"Pierre!" he yelled. "Oh no," he said to Émil, his voice cracking, "this can't be! What's happened?"

"I don't know, Jacques." The old restaurateur laid a heavy hand on St. Clair's shoulder. "Francis said he saw him stop rowing and slump over, and we ran out here just a minute ago."

"Has he looked up?" St. Clair felt panicked; he wanted to dive into the water.

"We have to hope it will be all right. Look, Francis is almost there."

As they watched from shore, Messerli brought his bow around and steered his skiff to draw up against Coubertin's so he'd be face to face with the baron.

As soon as he was within arm's length, he dropped the oars and pulled the boats together. Throwing a leg across the gunwales to brace the boats, the doctor lifted Pierre into a sitting position. The baron's head lolled and fell forward, but he seemed to lift it again and it appeared that he and the doctor were talking. In a few brief but urgent moves, Messerli lowered the baron back down into a resting position, tied the end of the boats together, and began rowing back to shore, lurching against the oars as Pierre's skiff trailed on a strand of rope.

A small cluster of onlookers had gathered on the rocks. St. Clair was in the water up to his waist, attempting to pull Coubertin's boat alongside the doctor's. Drut and a few others dragged the front end onto the bank—and as Coubertin was lifted past St. Clair, their eyes met and the baron, his mouth stretched low on one side, tried to say something. St. Clair strode out of the water, retrieved his satchel, and caught up with Messerli, who was directing four men, their arms linked in a hammock to carry the baron to the doctor's car.

"I'm going to take him up to the hospital, Jacques," Messerli said. "I'll call you once I've had a chance to evaluate his condition."

○ ○ ○ ○ ○

The news shook Juliette, who was just leaving for her studio when Jacques came home. She tried to comfort him to no avail, so she kissed him goodbye and went up the hill. St. Clair stayed at the cottage all day, sitting on the terrace, making notes and plans for the next set of interviews in the months ahead, and drinking a bottle of wine. Each minute, he hoped the telephone would ring. The French doors were open so he could run in for the call when it came, but the afternoon faded into a long August twilight without word. Juliette came home and sat with him as fleeting auras of red, pink, and orange colored the sky over the French Alps as the day dissolved into dusk.

St. Clair kept his mind on the work, on the last of their conversations, hoping against hope that the connection hadn't been broken. "Pierre formed two very close friendships in 1890 and 1891 ..." he said, unprompted, thinking out loud.

Juliette took his lead. "Two new allies, I suppose?"

"Brookes and Didon ... and we were going to talk about them both in our next session. He wanted me to fully understand their influence."

"I remember he mentioned Brookes when we talked about earlier editions of the Olympic Games."

"I remember that too ... when he was sitting for you."

"Is that where you're going to pick up the interviews?"

"Yes—" St. Clair said, but he got no further. The telephone rang, and he jumped to answer it.

"It was apoplexy, Jacques, but not severe, what we now call a mild stroke." Messerli's voice had a slight electronic buzz on the telephone line, a dull current of sound dropping as he spoke and rising between the words.

"Apoplexy—that's serious, isn't it?"

"In many patients, it is. It depends on the degree of severity, but Pierre possesses remarkable recuperative powers. His speech was garbled for about three hours, but he's already making sense."

"When can I see him?"

"Let me call you in the morning. I think you can come up tomorrow afternoon. The baroness and Renée are here right now."

"What's the prognosis?"

"We'll talk when you come up tomorrow. He's already asked for you."

"That's good to hear. How long will he be in the hospital?"

"A few more days just so I can monitor his recovery."

○ ○ ○ ○ ○

The nurses pointed St. Clair down the hall to a room on the right. He approached the door cautiously and peeked through its narrow glass panel. Pierre was sitting up in the hospital bed, writing on a table bridging his lap. Renée stood beside him, reading over a few pages like a secretary. To St. Clair's relief, there was no sign of the baroness—and the scene had a serene aspect. The white room was bathed in sunlight, and Renée's dress and Pierre's hospital gown were also white. The sheets looked fresh and crisp. From St. Clair's limited angle, the monochrome setting conveyed tranquility. He pushed the door open and walked in, smiling.

"Good afternoon, Pierre. Hello, Renée," he said, as they both looked up.

"Jacques St. Clair—as I live and breathe," said Pierre with nearly exaggerated delight, perhaps an effort, St. Clair thought, to overcome a very slight but noticeable droop on the left side of his mouth, a droop that slightly distorted his speech. The baron dropped his pen and stretched both hands across the table in an embrace that St. Clair gratefully accepted. He felt Coubertin's whiskers brush his cheek as they hugged, and the old man hung on to him for a beat or two longer than usual.

"I'm glad to see you too," said Renée, coming around the bed. St. Clair took her shoulders. She glanced away as their eyes met, but they kissed three times on the cheeks before she retreated.

"Should you be working, Pierre?" St. Clair rested his hands on the metal frame at the foot of the bed. "Hasn't Dr. Messerli prescribed rest?"

"This is restful, Jacques—the usual routine." As he spoke, St. Clair again noted a slight difference in pronunciation as each word seemed to slide out of the side of his mouth. Taking up his pen and pointing it at Renée, the baron said, "This little episode has brought me the benefit of an exceptional assistant."

"Well, for a few days, anyway. Mother needs my help as well and Father will be back on his feet tomorrow."

"Tomorrow?"

"We have work to do, Jacques." He handed the small table to Renée, threw back the sheets, and lifted his legs over the edge of the bed. St. Clair moved to assist him, but the baron held up his hand and stood, facing him. "I owe you an apology, my friend," he said.

"Pierre, please, that's not important."

"Oh yes, it is." He walked around the bed, suddenly animated and energetic again. "I'm sorry I didn't respond to your calls or notes, but I had to think through a few things and ... well ..." He paused and looked at St. Clair. "I hope you can forgive me."

"You're completely exonerated from any and all slights," St. Clair said, and they both smiled.

"Renée, please get the box for Jacques." She retrieved a cardboard box from the corner and set it on the bed. "Last week, I gathered the files you'll need on everything from Brookes and Didon up through the Paris Congress in 1894." He lifted the lid. "And this," he said emphatically, withdrawing an old notebook with a marbled cover, "is my journal from late 1890, starting with the trip to Much Wenlock and going through 1892."

"That's excellent." St. Clair took the journal and leafed through it. He stopped at a page in December 1891 that began "When Bertha and Arthur returned from Rome, they presented me with a list of the formal resolutions of the Peace Congress ..."

"You'll find some unvarnished thoughts in there," Coubertin said, sliding a visitor's chair toward Jacques. "Here. Take a seat and get out your notebook."

"Are you sure you want to begin right now?"

"Yes! Last time you said you wanted to cover William Penny Brookes and Henri Didon, so let's do that now." He climbed back into the bed. "But, there is one thing I want you to see first."

"What's that?"

"Renée, please show Jacques the letter from Carl Diem." Coubertin's voice took on a different tone. "The Nazis are coming, Jacques. Carl and von Tschammer want to deliver my copy of the final report from the 1936 Olympic Games in person."

"The final report?"

Coubertin motioned to Renée, and she replaced the writing table across his lap. "Yes, they've just finished the final official summary of the Games," he said with a dismissive wave of his pen, taking up a stack of papers and shuffling them. "It's the last formal reporting requirement of every organizing committee."

St. Clair read through the letter with a sense of disbelief. He'd imagined that Pierre—through the creation of the Commission on the Future of Olympism— had delayed further interaction with the National Socialists. The letter had clearly stated that no decisions would be taken on their proposal at least until the IOC executive board meeting, which St. Clair knew was scheduled for late September.

"Is it essential that they deliver it in person?" he asked, thinking Coubertin might delay them, wondering whether hosting a vanguard of men intent on taking over *his* movement might jeopardize his health further.

"On the surface it's a courtesy, but anyone can see it's a ruse. There's no necessity to provide me with a copy. They just want to come and put me in a vise—try to soften me up on their nine-point proposal."

"Can't you delay the visit on the pretense of waiting till the executive board meets?"

"Perhaps, but I'd just as soon meet them on our home court." There was a note of conviction in his voice. "We'll have to get ready for them, Jacques— with a clear strategy. I'll need you and Francis in my corner."

"What do you want me to do?"

"Right now, just take notes. We'll get to the Nazis later. Now what did you want to know about Brookes and Didon?"

After a few minutes of discussion about his old colleagues and friends, Coubertin sat up straighter and offered St. Clair credit for insisting on this particular conversation. "I think you were right to give these relationships their due. There is a distinct thematic thread that runs from Sloane to Brookes to Didon and back to Bertha."

"Yes," St. Clair said. "I see the possibility of a chapter called 'Allies' that bridges from Simon to Didon and links them all to the Sorbonne Congress."

"They were allies, all of them, and you can't launch a movement without strong and staunch supporters," Coubertin agreed. "Each of them helped me through hard times. I've no doubt that providence lined them up to help guide me along the way. Sloane was the strongest, of course, and most constant, a true partner, but they were all important to my work and vision."

"Let's turn back to Dr. Brookes and your trip to Much Wenlock."

"You've read my account of the Games in Shropshire?"

"Yes—it's colorful and well written, and that's why I want to hear about it."

"Dr. Brookes was an inspiration to me in every way—on multiple levels. His Games were quaint, but they produced a spirit of community—a zeal for village life—unlike anything I'd ever witnessed."

"Start at the beginning. How did you meet him?"

Two hours later, after Coubertin had visibly tired and lost the thread of memory he had been following, St. Clair wrapped up the session and went looking for Dr. Messerli. He found him in his office.

"He insisted on working," St. Clair said, taking a seat in front of the desk, "and we talked for nearly three hours, but I'm worried. The way he's forming his words—with the lower side of his mouth—it's a little hard to believe he's okay."

"Listen, Jacques." The doctor rose and perched on the edge of the desk. "The truth is I'm surprised that he's bounced back this fast—perhaps a tribute to his overall fitness. It seemed more severe when I reached him on the water, but it must have been mild. His speech is coming back, and it doesn't seem to have had any impact on his writing—which is often a telltale sign."

"Are we in danger of another episode like this—or something more severe?"

Messerli sighed and looked down. "I'm afraid we are, but there's no certainty either way. Sometimes a mild stroke is a signal of worse to come, or he could recover completely and go on for years." He picked up a valise and headed for the door.

"It doesn't sound promising." St. Clair followed Messerli out, and they paused in the hallway before parting. Messerli rested a hand on St. Clair's shoulder.

"I will say one thing. The work you're doing is good for him. If he's motivated to keep the interviews going, that's therapeutic. It was one of the first things on his mind when he recovered. 'Where's Jacques?' he said. 'I want to see him.'"

St. Clair wanted to find solace in the idea that the interviews might keep Coubertin alive, but he couldn't suppress the fear that it all might end soon.

"Keep pushing ahead. You're getting close to Paris, aren't you—to the resurrection of the Games?"

"Yes, slowly, we're getting there, but now the Nazis are coming."

"Well, that will feed his motivation too. Just keep pushing."

58

THE DOCTOR
AND THE PRIEST

When he had what he needed from the interviews, St. Clair thought he could compress the story of Coubertin's encounter with Brookes into three scenes. As he began drafting, he realized he wanted to do the same kind of portrait of Didon and combine them into a single chapter.

In early 1889, an envelope arrived at rue Oudinot from the village of Much Wenlock in Shropshire County, England. It was from Dr. William Penny Brookes and included a pamphlet that described an annual festival—the Much Wenlock Olympian Games—that had been produced under Dr. Brookes's patronage since 1850, for nearly forty years. In a letter from Brookes, Coubertin learned that the doctor had written in response to an advertisement he had seen in the *London Times*—a notice about the upcoming Paris Congress on Physical Education—and Coubertin's circular questionnaire calling for information on the practice of sport. The doctor, only too happy to oblige, provided a long list of the traditions and athletic events staged during the annual festivals, alluding to the ancient Greek Games as the inspiration for his ideas on the development of his community. In fact, he referred Coubertin to the goals of the Games as enshrined in the statutes of the Much Wenlock Olympian Society, which stated that "The purpose of the society is to contribute to the development of the physical, moral, and intellectual qualities of the residents of Wenlock, through the encouragement of outdoor exercises, and through the annual competition for prizes and medals intended to reward the best literary and artistic productions, as well as the most remarkable feats of strength and skill."

Astonished by the notion that an "Olympian" athletic competition had been waged for forty years in relative obscurity in the land of Sir Thomas Arnold, Coubertin unfolded a large map of England and found Shropshire County near the Welsh border. He wrote back to Brookes, inviting him to attend the Paris Congress, and so began an active correspondence with a persistent invitation from Brookes for Coubertin to come see the Olympian Games. While Coubertin had initially planned to travel to Wenlock in the summer of 1890, his budding romance with Marie and his work on expanding sport participation in French schools delayed his trip until the fall.

In honor of his visit, Brookes decided to stage a single-day festival, on Wednesday, October 6th, to ensure that Coubertin gained a thorough understanding of what the Olympian Games meant to his small community—and gained a full measure of inspiration for his own work as well.

○ ○ ○ ○ ○

It was raining lightly late Tuesday afternoon when the train rounded a bend and pulled into the Much Wenlock station, a brightly painted white-and-red clapboard cottage surrounded by carefully cultivated floral planters. From his seat, Coubertin caught a glimpse of the impressive ruins of the high-standing stone walls and old turrets of the Wenlock Priory and the verdant beauty of the setting. Stepping out of the train car, he was met by the white whiskered eminence of Dr. Brookes, who bore a wide umbrella over his top hat, and a small delegation. Each person shook his hand in turn, and he caught the name of the vice president of the Olympian Society, a Mr. Andrews, who accompanied him and Dr. Brookes to the Gaskell Arms Hotel, where Coubertin was booked for two nights only.

Several hours later, Coubertin joined Brookes and Andrews at a corner table in the hotel restaurant, anticipating a long dinner discussion. Before they even lifted a glass of wine in a toast, the first of a steady stream of townsfolk arrived at the table to be introduced to Coubertin. They all knew who he was and all left saying they would see him the next day at the Games. Even their waiter, whom the doctor introduced as Young Robert Gibson, would be riding the next day in the tilting competition, an event Coubertin had never seen.

Over the course of the evening, after drawing from Coubertin a good overview of the Paris Congress and his travels in the United States, the eighty-one-year-old doctor, whose gray hair was matted along the sides of his head and whose eyes betrayed a deep fatigue, carried on a conversation about the history of the festival and what it had done for his community. He spoke passionately about his love of ancient Greece and his appreciation for Coubertin's books, the baron's eloquent writing, and his campaign to introduce British athletics into the French school system. They agreed fully on the benefits of sport for every man, woman, and child.

While Brookes was the epitome of humility and modesty, at one point he suggested that he might have gone a little too far in describing the success of the festival. "I'm just a soft-hearted old country doctor with an abiding love for this little green valley and the people of Much Wenlock."

Mr. Andrews interrupted. "You're anything but," he said. "You're an inspiring philanthropist who is deeply loved by generations of Shropshire families."

It was then that the doctor began to speak of his thwarted ambitions to export the Olympian Games to other cities and counties in England and even back to Greece—and Coubertin listened with rapt attention, hearing echoes of his own ambitions and his conversations with Sloane.

"We had one national edition of the Games at the Crystal Palace during the 1866 World's Fair. Highly successful, but no second generation, despite my letters and appeals. We had Birmingham host a festival one year and Shrewsbury afterwards and a few others, but none of them took root with the city folk. After that, I wrote to the king and queen of Greece and proposed an Olympian Games in Athens, but they demurred, although they did encourage us with a grand silver cup as a prize. They've had their own Olympic Games, you know."

"No, I did not," said Coubertin, and Brookes quickly delivered a disquisition on the Olympic Games in Athens of 1859, 1870, 1875, and 1889—all produced with funds provided by an endowment left by Evangelos Zappas, a rich Greek industrialist with a penchant for the past.

"A round of port," Brookes said as Young Robert lifted away some plates. The doctor raised his eyebrows and waited for Coubertin's reaction.

"Well," Coubertin said, "you're not alone in your ambitions, Dr. Brookes. The idea of bringing to life a modern edition of the Olympic Games seems to be bubbling up here and there." He informed Brookes about the fleeting proposals by Grousset and Saint-Clair and harkened back to the Olympic Games Napoleon had staged on the Champ de Mars before 1810. And then he spelled out his own ambitions. "But you will be most interested to hear, I believe, that my new American colleague, William Sloane of Princeton, and I have discussed this very idea. International sports competitions are not yet a *fait accompli*, but we both believe their arrival is imminent. Destiny has made it clear they're just offstage—and perhaps the guise of the Olympic Games could capture the public imagination."

The old man smiled broadly and his eyes watered as if he had just heard a moving song or poem. He wrapped his large hand around Coubertin's arm as he began to speak from the heart. "I had a premonition when your train was pulling in," he said, "but it was only confirmation of what I felt in your letters and your books. I think you are meant to carry my work forward, to take it across borders I have been unable to broach. You're a Frenchman in every respect, but you're clearly a citizen of the world and there's a mission before us that needs the energy of a younger man. You'll see what I'm talking about tomorrow."

○ ○ ○ ○ ○

In the midst of a heavy downpour, Brookes and Coubertin shook hands under the cover of their black umbrellas and took their places of honor in a long procession gathering in front of the Gaskell Arms. There were men, women, and children in medieval costumes and a small cavalry of tilters on horseback with long lances, some of them large, heavy men, some light, all appearing comfortable in the saddle if somewhat inelegant. Despite the rain, laughter rose amid the parade and Coubertin felt the mirth spread along the street.

"All part of our ritual," the doctor said, his eyes sparkling with pride undiminished by the weather. "A short parade around town to excite the locals and then off to the fields for the ceremonies and competition."

The herald—a young man dressed like a feudal royal attendant in a red velvet jacket, a black feathered hat with bells stitched in, and a pair of white stockings below his tight britches—appeared before them. A white fluted halo of ruffles circling his neck gave his pale cheeks a glow. He smiled and nodded to the baron. "Are we ready, sir?" he asked Dr. Brookes, who glanced back and forth at the soggy parade and said, "Proceed."

With a loud proclamation, the herald signaled the beginning of the march, and a group of young girls in peasant dresses carrying baskets of flower petals raced from the cover of the buildings and took their places behind the front line of horsemen, who lifted their trumpets and played in unison as the procession moved forward in step with flag bearers at the front. As the girls spread their flowers, a choir of boys in farm clothes took their places behind them and began singing an English country tune Coubertin did not know, but voices from the length of the line lifted in a cheerful community chorus.

As they circled the block and headed for the bowling green, Coubertin was surprised to see townspeople emerging from their half-beam houses to cheer as the parade passed by, getting drenched as they clapped and whistled, calling out the names of their friends. "The streets are usually crowded," said Dr. Brookes, "but this is the first fall festival we've organized and this rain ..."

"No apologies, please, good sir," Coubertin said. "This is an extraordinary show you're putting on ..." He was about to add "for me alone," but he stopped. Within minutes, however, they came to the edge of the bowling green, and the horsemen led the way through a triumphal arch that had been created out of branches, leaves, and flowers with a banner stretched across its top that said, in beautiful calligraphy, "Welcome Baron Pierre de Coubertin."

As they marched across a long field bordered with trees that formed a great square arena, Coubertin noticed that the grandstands on the opposite side of the field were already filling with umbrella-carrying spectators. Looking at the midfield, he noted parallel tracks he assumed were for athletics and equestrian events. As the horsemen in front turned and stopped and the boys and girls gathered around, he took a place next to Dr. Brookes and waited as the parade of people surrounded them.

The first order of business, it turned out, was planting a tree in Coubertin's honor, an oak sapling that would take its place in the row of the progressively older trees that defined the edge of the field. Dr. Brookes gave a speech extolling the Greek traditions of these Olympian Games and exalted Coubertin's position as a leader of innovation in world sport. The downpour showed no signs of letting up, but the tree went into the ground, bottles of champagne were popped, and the celebration continued regardless. From the grandstands, Coubertin watched as the athletics unfolded with footraces, several throwing events, and one weightlifting competition, the people cheering madly for every competitor. At the end of the finals of each event, Coubertin followed the doctor to the victory stand as one of the town's beauties, gowned for the occasion, stepped forward to bestow a wreath on the head of each victor, who kneeled and kissed her hand. The doctor and the baron bestowed the medals.

Brookes kept up a running commentary, explaining to Coubertin the curious blend of the traditional Olympic events and the chivalrous contests drawn from Britain's romantic medieval past. "*Ivanhoe* remains the most popular novel in our library," he said. "The people of this valley have far greater affection for Robin of Locksley and Richard the First than they do for Hercules, Ulysses, or Achilles. When I started this festival in 1850, I knew a little taste of the Knights of the Round Table would make the sports even more appealing."

The final event of the day, the tilting competition, created the greatest level of excitement, and it was soon apparent why. With horses thundering down a hedgerow parallel to the grandstands at full gallop, throwing up a cloud of mud, each rider rose in his saddle and lowered the long shaft of his lance. The objective was to spear a small golden ring hanging on a peg directly out from the stands. The clang of the lance against the post typically signaled a sharp ricochet that sent the spear flying and took more than one rider off his mount, but several succeeded in catching the ring, drawing appreciative cheers from the crowd. Coubertin marveled at the skill of the riders, who were a motley assembly of townsmen of all weights and sizes, but who clearly loved the taste of competition and the thrill of the moment.

The day ended in a private dinner at Brookes's home. The erudite doctor
expressed a sense of urgency in the development of a broader Olympic Games, and
Coubertin responded with enthusiasm but begged patience as he explained his
inchoate plans. "It's going to take a good bit of time to rally the right international
players to support the notion of a modern Olympics. And we have to conceive of
it—as you have your Games—as a force for education and character building, not
simply a series of world championships, but a means to foster friendship among
people everywhere."

○ ○ ○ ○ ○

A few days later, St. Clair was back in the familiar setting of Mon Repos, across
the desk from Coubertin, working diligently on the biography. He looked up
from his notes as Pierre offered a final assessment of the impact Dr. Brookes
had had on his thinking.

"My admiration for him grew with each moment I spent in that little village,"
the baron said with perfect enunciation. To St. Clair's relief, all traces of the
earlier slurs had vanished. "He wanted to see the Olympic Games resurrected
on a broad, international scale. Although his attempts to expand the playing
field didn't bear any lasting fruit, he kept the Olympic spirit alive in Much
Wenlock. And he certainly educated and inspired me in both theoretical and
practical ways."

"What would you say were the primary lessons you took from Brookes?"

"That the idea of reviving the Olympic Games had more proponents than
I had suspected. I gained a good education on what Zappas and the Greeks
had done and began to research it after I returned to Paris. But Dr. Brookes
passed along something far more practical during that visit. He showed me
that the traditions, rituals, and ceremonies of an event can produce the same
solemn respect on a smaller local stage as they generate on a large national
or international scale. In the idiosyncratic charm of his festival, I saw how
speeches, parades, medals, music and song, flags, and the conveyance of honor
can fill the heart with a hushed reverence and touch the soul as if time had
stopped. Much Wenlock confirmed for me many of the lessons of pageantry
and public celebration I had drawn from the ceremonies of the Paris Universal
Exposition. Dr. Brookes was more than a philanthropist. He was a messenger of
the gods as far as I was concerned, and his words of encouragement stayed in
my heart and mind for years."

"Why didn't he come to Paris for the Olympic Congress?"

"His health. He was eighty-one when I met him, and I sensed what he already knew—that he was starting to fade. He died the year after the congress, but he went knowing his work had a new champion—as he dreamed it would."

The two sat quietly while St. Clair completed his notes. When he lifted his pen from the page, he looked at Coubertin and said, "How would you compare the influence of Dr. Brookes and Father Didon on your Olympic work?"

"Well, my relationship with Dr. Brookes, although brief, cemented the idea— that we both shared—that he was passing a baton on to me, generation to generation, to carry on the Olympic mission. But we never collaborated on anything specific. Henri Didon, on the other hand, lived just south of Paris in Arcueil and adapted my ideas at his school. He helped broaden the engagement of religious and public schools in our work—and over the years lent his considerable oratory skills to the Olympic cause. But first and foremost he was a great and close friend, what you might call a running mate."

"You mean you ran together?"

"Oh yes. He was about fifty when I met him, and he could run a good long race—despite his stocky build and his white Dominican cassock. In fact, the first thing we worked on together was a paper chase at his school."

"Where did you first meet him?"

"I walked over to his office in the Latin Quarter one afternoon. Once a week he took the train into Paris to take appointments at a small office he kept on rue St. Jacques between the Luxembourg Gardens and the Sorbonne. There were a lot of demands on his time."

"He was a public figure?"

"Ah, you don't know his story," Coubertin said. "I guess my tribute didn't really establish his standing properly."

St. Clair thought about the short piece published after Didon's death in 1900. He had looked it up the day after Coubertin had asked Brundage if he remembered Didon. "I think your brief homage paid respect to him as a fine orator and a great moral man who lambasted his congregation for anti-Semitism. But I'm not familiar with his background other than the fact that he invented the Olympic motto—*citius, altius, fortius*."

Coubertin looked at the papers on his desk and moved his finger across them as if scribbling a note. He took a deep breath before he spoke: "Henri Didon was one of the most gifted and powerful orators of our time—and some would say an equally gifted writer. More than once he filled La Madeleine with throngs—standing room only—for his Lenten sermons. His voice had a deep vibrato he could play like a cello. His face was handsome, open, and evenly featured with a broad forehead under a thick black shock of hair that gave him an unmistakable look, recognizable all the way to the back pew of any cathedral.

"And he was a master of the physical gesture." Coubertin threw his arm into the air with fingers spread in a wide claw. As he slowly closed his fingers into a fist, he drew his hand back toward his heart, adding, "His gestures dramatically wrapped his rhetoric in the grip of the truth. His logic was inescapable—and the flame of his passion for Christ touched the sensibilities of every listener. He had a vehemence for social justice—a fierce adherence to what was morally right—that got him into trouble with the church more than once."

"Sounds like a crusader."

"No, not a crusader, just a philosopher called to preach and a teacher with an unwavering conviction about what needed to be said. He argued so forcefully for the indissolubility of marriage, at a time of laxity and the growing ease of divorce—I think it was the late 1870s—that a public outcry arose. Many prominent Catholics had been granted divorces by the church—and ultimately, the archbishop dispatched Didon to Corsica to quiet him. He was gone for seven years, but he traveled to Palestine and walked in the footsteps of Jesus and returned to Paris with the fully written manuscript of his *Life of Christ*. It was published in 1890, just before I met him. It created a sensation and sold as if Balzac and Hugo had collaborated on it—and vaulted him back into the public eye. When I read the reviews—and discovered he had been appointed head of the École Albert le Grand in Arcueil—I searched for more information and came across an interview that said he was developing a new curriculum for the school that included sport. I could hardly believe what I was reading—he already had a program of fencing, riding, and gymnastics. Yet the previous headmaster of Albert le Grand had rejected all my proposals on physical education."

"You had approached that *école* already? Was that part of your work with the Simon Committee and the USFSA?"

"Of course. I'd already canvassed and visited about one hundred schools in France under the auspices of the two committees—to assess the level of sport, if any, and propose the implementation of a basic athletic program. The Monge School and Alsacienne were the most advanced. But generally, the religious schools were the most difficult. The Jesuits rejected sport out of hand because they didn't want to compete with public schools. In fact, I'd had success with only two religious schools—Gerson and Juilly. From my perspective, it was a godsend to think that a Dominican headmaster as prominent as Père Didon was embracing sport."

"How did you approach him?"

"Full of praise and optimism, hoping it wouldn't take much persuasion. And it took none at all. Our connection was immediate—and it was clear from what he told me that our ideas were fully aligned."

"Do you remember the date?"

"Actually, I do. It was the day after my twenty-eighth birthday—January 2nd, 1891."

○ ○ ○ ○ ○

Coubertin was escorted into a corner office with a portrait of Jesus over the mantel of a blackened stone fireplace and took a seat to wait for Père Didon. The room was windowed but shadowy on the overcast afternoon. It was warm but spare with dark, wood-paneled walls and a small desk in front of a cabinet, the top of which was covered with a stack of copies of the freshly printed two-volume set of Didon's *Life of Christ*. Several copies were sitting on the desk as well, and Coubertin guessed that the priest must have been signing them for his guests.

Suddenly the door flew open, and Didon rolled in like a snowman in the bright blanket of his white robes, tightly bound at his portly waist by a black sash, his eyes sparkling with the joy of his smile as the baron stood and they met face to face for the first time.

"Henri Didon." The priest introduced himself in a deep voice and with the clasp of a strong handshake.

The baron introduced himself, and they looked each other in the eye, their faces no more than a half foot apart. "Thank you for receiving me—" he began, but Didon interrupted.

"Not at all." Didon moved around his desk, pushing up the sleeves of his soutane as he sat. "I'm glad to make the acquaintance of the secretary general of the USFSA. I admire Jules Simon and appreciate the work you've done to push sport forward in our schools. We need it," he said emphatically. "The children of France need it."

"How much do you know of our work?"

"When I returned to Paris and was named the new prior of Albert le Grand, I made the rounds of the headmasters to see what I could learn, who was innovating, who was leading. I heard the name Coubertin from several people—at La Monge and Alsacienne. I don't know much, but I'm willing to learn. Tell me more about yourself."

Coubertin wasted no time complying with Didon's request, summarizing his travels in England and the United States, the Congress on Physical Education, and, most meaningful for the discussion at hand, his work with Simon driving sport into the French education system. "We have about twenty schools integrating sport into their curricula and building or acquiring fields, but we've hit a wall of resistance in promoting inter-school sports."

"That's predictable. There's strong resistance at the religious schools to engaging with non-religious state schools. I'm familiar with the outdated attitudes of many of my colleagues," he said. "How can I help you, Baron? What's your most immediate goal?"

"I need a strong advocate for open competitions between the schools. It would obviously accelerate the process if I could find a school that would host a competition."

Didon rested his chin in his hands. "You have your advocate already. Now, what kind of competition did you have in mind?"

"Have you ever heard of a paper rally—some call it a paper chase?"

He had not, but within an hour the two had mapped out a route for a paper chase covering a nine-mile loop from the Albert le Grand campus. Coubertin explained how the race was akin to a hounds-and-rabbits chase. A group of men— the rabbits—set out on the run and laid out a course, a trail of scattered pieces of paper, that competitive runners—the hounds—had to follow. The papers were scattered in a way that made it easy to lose the "scent," and the hounds had to spread out and search in different directions until someone found the trail again—and everybody ran to catch up with the lead hound.

Didon had other appointments that afternoon but extended his meeting with Coubertin to two hours. They discovered a personal harmony, shared goals for education and sport, and a deep parallelism in their egalitarian values. Didon had listened carefully to Coubertin's overview of global trends in physical education and remarked that he saw sport and play as essential components of the student experience—"vital in building character and planting the seeds of respect, confidence, and fraternal affection." Coubertin was impressed with the creative ideas that Didon had already implemented at Albert le Grand—no uniforms required, and students treated as adults, trusted with individual and group responsibilities, allowed to make certain decisions. And all were involved with sports. It was a natural French approach to Arnold's disciplines.

They made plans for another meeting over the weekend in Arcueil so Coubertin could see Didon's sports program in action and finalize plans for the paper chase. As the priest walked him out that afternoon, Coubertin commented on the rapidly rising sales of his *Life of Christ*.

Didon surprised him again, saying, "If God blesses the sale of my book and the royalties amount to much, I'll spend it all on the development of the school—and the first thing I'll build will be a new gymnasium."

○ ○ ○ ○ ○

After that weekend and the announcement of the upcoming paper rally at Albert le Grand, word of Didon's commitment to Coubertin's program spread through the French school system around Paris and directly to the community of headmasters at both public and private schools, who had considered, but mostly spurned, Coubertin's efforts.

Didon was an effective partner in promotion who recognized the importance of staging a series of announcements. One week later, he told *La Croix*, the leading Catholic newspaper, that his school was forming the Athletic Association of Albert le Grand and applying for membership in the USFSA. Within days, Coubertin issued a statement quoting USFSA chairman Jules Simon as welcoming the AAAG as the twenty-first member of the organization.

On the day of the first paper chase at Arcueil, a crowd gathered on the lawn outside the courtyard of the school. Early-morning dew was still fresh on the ground, and mists rose on the fields of Laplace Park, which surrounded and belonged to the château on the adjoining property. Forty-eight boys were eager to run, and Didon's staff of priests in their white robes were ready to officiate. A few parents and neighbors had come out to witness the start. Coubertin addressed the competitors, explaining the rules. In his flannel running pantaloons, he was ready to lead the way, and he selected a small group of three boys—the rabbits—to go out with him. The competitors and crowd watched as they ran toward Laplace Park. Didon, who was deep in conversation with a reporter he had invited from *Le Petit Journal*, missed the start and ran out after them in his excitement, calling to Coubertin to wait for him. After the rabbits disappeared into the woods across the long, open park grounds, the larger group of boys—the hounds—were let loose.

Following the course that he and Didon had charted, Coubertin and the rabbits took a route directly across the château grounds toward Villejust, skirting the village and climbing a hill at Chevilly, then passing through l'Hay and Bourg-la-Reine, running along a dirt path to cross the train tracks at Sceaux. Twisting back in a wide loop, the route led over to the modest plateau at Bagneux and made a turn back toward Arcueil and Albert le Grand. Covering nine miles and more, the hounds took about two hours to find their way to the finish line—where they straggled in, some near exhaustion, and were greeted with great cheers.

By the time they finished, the sun had burned away the dew and given them a bright morning. The rally had been a smashing success. The story in *Le Petit Journal* the next day captured the spirit of the event well, made the effort of the boys seem heroic, and elevated the collaboration between Didon and Coubertin as something of a breakthrough in school sports. Within a week, headmasters across the region of Île-de-France were thinking about their own paper rallies. But the story made it clear that Didon and Coubertin were just getting started. Didon had let slip the news that the AAAG intended to host its first annual school championship in March—a paper rally that would be open to all schools in the region.

○ ○ ○ ○ ○

Giving St. Clair a grin, remembering those hearty moments as the hounds came across the finish line, Coubertin said, "That single race was the beginning of the USFSA's greatest success—and we owed it all to Père Didon."

"Did Didon run all the way with you?"

No, he took a few shortcuts, but he had a great time, even though we left him bent over, red-faced and breathing hard, a few times. At one point, we were laughing from the top of the hill at Chevilly as we watched the hounds searching for the trail. He was joyous. And I'll never forget the image of him leaping over the ruts of a harvested hill near Bourg-la-Reine, misjudging his landing, and getting his cassock all muddied. It was a brilliant day, and the paper rallies that followed were the true beginnings of cross-country running, which became a phenomenon of its own."

"I can see why you called him a godsend," St. Clair said.

"Yes, but his greatest contribution was yet to come. Two months later, at the end of March, we ran the first AAAG Championship—and it broke open the school sports competitions of Paris."

On the morning of the championship, Coubertin stood on a chair he had discreetly placed at the far end of the courtyard of Albert le Grand, a large rectangle formed by the four gray stone walls of the school, arcaded and festooned with banners and flags of all the participating schools. He looked out over a crowd of nearly three hundred with a sense of accomplishment, pride, and gratitude as they all listened raptly to the inspiring words of Father Didon's welcoming speech. He was speaking of the joys of developing the human body and of competition for the glory of God and the honor of each school. Coubertin knew what was coming, for he had heard Didon give an earlier version of the speech a few days before at a training session for his own team, where he had stirred them all with the introduction of the school's new motto, a call to give everything for the effort and for the joy the effort would give back.

"Today, as I've told the athletes of Albert le Grand—it is not for ourselves alone that we run. We take to the fields and to the woods to exercise all the gifts our heavenly Father has given us—all the gifts we can master by training harder to race faster, by lifting our eyes to the highest possibilities of the talents we possess, by muscling our strengths and drawing even greater strength from our teams. Individually and collectively, I say to you today, to each of you who is here to compete—you can go faster, you can reach higher, you can be stronger. *Citius, altius, fortius*—faster, higher, stronger—for the glory of God and the honor of your school. This is the new motto of Albert le Grand, but it is also a fresh call to each of you to be at your best as you run with your brothers in sport today."

Didon dazzled the boys, men, and women present and left them all feeling that by taking part in this championship, they were making history. When he finished, he called Baron Pierre de Coubertin, the race director, to the stage to review the rules of competition and to provide final instructions for each of the teams. Coubertin dispensed with the formalities, not wanting to diminish the emotions Didon had stirred up, and called for the 132 competitors to move to the starting line. The Dominican priests who were officiating lined the runners up by teams in rows. The boys bounced in anticipation of the start, looking out at the glistening fields of Laplace. As the rabbits set off, Coubertin was enthralled by the size of the gathering, the distinct colors of the teams, and the electric excitement that filled the air.

And out they went, jostling in their colorful jerseys and caps, running into the fields just as he had seen the boys do at Rugby. As they spread and thinned into lines and packs, Coubertin could name each school by its colors—Chaptal in black and red, Buffon in blue and yellow. A small group from Alsacienne was the first to reach the woods, the white stars on their red jerseys disappearing among the trees, the green and white of Louis le Grand right behind them. Condorcet's blue-and-white stripes and the white caps of Michelet were still visible along with the traditional Dominican black and white of Albert le Grand, which seemed to be running last. Coubertin wondered if this were a deliberate strategy to conserve their energy. He missed the boys from Monge and Sailly but knew they were in the mix.

The course laid out by the rabbits went in a different direction this time, covering nearly ten miles across Meudon, Villebon, Vélizy, Viroflay, and Chaville. Whatever happened during the race, Coubertin knew that he and Didon had already succeeded, having created the first major competition between religious and state schools, private and public, finally breaking down all the barriers he had so fervently pushed against for years. This was a new beginning—and while it appeared to be only a local innovation—Coubertin was certain it signaled something far more. He knew on that day that other barriers, broader and more entrenched, would fall before the unifying power of sport. From local innovations, he thought, come the beginnings of global movements.

○ ○ ○ ○ ○

"What was it that made Père Didon such a vital and willing partner?" St. Clair asked.

"His belief in the power of sport," Coubertin said without hesitation. "With that first championship—that first taste of success—we both recognized that sport could do much more. While he continued to build Albert le Grand into an innovative center of sport and education excellence, he also became something of an apostle of my Olympic dream. Along with his brilliant motto, he lent the power of his voice and his vocation to the cause I was espousing. In fact, his encouragement drove my first proposal to restore the Games."

"Did you share your dream with him the first day you met him?"

"No, but it wasn't long after we met that the subject came up naturally," Coubertin explained. "As a teenager, he had studied in Grenoble at the Rondeau School under Father Lacordaire, a famous teacher at the time—and every year they held an edition of the Olympic Games."

"When was that? What years?"

"I'm not sure when Didon was there, but I think Lacordaire started the tradition in the 1830s."

"So it predated Much Wenlock?"

"Yes, I suppose it did." He sounded hesitant, as if he hadn't considered that fact before. "Sport in education was ingrained in Didon's heart. He saw himself as a servant of God, and true to his word, he spent all of his royalties on that school—essentially turning it into a sports academy."

"What did he build?"

"He built a new gymnasium, but first he acquired seven hectares from the Laplace Château next door. He bought the whole park. Then he built a riding hall that also hosted banquets and conferences, installed a track with a field house, and built a great swimming complex."

"Did the annual championship grow?"

"It became one of the best and most competitive of all. The year before the Olympic Games in Athens—the year I was married—the meet drew teams from all over the countryside. Stade Français, FC Lyon, the Cosmopolitan Club, and sports associations from Chartres, Montmorency, Versailles, and Montrouge all sent teams. I think there were thirty-two that year. Even the Anglo-American Athletic Club in Paris sent a team."

"You two built quite a legacy on the competitive front in Paris."

"Yes, but our greater legacy was carried out through the work of the USFSA. Within a couple of years—by about 1894—we had seen more than one hundred sporting fields or facilities installed in French schools."

"Quite a partnership."

"And an even deeper friendship. He brought twenty students on a caravan to Athens to witness the first Olympic Games."

"Let's jump ahead. You said Père Didon encouraged you to make your first public proposal to restart the Games. I've already talked to the baroness about this, but tell me about it and why it failed."

59

THE OLYMPIC IDEA

With everything he had learned in the interviews and gathered through research, St. Clair prepared a draft for Messerli's review on the origins, evolution, and final development of Coubertin's Olympic idea:

○ ○ ○ ○ ○

As far back as 1887, Baron Pierre de Coubertin had mentioned the Olympic Games in his writings. Thinking about the young boys of his country imprisoned in a school system that denied them the opportunity for exercise, he had written: "What they need is the dust of Olympia to excite them." He wasn't thinking then about resurrecting the Olympic Games. He did not know at the time that rising in his breast was an idea that would open the doors of the temple of sport for young people everywhere. He knew only that from his own experience—from the inspiration he drew from ancient Olympia—there was something in physical exercise that led to liberation, that freed the individual to discover within himself new dimensions of the gift of joy, a fresh wellspring of identity, a chance to run with confidence toward a new future. His compassion for the children of France— locked in an intellectual system he had survived—extended beyond his own understanding then. But after his trip to America and his discussions with Sloane, as he began to work on the first international rowing competitions between France and England—with Ambassador Waddington pulling strings to engage the powers of the Henley Rowing Club—the Olympic idea began to form, presenting itself again and again with an urgency that suggested it could be a calling, his calling. It was an idea that reached well beyond the confines of his country, an idea that would speak to a population he now described as universal youth.

In Coubertin's conversations with William Sloane, the idea of resurrecting the Olympic Games surfaced often as a vehicle to popularize moral sport, but they had not spent any time on the concept of organizational mechanics. In his visit to Much Wenlock, the Olympic idea took on crystalline form in the charming rituals of the Shropshire festival Dr. Brookes produced in his honor. But despite their shared passion, neither Brookes nor Coubertin could see a clear path to elevate those local contests to an international stage. In the persistent encouragement of Bertha von Suttner and others, Coubertin saw the possibilities of integrating a bridge of peace and even higher moral values into the celebration, but he doubted he could draw support from governments for such a vision in an era of realpolitik.

And then one day the doubt gave way to conviction, and he suddenly knew with a certainty that his life had one clear purpose—one clear calling. The ancient world was reaching out to his family once again; the mythical hand of Zeus was at his back, urging him forward, prodding him to recognize what he alone had been put on this earth to do. He was meant to resurrect the Olympic Games. As the conviction settled into his breast, he could see clearly that all of the experiences of his life had prepared him for this moment, this campaign. And he could feel that the roiling passions that were pushing him toward sport would not relinquish their demands. His skills were a match for the opportunities of the time. Sport was emerging as an international force without a steering committee, racing toward an uncertain destination like a horse that had thrown its jockey. Someone, somewhere had to step forward to offer a vision that could coalesce the powers at play; someone with the right idea—and the force of will to match—had to impose order.

While Hugo's great refrain, "Nothing is so powerful as an idea whose time has come," had suggested itself as a guide for his mission, he found more clarity for what he was about to do in the novels and essays of Anatole France. At night by candlelight, reading as he fell asleep, he found that Monsieur France spoke clearly to his ambition. "It is by acts and not by ideas that people live," he had written. But another quote became his slogan. He wrote it out and tacked it to the wall beside his desk: "To accomplish great things we must not only act, but also dream; not only plan, but also believe."

And so he dreamed of a modern Olympic Games and began to plan for their introduction. The circumstances favored action, but there was no opening. Coubertin would have to create one.

○ ○ ○ ○ ○

In the middle of November 1891, the Third Universal Peace Congress in Rome ended, and a few weeks later Baroness Bertha von Suttner stormed back into Paris like a hurricane of pacifism. Her arrival was greeted with newspaper reports of the impression she had made with a rousing keynote speech on the opening day of the congress. Already well known for the popularity of her novel, *Lay Down Your Arms*, by all press accounts she turned out to be an equally compelling public speaker. In the two weeks of the congress, she emerged as the burgeoning peace movement's first major female leader, a propulsive force whose moral magnetism became a focal point in clarifying the resolutions the Rome conference would put forward.

Anxious to hear about the proceedings, Coubertin called on Bertha and Arthur twice within a week of their return, but he missed them both times. He left his card and they sent apologies—the second of which included a separate envelope from Arthur, an invitation to a small dinner he was hosting to honor his wife's performance and leadership.

When Coubertin picked up Marie at her home, she looked ravishing in a white evening gown and pearl necklace—and her kiss told him she was delighted to be going out to a formal event with her new beau. Arriving at la Grande Cascade in the Bois de Boulogne, they disposed of their overcoats and his top hat at the cloak room, but he kept his white silk scarf on against the chill. Following a hostess, they were guided through the packed restaurant toward a private dining room for twelve. Arthur met them in the hall, apologizing again for missing Pierre's visits.

"Bertha has been leading the charge in the development of national peace chapters in Austria and Bohemia," he explained. "We came back with a renewed sense of urgency."

Arthur opened the door as Marie preceded Pierre inside. As they entered, Bertha turned from her conversation with Jules Simon to call their names and extend a hand. She was dressed in a violet gown with a delicate gold lace cape over her shoulders, and a black tiara nested above the crest of her coiffed hair. With Marie on his arm, Pierre moved to join them by a fireplace crackling with warmth. Looking across the room, he nodded to two men and women he did not know—one of whom turned out to be Élie Ducommun, another peace pioneer.

"Bertha," Pierre said, kissing her cheeks, "the press won't stop singing your praises."

"Nor should they," Simon added as they all greeted one another.

"Well, as Marie can attest," Bertha said, "it isn't every day that a woman makes the news if she's not singing, dancing, or matching wits with Sarah Bernhardt."

"Don't be self-deprecating, Baroness," Simon said. "You are not a novelty. What you've done is worthy of headlines."

The baroness graciously demurred as Coubertin added, "You certainly brought the congress to its feet in Rome, from everything I heard."

"Well, yes, my speech was well received."

"Pierre had a letter from Rome full of high praise for you." Marie nodded at Pierre. "From an American, I believe."

He picked up the point. "In fact, it was from none other than Daniel Gilman, the president of Johns Hopkins, who said—"

"Gilman! We're expecting him here tonight," Bertha said.

"What a surprise—and excellent news. I missed him when I visited Hopkins two years ago—and I was hoping to meet him as he passed through Paris."

Arthur called from the door just then and they all turned as Frédéric Passy, the doyen of peace, entered the room, his flaring white beard and silver-framed spectacles giving him the appearance of a sage. Simon and Bertha welcomed him as Coubertin whispered to Marie, "Well, the prime mover himself. It seems this is more a leadership conference than a quiet celebration."

"My, that's an impressive beard," she said. "Is he as old as Jules?"

"No, not quite. I'm pretty certain Jules is five or six years older." He remembered the two of them joking about the time they might have remaining when they were all working on the Paris Peace Congress.

Passy briefly greeted Pierre and Marie as he made his way around the room. Gilman and the last two guests arrived, and just as he and Coubertin were embracing over the pleasant coincidence of their meeting, Bertha called everyone to the table. Once they were seated—with Bertha and Arthur at either end and the two elder statesmen, Passy and Simon, across from each other at the center— Coubertin was pleased to find himself opposite Ducommun.

As the waiters swept in, Arthur wasted no time in singing the praises of the love of his life. Standing with champagne in hand, he led the room in a toast filled with genuine affection. "To the most talented author, most passionate patron of peace, and most beautiful woman I have ever known. We are all your admirers, Bertha, and all ready to march with you, shoulder to shoulder, in the cause of peace."

Voices rose in acclaim, and Bertha responded from her seat. "Arthur, you're always too generous in your praise, but I'm delighted to be the center of attention in such august company." Pointedly, she tilted her head in deference to both Passy and Simon. "We did accomplish much in Rome together, but there will be no respite from the work of building a better world."

As the guests settled in for the main course, Simon moved the conversation back toward Rome after apologizing for his absence there. "Frédéric, I followed the proceedings closely in the press, but I would be interested in your summation of the resolutions."

Dabbing his mouth with a napkin, Passy cast a glance at Bertha and Ducommun. "There can be no question, Jules, that this Third Universal Peace Congress ended with genuine advancements. We were able to build on the momentum we started in Paris and meet the difficult challenge of producing concrete measures showing progress for the peace movement—and for arbitration as well. Our resolutions were far-reaching, practical, and, I have to say, actionable. I think you would all agree that the creation of the permanent International Peace Bureau is our single greatest achievement."

"Bravo," Simon said. "And it seems to me your decision to place its headquarters in Switzerland is also telling."

"We had to signal the bureau's neutrality from the beginning," Passy said. He looked at Ducommun. "Perhaps you haven't heard that Élie has agreed to serve as our president and will be taking the reins immediately."

The din of approval rose around the table. Simon was first to pick up his glass. "Congratulations, Élie. Where will you open the office?"

"We considered Geneva, but since I work in Berne with a good corps of supporters, the Swiss capital is our choice. Our immediate priority—as I suspect you've seen in the press—is to have parliamentarian peace representatives appointed from every country. We're going to push the formation of national peace committees around the world—and Berne is fertile ground for both initiatives."

"Bertha has already begun the formation of several NPCs," Arthur added, prompting his wife to interject.

"We found great allies in both Vienna and Prague," she said. "The formation of both committees and the political outreach are already under way."

"And when do you plan to launch your annual international conferences?" Coubertin wanted most to ask about sport, but he held back.

"That's probably our most exciting initiative," Passy replied. "Hodgson had the idea of hosting it in a different country every year. We haven't put the first one on the calendar yet, but Hodgson is leading the charge there—along with a host of recommendations on education reform."

"Such as?" Simon asked.

"Making a foreign language an essential part of every school curriculum," Bertha said. "All in the interest of promoting international understanding among the young."

Gilman spoke from the other end of the table. "Education is the long-term path to peace." As heads turned, he added, "In the United States, we're already moving to make a foreign language mandatory for undergraduate degrees—and for admission to graduate school."

"There's a growing consensus on that point," Passy said, "and our international student conferences will promote friendships and cultural exchange across all borders."

"And do we understand correctly that sporting events will be part of the exchange?" Simon inquired.

"Most definitely."

"Frédéric," said Bertha, "Pierre and Jules have been discussing international competitions for some time, and Pierre has already organized several international rowing events."

"Along with our British and American friends," Coubertin said, "and I'm anticipating our first international athletic meets this summer in Paris. Racing will host."

"We should discuss our mutual interests there," Ducommun said, looking across the table to Coubertin.

"I'd welcome the opportunity."

With Marie now engaging—and sustaining the focus on Pierre's sport promotion plans—Coubertin took the opportunity to set forth his idea that sport itself could be the central organizing principle of an international festival of youth from all nations. He concluded by saying that he believed athletes of every nation could be cultivated through such a festival to serve as ambassadors of friendship and peace.

As he finished, it fell to Passy to respond. "That's a more narrow focus on sport than we have in mind," he said through his great white beard, "but I applaud your thinking. Athletes could play a vital role with sport rising as it is." He looked around the table and drew affirmation.

"The popularity of sport in America has already given it a more pronounced social role than it has in Europe," Gilman said. "It will be a tremendous international force in the future—as Pierre made clear in his *Universités Transatlantiques*."

Passy nodded as dessert arrived and the din of conversation engulfed the table again. Before they departed from the restaurant, Coubertin had arranged a meeting with Gilman the next day and a further conversation with Ducommun before he left Paris. Pierre's ties to the peace movement and to the leadership of higher education in the United States would be strengthened before he brought his ideas forward.

On the way to the Place Saint-Georges in the carriage that night, bundled with a blanket over their laps and their arms around each other, Pierre told Marie that he believed a full marriage of peace and sport was possible—through the Olympic Games.

"I'm sure they'll support you, Pierre. The Olympic banner could lift their annual student exchanges to new heights."

He kissed her, pleased with her encouragement. "I hope so. But sport must be given the lead. It has the power to unite like nothing else."

○ ○ ○ ○ ○

After that dinner, Coubertin's vision for the resurrection of the Olympic Games began to take on more substance, which allowed him to make more definitive plans. Several organizational issues that he and Sloane had wrestled over were easily solved through the initiatives of the peacemakers. The idea of an International Olympic Committee guiding the work of national chapters—he'd call them national Olympic committees—had immediate appeal to him. Dozens of other international organizations were flourishing at the time—including the Red Cross and the Universal Postal Union—each spreading their services and expanding their footprint nation by nation. He knew that Sloane could form an American committee, that Major General Balck would lead the development of a Swedish Olympic team, and that his old schoolmate, Ferenc Kemény, was ready to take the reins in Hungary. Each committee, he thought, would become the premiere national sports organization in its country—serving the ideals of peace, building stronger republics, with sport as a catalyst for social cohesion, and enhancing international comity and contact through Olympic competitions. He decided to discuss the idea of hosting an Olympic Congress with Georges de Saint-Clair under the auspices of the USFSA—and he realized, now that the union had grown to nearly seven thousand members in almost seventy sports clubs and societies, that a celebration was called for. Tracing the roots of Saint-Clair's organization back to 1887, he thought they could justify staging a congress in Paris and labeling it the USFSA's Fifth Anniversary Jubilee. He wrote to Sloane immediately and decided to ask White, Gilman, and Eliot, among others, to serve on his host committee.

○ ○ ○ ○ ○

A few nights later, however, troubled by a nagging worry that he might offend his peace allies, Coubertin found himself standing in the shadow of La Madeleine, looking across the plaza up to the fifth-floor windows of Jules Simon's apartment. The hour was late and no lights were on. He decided to climb the stairs anyway and risk waking his mentor. He needed counsel and it could not wait—he was anxious about how Passy, Pratt, Ducommun, and others would react to his announcement of an international Olympic Games in light of their own plans. Would they feel betrayed, as if he were stealing their thunder? How would he be able to gain the full patronage of the peace movement? How could he help the leadership understand that they were working for common goals? The Olympic Games, he believed, could do more to popularize international sport and strengthen its work for peace than their as yet undefined—and still unproduced—peace festivals.

On the third knock, Simon yanked the door open. He was dressed in his nightshirt, bearing a candleholder, and his uncombed hair was splayed wildly against the darkness behind him. His eyes flashed with anger. "It's awfully late for a social call," he said, giving little ground.

"My apologies, Jules. I must have your advice on a few urgent issues." He'd been fighting his anxieties for hours now, and decided he would beg if necessary.

"Too urgent to wait till the morning?" Despite his tone, Simon relinquished the space to allow his forceful young protégé in. "To the library," he said, and Pierre led the way down the hall.

They settled in, and Coubertin described the disquietude that had been gnawing at him. He felt embarrassed when Simon waved his anxieties away.

"Pierre, there's no reason for doubt or remorse. You've been working on these goals for national and international sport for a long time. Don't worry about Passy and Pratt—just act. If they object, I'll take care of them."

As their discussion wore down, Simon approached the window to gaze beyond the moonlit roof at the statue of La Madeleine across the square. Pierre followed his gaze. After some minutes, Simon turned and pointed to a bookshelf. "Pierre, would you retrieve that set of books on the middle shelf?"

The four volumes were bookended by two statues of knights on horseback. On his feet in an instant, Pierre lifted the set from the shelf. "Ah, *Don Quixote*—in Spanish." As he placed them on the desk, he felt a hole in the middle of the cover. "What's this?" he asked, his finger probing a gouge in the first volume. Opening the book, he saw that a wormhole bored all the way into the second volume, where a lead bullet was lodged.

"That's a souvenir from the bloody Communards," Simon said. "They shot through my windows."

"They were trying to kill you?"

"I was never sure whether they knew I lived here. But in their aimless violence they shot through the books that Thomas Jefferson used to teach himself Spanish. He had them here in Paris when he served as ambassador in France—and I bought a set of the same edition to savor the idea that I was connected to a better revolution."

"And you're making a point about violence—and peace."

"Exactly. The ideas you're generating—even those you feel are borrowed—must be put into action. They deserve the world's attention. For God's sake, this is about the right to play—about sport as a bridge of peace. It's everything we believe in. Don't let any doubts or threats stop you. If you don't act, someone else will— and the way they handle your ideas may be the death knell of everything you've dreamed about."

Despite his efforts, toward the fall of 1892 it became clear that Coubertin's plans for reintroducing the Olympic Games would have to move forward without much international support. His invitations and letters did not produce the outburst of enthusiasm he had anticipated in the sporting circles of England, the United States, or Europe. In fact, he had few confirmations from international sport or education leaders planning to attend his November congress. Undeterred, he turned toward France and moved to build momentum among his countrymen. Working with his loyal partner Georges de Saint-Clair, he drove the hierarchy of the USFSA to fill the Grand Amphithéâtre de la Sorbonne, where he intended to present his proposal on the night of November 11. Calling on Père Didon, he rallied the Dominicans and their family of Catholic schools to deliver a strong student contingent. He had the Russian aristocrat, Grand Duke Wladimr, preside. President Carnot was a lead patron. Jules Jusserand, a historian and future ambassador to the United States, lectured on medieval sport, and Pierre's brother, Paul, performed an entertaining skit on Dante and Virgil at the Union of Sports. Through Jules Simon and his aristocratic social connections, he was able to fill the dais and the front rows with an eminent cast of delegates.

Yet when the hour arrived and he stood on the stage, his heart sank. The audience was too French, he realized, too young, too oriented toward local and regional sports issues that had little to do with international amity and the greater cause of building sport into a force of friendship among nations. While he had achieved the goal of filling the room, he knew he had failed to serve his larger calling. As he stood to address the packed auditorium, he realized in a flash of insight that his greatest deficit—the key group missing from his audience—was the leadership of the peace movement. Though Bertha and Arthur von Suttner were in attendance and he knew they would carry his message back to Passy, Pratt, Ducommun, and the international peace network, it would have been far better to have all of them, along with the leadership of his international network, in the room at this moment.

He spread his arms expressively and spoke to the audience with full conviction. They were attentive and seemed to follow his logic as he arrived at the moment of revelation, the moment when he would first propose the advent of his great idea. "It is apparent that the telegraph, the train, the telephone, passionate scientific research, the international congresses, and the exhibitions have done more for peace than all the treaties and diplomatic agreements combined," he said. "I hope and believe that athleticism and sport can contribute even more. Let us export our oarsmen, our runners, our fencers into other lands—and they will become our ambassadors for peace. This is the true free trade of the future; and the day it is introduced into Europe, the cause of peace will have received a new and strong ally. It inspires me to touch upon a further step I now propose ... that together we may attempt to realize, upon a basis suitable to the conditions of our modern life, the splendid and beneficent task of reviving the Olympic Games."

A smattering of interest gave him brief hope, but despite his emphasis on sport and the strength of his appeal for bringing the youth of the world together in one great Olympic festival of friendship, despite his well-practiced pitch for peace through sport, despite his historic evocation of a modern form of an ancient event, the spirit in the room failed to rise. The atmosphere remained flat, the response polite, and his idea was launched without the essential acclaim or even the practical support it needed. As the magnificence of his dream faded, Pierre de Coubertin tasted the humbling bitterness of public failure.

○ ○ ○ ○ ○

As they discussed what had gone wrong that night, St. Clair discovered that the baron had obscured the depth of his disappointment in his own history of the event.

"In your memoir, you wrote that no one really understood precisely what you were proposing," St. Clair said.

"Well, that isn't altogether true. A handful of them did understand."

He was surprised at the contradiction. "Wait a minute," he said, pulling a copy of Coubertin's *Olympic Memoirs* from his pack. "Let me read what you wrote. 'Naturally I had foreseen every eventuality, except what actually happened. Opposition? Objections, irony? Or even indifference? Not at all. Everyone applauded, everyone approved, everyone wished me great success but no one had really understood. It was a period of total, absolute lack of comprehension that was about to start. And it was to last a long time.'"

"Yes, that's what I wrote, Jacques—and it may be half true. That's how I framed the story then, but the fact is that I made the critical mistake of hiding the true intent of the meeting until the very last minute. No one arrived that night expecting to hear a proposal to revive the Olympic Games, let alone join the campaign to find a host and help organize them. And there's a broader truth as well—the fact that we were unprepared to act if we had gained their acclamation."

"You weren't ready to move forward with the Games?"

"Well, maybe. But at that point, I didn't have the government fully on board, no support for including the Games in the Paris 1900 Exposition—and the lack of international support was very troublesome."

"So the dream died on that night."

"Not at all," the baron said emphatically. "The lessons were invaluable. That night, I finally learned what it would take to succeed."

○ ○ ○ ○ ○

In the fertile loam of failure, the seeds of success took root. And like the boxer knocked down, groggy for only seconds, Pierre was soon back on his feet, moving into the fray, his gloves raised, ready to swing again.

Marie was half right—the audience had been the problem. But Pierre had also learned that hiding his true ambitions could lead to devastating consequences. He decided he needed a more receptive international audience that would be prepared to act with force on his recommendations. And he also decided to make his intentions clearer and more broadly known. The next time he gathered an audience in the Sorbonne, they would know what they were there for. He decided to begin building his international support in the United States and England. The next world's fair—the 1893 Columbian Exposition—was opening in Chicago that next summer. He would gain the assignment from the Ministry of Public Instruction to attend as its official representative, and he would turn that assignment into a second tour of U.S. colleges and universities designed specifically to build support for the restoration of the Olympic Games.

THE WHITE CITY

I n early August, St. Clair finished his draft of Coubertin's second trip to the United States and felt as if he were building real momentum on the biography. He left the draft at Messerli's office for review, hoping his long treatment of Coubertin's visit to the Columbian Universal Exposition of 1893 and his interactions with the event's master builder would meet with the doctor's approval.

Up early and out for a run on his first morning in Chicago, Coubertin jogged north along Michigan Avenue, looking down into the broad gulch of train tracks that separated him from the great expanse of water to the east. The hot August air was dense with steam and smoke from the trains, their engines rumbling and steel wheels screeching as thousands of early-morning commuters arrived to take in the wonders of the Columbian Exposition and the White City. Like Pierre, many were arriving for extended stays in Chicago, and many more were making the connection to the ten rail lines that led directly to the exposition station in Jackson Park.

When he reached the Chicago River, he turned west, passing the Rush Street railroad bridge, crossing the river on the swing bridge at State Street, and admiring the ornamental ironwork on its piers. On the other side, he turned toward Lake Michigan, working his way through the cart-clogged madness of Streeterville, squeezed between the staid brick warehouses and the waterway, where cargo

424

steamships and sailboats were unloading their goods. Staying close to the riverbank, Coubertin marveled at the battalions of laborers swarming over the decks, docks, and wharves below, carrying farm produce and heavy crates on their backs, some hauling carts up the hills like horses in harness. In the congestion of vessels—many were roped together two or three deep against the wharves—the workmen were bearing their burdens across gangplanks between the ships, nothing slowing them down.

What a rough, robust city, he thought, turning north and weaving his way through the stately townhomes and mansions of the Gold Coast, eventually emerging on the seawall. Accosted by the cutting winds off Lake Michigan, he opened his stride and picked up the pace, not stopping until he arrived at Oak Street, where the coastline curved in and the pilings of two small rough piers enclosed a sandy beach. Coubertin stopped and let the sweat dry on his face, marveling once again at the immensity of this great inland ocean, looking for land across the horizon and knowing he wouldn't see it. It was as if someone had pulled the edge of the Atlantic coast halfway back across the continent.

A half hour later he was back at the Chicago Athletic Association in the sumptuous surroundings where he would stay for six weeks. Like the New York Athletic Club, the CAA was a sophisticated gentlemen's enclave with a luxurious hotel atop its eight floors. The club offered every form of exercise apparatus found in the finest gymnasiums. During his stay, he would swim, box, work the parallel bars and rings, lift weights, row on a contraption that mimicked the motions of a scull on water, cycle on a bike whose back wheel sat on two turning cylinders, and run on the indoor track, although he preferred the adventures of running through the streets.

Each morning as he stepped out onto Michigan Avenue for the thirty-minute carriage ride to the exposition, he made it a habit to check the size of the crowd gathered on the steps of the new Art Institute of Chicago, which sat alone like a forlorn ship on the edge of the railroad gulch. He knew the builders had raced against the clock to get it open on time for the fair and had barely made the deadline. The Beaux-Arts design seemed at first unfinished to Coubertin, familiar as he was with the opulence of the style found all over Paris, but as the days passed he began to see the façade as a successful modern interpretation that hinted at elegance rather than expressed it fully. The institute was not ready to present its art collection; instead, it was assigned as the major venue for all the congresses to be conducted during the fair—dozens of conferences that would examine everything from the depths of marine biology to the heights of high-rise architecture. The skyscrapers rising in cities across the country and continent were based on structural engineering concepts pioneered by Daniel Burnham in Chicago—the very man whose classical vision of the modern 'city beautiful' had been brought to life in this fair. Coubertin was hoping to meet him.

As much as the architecture intrigued him, however, Coubertin had come to the exposition for its congresses, particularly the Congress on Education, where he would present a paper on *The Sports Movement in France*. The Parliament of World Religions, an ecumenical conference due to start in September, had also sparked his interest because Monsignor Keane, whom Coubertin had met and admired on his first U.S. trip at the Catholic University of Washington, DC, was one of its leading conveners. He also intended to listen intently to a number of his friends at the Fourth Universal Congress for World Peace.

○ ○ ○ ○ ○

One of his first appointments—thanks to another letter from A.D. White—was with William Rainey Harper, the first president of the new University of Chicago, which had been founded only the year before in 1892. A few days before they were scheduled to meet, Coubertin was delighted to read that Harper was aggressively pursuing the development of the university's football team. According to a story in the *Tribune*, whose sports pages were dominated by the baseball exploits of the White Sox, Harper had engaged a highly regarded young coach, Amos Alonzo Stagg, to whip into shape "a football team that can tour the East and knock down every college we encounter."

Unusual, thought Coubertin, for a man of such academic prominence to allow himself that kind of boastfulness. Nonetheless, he enjoyed the sound of it. In the weeks ahead, he would hear a great deal of this kind of civic boosterism and come to recognize it as a habit of vernacular common to many Chicago leaders and working men. This city had a chip on its shoulder and it meant to find every means possible to prove its superiority to its East Coast counterparts, especially its archrival, New York City. While the exposition might have appeared to have larger aspirations—for instance, putting Chicago on par with Paris—the entire effort, he began to understand, was at heart motivated by a desire to show up New Damn York, as he heard it called over coffee, beer, wine, and stronger libations.

The carriage trundled around Washington Park, one of the beautiful southside parklands that had been taken over by the fair, and turned onto the Midway Plaisance—the long eastward extension of the exposition's temporary attractions. Harper's office was located in the university's new Cobb Lecture Hall, which faced the midway. As Coubertin stepped out to cross the open quadrangle and beheld the Gothic façade of the new building, he felt for a moment as if he were approaching a new Oxford University, for the architectural style echoed the capital of English education—less ornate, more utilitarian, but a tribute for certain. The midway itself was a temporal world full of extravagant buildings, exuberant exhibits, and titillating attractions. Coubertin gazed wistfully at the Ferris Wheel as he stepped inside to meet Harper.

The thirty-seven-year-old Harper had bulbous red cheeks that gave him a jolly round face, offset with a serious demeanor and piercing eyes enlarged by small wire-rimmed spectacles. Coubertin took in the high ceiling, oak-paneled office, and handsome stone fireplace as the president settled in behind his massive desk.

"White tells me you've written extensively about American collegiate sport," Harper said, tapping the letter in front of him.

Coubertin described his U.S. tour and the four-hundred-page assessment he had subsequently written.

"I'd like to see it," Harper said. "I take it you're here to attend the Congress on Education?"

Coubertin made a note to send a copy of his *Universités Transatlantiques* to Harper. "That's right. I'll be presenting a paper called 'The Sports Movement in France,' but I'll take in the whole exposition, of course, which is magnificent, and perhaps find a way to meet Mr. Burnham."

"Well, that's easy enough to do. I'll arrange the introduction. How long are you here?"

"Six weeks in Chicago, and three months elsewhere in the States, continuing my study of American sport."

"Then you must meet Alonzo Stagg as well. He's not only our football coach, he's a brilliant young man with a vision for sport. He's also coaching our baseball team, building a basketball team, and with my full support, planning for a regular national track and field meet on our grounds. And I suspect he's about your age—thirty-one?"

"Good guess. I'll be thirty-one in January."

Harper rose and invited Pierre to join him at the window to look out over the fantastical structures of the fair's grand midway. "This exposition, which, as you may know, we managed to build in three short years, is a signal to the world about Chicago's rightful place among the great cities."

"Indeed, it is. We put ten years into the development of the Paris exposition."

"And you set a high standard," Harper acknowledged, "which I humbly believe we have surpassed in several ways."

Coubertin accepted the assertion with a nod but no comment.

Returning to his desk, Harper continued. "My ambitions for the University of Chicago, sir, and for its sports program, are no less enterprising."

Coubertin opened his notebook again. Happy to maintain Harper's preferred protocol, he said, "If you wouldn't mind, President Harper, tell me about your full ambitions for sport—how you plan to use it to build the university's image and how you will balance its enthusiasms or check its excesses?"

"I'm glad you've brought up the challenges of managing student passions. I've given long thought to the role of sport in university life, and quite frankly, I'm not one to shy away from the rah-rah emotions. I want the Chicago Maroons charging onto the field with the full-throated backing of their classmates. Stagg and I have a theory—that the stronger the emotive roots of college life, the longer the devotion to the alma mater will last."

The interview went on for nearly an hour, filled mostly with Harper's oration on the virtues of sport for character building, the manly life, and social cohesion, echoing Coubertin's own Arnoldian philosophy and Theodore Roosevelt's vision of a sporting republic. Harper gradually moved beyond the campus into Chicago's broader sporting ambitions. "This city has the potential to become the American citadel of sport in the Midwest. Nearly thirty train lines merge here. We can draw athletes and spectators from the great expanse of the continent."

Coubertin closed his notebook and stood. "President Harper," he said, "I believe I have an international opportunity worthy of the great arena you have envisioned for Chicago."

"And what might that opportunity be?"

"The Olympic Games. A modern international festival of sport that attracts the greatest athletes in the world."

○ ○ ○ ○ ○

While his official business in Chicago involved attending the Congress on Education and delivering his paper, and while he was intent on compiling notes for another book on American education and promoting his vision of sport, Pierre loved all aspects of traveling, especially playing the tourist and discovering new things. The exhilaration of exploration resided in him like a character trait. New vistas and environments worthy of observation invariably produced an emotional response that seemed almost childlike to him, its effect as immediate and as pleasing as a fresh morning breeze on his face. He knew the feeling as well as he knew his moods and his attitudes. It was a gift rooted in his boyhood family trips and the walks with his father through Paris. He had learned a skill then that he had never forgotten—an ability to appreciate and absorb the power of new experiences and new visions. And so he took to the opportunities of the Chicago Columbian Exposition like an international *flâneur* of the first rank, a connoisseur of every street, corner, and cityscape visible. In his first week in Chicago, he spent nearly every day at the fair, arriving by every means available—carriage, train, ferry, and foot. He examined every building in scale and detail and took in nearly every exhibit and experience, matching his memories of Paris 1889 to the revelations of Chicago and finding both equally alluring.

It was the architecture that fascinated him most. Not just the exotic creations of the Egyptian Islamic world or the exuberance of the South Americans—Venezuela, Brazil, Colombia—or the elaborate Oriental rooflines of China and Japan, all of which drew his deep appreciation, but the differences and distinctions of the houses built to represent so many of the United States of America. The California House, done in the style of a Spanish mission, enthralled him, but he found the American colonial characteristics of the Pennsylvania House—with its Puritan white clapboard exterior and black louvered shutters—equally inspiring. He never thought he'd see again a building as voluminous as the Manufacturers' Hall of Paris 1889, but on the shores of Lake Michigan, a new palace of manufacturing and industry had exceeded its dimensions and taken the crown of enclosed space.

With eighty other people, all dressed as if they were attending a formal ceremony, he entered one of the glass-walled trolley cars of the Ferris Wheel, the world's newest engineering marvel, and rose again and again in perfect circles over the phantasmagorical creations of the exhibition, its chimeric atmosphere made even more otherworldly by the tranquil expanse of the great emerald lake serving as its backdrop. As the wheel carried their car up and over the zenith, the voices of men and women rose in notes of awe as they sought to express the wonder they were experiencing.

As Coubertin toured, he sought to summarize the value of this cosmopolitan expression of the diversity of human cultures and the glory of the human imagination. He felt it was impossible to walk through these precincts and not be affected by humanity's desire to find common ground. Amid the kaleidoscopic pluralism of national traditions mashed into this beautiful, whimsical utopian world, Coubertin realized that the language of form—the architecture, costumes, performances, rituals, and cultures on display—were as distinct as the dialects spoken by their denizens. The diversity of the world was worth celebrating, for it ennobled as much as it inspired.

The event itself produced a nearly inexpressible joy, a reaction Coubertin felt was universal, something that each participant experienced in their heart if not their soul—and that was a desire to share the moment, a palpable feeling that the privilege of this experience shouldn't be reserved for the few but should be broadened so that millions more could be inspired by its wonders and filled with its hope.

In the congresses and conferences he attended, the conversations were always animated by a common theme—the ideas being exchanged were alive with the belief that through the exposure of human differences, through the illumination of distinct ideas, a new pathway would be revealed, a transcendent route to a better world. Among all the things he saw and heard, nothing filled him with more hope than the Parliament of World Religions, especially the final scene of the masters of Christianity, Judaism, Islam, Buddhism, and Hinduism all standing together on stage in an ecumenical spirit of peace—all praying in their own languages of the soul, petitioning their gods to lift all mankind toward greater harmony and peace. As he left that day, he dreamed that sport would someday stand on this stage too, that sport would take its place among the great passions of man and offer its ideas for the development of a better world.

○ ○ ○ ○ ○

Burnham's physique put Coubertin immediately in mind of William Sloane. They were both tall, broad shouldered, and portly, but in a powerful way. Commanding, Coubertin thought, as he watched Burnham interact with a group of men around a wide table covered with plans of the exposition. In shirtsleeves under an open vest—exactly as Sloane had been attired the first time Coubertin saw him in Princeton—Burnham was pointing to different parts of the plans, dispatching the men one by one. His movements and the level of his voice conveyed urgency.

Burnham was not the commissioner of the exposition; he was its master builder. In its totality, the fair reflected his vision of an idealized urban capital, rooted in the classical, but futuristic in function. The White City, the most marvelous and magical monochromatic architecture Coubertin had ever beheld, had sprung from Burnham's imagination. He had recruited the finest architects in the United States to rush through this creation—and had given each their marching orders. Even the great Frederick Law Olmsted, who had designed the overall footprint, lagoons, and landscaping that surprised and delighted at every turn, worked under Burnham's creative sway.

The walls of the windowless room were covered with architectural drawings, colorful promotional posters, and an impressive lineup of finished paintings of each of the fourteen major buildings of the exposition. Coubertin took it all in. He was standing in the back of the room waiting for Burnham to finish when the big man approached him, buttoning his vest as he came forward.

After they had exchanged greetings, Burnham said, "You're from Paris, I understand." He placed a big hand on Coubertin's shoulder. "The most beautiful city in the world."

"Well, sir," Coubertin replied, "for sheer visual inspiration, I'm not sure mankind has ever seen anything to rival your White City."

"Thank you." Burnham guided him past his desk to a rectangle of couches and chairs. "I would say you're too kind but, at this point, that would be false modesty. I'm proud to say the exposition has lived up to our aesthetic expectations."

"I did a good deal of work on the 1889 Universal Exposition, assisting Jules Simon in evaluating the overall operations, so I know what it takes to produce the kind of environment you've created. I'm not offering idle flattery. It's clear to me there's genius at work here."

"Well, now I am genuinely humbled," Burnham said.

Coubertin studied his square face as an assistant arrived with a pot of tea and cakes. His black hair was parted high and swept across his forehead in a tight, low wave. The ridge of his prominent nose was broad and as straight as the steel beams in his buildings. His mustache matched Pierre's in width and depth, lighter than his hair, but his deep-set blue eyes, which burned with the intensity of his ambitions, were his true mark of distinction.

"Harper tells me you have some exciting plans for a new international event, to bring the Olympic Games back to life." Burnham lifted a hand to hold off two other men who had come into the room. "Give us ten minutes," he said, and they dutifully fell back, lingering around the worktable.

"Indeed I do, and I would like to discuss them with you." He decided to forgo the small talk given the pressure on Burnham's time. "But truth be told, I wanted to meet to hear your theories on public festivals, specifically how you arrived at the ideas for the spaces you created here. All of it—the midway, the lagoons, the waterways. I'm specifically interested in how you shaped the setting that produced the reaction you're getting from the public—that sense of awe people experience standing before the Grand Basin."

Burnham looked carefully at Coubertin for a moment before responding. "That's the heart of the matter, isn't it? This is a laboratory, Baron, an experiment in city planning—a large-scale test for a philosophy I'm developing about public spaces, how they're created, how they work, the effect they have on the citizenry."

"So you're using the temporary applications of the exposition to develop permanent plans for public spaces in Chicago?"

"Chicago, New York, Washington, DC. Anywhere and everywhere," Burnham said. "There are few borders to our ambitions. We're hoping that the ideas manifest here, which you can clearly see rooted in Classical Greece and Beaux-Arts France, become a movement. Not to be grandiose, but it's basically a new school of architecture we're calling 'The City Beautiful.' Think of it as a set of aesthetic standards, a sort of traveling palette for civic design."

"That's quite exciting." A commotion in the back of the room pulled Burnham's attention away momentarily. When he turned back, Coubertin put a request before him. "I wonder whether we might find a time to speak more broadly about this?"

"Of course, Baron. Created environments are my passion. I never tire of theoretical discussions—and I'm very interested in hearing about your Olympic plans as well. President Harper seemed to think Chicago would have an interest—"

He couldn't finish the thought. Three men were suddenly standing over them, one thrusting a newspaper in front of Burnham. "Sir, you told me to bring any negative stories to you immediately." Coubertin could see the photograph of a mass of people waiting in a long line winding around the edge of a building. The headline read, "Long Lines Turn Enchantment to Boredom."

Burnham's reaction was instantaneous. "Get me Paddy," he bellowed, standing. Coubertin also leaped up as the two assistants rushed from the room, yelling for Paddy. Burnham went to the worktable, where he threw down the newspaper. "Controlling the press is one of the most difficult parts of this job," he said. "Where were we?"

"I was wondering whether we might—"

"Yes, of course," Burnham said, pushing a hand through his hair. "Have you seen the view of the Grand Basin at night from the catwalk atop the Manufacturers' Building?"

"No, I haven't had that pleasure."

"Then let's have a working dinner Thursday night. I'm taking a ladies' auxiliary up there."

"It would be my pleasure."

"What is it, sir?" blustered a big Irishman who steamed into the room at the head of a group of assistants. His face was ruddy and red under a bowler hat, and he cast a curious glance at Coubertin.

"Have you seen this, Paddy?" Burnham smacked his hand down on the open newspaper.

Paddy leaned over for a second and popped right back up. "My God," the Irishman shouted, "it's a bloody betrayal, sir. That's Mickey O'Brien writing there." He put his finger on the man's name as if he were squashing a bug. "I bought the bastard a pint just two nights ago."

"Call him right now and get this straightened out. No negative stories. None!"

As Paddy and half the men in the room rushed off, Burnham turned back to Pierre. "My apologies, Baron, another appointment calls, but I'll see you Thursday night."

They shook hands and Burnham left with the two men who had been waiting for him. Coubertin was left standing at the worktable. He looked more closely at the newspaper that had triggered Burnham's ire. From the front-page headline— "Columbian Exposition 'America at Its Best,' Proclaims President Cleveland"—to its final daily ticket sales, the paper was full of nothing but praise. Why had that one small article set Burnham off? Coubertin guessed it was a theatrical overreaction to keep his team primed for problems.

As he left the room, a single phrase resounded in his head: "created environments." He was already envisioning the created environments Burnham might one day birth for a new worldwide festival of sport.

○ ○ ○ ○ ○

As twilight settled over Lake Michigan Thursday night, Coubertin moved through the crowds around the Grand Basin, arriving a little late at a side entrance to the Manufacturers' and Liberal Arts Building. Stepping inside, he spotted Burnham with a dozen women, all adorned in elegant dresses and broad hats, and half as many men in suits. They were standing at the foot of a zigzag stairway that climbed to the dizzying heights of the enormous steel shed.

"Ah, here's the baron now," Burnham said as Coubertin approached. Making the introductions to the Women's Auxiliary of the Police and Firemen's Ball, Burnham presented Coubertin as France's leading sports authority and a man of grand plans.

"Apologies that our elevator is out of commission at the moment," Burnham said, "but we can take our time climbing the stairs since the view is far more dramatic in the dark and the spotlights illuminate the scenery. Ladies, you may need to hold on to your hats if the wind is up—and please, everyone, stay close to the railing and be careful on the catwalk."

Emerging single file onto the linear metal grate that led to the observation platform, they were greeted by a cool zephyr rising from the dark expanse of Lake Michigan. Approaching the front railing and looking down on the Grand Basin, they were awestruck by the jewel-like illumination of the buildings, the light of a million bulbs outlining the classical façades that rose over the peristyle to the east and over the dome of the administration building to the west, all reflected in the shimmering waters of the basin, which glowed with a quavering image of the White City. Coubertin couldn't help but compare the site to the Ville-Lumière of Paris, and he had to admit this was far more elaborate—quite simply breathtaking. Suddenly a wave of symphonic music signaled the beginning of the water and light show, and fountains below spewed their foam ninety feet into the air. The fairgoers in the Court of Honor below signaled their approval with joyous shouts. Burnham directed his audience toward gigantic cylindrical searchlights mounted on tripods along the front of the building. On cue, men dressed like train conductors threw switches that emitted an electric buzz of carbon-arc lamps, sending shafts of blue, red, and white light flashing across the extravaganza. The men wielded the searchlights in a blazing sword fight of crossbeams that illuminated faces in the crowd. Coubertin wondered if they were blinded by the brightness.

At one point as the music rose, the lights converged on the great sculptural ship at the western end of the basin, drawing all eyes toward the figure of Columbus, the captain of destiny, standing on deck above his men as they labored to move the massive vessel toward the New World. Then the lights swept across the water, spotlighting, as the music crested, the goddess of fate—the golden Statue of the Republic—standing on the shores of the New World, scepter in one hand, globe in the other, beckoning Columbus as the future beckoned all explorers. That's what they're celebrating, thought Coubertin—the moment of discovery that opened the gates to the New World and produced everything on display in such abundance here. As the climactic moment passed, he noted they had struck the right thematic chord in this ceremony, bringing a static creation to life through the animation of water, light, and music. The show went on for the length of the symphony and ended with a booming fireworks display over the lake beyond the peristyle.

As his small delegation descended the stairs and the members of the women's auxiliary sought to outdo each other in their descriptions of the thrills the show had produced, Burnham took in the praise, laughing with pleasure beneath his fedora. Coubertin waited patiently as he bid each of his guests farewell, finally turning to him and wrapping an arm over his shoulders.

"I hope you're hungry," Burnham said, guiding Pierre toward the door. "We have a side of beef to consume."

"A side of beef?" Coubertin tried not to imagine a slab of meat fresh from the slaughterhouse laid across a table.

"If there's one thing we know how to do well here in Chicago, it's steak. I've taken the liberty of inviting President Harper to meet us at the California House."

They walked to the administration building, edging through the crowds along the basin with two of Burnham's close associates. As they jostled along, Coubertin had expected people to recognize Burnham, but none did. He had driven the creation of this extraordinary environment, and yet he was not a public figure. He had drawn millions to a single destination, and yet he went unrecognized. He was not a man of the people, but rather a servant of the city, maybe a captain of construction, and certainly a visionary architect, but obviously not someone looking to parlay his achievement into public adulation. At the administration building, Burnham went inside and gathered two more executives to join the dinner party.

Outside the California House, Burnham stopped to admire the mission style of the architecture, which he claimed was unique to the Spanish ranches of the West Coast. "The grand haciendas," he proclaimed, "sit like ships on waves over the rolling hills and valleys of our gold-rush state." And then like a football squad, Burnham and his men led Coubertin up the stairs and into a private dining room where Harper was waiting for them.

In total, eight men sat around the table, five of whom turned out to be members of Burnham's staff. For the first half hour, Coubertin and Harper, who were sitting at the end of the table, returned to their discussion on American collegiate sports while Burnham, with apologies, talked to his team about the priorities they'd face tomorrow.

Knowing not to interrupt Burnham, a steward introduced the featured wine to Harper, who asked Coubertin to do the tasting. It was a California cabernet sauvignon from the Beringer Brothers, according to the steward, grown by the Germans who had pioneered the vineyards of Napa Valley. To Coubertin's nose it was far too full of flavor, entirely too rich compared with the earthy, subtle French Bordeaux he preferred, but it was fresh and he nodded his approval, somewhat worried it might overwhelm the steak. However, that fear evaporated when the steaks arrived—twenty-eight-ounce bone-in ribeyes for everyone, crisply singed, covered with peppers and bloody rare to Burnham's orders.

Putting his international guest in the spotlight, Burnham led a conversation about the differences between the 1889 Paris Universal Exposition and the one at hand. Coubertin admitted the scale of Chicago far exceeded that of Paris but pointed out many of the similarities of the international houses and the emphasis he found in the Oriental entertainment, another version of Paris's Cairo Street on the midway. The regional differences were clear, with far more of a Latin American presence here. Burnham, with what Coubertin now recognized as characteristic modesty, heaped praise on Paris, acknowledging that no city in the world could rival the City of Light for its urban art and architecture, the balance and beauty of its boulevards, the majesty of its cathedrals, the allure of its public parks and gardens, and its mastery of artistic culture.

"It is the world capital of inspiration," he said. "Chicago aspires to become the Paris of the Prairies—but enough of comparisons. President Harper and I are intrigued by your notion of resurrecting the Olympic Games as an international festival of sport."

As the wine flowed and Coubertin spoke of his emergent vision of a modern Olympic Games, Burnham and Harper became more animated and more inquiring. Coubertin held their questions at bay while he described his plans for the Olympic Congress in Paris the following June, how he would gather the right assembly of international delegates to launch a modern Olympic Movement on a path of global expansion. He was reticent to promise them a Games in the United States too soon, for he believed it essential to establish the Olympics in Europe before leaping to the next continent. But their interest grew, and soon Burnham was questioning Coubertin about the stadiums, arenas, and facilities that would be required, about the housing, transport, public attractions, and conferences that might accompany the Games, and finally about the event schedule and the sports that would be included. Coubertin provided detailed answers, stimulated by the dialogue and the notion that he was in a room with men who knew how to produce spectacular events for the masses. When he began to describe his dream of teams arriving from Europe, Asia, Africa, and the Americas, Burnham could hardly contain himself.

"Clear these plates away, gentlemen," he said, standing and directing his men, "and get me that blue cloth from the sideboard." Coubertin and Harper also rose as Burnham spread the cloth along the length of the table. "Here's the shore of Lake Michigan," he said, pointing, "and here we are." He turned an empty water pitcher over and surrounded it with small glasses.

"That's the administration building," one of the men said.

"Exactly. Now, Baron, I want you to see that Chicago is a natural arena for the sports on your program. Let's start with rowing, which should be much closer to the center of the city." He laid three knives on the blue cloth to indicate the rowing lanes. "We'll put it right outside the train terminal, inside the jetties. It won't be a problem to clear the arena."

"Where would you put the main stadium for track and field? And I'm wondering whether the opening ceremony should be in the stadium itself, rather than at city hall."

"I'd build it at Washington Park," Burnham said, placing a bowl on the proper spot on the table, "and I'd put archery on the midway." He folded a napkin and created the footprint for the archery arena. "Start writing this down, Jacob. We're going to need a formal plan."

"I think we can anchor a lot of events at the university," said Harper. "What about football?"

"American football?" said Coubertin.

"Yes, of course. If we're hosting in Chicago, we must have football."

"I'm not certain you'll be able to raise any competitive international teams for such an indigenous sport. It's essential our competitive standards remain high. But rugby would be fine."

Sensing Harper's disappointment, Burnham said, "Don't worry, William. The Olympic stadium we build will become home to the University of Chicago's team after the Games."

As the wine flowed and the night rolled on, Burnham was a fountain of energy and ideas; he succeeded in placing a venue for every sport Coubertin named and found locations for accommodating more than five hundred international athletes. It was nearly midnight when they adjourned, with Coubertin promising that Chicago would be one of the first host cities on his agenda once the Games were resurrected. He left the California House knowing he had gained great allies in the heartland of America and had a host city waiting in the wings.

As he took a coach back up to the city and ruminated on the meeting, Coubertin was astonished at the effect the Olympic idea had had on Burnham's imagination—how quickly the idea had ignited the man's vision, animated his body, and moved him to dream of new venues for Chicago. The clip-clop of horseshoes and the rocking rhythm of the coach led Pierre into a reverie, wondering if there were men like Burnham in every city—architects, entrepreneurs, builders, industrialists, educators, mayors, and philanthropists—dreamers who would see the possibilities of harnessing the Olympic idea to reshape the cityscape and lead the development of a fresh civic agenda. He wondered whether every world capital held men who would take their turn in building new fields, arenas, and theaters of sport that could serve the ultimate goal of drawing the world's youth together for a festival of friendship and peace through sport. If he could find ten such men in world cities, his Olympic Games would have a stairway into the future, toward the pinnacle of worldwide sport, toward the success of his movement and the duration of his legacy. As the coach rolled onto the wide boulevard of Michigan Avenue, his imagination carried him to far-off capitals—to Paris first but then to London, Stockholm, Rome, Berlin, Budapest, and even beyond to Tokyo, Cairo, New Delhi, St. Petersburg, and Peking. If he could find ten men of imagination, ten dreamers who wanted greatness for their cities, his Olympic idea might be empowered to serve the cause of peace.

○ ○ ○ ○ ○

When Coubertin left Chicago for the West Coast—he had planned to see the whole country on this trip—he carried a sense of regret aboard the train with his baggage. Even though he wanted to cover the entire continent and to experience the romance of the West personally, even though he wanted to see San Francisco and California and travel through the Southwest, he felt he was leaving behind a chance at destiny. Harper and Burnham now occupied a new territory in his imagination, a blue-and-white landscape of Olympic possibilities. The vistas of the vast country and the charms of the new urban centers he saw were no match for the hold his new allies had on his thoughts and his plans. He could scarcely wait to get to Princeton and give Sloane a full report on Chicago and the men who would organize the first Olympic festival in North America. It seemed each passing day of his grand tour was another delay in the imminent work he believed he had been put on this earth to accomplish. After nearly two months and 7,000 miles he found himself back in Princeton, transferring his enthusiasm for his new American allies to Sloane.

61

THE FLYING WEDGE

s August baked Lausanne with a great deal of heat and humidity, St. Clair found himself growing impatient with the interview process. In the long, hot afternoons spent in the confines of Mon Repos, he began to feel the need to compress the story of Coubertin's American adventure. The fact that the baron had traveled across the full expanse of the continent was remarkable but had little impact on his Olympic plans.

"Let's get back to Princeton and the time you spent with Sloane," St. Clair said, abandoning Pierre's impressions of San Francisco and Stanford for the moment. "I'm assuming the two of you spent most of your time on plans for the Paris Olympic Congress."

Coubertin was making his own notes as he sat at his desk. He looked up. "Paris was a major focus, yes. But we were also intent on building support among America's current amateur sports leadership."

"The New York Athletic Club?"

"Yes, but we had problems in New York, which was surprising given my earlier meetings with Father Bill Curtis."

"Sullivan was the problem, wasn't he? Was it a personality conflict?"

"No, a conflict requires opposing forces. This was a personality problem, but it was all one-sided." St. Clair waited, wiping his forehead with the sleeve of his shirt. The heat didn't seem to bother the baron at all, but it appeared the memories did. "I don't think I ever met a more obstinate, manipulative, or ruthless man than James Sullivan," he said. "Maybe that's not fair. Paschal

Grousset probably had blood on his hands. Sullivan didn't kill anybody as far as I know, but he did engage in character assassination."

"By all accounts, he was a capable sports administrator. He certainly helped shape the American sports industry over the last forty years."

"Oh, he had talent, no doubt. He was a leader. Very forceful. Intimidating. Could stare down anyone. But he had no time for me—and he was a handful for Sloane for over two decades."

"Why? Weren't you offering him a chance to be on the ground floor of the U.S. Olympic team?"

"We were, but he was complex." Coubertin visibly wrestled with his thoughts. "He didn't trust anybody and he always wanted to be in control. American sports was a fertile but fractious field when Sullivan came up—and it was a fight for every inch of ground and every ounce of authority."

"Why didn't you ignore him?"

"We couldn't. He had become head of the AAU and the most powerful man in American amateur sport just as we were launching our Olympic revival. His endorsement would have meant the world to us, but he was too busy to meet. Sloane finally persuaded him to agree to a luncheon in New York City—at the University Club. It seemed like quite a coup because it was on Thanksgiving 1893, the same day Princeton was playing Yale, and Sloane wanted me to see the game."

○ ○ ○ ○ ○

As Coubertin entered Sloane's study, the big man finished a letter and rose from his desk, smiling. He said, "It's time for you to get a grip on our passion for American football, Pierre. We're going up to the Polo Grounds for the Princeton–Yale game on Thanksgiving."

"You won't be happy, will you, Will, until I'm completely indoctrinated into college football," Coubertin joked. "I thought we were going to spend the day eating turkey."

"Mary will forgive us. We're going to have lunch at the University Club with Sullivan and a good group of sports leaders to drum up some enthusiasm for our Olympic meeting in June."

"Sullivan's going to be there?" Coubertin was surprised—and relieved. He was planning to return to Paris in a week by way of London and desperately wanted the chance to expand his U.S. circle of support. Sullivan had been evasive, but Sloane had broken through.

○ ○ ○ ○ ○

The luncheon was officially being hosted by Sloane for Sullivan and the AAU, but when they arrived at the University Club, it was obvious Sullivan had gathered his troops in advance. When Coubertin and Sloane entered the room—where a long table was sumptuously set for twenty—groups of men in suits with drinks in their hands were already chatting amicably in the corners of the room.

Sloane caught Sullivan's attention and Coubertin smiled as the man approached for the introduction. Sullivan's face was sharply edged, the skin pulled tight around the cheekbones, the mustache trimmed to a slim shadow. He moved like an athlete, coming forward with assurance and standing close to Coubertin as they shook hands. Too close, causing Coubertin to look up awkwardly at the taller man.

Dispensing with the usual formalities, Sullivan said, "I trust the room suits you, sir," as if he were hosting, and then left no doubt that he was. Gesturing toward the end of the room, he added, "I'll seat you at the far end of the table, opposite me, and give you a chance to speak before the entrées are finished."

"That sounds like a fine plan to me, Mr. Sullivan." Coubertin glanced at Will, who offered no correction. "I greatly appreciate your taking the time to hear about our Olympic plans."

"The least we can do to promote competition between us," Sullivan said, his eyes darting around the room.

"The opportunities for international cooperation are just beginning. And I don't think there are two cities with a greater potential partnership than New York and Paris."

"I think Jim would have to agree with that point," Sloane interjected.

"Indeed, but we'll wait to hear what you're proposing." Sullivan offered no smile. "Now, if you'll excuse me, sir." He moved to the door to greet another arrival. His brusqueness was intentional, a signal to Pierre that the man had little interest in him or his mission.

Sloane turned to Coubertin. "Welcome to the AAU. Sullivan learned early that authority is 10 percent given and 90 percent taken. I suppose when he accepts an invitation to a luncheon, it becomes his event. Let's meet the rest of the crowd."

Approaching a circle of men near the fireplace at the end of the table, Sloane deliberately changed the tone, graciously introducing Coubertin as the leading proponent of physical education in France.

Pierre bowed slightly, melting the chill left by Sullivan. Just as introductions were completed, Sullivan called them to the table, and an hour later, as waiters were clearing the plates, he called Coubertin to offer his proposal.

Standing with his hands on the back of his chair, Pierre began with a general description of the work and the membership of the French Union of Sports

Societies—and the Paris Congress for the Olympic Games that the USFSA would be hosting in June.

"It is our intention to lift from the vaults of antiquity the greatest sports competition in the history of man. Gentlemen," he said, pausing to ensure they were all listening carefully, "we are going to resurrect the Olympic Games as the modern world's first major international sports competition, restoring them to their rightful role as the pinnacle of worldwide athleticism—the ultimate testing grounds for every generation of youth from every nation."

While he waited expectantly for a reaction, the men around the table cast glances at each other. Pierre imagined they were hesitating until they knew what Sullivan was thinking. Then he caught Sullivan's glare, a withering look full of resistance, exactly the opposite of what he had been hoping for—and so he pushed on, detailing the focus of the Olympic Congress, the current plans for the sports to be contested, his hopes for teams from twenty-five countries, the rules for eligibility, and a few broad strokes on how the first Games of the modern era would be staged in concert with the Paris Universal Exposition of 1900. He exaggerated the support of the French government for the concept.

"That sounds like a fine enterprise," Sullivan finally said, all the guests turning to look at him. "But what is it exactly, Baron, that you want from us?" His tone was filled with skepticism, but Coubertin responded as if this were the enthusiastic response he had been hoping for.

"I want you there, Mr. Sullivan," he said, putting his fists on the table. "Professor Sloane"—he nodded toward his chief ally—"will be leading the American delegation to the Paris Olympic Congress, but it is important that the full leadership of U.S. amateur and collegiate sport is well represented, and if word goes out that James Sullivan himself will be there, well, our success will be assured."

"That's very flattering, sir, but the Olympic Games are not yet on anyone's sports calendar—they're simply an idea at this point." Sullivan stood up and pulled his watch fob, glancing at the large timepiece. "An idea now scheduled to start, I believe you said, in seven years. Mr. Caspar, Mr. Kirby, and I have far more pressing matters at hand." Several men rose as if on cue.

"Well, Mr. Sullivan," Coubertin said, rounding the table to offer his hand to the man, "if you yourself are unable to join the U.S. Olympic Commission, perhaps you'll consult with Professor Sloane on an appropriate representative."

Sullivan shook Coubertin's hand, smiling dismissively. "Of course." He turned to the professor. "Will, I understand you're taking the baron up to Manhattan Field to watch Yale trounce Princeton today." A few laughs erupted.

"As a matter of fact, I am, but I think you'll be surprised by the strength of our team."

"I take it you haven't seen Yale in action yet this year. Perhaps we can continue the conversation at the game."

Within minutes, goodbyes were said and coats retrieved. Coubertin stood at the door, shaking hands with everyone, shielding his disappointment. It seemed they were all heading for the football game.

Out on Fifth Avenue, Sloane had a cab waiting. Although stores were closed for the holiday, the American passion for sport was evident on the sidewalks of the city. Groups of men in frock coats and hats strolled north, a few women wrapped tightly against the cold accompanying them. Knots of students with Yale and Princeton banners paraded about noisily.

"Manhattan Field," Sloane said to the coachman up on the box seat. "The new Polo Grounds."

The carriage jolted as they settled into cushioned seats and Coubertin spoke. "Was that as much of a disaster as I thought it was?"

"Sullivan is a street fighter," said Sloane. "I thought he would have seen the wisdom of signing up early to help build America's Olympic team, but he has other fish to fry. And if he gains control of collegiate sport through the AAU, well, he'll have a major role in any national Olympic effort anyway."

"What about Caspar Whitney? Could we approach him to join the delegation?"

"Whitney shares Sullivan's view and he's engaged in the AAU battle—writing his columns for *Harper's Weekly*."

Coubertin didn't fully understand the political struggle that Sullivan and Whitney were waging against the colleges, but he knew the stakes were high. "Well, if America sends only a delegation of one," Coubertin said, "at least we know we have the right man."

Sloane smiled and clasped Pierre's knee. "Don't worry, my friend. The divide between Sullivan and the universities may play to our advantage. We already have White, Eliot, and Gilman on our side—and you couldn't raise a finer crew. We'll be fine."

Coubertin looked out of the coach as they bounced north on Central Park West. All the way up to 155th Street, clusters of spectators, students, and fans were flowing along the sidewalks while coaches with colored streamers clopped along the streets.

As they exited the cab and joined the throng streaming toward Manhattan Field, Coubertin looked at the high palisades over the Harlem River, noting the cliffs were already packed with people—an irregular black line across the horizon formed by men in thick coats.

"I take it this game sold out," Coubertin said, pointing at the crowds.

"That's Coogan's Bluff up there—the public loves its free football grandstands.

But it's like watching a horserace run only on the backstretch."

Manhattan Field had been built originally as a baseball stadium for the New York Giants, but since 1890—when the Giants moved to the new Polo Grounds next door—the field had become a favored site for collegiate football clashes.

"If this were a true football stadium, this would be a bowl and we'd have grandstands in the outfield," Sloane said, leading Coubertin along the third-base side of the stands to join the stalwarts of Princeton.

Awed by the size of the crowd—twenty-five thousand filling the stadium and another twenty thousand packed along the shoulders of Coogan's Bluff— Coubertin marveled at this Thanksgiving Day festival of sport. They not only invent new sports here, he thought, they support them heart, wallet, and soul.

Under a deafening roar that fell only between possessions, Sloane tried to explain the formations and highlight the action, but for the most part Coubertin thought the game a slow, unrelenting grind. American football—as he witnessed it—looked more like a military competition than a sporting contest.

"That's the flying wedge," said Sloane as the Princeton men rushed into the Yale line like the point of an arrow, bodies clashing in clamorous struggle over a few feet of turf.

"Rugby is much more fluid—and apparently much less dangerous," Coubertin said as men with stretchers flew onto the field once again to carry off the wounded.

Princeton won the deadly match 6–0 for their first victory over the vaunted Yale Bulldogs in more than a decade. New York City filled with revelers post-game, and the campus of Princeton itself—90 miles to the south—erupted in a night of explosive and nearly uncontrollable celebration. The police had to protect the old town from the drunken student celebrants.

○ ○ ○ ○ ○

"So, you were trampled by Sullivan and then witnessed the flying wedge?" St. Clair said.

Coubertin laughed. "As it turned out, I witnessed the flying wedge at the height of its infamous glory. It produced so many devastating injuries, it was outlawed after only one more season."

"And Sullivan?"

"We never saw eye to eye. Although Sloane did finally manage to control him, essentially by empowering him to run the American Olympic Committee around 1916. Still, he remained an adversary throughout his career."

"I've read the letter Whitney wrote to the Brits right after the 1900 Paris Games."

"He proclaimed that neither I nor the IOC possessed any authority over the Olympic Games—and he proposed that Sullivan and the Brits form a new IOC to displace me. That battle lasted twenty-five years."

"It was a direct assault."

"Thank God the Brits disliked Sullivan more than I did. They ignored him, but that produced a terrible spirit of rivalry in the London events of 1908."

"What about Chicago? After you awarded them the 1904 Olympics, was Sullivan behind the plot that shifted the Games from Chicago to St. Louis?"

"I was never really sure of that. Perhaps, but it was President Roosevelt's decision. It may have been the men behind the World's Fair who persuaded him to pull the Games from Chicago."

"Harper and Burnham weren't happy, were they?"

"Harper offered to sue. He wanted to fight, but I asked him to stand down."

"So you left America with Sloane and a few college presidents backing you. What kind of support did Charles Herbert provide in London?"

"I went back to London in February for a meeting hosted by Sir John Astley at the London Sports Club, as I recall. They talked a good game, and Herbert agreed to represent England at the Sorbonne Congress. But most of the British athletic organizations were quite insular at the time, and they had no connections with the college and university sports structure. It wasn't hopeful. A little later Herbert introduced me to Lord Ampthill, who joined us at the Sorbonne and added his title to the original IOC membership."

62

THE SORBONNE

By the beginning of the second week in August, St. Clair felt as if he had crossed a crucial barrier in the writing of the biography. As he finished drafting the story of Coubertin's triumph at the Sorbonne, which he now recognized as the seminal moment in the baron's long life, he knew the end was in sight. He was certain, having come this far in six brief months, that he could finish the book. And yet he was troubled by the image of the old man slumped over, unconscious, in his skiff. St. Clair was haunted by the notion that Pierre might not have the stamina left to see it through. He pushed the thoughts aside and read once again Coubertin's story of that golden night so long ago.

As he ruminated on how to produce an event that would lift the spirits of his audience into Olympic fervor, Coubertin was once again aided by antiquity. In May of 1893—barely six months after his first failed proposal to resurrect the Olympic Games and just before his U.S. trip—a group of young French archaeologists, working on the outer wall of the ancient Athenian treasury in Delphi, discovered two extraordinary stone fragments engraved with curious letterforms. With the help of their Greek colleagues, they determined that the engravings were actually musical notations, one for instruments, the other for voice. They formed a hymn to Apollo. Dated within ten years of each other—from 138 to 128 BC—they had been written for the Pythian Games, an ancient festival of sport overshadowed by the far greater Olympic Games.

Fascinated by the idea that a two-thousand-year-old Greek hymn could be brought back to life, Coubertin followed the developments carefully—and he wasn't alone. By the time he returned from his American voyage, Henri Weil and Theodore Reinach, two enterprising French music scholars, had transcribed the hymn into a sheet music arrangement. It was first performed for King George I, Queen Olga, and the Greek royal court in March of 1894, creating a sensation that attracted the attention of France's greatest composer at the time, Gabriel Fauré.

With great fanfare, Fauré announced he planned a new arrangement, which was ready within a month. Set at an *andante moderato* tempo with a harp, a flute, two clarinets, and his own harmonium, Fauré's version was destined to be the most memorable of all. When it was performed at the École des Beaux-Arts in Paris in April, Coubertin was in the audience. His eyes filled with tears as the profound beauty of the ancient hymn stirred his soul.

Leaving the concert that night, Coubertin was certain that Fauré's new, evocative arrangement of the "Hymn to Apollo" could help transport his Olympic Congress back through time and bring history forward all at once, creating a mystical marriage of past and present that would lift his Sorbonne congregation into rapture.

When they met a week later in a small dressing room in the Paris Opéra, the silver-haired Fauré—a classicist at heart—was moved by the idea of the Olympic resurrection and immediately recognized the significance of the ancient music to the modern mission. With Coubertin looking on, he moved his hands through the air like a conductor as he thought it over before agreeing to repeat his performance two months later at the Olympic Congress, adding one startling innovation that surprised Pierre. For that evening at the Sorbonne, Fauré proposed a vocal performance by Madame Jeanne Remacle, the Parisian opera star who happened to be Fauré's favorite voice.

Coubertin almost danced away from the Fauré meeting, convinced the gods were with him this time, helping to orchestrate an event with the potential to bring the power of mythology to modern sport.

○ ○ ○ ○ ○

But the "Hymn to Apollo" wasn't the only godsend from Greece. Almost one month to the day before the opening night of the Olympic Congress, in May 1894, a letter arrived from Athens introducing Coubertin to Demetrius Vikelas, a Greek expat, literary scholar, and author living in Paris. The letter, sent by Timoleon Philemon, a former Athens mayor who had helped produce the last edition of the Zappas Olympic Games, indicated that Vikelas was expecting Coubertin's call and that he had already agreed to serve as the official Greek representative to the Sorbonne Olympic Congress.

Coubertin and Philemon had kept up an annual correspondence since the Greek had replied to Pierre's circular questionnaire on international sport in 1889. Although they had never met in person, Coubertin knew Philemon was respected in the royal courts because he also kept up a correspondence with King George to ensure the Greeks were fully conversant with his Olympic ambitions.

While the letter was signed by Philemon, Coubertin guessed it carried the blessing of King George—and he believed, therefore, that Vikelas was a royal appointment. This was good news because the Greeks were essential to Coubertin's plans, not only for the historic Olympic credibility but also for the imprimatur of one of Europe's most popular royal families. Both he and Sloane had been worried—since Philemon had repeatedly turned down his requests to travel to Paris—that they might end up convening the international Olympic meeting without Greek representation.

The next day, Coubertin put several documents and a notebook in a valise, donned his bowler, and called on Vikelas at his apartment on rue de Varenne, a convenient ten-minute walk from home. Vikelas warmly welcomed him into a commodious and stylish apartment. The bespectacled writer sported a neatly trimmed beard and curls combed across his forehead in the old style. He wore a gray morning coat and cravat that suggested he'd been expecting Pierre's visit. Smiling broadly, he led Pierre along a hallway covered with tapestries and paintings of ancient Greek scenes, crowded with sideboards and bookcases displaying busts of old philosophers and mementos from his homeland. Heavy drapes surrounded a series of doorways that revealed luxurious rooms and chambers on both sides of the corridor.

As Vikelas entered a wide parlor at the end of the hall, he opened his palms in a gesture of humility that immediately endeared him to Coubertin. "I must confess that I'm very excited about your Olympic mission, and I want to contribute whatever I can for my country, but I'm afraid I know very little about sport. As you can see, I'm no athlete."

Coubertin removed his bowler and pointed at the impressive wall of books behind Vikelas. "Well, sir, I'd say your knowledge of history and modern life, not to mention your Greek pedigree, makes you an ideal representative for your nation." Pointing his hat at Vikelas's slightly paunchy torso and smiling, he added, "And it won't take us long to get you into shape for your duties."

"Oh no you don't." Vikelas picked up a bell from his desk and shook it. "I'm honored that the king has called upon me—I am at your disposal. But don't expect to see me jogging through the Bois de Boulogne."

Coubertin laughed. "Fair enough." He was happy to have his suspicion confirmed that King George had appointed Vikelas. He now had two lines open to the royal family.

Vikelas cast him a serious look. "The very prospect of bringing back our great legacy and organizing the Olympic Games on a modern, international basis ignites in me a sense of pride I don't think I've ever felt before."

Coubertin glanced at the pen lying in an open notebook on the desk, half a page filled with a neat script, obviously interrupted by his arrival. "What you're feeling, Demetrius, is something more than pride. It's the call of destiny, the ancient spirit of the Games rising in your heart."

"I'm not sure it's an incarnation, as you suggest. But I'm deeply touched by the idea. I've been thinking about it ceaselessly since the moment I received the king's letter."

They paused as a servant brought tea into the room. Not wanting to lose the moment of conviction, Coubertin put his hand on Vikelas's shoulder and said, "Our shared mission will lead not only to the restoration of the Games, it will lead, in some ways, I believe, to the resurrection of the glory of Greece."

"I hope that's true," Vikelas said, gesturing at the tea table. "Shall we sit and discuss the prospects? I'm anxious to hear how I can help."

Placing his valise and bowler on the table, Coubertin took in the room, thinking it would be perfect for planning sessions with Sloane and Herbert when they arrived for the congress. It was a long, rectangular space with a set of French doors leading to a balcony overlooking the street and an alcove of windows on the other end of the room, where a mahogany dining table stood, ready for a party of ten. A fireplace with a carved mantel graced the wall across from the desk—with another famous ancient Greek scene framed above it.

Coubertin pointed to the work. "*The School of Athens*," he said as he sat.

"A rather poor imitation of Raphael's fresco, I'm afraid," Vikelas said. "But it's an ideal many of us are still striving to live up to."

"Your deep affection for your country is obvious. So what brought you to Paris, if I may ask, and when did you move here?"

"The allure of opportunity." Vikelas poured tea and offered Coubertin a cup. "My novels sold well here when I started writing in French, and I took this apartment about five years ago."

After exchanging personal details and discovering immediate affinities in their love of literature, art, and culture, they turned their attention to the work at hand. Coubertin provided a brief rendition of his Olympic journey as Vikelas took notes— from the German archaeology of his boyhood to the first failed proposal at the Sorbonne eighteen months earlier up to the significant support he had secured through Sloane during his second trip to the United States and in England with Herbert.

"You'll meet Will and Charles when they arrive in about two weeks, and we'll finalize the planning for the congress together." Pierre handed Vikelas the official ten point-agenda for the opening session. "This is the latest invitation with a full agenda," he said. "The first version of this went out in January to more than two hundred sports leaders from the United States to New Zealand. I sent this edition in March. It's more emphatic about our purpose: we are meeting to restore the Olympic Games."

Vikelas skimmed the document. "Hmm. It seems to put more of an emphasis on defining amateurism. Only the last three points—out of ten—concern the Olympic Games."

"It's a complex issue, but let me give you a shorthand education." Coubertin provided Vikelas with a brief overview of the historical problems of amateurism, going so far as to call it class warfare—and then branched into his philosophy of Olympism. Given Vikelas's background, he positioned it as a new form of Hellenism, marrying sport and peace in the modern world as it was in the ancient world.

Vikelas looked excited by the prospects. "It is the Greek Olympic ideal," he said, "the Ancient Truce of the Gods. Peace through sport." He opened his notebook. "It's a far greater mission than I thought—far more challenging, but even more inspiring."

Coubertin was thrilled that his new ally was an intellectual who embraced the ideas behind the event as much as the event itself. "We're committed to developing a republican form of the Olympic Games, to be as inclusive as possible, to knock down the walls that keep people out and expand the circles that allow them in."

"You're saying the Olympics will be a force for democracy, and that's the greatest of all the gifts the Greeks gave our world."

"Absolutely, in every way. The ethic of our movement will be sport for all. Talent will be the only admission to entry."

"I want to know three things," Vikelas said. "First, what kind of response have you had to the invitation? Who might attend? Second, how will the congress actually perform its work—what will the mechanics be? And third, where will the first modern Olympic Games be held—and when?"

Coubertin was inspired by the direction of the questions. He felt he had just gained a surprisingly insightful partner in his effort to launch the Games. Three hours passed as he gave Vikelas a full overview of the current state of his plans. Describing the positive and negative responses to his invitation, he said he was expecting representatives from more than a dozen countries. Although the

Belgians had denounced his efforts, claiming international standards would weaken sport, and the French Gymnastics Society threatened to withdraw if the Germans participated, he explained how he had managed to build sufficient momentum to ensure the Sorbonne would be filled on opening night. Georges de Saint-Clair, his partner in the USFSA, would lead the effort to organize sports demonstrations and several public events across the seven days of the congress, and Marie Rothan, his fiancée, would help plan the banquets, dinners, and receptions on the schedule. As Coubertin reviewed the list of official delegates, he stressed the broad participation of peace advocates. He wrapped up by saying, "You're going to meet some interesting people in this campaign, Demetri." Already, he felt comfortable dropping the Greek's formal title and full name.

In the second hour, they moved to the dining table, doffed their jackets, and worked through lunch. To answer Vikelas's second question, Coubertin outlined his plans—all developed in concert with Sloane—to form two committees to undertake the work of the congress. The Committee on Amateurism, which would be chaired by Sloane, would again wrestle through the difficult questions of eligibility and general participation. The Committee for the Olympic Games, whose chairmanship would fall to Coubertin if necessary, would address all the issues relevant to resurrecting the Games and would announce the name of the first host city and the date of the first modern Olympic Games.

"So Sloane will shoulder the heavier burden," Vikelas said, lifting a glass of Chablis.

"Sloane is a natural leader and a gifted administrator. He'll be more than a match for the controversies his committee will face. It's more a matter of management than vision. Vision is what I require for the leadership of the second committee."

"What about Charles Herbert, your British colleague?"

"No, I need Herbert to act as a floor manager. He's built a pretty good sports network across England, apart from a gap with the universities. He's forceful in person, has command of several languages, understands publicity, and is astute in the use of the media. I see him as what the parliamentarians would call a whip on the inside, and he can help me with the press on the outside. He'll have to have a certain amount of freedom since Sloane may need him to help build consensus on his committee. I have several other candidates in mind for the Games Committee." What he had in mind was Vikelas himself, but he didn't want to scare him off. He thought it would send the right signal back to Athens to have a Greek chairing the most important decisions the congress would make. While he briefed Vikelas as fully as necessary, for the moment he kept a few major points of strategy off the table.

"And to address your last question," he said, "my plan is that the first Games will be held right here in Paris." He noted a slight look of disappointment in Vikelas's expression. "In 1900—six years hence—they'll be part of the World Exposition. Georges de Saint-Clair and I have already secured the support of President Carnot and a few other government figures."

"Have you discussed it with Commissioner Picard?"

Suddenly Coubertin wondered if Vikelas knew more than he seemed to. Alfred Picard, who was running the development of the 1900 World's Fair with an iron fist, was no fan of Coubertin's. "No, we have not yet discussed it with Picard. In fact, he's a bit of a challenge for us. As we understand it, he's not enthusiastic about sports. But President Carnot assures us he will bring Picard into line."

"I feared as much. I was at a dinner party some weeks ago where Picard held forth on his plans. He was adamant that he wouldn't have any—what was his term?—sideshows to distract him from his vision."

"But he wasn't referring to sport as a sideshow, was he?" Pierre felt alarmed.

"I'm afraid that was precisely his point. He was responding to a question about international sports. I paid little attention, but I remembered it with some concern when the king's letter arrived."

Despite the daunting prospects of Picard's resistance to the inaugural Olympics in Paris, Coubertin left the meeting with Vikelas that afternoon believing his cause had just vaulted over a high bar. If Paris was going to be a problem, perhaps the Greeks were the solution—and Vikelas might just be the messenger he needed, a Nike to herald the rebirth of the modern Olympics from its ancient cradle.

$$\circ\ \circ\ \circ\ \circ\ \circ$$

As he worked nearly nonstop on the event preparations for the next two weeks, Coubertin drew the strings of his various networks tightly together, aligning his allies in sports, politics, education, culture, and peace with his aristocratic friends and organizing assistants. He met every few days with Georges de Saint-Clair and members of the USFSA to discuss the sports events to be staged during the congress. His *coup de gras* would be a run around the banks of the Bois de Boulogne lake at night, illuminated by a long line of torches that he had conceived as a magical expression of the theater of sport, runners moving in and out of the shadows, their images reflected back to the spectators in the shimmering waters. He went with Marie to the Jardin d'Acclimatation to review the details of the banquet planned for the closing evening, June 23. With Jules Simon at his side, he met twice with the rector of the Sorbonne, Octave Gréard, to ensure the opening ceremony would be flawless. Arthur and Bertha von Suttner were fully engaged in ascertaining that the leaders of the peace movement would be present at the opening of the congress. With tireless devotion, Coubertin recruited Baron de Courcel, France's ambassador to Germany, to give the opening keynote address, and Jean Aicard to present an inspiring ode to sport. With Fauré and Remacle delivering the "Hymn to Apollo," he was confident the evening would reach a high note, and, if his dreams reached fruition, the audience would respond in acclamation to his proposal.

The frequency of his correspondence with international guests increased in the closing months. He anticipated having representatives from more than forty sporting organizations from a dozen countries. His list of honorary delegates had grown to nearly seventy names—half of them connected to the peace movement. A further array of aristocrats—counts, dukes, and barons from across Europe— had expressed interest, and Père Henri Didon had drawn a large contingent of Catholics and some public school coaches to commit to dress for the occasion. The USFSA, with its seven thousand members, would ensure that the Sorbonne had at least two thousand people in the room by the early evening of June 16th.

Sloane and Herbert arrived one week before the congress. They engaged in a series of daily meetings at Vikelas's apartment, their afternoons filled with feverish details of planning as associates came from across the city to deliver their reports and receive final instructions.

○ ○ ○ ○ ○

Two days before the congress opened, at the last preparatory meeting in Vikelas's apartment, Sloane and Coubertin stepped out on the balcony overlooking rue de Varenne to take in the sunlight. In shirtsleeves, they had just finished discussing— for the fifth time—the agenda for the opening night. Coubertin had again stressed the importance of creating the right atmosphere in the Grand Amphithéâtre, emphasizing how Chavannes's new mural—already a cultural classic in France— would awe the arriving crowd and set the right tone before a word was uttered.

His elbows on the iron rail, Sloane said, "You know, Pierre, I haven't yet had the opportunity to see Chavannes's mural. I missed it when it was installed in 1889, and I never got around to seeing it on the last two trips. And I've heard more than once that the symbolism deserves a close inspection."

"It's a wonderful work," Coubertin said. "It covers the entire wall behind the dais, giving everyone in the auditorium a sense that they're part of a long tradition that places the humanities, sciences, and the law at the heights of human thought."

"So I've heard. I'm going to go over tonight to have a good look at it—while the amphitheater is empty—perhaps take a few notes."

Pierre smiled. "Excellent idea. I'll meet you there at seven, and I'll be happy to explain anything you don't understand."

"Why, thank you." Sloane swung his arm around Pierre's shoulders in an exaggerated fashion and pulled him in. "I'll be eternally grateful for your guidance."

○ ○ ○ ○ ○

Sloane was waiting in front of the great arched niche that held a marble statue of Homer as Coubertin crossed the Sorbonne's long vestibule. They stood together in silence for a moment, contemplating the posture of the poet, seated on a pedestal above a balustrade, a lyre nestled on his left thigh. Homer's right arm stretched into the air—a gesture of emphasis or the sweeping end of a strumming motion.

"I never tire of looking at old Homer," Sloane said. "It's remarkable that two thousand years later, we're still paying homage to the songs he sang."

"His poetry emerged in the same centuries as the Olympic Games," Coubertin said.

"Literature destined to endure. And sport destined to be resurrected."

"Homer's presence here is something of a consecration for us."

"Indeed," Sloane said. He placed his hand on Coubertin's back as they climbed the marble steps. "Consecration seeps from the walls of this magnificent cathedral of learning. I'm always awestruck when I'm here."

They entered the Grand Amphithéâtre, climbed past twenty-five rows, and turned down the aisle to sit in the center of the room, facing the large mural covering the wall behind the stage where they would be seated two nights hence. After a few minutes of silence, they discussed Chavannes's allegorical composition, which postured France and the Sorbonne as the font of knowledge—sages, muses, teachers, and students in every discipline of learning spread across the canvas.

"It's nothing less than a depiction of the history of education," Sloane said. "The young and old both drinking from the river of knowledge. And every form of study is represented—literature, art, science, medicine, math—each drawing from their own muses."

"Yes, every field of knowledge provides its own inspiration to the mind of man. Note that small temple in the middle—it's the old, original Sorbonne."

"The Greeks might give you an argument about where advanced education began, but I'm not unsympathetic to the artist's intentions."

"This is painting as patriotism. That's why we call Chavannes 'the Painter for France.'"

"Well, it is a masterpiece—but he forgot to include a sport or two."

Coubertin laughed. "I'll speak to him about a revision once we've used his enchantments for our Olympic mission."

They spent a further hour on the stage going through the program, Coubertin acting out each part and gaining Sloane's affirmation that the plan was perfect. They left confident that destiny was at the door.

○ ○ ○ ○ ○

In the early evening of the Golden Night, the name Coubertin had given it, he and Sloane greeted the honorary delegates as they arrived in the reception room across from the Grand Amphithéâtre—men in tuxedos, women in gowns, their jewelry glistening in the chandeliers' light. As the room filled, a circle formed around the Grand Duke Vladimir of Russia and Baron Christian Eduard von Rauffenstein of Germany, each sporting enough medals on their chests to form breastplates, each offering their observations on a new age of international sport. The von Suttners, Jules Simon, and Fredrik Bajer from Denmark had formed another circle, discussing the prospects of friendly sport competition as an avenue of peace, with Baron Rochefoucauld and his son, the rugby-playing banker, lifting their champagne glasses in agreement. The grand stairways just outside the doors were already filled with people streaming into the auditorium and continuing up the stairs to fill the seats in the galleries.

Taking Sloane by the arm, Coubertin left the greeting line and moved swiftly through the crowd, politely declining numerous requests to stop and chat. When they reached the arched windows that fronted the Sorbonne, Coubertin said, "Just what I was hoping for. Look, Will, the carriages are backed up well around the corner." On rue des Écoles below, a line of horse-drawn coaches of every make, model, and size stretched down the street and curved out of sight on boulevard Saint-Michel while a loose procession of couples and groups made their way along the streets and up the stairs.

"They're lining up to make history. Your Olympic Movement will soon be a reality."

"*Our* Olympic Movement, Will," Coubertin said, taking two glasses from a waiter and acknowledging Sloane's support with a toast. "If I didn't have your friendship, the Olympic Games would still be buried in an ancient vault."

Sloane bowed his head slightly. "Thank you. You're always too gracious, but it is one of your better qualities." Pulling the fob of his watch, he checked the time. "We've got another half hour to mix." He joined Jiří Guth-Jarkovsky and a small group.

Meanwhile, Coubertin spotted Vikelas coming toward him across the room. "A message from Athens," Vikelas whispered. "The king believes the first Olympics belong in Greece."

The news sent a wave of pleasure through Coubertin. His stratagem had worked, masterfully, he thought, since no one but Sloane knew about it. He stepped back and held his glass up to Vikelas, hoping his expression conveyed his full approval of the idea. "Well, Monsieur Chairman, that should help your committee complete its work." Two days earlier, Vikelas had agreed to lead the Committee for the Olympic Games.

Within minutes, Coubertin had taken his seat on the dais in the middle of his performers and key allies. The Grand Amphithéâtre brimmed with passion, the air seeming to crackle with electricity, and a murmur of anticipation filled the room. His audience was ready. Stepping to the podium, the trifling anxiety he had felt upon entering the room melted away.

"Ladies and gentlemen," he began, "we are gathered at this historic congress to recognize and elevate the role of sport in international relations. Tonight, with your approval, we will give birth to a modern movement that will spread from Paris to the corners of the world, soaring on the wings of man's passion for sport. It will unite humanity as nothing before through a modern incarnation of the ancient Olympic Games."

The audience sent forth an immediate burst of applause. Coubertin, his eyes suddenly watery in gratitude, waited until the din settled before going through the formalities of protocol, introducing everyone on stage and a few peace luminaries in the front row. He ended the introductions with the first speaker of the night. "And now, I have the pleasure of inviting to the podium France's distinguished former ambassador to Berlin, and just this year, our new ambassador to London, the distinguished Baron Alphonse Chodron de Courcel, who will offer us a diplomat's perspective on the potential power of sport to foster greater amicability in the international arena."

As Courcel began his speech, Coubertin returned to his chair between Simon and Sloane. The ambassador was brief and formal and delivered the requisite notes on the necessity of recognizing and harnessing the growing role of sport in world affairs. Back at the podium, Coubertin saw the fire in the eyes of his friend, Jean Aicard, who gazed back like a horse in the gate, ready to run. Coubertin knew Aicard would break through the tone of formality that Courcel had imposed.

As soon as he was introduced, Aicard jumped from his chair and ran to the edge of the dais, looking wildly at the crowd, casting his piercing gaze back and forth, left and right, until he had seized their full attention. He willed the room to absorb his energy, his verve, his charisma. It was the kind of animated performance Coubertin had hoped for—and expected. Aicard's voice boomed as he declaimed his poetry, rapidly, then slowly, modulating his tone line by line to fascinate and seduce.

And what of our muscles, our bodies, our physical lives,
And what of our bones, our hearts, the blood in our veins
The air we breathe that makes us all one
We are one—one and the same
And there is a world in each of us
Shall we lift that world into a new age
Shall we challenge ourselves to be stronger
Shall we be the heralds of a new era
Indeed, we shall be
Let us create then, a new republic of muscles
A new world of sport to which everyone belongs
A new country of all countries
A fresh parade with every flag
Every costume, every culture
Let us bring back the lost world of humanity
The gift of the Greeks
The tales spun by Homer
The labors of Hercules
The arena of heroes
Let us make Olympia today what it was once
The shining star that drew everyone together in peace
A place in timeless time
The holy ground of ritual
Where athletes writers philosophers artists and pilgrims
Joined in the celebration of agon
The contest
Where men subdue men
Not for conquest, not for war
But for glory and for wonder
To the amazement of one and all
We are one—one and the same
Let us bring back what has been lost
Let us find what is good between us
Let us compete for each other
Let us find peace in competition
Let us resurrect the Olympic Games

As spontaneous applause erupted and Aicard bowed from the waist with a dramatic swoop of his great pompadour, Coubertin returned to the podium.

Signaling to Gabriel Fauré to be ready, he waited until the noise faded, then said, "Two thousand years ago, the spirit of sport rose in a hymn to Apollo that our own French archaeologists uncovered last year. The great maestro, Gabriel Fauré, and our cherished opera star, Madame Jeanne Remacle, will now reach back across the centuries and bring that music to you—just as you will help us bring the Olympic Games back to life."

The orchestra began to play, and the sound of the ancient rhythms produced a tactile shift in the room, as if it wasn't music emanating from the instruments but a wave of history, an incarnation of the living past. Then Madame Remacle began the angelic procession of notes that carried the weight of the ages up into the galleries.

The room stirred, emotions flared, and the air filled with electric anticipation as if a spark might suddenly ignite. Pierre knew the feeling was evanescent, ephemeral, momentary, and yet he could see the music was transporting them, lifting them all into a rarified realm. He could feel the visceral atmosphere, and he saw that Sloane felt it too, his eyes closed, his body swaying. He looked from Simon, breathing deeply, to Bertha in the front row, her mouth open in awe, nearly swooning. Arthur, Passy, Pratt—each was mesmerized. He looked from face to face, his eyes sweeping across the auditorium and up into the galleries—everyone enraptured, seized by the unknown, the unexpected, the inexplicable, the reaction of the human soul to sounds sent by ancestors from a classical age, a message about the eternal yet transient lives we live.

The sound grew in intensity, its elemental cadence creating the profound sensation of an eternal march forward, a movement of chords in an inevitable progression, every soul in the room carried toward a threshold of expectation, bound to one another by an experience of music and voice as ancient as the bones and blood of their being. At its climax, the crowd was fully enthralled—and as the final notes softened and released them from the music's spell, they applauded again in a collective accolade of joy, affirmation, and deep appreciation.

Coubertin moved to the podium again and raised his hands to quell the murmur.

"The gods have spoken," he began. "For two thousand years, that hymn went unheard, hidden from our hearts and minds. But now its voice is restored to us. We have heard its message—and we are richer for it. We have been moved by the ancients and called together to take up their legacy—a legacy whose power we can deny no longer. Our modern world has taken up the clarion call of its greatest gift—democracy—and now we must take up its greatest celebration—the Olympic Games. Each of us here tonight—we who understand so fully the power of modern sport—must do our part in the resurrection of an institution that once found the power to bring peace in a time of war. Our modern world—so divided and so threatened—needs the power of sport to unite us, to foster friendships, to serve the modern cause of peace.

"Through the modern Olympic Games, we will bring the world together in friendship every four years. Every four years, the Olympic Games will call us to a new world capital where we will celebrate the triumphs of the best young athletes from every nation, all competing by the same set of rules, all upholding an oath to honesty and integrity for the honor of their countries and the glory of sport.

"I call upon you now to fulfill the destiny that guided you here tonight—to this moment of history—to be rebels and pioneers and the first true believers of the revelation that sport can serve society and unite our world for the greater good. Please signal now your approval of our proposal to restore the Olympic Games in modern form so we can begin our work in earnest."

He was ready to go on, but the acclamation was deafening, two thousand men and women rising to their feet, fully engaged in the idea that they were chosen for this moment, that they were making history—and at that instant, the Olympic Games were reborn.

○ ○ ○ ○ ○

The week rolled on, seven days of events, banquets, and sports demonstrations fueled by the certainty that the Olympic Games were meant to be resurrected—that history had called these delegates together as if Zeus himself had summoned them. The committees did their work. Vikelas became a modern Nike, sending and receiving telegrams to and from Athens, conferring on the proceedings the full blessings and support of King George and the royal family, working with Philemon to orchestrate the strategy that Coubertin had developed. On the night the location of the first Olympic Games were announced, the acclaim rose yet again. There was a certainty of the rightness of the decision to stage the first Games two years hence in Athens in 1896, with the second Games planned for Paris in 1900. Rules were agreed upon, and the new International Olympic Committee was charged with carrying forth its mission with haste and supreme authority. In all, seventy-eight official delegates—thirty-five of whom were peace activists in one way or another—representing forty-nine societies from eleven countries, approved the work of the congress.

On the final night of the congress, June 23, Coubertin hosted an elaborate banquet in the Jardin d'Acclimatation in the Bois de Boulogne. A procession of torchbearers illuminated the night as the guests arrived. The week had been the triumph that Coubertin had planned for. He had succeeded in convincing the leaders of sport and an international, influential audience that the Olympic Games belonged at the pinnacle of worldwide rituals in the modern era. His audacity was such that on June 15, the day before the congress had even started, before his assembly affirmed his vision, he had placed an article in *Revue de Paris* announcing the reestablishment of the Olympic Games.

The time had now come to summarize for his guests what they had achieved together. In the candlelight, he thanked them with a moving speech that ended in a toast. "Hellenism has returned. Classicism lives. And we are responsible. In this year of 1894 and in this city of Paris, we were able to bring together the representatives of international athletics for the restoration of a two-thousand-year-old idea, which today as in the ancient past still quickens the human heart. And so with all of you, with the deepest sense of gratitude, I lift my glass to the Olympic idea, which has traversed the mists of the ages like an all-powerful ray of sunlight and returned to illumine the threshold of the twentieth century with a dream of joyous hope."

As he sat down amid a round of applause, a sense of completeness filling his being, Marie clutched his hand and looked into his face with an expression full of love and admiration. It was a sweet moment for him. And when he looked across several tables, he saw that Sloane was smiling broadly at him, nodding in approval, conveying the pride he surely felt at that moment in their partnership. Ignoring the excited chatter around them, the two men held their stare for a moment of private recognition, a satisfying acknowledgment from the great professor that his faith had been rewarded, that the work they had done together had produced the results they had both dreamed of.

Then Sloane stood and created a sharp clinking sound, tapping his knife on the side of his champagne glass. The din of conversation stopped as everyone looked up at him, standing in the full eminence of his reputation, his tuxedo open, revealing the girth held back by his white waistcoat. He raised his glass and said, "We are fortunate, ladies and gentlemen, to have among us a man of international vision, who rose like a Napoleon of sport ready to conquer—not with an army, but with an idea. The very idea we are celebrating here tonight—that sport could and should play a vital role in building a better society and amity among nations."

Sloane carried on in high praise for some minutes in flawless French and concluded by drawing the crowd to its feet, as he said, "Ladies and gentlemen, please join me in lifting your glasses in a toast to an inimitable son of France, an education reformer who must now be counted among the world's leading sports entrepreneurs, the Baron Pierre Frédy de Coubertin. May his ideas—and his modern Olympic Games—become our cause and our legacy."

○ ○ ○ ○ ○

Over the next few days, Coubertin, Sloane, Herbert, and Vikelas worked tirelessly in the Greek's apartment to summarize the decisions of the congress and establish the bylaws, principles, practices, and procedures that would guide the work of the IOC and its organizing committees. It was Coubertin's idea to have the presidency of the IOC rotate every four years with the Games—and so, as part of the honor of naming Athens the inaugural host city, Vikelas agreed to serve as the first president of the IOC. Coubertin was named its secretary general. When the time came to discuss the membership of the IOC, Coubertin produced a list of those he wanted appointed—and that list was approved unanimously without discussion.

To establish an effective range of geographic representation, Coubertin had named thirteen members, six of whom had been present at the congress, plus seven more who had also agreed to carry the message of Olympism into their countries and form national Olympic committees. Vikelas would represent the IOC in Greece; Coubertin and Ernest Callot, who would also serve as treasurer, would be members in France; Sloane would serve in the United States; Herbert and Lord Ampthill in Great Britain; General Viktor Balck in Sweden; Ferenc Kemény in Hungary; Jiří Guth-Jarkovsky in Bohemia; Alexei de Boutowsky in Russia; Mario Lucchesi Palli in Italy; José Zubiaur in Argentina; and finally, Leonard A. Cuff in New Zealand.

Coubertin drafted the first Olympic Charter and Sloane contributed statements of purpose and membership. Within a few days, the fledging IOC was defined and operating around the vortex of its French founder. And in Athens, the first Olympic Games of the modern era were already animating a heated public discussion and political debate.

63

RESURRECTION REDUX

A s the heat of mid-August baked Lausanne and a humid pall hung in the air, St. Clair was intent on gaining a fresh take from Coubertin on the story of Athens, beginning with the tumultuous organizing period that preceded the Games. They were both in shirtsleeves, seated in their usual positions in Mon Repos, the windows open as if begging for a breeze that wouldn't stir. St. Clair wrote swiftly to keep up with Coubertin's long response to a question about what happened in the immediate aftermath of the Sorbonne Congress.

"Once we had raised the Olympics from the dead and the Greeks agreed to host the Games, I knew the organizing work would be well in hand in a month or two, and I thought I could attend to a few other things without worry about the effort now under way. I had seen the fire in Vikelas's eyes, and I knew he believed he had been chosen for a mission to restore the glories of Greece. We had a final telegram from Crown Prince Constantine on behalf of King George, indicating their full patronage, and Vikelas left for Athens almost immediately. He was returning home in triumph, knowing a hero's welcome awaited him—at least in some quarters. At the time, my heart was full of gratitude and I wanted to give my full energies to two things I'd been neglecting—my love for Marie and my love for France.

"Within a week, I had drafted the first set of letters to all sporting leaders of the day, informing them of the resurrection of the Games and asking them to prepare their national Olympic teams. I also set up a series of meetings through the USFSA to make advances in the standardization of a set of international rules for each sport and to draw up the competition schedule for each sport. I knew I could accomplish all this work—and stay in touch with Vikelas and Athens— while giving rein to my two other passions. I cleared the rest of my schedule so I could concentrate on writing the book I had long planned—*The Evolution of France under the Third Republic.* While sport was the centerpiece of my work, I felt I had enjoyed a privileged position in the halls of power in the critical years of France's re-emergence as a Republic, and I owed my country nothing less than a full account of the dynamics that changed the nation. And more importantly, I planned my formal proposal of marriage to Marie.

"For two months, everything seemed to flow in a high tide of perfection. I took Marie out to La Pavilion of the Grande Cascade and after a candlelight dinner, as we walked near the waterfall under a full moon, I stopped on the path and kneeled before her without saying anything, just looking up and waiting for her recognition. At first she looked askance, as if embarrassed by my position on the ground—and then she realized that this was the moment, and I asked her if she would consent to become the Baroness de Coubertin. She was overjoyed, and before I could rise she fell on me in a heartfelt embrace, and we rolled on the soft earth in the bliss of our love and a future so filled with promise.

"My writing on France flowed from a well deep within with an eloquence and felicity, I believe, that I was never quite able to match again. The history leaped forward just as I needed it, the references were always at my fingertips, and the perspective and explanations all amounted to a compelling case for the progressive if sometimes disruptive and acrimonious path that drove the Third Republic forward. I had great hopes then that my political insights and literary talents would align with my Olympic quest and my family life to form a grand triangle of purpose, like the head of an arrow pointing to the future. While the book moved forward and even found favor with an American publisher, those months of happiness were soon quelled by the demanding reality of the web I had spun."

○ ○ ○ ○ ○

Later, St. Clair composed a draft of the crisis that unfolded in Athens and Coubertin's response, which seemed to him to prove that in the face of adversity, the baron was an audacious man of action.

○ ○ ○ ○ ○

The first major shock came wrapped in a package from Vikelas in October. His cover letter was full of alarm and an urgent appeal for Coubertin to travel to Athens immediately. Coubertin understood why when he read the attached letter from the Greek prime minister, Charilaos Trikoupis, which brought down the hammer of political rejection. Announcing that while his nation was honored by the IOC's choice of Athens for the inaugural modern Olympics, he simply did not have the funds to underwrite such an ambitious undertaking. Greece had no choice but to decline.

Begging Marie to forgive his departure just as they had begun the planning of their nuptials, Coubertin took the train from Paris to Marseille and boarded the *Ortegal* for Piraeus, the port of Athens, at the beginning of November. As the vessel steamed toward Greece, he had four days to consider the options and to read through his Athens files. He looked closely at the latest correspondence from Vikelas, realizing it was filled with increasingly foreboding reports of economic hardships and the loss of political will summarized in the prime minister's letter. It seemed hopeless, but Coubertin believed he had a strong ally in the royal family if not the business community; moreover, the pride of Greeks was famously volcanic. His file was thick. He had newspaper reports on the growing political opposition to Trikoupis's conservative government, including bitter admonitions to loosen the purse strings from his leading adversary, Theodoros Deligiannis, a former prime minister and head of the Nationalist Party. Coubertin also had two cards he would play if needed—a telegram from King George and Crown Prince Constantine that had arrived at the beginning of July, just after the election in Athens, praising the decision and offering their full support. And, he thought, lifting a letter from the file, he had a trump card in an offer from his friend, the Hungarian IOC member Ferenc Kemény, describing Budapest's desire to host the Games in 1896 as part of Hungary's Millennium Celebration.

Coubertin also believed that the Zappas Commission, which Vikelas had appointed as the organizing committee for the Games, would rally to his cause. If necessary, he would find a way to turn up the political heat by inspiring the people to embrace their destiny. Originally, he had wanted to put the first Games in Paris in 1900, but he had yielded to the desires of the royal family to let Athens have the glory. Now, he had to make the most of a bad situation. Accustomed to opposition as he was—and full of fight—he refused to let his anxieties rise too much in advance of his arrival. For most of the voyage, he concentrated on adding pages to his *Evolution of France* manuscript and tried to enjoy the Mediterranean passage. While his mission was an emergency, the ship seemed to move with excruciating slowness. He wouldn't arrive until the second week in November.

When the ship docked in Piraeus at three in the afternoon, Vikelas was waiting for him with a two-horse carriage and a coachman. Stepping up to greet Coubertin as he came down the gangplank, Vikelas forced a smile but his face conveyed defeat. They did not embrace. Although they were friends, they had known each other for only six months. As they rode the dusty route toward Athens, Vikelas suggested they stop at the ruins of the ancient stadium, but Coubertin dispensed with the strained niceties and said, "We can get to the sightseeing once we reach the city. What's the latest news?"

Vikelas pulled a letter from inside his coat. "To be as forthright as possible, we've lost almost all of our support. The Games are hopeless."

"Who's this from?" Coubertin opened the envelope impatiently and unfolded the letter.

"Stephanos Dragoumis, the real political head of the Zappas Commission." A scowl crossed Vikelas's face as he looked out the window.

"He says we've lost the Zappas Commission, Demetri. I thought they were going to be our organizing committee."

"I did too, but they were controlled by Trikoupis through Dragoumis—they're allies—and they turned it into a study commission. This letter formalizes their decision to decline the Games."

"I can see that," said Coubertin, reading aloud in disbelief. "'This severe economic crisis ... leaves us ... burdened with the conviction that the task is far beyond the available means.'"

"They meant to send it to you before you left Paris."

"Yes, to stop me from coming, I'm sure." Coubertin felt betrayed. He was furious. "'We have no liberty of choice but to reject this generous offer,'" he read, then said, "that's the same language Trikoupis used." He fell silent.

Sitting shoulder to shoulder in the jostling cab, they were sealed together in the discomfort of the idea that their grand vision had failed. Removing his spectacles and rubbing his forehead, Vikelas said, "There's no chance, Pierre. I've met with the prime minister and begged him to reconsider, but he is adamant. He's planning to see you tomorrow morning at the Hotel Grande Bretagne. He wants to explain the impossibilities in person."

"Well, that's an honor—and certainly outside the usual protocol. I will receive him as a gentleman with all due appreciation, but Demetri, the Games cannot be stillborn, for God's sake. We've given our lives to their resurrection," he said, as if Vikelas had been working with him for years. "We *will* find a way; we will find allies. When we get to the hotel tonight, I want you to give me a full briefing on what you've done, who you've assigned to committees, who your strongest advocates are, where the king and the prince stand in this controversy—and most of all, who Trikoupis's major political opponents are. There's an election at hand, isn't there?"

"Yes, Deligiannis and Trikoupis are campaigning right now. They're at each other's throats almost every day. But it's not simply a matter of politics, it's the economics."

"It can't be the economics. That's a false fear. The Games will cost only two hundred thousand drachmas."

"What? Where are you getting that budget?"

"That's the operational budget I've constructed. What does Trikoupis think they'll cost?"

"Millions. At minimum."

"Then we'll give him a million reasons why he's wrong."

As the coach crested a hill and swung westward, the Acropolis came into view through Coubertin's window. He looked in awe at the Parthenon for the first time.

"My God," he said, "there's two thousand years of Greek glory on that hill, and we're worried about a few drachmas. Can we go see the stadium and a few sights before the light fades?"

○ ○ ○ ○ ○

Even though he knew it was coming, the meeting with the prime minister at the Hotel Grande Bretagne the next day surprised Coubertin. He knew very few politicians, if any, who would have cast protocol aside and met with a foreigner from an opposing camp without an entourage—and yet Trikoupis walked into the dining room of the hotel alone. Coubertin rose to greet him, and they stood face to face for a moment. They were nearly identical in size and weight—the prime minister looked fit but his mustache, nearly a match for Coubertin's, was silver gray and less neatly groomed and his pate carried only a bare wisp of hair. Although he was sixty-two, his eyes sparkled like a younger man's, and he seemed genuinely enthused to be meeting Pierre.

"It is a great thing you have done, sir, reviving our ancient Olympic Games," was the first thing he said. "I only wish I could be a more inviting host."

As Coubertin followed him to a quiet corner, he regretted momentarily that they were in conflict, but it soon became clear there would be no meeting of the minds that day. Trikoupis dismissed Coubertin's budget with a grunt and parried away each of his other ideas for funding the Games. There would be no lottery, no stamps, no search for rich Greek investors. In short order, each man fell into his entrenched position. The meeting ended with the prime minister inviting Coubertin to "take a good look around and assess our city for yourself. You'll see we can't possibly afford the expense of hosting the Games, which will cost, I believe we both know, far more than your optimism would suggest."

"I will do just that," Coubertin said. "George Melas and Alexandre Mercati will be here within the hour to guide me on a tour." He deliberately dropped the names of the son of the mayor and the son of one of Athens' most influential bankers.

Both names also conveyed connections to Trikoupis's political opponents, but he showed no concern.

"Well then, enjoy the sights," he said, turning to go.

"Mr. Prime Minister—wait, please." Coubertin advanced with his hand extended. "Let me just say again that despite our differences, I deeply appreciate the personal effort you've made to explain your position."

"We must honor the memory of our glories," he said, "even if we can't serve them as we wish we could."

Within an hour young George Melas and Alexandre Mercati were riding with Coubertin in a caliche with the top down. The baron was pleased to be in their company. Melas was a charming, intelligent young man and Mercati, the older of the two, had helped organize the last Zappas Olympics and was a childhood friend of the crown prince. The day was clear and bright, and Coubertin was awestruck as he gazed up past the ancient arched wall of the Theater of Herodes Atticus to the Acropolis. Heading toward the south side of town, they skirted the ruins of the Temple of Zeus and he breathed in the glories of the past, imagining the site filled with a crowd of enchanted international Olympic guests. They had a busy afternoon ahead, with appointments at two gymnastics clubs, an athletic club, and a cycling group, but for now they were on their way to the Panathenaic Stadium so Coubertin could assess the state of the structure, which would have to be restored for the Games.

Engaging his new colleagues in his plans, Coubertin recounted his discussions with Vikelas from the night before. "I know the king left last week for the funeral of Alexander III in Russia, but I understand the crown prince is serving as regent in his absence. That may work in our favor."

"Undoubtedly it will. He's very enthusiastic about the Games," Melas said. "He sees the opportunity to connect with the people through the Games."

Mercati nodded in agreement, squinting as the carriage described a half circle and placed him in the sunlight. "George is right. The royals have an acute sense of public symbolism. They're sensitive to their distance from the populace and yet intimately attuned to them—and they know public sentiment is strongly in favor of these Olympics. The people want the Games."

"Huh! Indeed they do, sir," called out the coachman, a burly, unshaven, and clearly opinionated man who surprised Coubertin by inserting himself in the conversation.

"Thank you, Yannis," said Melas, frowning. His tone suggested he wanted to quiet the man.

"I've asked Demetri to arrange a meeting with the crown prince as soon as possible. Is there anything you can do to assist him?"

"We'll make sure it will happen within a day or two," Melas said. "There's daily contact between the mayor's office and the royal court."

They arrived at the old stadium, which opened before them like two hills rising from a narrow, short valley. Coubertin noted that the irregular grassy shoulders on each side of the stadium floor had held their form, and although the stepped structure of the seats was only partially visible—along with traces of old stands and a rare piece of glinting white marble—the restoration could likely be completed without having to excavate too deeply or cart off tons of earth.

"This restoration is a question of labor above all else," said Melas. "Wooden stands will do."

"And labor is what we need here, jobs for the people," Mercati added.

They all smiled at each other as Coubertin walked through the opening onto the muddy, uneven stadium floor. Its plain was wide enough for a narrow oval track.

"History is going to come back to life here," he said.

○ ○ ○ ○ ○

As they continued their schedule over the next few days, moving from club to club, venue to venue, Coubertin realized that he had become something he had never been before—at least to this extent—a public figure. People pointed at him from the sidewalks around the Plaka as his coach whisked him along the rutted roads from meeting to meeting. Generally preceded through the door by Vikelas, Mercati, and Melas, he was aware that his arrival was anticipated and that he was the center of attention in every room he entered—with the exception of his seemingly confidential session with the crown prince and his brothers.

He had been in the spotlight in Paris during the Olympic Congress but had never truly reached center stage in French society. But in Athens the newspapers covered his movements and quoted him as if he were a visiting head of state. When the third successive coachman offered an opinion on how to win the Olympic campaign, saying, "Sir, I'll tell you just how to deal with that tightwad Trikoupis," as Melas translated, he began to understand just how deeply the people of Athens wanted the Olympic Games to succeed—and that he represented, above all else, their present hope and best chance to overcome the objections of the city's politicians.

To fire the people's passion further—and to gain some political advantage—he wrote an open letter, which was translated and published in *Asty*, a leading Athenian newspaper, challenging the nation to embrace the honor of leading the world into a new age of sport—as their forefathers had so long ago. "Greek glory has been lost nearly as long as the Games, and it is time to burnish it again to its rightful glow." The effect was evident on the streets the next day—a shopkeeper patted him on the back as he walked by, and a baker presented him with a loaf of dark bread.

It was late at night when Mercati and Vikelas picked up Coubertin in an enclosed carriage and took a circuitous route to the royal palace, where they were met in the torch-lit courtyard by uniformed guards and led into the private quarters of Crown Prince Constantine. The doors opened to a lavishly decorated salon, filled with luxurious furnishings and historic paintings cast in a golden light—and there stood Constantine and his brother, George, two tall, broad-shouldered royals in belted military jackets, looking ready for battle. They each had wide foreheads, thick mustaches, and gleaming smiles.

"So here, finally, is our great French friend, the hero of Paris," said Constantine, crushing Coubertin's hand in a tight grip only to be surpassed by his younger brother's. "Gentlemen, please be seated. Brandies all around, Yorgo." Brandy snifters were set out almost instantly.

Coubertin offered thanks for the audience and allowed Vikelas and Mercati to provide a confidential campaign briefing on the activities of the last few days, emphasizing the breadth of support for the Games at the highest levels of business, sport, and the public realm.

"At Pierre's direction, we're forming a new committee to replace the Zappas Commission," said Vikelas. "It will be filled with our allies."

"We'll be meeting with Deligiannis and his team in three days," Mercati concluded, falling silent as they awaited the crown prince's reply.

"That was a stirring piece in *Asty*, Baron. I could feel my Greek blood rise," Constantine said with exaggerated seriousness, and he and his brother laughed. "No, I mean it. It was quite moving, and I'm sure you'll be happy to repeat that message to an influential group."

"By all means, Your Highness, I am at your disposal." Coubertin was immediately taken with Constantine's composure and presence. He saw no shade of doubt or deliberation in the prince's eyes, only conviction.

"You know our position on this matter, Baron," Constantine said. "You have my telegram, sent on the king's behalf. The Olympic Games are important to us for many reasons, but most of all as a focal point for the people, to restore a measure of our Greek pride—as you well put it in the paper. Meanwhile, the prime minister and his government have diverted funds intended for public works for a military buildup." He looked at his brother, who picked up the point.

"Our security is critical, of course," Prince George said. "And our family can't publicly criticize the spending, but be assured we want to change course."

"In fact, we want a change of government." Constantine paused to let this sink in. "We know this is treacherous ground for our Olympic dreams. But you'll find Mr. Deligiannis ready to cooperate fully with your plans—or shall I say, your campaign."

"You are correct, Your Highness, in calling it a campaign," Coubertin said. "It's been a long campaign, and while I would prefer to hold sports above politics, I'm not willing to let this moment of opportunity pass. We cannot let the Games die now that they are breathing again."

"They will not die, sir. There will be an invitation issued in a few days. You'll be asked to speak to the Parnassos Literary Society—and I hope you'll reprise the themes of your editorial."

"An excellent stratagem," said Vikelas. "I must say, my hopes are now revived. At your invitation, we can draw the crème de la crème of Athens."

"It won't be my invitation, Demetrius. I won't be there, my name won't be associated with the event, but my presence will be felt."

"We understand," said Coubertin.

"Now tell me," Constantine said. "How did you arrive at this figure of two hundred thousand drachmas?"

The conversation lasted more than an hour, twice as long as Mercati and Vikelas had suggested. Coubertin was impressed with the royal brothers, their energy and attention to detail, and, most of all, their firm grasp of the requirements of organizing such a massive event. They were clearly familiar with the challenges from their engagement with the most recent Zappas Olympics and were not intimidated by the risks. They both responded positively to almost all of Coubertin's recommendations on the formation of committees and the delegation of responsibilities. When he said he believed a good many rich Greek industrialists living abroad would want to help their fatherland host the Games, the crown prince immediately agreed.

"I am certain we can find support among the diaspora," he said. "I know a merchant or two who might be willing to extend a generous hand. I'll have my father call on them on his return."

As they spoke, Coubertin could not escape the notion that they intended to use the Olympic Games as a visible platform for royal patronage, to assert their presence as the champions of the people. He decided to take an even bolder step. "If I may, Your Highness," he began, searching Constantine's eyes for a reaction to what he was about to propose. "If you will consent to serve as the president of a new organizing committee, if you will take a visible leadership role and apply your talents and skills to the effort, I'm confident we will succeed."

The crown prince could not hide the smile that creased his face as he looked at his brother first, then at his boyhood friend, Mercati, and the others. "Let me take this under advisement for now. I would, yes, of course, if Greece needs me, but the timing of an announcement is critical."

He has all the right instincts, Coubertin thought. He left the meeting with a sense of achievement, as if this had been the breakthrough he was hoping for on this trip. He was nearly certain that with such capable patrons, the Games would find the resources they needed.

In the antechamber as they left, they encountered a tall, middle-aged man in a top coat and suit, hat in hand, with a frown on his face, perhaps displeased that he'd been kept waiting. He had a thick black mustache and piercing eyes. Mercati and Vikelas reacted with enthusiasm to his presence, but he did not return their smiles.

"Timoleon Philemon," said Mercati, "I have the honor of presenting the Baron Pierre de Coubertin. Baron, our former mayor and one of the king's most trusted civic leaders."

Surprised that this was the man with whom he had corresponded for many months, Coubertin smiled and was about to say, "At last, we meet." But before he could respond, Philemon looked down at him coldly, with clear condescension.

"Ah, the little French baron who has come to take over our Olympic planning," he said in a mordant tone, bowing in feigned respect. His resentment was scarcely concealed.

Coubertin was surprised, but he refrained from taking umbrage or parrying the smart remark. A difficult character. "Not at all, sir, only to assist."

"To assist," Philemon repeated as he walked toward the door just opened by an attendant. "Not the impression one gets from all the stories in the press." He glanced back before striding off, and he and Coubertin locked eyes for a moment.

"Not a pleasant man," Coubertin said.

"It takes some time with Timoleon," said Mercati. "He's a fierce patriot and he's always outspoken on our national capacities. He resents the European perspective that Greece is a problem child."

"I hope I won't have trouble with him." Coubertin was a bit shaken by the encounter, realizing there might be a reservoir of pent-up animosity in the nation against international influence.

"Don't worry, he'll come around. He's a very capable leader, widely respected. He'll be good for the Games."

"Oh? He'll be working on the Games?"

"I think Constantine intends to give him a leading role. I suppose that's why he's here."

○ ○ ○ ○ ○

After that inauspicious meeting, several days flew past with success piling on success. In two meetings with the new organizing committee, Coubertin's program for the Games, his detailed competition schedule, and his international rules were accepted without revision. He offered sketches for a velodrome, promising to send detailed drawings and plans from Paris.

Deligiannis and his opposition party leadership heartily welcomed Coubertin and his small delegation. As the prince had promised, they were fully supportive, and somewhat to Coubertin's concern, almost too willing as conspirators. They too had other objectives the Olympic Games could serve. Despite his reservations, Coubertin suggested Deligiannis make a strong public statement in favor of the Games—and the politician jumped to the task and the next day landed in the headlines with a statement attacking Trikoupis.

Even as things rolled along smoothly, Coubertin had a nagging sense of suspicion that Philemon was hovering somewhere in the background, but he did not appear at any meeting until Coubertin spoke at the Parnassos Literary Society. The invitation arrived at his hotel two days after he met the crown prince. He was scheduled to speak a week from the following Thursday night, which meant his trip would keep him in Athens for nearly three weeks—longer than he had planned for. He hoped Marie would forgive him.

The Parnassos Literary Society had secured the rotunda of the Zappeion, one of the finest new buildings in Athens, built from the same fortune that had underwritten four editions of the Zappas Olympic Games. While Mercati, Melas, and Vikelas were filled with anticipation for this most visible public event of their campaign, Coubertin found himself homesick. By the time he entered the rotunda that night, he was longing for Paris and the love of Marie.

In a room full of a hundred men, Coubertin was treated as a celebrity guest. By the time they settled into their seats and the protocol announcements began, he felt as if he had shaken hands with almost everyone. At the podium, he was as certain of the arguments he was about to present as he had ever been. Feeling as if he had the mantle of the royals over his shoulders, he decided to begin by exaggerating and dismissing the arguments of the naysayers. As he spoke, Mercati translated in a fiery style that conveyed the emotion of the moment to those gathered.

"They told me you had no sporting tradition and no facilities. But I had the pleasure of spending a few days on tour with George Melas, your mayor's own son, and my distinguished colleagues, Alexandre Mercati and Demetrius Vikelas, and I'm afraid the evidence of your sporting life is impossible to hide. In two days, I could see exactly how and where the Games could be staged. And I must emphasize that my judgments are based on tours of the finest facilities of France, Britain, and the United States—so I am speaking to you as an expert in these things.

"I have already met with club leaders and representatives of your gymnastics, athletics, rowing, fencing, running, swimming, cycling, shooting, and equestrian societies. The ancient stadium must be restored for athletics and gymnastics, but the structure is in place. It's only a matter of labor. The cavalry grounds are perfect for the equestrian events, and the Zappeion Rotunda, as can be clearly seen, provides a magnificent setting for fencing and perhaps tests of strength. I've seldom seen a sailing and rowing site as lovely as Paleros Bay or a natural setting for swimming and diving to match the Bay of Zéa. A velodrome must be built, yes, and the proposed site at Neo Phaleron is perfect. When I look at the possibilities and the potential, and when I think about all those rich sons of Greece around the world who would be proud to invest in the restoration of the Games—as the Zappas brothers' patronage and legacy assure us—I'm confused by the fears of the naysayers. It may be easier to produce the Olympic Games here than anywhere else.

"Yes, we have offers from other countries. But I refuse to consider the option of the Games being reborn in Hungary or anywhere else for that matter—because they belong to you. The first Olympic Games of the modern era must be Greek. They must be staged here to bring the dark cycle of fifteen centuries to a close—and to illuminate the future with a dream of joyous hope. As certain as I stand before you today, I know I am right in this—as King George, Crown Prince Constantine, and his royal brothers surely know—and as George, Alexandre, and Demetrius know"—he gestured toward the three men—"the inaugural modern Olympic Games must begin again here, in Athens, in Greece—and only here. The world will come to applaud your achievements and recognize your greatness.

"Sport is rising toward the throne of leisure in our modern world. From the playing fields of Britain to the far campuses of the United States, across Europe and into Asia, competitive passions have been unleashed. And those passions, gentlemen, will be the fuel that drives the formation of Olympic teams in every country and propels the ships that bring those teams to Piraeus. It is that passion that will restore your ancient Panhellenic stadium and fill it with fifty thousand on opening day of the Games. Do not neglect your patrimony. You are Greece.

"What is a nation? It is an idea that animates a people. It is the foundation of your identity. It is who you are—and are becoming. I believe Hellenism once again has a role to play in the world. Liberated to reach for its modern calling, it will fill the entire world with a new wave of inspiration.

"Sport has a mission to fulfill in modern times. It can ennoble, or it can debase. It can be used to perpetuate peace or prepare for war. It can serve to build international friendships or create international enemies. The Olympic Games that are revived here, in Athens, will define in many ways the role that sport is to play in our shared future. You, men of Greece, will set the course for sport worldwide—as your ancestors did. You will yet again show the world how sport can best serve mankind.

"Thus, you, men of Greece, must not let this glory slip from your hands. This is your birthright. This is your heritage. This is your destiny. Today, gentlemen, your past is your future. The Olympic Games, which you must host, will be a pilgrimage to the past and an act of faith in the future. The world will come to Greece again and marvel at your monuments, celebrate your traditions, share the joy of your spirit.

"The people want the Olympic Games, but a few politicians and economists do not. So we are left with a dilemma. Do we accept the judgments of our leaders or do we rise up and serve the greater cause?"

The audience's approval was deafening. Although he was suddenly exhausted, Coubertin knew his rhetorical skills had served him well. Afterward, his colleagues took him to a taverna in the Plaka, where they toasted one another until the middle of the night, making plans as they drank. Coubertin knew the royal palace would already be full of the news of his success.

○ ○ ○ ○ ○

On the day he was to depart Athens, December 2, 1894, Coubertin had a final breakfast meeting with Melas, Mercati, and Vikelas. At the table, the three of them began to praise him again, but he cut their encomiums short.

"Thank you, Demetrius, but we have celebrated enough. We still have planning to do." Although he had achieved everything he needed to—there was no question that preparations for the Games would be driven forward by the crown prince and the royals with the assistance of Deligiannis and Mayor Melas—he nevertheless felt some anxiety about the need for funding and the final formation of all the organizing committees.

All three rode with Coubertin in the coach to the train station. They sympathized with his urgent need to return to Paris to tend to his fiancée and their wedding preparations, but they admired him all the more because he had decided to make his first pilgrimage to ancient Olympia on the way home. They bid one another fond farewells, and he left them standing on the platform as he boarded the train for Patras.

○ ○ ○ ○ ○

Jacques St. Clair and Coubertin were enjoying the afternoon sun after a late lunch at the Château d'Ouchy, walking along the quay of Lake Geneva at an easy pace. St. Clair held a small notepad and had a pencil tucked behind his ear. Over the past two weeks, he had been through Coubertin's various accounts of the Athens organizational effort and the Games themselves several times in detail, and one thing struck him as odd, given Coubertin's devotion to the ancient world.

"You didn't write much about your first visit to Olympia on the way back from Athens. Why?"

"Well, I'd intended to. But on the way home—stopping at Brindisi, Italy, where I gave another speech—I was concentrating on follow-up correspondence to everyone in Athens as well as trying to attend to my book on the Third Republic, which I hadn't touched in well over a month. I was also giving a lot of thought to my marital plans and how I'd mollify my family over the ceremony in a Protestant church." He paused and turned from gazing at the lake to look at St. Clair. "But the time in Olympia was as magical and meaningful as any experience I've ever had, including Rugby."

St. Clair faithfully recorded the baron's words in shorthand. They came to a bench and Coubertin sat down.

"I arrived late at night in Olympia on the overland passage from Patras," he said, "and I remember the gorgeous vista of Mount Kronos when I opened the windows in the morning. So many shades of green, verdant and varied, different from most of the Greek landscape, more fertile and fecund. I was completely surprised by the intimate scale. It took me a minute to realize I was looking at Kronos and not simply some small hill. And when I walked down into the ruins, it was a revelation of both the sacredness of place and the historic power of an eternal ideal."

As they walked back along the lake, St. Clair posed a final question on the subject. "What seems most significant to you about how the Greeks prepared for the Games during 1895? Is there anything else you want to add to what's in your *Memoirs*?"

"You know, I don't think anyone has given them the credit they deserve for how well they did the job. Yes, they fell behind schedule on the restoration of the stadium, but overall they set a very high bar for an effective organizational structure—and to this day their fundraising acumen remains unmatched."

○○○○○

Back in Paris, Coubertin received weekly letters from Vikelas and others, and while some minor problems persisted, the accumulated news rose like a new Mount Kronos of optimism. By January, the writing was on the wall—Trikoupis had resigned and Deligiannis had formed a new pro-Olympic government. The voice of the people had been heard, and the royal family was at work. The announcement that the crown prince would lead the organizing effort was popular with the people, and he proved to be an effective administrator. Nearly every letter reported another decisive move that reflected ideas and advice the baron had articulated in their single meeting. His reaction was mixed at the news that Constantine had appointed Timoleon Philemon as secretary general, but he was impressed with the alacrity with which the prince dropped people from committees when they didn't produce the results he wanted. One swift action followed another as committees on ticketing, athlete accommodations, Greek team development, and venue construction were formed and empowered for action.

As a former mayor of Athens, Philemon's broad business network helped him solidify his new position and extend his power by producing the first large gifts for the Games from the Hellenic diaspora—a total of 130,000 drachmas by mid-February. Vikelas let Coubertin know that Philemon was in the middle of a dramatic appeal to the richest of all Greeks living abroad, George Averoff of Alexandria, Egypt, who had already spent millions in philanthropy for new schools and a military academy in Athens. German archaeologists and diplomats in Greece, proud of their contribution to Greek history through their digs at Olympia, had encouraged the king and the crown prince to restore the Panathenaic Stadium to its original glory with exquisite marble from Mount Pentelicus. Plans were produced by the famous Greek architect Anastas Metaxas, and Philemon put together a presentation package, which included a restoration schedule, sending it off to Averoff with a price tag of 585,000 drachmas.

Although he was known to be withdrawn and humble, the rich man clearly saw the historic opportunity and didn't hesitate. The news of Averoff stepping forward as the new Herodes Atticus—the man who had originally built the stadium in 140 AD—sent waves of joy through the nation and triggered the generosity of the community of Greek merchants around the world. As the money flowed in from overseas, everyone at home bought stamps and contributed what they could. The Olympic treasury was soon overflowing, and the fine white marble of Mount Pentelicus was again being carried out of its quarry. Five hundred men were put to work at the stadium on day and night shifts. The velodrome and all the other venues were under construction.

Greece had risen to the occasion. Its moment of modern destiny was at hand. Patriotic pride and nationalism began to soar among its Olympic leaders, which in turn produced a backlash against the IOC. Vikelas sent Coubertin a series of ominous warnings about Philemon's campaign to discredit all outside influences. It seemed the Greeks, deeply proud of their organizational effort, bristled at the very idea that anyone else deserved credit for resurrecting the Games, particularly those who staged the Paris Congress. Excited with the momentum the Greeks had achieved, Coubertin dismissed the concerns, believing he'd be able to resolve any conflicts once he arrived in Greece.

64

THE NAZIS

oubertin was talking to Dr. Messerli on the telephone while St. Clair looked over his notes in the Mon Repos office. They had spent the better part of the day covering the baron's trip to Athens in 1896 for the inaugural Olympic Games. He and Marie had traveled together, just after their first anniversary, to a festival that was a grand public triumph but a personal humiliation for Coubertin and his IOC colleagues.

"Francis will join us here tomorrow late afternoon," Coubertin said, hanging up. "We'll finalize our preparations for dinner with Diem and von Tschammer then."

"Do you know what time they're arriving?"

"Diem said early evening, and they're usually punctual. I want to make sure we're prepared to parry the questions about their IOC proposal and the work of my commission." He smiled. St. Clair surmised he was satisfied with the measures he had implemented to protect his movement, at least temporarily. "Have we covered enough ground today? Did you get enough on our wedding in our last session?"

"Let me check." St. Clair opened his notebook as Pierre turned back to his papers. Shielding a few typed pages from Coubertin's view, St. Clair read through a passage on the wedding he had finished a few days before.

○○○○○

The marriage of Pierre de Coubertin to Marie Rothan took place on March 12, 1895, in l'Église Protestante Réformée de l'Oratoire du Louvre, a beautiful seventeenth-century church given to the Protestants by Napoleon in 1811 to provide an appropriate spiritual home to Paris's most progressive religious minority. The wedding ceremony bridged far greater distances than the gap of faith between the betrothed. The dispossessed mixed freely with the disenfranchised as the older generation of Coubertin Catholics, Bourbon royalists to the bone, met with the Rothan cadre of Second Empire outcasts, equally outside the power structure of the Third Republic. With Jules Simon and Henry Waddington in attendance, the ceremony enjoyed a flavor of the future. Jean Aicard, Lucien Drussard, and Georges de Saint-Clair kept a motley group of sportsmen in place while the Rothschilds, Sagans, and other aristocrats murmured about the unusual blend of the old and new, the hoi polloi and the bourgeoisie, the brilliant and the bitter, the promising and the fallen.

At the height of the ritual, with the church in a hush, Pierre lifted Marie's veil and whispered, "We will always be rebels." He kissed her passionately on the lips before they turned to a congregation filled with enthusiasm, the one moment when all present shared a sense of joy.

○ ○ ○ ○ ○

St. Clair decided not to share the scene with the baron—even though he had brought it along for that purpose. "I have more than enough to cover the wedding and your first year of marriage," he said.

"That first year was our happiest," said Coubertin. "I was working on *The Evolution of France*, Marie was drawing a fresh set of social contacts into our sporting circle, and we were attending dinner parties, dances, salons, and soirées at a breakneck pace. There was a sense in Paris, I think, that La Belle Époque was winding down, but most people didn't want to see it go."

St. Clair felt he'd written enough about the baron's social life at this point—and he didn't want to revisit the confessional and the tragedy of the baby boy or the baroness's breakdowns. He wanted to concentrate on the baron's ambitions. "Why do you think the French spurned your book? I think it's your best work."

"They felt it was too optimistic, too dismissive of the cracks in the façade, too forgiving of the constant crisis and the changes in government," Coubertin said. "And they were right, Jacques."

"Not in my assessment."

"Well, forty years have passed. You have to view it from their perspective. The truth is, I wrote it for Americans, and the French probably resented that.

And even so, all I heard from my U.S. academic friends—and the students participating in our debates at Harvard, Princeton, and Johns Hopkins—was that the instability of the Third Republic was its greatest weakness. It was, but I decided to present it as a vibrant expression of democracy."

"Political change as innovation?"

"Yes, as if every swift shift were a move toward better government, a natural characteristic in the evolution of a young republic."

"That's precisely what I took from the book."

"Still, the French considered it a whitewash. It had an educational purpose, but that wasn't a worthy defense at home—and I knew it."

○ ○ ○ ○ ○

Later, St. Clair left Coubertin at his desk and went down to the ornate lobby of Mon Repos. Standing between two Greek goddesses sculpted on opposing walls, he fixed his satchel over his shoulder, gripped the handlebars of his De Dion-Bouton, and walked it into the driveway. The sky was dull gray, the air still but fragrant as he slipped his foot onto the pedal. Just as he was about to descend the hill, a low, mechanical rumble rolled through the park, and he saw the front end of a sleek black car edging through the upper gate. It stopped halfway through the entrance, its engine growling in place, its large chrome headlights taking in the park like a pair of eyes, its silver grille shining like a shield about to advance. St. Clair turned his bike toward the fountain and pedaled easily to get a better look. A driver came into view, clouded by the sky reflected in the windshield. St. Clair could see the man talking to other passengers. He was wearing the black military hat of the Nazi SS.

With a jolt the Mercedes—an open convertible—slid through the gate, its immense black fenders swinging toward the château, revealing two men sitting in the back, both wearing Hamburg fedoras, neither in uniform. St. Clair recognized Diem. He dismounted and parked the bike as a movement caught his eye above. Coubertin stepped back from the window on the third floor; he had seen them coming. St. Clair walked out to greet them, standing in the driveway as the car thrummed down the hill. It came directly at him, and he decided not to move. The SS officer glared at him without turning the wheel and brought the car to a halt, the bumper just inches from St. Clair's knees as his gaze fell on the hood ornament—a red, white, and black swastika.

Diem stood up and stretched, his suit coat unbuttoned, his tie held loosely by a Nazi clasp, his size exaggerated by the height of the car. "Good evening, Monsieur St. Clair," he said. "What a pleasure to find you here."

"Hello, Herr Diem." St. Clair approached as the big man stepped down from the running board. They shook hands. "I thought you were coming tomorrow night."

"We were making good time and decided to push through in hopes of hosting the baron at dinner tonight instead. Is he here?"

"Yes, he's upstairs, but I'm not sure what his plans are."

"Well, we'll see. May I introduce our *Reichssportführer*, Hans von Tschammer und Osten." Diem indicated the man at his shoulder, also dressed in a gray suit. He was a few inches shorter than Diem, but tall and thin, his eyes narrow and darting, his cheeks clean shaven, his chin pointed. He stretched out his hand.

"So I meet the famous biographer," he said, unsmiling. "How does the work proceed? When will we have a draft to read?"

St. Clair ignored the presumption. "We're making progress," he said, aware of the boot steps behind him.

"And may I present Herr Heydrich." St. Clair found himself awkwardly close to the SS colonel in his imposing black uniform, a Luger in a holster on a thick leather belt, the brim of his hat hovering between them. "Stefan insisted on coming," Diem continued. "He is among Germany's most avid Olympic fans."

"I'm sure we have much in common," Heydrich said, gripping St. Clair's hand tightly. They were the same size, and St. Clair reacted to the sour smell of tobacco on his breath by squeezing back and holding him at bay, regretting the need to respond.

"What's your favorite sport?" he asked, noticing a small cleft in the ridge of Heydrich's upper lip.

"Cycling, of course," Heydrich said, releasing his grip. "Perhaps we can take a ride together." Without looking back, he motioned over his shoulder, saying, "Is that a Dion-Bouton you're riding?"

"It is." St. Clair realized with a twinge of unease that they all knew a good deal about him.

"Let's go and see the president," Diem said, and they all fell in behind him. On the stairway, St. Clair noticed that Diem and von Tschammer were each carrying heavy briefcases. He resisted the urge to look back as Heydrich trailed uncomfortably close behind him.

St. Clair was surprised that soon after bursting into the room and nearly smothering the baron in his embrace, Carl Diem conducted a rather stiff, awkward introduction of von Tschammer and Heydrich. As soon as the handshakes were over, the three Germans withdrew to the back of the room. They huddled together unpacking their briefcases, hiding their preparations, their backs to Coubertin and St. Clair, their whispers audible. After a few minutes, they turned in unison, each bearing an oversized book wrapped in silky brown paper.

They came forward like soldiers and aligned in front of the desk, pausing to allow the baron to absorb the image before him. Standing beside Coubertin, St. Clair noted that each book was bound by a black, red, and white ribbon with a swastika seal in the middle of a shiny ring—gold, silver, and bronze for each book.

At center, bearing the gold-sealed book, Diem said, "Mr. President, if we may, a brief message." He waited for Coubertin's approval before pulling from his suit coat a sheet of paper.

"'On behalf of the Third Reich,'" he read, "'this final report of Berlin 1936 is presented to the Honorable Baron Pierre de Coubertin, the founder of the glorious modern Olympic Games, the pinnacle of competition in the world of sport. With hearts full of gratitude, the Führer, the organizing committee, and the people of Germany offer their solemn respect and eternal appreciation for the opportunity you have given us to move your great work forward.'"

With that, Diem handed the gold edition to the baron while von Tschammer and Heydrich laid their packages on the desk.

Coubertin looked at each of them in turn as he said, "Thank you, gentlemen, for this elaborate presentation and for the genuine sentiments expressed. Of course, your gratitude truly belongs with the IOC, which awarded the Games to Germany, and not to me. However, I accept your homage in the spirit in which it was delivered. And I recognize that you have gone to great lengths, driving all the way from Berlin, I take it, just to deliver this report to me. I shall read it with enthusiasm."

"Please open it, Pierre," said Diem, dropping the formality. "There are a few touches I want to show you."

The wrapping paper tore away and the ribbon slipped off easily. Coubertin opened the book to the middle and began fanning through the pages, turning slightly to show St. Clair the contents. He stopped at the report on the Olympic Village.

"There's certainly a lot of detail on the architecture," Coubertin said, flipping to a series of shots of the construction of the massive Olympic stadium.

"We tried to be thorough and document everything," Diem replied.

"See if you can find Jesse Owens," St. Clair said, "or the cycling competition."

"Track and field is at the end of the book. Cycling is in Volume II."

Coubertin found images of Owens on the field and off. In one, he was seated at a desk, responding to letters from his fans, wearing a laurel wreath like a Greek god.

"These are excellent photographs, Carl." Coubertin pointed to a series of time-lapse shots of runners on the track.

Diem came around the desk and took the book in hand. Von Tschammer followed but Heydrich drifted over to Coubertin's side table, examining the bronzes and smaller mementos.

Opening the report to its first few pages, Diem held the book flat. A large photo of Hitler in a black suit glared back at them. "Read the Führer's quote, Pierre."

"Jacques, please," said Coubertin. "Let's hear it in a youthful voice."

"'Sporting and chivalrous competition awakens the best human qualities. It does not sever, but on the contrary, unites the opponents in mutual understanding and reciprocal respect. It also helps to strengthen the bonds of peace between nations. May the Olympic flame therefore never be extinguished.'"

"That sounds like something I would say," the baron said, grimacing.

"It was meant to sound like you—that's how I wrote it. A marriage of two great leaders. Look at this," Diem said, flipping the page to reveal a photo of the aged baron, standing in profile, looking away.

"You included me in this report?" Coubertin was clearly baffled. "This is Baillet-Latour's place, not mine."

"Henri is on the next page. We gave him his rightful place, but we wanted to honor you." Diem was beaming. He paged ahead to show Coubertin the story of the torch relay, his great innovation. The presentation went on for another half hour before the baron began to slump in his chair.

Diem took the hint. "And what about dinner tonight? Perhaps we can wrap up our work early and be gone in the morning."

St. Clair noticed Coubertin was tiring, and the idea of dinner with the Germans seemed like a bad idea.

But the baron rallied. "All right," he said. "I'll see whether Francis can join us. Give me an hour to wrap a few things up. Shall we say the Beau Rivage at eight o'clock?"

Clearly satisfied with the first phase of their visit, the Germans left in minutes. St. Clair followed them into the hallway to see them off, and when he returned, the baron was sitting with his forehead in hand, his eyes hidden.

"Are you all right, Pierre?"

"My final legacy—stamped with the imprint of National Socialism."

"Where did they obtain that photo of you?" St. Clair reopened the report. "It's not very flattering."

"I had it taken last year, when I did their radio broadcast. Carl asked for it, but I never thought I'd see it counterposed with Hitler. Damn it. They're relentless."

"They'll want to talk about their proposal tonight, won't they?"

"Of course. That's why they're here. They'll want to know all about the work of the Commission on the Future of Olympism."

"What will you tell them?" St. Clair was almost certain nothing had been done since Brundage had left Lausanne.

"That we're making great progress, but I'll tell them the commission's work is strictly confidential. I need to call Messerli." The baron reached for the telephone but paused for a moment. "Jacques, why don't you bring Juliette to dinner tonight?"

"Juliette? With the Nazis? I'm not sure she'll want to—"

"Of course she will. She'll be a great distraction. Tell her she can ask them anything."

"I'll ask, but don't expect the Duchess of Langeais to show up."

○ ○ ○ ○ ○

The twilight sky was filled with bands of soft red and orange as St. Clair and Juliette walked up the garden path to the Beau Rivage's restaurant. Coubertin and Messerli were waiting for them. Juliette's appearance drew a nod of approval from Coubertin. Wrapped in a black skirt, wearing high heels that made her taller and accentuated her shape, she looked like a gypsy princess. A flowery peasant blouse with a wide, tented collar and plunging neckline completed the ensemble, with a red headband that disappeared beneath her black tresses and large gold rings dangling from her ears. As they approached, she turned to them with a warm smile.

Coubertin greeted her graciously, but after the exchange of kisses, he turned serious. "Our guests are inside at a table for five. They obviously weren't expecting you to sit in, Jacques. Come with me. We're going to make them move."

St. Clair followed Coubertin inside. "There's a balmy breeze outside," the baron said as the three National Socialists rose. "Let's move the party out there? We can't fit the seven of us at this table anyway."

"Seven?" Diem exchanged frowns with von Tschammer. "I thought it would be only the four of us and Dr. Messerli. This is business we're discussing."

"I've asked Monsieur St. Clair to sit in—this is an important meeting for my biography—and he has invited his fiancé, Juliette Franklin, who is painting my portrait. I'm sure you'll find her charming."

Coubertin took Juliette's hand and made the introductions. Diem, von Tschammer, and especially Heydrich all bowed before her beauty. St. Clair stood back and absorbed the scene with Messerli.

Heydrich took Juliette by the elbow and guided her to a seat next to him as they settled at a round table. St. Clair sat right of Coubertin as instructed. He tapped his tablet with his pencil, impatient to get the conversation started, watching the SS officer engage in what appeared to be pleasant badinage with Juliette. Diem sat on the baron's left with von Tschammer next to him, and Messerli filled the empty seat between St. Clair and Juliette.

Drinks and food came but no serious conversation started. St. Clair noted that everyone seemed intent on avoiding tensions. The baron appeared content to let the evening pass without addressing the Nazis' proposals, first deliberately focusing the conversation on Olympic heroes, then asking Diem to recount the origins of the torch relay idea and its stages of implementation. When Diem attempted to summarize the story, Messerli chided him for being so humble.

"Carl, please," the doctor implored, "make no mistake. We're all vitally interested in how you managed to create such a masterpiece of symbolism."

Diem took the bait and regaled the table with his own imaginative autobiography of the Olympic flame. St. Clair thought he likely would have gone on until midnight, but when von Tschammer cleared his throat several times, Diem eventually wrapped up.

Juliette wasted no time in taking advantage of the lull. "How long will you be in town, Herr General?"

"Unfortunately, we don't have as much time as we planned," von Tschammer said. "We have been summoned back to Munich tomorrow."

"Oh, that's too bad," Juliette replied before Heydrich distracted her with a *sotto voce* comment.

"So you've been called back early," said Coubertin. "I hope it's nothing pressing."

"Baron, the only pressing matter, from my perspective, is the status of our proposals."

"Well, as you know, our commission is currently reviewing each point of your proposal to Baillet-Latour, and we'll be issuing a report for the executive board's consideration."

"Your Commission on the Future of Olympism?" von Tschammer said, a faintly disdainful tone emphasizing his remark. "Where exactly are you in your evaluation?"

"I'm afraid that's confidential, gentlemen," Coubertin said, "but I assure you our report will be thorough." St. Clair was impressed. The question was harsh, but the baron hadn't flinched.

Given von Tschammer's tone, St. Clair wondered whether he knew that no work had yet been undertaken, that in fact the commission had never been convened. He wondered whether the Nazis had probed the issue with Edström or Brundage or even President Baillet-Latour, and he was suddenly concerned that Coubertin's stratagem might backfire.

"May I ask where you stand, personally, on the issues?" von Tschammer said, his eyes narrowing into a glare.

"I'd rather not say."

"In that case may I offer you some advice?"

"A wise man always seeks sagacious counsel."

"You would be wise, Baron ..." Von Tschammer spoke with conviction, but he paused as Diem shifted uncomfortably in his seat. Even Heydrich turned away from Juliette for a moment to take in the general's pronouncement. "You would be very wise," he continued, "to look favorably upon the Führer's generous offer to assist and strengthen the IOC."

"Would I?" Coubertin seemed undaunted.

"For the sake of your movement, and for the future of the Olympic Games," von Tschammer continued, "you'd be very wise to approve all the points. Germany would be an ideal headquarters for the new IOC."

"But I moved the headquarters here, to Switzerland, in 1915—as Carl well knows—to ensure their neutrality as the war broke out."

"Well, if there is another war, your safest home would be in Berlin."

"Oh, there will be a war, we all know that," Coubertin said. "We just don't know when."

Just as von Tschammer was about to respond, a sharp slap turned everyone toward Juliette and Heydrich. His hand covered his cheek, where she had stung him. St. Clair leaped up but Messerli stood to restrain him.

"Miss Franklin," Heydrich said, "please don't misinterpret my remarks." He drew his hand away, and the pale skin of his cheek was imprinted with the image of a red hand.

Heydrich rose, glowering at St. Clair.

They were all on their feet by then. "Under these unfortunate circumstances," said Coubertin, circling the table, "it's probably better if we call it a night." He took Juliette's arm and drew her away. "I'm so sorry," he said, handing her off to St. Clair.

Turning back to von Tschammer, the baron said, "The report of the Coubertin Commission will be submitted to the executive board within a week—and it will be conclusive." He nodded goodbye to Diem, and he and Messerli hurried away to catch up St. Clair and Juliette.

As they walked swiftly down to the quay, St. Clair holding Juliette close, he felt as if they were escaping a grave danger. He was sure that he and Heydrich were destined to fight. His nerves were on edge as Coubertin caught up and began apologizing profusely to Juliette.

"It's all right, Pierre," she said, "I knew the kind of man he was from the moment we met."

"I wanted to kill him," St. Clair said, and they all fell silent.

"It was unfortunate," Messerli said, breaking the spell, "but at least it brought that tense discussion to an end. But Pierre, how are you going to get the commission's report done in a week? We haven't even had the first meeting yet."

"There won't be any meetings," Coubertin said. "That's why I called it the Coubertin Commission tonight. The report is nearly finished."

St. Clair realized that Coubertin had been working on the draft off and on all day.

The tension had abated as they stopped at the Château d'Ouchy, and Coubertin and Messerli turned to say goodbye, the four of them in a small circle.

"Pierre," said Juliette, "Let's put all this behind us. There's no need to apologize again. But I have a favor to ask—a very personal favor." She smiled brightly, her eyes dancing.

Bowing slightly, Coubertin said, "If there's anything I can possibly do for you, my dear, your wish—"

"Be careful," St. Clair interjected, "you don't want to give her that much power."

Juliette elbowed Jacques and he bent in mock pain. "I've finished the portrait, Pierre, and I'd like to have a little soirée at the studio to unveil it."

"A public unveiling?" Coubertin feigned alarm. "You mean I don't get a look at it before the curtain is lifted?"

"No preview for you or anyone. I'd like you to bring the baroness and Renée, and we'll ensure a select few attend." She nodded at Messerli and smiled.

65

ATHENS 1896

A s St. Clair finished drafting the scenes of Athens, which to this point had become the longest chapter in his biography, he was particularly satisfied with his descriptions of the abysmal treatment of Coubertin and the IOC at the hands of the Greeks. In Athens, Pierre entered a city full of patriotic pride that left no room for shared glory. In one of the least perceptive judgments of his career, Coubertin led his colleagues into a storm of opposition and humiliation in Athens—even as his inaugural Olympic Games soared to heights of success he could hardly have imagined.

Athens looked like a different city when Pierre and Marie arrived at Constitution Square in late March and checked into the Hotel Grande Bretagne. The heart of the metropolis had taken on a festive, colorful atmosphere—and had been scrubbed and polished by an energetic and patriotic populace getting ready for their moment on the world's stage. The streets were festooned with banners and flags, and bunting hung from buildings and houses. Like a ubiquitous mythic signature splashed on the city by Zeus, the Greek letters *OA*, the symbols for the Olympic Games, and the dates 776 BC–1896 AD, seemed to be everywhere, a reminder that the ancient past was about to be resurrected before a full stadium of witnesses. The streets pulsed with men and women adorned in their finer suits and dresses, strolling about in the gay air and seeing who was there to be seen. Soldiers in uniform mixed with villagers in their traditional costumes. Farmers in their fustanella—the white-vested, skirted, and stockinged outfits worn in the countryside—added a touch of folklore to the scene. Wandering bands of minstrels boosted the sense of merriment with song. Men and boys staged impromptu foot races on the plaza in front of Parliament—as if the capital had no greater business than the business of sport. A crowd gathered and cheered as gymnastic acrobats cartwheeled across the square.

Word at the hotel had it that among all the athletes who had arrived so far, the Hungarians had captured the hearts of the Greeks, strolling about in their dashing white-and-blue striped shirts, greeting their hosts with expressions of gratitude and high expectations. Coubertin couldn't wait to see Kemény and learn whether it was an intentional mission or a spontaneous act. He knew that a freshly independent Hungary believed a national team at the first Olympic Games was a simple move of political legitimacy.

Keenly aware of the press of history, Coubertin had instructed Vikelas to engage a photographer for the first formal photograph of the members of the IOC at the inaugural Olympic Games. Once he had Marie settled in their suite, he left for the Zappeion, the handsome arcaded building left by Zappas as a legacy of his earlier version of the Olympic Games. It was a brief walk across Constitution Square and down through the national park. As he strolled and his excitement grew, he experienced a single, pointed pang of regret. In the face of the massive editorial demands on the imminent publication of his *Life of Napoleon*, his dear friend, Will Sloane, had had to cancel his trip to Athens, leaving the fledgling U.S. team on its own. *I wish you could see what we've created, Will.*

When Coubertin entered the nondescript room, Vikelas's back was turned. He was holding a large notebook and discussing the setup with the photographer, motioning toward a small desk and three chairs that would serve as props for the shoot.

"Perhaps five or six men," Vikelas said to the photographer. "I'm not sure who will show up today."

"Well, Demetri," Coubertin said, circling a large tripod and boxy camera and taking his colleague's hand, "it's time for us to make our own history."

"Welcome, Pierre," said Vikelas, a broad smile on his face. Laying his notebook on the desk, he embraced Coubertin. "Welcome to your Olympic Games."

"How are the preparations going?"

"Very well, if you can ignore the fact that we—the IOC—are being treated as just another commission."

Coubertin knew the slights were coming, knew they would be sidelined, but he thought he might be able to restore order. "Perhaps if I have a word with the king or crown prince?"

"I don't think they'll see you."

"Why not?"

"It's complicated, but Philemon has been very effective in fostering animosity against internationals. At this point, I'm treated like a secretary."

The jangle of a sheathed sword and heavy boots turned them toward the door as Major General Viktor Balck of Sweden stepped into the room with General Boutowsky of Russia.

"Gentlemen," Balck said, advancing with his hand out, "this is an impressive event we've triggered."

"I didn't realize," said Boutowsky, "that the Olympic Games would ignite such a communal celebration."

"Oh yes," said Vikelas, "we Greeks have waited fifteen centuries for this party to resume. We were not about to miss a trick now."

They were soon joined by Jiří Guth-Jarkovsky of Bohemia, Ferenc Kemény of Hungary, and finally Dr. Wilhelm Gebhardt of Germany, who had miraculously managed to produce a German team for the Games at the last minute.

After they established their collective enthusiasm for the scene in the city, they prepared for the photograph. Coubertin and Boutowsky sat at the desk flanking Vikelas, books open in front of them, Coubertin poised with pen in hand as if taking notes, and the other four standing behind and looking at the books as if a decision was being recorded.

Once the photograph was taken—recording forever an image of the first meeting of the IOC at the Olympic Games—they arranged seven chairs around the desk and began their first Olympic session. Since the Greeks had reduced the IOC's role to observer status—with no authority over the Games—it wasn't long before their displeasures surfaced. They discussed the press coverage and Philemon's campaign to rob the IOC of any credit or credibility.

"Greek pride is fine—they should be proud of their efforts," Balck said, "but they're wrong to diminish our leadership."

"They've called you a thief, Pierre," said Kemény. "My team showed me the article—accusing you, accusing us, of stealing their glory."

The complaints flowed amid proposals for confrontation. "We should refute their accusation in the press," Boutowsky said. While his colleagues demanded the restoration of respect for the IOC, Coubertin said little, letting the membership roil until Vikelas pleaded for patience and understanding.

"We'll have to follow the wishes of the sovereign," he said. "The king has taken great pride in the role the crown prince has played in leading the organizational effort. He sees this as a public coronation of his son—and doesn't want anyone to denigrate Constantine's achievement."

Coubertin finally spoke. "We must respect what the Greeks—what the royal family has achieved here. If you've been following the progress through Demetri's reports, you know that pride over the Games has grown with each drachma donated, each brick put in place. The truth is that the Greeks have done a magnificent job with little help here on the ground from us. The idea that the Games belong to Greece and Greece alone is a natural outcome—and it has spurred them to this great moment. We will not argue, and we will not intervene. We may relinquish control of these Games, but we will not relinquish our ownership. In the end, the glory of Greece will accrue to us."

"Pierre is right," said Balck, "we can't win an argument against our hosts."

Within a short time, the members all agreed on the wisdom of holding their tongues.

"I know this is not what we expected," Coubertin said, "but let's swallow our pride. Let's play the role they've assigned to us and be keen observers. We need to diligently record everything that happens here. Manage your teams and instruct them to be gracious guests as well. Let's make the most of this, gentlemen, and resist the temptations to assert control. In the end, control will come back to us."

Even as he spoke, Coubertin knew it would be difficult for him to assume such a humble position, especially with Marie and her fiery temper at his side.

○ ○ ○ ○ ○

Late on the night before the Games, returning from a banquet at city hall in which toast after toast had been offered but not a single word of recognition of the IOC, Pierre and Marie walked to their hotel room in silence. The evening had opened a gulf between them. She had been inflamed with anger over the accolades offered to every politician, bureaucrat, and sportsman in the room, growing increasingly incensed as the night wore on and she watched her husband applaud dutifully and nod and smile as if everything was perfect. Finally, as the highest praise was lavished on the royal family—represented that night by Crown Prince Constantine and his brother George, who had avoided looking in their direction all night—she began to curse under her breath, whispering to Pierre, "This isn't right. They're the thieves, taking all the credit. How dare they ignore you."

"The crown prince and his family do deserve the credit, Marie," he said with *sotto voce* impatience, glancing around the table and hoping no one had heard. "This is not the time for us," he added. "Our day will come." He stared at the front of the room and smiled, lifting his glass in a silent tribute from Vikelas, who was looking back at them from his table on the dais, subtly signaling his solidarity as if subterfuge were called for and the baron was best seen and not heard.

The baroness seemed to relax, but only for a moment. "Everything you've done for them—it all seems to count for nothing. Is this the future our sacrifice will bring us?" He gazed at her in anger, but then softened his look to show her that he too was crestfallen. He put his hand over hers and squeezed, but she turned away.

Now, as he placed the key in their door's lock, she said, "Wait. Let's go up on the roof for a drink and look at the Parthenon. This is your night, Pierre, the eve of your great triumph—and if the Greeks won't toast you, I will." She raised her hand to his cheek. "I'm sorry, darling. I just can't stomach the injustice."

"I know, darling. Thank you." His eyes moist, he offered her his arm. "Your outrage is all the affirmation I need right now."

They sat at a table for two and gazed out at the torch-lit spectacle of the Parthenon, sitting atop the citadel of the Acropolis like an eternally scarred and perfectly broken crown.

The baroness ordered two ouzos, and when they came she lifted her glass and said, "On behalf of the nation of Greece and sportsmen around the world, I wish to thank above all others the man who brought the Olympic Games back to life for all of us to enjoy—who gave us a new-found sense of pride in our country and our abilities—*le Rénovateur* himself, the good and ever forgiving Baron Pierre de Coubertin."

He laughed out loud and enjoyed the drink. "The world has gathered here, Marie, and I cannot let the misery distract me from the joy."

○ ○ ○ ○ ○

The Games were set to open on Monday, April 6, the day after Easter Sunday, which also happened to be the country's Independence Day. For a Greek nation schooled in the ancient mysteries of mythology, the combination of religion and patriotism infused the event—and Olympic sport—with a deeper meaning and an animated sense of destiny. In some inexplicable ways, the Games swept like a mistral into the Greek consciousness, carrying with them the eternal verities from ancient gods that still held a prominent place in the present.

Along with these blessings, however, the calendar produced a set of remarkable conflicts. The Greeks still used the old Julian calendar, which dated from the time Caesar crossed the Rubicon. The rest of the world operated on the Gregorian calendar, which was twelve days ahead. While most figured this out in advance, the American team, which Coubertin was anxiously awaiting, didn't arrive until April 5th, the day before the Games began.

On Easter morning, the Coubertins took in an early mass to hear Père Didon deliver a stirring sermon on the Olympic moment—exalting men to live at their best. Didon had been invited by the Orthodox Bishop of Rome to share the pulpit at the grand cathedral, a gesture of unusual spiritual collaboration produced, the baron was certain, by the amicable spirit engendered by the Games. King George and his entourage were in attendance for the *Te Deum*, but Coubertin could not make eye contact and had the impression that Crown Prince Constantine was deliberately evading his gaze.

They walked back to the Grande Bretagne in a light rain. Under a wide umbrella, the baroness clutching his arm, Coubertin let a note of irritation slip. "They won't even look at me in church."

"As much as we are ignored," Marie said, "your Dominican friend is celebrated. Have you noticed? It's as though he has been installed as the Catholic counterpart to the Orthodox Bishop of Athens. They're in the papers every day, appearing everywhere together, side by side in their black-and-white robes."

"They're blessing everyone and everything. Perhaps this is the first great irony of modern Olympic history—two Christian priests, both men of genuine piety, blessing every ritual and event declared pagan and stopped 1502 years ago by Rome's Christian emperor."

○ ○ ○ ○ ○

The newly restored Panathenaic Stadium opened for seating on the first day of the Olympic Games at noon, and people began to stream in. The step-seats on both sides of the arena were of freshly polished white Pentelicus marble, but the back end was ringed with wooden seats. The laborious restoration effort had fallen short of the timetable but no one seemed to mind. There had been some public complaints about the price of tickets, but plenty of free open seating was available for spectators on the hills around the stadium. Few people were worried about missing the events. The public sphere was marked by a ubiquitous gaiety and a relaxed sense of order. A spirit was in the air, an unmistakable mixture of Greek pride and historic anticipation.

Coubertin and his colleagues, having their last pre-Games conference at the Hotel Grande Bretagne without Vikelas, who was tending to his organizational duties, speculated at the size of the crowd that would show up.

"Vikelas says it will be a sellout—and the largest single gathering of people in the history of Greece," said Guth-Jarkovsky. Coubertin's heart leaped and he wanted to shout for joy, but he held his breath instead. He couldn't help but be thrilled by the speculation. If his first Games produced record crowds, the second edition would do even more. Today was the day that all of his dreams and plans would be tested in the fertile soil of Hellenic myth. In a few hours, he would know how successful his vision had been.

Marie approached the table. "Every day we've been here, the streets have been crowded." She looked charming, dressed in pink with a white plumed hat over her hair. Coubertin rose and kissed her cheeks, and after she had greeted each of his colleagues in turn, he settled her at the table.

At the time, Athens was a city of about seventy thousand residents, and the port of Piraeus to the south had another forty thousand. All morning, full trains from Piraeus unloaded at the station, and it seemed that almost every Greek in town was making his or her way toward the restored stadium. The streets outside the hotel in Constitution Square were thick with parades of pedestrians, the men mostly in dark frock coats, the women in colorful gowns, many bearing parasols against the hovering clouds. Pierre could see that his colleagues wanted to get out into the mix—and he was almost ready.

From Vikelas's updates, he knew the travel plans of the royal family, and despite the fact that they had snubbed him, he wanted to ensure that the IOC would be part of the official delegation that entered the stadium with the king. "King George and his entourage should arrive at the square in front of the gates at about three o'clock," he said. "That gives us two hours to walk down, survey the final preparations, and be in position to greet the royal family."

"I'd like to head down there now," Kemény said. "I'm anxious to check on my team and ensure they're focused on the events and not parading about as they have been."

"All right," said Coubertin. "Let's make our way down to the stadium. Please be observant and take notes on the organizational effort. We're going to write a detailed report after these Games, and I'll want your thoughts."

With that, he turned to Marie and offered his arm. "Let's take a walk into history, madame," he said, glad she was in a good mood. Out the door they went, six IOC members on their way to the first modern Olympic Games.

They joined the flow of people across Constitution Square as competing strains of festive music from a number of roving bands filled the air. Enjoying the public theater, they crossed in front of the steps of Parliament and strolled under the spring leaves of the national park along a broad alley with hundreds of Greeks and internationals heading toward the stadium. They passed through Zappeion Park, circling the building, and the crowd began to slow, but with each step Coubertin felt a growing confirmation that his ideas and his judgments and decisions had mostly hit their mark.

As they emerged at the square that led to the stadium gates, soldiers were visible everywhere in the mass of humanity, ready to push back the crowds for the carriages of the dignitaries—the only ones allowed along this Olympic route—and at the gates collecting tickets and pointing everyone toward their seats.

"Smart use of the military," Coubertin said to Gebhardt. "The crown prince is an effective planner."

"Yes, it's a very effective measure—serving as ushers and imposing control at the same time."

Anxious to locate his team, Kemény quickened his pace, but Coubertin called him back. "Gentlemen, let's meet under the statue of Averoff," he said, pointing toward the entrance, "at two forty-five sharp. Please don't be late. I want the royal family to see that we're honoring them with our presence."

ooooo

Balck was the last one back at the statue, but he was on time. The soldiers had already cleared the street for the royal caravan, which, from the sounds of the shouts erupting beyond Coubertin's sightline, must have been approaching. Under the direction of a captain clearly briefed on protocol, soldiers arranged the dignitaries in several long greeting lines leading to the entrance. Coubertin led the IOC delegation toward the front of the line and was about to engage the captain when Timoleon Philemon appeared at his side.

"Captain," Philemon said to the soldier, casting a cold glance at Coubertin, "these gentlemen are leading their national teams to the Games. Please put them at the end of the line." He pointed to a place far from the gate and Coubertin followed his gaze.

The captain stepped forward, saying, "Right this way, please."

"Oh my God," Marie said. They had little choice but to obey his orders, and she said nothing more as Coubertin's cutting glance silenced her for the moment.

The clip-clop of horse hooves filled the air as the din rose and the crowd cheered the arrival of the royal coach behind eight white horses. The king's carriage was an impressive sight, Coubertin thought, gold-enameled and bearing the royal coat of arms in a handsome crest on the doors. Six carriages made up the royal entourage. The king, queen, and crown prince emerged to wave from the steps of the carriage as a wave of applause resonated across the square. The king led the way down the long line of dignitaries.

Reaching the IOC members at last, the king was first to greet Pierre. He said nothing, giving only the slightest nod of recognition and a faint smile.

"Congratulations, Your Majesty, on the great work you have done—" Coubertin said, but the king moved along before he could complete his compliment.

And then the crown prince was directly in front of him, shaking his hand vigorously, looking into his eyes with an intensity that might have been a plea for understanding. Coubertin repeated the same compliment, and as Constantine moved swiftly past the baroness, he noticed she was again wearing disappointment on her face.

Suddenly, a fanfare filled the air and the strings of the royal hymn rose. The king and queen promenaded toward the gates for their ceremonial entrance. As the entourage amassed behind them, soldiers under the direction of Philemon organized the procession using the usual Greek protocol, with ministers, diplomats, legislators, and government officials from cities across Greece filing in directly behind the royal family. Behind them came the decorated military officers and the clergy. The members of the Olympic Organizing Committee fell in line next, Vikelas among them—and then, and only then, was the IOC invited to follow at the back of the parade along with nameless members of numerous international commissions and members of the press. Coubertin was particularly chastened to see Hugues Le Roux, a writer from *Figaro* in Paris who had been particularly unkind to Pierre and the very idea of the Games, five rows in front of him. The soldiers formed a funneled column around the entrance as the parade carried on.

In a fleeting moment of pride, Coubertin noted as they passed through the gates that the six members of the IOC were marching in unison, in a single line that held the true power behind these proceedings—despite the lack of recognition. It seems Balck's military bearing had an effect on them for they stepped with a crispness that denoted their collective integrity as the group most responsible for the glories of the moment. But then Coubertin's gaze moved up to the stands and he beheld the white marble thrones of the monarchs, draped in red satin and pillows, and he couldn't help but think his fledgling organization belonged in the tribune with the royalty—at minimum. But with discipline and drive, he pushed away the distractions and soaked in the achievements of the moment and the fact that the first Olympic Games of the modern era were about to begin.

He climbed the stairs behind Marie, lightly guiding her by the elbow, the hem of her dress dusting the marble steps of the stadium. He nudged her forward when he saw her glance at the royal tribune, certain they would not be acknowledged, knowing the humiliation weighed more on her than it did on him. They rose past the boxes of the honored and finally reached the rows of commissioners, excusing themselves repeatedly as they bumped the knees of functionaries and bureaucrats, jostling into the crowd among their unknown collaborators. Pierre forced a smile and thanked a few of them, knowing the Games were dependent on these volunteers who had organized some aspect of the events.

As they took their seats, Marie's eyes conveyed her disbelief and deep regret, and he looked away. This was not what she had expected. Pierre knew what she was thinking and feeling because he could feel it too. He was trying to see a path forward through the emotional conflicts of the moment but was having trouble clearing his mind of undeniable reality that the Greeks, whose claims to ownership of the Games were growing by the minute, had succeeded in reducing his International Olympic Committee to just another commission—for the moment, at least.

This wasn't what he had expected either. I am now one of the workers, he thought, weighing the idea slowly. He realized he had become what he had wanted to be, a true republican, not just a man of the people, but one of the people.

Suddenly, the reality of the spectacle filled him with a pure joy. He pulled Marie to him and kissed her, then held her gaze as she opened her eyes.

"They can deny us all they want, Marie," he said, "but there is no denying what we've done. We have rallied the nation and its people and in some small way our whole world to a revival the likes of which no one has ever seen."

She smiled unconvincingly and looked away, gazing at those seated ten rows below them. Meanwhile, he tried to take pleasure in being among the workers who had made it all happen, but he couldn't sustain the feeling for he knew it wasn't enough, it wouldn't do, and the disquietude roiled inside him like an unruly sea as it plainly did in her. Despite what he had said to his colleagues, despite his pleas for humility, he did expect some recognition—if not honors, at least acknowledgment. And he decided at that moment that if honor wasn't going to be conferred—if the Greeks wouldn't give him the satisfaction—he would take it himself. He felt the sense of conviction that by now he knew so well rise within, a feeling of potency returning. He would claim it as surely as he would take back the Games when this mighty celebration was over.

And then, in a flash, the spectacle returned as the babble of thousands of voices broke through his consciousness—musicians began to fill the field below and a grand choir of three hundred in white robes assembled in their midst. A podium was set out and the crown prince suddenly appeared—tall, nearly massive among his subjects, the dress uniform giving him authority. He lifted his hands and silence finally settled over the crowd. His voice rose in a proclamation everyone strained to hear. Coubertin caught only a few phrases, parts of the message as the prince turned to shout to the fifty thousand in the stadium and the forty thousand gathered in the hills beyond. It was a paean to Greece, mixing patriotic pride with Christian and pagan myth, much of it lost in the vast space, but the last line was an unmistakable statement of praise for the king, who then rose on his throne and clearly said, "I hereby proclaim the opening of the first modern Olympic Games in Athens."

A swell of music rose from the orchestra and the choir began to sing the moving "Cantata of the Olympic Games." Coubertin felt a stirring in his soul as the lyrics flowed over them like a wave of affirmation, a language of solemnity and celebration written by an unnamed Greek: *Immortal spirit of antiquity / father of the true, beautiful, and good / descend, appear, shed over us thy light / upon this ground and under this sky / which has first witnessed thy unperishable fame.* The beauty of the words and the perfection of the music and the moment relaxed him, and he felt joy radiating from the humanity crowded around him. He glanced at Marie and Balck and Guth-Jarkovsky and saw that they were transfixed. He saw the same expression of awe on the faces of Gebhardt and Kemény to his left and he thought, brilliant, the Greeks have done it—and we've done it. The joy was so palpable that as soon as the last note rang through the air, the king was cheering, and the desire of the crowd—shouting "again, again, again"—for a repeat performance became evident. Yielding to the public demand, the conductor turned to the orchestra and raised his baton, and the crowd fell silent as the first plaintive strings of the Olympic cantata began again.

When it was over, the musicians and the chorus took their reserved seats to witness the beginning of the competition. All attention focused on the tunnel as a line of twenty athletes marched onto the field for the four preliminary rounds of the hundred-meter dash. Almost all were dressed in white shorts and loose cotton shirts and spikes—the leather track shoes that had become *de rigueur* for sprints. Spectators searched their programs for the numbers of the competitors and noted—as the heats went off in quick succession—that the Americans, who crouched to the ground with their hands on the starting line, bending low before the gun went off, easily outclassed the athletes who stood erect or leaned for the start. Coubertin was quick to note the differences in techniques and the advantages won by different positions, and later he would discuss with his colleagues the need to publicize the styles practiced by the finest performers. Along with their technical excellence, the Americans seemed to have the largest— and loudest—cheering sections in the stands. God, he wished Sloane were there. In the third heat, Pierre and Marie cheered after spotting the French sprinter, Albin Lermusiaux, at the starting line, and they shouted, "Vive la France!" when he qualified for the finals three days later.

And then came the first medal event of the day, the triple jump, popularly known as the hop, skip, and jump. The Greeks had two favorites in the event, but after the first few rounds it was clear that a Frenchman from Athens named Alexandre Tuffère and the American James B. Connolly were the true talent in the field. Coubertin was on his feet—and a good scattering of French patriots in the stands cheered with him—as Tuffère made a fine jump, the longest of the day, well beyond the best of the Greeks but just beyond where Connolly had last landed. Coubertin knew from Sloane's letter regarding the U.S. team that Connolly was a spirited young man who quit Harvard to travel with the Boston Athletic Association to compete in the first modern Olympics. And now, Coubertin drew

Gebhardt's and Marie's attention to Connolly, who walked the length of the track, stopped along the sand pit, and astonished the crowd by throwing his hat in the sand a full meter beyond Tuffère's mark. Looking at the crowd, Connolly solicited a chorus of "B-A-A! Rah, rah, rah! B-A-A! Rah, rah, rah!" from his supporters.

The odd staccato sequence of the cheer—familiar to every U.S. college crowd, but new to the ears of the internationals—turned almost all eyes toward the American fans and then to the field again as Connolly jogged back to the starting line.

"What is he doing?" Marie asked.

"Showing off," said Coubertin.

"I doubt he can make that jump," Balck said.

"It would be a record."

They all watched, riveted, as Connolly rolled into the fastest sprint of the day, made great distance with his hop, skipped better than his last attempt, and soared through the air above the pit, landing just beyond his hat.

Another cheer emanated from the top of the stadium and swept across the stands like a wave. Coubertin saw a group of uniformed sailors from the USS *San Francisco* lining the top tier. Their captain had decided to keep his ship anchored in Piraeus for the duration of the Games, and they would soon become one of the most familiar American cheering sections. Then the collegiate cheers resumed, morphing from "B-A-A, B-A-A" to "U-S-A, U-S-A" as students from the American University in Athens formed another enthusiastic unit.

In honor of Connolly's magnificent leap, which officials had registered at 44' 11¾", a new world record, the U.S. flag was raised in a brief victory ceremony as the national anthem was played. The Boston Athletic Association and Princeton sections vied with the sailors for loudest cheers.

The crowd was still abuzz with "the miracle" of Connolly's triple jump when the first of two eight-hundred-meter heats was run. Seven runners gathered at the starting line, and Edwin Flack, a swift Australian who was a member of the London Athletic Club, and therefore part of the modest British Olympic team, easily outclassed the field.

Flack's triumph brought consternation to the IOC camp. Coubertin was reminded of his disappointment in the two British IOC members, Charles Herbert and Lord Ampthill, who had failed to recruit a competitive team of British athletes. There was no excuse for a six-man British team when everyone knew the talent was certainly available. Watching Flack, Coubertin was pained by his own failure as well. He had realized much too late that neither Herbert nor Ampthill had the appropriate connections to Oxford, Cambridge, and other universities that could have sent teams to demonstrate the reach of Thomas Arnold's great legacy. Too late, Coubertin had sent open letters and appeals to the *London Times* and other papers in an attempt to increase British participation. Neither Herbert nor Ampthill had traveled to Athens, a fact that only reinforced the resentment of their hard-working colleagues.

But then Coubertin was on his feet for the next eight-hundred heat, in which the diminutive Frenchman Lermusiaux captured the second preliminary.

Clouds were darkening the sky and the wind brought an early-evening chill when the predominantly Greek crowd welcomed into the arena a broad international field of discus throwers. Eleven athletes from seven nations—Greece, Denmark, Germany, England, France, Sweden, and the United States—lined up to compete. Hopes ran high in the host nation. With two well-known and respected regional champions—Sotirios Versis and Panagiotis Paraskevopoulos, who had entertained crowds in their public practice sessions for months—the Greeks believed this event might belong to them. Their expectations were deeply rooted in the national psyche. Every Greek child grew up admiring the graceful, muscular lines of Myron's *Discobolus*—and thousands of young Greeks had thrown the discus in the run-up to the Games, trying to imitate the classical sculpture that revealed the possibilities of sport as artistic dance. Thanks to the endless stream of Roman reproductions over the centuries, the image of *Discobolus* resided in the Greek imagination as an idealized symbol of the past—and all the Greeks present longed for the triumph of their two finest throwers.

In short order, the field fell away and Versis, the leaner of the two, took the lead with a brilliant second throw of 91' 1". Knowing he had done his best, Versis waved that he was finished and would forgo his third throw, and the crowd cheered. But then Paraskevopoulos, his larger, stronger compatriot, unleashed his finest throw of the day and took the lead at ninety-five feet.

But while the Greeks and most of the internationals twisted their bodies into a spring but kept their feet planted, throwing on the strength of their arms alone, the lone American in the contest had developed an entirely different technique. Using the full length of the approach, Robert Garrett of Princeton coiled his body at the back of the throwing ring and spun forward in two complete rotations. As he did, beautifully maintaining his balance, he extended his arm, and like the end of a whip it brought the discus around with great force. The crowd gave a collective gasp as the plate soared through the air and landed inches beyond the best Greek throw. It was marked at 95' 7", achieving another victory for the Americans.

Garrett's teammates and friends unleashed another staccato cheer: "P-R-I-N-C-E-T-O-N." The sailors and other Americans soon joined in, and Coubertin worried that the boisterous response might offend their Greek hosts. But at that moment, the Greek spectators revealed the magnanimity that would characterize the Games. They rose en masse and cheered for the new Olympic champion.

Dusk was settling in, and everything stopped for a moment as the orchestra played the royal hymn, and the royal family departed with appropriate pomp and circumstance. The crowd began to drift away. With the temperature dropping, the last event of the day—the preliminary heats for the four-hundred-meter race—offered the Greeks little hope of victory. The Americans didn't seem to mind, however, with Tom Burke and Herbert Jamison of Boston winning the heats before a half-empty stadium.

○ ○ ○ ○ ○

As darkness fell, torch-lit parades illuminated the streets of the city, and celebrations filled every plaza, restaurant, and taverna. Everyone knew the first day of the modern Olympics had been a grand success, exceeding all expectations and proving the Greeks were marvelous hosts. The credit truly belonged to them, Coubertin thought. The joy in the air was palpable. Vikelas joined his colleagues for a hearty round of congratulations as they strolled back to the Hotel Grande Bretagne and discussed the day. What most impressed Coubertin was how the Greek spectators had responded to America's victories, cheering in appreciation of the achievement even while enduring their own losses. The Greeks embodied the internationalism he had hoped for—and it filled him with pleasure.

Back at the hotel, Marie whispered that she was tired and bored with the minute examination of the day's events, so Pierre escorted her up to their room to retire for the night. He knew her disappointment had abated somewhat in the excitement of the day.

"What a privilege," she said, "to witness this marvelous resurrection. But I still believe some of the spotlight should have been on you, Pierre." She embraced him. "I'm proud of you, darling."

When he returned to the table, Vikelas suggested they all go out and enjoy the celebrations and merriment in the streets. "If we miss the atmosphere of this opening evening, we'll miss half of the joy that we produced."

"I agree," Gebhardt said, "but before we go, gentlemen, I would like to propose a toast." The seven members of the IOC immediately stood, ready to lift their glasses to their mutual success. "We have much to be thankful for today," Gebhardt began, "for our magnificent Greek hosts and particularly the royal family, for the tireless work of Demetrius and his colleagues, but above all—to the man who made all this possible." He pointed his glass toward Coubertin. "Pierre, all this is your work and vision."

Coubertin bowed graciously, knowing these modest moments of recognition would give him the strength to resist confronting the Greeks.

They followed Vikelas out of the hotel, and within minutes they were jostling their way through the narrow, twisting lanes of the Plaka, absorbing the boisterous spirit of the street party. Kemény wrapped his arm around Coubertin's shoulder and pointed up—directly above them stood the torch-lit Parthenon, a magical, millennial apparition. Two blocks farther, they came upon a knot of people in front of a corner taverna. Laughter erupted among them, and they all cheered and lifted their glasses. In their midst, Garrett and Paraskevopoulos were saluting each other, the Greek stating that if he'd had one more throw, he might have tried Garrett's spinning approach.

Observing without interrupting the gaiety, Coubertin said to Kemény, "This, Ferenc! This is just what we have been striving for—friendships fostered by sport."

○ ○ ○ ○ ○

The week rolled on, with a crowded schedule of competitive events in the stadium one day and at venues around the city the next. Coubertin and the other six members of the IOC attended events both together and apart, and they held meetings in the evening or morning to discuss their observations and make notes on the organizational aspects of the Games. Although they were sidelined, they were active and, truth be told, deeply impressed and inspired by the quality of the Greek effort to stage an event worthy of their Olympic history.

For Coubertin's benefit, Vikelas reviewed the king's schedule, explaining how it was planned to ensure that the presence of the royal entourage graced the most significant events of each day, helping to inaugurate each of the new Olympic sports at the very beginning of the competition. The baron followed King George and his entourage to various events, observing how the arrival of the royal family immediately lifted the atmosphere of the competition and filled each venue with historic meaning. The first fencing competition was staged on a raised platform in the Zappeion's colonnaded courtyard. As the king arrived and climbed the stairs to the crenelated royal tribune, the event took on an air of commemoration. Coubertin was delighted that the French foil masters dominated the competition— with two of his countrymen, Gravelotte and Gallot, taking the top medals and enjoying the king's personal recognition.

That night at the IOC debriefing, Coubertin said, "It seems our Olympics have given the monarchy a new vitality if not a greater sense of purpose." Indeed, while their roles were beneficial to the Games, the Games also served to enhance the image of the royal family. Through their highly visible engagement, the king and his three princes endeared themselves to the public and won the affection of their people in ways that would have been appreciated in the *Ancien Regime*. Although the Games embodied the spirit of democracy—the republican urge toward equality was at their heart—the demands of ritual and protocol created room for the monarchy and validated its worth in social terms at least. Coubertin and his colleagues spent a good deal of time discussing the symbolism of the processions they witnessed and the moments of ritual created. They were satisfied that Athens was creating a symbolic legacy whose significance would transfer to and grow with each successive edition of the Games.

In particular, by the end of the fourth day, Coubertin was pleased that the multiplicity of events and the diversity of sports had contributed to the sense of festival he had hoped for—and that the breadth of inclusivity had given the Games a distinction no past event had ever achieved.

On the competitive front, it was clear from the beginning that despite their modest size, the American team had skills and techniques no country could match. With only four of Sloane's most athletic students from Princeton and ten others from the Boston Athletic Association—plus a coach and a trainer—the Americans were simply dominant. They won every track and field event except the eight hundred and fifteen hundred meters, both of which were won by the Australian Flack, who barely nipped Boston's Arthur Blake at the line of the fifteen hundred. The marathon was still to come, but the Americans had already emerged as the most heroic team at the Games. Among the fourteen of them, they carried home twenty medals.

But there was still enough magic to go around. The marathon, which by all eyewitness accounts including Coubertin's, turned out to be the greatest event of the Games, was not simply a victory for Greece, but full redemption for every other Olympic dream that fell short.

○ ○ ○ ○ ○

On the afternoon of the fifth day, as the packed crowd awaited news of the marathon, the sound of a faraway cannon shot reached the stadium, indicating the runners had breached the city limits. And then another softer sound filtered into the stadium from a great distance, like the echo of a shout from a far-off chorus. And then it came again, a little louder, and again, a little closer, and heads turned in search of something to behold. And then it became clear that it was a roar of ecstatic cheers, a succession of euphoric shouts from people lining the course, becoming progressively louder as the leader ran toward the hundred thousand waiting in the stadium and on the hillside. Suddenly, it seemed, everyone realized the cheers had a national bearing, an unmistakably Greek accent, citizens straining to proclaim their adulation for someone moving toward destiny, like a gathering of witnesses spurred on by ghosts of the gods. The volume continued to mount, a wave of sound becoming ever more powerful as the vaults of history opened and the modern Games called forth the spirit of Olympia. Suddenly the word "Hellene, Hellene" began to course through the crowd—and a din of anticipation rose in the stadium that a Greek was indeed leading the marathon. And then like an apparition he was before them, emerging from the archway of the tunnel, a lone runner in the white skirt of the Greek fustanella sporting a gold headband above his black vest, the garb of a peasant who had just become a hero. As he made his way onto the track, Greek spectators could not contain their pride—and their voices rose even higher. A native son was about to win the greatest race in history. Their Olympic Games had come back to life, not in a museum or some static exhibit but in the living, breathing moment that filled their lungs and pushed the blood through their veins.

The crown prince and his brother George ran onto the track, circling the oval like escort runners alongside the soon-to-be-famous Spiridon Loues, whom the gods had granted the gift of speed over distance.

○ ○ ○ ○ ○

Two days later, on the morning of Sunday, April 12, King George invited three hundred guests—including every visiting athlete and all the international journalists in town—to join him for breakfast in a ballroom at the royal palace. Still angry, Marie refused to attend, but Coubertin and his colleagues occupied a table amid the opulence. Despite the early hour, guests milled about the room with champagne in their hands, freely interacting with the king and the royals and their great guest of honor, Spiridon Loues.

Once they were all seated, the toasts began and rolled on endlessly, it seemed to Coubertin, who suspected what was coming. The true believers and sycophants stood one after the other, heralding the birth of a new age of sport, trumpeting the magnificence of their sovereign and his sons. Still full of fervor from the miraculous marathon triumph, the crowd reveled in the presence of the king and implored him to take the floor himself, which he finally did.

Vikelas glanced at Pierre as the speech began, and Coubertin was aware that the Greek was carefully observing his reaction to the words that spilled from the royal tongue, obviously written in advance:

"Greece, the mother and nurse of the Olympic Games in antiquity, has labored to celebrate the Games once more before the eyes of Europe and the New World. Since the success of the Games has passed all expectations, we hope that our guests, who have honored us with their presence, will select Athens as the peaceful meeting place of all nations, as the stable and permanent seat of the Olympic Games."

So there it was. Coubertin felt his blood boil as if anger had heated his marrow. Vikelas was still eyeing him, and he felt his expression betray his emotions.

As approving replies came from Philemon and others, his agitation mounted. Not once had they mentioned his name, not once had they acknowledged that he had saved their Games after resurrecting them in the first place. He had built the committee that put on the Games, yet the king was proclaiming that the world should now recognize that the Olympics belonged to Greece permanently, and would be celebrated henceforth in Athens every four years and nowhere else. The moment presented more than the greatest challenge to his work, it signaled the complete loss of his authority, the end of his life's work just as it was beginning, the failure of his vision, and the dismissal of his leadership. He would not have it. He decided to offer his own response, to let the king and all the guests present know that he, Baron Pierre de Coubertin, and the IOC would gladly welcome them to the next celebration of the Olympic Games in Paris in 1900.

But as he reached for his glass, Vikelas laid his hand across Pierre's arm, holding it down with some force, preventing him from rising. He glanced around. All of his colleagues had noticed, including Gebhardt. They understood what was coming.

"We cannot argue with the king now," Vikelas said, his mouth close to Coubertin's ear, the soft words urging wisdom, restraint in the face of Greece's euphoric pride. He looked at his friend, then at Gebhardt and Kemény, who shook their heads, and then put his drink down. He knew Vikelas was right, they were all right. He couldn't blemish the ethic of friendship through sport and destroy what he had set in motion. And so he decided to withhold his challenge for now, to let them have their illusion, to let them think public sentiment would bring the Olympics back to Athens.

"You're right, Demetri," he said. "They should have their day."

○ ○ ○ ○ ○

The marathon had been the final event of the athletics competition. Gymnastics concluded on the same day, and weightlifting, tennis, and fencing were already finished. Wrestling, cycling, swimming, and shooting events were still to be contested, but yachting was canceled because storms produced high seas that would not relent. The competitions went on until April 13. The last event was a twelve-hour cycle race in a nearly empty velodrome. Six contestants started out at five o'clock in the morning, and by mid-afternoon only two continued to pedal, an Englishman named Kiping and an Austrian named Schmall. Enduring pain, swollen limbs, and exhaustion, they fought for the last gleam of Olympic glory, passing each other again and again until the Austrian won, having circled the track nine hundred times, exactly one lap more than his English competitor.

In the end, as the IOC compiled its analysis, heroes emerged from almost every competing country. The Germans and Swedes dominated gymnastics, the Hungarians captured the swimming glory, the Americans ruled track and field, and the French excelled at fencing and cycling. But in Flack, Australia and England found a great champion. And beyond Spiridon Loues, the Greeks captured more medals overall than any of their guests.

After another weather postponement, the very last event of the 1896 Athens Olympic Games—the awarding of the prizes—took place before a full stadium on Wednesday, April 15. All winners received a silver medal, an olive branch from Olympia, and an engraved certificate. Second-place finishers received a bronze medal, a laurel branch, and a certificate as well. Third place went unrecognized. The gold, silver, and bronze Olympic era would begin in Paris four years later.

On the field in the Panathenaic Stadium that day, Coubertin stood quietly with his colleagues in a wide circle of officials watching King George standing before them on a raised platform as he greeted each athlete and bestowed their awards. Rich patrons added several silver cups to the ceremony for outstanding performances, the largest by far presented to Loues as his marathon exploits were recalled.

As the ceremony brought an end to the glories of Greece, Coubertin and the IOC were faced with the challenge of countering the king's claims to make Athens the permanent home of the Olympics. A further blow occurred when a petition surfaced signed by every member of the U.S. Olympic team, supporting the royal family's wishes to make Athens the world's Olympic host for all future Games.

○ ○ ○ ○ ○

It was the end of another long day at Mon Repos. Coubertin seemed to be tired of the memories of Greece, of that long night of humility. He asked St. Clair if he had heard enough about the Athens Olympics.

"I think I've had enough of the ignoble treatment you endured," St. Clair said. "The only question remaining for me is why you were so generous with the Greeks in your *Memoirs*, why so forgiving. Despite the continual slights, I can find no objection to their behavior in your writings—and no bitterness."

Coubertin didn't ruminate long on the answer. "I didn't want to dampen in any way the immense pride the Greeks deservedly took in their achievements— or diminish the unique bond that developed between the royal family and the people through the Games. They had raised the money, restored the stadium, organized the events, and welcomed all competitors with true hospitality. They deserved the adulation that followed. If I had attacked on the basis of their slights—and that's what they were to me, slights, not the humiliation Marie felt—the reaction might have produced an irredeemable split in the still fledgling Olympic Movement."

"But were you not worried that the political power and popular support they amassed—the support they had for making Athens the permanent Olympic host—might rob you of your authority to organize the Games elsewhere?"

"At first, yes, I was angry. But I quickly realized that if I had fought openly, the world of sport might have been divided between Greece and its supporters and our small band of IOC administrators. The odds were against us coming out on top. I was certain that if I had engaged in any battle in the public realm, I would have lost control of the movement and the Games. I'm still certain of that. I had to be gracious, and I had to bide my time."

"And you had Paris waiting in the wings."

"I thought I did, but it wasn't long before I realized Picard held all the power in 1900—and in the end the French did as much to shunt us aside as the Greeks had."

66

THE UNVEILING

L ate on a Friday afternoon at the beginning of the third week of August, Pierre experienced a sense of youthful anticipation that was once as common as the air he breathed, but had been beaten into the background by the difficulties of his last decade. He looked in the mirror and tightened his tie, wondering if Juliette's portrait would restore some youthful optimism to the worn countenance staring back at him. He winked at himself, delighted that the night ahead belonged to him. Marie and Renée were stirring in the hallway, waiting for Dr. Messerli and his wife, who were going to drive them to Juliette's studio for the unveiling of the portrait.

Fifteen minutes later they all climbed the stairs to Juliette's sunlit atelier. Even before the doctor opened the door, Pierre could hear the buzz inside. The room was full of vitality and laughter, but once they entered, it fell into a momentary hush as Juliette announced, "Ladies and gentlemen, our guest of honor has arrived." Pierre was surprised to see Arthur Maret, the mayor of Lausanne, and several municipal dignitaries along with Émil Drut and a few other restaurateurs—each of whom looked after the baron as part of Messerli's long-standing social conspiracy.

Turning toward him en masse, the guests clapped or clinked their glasses in welcome. Two of Drut's waiters offered champagne to Pierre and Marie as the room fell back into the din of conversation. St. Clair and Juliette greeted them, and Juliette drew Renée from behind the baroness and held her hand as they talked.

"This is quite a gathering of luminaries," Coubertin said, smiling and nodding at people across the room.

"They're here for you, Pierre," Juliette replied. Turning to Marie, she added, "To honor both of you."

"Indeed," said the baroness with a half-smile, clearly struggling to be gracious, "it is an honor to have a portrait painted by … an American artist. I can't wait to see what you've done." Her half-hearted tone belied her words. She looked to St. Clair and they each nodded politely.

Motioning to the platform where the portrait was covered by a gold silk sheath, Juliette addressed the baron, "I hope you won't be disappointed by my humble work."

"I know the painting will be brilliant," he said. "I just hope the subject does not undermine your intent."

"The subject, my dear baron, is the shining star of this show."

"Let's go greet your audience," Messerli said, guiding Pierre and Marie toward the mayor. St. Clair, Juliette, and Renée trailed behind them, but Renée tugged on Juliette's arm to hold her back for a moment.

As their eyes met, Renée held her gaze. "I just wanted to thank you for everything you and Jacques have done for Mother and Father. This means so much to them."

"You're welcome, of course," Juliette said and they embraced. A chorus of laughter turned them as the mayor, Messerli, and the Coubertins shared a moment of some hilarity. People clustered all around them, waiting to greet the baron and the baroness. The night was off to a fine start.

An hour later, as twilight darkened the garret's window wall, St. Clair turned on all the lights as instructed, and Juliette took to the stage. Pierre took Marie's hand and they made their way to the front and up the single step of the riser.

Juliette positioned them on the other side of the draped portrait before beginning her speech. "More than six months ago, at the invitation of Dr. Francis Messerli, Jacques St. Clair and I moved to your community, and we have felt at home here ever since. You have embraced us as members of your family—and we will always be grateful for the generosity of Lausanne. The natural beauty of this city is exceeded only by the warmth of its welcome. I want to thank Mayor Maret for joining us tonight. And our dear friend Émil Drut for robbing La Nautica's kitchen and staff for our benefit."

Looking out at all the expectant faces, Pierre felt that sense of youthful anticipation again; he looked at Juliette in gratitude as she continued. "As some of you know, we came here with a mission, to tell a story that has never been properly told. Jacques has been writing the life story of the Baron Pierre de Coubertin and his quest to give our world one of its greatest modern gifts, the Olympic Games." She went on to praise him and his great creation, stating that his legacy was worthy of a great biography—and perhaps something more. "And like Jacques," she said, "I wanted to contribute to our mission. And our friend Pierre consented—with some reluctance—to sit for me and allow me to paint his portrait. And so, ladies and gentlemen, I am honored to present to you tonight another look at our resident genius of sport—the Baron Pierre de Coubertin."

Taking the hem of the silk cover, Juliette swirled it away from the painting to dramatic effect. A collective intake of breath indicated the crowd's positive reaction. Shouts of "Bravo" punctuated the applause, and whispers of approval continued after the clapping receded. The symbolism of the old Greek temple, the ruins of what might have been an ancient stadium, and the Olympic rings floating in the clouds added meaning to the baron's impressive visage with its shining eyes and hint of a smile.

Pierre took Juliette's hand and stepped forward with Marie. He felt the crowd's eyes on him as he inspected his image, noting Juliette had restored a hint of youth and rosy health to his otherwise aged face. He was handsome again. On canvas, he had regained what the years had taken away. His eyes felt moist when he looked at Juliette, who was beaming. Turning to the crowd, his voice cracked in humility as he thanked Juliette and Jacques and Francis, but he couldn't make a speech and didn't want to. Deeply honored, he tried to show his gratitude by dropping his head and embracing Marie—something he had not done in years—hiding his face in her shoulder. The gesture, and Marie's acceptance of it, seemed to endear him to his audience all the more.

Marie pulled away from Pierre's grasp a little too soon and stood for a moment looking at the painting. "It is a remarkable likeness and full of the spirit that my husband has sought to spread all over the world—the spirit of sport and the timeless gifts it bestows on all those who seek its rewards." Pierre appreciated the effort she was making, knowing she had long ago grown to detest almost any public celebration.

"Bravo," Jacques shouted, leading another round of applause.

As the celebration wound down and the mayor took his leave, Pierre, Émil Drut, and Jacques stood by the bar. "Jacques, you are a very lucky man," Drut said. "Your Juliette wears the tiara of a goddess. What a beauty she is."

"Thank you, Émil." Jacques laughed at the restaurateur's passion. "I can't argue with you. I am lucky."

Messerli called them over to a circle of men. One of them, Ferdinand Carrard, insisted that Pierre accept his offer of a week at his chalet in the mountains of Verbier because the heat of late August had become nearly unbearable. Carrard was a large man with a pointed chin and close-set eyes who had done well as an attorney. "Anyone who has been there," he said, "will tell you the air will restore your health, and the vistas will inspire your dreams."

Pierre wasn't at all sure he had the time to get away, but before he could respond, Messerli said, "It might do you some good to spend a week relaxing in the mountains. Perhaps Jacques could go along."

St. Clair raised his eyebrows at the prospects just as Émil Drut seized the conversation. "That's an excellent idea, but if you're going to the mountains, why not go all the way to Zermatt."

"To the Matterhorn," Messerli said with some enthusiasm.

Carrard nodded. "I have no objection to that."

"You can take my chalet. It's open this month," Drut said, "and Frau Schneider, the innkeeper who manages it for me, will take good care of you. You'll enjoy her hospitality."

"That's very kind of both of you," Pierre said, "but I don't think it's possible—"

Messerli interrupted. "Of course you can find the time, especially if you invite your biographer to go along for the trek. Doctor's orders," he added, nudging St. Clair.

"I'd love to go along," St. Clair offered. "I've written about the Matterhorn but have never seen it."

"It is something to behold," said Carrard. "Nothing else quite so dramatic in the Alps."

Pierre reconsidered. "Well, perhaps if I had Jacques along … it might be nice to break the routine for a few days and get out of this heat."

Drut seized the opening with Messerli's encouragement and before long it was settled. Pierre would spend a week with St. Clair in the valley of Zermatt, relaxing and enjoying the alpine environment. They would leave on Sunday, two days hence.

67

THE MATTERHORN

The train clattered through the hillside vineyards beyond Montreux, and Lake Geneva took on a cerulean hue below the clear August sky. St. Clair turned from the view to open the Swiss mountain rucksack he had acquired for the trip, loosening two leather straps holding the top closed.

"That thing has more belts than a coach and six," Coubertin said.

"Yes, it's practical like the Swiss." St. Clair removed a large wedge of gruyère and fished deeper for his fruit. "And perfect for my notebooks." He found two Swiss apples and handed one to Pierre, who lifted a small wooden table into place and pulled his own Austrian rucksack from the floor, which had one more pocket and one less strap than St. Clair's.

"I far prefer the greater simplicity of the Austrians," Coubertin said, spreading a white-and-red checked cloth over the table and placing a bottle of Swiss white between them.

"To each his own." St. Clair cut his apple into wedges. "Let's get this trip started."

"The Château de Chillon," Coubertin said, pointing down to the old stone castle on the lake. "Where Bonivard walked in his chained circles for six years—immortalized by Lord Byron."

St. Clair looked up too late and caught only a glimpse of the round tower before it disappeared from view. "Missed it," he said, "and I've never read Byron."

"Well, you have plenty of time left for the Romantics," the baron said, polishing his apple before biting into it.

They consumed the lunch and a few glasses of wine as the train rolled into the mountain valley at the east end of Lake Geneva, moving steadily south toward Visp, where they would change trains for Brig. Clearing a spot, St. Clair placed his tablet on the table and bent over it.

"Back to work so soon?"

"If you don't mind, just a few questions about the Le Havre Congress of 1898 and what really happened with the Paris 1900 organizational effort."

By the time they changed trains, taking the funicular up through the narrow alpine valley into Zermatt, Coubertin, stimulated by the travel, had talked incessantly for well over an hour. St. Clair had nearly two dozen pages of shorthand and a clear understanding of how Coubertin had used the Congress of Le Havre to reassert his control over the Olympic Games, but how quickly the ground shifted again as he lost control of the organizing effort in Paris and the Americans, led by the ambitious James Sullivan, launched an attack to take over the movement.

The funicular ground slowly up the steep grade, passed under a few snow sheds, and finally began its descent into the valley. On the platform at Brig, St. Clair had noted the language had changed from French to German, and now the conductor walked by, repeating, "*Meine damen und herren, Zermatt ist endstation des zuges.*"

At Zermatt, they stepped off the train with their bags, the fresh, cool air enlivening the moment.

"Ah, that's lovely," Coubertin said, shouldering his rucksack and breathing deeply. "It's good to be back here again after so long."

Looking up over the village, St. Clair searched the horizon for the signature summit. "Where's the Matterhorn? I thought it stood above the village."

"Patience, young man," Coubertin said, lifting his second bag. "You'll see it soon enough."

St. Clair insisted on carrying Coubertin's duffel, which the old man relinquished without protest. "What do you have in here? A couple of bricks?"

"Books, boots, and my wool britches. If it's too heavy for you—"

"It's not too heavy," St. Clair said, swinging it away as they heard the distinct clink of glass. "Did you think it necessary to bring wine up here, Pierre?"

"Well, you never know the state of an alpine cellar. Let's go." The baron turned and set off at a quick pace, heading down the dry dirt road toward the picturesque village, which was bathed in a valley of shadows under the sunny sky. Zermatt was crowded with classic Swiss chalets and surrounded on the mountainsides with clusters of dark brown hand-hewn wooden huts. As they edged onto the main road, they saw the white steeple of the church standing above the roofs straight ahead. Émil had given them instructions to turn left at the church, follow the road across the river, and continue as the path began to rise. "You'll find my chalet 100 feet up the hillside, just next to the Schneiders' Gasthaus."

Old Frau Schneider was the widow of a Bavarian farmer who had built by hand their Zermatt inn and the chalet she sold to Émil. She always had it cleaned and ready on his arrival. As they walked by the small, crowded graveyard behind the church, Coubertin said, "It began as a romance, you know, Émil and Frau Schneider."

"Émil, in a romance?" St. Clair was surprised, trying to imagine the portly proprietor of La Nautica winning any woman's affection.

"Yes, he came down for a few weeks of mountain air ten years ago, saw the sale sign, and ended up staying a month. We were afraid we were going to lose him—and his restaurant—but they've managed to keep the romance going in a long-distance fashion. I think she comes up to Lausanne in the spring and he comes down three or four times a year."

They paused on the bridge over the Vispa River, a pleasant spray rising as the water rushed through the narrow, rocky sluice below. Feeling the fresh vapor on his cheeks, St. Clair instinctively turned his face to the sky. And there was the Matterhorn, standing over the southwest horizon like a mighty fortress. Shadows on the western rim of the caldera were just beginning to appear at its base, and it rose to its point as if carved by the gods into an arrowhead.

"It's breathtaking, isn't it?" Coubertin said. "One of nature's most magnificent citadels."

"My God, yes. What a vision."

The valley of Zermatt turned west at its southern end, where the rounded shoulders of the lower mountains plunged, like monks kneeling before their lord, opening a wide vista below the point where the Matterhorn's pyramid of solid gneiss rock rose to 14,692 feet above sea level.

"I think we simply must climb it tomorrow," Coubertin said solemnly. Then he burst into a laugh. "Don't get any ideas about dragging me up that mountainside. I'm here to relax and contemplate the beauty, not risk my life on that treacherous shark's fin."

"Then who's going to carry the camera and take my photograph on the peak?"

"Maybe Frau Schneider."

Coubertin and St. Clair followed the trail up the rise. Within a few minutes, as the angle of incline steepened, St. Clair drew a deep breath and felt the old familiar joy of effort enter his breast, a slightly lightheaded sensation of contentment. It felt good to be in this place at this moment with old Pierre.

A voice called out to them with a thick German accent. "Is that the famous Olympic baron and his biographer coming up my path?" St. Clair looked up and saw, standing on a porch beneath the sign for Schneiders' Gasthaus, a large, voluptuous woman in a blue-and-white dirndl, an apron drawn tight around her waist, her brown hair stacked in a bun above her wide, smiling face.

Coubertin paused as St. Clair continued to climb. "You've identified us, correctly, madame," the baron called. "And it could not be more obvious that you are the beautiful queen of Zermatt, Katarina Schneider."

"A charmer to boot," she said, offering her hand to welcome St. Clair.

"Just repeating what Émil Drut has often said." Coubertin huffed as he came up behind Jacques. "He's been singing your praises for years."

They followed Frau Schneider the twenty steps up the path to the chalet, which was built from the same dark-stained wood that marked most of Zermatt's structures. Its front balcony was brightened by lush red impatiens spilling from planters. Firewood was stacked on the landing. Inside, the front of the chalet opened into one large room, with a kitchen, table and chairs, a large stone fireplace, and a couple of overstuffed sofas, all framed by the windows and door of the balcony. A blue-and-white checked tablecloth, which Coubertin recognized as the flag of Bavaria, covered the table and presented a plate of sliced meats, gherkins, a block of cheese, and a basket of bread. An envelope marked "Pierre & Jacques" was propped against the basket.

Frau Schneider lifted two bottles. "Do you prefer the red or the white?"

"The red," said the baron. "You have a lovely place."

Frau Schneider uncorked the bottle. "The bedrooms are in back and the privy is out the side door." Coubertin and St. Clair made a quick inspection of the premises as she poured three glasses, raising a toast as they returned.

"Delicious," said Coubertin, looking at the label.

"Émil keeps an excellent cellar. Now, let me show you the best feature of the place." She opened the door to the balcony. They stepped out onto a rough-hewn wood floor under extended eaves, and there in the distance, framed in the center of their vista over the blooming wisteria, stood the majestic peak. "You'll never tire of sitting out here," Frau Schneider said. "My husband built this chalet for this view alone."

"He obviously wanted to leave you an inspiring legacy," St. Clair said, noting the woodshop craftsmanship of the two chairs and the table they'd be using. "Did he climb the mountain?" He stared wistfully at the massive gray monument, taken with the notion that he should make an attempt.

"Oh, he went up to the Hörnli Hut many times," she said, pointing at a spot on the Matterhorn, lowering her eyes along her arm as if aiming a rifle, "but he was not a man to take risks."

St. Clair remembered the Hörnli Hut from his story of the Latin Quarter baker and alpinist dreamer. "That's the cabin that is the last stopping point for the final ascent, isn't it? Can you see it?"

"If you know where to look." She extended her arm in front of him. "Follow the ridge line down from the bend below the peak. See where it meets the shoulder? There's a speck of white just out from the base ... with a tiny patch of black ... that's the roof."

"I see it," said St. Clair. "Pierre, perhaps we should give it a try."

"My days of Olympian efforts are past, Jacques—but you should go, by all means."

Late that night, under candlelight, St. Clair worked through his first draft of the post-Athens period.

○ ○ ○ ○ ○

Two weeks after they returned home from Athens, Coubertin and Marie left the heat of Paris and moved up to the Château de Mirville in Normandy for the spring and summer months. What was to be their first vacation together soon turned into a base of operations for the Second Olympic Congress, to be held in the summer of 1897 in Le Havre. Coubertin went back and forth weekly between Mirville and Le Havre. After the challenges to the authority of the IOC in Greece and the difficulties he was beginning to have in Paris with Picard and even with his own allies in the USFSA, he had decided to use the platform of another congress to buttress his control and move his agenda forward.

In his emergent plans for strengthening and growing the Olympic Movement, Coubertin could see the potential value of two distinct kinds of Olympic conferences between the editions of the Games. First, there would be the annual IOC sessions, essentially planning meetings for the members and the leadership of the international sports federations and national Olympic committees. The sessions would be preoccupied with the business of organizing the Games, deciding on the next host cities, and reviewing progress reports from the organizers. The Olympic Congresses, on the other hand, would provide intellectual amplitude, the opportunity to bring together the Olympic Movement and the best minds of civil society to address broad social issues on the impact and values of sport. The latter would be a chance for him to explicate the philosophy of Olympism, engage in public debates to refine it, and ultimately develop it into the modern philosophy he intended it to be. The congresses could also address persistent technical issues such as the amateur code, the rules of each sport, and the role of arts, music, and letters in the Olympic Games—a subject close to Coubertin's heart and vision for the Games' future.

As history has noted, the theme of the First Olympic Congress at the Sorbonne in Paris had been nothing less than the establishment of the modern Olympic Games. Coubertin decided that the theme of the Second Olympic Congress in Le Havre would be sport and education. He was not finished with his drive to spread sport through the schools of France—and his colleagues in the IOC all responded positively to the idea. In fact, Wilhelm Gebhardt made overtures to host the congress in Berlin.

But Le Havre was Coubertin's home court. And since he intended the next Olympic Games to be held in Paris, he moved quickly to consolidate support. Within a few weeks, his allies in Le Havre—the mayor, several members of city council, and the manager of the Hotel Frascati, a beachside resort—had rallied to his calls. From the years he had spent in Mirville and Étretat, he was well known in the city, and the facilities of the impressive town hall were soon at his disposal.

His sense of urgency increased when Vikelas betrayed him in a letter to all IOC members. As a proud son of Greece, it may have been predictable that Demetrius would align with the royal family in hopes of making Athens the permanent home of the Games. But calling upon his colleagues in the IOC to convene a congress for the purpose of acceding to the king's wishes was too much of an offense to tolerate. Coubertin had assumed the presidency of the IOC as he left Athens, and now he would act with force to defeat Greek designs on the Games.

That next summer as the Le Havre Olympic Congress opened, no Greeks were in attendance. But Coubertin's allies—old and new—paraded to the podium one after the other. The president of France himself, Félix Faure, served as the honorary president of the congress. Henri Didon gave a keynote on sport and education—summarizing the positive impact of games on the development of the young—while celebrating the call of *citius, altius, fortius* and the success of the first Olympic Games. From across the Channel, Coubertin drew upon British eloquence in the form of an Anglican minister and headmaster who counted sport among God's greatest gifts to humanity. The Reverend Robert S. de Courcy Laffan would stir the congress with a testament of the power of sport—delivered in flawless French. Laffan was soon to join the ranks of Coubertin's greatest allies and advocates, friends he would dearly need in the years ahead.

When the gavel fell at the last session of the congress in Le Havre's town hall,

there was no question about who held the keys to the future of the Olympic
Movement or where the next Games would be held. What was in question, despite
President Faure's endorsement of Coubertin's vision, was how much authority, if
any, the IOC would exercise in Paris in 1900.

○ ○ ○ ○ ○

All week long, they fell into the same pattern, working in the mornings, and
taking leisurely walks in the afternoon, never moving very fast but always
uphill, taking the trails on both sides of the valley. Stopping to catch his breath
one afternoon, Coubertin mused that in Zermatt there was nowhere to go but
up. Gazing wistfully at the magnificent peak that would disappear behind
shoulders of land and trees and then suddenly sweep back into view, St. Clair
yearned to go farther. But he was constrained by Coubertin's limitations. The
baron's capacity reflected his age, and perhaps his health. While they coursed
through the village of Zermatt, his pace was as quick as it was in Lausanne, and
although he was used to the hills—up and down from Mon Repos almost daily—
he did not have the stamina to attempt a serious alpine trek. As soon as they
began ascending any path, his step slowed and his breathing became labored.
His pattern was stop and go, fifty feet, one hundred feet, never venturing very
far without pausing to give his heaving chest a break. Again and again, St. Clair
suppressed his desire to suggest going farther, catching the words on his lips
as he gazed at the challenge of the Matterhorn, remembering that his climbing
partner could no longer climb.

   In the waning afternoon light on the second day, they made their way back
down to the village and stopped in the little cemetery behind the church.
The inscriptions on the gravestones revealed the deadly legends of the great
mountain. A young German man of nineteen had lost his life on his first attempt
to reach the Matterhorn's summit, joining this small community of the dead
who had come to Zermatt to test their skills on the great rock face. Coubertin
and St. Clair were surprised at the number of young men who had traveled
great distances to meet their fates. Seven men formed the first group to reach
the summit in 1865, and only three of them survived. Led by an English painter,
four Brits plunged to their deaths on the descent when one fell and three were
dragged over the edge by the rope that linked them. All seven would have died,
but the rope snapped, leaving the painter and the father and son guides from
Zermatt clinging to rocks above the tragedy.

   Out of curiosity, St. Clair led Coubertin into one of the alpine shops in the
village and asked the proprietor about the best routes up to the Hörnli Hut.

While St. Clair and the man examined a map of the trails, Coubertin fooled with ice picks, examined the steel points of a set of crampons, and marveled at the lengths and weight of ropes that bound climbers in their risky schemes.

As they left, Coubertin said, "You know, I wanted to give an Olympic medal in Stockholm to the greatest alpine feat of the time."

"It sounds faintly familiar. Who won?"

"No one. The Stockholm committee decided it was too difficult to judge among the entries, especially since several of the stories submitted were for climbers who had died on their adventures."

On their fifth day, over a leisurely breakfast, Coubertin said, "I know you want to try your legs on the higher elevations. Our time is running out, so why don't you start out early tomorrow morning and see if you can make it to the hut? There are too many gravestones to try anything more without a guide and the right equipment, but you can likely get to that hut with little more than a staff."

○ ○ ○ ○ ○

St. Clair left before dawn, while Coubertin was still asleep, just as the first hint of light was spreading across the sky. Following the trail out of the south end of town toward Schwarzsee, he was full of energy, feeling as if he could climb all day. He was exhilarated, the walking stick he had carved the day before the perfect tool, his rucksack light with only a sandwich, an apple, and a bottle of water. Within three hours he had made it up to the ridge line and the chapel at Schwarzsee, and he was now no more than a few miles from the Matterhorn, which lay directly west, standing at the same elevation of the wide skirt of rock that formed its base. It looked even more formidable from this close a range.

On this bright morning, he could clearly see the true start of the ascent to the Hörnli Hut. As the shopkeeper had told him, he came to a stair carved into the stone that led to a rock face around which a slatted wood and rope bridge clung like an apron and swayed beneath his step. The path entered a snowfield in the shadows beneath a bluff, and the footprints of a hundred hikers showed him the way across. The white field stretched for a hundred yards and spilled into a steep, narrow ravine that disappeared over a cliff. He knew if he slipped there would be no way to stop his slide. Carefully probing with his staff, he discovered a point just off the path where the long stick found no ground and plunged all the way to his wrist. He verified the solidity of each step beyond that point. Once he was through, he traversed a long field of shale, drawing closer to the mountain, which now loomed above him ominously. He heard voices, and two young Germans approached from behind as he came to a wall that required scaling. Although it was not particularly risky and the drop would have been only a dozen feet, he was careful. By the time he reached the top the Germans were on the wall, so he waited for them to pass. The hut was now clearly visible; he knew he would reach it in a half hour and wanted to take his time.

As he climbed toward the Hörnli Hut, St. Clair stopped several times to survey the 360-degree views. The shape of the caldera was clear. The Matterhorn was the highest peak along the roughly defined rim of an enormous bowl, a gaping mouth left by an ancient volcano that had once spewed smoke and lava into this dazzling blue air. Sitting at the hut, eating his sandwich as the sun passed mid-day, he was satisfied with his effort. In front of him, the massive rock face rose toward wisps of cumuli, and he knew the climb would become too technical from here and far more daring than his appetite for adventure would allow.

Resting for a final moment before descending, St. Clair spotted a wide-winged bird riding the wind rising from Schwarzsee. As it soared away to the south, he felt his spirit lift with it, alone and grateful for the experiences he had had, not only on this day, but on his entire journey with *le Rénovateur*. He felt as if he had gained more than a friend; in fact, it felt as if he had gained a new father.

It was dinnertime when St. Clair trudged up the path toward the chalet. Coubertin and Frau Schneider emerged from the inn and called to him from the landing. His feet hurt and he was exhausted but eager to join them at the table and regale them with stories of his day. His mouth watered when he stepped inside the inn and absorbed the aromas of the oven. Frau Schneider served large portions of *Schweinshaxe*—roasted ham hock—potato dumplings, and sauerkraut. As soon as he'd had his fill, St. Clair walked stiffly up to the chalet and collapsed on the bed while it was still light out.

○ ○ ○ ○ ○

He woke in the middle of the night and couldn't get back to sleep. In the kitchen, pouring a glass of water, he noticed the balcony door was open and saw Coubertin sitting there, illuminated by the moonlight in his white nightshirt, sipping a glass of wine.

St. Clair stepped out and Coubertin said, "It's even more astonishing at night," motioning to the mountain. Indeed, the east face was radiant with moonlight, its wide descending surface cast from the shadows in relief, the distinct shape of a new image revealed in the night.

"What do you see, Jacques?" Coubertin asked. "What does it look like to you?"

St. Clair took a seat. "A spectacular rock face in the moonlight."

"Yes, but look at it upside down. I saw it as soon as I came out here."

"You couldn't sleep?"

Coubertin's features were indistinct, half shadowed, blurred by small movements. "No, but that's not unusual," the old man said. "I seem to need less sleep these days. I had a lot on my mind this evening."

St. Clair had an impulse to retrieve his notebook. He couldn't help but ask, "What was on your mind?"

"Look at it upside down," Coubertin said again. "It's very distinct."

St. Clair puzzled over the image for a moment. "I don't know, Pierre. What do you see?"

"It's a footprint, Jacques, the sole of a shoe—and it looks to me like a track shoe."

St. Clair saw it. The thin heel at the top of the face, the wider part of the shoe lower down. "Yes, I see what you mean."

"It's like the foot of a runner—a sprinter—set to take off."

"That would be one gigantic sprinter," St. Clair said. "He'd cover the Alps in a few strides."

"A Titan could have left a footprint like that. But I think it must have been an Olympian. Maybe it was Zeus, his knee bent over Zermatt, his first stride carrying him into the Balkans."

"I'll leave it to you to determine which god left that footprint. But kindly tell me what was on your mind tonight."

"It's strange," said Coubertin, "but when you were gone today, I found myself worrying about you, thinking the worst might happen. The fear was persistent, and I couldn't draw my mind away from it."

"There was nothing to worry about. I wasn't taking any chances."

"I know." The old man shifted in his chair and took another sip of wine. "But I couldn't shake the notion that the mountain was dangerous. And then I realized it had to do with the cemetery at that little church. It's ironic, isn't it, that in this beautiful valley, filled with sunlight and stirred by the majestic power of nature—the imprint of death is never far removed. It lingers, it haunts, it worries us."

"That's what you were thinking about all day? Death? That must have been depressing."

"No, it wasn't death troubling my mind." His voice dropped to a whisper. "It was religion. Death was only a reminder that I had something more to say to you. We haven't talked enough about my religion—the religion of Olympism."

"You're right, we haven't. We should focus on it tomorrow."

"I don't want to wait. I've been thinking about it all day." He began to talk, not stopping for a long while. St. Clair listened carefully and refrained from interrupting.

"I'm sure you've heard me say that Catholicism, like Christianity, the faith I was raised in, is a religion of the dead, a philosophy of death, because it forces us to dwell on the life after this life," he began. "That's why we bury the dead in the churchyard. At church and in school, we were taught to divide the body and the spirit, to subdue the flesh and our natural physical impulses, essentially to split ourselves into warring factions. The Catholic Church led our society to develop an asceticism—an aversion to the physical nature of man—that was unhealthy.

"But in the Hellenism of the ancient Greeks, there was clearly a celebration of this life. Hellenism was, in fact, a cult of humanity, and the Olympic Games were the pinnacle celebration of the physical achievements of man. For me, Olympism is a counterpoint to the religion of death. But I don't think of it as a rejection of religion, I think of it as a philosophy of life—a focus on the joy of life God has given us. All of this made sense to me personally because I had experienced early on—as a boy—the sheer joy that came through play."

"I knew modern sport needed the characteristics of religion, the spiritual dimension that would lift the emotions and produce joy and celebration again, would unite people in awe of the athletes who emerged like heroes on a stage, and would fill their countrymen with a healthy, nationalistic kind of pride."

St. Clair thought about the solemnity of the opening ceremonies he had experienced at the Olympics. "So you set about to deliberately add the rituals of religion to sport?"

"In part. But I drew from the state as much as the church. I realized that sport was not popular enough, not widespread enough yet to command that emotional power that religion had on its own, but that patriotism was. Patriotism was the key. It had the requisite spiritual power, the ability to inspire pride, healthy or unhealthy, to produce sweeping emotions, to unite and rally and overcome differences and intellectual objections through the force of will. I saw the possibilities of linking sport to patriotism to create a new religion, without any deity but man, for modern times.

"In England and in America, you could not fail to be aware of the intense identification of each team through its symbols and uniforms. The caps of the English schools were badges of honor to those who wore them and those who cheered the players on from the sidelines. But there was no power like the power of the national flag. It was so evident in Athens when the American flag was raised on that first day that modern sport had the power to instantly ignite national passions, to bring forth the core emotional allegiance that every individual feels for his country. And I wanted that power for France—because we needed it.

"The Third Republic was a young democracy sailing toward the future like a galleon being tossed by high seas on its way to a promising new shore. There was a sense everywhere in France that we were all pioneers together, that we were creating a new nation, giving birth to a new world, and that we were all responsible for the direction of the country.

"In the Third Republic, patriotic emotion was present in every conversation, always roiling just offstage and ready. Raising the Tricolor at any public gathering was like lighting a flame as night was falling. And sport, I knew, had the power to focus that emotion, to unite people in national pride, and to celebrate the common good."

The old man finally stopped. The river's gurgle rose through the silence. St. Clair looked again at the moonlit footprint above the valley and said, "Your religion has certainly made its mark, Pierre."

A few days later, nearly the end of August, they returned together to Lausanne.

DEATH AND HONOR

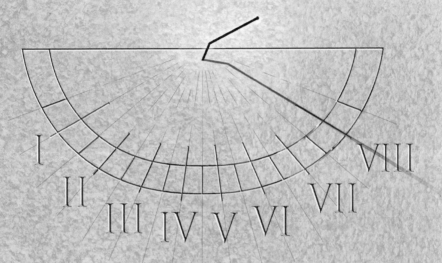

68

DEATH AND DEPARTURE

On the morning of Thursday, September 2, St. Clair and Juliette lingered over breakfast on the terrace, enjoying the rise of the crisp air off the lake in the warming sunlight. Afterward, he left for Geneva on his Dion-Bouton. He and Coubertin had agreed to meet at Pension Melrose at ten o'clock—after the old man's regular four-mile walk around La Grange Park—and spend the day together.

Flying along the road through Nyon toward Coppet, St. Clair pushed the pedals hard, feeling the exhilaration of the moment and the satisfaction of his accomplishments. With the drafts of Athens 1896 and the Le Havre Congress behind him, he felt he had the hardest part of the biography written. The story of the growth and evolution of the Games from Paris 1900 through Berlin 1936 was well documented. The official reports, the record books, the Olympic Revue, and the press coverage of the Games, especially the feats of Olympic heroes, would provide a rich trove of information to color the rest of Coubertin's story.

Like so many endurance athletes, St. Clair found clarity of thought in intense exercise. He pushed harder as he neared the outskirts of Geneva, the wind from his speed causing tears to stream on his face while he considered the structure of his story. He knew already that the rest of the biography would be marked by the triumphs of Stockholm 1912, the first nearly perfect Games of the pre–World War I period, and Paris 1924, the real culmination of Coubertin's career. As St. Clair saw it, the resurrection of the 1896 Games, which were dead on his arrival in Athens in 1894, was nearly as important as the Sorbonne Congress that had first raised the Games from oblivion. He intended to show that Coubertin had shaped history, that he had bent both the times and diverse cultures—particularly the Greek, Scandinavian, and French cultures—to his will through those three Games, which in scope and detail revealed the true force of his vision and his ferocious, relentless drive.

In St. Clair's view, it was the apogee reached in Stockholm that created the momentum to ensure the swift resurrection of the Olympics after World War I. In and of itself, the act of putting on the Antwerp 1920 Games was no small feat in war-ravaged Europe. But St. Clair's storytelling instincts told him the biography should dwell on the success of Paris 1924—the first he had covered as a journalist. They were a magnificent festival of youth that St. Clair now considered the zenith of Coubertin's career. He believed the sustained brilliance of Coubertin's Olympic leadership could best be measured by the three milestones of 1896, 1912, and 1924. As a writer, he knew he would also have to weave in the shortcomings, Coubertin's antiquated attitudes on women in elite competition and his seemingly endless parade of enemies, along with the personal tragedies and financial stress—all to offset and balance the overwhelming success of the Games.

As he crossed the pont du Mont-Blanc to the south side of Geneva, St. Clair realized he was a half hour early and decided to pedal up to La Grange Park to see whether he could catch Pierre on the walking paths. He felt some urgency in engaging the baron in a conversation on the repeated ruthless attempts of James Sullivan to displace Coubertin and seize control of international sport. He reflected on how the atmosphere of mistrust generated by those battles between 1900 and 1912 had failed to poison Coubertin's noble spirit or distract him from his mission—and realized in some ways that the ideology of Olympism was Coubertin's response to the enduring animosities he faced. The baron had used his pen to fashion a philosophy of sport grounded in friendship, transforming the conventional metaphor of competition as war into a metaphor of sport as peace.

Speeding along the quay bordering the seawall, St. Clair slowed at the corner of avenue William-Favre, dismounting and walking his bike through the half-opened gates of the park. He stepped carefully onto a muddy path beneath a tunnel of trees along the park fence and approached the field ahead. The leaves on the hardwoods hinted at fall colors that would soon be prolific. Two teams of boys were playing football in the open field under the eye of a coach, their shouts enlivening the sylvan arena, and St. Clair stopped to watch as they kicked the ball across the grass toward two stubbed markers where the goalie waited. One team wore whites, which reminded St. Clair of the stories and images Coubertin had recalled from his visits to Rugby. As the goalie dove to make a save, St. Clair walked his bike farther down the path until the La Grange Château came into view though a break in the tree line. A figure appeared on the path between the front of the old mansion and its expansive lawn, and St. Clair could tell from the brisk pace and distinctive gait that it was Pierre, who disappeared behind the glades. The path would bring him to the other side of the field where the boys were playing, and St. Clair decided to wait and watch the baron react to the game at hand. It was a decision he would regret for the rest of his life.

Coubertin soon reappeared and fixed his gaze on the boys at play as he approached the other side of the field. He had still not spotted St. Clair when he reached the edge of the pitch and stopped, bending over as if he had run out of breath, holding the position, his hands on his knees. Suddenly the baron's body lurched and he jolted upright. Alarmed, thinking the worst, St. Clair mounted his bike and began to pedal hard, watching in disbelief as the baron suddenly stiffened and his body seemed to convulse. His hands clutched at his chest and he fell sideways, not attempting to break his plummet but landing hard on the grass.

"Pierre!" St. Clair twisted his bike off the path and raced across the field. The boys and their coach ran ahead of him toward the fallen man, crowding around him as St. Clair arrived. "Call an ambulance!" he yelled, kneeling in the grass next to the gasping baron, whose eyes were bulging in desperation.

"Pierre! What is it?" He cradled the old man's shoulders and tilted his head up. "Are you all right? Look at me—the doctor is coming."

Coubertin did look at St. Clair then, held him in his gaze as if they were the only two people in the world. A faint smile creased his cheeks, a disheartening half-smile that dipped severely to the left. His lips moved as he struggled to form words, and then, in a whisper, he said, "Jacques. Jacques ... my son."

St. Clair looked up in desperation, hoping to see an ambulance coming, but they were on their own. He began to cry. "I love you, Pierre," he said. And then he felt Pierre's body contract in a paroxysm, his muscles as taut as a plank. His mouth pulled back in a reflexive grimace before his jaw went slack; his eyes were fixed on a site beyond this realm.

He was gone.

St. Clair lifted Pierre in his embrace, clutching him in disbelief as the sobs came in waves and he cried silently, *no, no, no.* The coach knelt beside him and laid his arm across St. Clair's shoulders. But there would be no solace for this loss, no way of closing the breach that had opened in his heart. He heard the echo of Pierre's last words again, *Jacques, Jacques, my son*, and knew he had lost his father—again.

○ ○ ○ ○ ○

Juliette stayed at her studio until late that afternoon, not expecting Jacques to be home until well after dark. When she arrived at the cottage at twilight, the Dion-Bouton was lying on its side and the front door was open. She called to him, but he didn't answer. She found him on the terrace, drinking wine from a bottle, his back to her.

"Drinking without me again," she said, but he didn't turn as she came up behind him, intending to tickle his neck. She stopped when she saw another empty bottle lying in the grass at his feet.

"Jacques, what's wrong?" she asked, taking his head in her hands and tilting his face up. She was shocked by his visage. His eyes were swollen and red, and his face was wet with tears. She knew before he said it.

"Pierre is gone," he uttered in a slur, his chest heaving with a great sob.

"Oh God, no!" She clutched him as his arms encircled her waist and he pulled her down. She began to cry too. "When? Today?"

He couldn't respond. She settled in his lap and buried her face in his shoulder, waiting until he was ready.

Fifteen minutes passed. As the light faded and his sobs became occasional sniffles, she asked again, "What happened?"

"I think … I think it was … his heart …" he mumbled. "In the park … kids playing … he collapsed … I raced to him."

She could picture the scene but hoped it wasn't what she imagined. He had once—and only once—talked to her about his father's death. "Did you speak to him?"

"I held him in my arms, Juliette, just like my …" He broke down, sobbing again, inconsolable, pushing her away.

"Oh Jesus. Jesus God." She found herself crying again, as much for Jacques as for Pierre.

○ ○ ○ ○ ○

St. Clair tried to ride off his hangover the next day, pushing himself down the coast to Montreux, but he couldn't find the solace that typically came from exertion. There was no refuge in the exercise. On the way back he turned up through the vineyards and found a new route to Grandvaux. Stopping at the same café where he'd had lunch with Coubertin on the day of their tandem ride, he ordered a carafe of wine, a baguette, and some cheese. Trying to focus on the goodness he discovered in the old man, he remembered Pierre smiling with delight and telling him he was an athlete indeed. The memory was pleasing for a brief time, but the pleasure vanished and the abyss of loss opened again.

He lingered for a while, finally deciding to return to Lausanne before he became too drunk to navigate. When he reached the city, he wasn't ready to go back to the cottage so he circled above the cathedral and down past Mon Repos over to rue de Bourg. He stopped and thought about going up to his little office, but it was filled now with books and magazines and files from Coubertin's life and work. Riding down to rue de Gare and on to avenue Ouchy, he realized everything in the city reminded him of Pierre—each site, each restaurant, each corner. That night, he couldn't sleep, read, or work. He was overwhelmed with grief again. He walked around the cottage with a glass of wine in his hand and finally passed out on the sofa, but he didn't sleep long.

The next morning he woke Juliette to the aroma of freshly brewed coffee, said he wanted to talk, and waited patiently while she donned her bathrobe and came out to the kitchen. He suspected she knew what was coming.

"What do you do when the race is over?" he said.

She made no reply, just looked away. But he pulled her back and repeated the question.

At last, her voice cracking, she said, "You go home."

"That's right. We're going home."

○ ○ ○ ○ ○

That afternoon, under the pretense of discussing funeral arrangements, he rode to the university to see Francis, dreading the meeting.

They embraced warmly without saying a word—they had talked it through amid tears when Jacques called him from Geneva. Staring at the doctor—this man who had shared his mission in a race against time—St. Clair thought Messerli looked heavier than usual and realized that his face was fatigued and puffy from strains of grief too.

Rounding his desk, Messerli spoke with some frustration as he sat down. "There's no news on the funeral, Jacques. Nothing's going to happen this week, maybe not this month. The mayor and the baroness are discussing a ceremony here. The French Olympic Committee wants to do something in Paris, and we're still waiting to hear from the Greeks."

"Who will take his heart to Olympia?"

"I don't know. The IOC is communicating with the Olympic Committee in Greece."

"That's disappointing. I was hoping we'd all have a chance to pay our respects publicly." St. Clair was unable to escape the sadness they shared. He wished he had something encouraging to say, but it wasn't in him.

"We will, Jacques. It's just going to take some time."

"Then we'll have to come back ..."

"Come back?" Messerli did not hide his surprise or concern.

"I can't stay here, Francis."

"But what about the book? You have more to do. We have more work to do."

"I'll work on it from Paris." With resignation, he added, "I just can't write about Pierre right now. I have to get away for a while—away from ..." He let the thought go, not wanting to say he couldn't cope with the memories of Pierre here in Lausanne—they were simply too vivid.

"Paris?" Messerli said. "You're not going back to *Le Petit Journal*, I hope."

"I'm going to need to work—we'll have expenses—and Edgar has offered me a position on the international desk."

"But Jacques, I'm paying you. And I will continue to pay you. You're so close—you were close to finishing the interviews, weren't you? You have what you need, don't you?"

"Yes, I have a lot of information, maybe enough. But I don't have what I need most. And I won't take any more of your money, Francis. I know I owe you a manuscript, and I will finish it but not until I'm ready."

"I'm sorry, Jacques. I don't mean to press but ..." He left the thought unfinished.

St. Clair looked away and bowed his head. He was certain Messerli was wrestling with his own pain. He could only hope the doctor would understand the extent of the loss he was feeling. Something was broken, something that couldn't be healed without some time and distance.

Messerli frowned. "When are you planning to leave? I hope this break won't derail the biography for too long. Now that Pierre's gone, it's even more important that we get the book done."

"Maybe a day or two. We have some packing to do."

St. Clair politely declined a dinner invitation and promised Francis he would call and write soon and they'd develop a plan for finishing the biography. The goodbyes were not as impassioned or as affectionate as their earlier embrace. St. Clair felt awkward and guilty. He was leaving Lausanne five months shy of the year he had committed to, but under the circumstances, he was hoping Messerli wouldn't hold it against him.

○ ○ ○ ○ ○

Near the end of the workday, another knock came on Dr. Messerli's office door.

"Yes?" he called from his desk, surprised when Juliette walked in. She pulled off a beret and let her hair fall free. She was dressed in paint-stained pants and an old jacket and looked as though she'd been working.

"Hello, Francis," she said in a sad tone as he rose to embrace her, touching her cheeks with his lips and wondering whether it might be the last time he would have that pleasure.

"Well, this is quite the day for goodbyes, I guess. Jacques was just here a few hours ago."

"Yes, I know," she said, "I left him at the cottage. He was already emptying the drawers."

They sat down facing each other and Messerli's worries spilled out. "I'm surprised you're leaving so soon. I mean, Pierre has only been gone a couple of days, and Jacques and I still have so much work to do on the book ..."

"That's why I'm here, Francis."

"What? You're here to say goodbye, aren't you? I don't suppose there's any chance—"

"No, there's no chance. And I'm here to tell you why ... why we're leaving so soon."

Messerli raised an eyebrow and looked at her intently.

"I don't suppose you know the story of Jacques's father, do you?"

"No, no I don't." Messerli's mind raced for a connection he couldn't find.

"Jacques never talks about him. I don't think he ever told Pierre about him, which is sad, in a way, because Pierre was like a second father to him. I don't think he'd been that close to an older man since his father died."

"Jacques's father died?"

"Long ago—right after Jacques turned thirteen."

"Oh, that is sad. What happened?" Messerli was beginning to guess.

"He was a carpenter in Paris, a respected craftsman, but he was also an amateur athlete."

"A cyclist?"

"Yes, a cyclist. He stayed in good shape and rode with a group of friends until Jacques came along. And then his greatest passion was training his son."

"And Jacques made it all the way to the Tour de France."

"That's right—and that was his father's dream."

"But he obviously didn't live to see it."

"No. One afternoon they were riding on the Left Bank, near Bon Marché, when something happened to his father. Jacques thinks it might have been a heart attack, but he lost control and skidded on the cobbles. He was having trouble breathing when Jacques reached him."

"Oh no, don't tell me. He died in his arms? Just like Pierre?"

Juliette nodded as Francis clasped his hands between his knees and looked down.

"His mother told me he didn't ride for a year—wouldn't even look at a bike—and wouldn't talk about what happened. He told me about it once—but never again."

"Oh dear," Messerli said, groaning. "He's a prisoner of guilt. Blames himself. A natural reaction for any boy. I should talk to him."

"You can't, Francis. I didn't come here on a rescue mission. He'd be outraged if he knew I told you. It's his burden—and he wants to bear it alone."

"Well then, he's never going to escape that guilt."

"He recovered once. He'll recover again."

Messerli stood and Juliette followed suit. After a quick embrace, he said, "I wish that were true, but it isn't. He never recovered the first time."

○ ○ ○ ○ ○

In a single day, Jacques and Juliette had boxed up all the supplies in her studio and, with the help of two of Messerli's students, closed out his office, moving all the books and files to Messerli's townhome. They had worked diligently and solemnly side by side, Juliette content to follow Jacques's lead in silence. They had a purpose, as if they were on a new mission already, and there was no time for light banter. Jacques had made it clear he didn't want to recount the memories of their Lausanne experience yet. But as Juliette began to pull the canvas from the frame, Jacques stopped her for a moment. Standing in front of the portrait, they absorbed it together, staring into those life-like eyes glistening with brightness, studying that emphatic, generous countenance.

"I've never had a friend like him, Juliette. I'll miss him till the day I die."

"I will too." They laid the frame flat on the floor, and she finished pulling the canvas out and cutting it from the wood. With his help, she rolled it up neatly in layers of white paper and sealed it in a tube she intended to carry on the train.

"We're going to find the right place for Pierre in Paris," she said, "and we're going to tell everybody about him."

St. Clair hugged her and said, "Yes, we'll tell everybody someday."

They left the gilt frame as a gift to the good doctor for all his kindnesses. And later, Juliette tacked eight of her best sketches of Pierre on the wall over the sofa, leaving them as a gift for Renée.

○ ○ ○ ○ ○

The next afternoon, after they finished putting most of their clothes into the same suitcases they arrived with, they decided to take the boat to Evian, have dinner, and spend their last evening looking at Lausanne from across the water.

The night was warm and cloudless. On the way back, they stood in the boat's prow, their arms wrapped around each other.

"Wherever we go from here, Jacques," Juliette said, still searching—as he was—for notes of comfort and solace, "this will always be one of the great adventures of our lives."

"I don't know if we'll ever encounter another man like him—or another story like his. There was so much more for us here. We were just getting started."

"Well, now we're going to start again. And you're going to finish his story."

St. Clair didn't reply, but he kissed her gently as the boat steamed toward Lausanne.

69

THE PACKAGE

Much to Messerli's disappointment, the communications from Paris through the last months of 1937 were scant, just a few brief, apologetic responses from St. Clair to the doctor's regular inquiries. Most were thin excuses about the burdens of deadline work for *Le Petit Journal*—and St. Clair's inability to find the time to dive back into the book. Each ended with the same promise of progress to come, but no manuscript arrived, not a chapter or a scene. In October and November, Messerli tried to reach St. Clair by telephone at the *Journal* without success. He was always out on assignment—and Edgar, his editor, while politely apologizing, was equally evasive.

In December, as the streets of Lausanne brightened with strings of holiday lights and the festive spirit of the season took hold, Messerli found himself despondent, deeply needing to know what St. Clair's intentions were. The idea of suing crossed the doctor's mind in the worst moments, but he dismissed it immediately, knowing litigation would be fruitless—and ruin the relationship they still had left. He wouldn't allow himself to believe the writer had completely given up on the biography—had abandoned the story of a man he claimed to love—but that was the doctor's persistent fear. He needed some kind of salve for his worry, some form of reassurance that a plan was in place—that St. Clair intended to honor their original agreement. It became painfully clear to him that they should have discussed how they would finish the book if Coubertin died, but Messerli forced himself to believe St. Clair would come around.

One afternoon the week before Christmas, he felt overwhelmed by his worries and decided to act. He called the studio in Paris where he knew Juliette was painting with a group. A stranger answered, and he waited, lulled by the telephone's static and clatter as the person sought out Juliette. After several minutes, her voice jolted him from his anxiety.

"Oh, Francis! I was wondering if you would one day call me. But I'm sorry—this telephone is in a hallway and I can't talk here. Can you give me a few hours, and I'll call you back at your office?"

When she telephoned back, her tone was so filled with empathy that he felt the urge to embrace her.

"Hello, Juliette," he said, nearly choking on the depth of his emotion. "I'm sorry to trouble you—"

"Please, Francis. It's no trouble. I've read all your letters to Jacques. I can't imagine how disappointed you must be—and how worried."

"You've read my letters?" He was surprised. He had sent everything to Jacques at *Le Journal*.

"Yes, of course. He shows them to me because he feels so terrible ... that he hasn't been able to continue the writing ..."

Messerli absorbed the news, which confirmed his fears. "Unable to continue? What do you mean? He's writing stories every week for the *Journal*. I've seen them."

"He's not the same, Francis. He's still not sleeping well and he's often so distracted I can't talk to him—as if he's in a trance. He's not exercising like he always did. He drinks too much sometimes. It's complicated."

Messerli couldn't avoid forming a diagnosis. "He needs counseling, Juliette. It's an emotional blockage." He had been speculating for months about St. Clair's psychological condition—about the impact of Coubertin's death on his psyche—and now he was hearing a list of predictable signs.

"I've told him that." She sounded resigned. "But he doesn't want to talk to anybody. He thinks he can break through if he keeps trying."

"Trying to write? The biography?"

"Yes. He tries to get going—every now and then. Last week, I came home and he was surrounded by his notebooks, reading his shorthand from the interviews."

"So he does want to finish the book." Messerli relaxed somewhat, realizing he had judged correctly—that St. Clair was still committed to the work.

"He intends to finish it, but he hasn't been able to concentrate on it—or write anything more than a page or two before he ..."

"Breaks down?"

"I don't know. I just know it's difficult for him to go back to those memories with Pierre right now ... but I do think he will eventually figure it out."

Reassured, Messerli decided not to write any more insistent epistles. Instead, he would wait a month or two to see whether Juliette was right. He turned to small talk, and Juliette asked about his grandchildren.

When he finished the full update, she said, "I'm so glad your family is doing well. I know you've always been a good father—and grandfather—and I know Jacques will be too."

It took Francis a moment to realize what she was saying. "My heavens, Juliette! When did you find out?"

"Just last week. The baby is due in July."

When he hung up, Messerli's anxieties had for the most part evaporated. Though he knew the sentiment was selfish, he imagined a child would be more than enough to reawaken St. Clair's ambitions.

○ ○ ○ ○ ○

By mid-February of 1938, Marie de Coubertin and Olympic officials in Paris, Lausanne, and Greece had finally set a date in March for three simultaneous ceremonies that would serve as funerals and celebrations of Coubertin's life. The baroness asked Dr. Messerli to carry Coubertin's heart to Olympia—and he agreed immediately, as honored by the request as he was duty-bound to fulfill it.

As he prepared for the trip, he considered writing to St. Clair, thinking the ceremonies might be the prompt to action he needed. But before he had composed a letter, a package arrived from Paris. Disappointed by its weight, knowing it could not be a full manuscript, he was encouraged nevertheless and retreated to his study with a small measure of optimism.

Dear Francis,

When you receive this I will be on my way to Berlin. The Journal *is stretched for resources, and I've been drawn into the international fray once again. It seems the beat of the war drums in Germany deserves more attention than the bicycle circuits of France, so I won't be able to get back to work on the manuscript for a month or two. While my progress has been faltering—no excuses except the difficulties I've had thinking about Pierre since he died—I have made some limited progress lately. I'm truly sorry for the delays, but I do intend to fulfill our contract. In fact, I'm taking my last few notebooks and a few new pages of the manuscript with me. I left everything else in Paris for safekeeping in the event this trek proves more risky than it is supposed to be. But nothing is new in that hoard, just my notebooks and research and a few typed pages of transcripts capturing Pierre's voice on subjects we've covered.*

Over the last few months, I have become convinced that Pierre's story needs an introduction that summarizes who he was and what he left us. Since the Journal *asked me to write an appreciation for his funeral here in Paris—something more than an obit—I'm enclosing my first draft, which summarizes his life succinctly and should serve the purpose I have in mind for the book's introduction. I understand you are soon going to be traveling to Olympia with Pierre's heart— and all I can say is "Bravo!" You are truly his best friend—even now. Knowing how long you've been waiting to hear from me, I'm hoping this will reach you before you leave. If you have a chance, please send your review to Paris so Juliette can forward it to me in Berlin.*

I know how anxious you are, Francis, to get the full manuscript, but there's still much work to be done to capture the drama of the story Pierre gave us. I know in my heart that you'd rather have it written right than shortchange him— and I'm still not able to give it what it needs, but I am coming around. So I leave you with this appreciation for now, which should be encouraging since it was probably the hardest single piece of writing I've ever done. And I'll also leave you with the promise that as soon as I get back to Paris I will drop everything else and work tirelessly until the manuscript is ready for your review.

Warm regards—Jacques

GENIUS OF SPORT
In Appreciation of Pierre de Coubertin
By Jacques St. Clair

The Greeks left Western civilization with a legacy based on the idea that man is the measure of all things. By that calculus, the dignity of humanity comes from the value of each man's life—and from the collective progress of every man's journey through our shared history. The Greeks themselves established the paragon that confirms their theory. We comprehend the meaning of their ancient world through the lives of the men who shaped their times. Homer, Pericles, Socrates, Plato, Aristotle, Euripides, Archimedes, Sophocles, Alexander the Great— the colossi of that nation's brief centricity on the world's stage have exerted an eternal hold on our imagination.

By that calculus, the central question of our quest to understand our own experience must be the measure of the lives of those who share the stage with us as the pageantry of life unfolds. Among us, in our time, there was a man whose measure the world has yet to fully comprehend. For his reach is already extending well beyond the horizon we can see to the most distant dates we can imagine. He has put an indelible imprint on the calendar of our future and left us to contemplate the power and promise of a worldwide movement that seeks to unite all humanity in a celebration of friendship and peace through sport.

That man is Baron Pierre de Coubertin, the French genius who reached into the vaults of antiquity, into the heart and soul of that ancient Greek world, and resurrected the Olympic Games in modern form. He passed away last September 2 in Geneva at the age of seventy-four, and the time has come to take the measure of his life.

○ ○ ○ ○ ○

He stood only five foot three, but by every measure, his achievements mark him as a giant of the last century. Born into the French aristocracy as it entered the late stages of its decline, he witnessed the national humiliation of the Franco-Prussian War as a boy and embraced the birth of the Third Republic and its egalitarian ideals as a young man. He drew inspiration from the transformation of Paris into the capital of modernity as an adult. At the age of twenty-six, he saw the glorious symbolic possibilities of international events as the Eiffel Tower rose above the Champ de Mars for the 1889 Universal Exposition of Paris. That historic event became a lifelong touchstone for Coubertin as he organized the world's first Congress on Physical Education as part of its program.

As a student of the Jesuits, fascinated with the classical world of the Greeks and Romans, he turned his back on his family's plans for a career in the church, the army, or politics and found his mission instead in a vision for turning sport into a worldwide force for good. In 1892, when he delivered his first public proposal to bring the Olympics back to life after fifteen hundred years, he said, "Let us export our fencers, our runners, our rowers to other lands, for therein lies the free trade of the future, and the day we do it the cause of peace will have received a strong and vital ally."

His audience didn't rally to the idea then, but he was not to be deterred. Once he fixed his course on resurrecting the Olympic Games, he proved to be a man of unbending will. His drive and determination were unwavering. His pursuit of his ultimate goal could serve as a worthy model of dedication, courage, and endurance for the thousands of athletes who have followed him into the Olympic arena, onto the stage he created.

A year and a half later, on June 23, 1894, in the Grand Hall of the Sorbonne, he led a gathering of more than two thousand to support his proposal to resurrect the

Olympic Games. The path that led to that moment, like the path ahead to the first Games in Athens in 1896, and the next three in Paris, St. Louis, and London, was filled with obstacles and adversaries, marked by failures, and followed by personal tragedy, but none of it deterred him. Opposed nationally and internationally by sports organizations resistant to change, sports leaders hungry for power, and politicians and governments unwilling to support his vision of a "festival of the springtime of youth," he met every challenge by redoubling his effort. At the heart of his vision was an unshakable conviction: that sport could bring "the joy of effort" to every individual life and could hold great promise for the future of the nations. "We shall not have peace until the prejudices which now separate the nations of the world have been outlived," he wrote. "To attain this end, what better means than to bring the youth of all countries periodically together for amicable trials of muscular strength and agility?"

While his movement prospered in the decades that followed and gained traction as a seminal event on the international sports calendar, his personal fortunes declined. Near the end of his life in 1937, he was living in Lausanne, Switzerland, in apartments generously provided by the municipality. Depressed and accosted by a wife embittered by their losses, he had exhausted his family's fortune—and hers—in underwriting his great campaign to put sport at the center of modern life and make the Olympic Games a permanent quadrennial celebration of humanity.

The last Games he witnessed from a distance were under the control of Adolf Hitler's National Socialists in Berlin in 1936. While those Games produced an unprecedented level of pageantry—and while a recording of Coubertin's voice echoed through the stadium during the opening ceremonies, saying, "The most important thing in the Olympics is not to win, but to take part, just as in life, the most important thing is not to conquer but to struggle well"—they were marred by Nazi racial hatreds and discrimination that were anathema to the Olympic ideals Coubertin had spent his life fostering. As the light of his life dimmed the following year, he was left to contemplate the tragic notion that his great movement for peace through sport had fallen into the hands of a madman leading the world to war.

As Messerli read through the familiar details of Coubertin's life, the 10,000-word essay revived his confidence in St. Clair's ability to draw an effective narrative from the baron's Olympic obsessions. Aside from the opening, there was nothing new here, nothing the doctor hadn't heard or spoken of himself, but it was all presented in a fresh telling—the aristocratic heritage, the childhood, the education, the early success at the Universal Exposition, the rise to prominence in the Third Republic, the alliances built at home and abroad, the rebirth at the Sorbonne, the first Olympic Games, and the clashes in Athens, Paris, and St. Louis. It wasn't a full biography, but it certainly encapsulated the remarkable life story Messerli yearned to share with the world. He returned to the reading.

After the 1904 debacle in St. Louis, Coubertin was looking forward to better days in Italy. He had longed to stage the Games in Rome—and had awarded the 1908 Games to the Eternal City before the competition started in St. Louis. With his classical education, he saw the possibilities of "sheathing the Games in the toga of ancient mystery," but his dreams were suddenly shrouded by dark clouds of ash. On April 7, 1906, Mount Vesuvius erupted in a disastrous calamity that strained Italy's already complicated finances and forced Rome to withdraw as host.

By this time, however, Coubertin had cultivated sophisticated sports allies in Britain, who stepped up on short notice to take over the organizational effort, essentially saving the 1908 Olympics. In the end, Coubertin was delighted at the turn of events that aligned the Games with the sporting legacy of his hero, Sir Thomas Arnold. Every organizing committee introduces a corps of talent to the Olympic Movement at all levels of sport from the political, cultural, commercial, industrial, and athletic arenas. It is not just great athletes who respond to the Olympic ideal but people from all walks of life, and Coubertin could readily see that the level of talent flowing into the organizing effort in London, with its pervasive sporting traditions, was destined to set a new benchmark for all future Games.

With the elegant and eloquent Reverend Courcy Laffan, who first stood up at the Le Havre Congress, delivering a series of inspiring sermon-like speeches on the potential of international sport as a foundation for amity between nations, the preparations took on a moral purpose. London seized the opportunity of the Games with relish. From the president to the laborers, the London team took to their business with unprecedented professionalism and moral conviction—like an army called up by Arnold to ensure that the Olympic Games finally gained the credibility and esteem they needed. Still, the vestiges of old animosities and patriotic fervor drove the Americans and Brits into such vehement competitiveness that fights broke out and accusations of cheating became rampant. The belligerent attitudes of James Sullivan, the American sport leader, seemed to bleed into his team, and some events were marred by bloodlust. While Coubertin knew the rancor of excessive nationalism was an ever-present threat to the Games, he believed the philosophy of peace he had ingrained into Olympic sporting values—and the admiration for human excellence across all cultures— would always triumph or at least emerge victorious in the long run.

As an Olympic sports milestone, however, the London Games marked a new level of success, the first since Athens 1896 to advance the cause and demonstrate that this quadrennial festival of youth could be the world's pinnacle of international competition. If London revealed the true power of the Games, the next edition in Stockholm unveiled its magical properties.

To add artistic stature to the Olympic celebration, Coubertin had convened in 1906 at *La Comédie-Française* in Paris a conference on sport and culture. He led an assembly of eminent writers, performers, sculptors, artists, architects, and creative cognoscenti to develop the idea of a multi-disciplined cultural Olympiad—a counterpoint to the sport competitions that would enhance the international prestige of the Olympics. The greatest works in architecture, painting, sculpture, music, and literature would be recognized with Olympic medals, thereby engaging the worldwide cultural community that had, up to this point, shown little interest in the sports. Conceived too late to introduce effectively as part of London 1908, Coubertin gained the support of General Balck and his Swedish colleagues to launch the cultural program at the Stockholm 1912 Games.

Led by the young Sigfrid Edström, the Stockholm Olympics would become the Games of Enchantment for Coubertin—the closest he would come in his career to the model of organizational precision and perfection he had always hoped for, with a balance of sport and culture that satisfied his longing for social relevance. And the competition produced the most extraordinary individual spectacle in the modern era. The American Indian Jim Thorpe arrived on the field of play at the height of his athletic powers. He possessed unmatched physical gifts and took such pleasure in his feats that Coubertin, watching him dominate both the pentathlon and the decathlon, decided he was the pure embodiment of "the joy of effort." Here was a hero for all time, an athlete who had found in sport the essence of happiness and mastered every discipline he took up with a finesse that even the ancients would have admired.

In the Cultural Olympiad, Coubertin himself won the poetry competition, writing under the dual *nom de plume* of Georges Hohrod and M. Eschbach, with his touching *"Ode to Sport."* The poem served as a litany of his belief in the power of sport. He sang its praises: "O Sport, thou art beauty ..." and went on to portray sport as justice, honor, joy, and peace.

With the harbinger of Stockholm elevating his sense of the international influence of the Games, Coubertin sought to put them to the ultimate test. Believing against all odds that his movement might actually have the power to ease hostilities between nations, Coubertin pushed to award the 1916 Games to Berlin, to a team led by Carl Diem, a young, dynamic German sports administrator and writer. Diem would become a dedicated and invaluable contributor to the Olympic Movement in the years ahead, before compromising his personal legacy as a minion of the Third Reich. But World War I came, bringing devastation in its wake, and the Games were canceled.

To protect the Olympic Movement and seek a neutral home in hopes the Games could survive the war, Coubertin, whose patriotism drove him to join the French Army at the age of fifty-one, moved the headquarters of the IOC from Paris to Lausanne in 1915. After the war, Henri de Baillet-Latour of Belgium, a true believer in the power of sport and an equestrian, who would succeed Coubertin as IOC president seven years later, stepped forward and offered Antwerp as a host site for the 1920 Olympic Games. Once again, a city saved a movement. With less than two years to organize the Games, Baillet-Latour and his team proved equal to the task, marshaling a modest but effective festival that reminded the world of the enduring nature of the Olympic ideal and the host site.

The Olympic flag with its five-ringed logo, designed by Coubertin and introduced to the IOC at the Paris Congress of 1913, flew for the first time over the Antwerp Games, marking the beginning of a series of innovations that would change Olympic history. Antwerp would also see the installation of the IOC executive board, the first time since the end of the Athens Games that Coubertin shared authority over the Olympic Movement. In Amsterdam in 1928, a cauldron was built in the stadium and lit for the first time in the opening ceremony, launching the tradition of the Olympic flame, which the Germans took to new heights and distances with the invention of the torch relay—a variation of an ancient religious ritual—for the 1936 Berlin Games.

In the midst of the Olympic Movement's robust recovery, growth, and continuing modernization after Antwerp, Coubertin realized the time to step aside was drawing nigh. Having led the movement for three decades, ensuring that it found its footing before the Great War, survived, and reached true international status in Paris in 1924, he retired at the Congress of Prague in 1925 and never attended another edition of the Games, despite the fact that he was made honorary president for life.

Like so many who are farsighted enough to earn the epithet of visionary, Coubertin also had his blind spots. He was adamantly and unapologetically opposed to women competing at the elite levels of sport, particularly in track and field. Although women competed in sports such as archery, tennis, swimming, and diving in every Games after Athens—and although he encouraged exercise and sport for all, including women—the baron stood as a bulwark against allowing female athletes onto the Olympic track. When the history of the modern Olympic Movement is one day written, some will recognize that it was Coubertin's inability to see the value of women in the Olympic arena that ultimately led to his downfall. When a group of women, outraged by the IOC's refusal to open Olympic track and field and some other events to them, produced their own version of the event—the Women's Olympic Games in Paris in 1923—the executive board had no choice but to move beyond Coubertin's obstinate position and conform to the times.

Their decision to dramatically expand women's events in the 1924 Games clearly signaled the beginning of a new era—and the end of Coubertin's reign.

Despite his blind spots, his fundamental values were as clear in his actions as they were in his words. He continued to push for equality through sport—at least among men. In 1923, Coubertin called on the colonialists of Africa to open their national competitions to the indigenous population and to create a continental championship open to everyone—a true Pan-African Games. He continued to promote that idea well into the 1930s, never wavering in his belief that sport could serve as a force for liberation everywhere. All his life, he remained committed to the working man. At the age of sixty-three, he and his friend, Dr. Francis Messerli, founded the Institute for Physical Education in Lausanne—an offshoot of his earlier Olympic Institute of Lausanne and his recent Universal Pedagogical Union. Its goal was to create more opportunities for the laborer, the plumber, the mechanic, the baker, and the tailor to engage in and enjoy the benefits of sport at a public gymnasium that offered intellectual stimulation and broader opportunities for learning.

○ ○ ○ ○ ○

What possesses a man to believe he can accomplish so much at such a young age? In Coubertin's case, it may have been the sense of mission he derived through recognition that his heritage—the aristocracy he was born into—had long oppressed men, and that was a tragedy he would spend his life trying to correct. He brought to the challenge a set of talents and perspectives ideally suited to the cause.

He had an intense and exquisite sense of history. The ancient past and the recent past were as real to him as the moment at hand. He melded an ethic of sport out of classical Hellenism and the emergent Anglo-Saxon sporting tradition that was well suited to modern times. Part of his genius was in finding a balance between the philosophic inspiration of ancient Olympia and the muscular Christianity that rose from the fields of Rugby. He took the best of both and blended them into the concepts of Olympism.

And it is clearly the ideology of Olympism that elevates the Olympic Games above all the other sporting events and leagues that compete for our devotion today. That ideology is one of the most valuable assets the IOC owns. And it is, in essence, the heart and soul of Coubertin's legacy, the philosophic foundation for the continuing expansion of his movement and the dissemination of its values.

He not only gave us the world's greatest sporting event, he gave us a philosophy of life designed to foster a better world. Among his other contributions to contemporary culture, Coubertin gave us the morality of modern sport. More than anyone else, he is the inventor of sport with a social purpose, the author of the idea of putting sport at the service of humanity on an international scale. For Coubertin, sport was always a means to a greater end—a platform for education, moral values, character building, personal excellence, mutual respect, friendship, and ultimately peace.

Coubertin saw the mythological and spiritual dimensions of the Games from the beginning. He knew intuitively that he had raised more from the earth than an ancient sporting tradition. Although he didn't fully understand it—couldn't explain it—he was certain the corpus of competition he had resurrected came out of the ground shrouded in mythology. He was convinced that he had set loose in the modern world a mythic reality that would one day be recognized by people everywhere. In Athens, as the rituals unfolded on the field before him—and particularly when the marathon runners closed in on the city—the presence of a new spirit, the Olympic spirit, was undeniable. Invisible but real, it moved like the wind, sweeping through the skin to touch the soul, a visceral, palpable sensation. They all felt it; they were all bound by it. No one could describe it, but everyone in the stadium knew something eternal had returned.

While his strengths as a promoter, producer, organizer, and sports administrator were nonpareil, his greatest weakness may have been that he tried to do too much, expending his energy along too many parallel tracks at the same time. He craved wider recognition as a scholar and a writer. In 1895 and '96, while the Athens Games were in the critical stages of preparation, he refused to give up his work on *The Evolution of France under the Third Republic*, a book whose optimistic view of the achievements and progress of the Third Republic was at odds with the prevailing notions of political struggle at the time. Absent from Greece for most of the year leading up to the Games, he faced the double disappointments of the poor reception of his writing and the Greeks' minimization of his contribution to the Games.

Still striving for intellectual recognition at sixty-four, he published the four-volume *l'Histoire Universelle* in 1927, hoping his integrated cross-cultural view of the history of nations would bring him accolades. It didn't—instead, it contributed to his nearly lifelong belief that his work never really gained the appreciation it deserved. A tireless thinker, writer, and campaigner throughout his life, he left behind more than sixty thousand pages of books, essays, campaign pamphlets, letters, and Olympic publications.

Until the very end, he rowed in circles on the blue-green waters of Lake Geneva off the quay behind the Château de Ouchy, at the point where Lausanne spills down from its high hills to meet the shoreline. Sport was a constant for him, a commitment to the joys of effort that served as a focal point through times of

prosperity and a long night of adversity. His deeply held convictions about sport
for all were founded in his personal experience with exercise. Like an anchor
holding a ship steady, sport became for him a refuge from the circumstances of
his life and a bulwark against the winds of opposition that blew so fiercely against
the Games he struggled to launch.

Coubertin is gone now, but his work lives on in a movement of friendship, peace,
and sport that continues to extend its reach around our world. In our time, few
men have produced more impact than this proud Frenchman. And yet, his story
is shrouded in anonymity. By the calculus of the Greeks, he is a modern colossus
in the world of sport, and some believe that his name will yet one day rise to the
pinnacles of fame, that future generations will be taking the measure of this man
as long as the Olympic flame continues to enlighten our world.

○ ○ ○ ○ ○

Messerli finished reading the appreciation and set it aside. He was moved by
its summary of Coubertin's life and thought St. Clair had done justice to the
story in the form of a newspaper profile. He was grateful that Jacques had
finally produced a fresh piece, however compressed, of Coubertin's story. But
he remained disappointed that this was all the progress they'd made. He
wondered yet again if they would ever finish the book.

70

THE FUNERALS

uneral arrangements were complicated by the number of people and committees who sought to pay tribute to the man, but even more by the logistics of fulfilling his wish to have his heart interred in Olympia. It took some months after his death for the International Olympic Committee, the French Olympic Committee, the Greek government and royal family, the Baroness de Coubertin, and the mayor of Lausanne to finally agree to a date for simultaneous ceremonies in Olympia, Lausanne, and Paris. The date was set for Saturday, March 26, 1938. Dr. Messerli agreed to accompany Pierre's heart to Olympia on behalf of Marie de Coubertin, and he carried a letter from her to be read at the ceremony.

On the boat to Piraeus, Messerli took a drink to the deck and watched the sun set over a calm Mediterranean. Sitting on a deck chair, he began to wonder and worry again about St. Clair—and the worry only deepened when he thought about Jacques's new assignment in Berlin. Strange and violent times were unfolding in Germany's capital, and Messerli, on his way to a funeral, wondered if *Le Petit Journal* had secured assurances for St. Clair's safety.

○ ○ ○ ○ ○

In Paris on March 26, the French Olympic Committee held a solemn ceremony before a full audience at the Roman Catholic Church of the Trinity. While the world outside seemed to be drifting inexorably toward another war, the French

NOC and Olympic officials remembered Coubertin as a visionary man of peace and friendship through sport. Seated next to the mayor in the Notre Dame du Valentin church in Lausanne, the veiled Baroness de Coubertin, with Renée and Jacques at her side, listened to a series of messages that proclaimed her husband's enduring greatness and the eternal quality of his legacy. Young people sang and candles burned as his body was buried in the Cemetery Bois-de-Vaux. In Olympia, the tribute and ceremony took on a spiritual quality that Coubertin himself had probably envisioned.

On the morning of the funeral, Messerli rose with the sunrise in Olympia and stepped out on a narrow balcony on the back of his small hotel room. The scene was almost wholly natural, with only one red-tiled roof accenting the lush green slope of Mount Kronos. His senses seemed unusually alert to the morning's birdsong, and with sudden appreciation he saw the variety of hues in the leaves of Olympia, the olive trees contrasting strikingly with the acacias and other trees.

He dressed and went to the lobby of the Hotel SPAP, where the IOC president and the Greek delegation were all staying for the ceremony. But aside from staff, the lobby was empty, as Messerli had wished it would be. He headed down Olympia's main street toward the ruins, hoping for a private moment of communion where he knew, for certain, the memories of Pierre would be intensely present. Turning down the hill, he followed the columns of the gymnasium and stood among the fallen pillars of the Temple of Zeus in the Altis, trying to imagine what the place must have been like in the ancient world. He felt a breeze coming up from the River Alpheus and wondered whether the spirit of his friend might be blowing through the air. He walked through the tunnel to the stadium and crossed the plain where sprinters had first competed 2,713 years before, running for the fleeting glory and fame that would disappear until a French visionary declared the glories of Olympia revived.

He climbed up the embankment where the spectators had sat, Plato and Pericles among them, then spotted the ceremonial monument the Greeks had set up for Coubertin's heart just beyond the end of the stadium. He walked down to the white marble column and examined the engraving of Coubertin's name just below a relief of Hercules's head. The proportions of the stele seemed just right to Messerli, its geometric sides and vertical height pointing symbolically toward the clear blue sky. Smiling to himself, he imagined the moment that would come later that afternoon when the Greeks interred Coubertin's heart in its base, finally paying homage to the man who gave them so much. Forty-two years after they had stood silently by as their countrymen denounced him as a thief trying to steal their heritage, the Greek royal family would finally recognize the greatest international sports ally their nation ever had. Messerli knew Coubertin had planned for this moment, knew his friend had a much clearer vision of the future than most men.

Retracing his steps across the open track and through the tunnel, Messerli stopped for a moment under the shade trees of the Altis. He gazed at the scattered ancient stone and crumbled foundation of the Temple of Hera, where the flame had been lit for the torch relay that preceded the Berlin Games, wondering whether that tradition would last. Sitting for a few minutes, he rested his hand on the cool surface of a broken block of white stone and immediately felt a set of depressions beneath his fingers. Looking closely at the stone, he realized that it was engraved with a list of names and had clearly been placed next to the bench for tourists to see. Although his Greek was barely passable and no visible dates were listed on the fragment of rock, Messerli knew he had rested his hand on the names of Olympic victors from one edition of the ancient Games.

In that moment of recognition, a wave of emotion flooded him. He realized Pierre must have known that in order for the Greeks to bury his heart in Olympia, his name would be carved in marble, linking him forever to those ancient names he brought back to life in the modern world. Messerli's eyes teared up, and he wished as deeply as he had ever wished for anything that St. Clair could have been with him to experience the same emotions. The loss seemed all the greater because St. Clair wasn't there. He bowed his head and wept silently for a few minutes.

As he walked back to the hotel to prepare for the ceremony, he looked again at the fallen pillars of the Temple of Zeus, two thousand years old, lying on their sides in disarray as if they had just crumbled. The Greeks could have rebuilt the temple by now, they could have picked up the pieces, he thought, and reassembled that magnificent building that had once housed one of the seven wonders of the ancient world. But that remained undone. In that moment, he realized that his great work, his dream of telling Coubertin's story to the world, might never be finished either. With St. Clair off in Berlin, the future was more uncertain than ever.

As he left the ruins, an undeniable sense of disappointment and regret crowded into his thoughts, the inescapable notion that some parts of Olympic history would always be lost to the world. The story of history's greatest Olympic hero, an athlete of ideas without peer, might never be told. He touched the pillars of the gymnasium one by one as he passed, feeling the cold stone of history and wishing for yet one more Olympic resurrection.

○ ○ ○ ○ ○

In the lobby of the Hotel SPAP, which was now crowded with IOC members, Greek ministers, and dignitaries from around the world, Messerli caught the eye of Baillet-Latour, whom he had known for years, and stepped over to shake his hand. It was just before noon.

Baillet-Latour greeted Messerli. "We're grateful you've made the trip, Francis. I know your presence would please Pierre."

"It's good to see you, Henri. And Pierre would certainly be pleased by the size of the crowd."

"Yes, we're just waiting for the crown prince to come down. Protocol, you know. He'll lead the caravan down to the stele."

"You have a copy of the baroness's message, I believe." Messerli pulled his copy of the letter from his breast pocket to show Baillet-Latour.

"Yes, I have it. Sauvigny's going to read it."

"Very good. Thank you. Pierre was an extraordinary person, and he had great affection for you."

They were interrupted by an American who introduced himself in perfect French as Lincoln MacVeagh, the U.S. ambassador to Greece. Messerli thanked the IOC president for carrying on Coubertin's work.

Just then, the din rose in the room and Crown Prince Paul appeared in Greek military uniform, complete with brocaded hat, high boots, and leather gloves. Baillet-Latour excused himself and left the ambassador to join the prince. After they had greeted each other, the procession began and the hotel lobby emptied quickly.

As the official delegation followed the crown prince down the main street in their funeral suits and uniforms, people from the village and nearby farms joined the procession, their country clothes adding touches of color and humanity. When they reached the stele, which was now surrounded by an iron fence, everyone formed a circle around it. Seven feet in height, the Hellenic marble monolith rose in two tiers. In the pedestal at its base, there was a door to a compartment designed to hold the baron's heart. At eye level, a tribute to Coubertin was engraved in Greek just beneath the head of Hercules. The Greeks understood symbolism as well as anyone and had prepared for the day with true compassion.

The grand marshal, Count Alexandre Mercati, who had been one of Coubertin's earliest allies in Athens and now served as the elderly IOC member from Greece, called the gathering to order, proclaiming the day a loss for all humanity and a profound moment in the history of Olympic sport. "Baron Pierre de Coubertin," he said, "was a Philhellene, a man who returned the Olympic Games to Greece during a difficult time for our nation. Our debt to him can never be repaid, but today we will make a down payment of royal respect."

The crown prince, who bore Coubertin's heart in a green marble urn Messerli had carried from Lausanne, joined Mercati, Baillet-Latour, and Count Albert Bertier de Sauvigny, another of Coubertin's oldest Olympic friends, to form a front line that approached the monument solemnly.

Together they faced the crowd, and old Sauvigny stepped up, opening a letter from Baroness de Coubertin and reading her regrets at being absent from Olympia on this day. "'Thank you to all who revere the name of Pierre de Coubertin,'" he read. In her message, the baroness called out Crown Prince Constantine, who had helped guide the first Games of 1896, and offered up a roll call of honor, paying tribute to the early pioneers who had helped bring her husband's dream to life—Vikelas, Balck, Sloane, Gebhardt, Boutowsky, Kemény, and finally Guth-Jarkovsky, the only survivor among them. Sauvigny closed with her final words: "'The torch has passed from Coubertin's hand to those who will hold it high and pass it on to others. Lift it for all to see. His flame will never be extinguished.'" Messerli listened with a sense of irony, knowing he might have been the only one present who knew the other side of Pierre's widow.

And then, on a signal, the Greek cultural minister stepped forward, and as Crown Prince Paul placed the urn in the base of the stele, he said in a loud, clear voice: "Your heart is at this moment deposited on the sacred soil of Olympia. A block of white Hellenic marble will forever mark your illuminated passage in this world and will consecrate the memory of your struggles for the Olympic Games."

Messerli was glad to hear the Greeks acknowledge that for Pierre, the resurrection of the Games had been, above all else, a struggle. A struggle, he thought, made all the more difficult by this argumentative nation. Other remarks and prayers followed from several priests before the closing moment came, and it was left to Baillet-Latour, who had been friends with Coubertin for thirty years, to deliver his final thoughts. He began by saying that an extraordinary man had passed through their lives and left nothing he touched unchanged. "The whole world now knows of his work," he said, "which fills the hearts of the young with dreams of bringing honor to their countries through the glories of sport." Messerli listened carefully to the song of praise for the man who had indelibly shaped the highest office in the world of sport. Baillet-Latour closed with an appropriately common but heartfelt goodbye: "Farewell, Pierre de Coubertin," he said, a catch in his voice. "May thy soul rest in peace."

After the ceremony was over and the crowd had dispersed, Messerli quietly moved to the stele, admiring the graceful carving of Hercules in cameo. He touched the cool marble, placing his fingers in the engraved name of his friend, feeling the permanence of the indentations he had felt that morning in the Sacred Grove of the Altis. The name of Coubertin was now added to the eternal list of Olympic champions who had once breathed, lived, and dreamed the glories of these hallowed grounds.

71

THE LAST LETTER

I n the daily press of life, Francis Messerli soon turned his energies back to his career and his family. As the quivering summer heat waves of 1938 rolled across the lake, he tried to stop worrying about his aborted passion. He had little contact with the IOC now and none with the baroness, and he slowly relinquished his preoccupations with Pierre. He had let his contact with Juliette in Paris drift away too, finding it difficult to ask if she'd heard anything, knowing the answer would bring both tears and silence. Jacques and Pierre were their connection and it was difficult to face the loss of both. But six months after his package from the writer arrived, almost on the anniversary of Coubertin's death, Messerli received a letter air mailed from the United States. He knew it was Juliette from the script in which his name was composed. The return address, in ink-stamped type, read Franklin, Philadelphia, and he knew before he opened it that Juliette had gone home, ending her Paris adventure as the hope for Jacques's return finally faded completely away.

Dear Francis:

I'm writing to you from my parents' home in Bryn-Mawr on the Main Line just outside Philadelphia. Jacques-Pierre Franklin St. Clair was born here almost a month ago, and he has become the center of the new life that my family has provided for us. They're doing their best to keep my spirits up, and I'm doing my best to let my hopes die.

It has now been almost five months since Jacques disappeared. In that time, I've had to come to terms with the truth. He's gone, and I doubt that we'll ever know what happened.

I'm sorry I haven't written you before this, but I left Paris in something of a hurry at the beginning of June. Without Jacques, life there had become difficult. I was having trouble keeping up the apartment, and my family began to worry about my state of mind. They became insistent that I needed their support for the birth, and my mother and brother came over to help me pack for the voyage. I'm not sure whose decision it was, finally, but I believe it was for the best.

I'm not painting anything right now, Francis, but I'm starting to dream of an image of Jacques in Lausanne—on the terrace of that cottage you gave us, the lake and the Alps in the background. Lausanne was the height of our romance, the place where our love reached its depths and its peak last summer before Pierre died. I want to paint something from those days so I have it while the memories are fresh—and so I have it when Jacques-Pierre is ready to hear his father's story.

Sometimes I still wake in the mornings and reach over for him. It's been almost a year since we left you and a half year since he left Paris for Berlin. Yet it's still so hard to understand ... and still so hard to find solace.

Although I do hope you find a way to finish the book, Francis, I know how distraught you must be as well. I sincerely hope your family is doing well and that you can still draw some sense of satisfaction from the work you and Jacques did and the good times we all spent together.

I wish I could see you and introduce you to our son soon, but it appears it may be some time before we return to Paris, let alone Lausanne. I will bring young Jacques over to meet you one day. That's not just a promise, it's a certainty. But it seems that everyone in America is convinced that war is coming to Europe soon. It's all the men talk about at dinner.

I hope it's not true—but if it is, and if you find it might be wise to move off the continent for a time, please know that you and your family will find a warm welcome waiting here at the Franklins' in Philadelphia.

I miss you, dear Francis, and hope it is not too long before we see each other again.

Warmest affections,
Juliette

○ ○ ○ ○ ○

Word came from *Le Petit Journal* a few weeks later. The silence from Berlin was more than likely permanent. They had determined that the last time anyone had heard from Jacques was the night he went to a dinner at the French Embassy a month after he arrived.

Messerli listened to Edgar's gravelly old voice, carrying resignation and deep regret over the telephone line. "Here's the problem. Our ambassador, André François-Poncet, had studied journalism before he became a diplomat and he liked to have writers at his dinner parties. He had two other writers there to introduce them to Jacques."

"Nothing wrong with that," Messerli said, unsure why he was making the point.

"Except for the fact that Hitler detested François-Poncet and distrusted all foreign journalists—and he had the residence under Gestapo surveillance for years. They watched everybody come and go."

"But I still don't see why anyone would care." Messerli felt a twinge of sickness in his gut. He knew the Nazis had put a lot of critics in prison, including a few foreign writers.

"The other two writers, a Czech and a Serb, had been outspoken critics of party policy and brutality. François-Poncet said the three of them left together. They've all been missing since."

72

FRANCIS ALONE

ate on a chilly Sunday night at the end of September 1938, Francis Messerli sat alone in the small office he kept on the back of the second floor of his home. His wife was already asleep. On his desk, a half glass of double malt in melting ice sat on a coaster next to the package he had just finished tying in rough brown twine. It was a bundle of every piece of writing he had collected from Jacques St. Clair, from those now wistful months the writer had lived in Lausanne to the progressively sparse epistles that had ceased arriving more than six months before. Like a faithful archivist, Francis had placed every page of the unfinished book and every scrap of handwritten notes he could find into a sheath and wrapped it tightly. And there it sat—the unpublished codex of Coubertin's life.

The writing he had compiled, he was certain, would form the foundation of a strong biography—a true telling of the life and times of the genius who had become his best friend—but he was at a loss as to how to finish the work. Critical pieces were missing—notebooks full of St. Clair's distinctive shorthand from the late interviews he had never typed up. But he had no idea where they might be since Juliette had failed to find anything more while she was in Paris, and since Edgar came up empty-handed as well. Messerli had thought about finding another writer to finish the work—and he might have pursued that route if the times had not turned so dark.

While he was on his way to Greece with Coubertin's heart, the Germans had marched into Vienna and annexed Austria in the Anschluss. And just a few days ago, in Munich, the Czechoslovak Republic had ceded the Sudetenland to Germany in an agreement also signed by Great Britain, France, and Italy—with Chamberlain proclaiming that "peace in our time" had been secured. But Messerli, like so many others, could already hear the drumbeats of war pulsating beyond the horizon. As if on cue, the wind began to pick up outside, and the branches of the locust tree over his terrace, stirred by the sharp gusts, slapped at the window of his office.

Messerli lifted the hefty package of papers, slid it into the bottom desk drawer he had just emptied, and turned the key to lock it away. Sadly, with a sense of resignation not unlike mourning, he studied the old key under his desk lamp, worrying the worn edge of the barrel with his fingers. He rubbed the gold until it shined. He was now the keeper of the flame—at least the keeper of this particular Olympic flame—but he was tired of promising himself he would do everything in his power to bring his friend's story to life when his plan had faltered so badly at the end. The same thoughts haunted him constantly now—if only he had started the year before, if only he had pushed St. Clair to write faster, if only he had known about Jacques's broken past. To escape the guilt and to preserve his own sanity, he told himself it was time to put the biography to rest for a while.

He lifted his glass and drained it, and then drew a small white envelope from a slot on the desk and wrote "St. Clair's Coubertin" on the front. Placing the key inside, he sealed it, running his thumb firmly along the joint to make sure the glue held. Sliding his chair back, he opened the shallow middle drawer of his desk and pushed the envelope deep in the back where he would never see it by chance. He leaned forward and rested his forehead on his folded hands. Hearing the wind again, branches brushing the house, he stepped over to the sideboard by the window and poured himself one more drink. Pulling the drape aside, he moved close enough to the glass to feel its chill on his cheek. Gazing across the dark expanse of Lake Geneva, a black slab of shimmering slate in the dull moonlight, he saw the lightning of a late storm thundering over the distant peaks of the French Alps. In that moment, he wondered whether the world would ever hear the story of Baron Pierre de Coubertin—or whether the movement he had launched would ever gain enough influence to stop the world's incessant march to war and engender the friendships and peace his brilliant little friend had dreamed of.

AFTERWORD AND ACKNOWLEDGMENTS

A Movement, Not Just an Event

My Olympic journey began, as so many have, through a friend.

In the spring of 1988, as I was beginning to train for a fourth marathon, one of my running buddies, Brad Copeland, began to talk to me about Atlanta's emergent bid for the 1996 Olympic Games. Brad, who bore a striking resemblance to a young Steven Spielberg, ran a small, award-winning graphic design studio, but couldn't usually make it beyond the ten-mile mark on the road. Nevertheless, as we jogged along, he talked enthusiastically about Billy Payne, a former University of Georgia football star who was chasing the city's unlikely Olympic dream. Brad wanted me to meet Billy and present my writing credentials for a major project called the "bid books." Although I was Brad's go-to writer for almost all of his creative projects—and often helped him pitch clients—I was busy with a lot of other work, including a few annual reports and a religious novel I had just finished after four years of work. An editor in Chicago wanted me to soften the sex scenes and I was thinking about it.

Truth be told, the Olympic bid sounded like a long shot. But then Brad won the design competition for the campaign logo and suddenly his passion became an obsession. He knew Billy and his team were searching for a lead writer for the bid, and he figured if we were hired as a writing/design team, it might open the door to a whole new world. How right he was.

On the day we met Billy, Brad and I were ushered into a boardroom on the 34th floor of the IBM Tower, at the time Atlanta's newest signature skyscraper. Billy and two of his advisors were seated at the far end of a long conference table built for twenty. Brad and I settled in at the opposite end and we talked across that awkward distance for some time. The conversation went well and when Billy finally asked why he should hire me and why I thought I could write the bid books, I reached into my portfolio and pulled out my *pièce de résistance:* a set of matching eighty-page brochures on Atlanta and Georgia that had recently won a good number of creative awards for First Union Bank. I laid them on the dark polished surface of the conference table and slid them toward Billy like a shuffleboard player.

Four months later in April of 1989, Brad and I were on a plane to Lausanne, Switzerland, as the Atlanta Organizing Committee's new creative team. Our assignment was to investigate Olympic history, analyze the bid books from past bid cities and come home with a proposal that would set a new standard for bid book writing and design. Our destination was the Olympic Library, which at the time was housed on the first floor of a modest building just west of the Lausanne train station, about 100 yards up avenue de la Gare.

Fifteen minutes after we entered the library, I was staring for the first time at the white mustache and kindly countenance of the founder of the modern Olympic Games, Baron Pierre de Coubertin, in the pages of an old bid book. A headline by his photo proclaimed that Coubertin had launched the Olympic Games as part of an international movement chartered to unite our world in friendship and peace through sport. I was stunned—and suddenly in the grips of a feeling of destiny, as if I was always meant to be in that room at that moment. The news that the Olympic Games were part of a greater movement, a movement driven by the values of friendship and peace rose from the page like poetry and stirred my heart and soul. *"Brad,"* I said, *"This isn't just a sporting event, it's a movement."*

○ ○ ○ ○ ○

In May of 1969, my brother, Gary, was wounded on Hamburger Hill in Vietnam. Five months earlier I had been in Washington D.C. to protest the war at Richard Nixon's presidential inauguration—and I returned the following November to march in the Vietnam Moratorium, the largest anti-war protest in U.S. history to that point. My brother came home and fully recovered physically, and the war in Vietnam eventually wound down. As the years rolled by my passion for peace took a backseat to raising a family and building a career. When I graduated from Temple University with a degree in journalism, my young wife, Carole, and I decided to move to Atlanta with our young son, Jason, to be part of the New South and help build a new future there.

We arrived in October of 1973 and I settled into a writing position with an ad agency in Colony Square in Midtown. But even as I succeeded in the advertising game, eventually becoming one of Atlanta's leading freelance writer/producers, I couldn't help but feel I had abandoned a far more important quest, that riveting earlier engagement with a vision for building a more peaceful world.

But suddenly, on that April morning in 1989, I realized that peace had come calling again and here, in the Olympic Movement, was a chance to rekindle my passion—not against something this time, but for something. The revelation led to the larger question, of course, *Who was this Baron Pierre de Coubertin and why hadn't I ever heard of him?*

○ ○ ○ ○ ○

Under the brilliant leadership of Billy Payne, Atlanta ran a very smart campaign. Mayor Andrew Young, the civil rights icon and one of the finest men I've ever met, stepped up to work shoulder to shoulder with Billy, telling Atlanta's story and conveying our vision to the Olympic Family all over the world. The two of them—white and black—embodied the best qualities of *the city too busy to hate* and helped turn the sentiments of the IOC away from Athens, Greece, the prohibitive centennial Olympic favorite, toward the capital of the New South. On September 18, 1990, in the ballroom at the Grand Prince New Takanawa Hotel in Tokyo, Japan, IOC President Juan Antonio Samaranch opened an envelope and pronounced, in his thick Catalan accent, that *Acklanta* had won the greatest civic prize in global sport. The wave of euphoria that followed was unlike anything I had ever experienced. On the flight home, Brad and I decided to form a partnership—and our new studio, Copeland Hirthler, became the leading design and communications firm in the Olympic world in the 1990s.

Within six months of our victory, it seemed every city bidding for the 2000 Olympic Games—Sydney, Beijing, Berlin, Manchester and Istanbul—made a pilgrimage to Atlanta to learn what Billy and his team could teach them. Billy graciously sent them all over to talk to his creative team. Before the Barcelona Olympics in 1992, Istanbul had hired Copeland Hirthler to write and design their bid books. In the end, Istanbul lost to Sydney, but the work we did for the bid, particularly the way we wrote about the idealism of the Olympic Movement and its promise for our world, garnered the attention of the IOC and opened other doors for us. Soon we were engaged in the Stockholm 2004 campaign, and then Klagenfurt 2006, a three-country Winter Olympics bid from Austria, Italy and Slovenia.

Brad and I went our separate ways in 2000 as I started a new company with Terrence Burns, and within a month Beijing engaged us to help with their campaign for the 2008 Games. We won that campaign and then went on to win the bid with Vancouver 2010. From there, on my own, I served as a lead writer or senior communications strategist for five more campaigns—New York City 2012, Salzburg 2014, Chicago 2016, Munich 2018, and the aborted 2020 bid for Rome, where I had the pleasure of reteaming with Terrence Burns, with whom I'm working once again part-time on the bid of Los Angeles 2024.

As I labored side-by-side with the teams for each of these aspiring host cities, I met men and women whose imaginations were fired by the magic of the Olympic dream. It became clearer and clearer that it wasn't only athletic talent that responded to the Olympic call to excellence, but people from every walk of life, every culture, nearly every occupation. Across ten campaigns my belief in the transformative power of the Olympic Movement deepened bid by bid— and my conviction that Baron Pierre de Coubertin was one of history's greatest forgotten heroes grew stronger year by year.

○ ○ ○ ○ ○

In February 1992 in the Main Press Center at the Albertville Winter Olympics, I came across a brochure that outlined the activities of the International Pierre de Coubertin Committee. On the way back to Atlanta, I decided to form a chapter in the U.S. With Billy Payne's full endorsement and the tireless help of Cindy Fowler and Susan Watson, we launched the United States Pierre de Coubertin Committee in 1993, seeking to promote the ideals of the founder and the values of the movement in the run up to Atlanta 1996. With Cindy leading the charge, we raised $500,000 and commissioned Raymond Kaskey to design and build a world-class statue of the Baron in Centennial Olympic Park. It became one of the most photographed and filmed landmarks of the Games— and it still graces the green lawns of the park. We also led the effort to translate approximately 800 pages of Coubertin's Olympic writings into English for the first time, working with the IOC and Professor Norbert Muller of the University of Mainz in Germany. The project eventually resulted in publication of the book *Olympism*, which the IOC printed in time for the Sydney 2000 Olympic Games—and has subsequently translated into several other languages.

Over the years, I've had the opportunity to deliver dozens of presentations on Coubertin's vision to Olympic assemblies and public gatherings. Invariably, when I'm finished, people express their surprise—sometimes about the movement behind the event, most often about why Coubertin's name is not more widely known. When you consider that 3.5 billion people—half the world's population—typically watch some part of the quadrennial Summer Olympic Games on television, it's stunning that the founder of an event with that kind of reach isn't part of the daily public parlance. Some years ago, I addressed one of the largest Olympic organizations in the world and when I was finished a gentleman came up to me and said, "I've been working here for seventeen years and I've never heard any of this." He had long been part of a global movement of friendship and peace through sport, but had never been taught about its roots.

○ ○ ○ ○ ○

In 2010, I decided I had to write a book about Baron Pierre de Coubertin. And as I began to search for the right approach—not only to tell his story, but to dramatize his achievements and paint a portrait of the extraordinary transformation of Paris that served as both backdrop and inspiration for him—I decided that historical fiction would give me the most leeway and license. Historical fiction uses fact to create a framework for imaginative interpretation. It allows the writer to surround real personalities with fictional characters—and to create conversations and actions that reveal the possibilities of past events with a telling immediacy.

In *The Idealist*, I wanted to remain as true as possible to Coubertin's history while building a compelling and hopefully inspiring narrative. While most of the events, dates and places that represent Coubertin's drive to resurrect the Olympic Games are accurate, the backstory and the description of the events and conversations themselves are all fiction. Some historic settings and dates have been shifted for dramatic effect. What we know of his life, we know mostly from the surface. Beneath that surface and the facts that shape it, I created a cast of characters who help draw from Coubertin his personal and professional history, interacting with him almost at the level of intimacy found within a family. They become his family in a way, burdened with a need to tell his story—and help the world remember a hero it had forgotten.

Acknowledging a World of Friendships

When you work on Olympic bid campaigns like I have, you have the privilege of traveling far and wide, covering almost all the world capitals over time.

In the international whirlwind of events that mark the Olympic Movement's annual calendar, you're constantly meeting people and networking, making connections, sharing information, finding mentors who can teach, counselors who can guide, colleagues who can help, learning, understanding and adapting to the rituals, customs and mores of a culture of diversity formed by people from all over the world—the people who are the Olympic Family. Like any family, it is an integrated coterie of people empowering each other in the shared ideal that individually and collectively they're building a better world. There is a common belief—a faith in the power of sport—that the Olympic Movement is planting the seeds of hope in young hearts and minds in every nation. That idea—and the idea that you're helping to make it happen—is inspiring in and of itself. There is satisfaction in the work because it seems so important, so valuable and so values driven. As the great John Furlong once said while he was leading the Olympic bid of Vancouver 2010, "The Olympic Movement allows us all to lead lives of greater significance." And that significance came down to us from Baron Pierre de Coubertin.

Every meeting you go to in a far-off city is, in its own way, like a family reunion. The longer you're in it, the more friends you make, and the more your affection grows for a good many of them. It's a traveling circus and a marvelous feast for sure, but the essential lesson of the Olympic Movement is friendship through sport.

It's not a perfect movement, of course, far from it. As this novel goes to press, the leaders of global sport are embroiled in a perfect storm of scandals that threaten the integrity of the Games. But the Olympic Movement will prove more resilient than the people who have comprised its ethics. Just as it survived two world wars, the Great Depression, terrorism, political boycotts and doping revelations in the past, it will overcome these challenges and draw from them the lessons necessary for reform. The Olympic ideal will emerge from these trials as inviolable as ever, the burnished golden standard of human excellence rising once again to the pinnacle of worldwide sport.

As you would expect, I've been encouraged and inspired on my Coubertin quest by hundreds of people in the Olympic Family. With all due apologies to those I inadvertently overlook, here are a few I'm deeply grateful to: Brad Copeland, Billy Payne, Terrence Burns, Cindy Fowler, Andy Young, Ginger Watkins, Charlie Battle, Linda Stephenson, Bobby Rearden, Susan Watson, Nancy Newton, Harry Shuman, V.V. Bock, Jean-Michel Bock, Doug Gatlin, Kay B. Lee, Dory Watkins, Elizabeth Clement, Jane Stewart, Chris Welton, Tim Smith, Chip Campbell, Michael Payne, Françoise Zweifel, Bob Cohn, Scott Goodson, Sead Dizdarevic, Alan Dizdarevic, Bob Fasulo, Bob Ctvrtlik, Markus

Kecht, Gernot Leitner, Mark Mitten, Scott Leff, Sergej Gontcharov, Jon Tibbs, Mike Lee, Sevi Hubert, Alex Corp, Chris Sullivan, Mark Lewis, Bill Scherr, Gordon Kane, Willie Banks, Anne Cribbs, Bob Stiles, David Woodward, Bob Heussner, Patrick Sandusky, Lars Haue-Pedersen, Richard Bunn, Penny Baker, John Moore, Simon Balderstone, Mark Jones, Marty Appel, Don Mischer, David Goldberg, Rich Godfrey, Todd Brooks, Anne Kelly, Kirsty Bonn, David Aikman, Martin Benson, Karen Webb, Liz McMahon, Steve McCarthy, Gillian Hamburger, Scott Givens, Rob Cohen, KieAnn Brownell, Steve McConahey, Gunilla Lindberg, Austin Sealy, Arne Lungqvist, Dick Pound, Craig Reedie, Jean-Claude Killy, Gerhard Heiberg, Anita DeFrantz, Randir Singh, Larry Probst, Angela Ruggiero, Donna de Varona, Charmaine Crooks, Edwin Moses, Bob Pickens, Dick Fosbury, Svein Romstad, Dwight Bell, Carlos Nuzman, Leonardo Gryner, Leo Wallner, Peter Ueberroth, Darrel Seibel, Jim Scherr, Chris Coleman, Chip Hardt, Rick Ludwig, Jerry Anderson, Sharon Kingman, Scott Blackmun, Lisa Baird, Doug Arnot, Bud Greenspan, Johann Olav Koss, Stewart Binns, Rob Siltanen, Erwin Roth, Ed Hula, Brian Baker, Keith Ferguson, David Miller, Alan Abrahamson, Stratos Safioleas, Masanori Takaya, Asami Saito, Sinan Erdem, Atilla Aksoy, Tevfik Bilgin, Yalçın Aksoy, Rıdvan Mentes, George Courmouzis, Dimitri Tziotis, Peter Economides, Thoeore Mantzaris, Olaf Stenhammer, Bjorn Unger, Coco Unger, Lena Abrahamson, Eva Rodenstam, Tommy Gustaffson, Tomas Gustafson, Jomar Selvagg, Olle Johanson, Calle Hennix, Dieter Kalt, Franz Klammer, Heinz Jungwirth, Arnold Fellinger, Thomas and Lucie Rothhauer, Andreja Wieser, Heinz Schaden, Hannes Maschkan, Carol Chu, David Chu, Wang Wei, Han Wen, Liu Qi, Liu Jingmin, Pan Zhiwei, Zhenliang He, Curt Huang, Min Wang, Garson Yu, John Furlong, Jack Poole, Andrea Shaw, Marti Kulich, John McLaughlin, Terry Wright, Ali Gardner, Tim Gayda, Bob Storey, Steve Podborski, Dan Doctoroff, Jay Kriegel, Roy Bahat, Amy Stanton, Young-Sook Lee, Wendy Hilliard, Pat Ryan, Dave Bolger, John Murray, Lori Healey, Doug Neff, Jonathan Lewis, Jessica Fairchild, Diane Simpson, Jeff Stiers, Kimberly Meyer, Harold Gauthier, David Spiegel, Shirley Yang, Thomas Bach, Dieter Kuhnle, Bernhard Schwank, Simone Seefried, Lisa Geissler, Reto Lamm, Tobi Kuner, Katarina Witt, Katrin Merkel, Claudia Bokel, Judith Bongard, Stefan Klos, Jochen Färber, Michael Vesper, Willy Bogner, Heike Marie Boch, Christian Klaue, Richard Adams, Karen O'Neil, Mike Fennell, Mike Hooper, John Fish, Michael Lenard, Wayne Wilson, Harvey Schiller, Mike Plant, Michael Pirrie, Oscar Lopez, Michael Schmidt, Don Porter, Greg Harney, Francisco Campo, Joe Torsella, Greg Cuchard, Vin Lanana, and my newest Olympic friends Mark Davison Smith, Brock Park, Janet Evans, Danny Koblin, Matt Rohmer, and Jeff Millman.

And I must acknowledge the specific help I've had from a number of passionate people: first, the late Geoffroy de Navacelle, the great nephew of Baron de Coubertin, who invited me into the Château de Mirville and schooled me in the family background, and to his son, Antoine de Navacelle, and his nephew, Yvan de Coubertin, for further encouragement and family insights.

There are numerous scholars who have sustained Coubertin's legacy over the years, but three must be regarded as giants of erudition: Professor John MacAloon of the University of Chicago, for *This Great Symbol*, his masterful psychological study of Coubertin's complex motivations in founding the Games; and Professor Dr. Norbert Müller, formerly of the Johannes Gutenberg University of Mainz, who has probably done more than anyone to keep the spirit of Coubertin alive. Over the years Müller has taught courses in the Olympic history to more than 10,000 students. Today his work is being carried on admirably by Professor Dr. Stephan Wassong, Director of the Olympic Study Center of the German Sports University Cologne, whose writings on Coubertin's two trips to America broke new ground.

Special recognition must go to my longest-standing colleagues on the International Pierre de Coubertin Committee, including the late Yves-Pierre Boulongne, the late Don Anthony, Professor Dr. Otto Schantz, Jean Durry, Professor Dr. Jean-Loup Chappelet and Dr. Christian Wacker, all of whom strive to keep the legacy alive.

For years of support at the Olympic Study Center at the Olympic Museum in Lausanne, Switzerland, I must thank Regula Cardinaux and her entire team. And thanks as well to Christian Zutter of the city of Lausanne for his detailed tour of Mon Repos, to Yassine Yousfi of Olympic Solidarity for additional Mon Repos insights, and especially to Marcel Ruegg at the Lausanne City Archives.

I also want to thank Rachel Kaplan and Ilham Nassor at French Links Tours and especially their colleague Arthur Gillette for his walking biographical tour of Paris; Kim Dorman at the Princeton Library; and Claire Potvin for translating Marie-Thérèse Eyquem's *Pierre de Coubertin: L'Epopée olympique* and Sara Appino for other translations.

For editorial work: Perry Mitchell, Arlene Prunkl, Patricia MacDonald and Karen Rosen; for book design, David Laufer; for the painting and illustrations, David Gaadt; and for photography, Alexander Herring.

Special thanks go to my daughter, Jamie, for her historical research, my son, Jason, for his precise editorial suggestions, and finally to the love of my life, Carole, for five decades of unwavering belief in my literary dreams.

GH, Atlanta, 2016

Colophon

Text set in Bitstream Bodoni Book with
The Mix Light for St. Clair's biographical drafts and
Trajan Bold for part titles;

Illustrations by David M. Gaadt, Greensboro, North Carolina

Designed by David Laufer, Atlanta, Georgia

Printed on archival paper made by
American Eagle Mills, Tyrone, Pennsylvania

Printed and bound by Thomson Shore, Dexter, Michigan